Joy Fielding is the author of nine previous novels, including the bestselling *See Jane Run* and *Tell Me No Secrets*. She lives with her lawyer husband and two daughters, dividing her time between Toronto, Ontario and Palm Beach, Florida.

Praise for Joy Fielding's novels of psychological suspense:

'Runs rings round Mary Higgins Clark. Don't even think of starting this anywhere near bedtime' *Kirkus Reviews*

'Compulsive reading' *Company*

'Joy Fielding tightens suspense like a noose round your neck and keeps one shattering surprise for the very last page' Netta Martin, *Annabel*

The Other Woman

Joy Fielding

First published in Great Britain in 1983
by Macdonald & Co (Publishers) Ltd

Reprinted in this edition in 1994
by HEADLINE BOOK PUBLISHING

A HEADLINE FEATURE paperback

10

ISBN 0 7472 4435 9

Typeset by CBS, Felixstowe, Suffolk

Printed and bound in Great Britain by
Mackays of Chatham plc, Chatham, Kent

HEADLINE BOOK PUBLISHING
A division of Hodder Headline PLC
338 Euston Road
London NW1 3BH

www.headline.co.uk
www.hodderheadline.com

To Warren

Chapter One

'Excuse me, Mrs Plumley?'

The girl was young and pretty, with large breasts and a surprisingly husky voice. Jill Plumley shifted uncomfortably, the heels of her shoes making fresh holes in the uneven knoll of newly manicured grass. She had wanted to wear flat shoes – it was an outdoor picnic, after all, even if it *was* being held at the chic Rosedale Country Club – but David had insisted that all the other wives would be more formally dressed, and he was right. Except for this girl, who wore a casual red T-shirt and a pair of defiantly non-designer jeans pulled tight across her equally defiant young bottom. Whose wife was she anyway?

Jill smiled, quickly taking in the girl's violet eyes and flawless skin, artfully made up to look as if she wore no makeup at all. Her discomfort increased when she realized she was being similarly inspected. She felt instantly self-conscious about her hair – it always looked as if she were just about to comb it – and her height – five feet nine inches. This girl had silky black hair and stood a more reasonable five foot six, or so Jill quickly estimated, feeling her own shoulders slump instinctively to compensate for the difference in eye level,

1

feeling generally awkward and too large, the bull in the china shop confronted by the porcelain doll.

'Yes?' It was half-statement, half-question. Yes, I am Mrs Plumley; yes, what is it you want? Jill was surprised at how husky her own voice had suddenly become.

The girl's face lit into a broad, perfect smile. 'I'm Nicole Clark,' she said, extending her hand. 'I'm going to marry your husband.'

Everything stopped. Like a movie which suddenly snaps in mid-reel, the annual firm picnic of Weatherby, Ross jerked violently out of sync and was abruptly pulled from view.

It was one of those days. She'd known it from the minute her stomach had catapulted her out of bed toward the bathroom at not quite seven that morning to rebel against the shrimp dinner of the night before. David had followed her with his spray can of Lysol and there they had remained, alternately heaving and spraying, until Jill was able to sustain sufficient breath to yell at David to kindly stop that damn spraying – the smell was making her sick. He, in turn, wished her a happy anniversary – their fourth – and got back into bed, leaving her to contend with the final arrangements for picking up the two children from his previous marriage and bringing them to the picnic, an event they looked forward to with almost as much anticipation as a trip to the dentist's. Or a visit with their stepmother. On top of all that, Her Royal Highness, the first Mrs Plumley, had greeted Jill at the door to David's palatial former home – looking just past her as if she really wasn't there – to request that David and Jill also feed the children supper – she had a date.

An anniversary, an upset stomach, two hostile stepchildren,

her husband's ex-wife, and now this. Jill stared wordlessly at the girl, this Nicole Clark, who stared back as directly and pleasantly as if she'd just asked for her the correct time. Slowly, the scene around her began to re-form, regain its shape and colors, impose its reality on the absurdity of the situation. She was standing in the middle of some one hundred lawyers, all members of one of Chicago's largest and most prestigious law firms, their various spouses and offspring. It was a white-hot day in the middle of June; her sundress was sticking to her back and underarms; her white shoes were slowly burying themselves into the soft earth beneath her, and she was talking to a girl at least a decade younger than herself, with perfect skin and hair that didn't frizz up with the humidity, who had just informed her that she was going to marry her husband.

It had to be a joke. Someone – possibly even David – had put the girl up to it as a gag on their anniversary. Jill allowed her mouth to relax into a friendly grin, feeling a little foolish at having taken so long to catch on to what was happening.

'This isn't a joke,' the girl said, reading Jill's mind. 'I'm very serious.' Jill's grin stretched even farther across her face. This girl was good, whoever she was. Maybe even a professional actress brought in especially for the occasion. Or possibly she was a client of David's. That thought made Jill vaguely uncomfortable, recalling as it did a remark her mother had made to her once long ago and one she had confronted David with on their first memorable meeting. Then she had appeared in her role of brash young television producer and he as the ever-cocky, potential interviewee, one of the city's most successful divorce attorneys and quite probably the most gorgeous hunk of legal training she had ever seen. Without seeming to move her eyes, she had taken in his artistic face, his athletic body and his plain gold wedding band, and thought of her mother's caustic observance when her cousin Ruth had begun dating the divorced divorce attorney who had handled Ruth's own recent separation. Is it true, Jill had asked David almost six years previously, wishing that her mother's casual observations weren't so frequently uncannily astute, that divorce lawyers who are themselves divorced often fool around with their clients? I couldn't answer that, he had stated, a wicked half-smile slowly curling the corners of his mouth, I've never been divorced. How long have you been married? she pushed, knowing the question was irrelevant, not anywhere in her notes. Fifteen years, he said, his face suddenly without expression.

Jill continued grinning at Nicole, hoping nevertheless that she wasn't a client. She had also had enough of the gag and wished fervently that the girl, whoever she was, would just take her magenta fingernails and go home.

'I thought it was only fair to warn you,' Nicole continued, about to say more.

'That's enough,' Jill said, cutting her off abruptly, surprising them both with the sudden fierceness of her tone, the soft huskiness having disappeared altogether from her voice.

'I mean,' she continued, softening, 'you had me going a bit there, I admit it. So it was a cute gag and I'll get a good laugh out of it when I tell my friends, but the trick is to leave 'em laughing—'

'This isn't a joke,' the girl repeated.

Jill's mouth closed tight. Her voice turned low, barely audible against the sound of her heart pumping fresh blood past her ears. 'Then I think you better get the hell away from me.' Jill drew her body up to its full height, pushing her shoulders back as proudly as if she had just been named this year's Posture Queen, and stared down at Nicole Clark. I am not afraid of you, she shouted wordlessly. I am not afraid of you or your youth or your threats.

Nicole Clark shrugged, her smile undisturbed. With almost deliberate slowness, she turned in a half circle and disappeared into the well-dressed crowd.

Where was David? Jill suddenly wondered, spinning around quickly, feeling her body shaking with sudden indignation as she searched the crowd, recognizing that despite her earlier self-assurances, she had never been so afraid in all her thirty-four years. Her eyes narrowed as she caught sight of Nicole snaking her way languorously through the crowd, smiling comfortably at those she passed, obviously headed in a specific direction. Where? Jill watched her with fresh intensity.

'Jill Plumley!' The voice was male and carried with it a recognizable insistence. Reluctantly, Jill turned in its direction. 'I said to Harve, if anyone knows the answer to this one, it's Jill Plumley. Jill knows *trivia*.'

Jill smiled at Al Weatherby, the firm's original founding father, though he hardly looked the role with his wiry boy's body and wavy brown hair, and subtly angled her glance back toward the crowd. She couldn't find Nicole.

'Who's the girl who starred with Dick Benjamin in *The Marriage of a Young Stockbroker*?' he asked, his broad smile filling his face. 'I bet Harve Prescott fifty dollars you'd know the answer.' Harve Prescott hovered anxiously nearby.

'Joanna Shimkus,' Jill answered absently, her body shifting slightly.

'No, not the wife. The other one – you know, the other woman, the real sexy one who sprawled out on the bed and lifted her skirt—'

'Tiffany Bolling,' she answered, feeling her body being pulled like a magnet toward the crowd.

'Right!' she heard him call after her as she moved away. 'You're terrific! I knew you'd know! Did you hear that, Harve?'

Jill hoped she hadn't been too noticeably rude as she pushed herself farther into the crowd. Al Weatherby was more than just the kingpin of a successful law firm who had single-handedly built his own legal empire from its humble beginnings over a drycleaner's shop. He was the man most responsible for her husband's own rapid rise to prominence, the one who had recognized David's early potential and first brought him into the growing firm, nurturing and guiding him along the way, and in the process becoming a close personal friend. He had even taught the two wary novices to play bridge, displaying at all times the legendary patience he was noted for. She heard him laugh, turned in his direction in time to catch his playful wink, and realized she needn't have worried. Al Weatherby was not a man who took easy offense. Her mind returned quickly to the girl in the red T-shirt.

Nicole Clark had disappeared. Maybe she went home, Jill hoped, taking a deep breath and doing a quick turn. She caught sight of David's daughter, Laurie, sulking over by the dessert table (though she would never touch a bite of anything on it), and his son Jason halfheartedly deigning to participate in an impromptu game of hide-and-seek with some of the other, more animated youngsters. Were all teenagers this sullen? Jill found herself suddenly smiling, the thought of Nicole having to contend with these two delights making her feel instantly better. Laurie's younger brother, though not yet into his teens, bore an uncomfortable resemblance to his mother, and was almost unbearably shy. If either youngster smiled at all, especially in her presence, it was usually to the accompaniment of news that their mother was going back to court to ask for an increase in alimony payments or that she was about to recarpet the entire house in white plush because she was feeling a little low since her return from her holiday in Europe and was in need of perking up. For a man of David's considerable reputation, he'd certainly been taken for a royal ride when it came to his own divorce. Judges were always toughest on members of the legal profession, David had explained, quickly bypassing seventeen years of marriage, two children and an undisclosed number of illicit liaisons, their own included.

Laurie looked directly at her, shooting her a look filled with such perfect disdain that Jill almost had to admire the skinny child's skill, for it told her in a glance that not only was she still considered a homewrecker six years after the fact, an interloper, an outsider, a temporary inconvenience who would surely be discarded when their father came to his senses – in short, a total yuck – but she was also weird, dumb, gross and all those other peculiar adjectives fourteen-year-olds seem so drawn to.

I did not break up your parents' marriage, Jill tried to

communicate to the young girl with her eyes, recalling Elizabeth Taylor's choice remark when Eddie Fisher left Debbie Reynolds to her diaper pins and pigtails – you can't break up a happy marriage. Laurie turned away from Jill's gaze. Sure, she thought, expect a fourteen-year-old girl to buy that one! Did Debbie Reynolds buy it?

Jason appeared, accidentally brushing up against her side, the heel of his shoe jamming into her exposed toes. 'Oh,' he said, recognizing her. 'Sorry. Did – did I step on you?'

'It's all right,' Jill told him, trying subtly to extricate her right foot from the earth which now covered it. 'I have another one.' Jason looked close to tears. 'Sorry, old joke,' she continued, forcing a chuckle. 'So – are you having a good time?' Why was she asking that? Any idiot could see the answer.

'It's okay,' he answered slowly, so as not to stutter, a stutter which Elaine had been quick to point out had only developed *after* his father had left home, and which served as a constant reminder to David of his failure as a parent. The boy had lately taken to talking more slowly in an effort to control it. If only David's guilt could be as easily controlled, Jill thought, watching Jason, who always appeared so much older than his years. She could almost hear his mother's voice – you're the man of the house now, Jason.

For an instant, Jill felt the overwhelming urge to throw her arms around the young boy, but the look in Jason's eyes suddenly hardened and Jill felt herself pull back as Jason shuffled away, his growing boredom reflected in his walk. Maybe he'd find his father, persuade him to leave the picnic early.

Where was David?

Jill found him posed beneath a monstrous weeping willow – an appropriately dramatic setting, she thought – engaged in what even from this distance she could recognize was an earnest, and therefore, probably long, conversation with one of his partners, a conversation nobody would dare to interrupt. She felt her body relax a little, the acid in her stomach gamely trying to return to its normal level, admittedly never low.

Just looking at him made her feel good. People were always telling her he looked like Robert Redford, but even with his wheat-blond hair falling carelessly across his forehead and his mischievous pale green eyes, she thought that was stretching things a bit. What he was, however, was absolutely, unquestionably handsome, and if he lacked the singular presence that went into the making of a major movie idol, well, so what? She doubted that Robert Redford knew the difference between a tort and a tart. She only hoped David would remember, thinking unwillingly of Nicole Clark.

Undoubtedly, if you were going to be objective about it, they made the more appropriate-looking couple, her husband and this other woman. They complemented each other well, both sculpted from the same mold of casual perfection. Even her black hair co-ordinated with his blondness, each accenting and highlighting the other. The hell with being objective, Jill suddenly decided, shaking her own reddish mane, feeling several stray hairs sticking spitefully to her back. In happier moods, she told herself she looked like Carly Simon, but as no one else had ever commented on the resemblance, she had concluded that it must be somewhat subtle. At any rate, it didn't really matter. *She* was the one David had married – and he'd left one conventionally attractive woman in order to do so. Somehow the thought of her husband's earlier infidelity and divorce didn't make her feel any better. She wanted to go home. Perhaps she could plead illness – her stomach, the heat—

'So, how's university life?'

The voice startled her and she visibly jumped, turning to confront Beth Weatherby, wife of Al and one of the few office wives with whom she felt any sort of kinship at all.

'Fine,' Jill lied, seeing instantly that Beth didn't believe her.

'The hell it is,' laughed Beth, who was, at forty-five, twelve years younger than her husband. They had been married twenty-seven years, a fact which constantly amazed Jill: to know what it was you wanted when you were eighteen and to still want the same thing almost three decades later. 'I saw Al trying to corner you before,' Beth said, as if recognizing Jill's sudden change of thought. 'Honestly, a grown man and he's just like a kid. He sat up half the night trying to think up movie trivia that would stump you.' Jill laughed. 'You really miss it, don't you?' she asked suddenly.

'Miss what?' Jill asked, although she already knew the answer to the question.

'Television,' came the expected response.

'Yes,' Jill said simply, her attention suddenly diverted anew by the sight of Nicole Clark re-emerging and maneuvering her way toward David. Jill watched as her husband moved to include the newcomer easily in the conversation.

'Who is that?' she asked Beth Weatherby.

Beth looked toward the towering weeping willow. 'The girl

talking to your husband? I can't remember her name, but she's new. One of the law students, I think, working at Weatherby, Ross for the summer.'

'She's going to be a lawyer?'

'Al says she's very good. Very smart. In fact, now that I remember it, he hasn't spoken as highly of anyone since he met David and asked him to join the firm. He says she has an absolutely brilliant future ahead of her. Wouldn't you know she'd be absolutely gorgeous to boot!'

Jill felt her stomach beginning to turn over. 'Excuse me, I'm not feeling very well.' She retreated to an unoccupied corner of grass. She felt her heels submerge, locking her in place. Beth Weatherby was instantly at her side, pulling some large white pills from out of her yellow straw bag.

'Antacid,' she explained before Jill could ask. 'Take a couple.'

Jill did as she was told and put the two tablets in her mouth.

'Chew them.'

Jill began to chew, her face reflecting growing displeasure.

'I know, they're terrible. Taste just like chalk. But they work. I've been taking them for more years than I can remember. Ulcers,' she said, again not waiting for the obvious question.

'Why do you have ulcers?' Jill asked, genuinely surprised.

'Occupational hazard,' Beth said, smiling. 'Lawyer's wife.'

Not to mention having raised three children, Jill thought, remembering that David had recently told her that the youngest, a boy of seventeen, had dropped out of school to join the Hare Krishnas. At the same time David was telling her this, he had given Jill permission to shoot his own son should a similar insanity ever overtake the boy.

'Here, *this* should make you feel better,' Beth announced, pulling what Jill assumed was another pill out of her purse, and putting it into her outstretched hand. Jill looked at her palm. Not pills. Instead she saw a plain white envelope addressed to herself in Beth Weatherby's backhand scrawl. 'I thought you'd appreciate it,' Beth said, giving her a sly smile and then moving over to join a small cluster of other wives who promptly shifted their bodies to admit her. Like an amoeba swallowing its prey, Jill thought, seeing Beth virtually disappear, and turned her attention to the letter in her hand. She tore open the envelope and pulled out its contents.

The letter was to the point and neatly typed. Only her name had been written in by hand. She read it quickly and then read it again.

Dear *Jill*,

Are you bored in bed? Tired of waking up every morning to the same assortment of grunts and smells and complaints? Do you miss the excitement of those bygone days when his heart was bigger than his bald spot?

We know how you feel. We feel the same way. So we have devised a plan. Simply send your husband to the first name on the list below, cross that name off the list, and then add your own name to the bottom. Then make copies of this letter and send it to five of your friends. Within six months, you will receive 40,000 husbands.

But be careful – YOU MUST NOT BREAK THE

CHAIN! Two years ago, Barbie Feldman broke the chain and not only has she been stuck with poor old Freddie ever since, but her GE toaster-oven broke down and she was raped by her Maytag repairman! We don't want this to happen to you!

Why take a chance on misfortune? Come on – it beats ironing shirts. Just send your husband and add your name. Then do a favor for five of your friends. DO NOT BREAK THE CHAIN!

It was followed by a list of five names, Beth Weatherby's being the new addition at the bottom.

She laughed out loud, feeling instantly better. Leave it to Beth, she thought, looking toward the weeping willow, seeing her husband now alone in conversation with Nicole, feeling instantly worse.

She watched them talking, unaware of her attention. David seemed relaxed and happy. Even from this distance she could make out the roguish twinkle in his eyes. Suddenly, he threw his head back in laughter, undoubtedly the result of a hopelessly clever remark Nicole Clark had made. He caught her eye as he turned his head to push back the hair that had fallen out of place. Immediately, he smiled warmly, lifting his wine-glass in her direction for a silent toast. As she watched, he lowered his head toward Nicole, whispering something while the girl nodded acknowledgment. Jill's eyes traveled immediately to Nicole, who quickly trapped her gaze and returned it, lifting her own glass into the air in a toast exactly like David's. Her lips moved silently. 'Happy anniversary,' she said.

Chapter Two

The offices of Weatherby, Ross occupied two full floors of the ninety-four-story John Hancock center, and they were everything a Hollywood set designer could imagine – thick beige Berber carpeting against caramel suede walls covered with modern lithographs and tapestries, and corridors that wound their way lovingly in all directions, stopping at suitably spaced intervals for spacious offices with floor-to-ceiling windows and views appropriate to the rank and stature of the various inhabitants.

David Plumley's office was located just past the wide, interior, circular stairway and almost directly across the hall from the boardroom. His view – from the fifty-eighth floor – was spectacular. The office itself was a mess.

Jill Listerwoll had been ushered in politely and told that David Plumley would be in to see her momentarily. That had been almost twenty minutes ago, but Jill didn't mind, using the time to go over her notes and reread the information she had gathered from those lawyers she had already interviewed. Of all the offices she had been in that afternoon, this was by far the most disorganized. She had never seen so many papers or law books scattered about in so seemingly chaotic a fashion. The large oak desk was completely swamped, as were the bookcases, filled to bursting. Even the visitors' area – two blue-and-green-striped chairs hugging a round glass table – was piled high with legalese, and stacks of papers grew like ivy from the base of the walls. The artwork was interesting, detached in its blatant modernity. The only hint of a sense of humor lay in one of the lithos – a stark re-creation of a parking meter registering 'Expired,' which hung directly behind the desk and which, she surmised, was meant to serve as a subtle reminder to tardy clients that their time was up. There were no family portraits – appropriate, she thought, for one of the winningest divorce lawyers in town.

David Plumley walked into his office and sat down behind his desk. Jill took quick note of his blond hair, green eyes and boyish I-know-I'm-a-handsome-devil grin, felt the meter ticking behind him, and plunged right away into her first question, the one she had told her mother, with just the proper degree of disdain, that she had absolutely no intention of asking.

'Is it true that divorce lawyers who are themselves divorced often fool around with their clients?'

His mischievous grin grew wider. 'I couldn't answer that,' he said simply. 'I've never been divorced.'

'How long have you been married?' she continued, aware of the antique gold band on the appropriate finger of his left hand. It was an unnecessary ornament, she felt – everyone knew that the ones who looked like he did were invariably married.

'Fifteen years,' he said. His face and voice were suddenly flat. 'I'm sorry I kept you waiting.'

'Waiting?' For one crazy second, Jill felt he was in some way still referring to his marriage.

'I got tied up in the boardroom.' The mischievous grin was back on his face. Almost as if he could read her thoughts, as if he could sense the confusion into which her whole body had suddenly been thrust. 'Can I get you a cup of coffee?'

'No, thank you,' she said, looking around, hoping to avoid his eyes. 'I've had three cups already.'

'Then I'm not your first – interview, that is,' he continued coyly as her eyes crept slowly back in his direction.

'No, you're not,' she answered sharply. Surely they were both too old to be this cute. 'Is your office always such a mess?'

His voice was equally sharp, his answer as precise as her question. He needed no second hints. 'Yes,' he said. 'Now, what exactly can I do for you?'

She told him, slipping comfortably back into the role of TV producer, distancing herself from his cool green eyes. She was doing a news show on the elite of the Chicago legal profession, interviewing the three top firms (he questioned the other two choices) and trying to gain some insight into the way a firm of the size and scope of Weatherby, Ross functioned on a daily basis. Al Weatherby, whom she had interviewed first, had taken her on a general tour of the offices, had explained that the eventual goal of the large firm was to be even larger still, indeed the largest law firm in the city. There were eighty-five lawyers on staff, he had proudly explained, predicting an increase to one hundred within five years, and beyond as the firm expanded with time. Of the eighty-five lawyers, almost thirty were senior partners, the remainder consisting of juniors and associates. Each lawyer employed one full-time secretary, and there was an additional coterie of general office staff and law clerks. In addition to the individual offices and boardroom, there was a library, a cafeteria and two staff lounges. Al Weatherby had estimated their annual rental at around one million dollars.

The lawyers themselves fell into different categories. Basically, in decidedly non-legal terms, if there was a problem, there was also a lawyer to solve it. Corporate, criminal, tax, family, litigation, real estate – *et al*. They were all here. And doing very well, thank you.

'How much money do you make a year?' Jill asked David Plumley, trying to catch him off guard.

'Is that relevant?' he asked.

'I think so,' she said, looking directly at him. 'Considering that this *is* a show about the highest-paid members of your profession. I like to know roughly what I'm talking about.'

'Don't we all,' he mused, almost to himself. 'Six figures.'

'Over a hundred thousand dollars a year?'

'Six figures,' he repeated.

'Do you work on a contingency basis? The higher the settlement, the larger your share of the profits?'

'No, that's not my style.'

'Why not? What is your style?'

'I prefer to charge according to the amount of work I do, the time I spend. Contingency fees aren't always fair, in my opinion, although there are a great many highly reputable lawyers who would give you a good argument on that point.'

'But you don't like that system—'

'I prefer another method.'

'Moral ethics?'

'Possibly. We lawyers do have them, you know.' He smiled for the first time in several minutes. 'I feel like I'm being cross-examined.'

'What sort of day do you put in?' she asked, suddenly switching gears.

He shrugged, a touch of irony creeping into his voice. 'Oh, just your average fifteen-hour day – in by eight a.m., home by ten p.m.'

'That's only fourteen hours.'

Again he smiled.

'Do you feel it's "fair" – your word – to be making so much money from other people's misery?' she brushed on.

'I like to feel I'm putting an end to the misery. And yes, I think it's eminently fair. I work very hard.'

'What do you think of the charge that's been made by many parties involved in divorce actions that everything goes along fine until the lawyers get involved?'

'I think you've been talking to a lot of losers.'

Jill tried not to smile. 'You don't think it's true, then,' she began, shaking her head back, throwing off the temporary invasion of his charm, 'that a lot of women are really out for blood and that they often take the poor guy for everything he's got—'

'It may well be true,' he answered honestly. 'It's also true that a lot of men will try any number of dirty tricks to get away without paying their wives what they rightfully owe. And that's one of the problems. I think that a lot of women still don't understand all their rights under the law, despite the advent of women's liberation, and they don't realize just what they're entitled to. I *tell* them what they're entitled to.' He paused. 'And then I get it for them.'

'Are most of your clients women?'

'About two thirds.'

'What first interested you in the law?'

'I like to give advice.'

'And family law?'

He paused. 'I'm not really sure.' He shrugged. 'I tried out the various alternatives, didn't like real estate or criminal law, hated corporate and tax law although I was very good at it. I guess I just kind of drifted over to divorce. Are you married?'

'No.'

'Divorced?' An engaging tilt of his head.

'Single,' she stated with a touch of defiance. 'Never married. Spinster. Old maid.'

Her eyes challenged his – okay, buster, you started this. Where are you headed?

For his part, David Plumley saw a woman with large brown eyes and frantic reddish hair who took almost a perverse delight in downplaying how attractive she really was, hiding behind baggy pants, a shapeless shirt and a rough, even abrasive manner. He saw an independent, slightly fey kind of woman with an important, even glamorous, job who was trying very hard not to be attracted to him, and despite the fact that she was far from the prettiest woman he'd had in his office that day, she was as appealing to him at that moment as any woman he'd ever met.

The knock at the door interrupted their thoughts. Al Weatherby popped in to whisper that Warren Marcus was getting a little hot under the collar about everyone's tardiness and kindly requested that he please have all his dockets in by five o'clock.

'What are dockets?' Jill asked as soon as the door closed again, feeling grateful for the interruption, her pencil poised.

His answer was precise and well thought out, as if he were used to explaining things to novices, and enjoyed doing so. 'Dockets are time records that every lawyer keeps which set out, one, how long he worked on a particular matter, and two, what the matter was about. It's what I was mentioning briefly before when you asked about my style. Say, you come to me for a divorce and we spend two hours discussing it. When you leave, I get out my file marked Listerwoll, Jill, and I fill in "Two hours: discussed divorce petition." A few days later, you call me on the phone, you're worried your husband's going to sue for custody of the children. We talk for thirty minutes. When we're through, I get out your file and fill in "Thirty minutes: talk re custody." At the end of three months, I take your file and add up all the hours I've spent on your messy little marriage and multiply them by my hourly rate, so I can then send you a bill which also lets you know exactly what I've done. That is a docket.'

Jill smiled widely, immensely pleased he had remembered her whole name. 'You're cute,' she said, feeling herself suddenly relax, and they both laughed, Jill aware that this extraordinary-looking man could be had for the asking, feeling inexplicably very sorry for his wife. I wouldn't want to be married to a man

21

like this, she found herself thinking. A man you'd have to share with the world.

'What are you thinking about?' he asked.

She looked into his eyes and said nothing. He knows, she thought.

'Oh, you smell good,' he said, coming up behind her in the small bathroom and kissing the nape of her neck. Jill's back moved up against him instinctively, hoping for more. 'You almost finished in here?' he asked.

Jill put down the mascara she had been holding and looked at his reflection in the mirror. 'You know what my idea of luxury is?' she asked, not waiting for him to answer. 'Two bathrooms.'

He turned her around and kissed her on the mouth. 'You almost finished?' he asked again, smiling.

She groaned playfully. 'I guess I can brush my hair in the bedroom.'

He looked at her quizzically. 'I thought it was brushed,' he said.

'Thanks a lot.' She grabbed the brush and headed out into the hall.

'That was a compliment,' he called after her.

'Sure it was,' she said, plopping down on their queen-size bed and staring at herself in the mirror over the dresser. What had ever possessed her to paint the walls yellow? It was definitely the wrong color for her complexion, not to mention her hair. She ran an indifferent brush through the tangles, then got up from the bed and moved toward her image, stroking her hair with greater concentration and determination. When she was satisfied, she put the brush down and returned to the bed, trying to decide on what to wear. She'd narrowed her choice down to two outfits – a pink sundress or white pants with a lime-green halter top. She decided on the pants since it was foolish to wrinkle an expensive new dress on three hours of bridge. I've become so practical, she minced, thinking that the dress was, in fact, a year old. David walked into the room looking appealingly disheveled. Could this man never look less than gorgeous? she wondered. And what on earth did he see in her? It was a question she knew was in the minds of whoever saw the two of them together, of all the office wives, excepting Beth, who could never understand why he had discarded Elaine (why, Jill isn't even pretty, she had once overheard). Undoubtedly, Nicole Clark had asked herself that very question.

'Where's the brush?' David asked.

'On the dresser.' She pointed. 'Go ahead. Take it.'

'That's all right,' he said, good-naturedly, 'I'll wait until after you've used it.'

'Great.'

'What's the matter?'

'I just used it, you turkey!' she said, jumping up, the belt on her bathrobe coming loose to expose the naked body beneath it.

In a flash he had thrown her back across the bed and was scrambling on top of her, the two of them laughing so hard it was impossible to do anything else.

'I was just teasing you,' he said, throwing her arms up behind her head and pinning them there. 'You look magnificent. I think you are absolutely terrific-looking.' He started kissing her in earnest now and their laughter ceased as his hands moved expertly down her body.

The phone rang.

'It's for you,' she said. 'Guess who?'

'What makes you so sure it's Elaine?' he asked, stretching his arm across her to the telephone, without moving the rest of his body.

'Because she always calls at moments like this and besides, the dear thing only phoned twice today already. I take it you didn't return her calls?'

'I never return her calls.' He picked up the phone. 'You could be wrong, you know. Hello.' Jill waited for the inevitable, oh yes, hello, Elaine, and it followed immediately. She gazed up at the cracks in the ceiling while her husband, still lying on top of her, talked with obvious exasperation to his first wife.

'Yes, I saw your messages; no, I didn't bother returning your calls. I didn't have time for another argument about nothing.' He looked down at Jill, kissing her nose. 'I don't have the time now.' He paused long enough for Jill to catch the whine in the other woman's voice. The passion had left her, she realized with only a modest degree of surprise. The woman must have a television camera hidden somewhere in the room, Jill thought, so she knows each time exactly when to call. Pushing David aside gently, she maneuvered her body free of his and moved toward the walk-in closet, opened it, stepped inside and pulled out her white pants and green halter top.

'Of course I know Jason is going to camp at the end of next week. Who do you think is paying for it?!'

Jill went to the dresser and took out a pair of white panties.

'Why does he need a new sleeping bag? He has a perfectly good sleeping bag. So what if it's five years old? The parts don't stop working!'

Jill stepped into her panties and slipped into her lime-green halter top. She stared in the mirror. Who was she kidding? If you wanted to wear halter tops, you needed boobs. She thought of Nicole Clark, who'd have no trouble holding the damn thing up. She looked over at David. She hadn't told him of her conversation with the younger woman. What was the point? If anything, it would only perk his interest. What man wouldn't be intrigued by the sheer audacity of such an unprovoked declaration? Especially when the declaree looked like Nicole Clark. Especially when the man was David. She discarded the green halter top and returned to the closet.

'I don't care if the damn thing is ripped to kingdom come, I am not paying for a new sleeping bag. It's a thousand dollars a month at this camp you're sending him to – don't they have any beds?'

Jill selected a hot pink oversized shirt and threw it over her head, poking her arms through the wide sleeves.

'Look, Elaine, I'm not going to discuss it further. You think the kid needs a new sleeping bag, *you* buy him one – with the seventy-five hundred dollars a month I'm already paying you!'

Jill looked in the mirror. She looked pregnant, she thought, feeling suddenly light-headed at the prospect. Maybe, she hoped, silently calculating the number of days till her next period. She looked over at David, a shiver running through her.

He shook his head, covering the receiver with his hand. 'You look pregnant,' he whispered, obviously displeased by the notion. Of late, she had noticed his increasing reluctance to start a new family or even to discuss the possibility. Quickly she removed the pink shirt and returned it to the closet. David's voice brought her running back.

'What?' he yelled, raising his voice for the first time in the conversation. 'You're crazy, Elaine. Do what you want! You want to go back to court? Fine. We'll go back to court!' He slammed the receiver.

'She's going back to court?'

'She's making threatening noises.'

'What for this time? My God, don't tell me she heard I saved enough money to buy a new sweater?!' Jill was only half joking. Alimony, child support and taxes depleted the lion's share of David's income, making her job at the university not only one of convenience, but one of necessity. You're a kept man, she would sometimes tease her husband, trying to mitigate her hostility by laughing at what was eating at her, namely that all David's money seemed to go to his ex-wife and kids while all her money went to support the two of them. She'd been paying the rent on their downtown apartment since their marriage four years ago, despite the fact that the arrangement had supposedly been temporary. Not quite the life-style she'd envisioned.

'She says that she's thinking of asking for a cost-of-living clause because, well, you know, inflation.' Jill stared at her husband with blank eyes. She couldn't speak without risking anger, and what was the point of getting angry at David? It certainly wouldn't help matters. 'Is that what you're going to wear?' he asked. She looked down at her naked breasts and white slacks. 'Why the hell doesn't she get married again?' he asked, throwing up his hands.

Jill found herself back at the closet. 'Are you kidding?' she asked scornfully. 'That woman will *never* get married again. She's having much too good a time pulling the strings – purse and otherwise.'

David laughed ruefully. 'It would have to be a pretty special kind of guy – one who only likes to screw twice a year.'

Jill ran a hasty hand through her blouses, seeing prominent stains on the few she would have considered, wondering why she had ever bought the others to begin with. They were awful. 'Wear the green halter,' David said, squeezing past her to get at his own clothes. 'It looked cute.'

Jill grabbed the skimpy top, her thoughts immediately back on Nicole. She lowered it and turned to David. 'What do you think,' she asked, 'do we have time to finish what we started before?'

He checked his watch. 'We're due at the Weatherby's in exactly thirty-five minutes and Lake Forest isn't exactly around the corner.'

She dragged the green halter top down over her hair – what difference did it make? – and firmly closed the door.

'We'll finish when we get home,' he called after her. She nodded though she knew he wasn't looking. What made people live in the suburbs? Jill wondered, feeling frustrated and annoyed as she plopped on the bed and waited for David to finish dressing. She looked over at the phone. She always knows just when to call, Jill thought. Somehow, she knows.

Chapter Three

'One no trump.'

  'Pass.'

  'Two hearts.'

  'Pass.'

  'Pass.'

  'Pass.'

'Two hearts it is and my beautiful partner is playing,' said Al Weatherby, looking across the table at his wife of twenty-seven years. David led the king òf spades and Al Weatherby laid down his hand as dummy. 'Eighteen beautiful points. Too bad you don't have anything to go with it, honey,' he said, walking around the table to see what Beth had in her hand.

'Oh, Al, I'm so sorry,' Beth said, paling noticeably. 'I don't know where my mind was.' She laid her cards against her chest, hoping Al would choose not to look, and when he chose otherwise, she reluctantly brought her hand forward for him to see. 'I forgot everything!' she moaned.

'My God, look at what you've got here,' he said, his voice registering more shock than anger.

'I know. I know.' Beth's voice was barely audible.

'We've got at least a small slam between us and we're playing two hearts! Where are you tonight, honey?' Beth's eyes filled with tears. 'Oh, please don't cry, sweetie,' he said quickly. 'It's only a card game! I'm not angry. In fact, now that I see your cards better, I can see that two hearts is the perfect bid. I would have said exactly the same thing.'

Both David and Jill laughed and Beth tried to laugh too, but couldn't. Jill felt so sorry for Beth – she'd been playing very badly all night despite her years of experience at the game. At least Al was the kind of partner who never lost his temper. It was, as he had said, just a game.

'Just play it, honey,' Al said, returning to his seat. 'You can't go wrong.'

Beth played out the hand in silence, missing only one trick and easily making the small slam she should have bid. She smiled over at Al sheepishly at the hand's conclusion.

'You should have finessed the king at trick three,' he said patiently, gathering up the cards. 'That way you would have had them all – you had nothing to lose.'

'Let's have some coffee,' Beth said, getting up from the table and bumping into Jill's chair. She let out a short, involuntary gasp.

'Are you okay?' Jill asked, concerned.

Beth nodded. 'Just that I keep hitting the same spot all the time. You know what they say about open wounds.' She stopped. 'Do they say anything about open wounds?' she asked and everybody laughed. Jill's offer of assistance in the kitchen was turned down as they moved from the card room to the large

30

and comfortable living area, filled to overflowing with expensive antiques.

'I'll help Beth,' Al volunteered, making sure his guests were comfortable first. 'That was a real cute chain letter Beth sent out, wasn't it? God, I had such a good laugh about it. By the way, Jill,' he said suddenly, a mysterious glint creeping into his eyes, 'who were the three women who starred in *A Letter to Three Wives*?'

'Jeanne Crain, Ann Sothern, and Linda Darnell,' Jill answered without a moment's hesitation. 'You want the men's names, too?'

'Are you kidding? A good lawyer always knows when to quit. Isn't that right, David?'

David nodded. 'She's the champ.'

'Thought it might be before her time.'

'I watch a lot of old movies,' Jill said, remembering the days when it had not been uncommon for her to watch a whole string of late-night features only to stumble in to work on an hour's sleep, fresh images of Joan Crawford rolling around in her brain.

She didn't stay up all night watching old movies anymore. David started his day at six-fifteen in the morning. He liked to be in bed early, and he claimed he couldn't get to sleep if she wasn't in bed beside him.

'Let's see, David, you like cream, no sugar, right?' Al Weatherby asked, already heading toward the large hallway. Jill thought that you could pick up their whole apartment and plop it right in the middle of that hallway and still have lots of room to move around.

David nodded. 'And, Jill, you like yours black.' It was a statement, not a question.

'Please.'

'I think Beth made an extraordinary blueberry flan,' he said. 'If you'll excuse me, I'll go help her and be right back.'

Jill watched Al Weatherby leave the room. He was only minimally taller than herself, an elf-like man of seemingly boundless energy and patience, his thin body made surprisingly muscular because of an early and deep interest in lifting weights. It was said he could survive on virtually two hours' sleep a night, and David had once commented that in the fifteen years he had been with the firm (the last eight as a senior partner) he had never seen Al Weatherby lose his temper. Al also made a point of ferreting out as much information as he could about the spouses of the lawyers in his corporation. When he'd learned that Jill was as addicted to trivia and the Classified Ads section of the morning paper as he was, she'd become his special favorite. His acceptance of her had made her acceptance by the other lawyers and their spouses (especially those who had known and liked Elaine) infinitely easier.

'What letter is he talking about?' David asked, settling back comfortably into the soft velvet of the old Victorian sofa. For an instant, Jill thought he must be talking to someone else.

'Oh, the chain letter – about the husbands. You know – didn't I show it to you?' He shook his head. 'Oh, well, I still have it – somewhere. Beth gave it to me at the picnic.' Her voice faded away.

'The picnic,' David repeated ominously. 'Are you going to tell me what happened at the picnic?'

'What are you talking about?'

'Something happened at that picnic that you won't tell me about, and every time I mention it, your face goes kind of funny and your eyes get this curious kind of dazed look about them – there, they've got it right now.' Jill blushed. 'And you're blushing! You never blush.'

'I'm not blushing,' Jill said, trying to laugh away the truth of his words. 'You're crazy.' She looked around. 'Such a huge house for just the two of them.'

'A not very subtle attempt at trying to change the subject,' he winked.

'They have such gorgeous kids,' she continued, ignoring him and concentrating on a beautifully framed portrait of the three Weatherby offspring which hung above the large marble fireplace.

'Not exactly kids anymore,' David reminded her. 'The youngest is seventeen.' David shook his head in obvious dismay, his mouth opening again to speak.

'I know,' Jill interrupted. 'If Jason ever starts reciting the Moonie alphabet, I have your permission to shoot him.'

'Is that what they recite?' he asked. Jill shrugged playfully. 'Smart-ass,' David said, pulling her closer beside him, about to kiss her.

The scream from the kitchen sent them scrambling to their feet. Jill made it to the kitchen door only seconds before her husband, and both rushed immediately to Beth Weatherby's side when they saw the blood.

If anything, Al Weatherby was even whiter than his wife. 'What the hell happened, Beth?' he was saying, his voice almost icily calm. 'Christ, I turn my back for two seconds and you almost kill yourself—' He turned on the cold water tap and grabbed Beth's arm, thrusting her blood-covered hand under the flow. She screamed again at the sudden impact of water on flesh, the force of the spray quickly washing the blood away to reveal a deep cut that ran almost like a second lifeline across the width of her hand, just below the base of her fingers.

'I don't know how I did it,' Beth was saying, holding back the tears. 'I was cutting the flan and I must have made the crust too hard because – ow! – the knife kind of caught, and so I jiggled it, and the next thing I knew, wham, right across my hand. Jesus, that hurts!'

'Hold still,' Al Weatherby said calmly, the color returning to his face. 'There's a lot of blood. I don't know. Maybe we should take you to the hospital.'

'No,' his wife insisted. 'Please, I'll be all right. There's some gauze upstairs—'

'I'll get it,' David offered, already out of the room.

'First bathroom on the right,' Al called after him. 'It's that damn phone call from Lisa, isn't it?' he stated more than asked. Then he turned to Jill. 'Having a bit of trouble with our daughter,' he explained, still keeping his eye on his wife's bleeding hand. 'Seems she's gotten herself involved with some musician – married, naturally.'

Naturally, Jill thought.

'Little children, little problems,' David said in the car on the long drive home. 'Big children, big problems. It's not worth it, Jill, believe me. It's just not worth it.'

* * *

They'd been driving for some twenty minutes.

'It's just around the corner – there, that house on the left, number ninety.'

David pulled the car into the first available space. The street was narrow and dark, lined on both sides with semi-detached homes which had probably been quite elegant in their day but which were now showing definite signs of neglect and the decay wrought by the onslaught of the Chicago weather. 'It doesn't look very safe,' he said, bringing the car to a halt.

Jill smiled. 'Oh, it's safe. I'm on the second floor and my landlady lives down below with her two pets – a Doberman and a shotgun.'

'The American way,' David laughed.

Jill was about to open the car door when she hesitated, realizing how reluctant she was to leave this man. 'I want to thank you,' she began.

'Don't thank me,' he interrupted. 'It was a purely selfish gesture on my part. I'm only sorry you don't live farther away; then I'd get to enjoy your company a little longer.'

Jill smiled, thinking back over the afternoon in his office. She had finally stopped acting so belligerent, and had listened to what David Plumley was saying, allowing his humor and his personality to temper her hostility, a hostility which she knew had only developed when she felt herself so instantly attracted to him, when she realized he knew exactly what she was feeling, and she was embarrassed and afraid. She'd accepted his offer of a cup of coffee, and listened to him hold court on everything she could hope to know about the legal profession and the people who practiced it. One hour quickly became another, as all calls and other appointments were put on hold or canceled. It was close to 6 p.m. when she realized with some disappointment that any further questions she might ask would have absolutely nothing to do with law and everything to do with his wife and family and the obvious possibility of other women. He, in turn, offered to drive her home, and she readily accepted, despite the fact that her car was parked in the underground parking lot. What the hell, she'd go back for it the next day.

She pushed open the heavy car door. 'Well – thanks again – for everything.' She stopped, once more turning in his direction. 'I feel kind of guilty about having taken up so much of your time,' she lied, deciding that having come so far, she might as well push ahead all the way. 'If you weren't married, I'd invite you inside for dinner.'

His answer was simple. 'I'm separated,' he said, neglecting only to mention that by separated, he meant his wife was at home with his children while he was here in his car with Jill.

'I'm sorry,' he said, abruptly sitting up in bed. 'I know I'm keeping you up. I just can't seem to get comfortable.'

Jill sat up beside her husband and peered over at the clock. It was almost three-thirty in the morning. 'We shouldn't have had all that coffee,' she said, thinking back to the large pot they had brewed and drunk as soon as they walked through the door of their apartment. They had left the Weatherby house when Beth's bleeding had stopped and her hand was safely bandaged up. Al had suggested his wife go right up to bed, and though

Beth protested, Jill and David had thought it best that they leave. The blood had made Jill vaguely queasy herself, and David's vehemence in the car about not fathering any more children had upset her further. Coffee seemed the only viable solution. They had finished the pot, gotten undressed and into bed, and drifted into a restless and unsatisfying sleep, forgetful of their earlier desires, wanting only to disappear into their pillows until morning.

'Do you want anything to eat?' she offered.

'What is there?' he asked, straightening his shoulders.

'Some cheesecake—' He shook his head. 'Some of that rice pudding I made from the other night—'

'No.'

'Do you want to call in for a pizza?'

He laughed quietly. 'No – food's not the answer.'

'Ginger ale? Juice?'

'No.' He peered into the darkness. 'Shit,' he muttered with frustration.

'You want me to rub your back?'

He tilted his head. 'Yeah, that's what I want,' he smiled, flipping over. Jill immediately climbed on top of him, her hands working on his shoulders.

'How's that?' she asked after several minutes, her hands tiring.

'Awful,' he said gently. 'You always did give the world's worst backrubs.'

'Oh, is that so?' she asked, suddenly pounding on his back. 'Well, how's this?'

'Better,' he laughed, flipping her over and crawling on top

of her, quickly entering her and starting to thrust. 'Much better.'

Later they lay very still, side by side, their breathing even, their eyes open, relaxed but still not sleepy.

'So,' he said suddenly, 'are you going to tell me what happened at the picnic?'

'What do you mean?' she asked, startled.

'Jill,' he said, patiently, 'you haven't been yourself the last few days. You're as bad as Beth Weatherby – walking into walls, changing your clothes fifty times a day—'

'I am not. I haven't been—'

'How many times did you change tonight?'

'I don't know what you're getting at. The picnic was fine. Nothing unusual happened.' She felt herself beginning to blush. 'Why do I feel like if I tell one more lie my nose will fall off?'

David laughed. 'Because you're as transparent as Pinocchio, that's why. Now, tell me what happened.'

Jill sat up, bringing her knees to her chest and leaning her head against them. 'I don't understand how you always know what I'm thinking.'

'I don't know *what* you're thinking – only that you *are* thinking. Come on, you know you can never keep anything from me. Are you going to tell me?' He waited, saying nothing.

Jill tried to choose her words carefully. What could she say? How could she tell him without maximizing the inherent appeal her words would carry? Listen, David, you know that brilliant and beautiful law student that's working for the summer in your office – the one with the big tits and the flawless complexion – well, she wants to marry you. She tossed the words around in her head a few more times, trying to make them sound funny, casual, non-threatening. Guess what? she tried silently, there's another woman in love with you—

'Well?' he asked.

'This is going to give your ego a real boost,' she began nervously, wondering why she was so afraid of telling him. 'I'm just telling you this because I trust you so much—'

He laughed. 'Oh, lay on the old guilt,' he bellowed. 'Make me feel so guilty in advance, I won't be able to enjoy it – whatever it is! Are you going to tell me?'

'It's about Nicole Clark,' she stated directly, plunging right in.

'Who?' he asked earnestly.

'Nicole Clark,' she repeated.

He looked genuinely puzzled. 'Who's Nicole Clark?'

Jill's face broke into a wide grin; she felt instantly better. 'You really don't know? She works in your office. Or at least, she's there this summer – she's a student. Dark hair, young – pretty, if you like that perfect kind of type – you were talking to her for quite a while at the picnic—'

David's eyes reflected his confusion. She could actually see him trying to piece together the various parts of the invisible puzzle, trying to put a face to the name Nicole Clark. Pretty . . . dark hair . . . student . . . 'Oh, Jeez, Nicki, of course. Nicole Clark! You made her sound so formal. Pretty, you said? She's gorgeous!'

He obviously liked that perfect sort of type. Jill felt her face muscles tense. 'So, you know who I mean,' she said unnecessarily.

'Of course. Bright, *bright* girl. Nice, too. Very sensitive.'

'I'm sure,' Jill said, flopping backward onto her pillow, her back rigid.

'What's the matter?'

'Oh, nothing. Just that that gorgeous, bright, nice, sensitive person informed me at the picnic that she intends to marry you.'

For several seconds, David said absolutely nothing. Then he started to laugh.

'I'm not sure I see what's so funny,' Jill said quietly, trying not to pout.

David kept laughing. 'Well, it was a *joke*, for heaven's sake.' He laughed even louder. 'That's very funny. I didn't realize she had such a sense of humor.'

'Now she has a sense of humor too. Wonderful,' Jill muttered.

'Jill, come on, you're not really upset, are you?'

Jill's voice was louder than she had intended. 'Why shouldn't I be upset? Some girl tells me she's going to marry my husband and my husband makes me feel much better by telling me she's a) gorgeous, b) smart, c) sweet and d) sensitive. Oh, and I almost forgot e) she has a wonderful sense of humor.'

David was suddenly all over her, kissing her face and neck, tickling her sides. 'Come on, you silly goose. What are you upset about, huh? You know I love you. Well, don't you?' Reluctantly, she found herself nodding. 'So, why do you let a silly little joke upset you?'

'Because it wasn't a joke. She told me that. She made it very clear.'

David sat up. 'Tell me exactly what she said.' Jill related the Sunday afternoon conversation to the best of her ability, trying to keep her voice as flat as possible.

'Still think it's all a joke?' she asked.

David's voice was suddenly very serious. He looked directly at his wife. 'I love you,' he began. 'I love you very much. It's why I married you. And I have absolutely no intention of marrying anyone else. Do you understand? Or even looking at anyone else. You are the only one I want or need or will ever want or need. In other words, you, lady, are stuck with me. For keeps. If Nicole Clark was serious, she's a very foolish girl and I'm extremely disappointed in her behaviour.'

Jill felt her eyes fill up with tears of love and gratitude. She repeated his words over and over in her mind, trying to stop herself from wondering if he had ever said anything similar to Elaine, trying to stifle the sound of her mother's initial warning when she had told her she was involved with a married man: 'If he'll do it to one woman,' she had said plainly, 'he'll do it to you.'

'Go away, Mother,' she muttered.

'What?'

Jill laughed. 'Nothing.'

'Why are you crying?'

She shook her head. 'I love you,' she said as he kissed away her tears.

'Well, then, do me a favor,' he said, kissing her nose. 'Keep remembering that *I* love *you*, and that you're as beautiful as any woman I've ever known.'

He kissed her mouth. 'Now hold me,' he commanded gently, turning over and feeling her crawl into the space around him, their limbs resting comfortably against each other. She was almost asleep when he started to laugh. 'I can't believe Nicki actually said that!'

Jill said nothing, feigning sleep. Instinctively, her body moved closer, hugged him tighter to her. Damn him, she thought sullenly, any hopes she'd had for sleep vanishing, he's interested.

Chapter Four

Jill tossed restlessly, vaguely aware that it was morning and probably time to get up. She wasn't ready yet – her eyes were still unwilling to open themselves to the light she knew was trying to crawl beneath the bedroom curtains, and her body was tense and sore from lying in all the wrong ways. If only she'd been able to sleep for a few hours, she thought as she reluctantly opened her eyes, swallowing the nausea that always developed when she didn't get enough rest, and looking over at the clock radio which was mysteriously sitting on the end table beside her. What was it doing there? she wondered, feeling suddenly disoriented. It was always on David's side of the bed. At precisely 6 a.m. every weekday morning, David's hand would blindly reach for the right button, his face remaining submerged beneath the blankets, and abruptly silence whoever was rocking them awake. With no need for further alarms, David would sit up in bed fifteen minutes later, and head for the bathroom. Whatever it was he did in there took exactly one hour. (She had once timed his activities – five minutes in the shower, ten minutes to shave, thirty seconds to brush his teeth, and another five minutes to blow-dry his hair. That left thirty-nine minutes and thirty seconds unaccounted for, and when she once asked him, 'What is it that you *do* in there for so long?!' he had winked and said, 'Ask my mother. She trained me.') Men put such a premium on their precious bowels, Jill thought, closing her eyes again. Every morning like clockwork or you'd think the world was coming to an end. Jill thought quickly of the large container of Metamucil on the bottom shelf of the medicine cabinet. It was there for just such an emergency. She laughed silently. She was the one who should be taking it, with her regular irregularity. She often went as long as three or four days without— Her eyes opened suddenly, shooting back at the clock. It was after eight! David was usually long-gone by this hour. Perhaps he had already left, having completed his morning rituals in absolute silence. Had he come in to wake her up at seven-thirty the way he always did? She couldn't remember his mouth grazing the side of her cheek the way he did to say good morning and have a good day. She couldn't remember anything having happened at all.

And if it hadn't – if the alarm hadn't gone off for the first time in four years (probably because whoever moved it had loused up something inside) – that meant that they had overslept and David would be late for court that morning. She remembered he had to be in court by nine o'clock. Frantically, she turned towards her husband.

'David—' She stopped short at what she saw.

They were lying together beside her, wrapped up in each other's arms, their legs encircling each other's hips which were rotating grotesquely, their hair falling across each other's faces, so that at first she couldn't make out who exactly they were. Jill sat up in bed and moved closer to the couple who were obviously ignorant or unmindful of her presence. She pulled back the blanket and watched in wonderment as their bodies slapped against each other, flapping like fish at the bottom of a rowboat, colliding and retreating in endless repetition. She saw the woman's ample bosom squashed beneath the light blond hairs of her husband's chest, heard her husky voice whisper something in David's ear. 'She's watching,' she knew the girl had said, wondering why she was able to hear so clearly. David laughed and swung their bodies around so that the girl was now on top. His hands reached up and suddenly pushed the girl's body away, so that the large breasts and effortlessly flat stomach were thrown back, arching up toward the ceiling. They remained locked together as her black hair fell away from her face. She was laughing. Slowly, she turned her head to stare directly at Jill. It was her mother!

Jill sat up in bed with a start, a loud gasp escaping her mouth, her eyes fully open and on the alert. In the next instant, David was awake beside her.

'My God, Jill, what's the matter? Are you going to be sick?'

Jill's eyes moved immediately to her husband's startled face. He looked terrified.

'Jill?' he asked. 'Answer me – are you going to be sick?'

It took a minute for Jill to come to terms with the fact that she and David were alone in the bed and that what had transpired had all been a peculiar dream. It had felt so real.

'I had the most ridiculous dream,' she said slowly, in amazcment.

'Jesus,' David muttered, falling back against his pillow. 'Jesus.'

'Well, I didn't do it on purpose,' Jill said in her defense. 'Wow, was it strange! And in such detail.'

'What time is it?' David asked, retreating under the covers.

Jill looked over at the end table beside her. The clock radio was gone.

'Where's the radio?' she asked in alarm.

Once again, David shot up in the bed, looking at the table to his right. 'What's the matter with you? It's right here. Where it always is.' Jill looked over in his direction. 'And it's five to six, for God's sake. I could have slept five more minutes.' He looked anxiously at his wife. 'Is there any point in my trying to lie down again?'

'I should have known it was a dream when the clock was on the wrong side of the bed,' she said, watching David lie back and roll over. 'That was the tip-off.' She lay down beside her husband, hugging his back to her stomach. 'Not to mention my mother.'

'What are you muttering about?' he asked, his voice muffled against the pillow.

It was a question that required no answer. Indeed, it was a question that precluded any answers, that almost dared her to try. She recognized the tone. It meant be quiet and let me get some sleep. Jill felt herself going over the events of her dream, losing them as they ran to get away from her conscious self. By the time David's hand reached up to silence the musical alarm (Barbara Streisand and Barry Gibb doing 'Guilty'), all but the image of her mother's face on Nicole's body – she knew it was

Nicole's body welded to David's groin – had disappeared.

David sat up in bed and stretched. Jill waited for the feel of the bed emptying as his body moved quickly out, but instead she felt cold, a draft, like her blanket, reaching up and covering her from her feet to her shoulders.

'Out of bed,' he said, playfully, pulling at her arms, her completely exposed body curling into itself against his sudden invasion. 'Come on, you cost me five minutes of sleep. Time to pay the penalty.' He let go of her hands and began pulling at her feet.

'What are you doing?' she laughed, kicking at him. 'Go away. You know I have another hour and a half! What are you doing?' She screamed, laughing helplessly, as she felt herself being tugged onto the floor. He grabbed her ankles. 'What are you doing? Where are you taking me?'

She opened her eyes, tears of laughter running down her cheeks, and watched his nude body (magnificent, she told herself, even at six in the morning) dragging her nude body (less than magnificent, she thought, trying to cover the slight rounding at her belly) across the bedroom carpet. 'Watch my head!' she shrieked, as they rounded the corner and moved out into the hall. 'Where are you taking me?'

'You need a shower,' he said.

'Oh, no!' Jill screamed, starting to struggle in earnest. 'Not at six in the morning, I don't need a shower! No!' She yelled again as David pulled her into the small washroom.

'You're lucky this floor is carpeted,' he said over her squeals, one hand holding firmly onto her foot, as he reached up and, leaning over the tub, turned on the shower. Jill kicked at him frantically with her free leg before she felt his arms grab her around the waist, lift her struggling body up into the air and deposit her with seemingly no effort at all under the forceful spray of the shower.

'Shit,' she screamed. 'It's freezing!'

'Sorry,' he said, quickly adjusting the taps and climbing in after her.

'You're getting my hair all wet,' she yelled, starting to laugh again.

'It needs washing.'

'I just washed it!' She squirmed along the side of the tub.

Again David picked her up and deposited her directly under the flow. Every time she tried to protest, her mouth filled up with water, so she stopped trying to speak and recognized that she was actually enjoying the water and the sheer force of it as it pelted her body. She was aware of his hands now on her breasts, soaping them with a gentle massage, moving down to her stomach. In another few seconds, he was inside her, pounding her back against the tile, moving her up and down against the taps. If this is another dream, she thought, it sure beats the last one.

Her mind flashed back to almost five years ago, the night he had come to her door at two in the morning, drunker than she had ever remembered seeing anybody – the only time during their illicit romance that he had stayed till the morning. Abruptly, she was back in the present, the water stopping as David maneuvered his wet body away from her own, kissing her sweetly on the lips. 'Get out of here,' he whispered. 'I have work to do.'

She laughed. 'You always were terrific under water,' she said, confident he would understand her reference. He gave her backside an affectionate pat as she struggled out of the tub and into a waiting towel. 'I'll make some breakfast,' she said.

'I'll be a while,' he answered.

'Yes, I know,' she said, backing out of the room, closing the door behind her and heading down the familiar hallway.

It was six thirty-five. She had an extra hour before she really had to be up. David would be in the bathroom for another forty minutes. She could crawl back into bed and try to get some more sleep. Or she could do some exercises, she thought, drying herself off and dropping the towel to stare at herself nude in front of the mirror. Definitely some exercises, she decided, lying on the floor and bringing her knees to her chest, rolling them back and forth from side to side. Beth had told her about an exercise class and suggested that the two of them join. She'd have to call Beth and ask her about it. She'd definitely like to start. Her body was falling apart. Had David noticed?

Jill kept her knees bent and put the bottoms of her feet on the floor. Cupping her hands behind her head, she tried to sit up. 'Oh, my God,' she said, 'this is ridiculous.' She managed to get herself in a sitting position. Beth, she thought, visions of Beth's bleeding hand before her eyes. She wondered how she was this morning, if the bleeding had stopped. The cut had been deep, very unpleasant-looking. She'd call Beth after her nine o'clock class.

The thought of her morning class made her instantly depressed, all those bright, young faces waiting eagerly for her to unleash the vast secrets of her experience and expertise. She hadn't even thought about today's lecture, what she was going to say to these youngsters who still thought that all you needed was a college degree and a love of film to be able to walk up on the stage and collect your Academy Award. They would all be in her classroom at the sound of the bell, waiting for her words of wisdom. What could she tell them? That she was bored to tears and wished she were anywhere else? What was she doing stuck in a classroom? She was meant to be out there in the real world, directing its violent outbursts and capturing history as it stumbled forward in all its trivial displays. She was meant to be moving!

What was she doing here on the floor? she wondered suddenly, pushing her body up with her elbows. This isn't going to work, she told herself, standing·up. She needed the discipline of the classroom she hated if she was going to get her body back in shape. She selected a mauve cotton dress from her closet and put it on, wrapping the towel around her head as she moved from the bedroom, down the hall to the front door.

The morning paper was waiting. The paper boy was always very prompt – he must get up at dawn, Jill thought, bringing the paper into the kitchen and laying it on the counter as she poured some coffee into the percolator. The headlines were as depressing as usual – the economy was going all to hell; they were in the midst of a recession which was in all probability leading them toward a depression; the arms race was back in bloom; the IRA and the PLO were doing business as usual. Wonderful, she thought.

'Do you want some eggs?' she called toward the bathroom.

'No thanks,' David yelled back. 'Just toast and coffee.'

Jill reached for the bread basket and took out several pieces of white bread. David was always telling her to buy whole wheat, but she hated the taste, and stuck stubbornly to the Wonder Bread she had known since childhood. Leaving the coffee to perk and the bread to sit until David was ready to toast it, she picked up the paper and went into the den.

The large leather chair beckoned invitingly and she plopped herself down, flipping quickly through the paper. She felt strangely assured to note that in addition to the latest in floods, fires and other natural disasters, Chicago could still be counted on to produce its share of murders, rapes and robberies. Jill moved directly to the Classified Ads and Companions Wanted columns. She settled comfortably back and began to read.

The ad caught her eye immediately:

WANTED

Black, attractive man, 6'1", professional banker, separated, no ties, from upper middle class family, planning to return home to West Indies in December, seeks attractive, exuberant, intelligent, plump, sensuous Caucasian female accountant.

Now, that's telling them, Jill thought, laughing out loud. No room for error here. It was all spelled out perfectly clearly. Exactly what the man desired. Her eyes quickly ran down the rest of the Companions Wanted columns. It seemed that all sorts of gorgeous, intelligent, successful people were out there looking for friends. Friends? she asked herself. An interesting choice of words.

Sensuous, caring professional man desires to meet beautiful, shapely sylph with warmth and rhythm.

Rhythm this one wanted, not friendship. What motivated these people? she wondered. Who were the faces behind the often bizarre requests? More to the point, did they really get everything they seemed to want? Do any of us? she wondered skeptically, flipping over the page to the Birth and Death Notices. All she needed was one really gross announcement to make her day. She found it.

Frey, Joel and Joan (nee Sampson) are thrilled to announce that Joel wasn't just shooting blanks all those cold winter nights! Twins Gordon and Marsha greeted the new day at a very respectable 6 lbs. and 5 lbs. 10 oz. respectively, shrieking their approval of the pains to which their parents had gone. (Especially Mom!) We thank Dr Pearlman and the entire staff of Women's College Hospital.

Jill closed the paper, hearing her coffee beginning to perk in the kitchen.

The phone rang just as she finished pouring herself a cup. Jill glanced automatically at the clock. It was barely 7 a.m. Even Elaine wouldn't have the nerve to call this early. Unless it was an emergency. Jill reached anxiously for the phone.

'Hello?'

'Is David there, please?'

The voice was dark and husky and definitely not Elaine's. Jill recognized it immediately. 'Who is this?' she asked anyway.

'It's Nicole Clark,' came the reply. 'I hope I'm not disturbing you.'

I'm sure, Jill said silently. 'Is something wrong?' Jill asked.

'No,' the voice replied quietly. 'I just wanted to make sure I talked to David before he left. I know he leaves very early in the mornings.'

'Well, he's in the bathroom,' Jill said in distinctly businesslike tones, trying not to sound too territorial. 'He can't come to the phone right now.' Your fiancé is taking a shit, she wanted to yell. Instead she said, 'Can I take a message?'

There was a moment's hesitation. Then Nicole's soft tones floated gently to Jill's ears. Each word stuck against her scalp like a pin on a paper donkey's tail. 'It's kind of a complicated message. Maybe he better call me back.'

I'm not exactly an idiot, Jill told the other woman wordlessly. I know how to take a message. Aloud she said, 'As you like. What's your number?'

Nicole Clark began to recite her phone number as Jill looked frantically by the phone for a pencil. 'Just a minute,' she interrupted. 'I can't find a pencil.'

'Who is it?' David shouted from the bathroom.

Jill paused. 'Nicole Clark,' she called in his direction, wishing she could see the look on his face.

It was David's turn to pause. 'What does she want?'

'She wants you to call her back.'

'Okay. Get her number.'

Good idea, Jill decided, rummaging through a drawer and finally locating a pencil that wasn't broken.

'All right, I have one,' she said into the phone. '531—?'

'1-7-4-1.' Nicole completed.

'He'll call you,' Jill said.

'Thank you,' the other woman purred.

Jill replaced the receiver and growled at the telephone. 'Keep your legal little fingers away from my husband,' she whispered, picturing Nicole's long purple nails and comparing them to her own short, chewed and tattered ones. Her embarrassed fingers, the obvious loser in any contest, encircled her coffee cup, and she quickly lifted it to her mouth.

Why had Nicole called? Did she really need some early-morning information or was it all a ploy, a simple part of her master plan to capture her husband and ferret him away? Keep the little wifey nice and edgy, she thought.

Jill took a long, slow sip of her coffee and opened the pantry door, coming face to face with at least half a dozen stale donuts. She reached up and grabbed two of them. Just what I need, she thought, trying to figure out exactly what it was that Nicole was doing. 'Enough of this,' she said aloud, then finished the rest of the thought in silence. If I'm going to worry about every little number who looks lustingly after my husband, I'm going to drive myself nuts. Probably exactly what she has in mind, Jill decided, taking a big bite out of one of the donuts, thinking at the same time that Nicole Clark – Nicki to her intimates – had done more than just look. She had brazenly announced her intentions. Jill swallowed the rest of the donut. The hell with it, she thought. That's her problem, not mine. She took a bite out of the second donut. She'd definitely have to phone Beth later about that exercise class.

She heard the bathroom door open and once again looked up at the clock. David couldn't be finished in there already – it was too early. He appeared in the doorway draped in a towel.

'She wouldn't say what she wanted?' David asked, carefully avoiding the mention of her name.

'Apparently she doesn't trust me to take a message,' Jill answered, automatically pouring David a cup of coffee and adjusting it to his specifications. 'There's the number,' she said, pointing to a piece of scrap paper. 'You're finished early today,' she noted.

'She probably wants to know what courtroom,' he said, almost absently. 'She asked yesterday if she could sit in this morning, you know, to observe.'

'Of course,' Jill said, finishing off her donut and walking toward the den. 'I'll leave you two alone.'

David laughed and picked up the phone. Jill heard him dialing as she walked into the den and sat back down in the leather chair. The morning paper was where she had left it. She retrieved it and began perusing the real estate section. From the kitchen, she heard David's voice. 'Hello, Nicki. It's David Plumley.' Both names, she noted. He's keeping it formal. 'What can I do for you?' I'll tell you what you can do for me, Jill said silently, and then shook her head to free herself of the thought. The towel that had been wrapped around her hair fell to the floor. 'Great,' she said, bending over to pick it up, and dropping the newspaper in the process. 'This is starting to feel like a bad comedy,' she muttered, grabbing the newspaper and watching it come apart in her hands, loose pages all over the floor. She got down on her hands and knees and began noisily piecing the pages together again, folding one inside the other. She realized as she was doing this that she couldn't hear anything that David was saying, and decided that was probably why she was doing it, so she wouldn't have to.

'What is all the rustling going on in here?' David asked from the doorway.

'I dropped the paper.'

'So I see.'

'What did Snow White want?' Jill asked, getting awkwardly to her feet.

'What I thought. She wanted to know what courtroom to meet me in.'

'And you told her, of course.'

David smiled indulgently. 'What choice did I have?' He moved toward Jill. 'If you had told me yesterday what she'd said to you at the picnic, I could have thought of some excuse to tell her not to come. But it's too late today.' He kissed her. 'That'll teach you to keep things from me.' He started toward the bedroom and then stopped. 'Do you want me to say anything to her?' he asked.

Jill shook her head. 'What can you say? No, just ignore it.' She smiled. 'Besides, she'll be gone at the end of the summer anyway.' David said nothing. 'Won't she? I mean, Beth told me that she's just there for the summer.'

David lowered his head. 'There's a good chance she'll be joining the firm after she's called to the bar in September,' he said. 'A few of the partners have talked about asking her.'

Jill nodded. 'I understand Al Weatherby thinks she's pretty terrific.'

'She is,' he said. 'Legally speaking.'

'I always speak legal,' Jill joked, stepping into David's outstretched arms.

'I love you.'

'I know you do.'

'Do you want me to say something to her?' he asked again. 'I will, if you want.'

'Actions speak louder than words,' she told him.

He smiled. 'Right you are.' He kissed her nose, signaling the end of the discussion, and Jill watched him move down the hall before she went quickly into the bathroom to dry her hair and brush her teeth. She had just closed the bathroom door when she was aware David was speaking.

'What did you say?' she called, opening the door.

'I said why don't you come down to court this morning and watch me too?'

'I have a class.'

'Only at nine o'clock. Then you're free till two. Isn't that Thursday's schedule?'

'Yeah,' she said, mulling over his suggestion.

'So, come after ten and watch me, then we'll go to Winston's for lunch. How does that sound? '

'Sounds fantastic. You got yourself a deal.' She retreated into the bathroom and plugged in the hair dryer, immediately feeling the hot air as it blew against her skin. What would Nicole think of her suddenly showing up at the courtroom? Would she interpret it as a sign of insecurity, a show of weakness? the mother hen protecting her chick, making sure he didn't stray too far from the fold?

The hell with what Nicole thinks, she told herself, watching her hair curl stubbornly away from the style she was intending. She can think whatever she wants to think. Nicole Clark was simply not one of her concerns.

Jill looked down at what she was wearing. Just the same, she thought, maybe she'd change her dress.

Chapter Five

'Just when was it you discovered your ex-wife had a lover?'

'Six – eight months ago, maybe.'

'Maybe? You're not sure?'

The witness – a good-looking man approximately the same age as David Plumley, who was conducting the cross-examination – squirmed uneasily in his seat.

'I'm sure she has a lover,' the man said evenly. 'If you want, I'm sure I can pinpoint the exact time of my discovering this fact.'

'That would be nice,' David remarked obligingly, moving back from the witness stand and closer to the table and chairs he occupied when not questioning a witness. From her seat in the courtroom, Jill watched her husband as he moved, conscious, as the witness was not, that by seeming to back away, David was, in fact, only playing with his prey, the deadly panther seeking merely to improve his position before rushing in for the final, killing stroke.

The witness paused for several seconds, his eyes obviously retracing time, finally locating the date he sought. 'October seventeen,' he said, not without a touch of smugness. 'I remember the exact date because it was a surprise birthday party for a friend of mine.'

David paused for precisely the same length of time as had the witness. Then he spoke. 'October seventeen? That's nine months ago, almost ten.'

'Yes,' the witness agreed. Then he smiled. 'I guess it's been going on even longer than I realized.'

David returned the man's smile. 'You don't feel your ex-wife is entitled to have a lover?'

'Not that I have to support,' the man shot back sharply.

'Tell me, just as a matter of interest,' David asked almost lazily, 'did you have a date for this surprise party?'

'Yes,' the man answered. 'Aren't *I* entitled?'

'Is it fair to say that in the five years you and Patty Arnold have been divorced you have had a substantial number of "dates"?' David asked, ignoring the man's question and putting a noticeable stress on his final word.

'As you already noted,' the man replied, 'I've been divorced for five years. I thought that gave me the legal right to "date" anyone I wanted to.'

'Exactly so,' David said, brushing up against the table, where Nicole Clark sat beside his empty chair, observing him intently. 'You don't feel your wife is entitled to the same privileges?' Jill watched as David moved away from the table. She could feel Nicole's eyes riveted on his back. He must feel like he's back in high school, Jill thought, trying to impress the girl in the last row. Was that why he was coming down so hard on this man, this man who on more than just a superficial level so closely resembled himself? And which girl was he trying so hard to impress?

'My *ex*-wife,' the witness spat back defiantly, the words suddenly pouring out of his mouth like spilt milk from a pitcher, 'and she's entitled to do any goddamn thing she wants as long as I don't have to support her!' The judge banged his gavel, reminding the witness that such language would not be tolerated in a court of law and cautioning him to refrain from further outbursts. From her seat several rows behind the rectangular table, Jill Plumley knew the man had already lost, for as good as such histrionic outbursts looked in the movies, as bad did they appear in front of a judge. A good lawyer, David had once told her, always impressed upon his witnesses the importance of staying calm. On the other hand, if you could provoke the other side to anger, it greatly improved your own chances of success. The man on the witness stand looked helplessly around the room and finally brought his eyes to rest on Nicole, speaking his next words as if directly, and only, to her. 'Look, I'm not saying that she's not entitled to have any friends or lovers. I'm just saying that for the past five years I've been busting my— working very hard to try and live a reasonably decent life and still keep up with all my alimony payments. She got the house, the furniture, the car, the kids, everything. I walked out with the suit on my back and my briefcase. For the past five years I've been paying her a thousand dollars a month in alimony and a thousand in child support. Now, I have no objection to the child support – I'll support my kids for as long as they need me – but why should I have to pay for my wife to set up house with some other guy and give this jerk my hard-earned money so that he can start a new business?'

Again David ignored the man's question. 'How long were you married, Mr Arnold?'

'Twelve years.'

'Two children?'

'Two boys.'

'So, what you've just told me is that after twelve years of marriage and two sons you just walked out!' He paused. 'With the suit on your back and your briefcase, of course.'

The man wasn't sure he liked the way the facts had been restated but he answered in the affirmative.

'What was in the briefcase?' David asked suddenly. Jill found herself smiling. 'Stocks, as I recall,' David continued, answering for him. 'A few mortgages, wasn't it? The deed to some property in Canada?' The man said nothing. 'So, you weren't quite as empty-handed as you'd have this court believe.'

'That was five years ago,' the man said, resuming his squirming. 'I'm talking about today.'

David nodded. 'And today you say your ex-wife is living with another man and has been for the last ten months—'

'Well, I heard about their affair ten months ago at this party—'

'October seventeen—'

'Yes – October seventeen.' He stopped. 'I'm not sure exactly when they started living together.'

David returned to his table. 'What makes you so sure your ex-wife is living with this man?'

'I followed them on numerous occasions. His car was parked there day and night.'

Jill listened as intently as she knew Nicole was listening, as the witness parried with the lawyer, exchanging thrusts along with information, hearing as David produced evidence that the lover in question continued to pay rent on his own apartment – indeed to visit it daily – to explain that Mrs Arnold was entitled to spend her money in any way she saw fit and that if she chose to invest in her lover's business as a way of potentially increasing her own capital, she was as entitled as the witness himself with regard to his own investments. Then she stopped listening, knowing David had won his case, that the man squirming uncomfortably on the chair would get no reduction in the amount of his monthly alimony payments and that it was unlikely Patty Arnold would be threatened in this manner again. The world was once again safe for ex-wives and lovers.

He was a brilliant lawyer, she thought, always knowing just how far he could go, when he had to stop and pull back, when he could plunge full-scale ahead. She'd forgotten how impressive he was in a court of law, not just the way he looked which was glorious, but how he moved, the way he spoke, his choice of words. In the early days of their affair, she'd come often to watch him work. He obviously loved what he was doing, his eyes sparkling with the excitement of the challenge and the ultimate certainty of conquest. Her schedule, erratic as it had been, had filled certain of her weeks to overflowing, and left her at other times with virtually hours to spare. She had spent as many as she could watching this man. Any chance at all to be with him.

David walked past the rectangular table where Nicole sat watching, and winked – his victory wink, he had once told her. Except that this time, the wink had been for Nicole. Jill wondered if David even remembered at this moment that she was there, feeling suddenly very much the outsider, knowing that as close as she usually felt to him, as close as he professed to be to her, she could never completely understand the sense of victory he must be feeling at this time, she could never fully share in moments like this one. The way Nicole undoubtedly could.

Jill watched as her husband crossed back in front of the table, his deep voice dismissing the man on the stand, his body lean and striking in his dark navy suit. He suddenly caught her stare and smiled widely before returning to his table and sitting down beside Nicole. The other woman leaned toward him and whispered something in his ear. Congratulations, no doubt, on a job well done. You were wonderful, David. Really wonderful. David smiled guardedly, undoubtedly realizing Jill was watching him.

She couldn't blame David if he did find himself attracted to Nicole, Jill realized, feeling the same sudden intrusion of objectivity she had felt at the firm picnic just last weekend. Aside from the younger woman's obvious physical beauty, she was bright – no, *bright*, David had stressed the night before – and she was glamorous and held down a challenging job, or would very soon anyway. And they had the law in common. They could probably sit for hours and discuss their various cases. Her own job at the university rarely provided anything worth talking about anymore. They'd given up the pretense.

It had been interesting at first, something new, something different. She had told herself it would be challenging to try and train new minds. She pictured herself as Miss Jean Brodie in her prime. Or more precisely, Maggie Smith as Miss Jean

Brodie in her prime. 'Give me a girl at an impressionable age and she's mine for life,' she whispered. Something like that. Except that her students turned out to be long past impressing, and she'd discovered all too quickly that she hated teaching. Beth Weatherby had been right – she missed television, its excitement, its deadlines, its danger.

What she didn't miss were the problems it had created in her marriage. At least most of those had been solved when she had informed the network she was leaving. David was right – it was crazy for her to keep putting her life in jeopardy, leaving him to expose herself to bullets and disease all over the globe. Besides, he missed her when she was gone, and he worried about her. His worry interfered with his work. He needed her support. He couldn't feel it when she was half a world away. Didn't she think she could find something more sedentary, something closer to home? Didn't she want to start a family? Yes, she did. She didn't like the separations any more than he did. She missed him terribly. And a man like David needed a lot of ego gratification. If she wasn't there to provide it, she knew there were many who would be only too delighted.

Still, it didn't seem fair. His life, despite a change in wives and the reduced time with his children, had remained remarkably unchanged to all outward appearances. True, he'd exchanged a large house for a small apartment, but it was still a prestige building in a prime location and there was still someone waiting with a hot meal when he finally walked through the door at the end of the day, some nights as late as ten o'clock. Most importantly, he was still doing the work he loved.

Her life, on the other hand, had undergone a total transformation, from her surroundings to her marital status to her job. Instead of doing the work she loved, she was teaching others how to do it. TV journalism, the course proclaimed. Jill Plumley, professor. Her world was now confined to a classroom and she could invariably jump off in time to prepare dinner. Why, she'd become a regular little Betty Crocker in the kitchen. How had it all come about, she wondered, trying to get a fix on the subtle shifts that time had wrought. Temporarily forgetful of her surroundings, Jill pictured a David of approximately five years ago pacing angrily back and forth in front of her. That long ago, she marveled as his image became increasingly clear, his words gaining resonance and conviction. For several minutes, as the past overtook the present, the courtroom disappeared altogether.

She was obviously excited and he was just as obviously upset by her excitement.

'Why shouldn't I be happy? I've never been to Ireland before!'

'We're not talking about a sunny little vacation trip to Dublin – we're talking about bombs and snipers in Belfast.'

'I survived the Vietnam war,' she reminded him, trying not to sound too cute.

'I don't know why the network has to send you!'

'Because I happen to be a first-rate producer, that's why. And because I asked for this assignment.'

'You what?'

'I like to travel, you know that. And this is the kind of project I do very well. Besides,' she said softly, 'I don't think it would be such a terrible thing for us to take a two-week breather.'

'What do you mean?'

'You know what I mean.'

It seemed lately that's how all their conversations ended up. What do you mean? You know what I mean. It all means the same thing – you're a married man.

'All right,' he said, 'you want to go off for a few weeks, fine. Go to Los Angeles. Go to Bermuda, for Christ's sake. There's no civil war in Bermuda.'

'There's nothing in Bermuda.'

'You could get killed!'

'I'm not going to get killed.'

'Oh, you have that in writing, do you?'

She smiled and kissed him gently. 'Only a lawyer would ask a question like that.'

'Then do a show on lawyers.'

'I already did. That's why I'm in this mess. Remember?'

He sat down on the bed and watched her take out her suitcase and start to pack.

'This is the fourth trip you've taken in the last six months,' he said.

'You can't call a two-day stopover in Buffalo a trip!'

'You were away.'

He watched her throw a few cotton shirts and several pairs of jeans into the suitcase.

'You like it that I go away,' she said jokingly, before she realized that she really wasn't kidding at all.

'What are you talking about?'

'It's part of my mystique,' she told him. 'It's what sets me apart.'

'Apart from what?'

'From the others,' she said, knowing instinctively there had been. 'From your wife.'

He laughed. 'My wife's idea of an exciting holiday is two weeks in Las Vegas so that she can play the nickel slot machines and listen to Robert Goulet.'

'I was in Las Vegas,' Jill told him, 'a few years back. We did a story on those wedding chapels that are open twenty-four hours a day.'

'Is there anywhere you haven't been?' he asked her. 'Aside from Ireland, that is.'

Her face lit into a broad smile. 'China,' she said. 'Parts of Africa. But I'm working on it.'

'China, huh? I'd like to see China.'

'Well, you can come with me.'

'I love you, you know,' he said, his voice suddenly soft and serious.

Jill sat on David's lap and let her arms encircle his neck. 'Why do you love me?' she asked with genuine interest. 'Why does a man who looks the way you do fall in love with a woman who looks the way I do?'

'First of all because you're smart.'

'Oh, thanks. You're supposed to say there's absolutely nothing wrong with the way I look, that you think I'm pretty gorgeous.'

'I do, that's exactly right, and I love you because you're smart enough to know it.'

She laughed. 'Yes, okay, what else?'

'I don't know,' he shrugged. 'You're bright, sensitive, you know what's going on in the world, you do interesting things. You're smart.'

'You said that.' He nodded. 'Not smart enough to tell you to get lost when I found out your definition of marital separation.'

'I just couldn't let you walk out of that car,' he said, remembering.

She got up off his lap. 'I hate this situation. I hate the whole idea of it. I like women too much to be involved with a married man. I don't want to hurt your wife and I certainly don't want to get hurt myself.'

'What do you think I want?' he asked.

'I don't know.'

He exhaled a deep breath of air. 'Neither do I,' he said. 'I was hoping you could tell me.' He looked down at her suitcase. 'Is that all you're going to take?'

She went to the bathroom and opened the medicine cabinet, tossing a few items into a small kit.

'You're taking your birth control pills?' he asked, watching her.

He could see her smiling at him indulgently from the reflection of the bathroom mirror. 'You don't stop taking them, you know, because you're not going to be doing anything for a few weeks.' She came back into the room.

'How long have you been on them?' he asked.

'Eight years,' she answered.

'Isn't that a long time?'

'It's eight years.'

'Ever think about stopping?'

'All the time. But I don't think this is a particularly appropriate time in my life to conceive, do you? Much as I would very much like to have a child.'

'You should. You'd make a really good mother.'

'Yes. I think I would.'

The conversation halted abruptly. They were back at square one – she was going to Ireland and he was a married man.

'Will you call me as soon as you get back?' he asked.

('What do you mean you're involved with a married man? How could you let yourself do anything so stupid? You're a smart girl, Jill, how can you be so dumb? You think he loves you? Well, maybe he does. You think his wife doesn't understand him? Well, maybe she doesn't. You think he's going to leave her to marry you? Don't kid yourself, my darling daughter, it'll never happen. And if it does, if he does leave her for you, think about it for a minute – what kind of prize are you getting? A man who walks out on one woman when he finds one he likes better. A man who trades a slightly used family for a newer set. Is this someone you'll be able to trust? Believe me, Jill, if he'll do it once, he'll do it again. What do you need it for? Think about it, darling. Do you really need this kind of aggravation?')

'Will you call me as soon as you get back?' he repeated.

'Yes,' she answered.

There was a great flurry of movement around her, snapping Jill back into the reality of the present.

'Excuse me,' said a voice beside her, as a woman pushed her way past Jill and toward the middle aisle. Jill looked up at the clock on the wall. It was noon. Her eyes tried to find David and finally located him in a conference with several other men. The judge was gone. Obviously, court had been dismissed. And she'd missed the final verdict although she was sure she knew what it was. Still, if David should ask—

'Wonderful, wasn't he?' the voice asked huskily.

Jill looked to her right. Nicole Clark, her hair pulled back into a French braid, was smiling attractively at her, as if it was only natural that she do so. Maybe it was. Maybe she *had* been joking at the picnic. 'Yes, he was,' Jill answered, determined to be pleasant. 'It's been a while since I've had the chance to watch him. I forgot how impressive he can be.'

'That's not very smart,' Nicole said, her smile as bright as ever. 'It's something I never forget.'

Nicole turned and walked toward the rear door. Jill was about to go after her, put an end to the cruel joke once and for all with a simple blow on the head. Would anyone actually have the nerve to charge her? But David was suddenly at her side, his face flushed with victory, his arm around her waist.

'Ready for lunch?' he asked. Before she could answer, he was holding her tight against him and leading her out of the courtroom.

Chapter Six

'I felt a little sorry for that guy on the stand,' Jill said, taking a large shrimp from her bowl and covering it in sauce before lifting it to her mouth.

'Don't,' David said simply. 'Guy's a jerk. He's making three times what he was making five years ago and even then, he tried to get out of everything he could. He got off easy, I assure you.' He shook his head. 'Jerk. Doesn't even hire a private detective, he's so damn cheap. Follows them himself in his car for a few weeks. That's his idea of evidence. He's lucky the judge didn't *increase* his payments.' She laughed, helping herself to another shrimp. 'So, did you enjoy yourself this morning?'

Jill smiled widely. 'It was terrific. I'd forgotten how good you look in court.' She paused, recalling Nicole's words. 'Anyway,' she said, recovering quickly, 'I want to thank you for suggesting that I come. It was a good idea. You were really wonderful.'

David smiled. 'My pleasure. Very routine stuff.'

'Well,' she demurred, knowing his ego was searching for a few more strokes, 'you make it seem like it's all very routine, but I know how hard you work. And I know that behind that seemingly casual facade is a man with a map of his every move. And you're terrific, so what else can I say?'

'More of the same would be nice,' he smiled.

'And you look absolutely gorgeous,' Jill continued, not missing a beat. 'Actually, it was very interesting the way you let the poor sucker relax, then – pounce. Very exciting.'

'I'm glad you enjoyed yourself.'

'I enjoyed *you*,' she stated, finishing off the last of her shrimp, and smiling with her open mouth.

'You have sauce on your teeth,' he said.

Jill quickly brought her lips together. 'Wonderful,' she said. 'Someday, I'm going to learn how to eat these things properly.' She licked at her teeth without opening her mouth. 'Gone?' she asked timidly. David nodded. 'What can you expect from a girl raised on well-done roast beef and mashed potatoes?' she asked. 'So – what did Nicole think of your performance?' She tried to sound as unthreatened as possible.

'She didn't say much. Congratulations. Well done, that sort of thing. She thanked me, of course.'

'Of course.'

'I noticed the two of you were talking,' he broached. 'Anything interesting?'

'Very interesting.'

'Did she apologize for what she said at the picnic?'

'Not exactly.'

'What then? Tell you it was all a joke?'

'Not quite.'

'Jill—' he said, a touch of exasperation creeping into his voice.

'She said she thought you were wonderful. Well, no, actually her precise words were "wonderful, wasn't he?"'

David shifted uncomfortably in his seat. 'Well, she meant the way I cross-examined the poor bugger—'

'I agreed with her,' Jill continued. 'Then I said I'd forgotten how impressive you could be, and she said—' Jill paused, lowering her voice and trying to capture the other woman's tone. '"That's not very smart. It's something I never forget."' Jill stared directly into David's eyes. There was a second's silence and then he started to laugh. 'You're really enjoying all this, aren't you?' Jill accused him, trying to keep from laughing herself.

'No, of course not,' he chuckled.

'Oh, sure. You look like the cat who swallowed the canary.'

He shook his head. 'Well, you have to admit it *is* pretty funny.'

'To you, maybe.'

'Well, it's not often a man has two beautiful women fighting over him.'

'You've had it all your life,' she reminded him. 'And I'm not sure if I'm more flattered that you think I'm beautiful or more angry that you think she is!' David opened his mouth to speak, but said nothing. 'Anyway, let's change the subject. I spoke to Beth this morning.'

'Oh, how is she?'

'Well, she was apologizing all over the place, of course, for ruining our evening.'

'That's ridiculous.'

'That's what I told her. It's the last thing she has to worry about. But she apologized anyway. She said her hand finally stopped bleeding around three in the morning, so she didn't get a whole lot of sleep.'

'That's too bad. But it's all right now?'

'Apparently. I suggested she have a doctor take a look at it, but she said it's okay. I'm going to see her next week. We've decided to take an exercise class together every Wednesday.'

'That's a good idea.'

'You're supposed to say, what do *you* need to exercise for?'

'Everybody needs exercise,' he said.

'You never do.'

'I should.'

'When was the last time you played squash?' she asked.

'February,' he answered. 'And it's racquetball, not squash.'

'What difference does it make if you don't play?'

'I'm thinking of starting again.'

'You should. The club's right in your building. Do you still belong?'

He nodded. 'At seventeen hundred dollars a year,' he calculated, 'that was probably the most expensive racquetball game in history.'

'One thousand, seven hundred dollars a year?' Jill repeated. 'David, what we could be doing with that money—'

'I'll start using it again,' he promised. 'How was your class this morning?'

'You're changing the subject.'

'A good lawyer always knows when to change the subject.'

'And a good husband?'

'Especially a good husband.' He paused, reaching across the table and covering her hand with his own. 'So, tell me, were you brilliant as usual?'

'I was awful, as usual,' she said. 'I'm a rotten teacher, David. I know it and they know it. I'm bored to tears and so are they. One kid was actually reading the morning paper while I was talking.'

'What were you talking about?'

'How to conduct an interview.'

'Sounds interesting.'

'It's not. At least not talking about it. What's interesting is doing it.'

'You have to know how first.'

'I *do* know how,' Jill said, surprising them both with the passion in her voice. 'That's just the point. I should be out there, not stuck in some classroom. I feel sometimes when I'm talking that I'm going to burst wide open with—'

'With what?'

'Resentment,' she said quietly. 'I really resent those kids wanting to be what I was, knowing that a few of them will probably do well, become producers, filmmakers. Knowing that they think I'm a teacher because I couldn't make it—'

'That's not true. You know it's not.'

'*They* don't. They're all firm believers in the old adage: "Them that can, do. Them that can't – teach."'

There was a second's pause before David spoke. 'And me?' he asked. 'Do you resent me, too?'

She lowered her head, prepared to lie. 'Sometimes,' she

finally admitted, truthfully. 'I know it's not your fault, David. Honestly, I know that. It was an impossible situation. I was away too much. We hardly got a chance to see each other. Not that we see that much of each other lately, anyway.'

'Things will slow down again, Jill. It just got very hectic all of a sudden,' he apologized.

'Summer's usually the slow time, I thought,' Jill said quietly.

'Another few weeks,' he said. 'It should calm down a bit by then.' He looked around. It was obvious to Jill that this was not turning out to be quite the victory luncheon David had had in mind. 'What is it you want, Jill?' he asked. 'You want to quit work at the university? You want to go back into television?'

Jill recalled the early crises in her marriage. They had all revolved around her job. 'I don't know what I want,' she said at last.

'I don't want to be the heavy in all this,' David was saying. 'God knows I have nothing against your working. You know that. I don't even mind that you work in television. Christ, that's how I met you. And you were wonderful – you had such spark.'

'That's just it, David, I'm *losing* my spark.'

'No,' he argued sincerely. 'No. You're just hiding it temporarily.' He smiled at her and waited until she reluctantly returned his smile. 'Look, why don't you call the network, call Ernie whatever-his-name-was—'

'Irving,' she corrected. 'Irving Saunders.'

'Call Irving and see if he doesn't have something that wouldn't involve any traveling—'

'I asked him that two years ago when I left. There just isn't anything. Not in my field. I mean, there might be a few shows out of Chicago, but nobody's going to guarantee I won't have to do some traveling, or that I can finish up by five o'clock every night or won't have to work weekends or even all night sometimes.'

'So, what are you saying?'

'I don't know. I don't know what I'm saying.'

'You don't think it's worth a try?'

'David, what would you say to a potential lawyer, say Nicole Clark, for instance,' she offered, and immediately wished she hadn't. 'Anyway,' she continued, 'say she told you she'd be delighted to join your firm but she wanted it understood up front that she wouldn't work past 5 p.m., and that weekends were out of the question.'

'I'd tell her to find herself another law firm.'

'Exactly.'

'What can I tell you, Jill? I can't make up your mind for you.'

'I know.'

'Maybe you're getting your period.'

'What's that got to do with anything?'

'Well, you know how you sometimes get depressed when—'

'Everybody gets depressed from time to time! Don't start on my hormones—'

'I don't want to argue with you. I've made my suggestion. You can decide to act on it or not.'

'You wouldn't mind if I got my old job back?' she asked timidly.

'I didn't say that,' he answered. 'I'd probably mind it very much. As far as I'm concerned, all the old objections are still valid. But I also have to recognize that it's your life and your decision.' He shook his head. 'I don't happen to think that you're giving the teaching a fair shake. You decided almost at the outset that you hated it – although I think you hate the idea of it more than you actually hate the teaching itself – and you won't allow yourself to enjoy it. You feel it would be some kind of betrayal. To what, I don't know.'

'You're way off base, counselor.'

'Maybe,' he said. 'If I am, I apologize. I was just trying to give you my opinion.'

'You don't give opinions,' she said, sullenly. 'You give lectures.'

'Maybe I should be the teacher,' he said, smiling, his hand back on hers.

'Damn it,' Jill said, allowing a small smile to crease her lips. 'Why'd you have to be so charming? I'm sorry, David. I'm acting like a spoiled brat.'

'And I was probably lecturing. You're right. Sometimes I get awfully impressed by the sound of my own voice.'

'I love you,' she said.

David signaled the waiter for the bill. 'What do you think we should do with the kids this weekend?' he asked.

'I don't know. A movie, maybe?'

'Think about it,' he said. 'Jason leaves for camp in less than a week. Maybe you could make a special dinner for him.' Jill shrugged, thinking that all Jason ever ate was hamburgers and that Laurie never ate anything at all. David gave the waiter his gold American Express card. 'Come on back to the office for a few minutes,' he said. 'You've got time.' She looked skeptical. 'Come on,' he coaxed. 'We've made a few changes. It'll do you good.'

'Okay,' Jill agreed, thinking maybe David was right about her attitude toward teaching. Maybe she'd never given it the proper chance. She decided to try extra hard for her two o'clock class. No matter what she did, she knew, watching her husband sign the tab and tear off his portion of the receipt, anything was better than risking the loss of this man. He was better than a daily dose of Vitamin C. There was no way she ever wanted to live without him. It was as simple as that.

'Good afternoon, Mrs Plumley,' Diane greeted her pleasantly. 'How are you today?'

'Just fine, thank you,' Jill told her husband's secretary.

'Good. Been looking around?' Jill nodded. 'They made some nice improvements to the staff lounge,' Diane continued. 'And your husband chose all the new paintings.'

'He told me. They're lovely.'

The secretary smiled, turning her attention to her employer.

'Mrs Whittaker has been calling you all morning,' she announced as David walked past her toward his office. 'And Julie Rickerd has called twice. She says it's very important. And a Mr Powadiuk – I think that's how you pronounce it – he says could you call him, he came home from a fishing trip yesterday to find his wife had left and cleaned out their entire apartment. Didn't even leave him the paper plates.'

David thanked her, taking the messages from her outstretched hand and motioning for Jill to follow him inside. He closed the door behind them, sitting down immediately at his paper-strewn desk. Jill went to the window and gazed out at the tops of the city buildings. 'It's so beautiful up here,' she said. 'Like being in a different world.'

David smiled in agreement and pressed the buzzer for his secretary. 'Diane, get me the files on Julie Rickerd and Sheila Whittaker, please. And call this Mr Powa – whatever-his-name-is.' He flipped off the intercom. 'What's this?' he asked, sifting through the clutter of his desk and retrieving a delicate bud vase containing a single red rose.

Diane brought the requested files in immediately, somehow finding room for them amid the general clutter of his desk. 'I'll call Mr Powad – whatever,' she said, going out again.

David flipped absently through the files, then looked back at the flower.

'Is there a card?' Jill asked, a queasy feeling building in the pit of her stomach.

David searched the top of his desk. 'I don't see one,' he said. 'Probably Diane put it there.'

Jill walked over to his desk and reached into the stack of papers, pulling out a small lavender envelope. She handed it to David.

'Didn't see it,' he said, reluctantly taking it from her and tearing it open. He read it quickly and handed it to Jill. 'I'll talk to her,' he said.

Jill read the note aloud. 'Thank you again for a most interesting morning.' She lowered the note to the table. 'Nicki,' she said, repeating the signature out loud.

'I'll call her right now if you'd like. You can be here while I talk to her.'

'No. No,' Jill protested, 'let's just leave it alone, okay? If you bring her in here, it'll only embarrass everybody. It's just a thank-you note. A very nice touch, actually. Just ignore it. Maybe if she sees she's the only one playing this silly game, she'll get tired of it and go home.'

'That's fine by me. You're the one I don't want to see upset,' he said.

'I'm not,' she lied. 'If I can survive Elaine, I'm sure I can outlive Nicole. Nicki,' she minced. David laughed but the laugh stuck in his throat.

'Maybe we're reading too much into all this,' David offered. 'We're liable to get paranoid if we're not careful. She's really a first-class lawyer.'

David's buzzer sounded. 'I have Mr Powa – he's on the phone,' Diane said.

'I'll go,' Jill whispered as David picked up the receiver. She bent over and kissed his forehead, her nose immediately catching the subtle scent of the rose.

He waved goodbye as she closed the door behind her.

On the other side, her heart was pounding wildly. She stood for a minute at the doorway and tried to catch her breath.

'Are you all right, Mrs Plumley?' Diane asked.

Jill looked over at her husband's secretary, a pretty girl with dark brown hair and large blue eyes. David had always surrounded himself with attractive women. During his marriage to Elaine, he had often succumbed to their attractions. He lied easily and well, he had once told her. And often, she knew, when he was married to Elaine. Had he ever lied to her? Jill wondered, then threw the thought away with a toss of her head. It was something she preferred not to think about. Nicole might have grand designs, Jill decided, but that was all they would ever be.

'I'm fine,' Jill told Diane. 'I'll see you again.' She started down the long, winding corridor.

You had to give the girl high marks for trying, Jill thought. She was very clever. No doubt she would make a first-rate attorney. She was so bold, so brazen. Coming right out and stating her intentions. Putting the wife on immediate guard, on constant edge. Forcing her to imagine hidden meanings where none existed, perhaps causing unnecessary friction at home, laying the groundwork for small doubts to bloom into large ones. Bloom, Jill thought. Like a rose.

The best solution, short of murder, was simple indifference. She would not allow herself to get upset; she wouldn't even allow herself the luxury of sarcasm. Not in front of David, anyway. There would be no fights because of this girl.

And David would be extra cautious, she knew. But also very intrigued. How could he be anything less? Annoyed? Maybe. Indignant? Possibly. But definitely intrigued. All part of the master plan: the insecure and suspicious wife at home, the intriguing other woman at the office.

She was almost at the end of the hall when the voice stopped her.

'Jilly? Jilly, is that you?'

She stopped and turned around. There were only two men in the world who called her Jilly. One was her gynecologist. The other was one of David's partners, a highly esteemed criminal lawyer with a fondness for outrageous clothes and irritating nicknames.

His name was Don Eliot and he stood before her in blue jeans and a brown corduroy jacket. She was surprised to see he was wearing a tie until she saw that the figure embroidered at its base was Mickey Mouse. Hello, Donny, she wanted to say, but thought better of it.

'Hello, Don,' she said instead. 'How are you?'

'Just wonderful,' he said, taking hold of both her hands. 'How's Adeline?'

'Oh, fine. Great. The kids are driving her nuts, of course, but that's not unusual.' He looked her over. 'You look good,' he said, as if commenting on the quality of a sweater. 'A little tired, maybe. You getting enough sleep, Jilly?'

Thanks a lot for the compliment, Donny, she thought. His remarks were the last thing she needed to hear. 'Do we ever get enough sleep?' she questioned in response.

'No, I guess not,' he said. 'Certainly not around our house. Can you believe we had two of them up running around the bedrooms last night at four in the morning – the two-year-old, who's just learned how to climb out of his crib, and the four-year-old, who wanted to see what all the commotion was about. I tell you, Jilly, you and David have probably made the right decision not to have kids. It changes your whole life, I tell you. Of course, David already has two. That's plenty. We should have stopped at two. Five is crazy!'

Jill tried to smile, grateful that Don Eliot obviously required no comments from her end. She was afraid that if she did speak, she might cry. So David had discussed his intentions (or lack of them) with regard to future children with others. Indeed, had told them the decision had already been made.

'Well,' she said, finally. 'Few decisions are carved in stone. You never know.'

'Thatta girl, Jilly,' he said, patting her shoulder and starting to move away. 'Oh, by the way, now that I've got you here – Adeline's been after me for weeks to invite you two for dinner. How about a week this Saturday?'

Jill could think of nothing to say, so she nodded her head.

'Good,' he said. 'I'll have Adeline call you, set up a time.'

'Sounds good,' Jill lied.

'See you then.' He disappeared behind a curve in the wall.

Jill stood for a few seconds in the corridor, trying to collect her thoughts. Since that lovely episode in the shower, early that morning, the day had taken a distinct downhill turn.

'Looking for a way out?' the husky voice asked with just the hint of a smile.

Nicole Clark stood only six feet away. Jill stared at her with a look of what she hoped was calm superiority. 'Thank you,' she said. 'But I know my way around.' Gathering herself up to her full height, hoping desperately that she wouldn't trip over her own feet, she walked briskly by the other woman and out the office doors.

Chapter Seven

The picnic grounds were crowded and they had to circle the park for almost half an hour before someone pulled out and David found a place to park. By that point, David's mood was less than jocular, Laurie's pout was more prominent, and Jason's stutter more pronounced. Jill shifted the food basket on her lap, hoping that no one would remember that this afternoon's outing had been her idea.

'W-we'll n-never get a f-free barbecue,' Jason spit out, as they grudgingly climbed out of the car. 'There's a m-million people here this aft-afternoon. There w-won't be any b-barbecues left.'

'Then we'll have to share,' Jill told him, watching David retrieve the large thermos box from the trunk of the car. 'Let's go that way,' she said, pointing straight ahead at the crowded campgrounds. 'I think the whole city must be here today.' She hurried to catch up to David, his two children falling behind. 'Do you think we'll be able to find a barbecue?' she whispered once they were out of Jason's earshot.

'We'll find one,' he said, forced good will evident in every syllable.

They did. It took twenty minutes, and they had to share, as Jill had predicted, but at least it was already lit and everyone had worked up a considerable appetite in the interim.

'It's so hot,' Jason said slowly, as Jill handed him his second hamburger.

'What is? The weather or the hamburger?' Jill asked, feeling that the afternoon might not turn out so badly after all. They had found a comfortable spot which provided a hint of shade, and the people whose space they were sharing seemed pleasant and helpful, although their three-year-old was obviously not happy with the family's latest addition, an infant of only a few months who lay gurgling contentedly on the blanket.

Jason handed back his hamburger in silence, displeased by the amount of blood dripping from the pink meat.

'Hamburgers are better when they're not little black balls of charcoal,' David told him.

The boy was instantly apologetic. 'B-but I don't like it that way,' he protested.

'I do,' Jill said, taking it from him. 'We'll make you another one,' she offered, looking over at Laurie. 'What about you, Laurie? Another hamburger?'

'I haven't finished this one yet,' Laurie said, watching as the three-year-old ran by his younger sibling, his foot just managing to brush sharply against the baby's side.

'Martin!' the child's mother warned, scooping the infant into her arms and shooting a withering glance in her son's direction.

Jill's attention moved back from the young mother to Laurie's plate, which had barely been touched. She hasn't started, let alone finished, Jill thought.

'More Coke?' Jill asked.

'It's not C-Coke,' Jason corrected. 'It's P-P-Pepsi.'

'More Pepsi, then,' Jill stated.

Jason shook his head.

'Laurie?' her father asked. 'Some Pepsi for you, sweetie?'

'Nothing,' the girl said. Her eyes traveled back to the young family, with whom she would obviously have preferred to be, Jill thought, watching her, and then she too looked longingly at the baby in her mother's arms.

'How old is she?' Jill asked the young woman.

'Three months,' the woman answered proudly.

'It must be a hectic time,' Jill said, indicating the small boy watching enviously only several feet away.

'It is, especially with Martin being so jealous,' the woman nodded. 'He actually peed on little Pamela the other day. Stood over her and peed all over her little tummy. I thought I'd die!'

'Your classic case of piss-on-you,' Jill said, and the two women laughed easily while everyone else around them looked vaguely embarrassed.

'How can you talk to a stranger like that?' Laurie admonished.

'Why not?' Jill asked. 'I'm old enough.' As if to prove her point, she turned back toward the young mother and introduced herself. 'You look wonderful,' she continued. 'You're so nice and skinny.'

'I was lucky,' the woman said. 'I was all baby. And I've been exercising every day like crazy.'

Jill patted her stomach. 'I have to start,' she said. 'Actually, I'm going to a class this Wednesday. Rita Carrington's. Have you heard of her?' The woman shook her head.

'Can I come?' Laurie asked suddenly.

'Come where?' Jill asked in return, directing her attention to David's daughter.

'To the exercise class,' Laurie answered.

'Sure,' Jill said, surprised by Laurie's interest.

'M-Mom's getting one of those b-big gas b-barbecues,' Jason ventured timidly at his father.

Jill watched David's face tense. 'Is your mother also buying a cook to help her plop the hamburgers down on the grill?' he asked.

'Mom knows how to cook,' Jason said immediately in his mother's defense. 'She's a great cook. She makes way better hamburgers than these,' he added accusingly in Jill's direction. Jill noted the child had not stuttered once.

'So,' Jill said, hurriedly trying to change the subject. 'Are you looking forward to camp?'

'He better be,' David answered, before the boy had a chance. 'It's costing enough to send him.

'Mom says it's not costing half enough,' Jason said, again with no trace of a stammer, his anger seeming to smooth his tongue.

'She's thinking of having a pool put in for next summer,' Laurie contributed.

'What the hell does she want a pool for?' David questioned. 'She doesn't swim.'

'She says she'll take lessons.'

'Private, of course,' David added.

'She's entitled,' his son shot back. Jill could hear Elaine's

THE OTHER WOMAN

voice. I'm entitled, the other woman said.

'Your hamburger's ready,' Jill announced, wrapping the well-cooked meat inside a hamburger bun.

'Th-thanks,' Jason whispered, looking guiltily away.

David reached over and ruffled his son's dark blond hair. 'You're getting to be a good-looking little kid, you know that?' he said with pride.

Jason playfully knocked his father's hand from his head, shaking his head in the same way that David always did to get the hairs back in place. 'L-like f-father, like s-son,' he stammered shyly.

David laughed and put his arms around the boy's neck, bending over to kiss his forehead. 'What do you think of the Moonies or the Hare Krishnas?' he asked, seemingly from out of nowhere. Jill had to stifle a laugh.

'Which one?' Jason asked. 'Th-they're two c-completely d-different things.'

'Like Coke and Pepsi,' David said.

'Yeah,' his son concurred. 'Exactly.'

Laurie nodded in agreement, her plate still untouched.

Jill watched the young family beside them gathering up their now-screaming youngsters and bundling them off toward their car. Little children, little problems, she heard David's voice repeating. Then she looked back at Laurie and Jason.

'And one and two, that's right, ladies, to the right. And one and two. Now switch. To the left. And one and two. And again. To the left. The left, Mrs Elfer, that's the way. And one and two. Five more times. To the right now, ladies. The right, Mrs Elfer.'

Poor Mrs Elfer, Jill thought, contorting her body to the right, her hands stretched taut above her head. There's always one in every class who doesn't know her left hand from her right.

'And to the left, now, ladies. And one and two.'

The rest of the class of some twenty-five women was already on the second beat when Mrs Elfer finally found the first.

'Better, Mrs Elfer,' the instructor called out, not missing a beat. She seemed to speak as if every other word represented the clashing together or cymbals. 'Okay, one more time. Now, bend forward from the waist and bring your right elbow over to your left heel for two counts, then your left elbow over to your right heel. Got that, everybody?' she yelled above the music (Debbie Harry and Blondie singing 'Call Me,' which Jill recognized as the theme from *American Gigolo*). The instructor bent forward and peered back between her spread legs at the rest of the group. 'Ready? And one and two. Switch. One and two. Switch.'

She's trying to kill us, Jill decided, bringing her right elbow to her left heel in time to the blaring disco beat. Whoever said disco was dead obviously had never been to Rita Carrington's exercise class. Jill stared wonderingly at Rita's protruding rear end. The woman was an Amazon, at least six feet tall, with the kind of body that usually found itself in the centerfold of *Playboy* magazine. Indeed, it was said that Rita had once worked as a Bunny and had been prominently featured in the magazine's presentation of 'The Girls of Chicago.' It gave one something to aspire to, Jill thought. Better than some fat old lady in torn leotard trying to convince them that hers was the way to a better body. At least, with Rita Carrington leading the way, there existed the faint glimmer of hope that it was indeed these exercises – and not an act of God – that had produced those results.

Rita Carrington straightened up and shook her hair free of her face. The hair was a deep auburn color and cut into seductive layers. ('She'd look good wet,' Beth had commented when they first saw her.) Almost immediately, Rita Carrington was into the middle of another exercise. 'Okay, ladies, up into the jog,' she said, lifting her knees rapidly and jogging in place. 'Get those legs up. Good. Good. Let's get a little sweat going here, ladies, come on. Let's move.'

'She obviously hates women,' Beth whispered from beside her.

'Whose idea was this anyway?' Jill breathed heavily in reply.

'Laurie's doing okay,' Beth noted, indicating David's daughter in the front row.

Jill looked over at her husband's elder child. She still couldn't fathom why Laurie had expressed an interest in coming along. But since it was the first thing Jill had ever done that Laurie had been even remotely interested in, Jill did not feel it appropriate to turn down her request. Laurie had even called several times since the weekend to make sure the date was still on. And so here she was, all fourteen years of her, in the front row, twisting and turning her already skinny body, working as hard to trim off whatever fat she imagined she had as the rest of the women, who had, unfortunately, a good deal more excess flesh than imagination.

'You're doing pretty good yourself,' Jill told Beth sincerely.

Beth Weatherby, at forty-five, looked better in her black leotard and pink tights than most of the other women did who were many years her junior.

'No talking, ladies,' Rita Carrington cautioned. Jill felt suitably chastised, as if she were a child back in school. Beth made a face and turned her attention back to the instructor. 'Okay, ladies. On your backs.'

Jill crouched down, watching Beth do the same. When Beth put her hand on the floor, she winced. 'Still hurts?' Jill asked.

'I'm not sure if it's really the cut that hurts or just the memory of it,' Beth answered.

'Ladies, please, you can talk in the lounge later.'

'We can talk in the lounge, later,' Jill repeated under her breath.

'Feet up, knees bent. Bend from the waist. And one and two and three and four—'

'Oh, that tastes good,' Jill exclaimed, taking a long, slow sip of her Coca-Cola. 'There is nothing like the taste of pure sugar after an hour of torture.'

'It's better than sex,' Ricki Elfer agreed, tossing away her straw and lifting the glass of Coke to her mouth.

'Well, I don't know—' Jill protested.

'Oh, yes, take my word for it,' the slightly pudgy blonde protested. 'I may not know my left hand from my right, but the two things I do know are sex and Coca-Cola. Coca-Cola's better.'

Jill and Beth laughed at the woman who shared their table. Jill wondered if Ricki Elfer made the same distinction between Coke and Pepsi as did her stepson.

'I remember when I was in Rome,' Ricki Elfer continued. 'This is many years ago, remember. I was twenty. I'm thirty-six now. I was with a girlfriend. We'd been touring Europe all summer. You know, university kids on their summer vacation, and this was in the days of Europe on five dollars a day. And that was like all the money we had, so there was no such thing as little luxuries like a Coke, because we couldn't afford them. And this one day, it must have been a hundred degrees out and we'd been walking around all day looking at the Colosseum or whatever, and we were so thirsty, I thought we were going to die. Suddenly, this car pulls up beside us and these two Italian guys shout, "Americanas, Americanas." And my friend, who was getting a little tired of having her ass pinched every two seconds, shouted at them to keep driving. They yelled back that all they wanted to do was talk. So I said, "Buy us a Coke first, then we'll talk!" And they did. And we did. And later that night we did a little more. And like I said, the Coke was better.' She finished her drink. 'It always is.' She shook her head. 'At least you know what you're getting; it doesn't pretend to be something it's not. And it always leaves you satisfied.' She smiled. 'Oh, youth,' she said, still traipsing through the ruins of ancient Rome.

'Speaking of which,' Jill interjected, 'can you believe Laurie deciding to take another class?!'

'That skinny kid?' Ricki asked.

'My husband's daughter,' Jill nodded. 'She says her waistline's too thick.'

'How old is she?'

'Fourteen.'

'She's nuts,' Ricki said plainly, and Jill and Beth laughed. 'They're all nuts at fourteen. Then they get older, they get worse. Wait till *she* wants to go to Europe.'

'You have children?' Beth asked.

'Two boys,' Ricki Elfer answered. 'Ten and eleven. They live with their father.'

'You're divorced?' Jill asked, noting Ricki's wedding band.

'Several times, Paul, my current – I love that word, it makes him sound so impermanent – is my third husband. I'm trying to decide right now whether to have another baby or tie my tubes.'

'That's quite a choice,' Beth commented.

'Women are always faced with wonderful choices like that. But it's true. Part of me would like to have another child – which part, I'm not sure – and I figure, at thirty-six, if I'm going to do it, I better do it now. The other part of me – the sane part – says I've done my share and what do I need with the aggravation, not to mention the nausea and the discomfort and, lest we forget, the pain.' She signaled the waiter for another Coke. 'Not to mention what it does to your body. Can you believe that before I married my first husband – his name was Errol, his mother named him after Errol Flynn – anyway, before we got married, I weighed ninety-eight pounds. And I'm five foot four. Not exactly a shrimp.'

'You must have been like Laurie,' Jill remarked.

'No. I was skinny, all right, but Laurie's almost emaciated. You ever heard of anorexia nervosa?'

'Oh, no,' Jill said, dismissing the thought. 'She's skinny but I don't think she's deliberately starving herself.'

The waiter put a second glass of Coca-Cola in front of Ricki Elfer. 'Thank you,' she said, then turned her attention back to her new friends. 'This place used to be a real dump, but since they put in this lounge and everything, it's picked up a lot. Rita did that. Before she came, there was nothing.'

'How long have you been coming here?' Beth asked.

'It's been a second home for the last two years.' She looked at her body. 'Discouraging, isn't it? Especially when, after all this time, I'm still going one way when everyone else is going the other. Remember when you took ballet and there was always one kid in the class whose arms were going up just when everyone else's were going down? Well, that was me. I'm that kid.' She patted her stomach. 'I know that somewhere inside here, Jane Fonda is struggling to get out.' She shook her head. 'After thirty, boy, that's it. The body goes all to hell. Everything drops three inches. What doesn't drop, expands. And your skin dries up and pretty soon you're looking like a big, fat prune.' Jill and Beth started laughing again. 'Let's get back to sex; it's not quite so depressing.'

'How'd you meet your husband?' Jill asked.

'Which one?'

'The latest,' Jill smiled.

'I met him while I was married to husband number two. We were thinking of renovating our townhouse and so we called in a few architects to get some ideas. Paul was one of the architects; I took one look at him and got plenty of ideas. Now that I think of it, I probably should have my tubes tied instead of insisting that Paul have a vasectomy. If I tie my tubes, I can still fool around. If Paul has a vasectomy, it's another fifteen years on the Pill.'

'Do you fool around?' Jill asked her, amazed she was having such an intimate conversation with a woman who only an hour ago had been a total stranger.

'Not as much as I'd like,' the woman answered. 'Not as many cars pulling up beside me these days yelling "Americana, Americana."' She laughed heartily. 'What about you?' she said, turning to Beth.

'Me?' Beth smiled. 'Oh, no. I've never even been to Europe.' Both Jill and Ricki regarded her expectantly. 'No, I've led a very sheltered life. I met Al, my husband, when I was seventeen. I was working in a bank. I was a teller. He used to come to my window all the time. I thought he was cute, not very tall, slight of build, but cute anyway.' Jill giggled. She loved stories like this one and she'd always been curious about Al and Beth Weatherby. 'He was so full of confidence though, you would have thought he owned the bank,' Beth continued. 'He used to strut over to my window and deposit his money. After a few months he started talking to me. Told me he was a lawyer. I was very impressed. He said he liked the theatre and lifting weights and that one day he was going to head the city's largest, most successful law firm. I told him that when his bank balance hit ten thousand dollars, he'd have to marry me.' It was Beth's turn to giggle. Jill thought that when she did, she looked just like a little girl.

'And he did?' Ricki asked.

'The day after my eighteenth birthday,' Beth answered. 'My mother wasn't at all happy about that. She thought I was much too young, that Al was too old for me, that he'd always have more dreams than clients.'

'What does she think now?' Ricki wondered.

'She died about eleven years ago.'

Ricki was appropriately apologetic. 'So, you've been married how long?'

'Twenty-seven years.'

'My God! Amazing! Any children?'

'Three. Two boys and a girl. The oldest, Brian, is a doctor in New York; Lisa, the middle one, is a singer in L.A.; and Michael,' she sighed, 'Michael has fallen into the clutches of the Reverend Moon, or someone like that.' She looked past Jill into the open space behind her. 'It's funny,' she said, almost wistfully, 'how nothing ever works out quite the way you thought it would.'

Jill nodded her head in agreement. Her own life was certainly not what she had expected. 'How *is* Lisa?' she asked.

'Oh, fine. She's still not working, but at least she's trying.'

'And that married musician—?'

'Married musician?' Beth looked genuinely astonished. 'What are you talking about?'

Jill was confused. 'Al mentioned that night you cut your hand that you were upset because of Lisa's involvement with a married man, a musician—'

'Did he? I don't remember—' Her voice trailed off. Jill thought it best to drop the subject. There were several seconds where no one said anything at all.

'How about you, Jill?' Ricki asked suddenly, catching Jill by surprise. 'How'd you meet your husband?'

'Oh, we met when I was interviewing him for a television show,' Jill began.

'You're in television?' Ricki Elfer asked quickly. 'What's your last name again? Are you someone I should know?'

Jill laughed. 'No, you wouldn't know me. My name was Jill Listerwoll before I got married. Now, it's Jill Plumley.' She stopped, thinking that her name had always been full of l's. 'And I'm not in television anymore. I'm a teacher at the university.'

The door at the far end of the lounge opened, and David's daughter Laurie came inside. For the first time since the three women had sat down, Jill allowed herself the luxury of taking a long, hard look at her surroundings. Rita Carrington had done a good job. The room was restful, almost soothing, with its deep burgundy walls and pink and mauve sofas. Even the bar area, where they were sitting, was well-appointed with attractive white tables and chairs with deep purple cushions. Just the right sort of room in which to pamper yourself after an hour with Rita Carrington. Jill watched as Laurie ambled toward her. The child was still in her pink leotard and leg warmers.

'Hi, Laurie,' she said pleasantly. 'How you doing? Want a Coke?'

'No, thanks.'

'Oh, you gotta have a Coke,' Ricki Elfer encouraged. 'It's better than—'

'So how was the second class?' Jill interrupted, cutting Ricki Elfer off just in time.

'Great,' Laurie said. 'Better than the first. It was a different instructor. This one really made you work.' Jill and Beth exchanged incredulous glances.

'You better watch that you don't exercise yourself into thin air,' Ricki Elfer cautioned.

'No, I really need the exercise,' Laurie insisted, then turned back to Jill. 'Is it okay if I take a shower before I go home?'

'Of course,' Jill said. 'I'll wait for you.' She paused. 'Actually, I thought that since David was working late tonight, you and I could have dinner together, maybe go to a movie—'

'Oh, I can't,' Laurie said apologetically. 'Ron's taking my mother and me out as soon as I get home.'

'Ron?' Jill asked.

'Ron Santini, my mother's new boyfriend.'

'Ron Santini, the gangster?' Jill asked, the words popping out of her mouth in astonishment.

'He's not a gangster,' Laurie answered indignantly. 'He's in fruit.'

'Oh,' Jill said, nodding. 'Sorry. There must be more than one Ron Santini in Chicago.'

'I guess so,' Laurie pouted. 'Ron's in fruit.' Jill nodded again. 'I'll go take my shower.'

'I'll wait for you here,' Jill offered. 'At least I can drive you home.'

'It's not necessary.'

'I'll drive you home,' Jill insisted. Laurie shrugged and walked away. 'I don't know,' she muttered, almost to herself. 'I try, I really try to be friends with that girl—'

'Shouldn't have called her mother's boyfriend a gangster,' Ricki advised.

Jill laughed. 'It just slipped out.' She watched Laurie make her exit. 'I thought everyone knew Ron Santini was a big shot

101

with the Mob. We did a show on the guy a few years ago. Those fruit stores of his are nothing but fronts.'

'I bet I know something you don't know,' Ricki chimed in a singsong-like refrain.

'What's that?' Beth asked.

'Well,' Ricki said, leaning forward, 'Ron Santini, reputed Mafioso, is also reputed to have a twelve-inch cock!'

'You're kidding!' Beth exclaimed, looking around her. None of the other women in the room seemed to have overheard, although one woman at the next table was leaning noticeably farther back in her chair.

'I'm serious,' Ricki continued. 'A girlfriend of mine once had a very brief fling with the guy – he really gets around, you know. Apparently he's Chicago's answer to Warren Beatty.'

'It can't be the same guy,' Jill said.

'Why not?' asked Beth.

'What would a playboy with a twelve-inch cock be doing with someone who only likes to screw on Christmas and Thanksgiving?'

'Who only likes to screw on Christmas and Thanksgiving?' Ricki asked.

'Elaine, my husband's ex-wife.'

'Who told you she only likes to screw on holidays?'

'My husband. He said that in seventeen years of marriage, he doubted they made love more than fifty times.'

'Never believe anything a husband tells you about his ex-wife,' Ricki advised.

Jill turned to Beth. 'You know her, Beth,' she said. 'What do you think?'

'Who ever really knows about anyone else,' Beth answered cryptically.

'True.'

'My first husband had a big dick,' Ricki said, loudly enough to attract the undivided attention of the women sitting at the next table. They stopped any further pretense at conversation. 'A big dick and thirty million dollars,' she continued.

'And you left him?!' the woman leaning back in her chair asked, almost falling to the floor.

'He was so boring,' Ricki explained, moving her chair in order to accommodate her new listeners. 'He was really the most boring person I have ever met. I knew he was boring when I married him, of course, but I thought that with a dick a foot long and thirty million dollars, I could learn to love being bored. Alas, such was not the case,' she sighed theatrically. 'That plus the fact that he caught me in *flagrante delicto*, or whatever you call it, with his stockbroker. Husband number two, incidentally.' She paused. 'God has to be a man,' she said, thinking out loud. 'Only a man could take such wonderful potential and make such a mess!'

Everybody laughed. 'They should only know how women talk about them,' Jill said, and everyone agreed.

One of the women at the next table stood up. 'Well,' she began, 'it's been a pleasure, and I hate to leave just when things are starting to get interesting, but it's late, and my husband likes his dinner on the table when he walks in the door.'

'So, let him put it there,' someone else said.

'The only bad thing about marriage,' Beth announced, 'is that it goes on for so long.'

'Not mine,' Ricki exclaimed, standing up as well. 'Actually, I should go too.'

'We all should,' Beth agreed. 'Much as I hate to admit it, Al also likes his food on the table as soon as he comes home.'

'You go,' Jill told her. 'I'll wait for Laurie.'

'You don't mind waiting alone?' Beth asked her.

'How long can it take to wash seventy-five pounds?'

'Anorexia nervosa,' Ricki intoned ominously. 'Goodbye, Jill.' She extended her hand. 'It's been lots of fun. Hope to see you here again.'

'Next Wednesday,' Jill told her.

'I'll be here,' answered the round little woman, bidding a similar farewell to Beth.

'She must be dynamite in bed,' Jill whispered under her breath, thinking that it usually took more than a sense of humor to attract three husbands, not to mention thirty million dollars and a twelve-inch cock. She thought immediately of Elaine. What was she doing with a man like Ron Santini? More to the point, what was he doing with a woman like Elaine?

'Jill? Hello, Jill, are you there?' Beth was asking.

'Oh, sorry, Beth. I guess I wasn't. You're leaving.'

'Yeah, I really should. You'll be at Don Eliot's on Saturday night?'

Jill looked pleasantly surprised. 'Yes. You too?'

Beth nodded. 'We'll be there.'

'Oh, good. See you then.' Beth turned and headed toward the door. 'And one,' Jill called after her, her voice a dead ringer for Rita Carrington's. 'And two. And one —'

Chapter Eight

Don Eliot's home was big and old and in as much a state of shambles as one might expect from a place that housed two adults, five children under the age of ten, and three cats. There were also the required number of gerbils and goldfish although they were too prone to unfortunate accidents and flushings to be ever seriously included in the family census. In short, the house looked exactly like the kind of house one would expect Don Eliot to live in – it rambled; it was messy; it was vaguely intimidating; it was very comfortable. Jill tried to reconcile the two final descriptions. How could a house that was intimidating be comfortable? she wondered, yet concluded that those were exactly the right words to use. Don Eliot was exactly the same way.

His wife was only comfortable. There were no airs, no pretenses about her. She was, plainly and simply, a woman with five children and no live-in help. A cleaning lady came twice a week, but both she and her husband had been unhappy with the notions of strangers sharing their house. And so, Adeline Eliot had done it all herself. ('What I really hate,' she had confided to Jill, 'is these single women who meet you at parties and ask you what you do, and when you tell them you're a mother, they stare and say, "Yes, but what do you *do*?"')

'I hope you don't mind, the children are all up,' Adeline greeted them at the door. 'They wanted to meet you before they went to bed.'

'Sounds great,' David said enthusiastically, kissing Adeline on the side of the cheek. 'Where are they?'

'Upstairs, for the moment – count your blessings,' Don Eliot's wife responded, her warm smile etching deep creases at the sides of her mouth. The combination of the lines and the many streaks of gray running through her otherwise dark hair, which she wore pulled back severely into a bun, contributed to the image of a much older woman, although Jill placed her age at somewhere between Beth Weatherby's and her own. 'I can't remember whether or not you've been here before,' she said to Jill.

'No, I haven't,' Jill replied, realizing Elaine obviously had been. 'It's lovely.'

'Well, it's a mess,' Adeline laughed. 'But then it always is. I've given up trying to do anything about it. Maybe when all the children are gone—' She ushered them into the large living room where Don Eliot was standing behind a makeshift bar serving drinks. Al and Beth Weatherby, their hands interlocked, sat as close as newlyweds on the tattered print sofa. Everybody rose immediately to say hello.

'Who starred with Richard Burton in *The Spy Who Came In from the Cold*?' Al asked instantly, releasing his wife's hands to take hold of Jill's, and kissing her on both cheeks.

'Claire Bloom,' Jill said, returning his kisses.

'Too easy,' Al muttered. 'I knew it was too easy. Wait, I have another one. Who was the male lead in *Them*?'

'In what?' asked Don Eliot.

'*Them*,' Jill repeated. 'It was a horror movie. One of the first about the possible results of nuclear testing, and one of my favorites.'

'Naturally,' Al sighed, playfully. He looked at Jill. 'So, who was the male lead?'

Jill smiled. 'Was it James Arness?' she asked.

'It was,' Al sighed. 'One of these days, I'm going to stump you.'

'Many have tried,' David laughed, squeezing Jill's arm and going over to Don Eliot.

'We intend to try harder – later on,' Don Eliot stated with a mischievous twinkle. 'What'll it be?' he asked, indicating the drinks.

'Scotch and water,' David said.

'White wine?' Jill asked.

'You got it,' Don answered.

'It's quiet,' David remarked, looking around.

'That's because we have all the kids locked up in a soundproof vault until everybody arrives.' There were a few chuckles. 'Seriously, they must be watching television. We told them if they kept relatively silent until we finished welcoming everyone, they could come in and do their little Von Trapp number.'

'Who else is coming?' Beth asked.

Jill suddenly sneezed.

'Catching cold?' Don Eliot asked. Jill shook her head.

'Cats bothering you?' David asked, taking his drink from Don's hand.

'I guess so,' Jill said, sneezing again. 'I have a slight allergy to cats,' she explained. Slight? she questioned herself. She'd be lucky if her eyes didn't swell up and close over by the time the evening was finished. If she was really lucky, she might even be able to breathe by the following morning. She pictured the long night ahead.

'I should have told you about the cats,' Adeline whispered. 'A lot of people have allergies to cats these days. I could take them outside, if you'd like.'

'No, it's the hair,' Jill explained, seeing one cat curled up on the sofa and another in a chair by the windowsill. The third was undoubtedly warming her seat in the dining room. 'It gets in everything.'

'Especially in this house,' Don Eliot said, handing Jill her drink. 'There you go, Jilly. That'll make you feel better.'

'I'll be fine,' Jill said, sipping the clear white liquid. 'It's probably just the initial contact.' She hoped she sounded more confident than she felt.

Don Eliot looked around the room. 'Anybody else?'

Beth shook her head. 'I'll have a refill,' Al Weatherby said. 'You didn't answer my wife's question. Who else is coming?'

'Oh,' Don Eliot said, returning to the table where the liquor was all set up, 'I invited Nicki Clark.' Jill sneezed violently. 'You all right?' Don asked her. Jill buried her face in the Kleenex which Beth thrust suddenly under her nose. 'She's been helping me the last few weeks with a case I've been working on. I thought it would be nice to include her. She lives alone, you know. Her father lives in New Hampshire with his wife, who apparently is only a few years older than Nicki. Her mother died of cancer some years back. Kind of sad. She's a real nice kid, but I don't think she has a whole lot of friends.'

I wonder why, Jill thought, glancing over at David. He was looking at her as if to explain he was as surprised as she was.

'I'm sure she's given up on the whole thing,' he said a few minutes later, walking over to Jill and whispering from behind his drink.

'Oh?' Jill questioned, trying hard not to sneeze again.

'I haven't seen her all week. I think she's been avoiding me. Probably embarrassed.'

'Maybe,' Jill said. 'Don't worry about it. I'm not.'

David smiled. 'Good girl.'

'So, is Nicki coming alone?' Al Weatherby asked in a temporary lull in the conversation.

'No. She phoned Adeline and asked if she could bring a date.'

Jill watched David's face. He smiled at her, as if to say, there, you see? Well, maybe he was right. Maybe the game was over. She sneezed again, her eyes beginning to itch.

The doorbell rang again and suddenly everything began happening at once. The third cat appeared and began running through everybody's legs; the five Eliot children exploded into the room, chasing the cats, grabbing at the fresh vegetables and dip Adeline had prepared (God only knew when), playing hide-and-seek behind the liquor table and screaming loudly at no one in particular. 'Home sweet home,' Don Eliot mused, re-entering the room with Nicole Clark and a young man who looked enough like her to be her brother. 'Nicki,' Don said, his right arm sweeping across the room as if to bring everyone closer together, 'I think you've probably met everyone – at least, the gentlemen. Do you know Al's wife, Beth?'

'I think we've said hello,' Beth said graciously. 'At the picnic.'

'Oh, yes,' Nicole said in her deep voice. 'Of course.'

'And David's wife, Jill?' Don continued.

'We've met,' Jill said.

'Nice to see you again,' Nicole said, as if she meant it.

'And, of course, my wife you met at the door,' Don concluded. Nicole nodded. 'And this is Nicki's friend, Chris Bates, right?'

'Very good,' the young man smiled, confidently.

'Chris is one of the new lawyers at Benson, McAllister.'

Everyone agreed it was nice to meet him. Jill sneezed.

'Do you have a cold?' Chris asked over the general shrieking of the children.

'A slight allergy,' Jill said quietly.

'To cats or children?' Nicole asked. Everybody laughed, including David.

'Cats,' Jill answered.

'I always thought allergies were psychosomatic,' Nicole said cheerfully, before turning her attention back to her date.

'Okay, kids, line up,' Don Eliot ordered the children.

It took several minutes but then there they all stood, arranged according to height, before their captive audience. 'We'll do this as fast as we can,' Don said, starting at the tallest head. 'Jamie, Kathy, Rodney, Jeremy, Robin,' he said, tapping each head in turn. 'Are you going to sing or dance or what?' he asked.

'Or what!' the oldest, Jamie, yelled out, and everyone went wild.

It took almost ten minutes before calm was restored and the children were herded upstairs. 'We have a surprise for you,' Don said, leading his guests toward the dining room. 'It's a game we made up in honor of Jilly. She's our movie buff. I'll explain it at the table.'

'Oh, good,' said Nicole Clark, looking directly at Jill. 'I love games.'

The guests sat at the long, heavy oak table and eyed each other warily over their steaming bowls of mock turtle soup.

'This is delicious,' Jill said, breaking the silence. Was everyone as nervous as she was? And why was she so nervous? It was just a game, a harmless little parlor game. It didn't matter who won or lost. Jill looked across the table at her husband, who was sandwiched between Beth Weatherby on one side and Nicole Clark on the other. What was making her more nervous – the silly game or her husband's proximity to the woman everyone at the table, except herself, casually, even affectionately, referred to as Nicki? Jill looked over at Nicole's perfect profile. The girl was quietly engaged in a conversation with her host, and except for a smile in David's direction when he'd passed her the bread basket, she had largely ignored the fact that he was seated beside her. Jill tried to reach her husband's feet with her own but the distance between them was too wide. Instead, she collided with one of the table legs. She winced, realizing with some relief that her nose felt less stuffy in this room. We never allow the cats in the dining room, Adeline had told her as they'd crossed the wide center hall.

'Jill?'

Jill's eyes suddenly focused on her husband's. He had been saying something to her. She hadn't heard a word.

'I'm sorry,' Jill apologized, realizing everyone was watching her.

'Trying to figure out how to get your line in?' Don Eliot asked gleefully.

'I guess I was,' Jill lied, thinking quickly of the game they were supposed to be playing and the line she had been assigned to deliver.

'Adeline asked if you'd like the recipe,' David told her, in a suitably subtle admonishment.

'For the soup,' Adeline added.

'I'd love it,' Jill said enthusiastically. 'If it's not too hard—'

'Hard? Are you kidding? Do I have time to make hard?'

'I don't know how you have time to do anything,' Beth said, echoing Jill's feelings.

'It's all a fake,' Adeline continued proudly. 'You just mix Campbell's tomato soup with Campbell's green pea soup, add a little milk and a lot of sherry, and presto, mock turtle soup.'

'I'll have to try it,' Jill promised.

'I'm hopeless in the kitchen,' Nicole Clark interjected. 'When I get home, I'm usually so tired, I just call in for a pizza or something.'

'She calls in for pizza, and look at her,' Beth said innocently.

'Jill and I would have to go to exercise class every day for a month before just calling in for a pizza!'

Nicole Clark smiled sweetly at Jill. 'Oh,' she said, 'I think you're exaggerating.'

'Has your wife been complaining all week too, David?' Al Weatherby asked. '"This hurts, that hurts. Don't touch me here. Don't touch me there."' He laughed.

'I've heard the odd complaint,' David confessed.

'They go to one exercise class,' Al continued. 'You'd think they'd been to the wars.'

'What exercise class do you go to?' Nicole asked.

'Rita Carrington's,' Beth explained. 'Over on Warden Street. We joined last week. A humbling experience, wouldn't you agree, Jill?'

Jill nodded, trying to smile.

'I've never been to an exercise class,' Nicole said. 'I guess I should, though, *before* my body starts to fall apart.'

Jill finished off the last of her mock turtle soup quickly before the urge to hurl it across the table completely overwhelmed her.

'Exercise takes a lot of self-discipline,' Chris Bates began. 'A lot of self-control. I'm not big on control.'

Jill's eyes shot directly to his. '*Ordinary People*,' she spat out suddenly. 'The psychiatrist, Berger, I think.'

'Right you are!' Don Eliot applauded. Everyone else looked vaguely startled.

Chris Bates lowered his head and laughed. 'I rushed things,' he said. 'I shouldn't have been in such a hurry to get the line out.'

113

'It was the perfect time,' Adeline said, disagreeing. 'But you're up against the master.'

'One for Jilly,' Don Eliot said and everyone smiled.

The next course was less successful than the first, the salad too wet and lifeless, the roast beef too tough, the potatoes too bland. For a few minutes, Jill felt as if she were back at her parents' home. It was the kind of meal she had grown up on. She was starting to relax more with the game, however, having decided she couldn't be any more clumsy than anyone else. The game consisted of simply being able to identify lines from famous movies. Each person at the table (with the exception of Don and his wife, who had devised the game and therefore knew all the answers) had been assigned a line of dialogue, and it was everyone's responsibility to inject this line into the conversation without detection. It was up to everyone else to do the detecting.

So far, Jill was batting two out of three, having successfully identified Chris's earlier attempt from *Ordinary People* and Beth's subsequent exclamation of 'Oh, we're fertile, all right,' which Jill recognized instantly as a line from *Rosemary's Baby*. Nicole Clark had guessed the third, Al Weatherby's vain attempt to disguise Faye Dunaway's line from *Bonnie and Clyde* ('We rob banks') in the middle of a long anecdote which Jill had been waiting for him to complete before unmasking him. Nicole, however, chose not to wait. She jumped right in.

The dessert was a soufflé which had fallen somewhere between its removal from the oven and its presentation at the table. It was served without apology and tasted as good as Jill imagined it would have anyway. She finished it all and asked for seconds, realizing that the rest of them had to get their lines in before coffee was concluded.

'How's the Rickerd divorce coming?' Al Weatherby asked David.

'Messy. The stuff of front pages.'

'I just want to know who's got that gorgeous house,' Beth said.

'I've seen it,' Nicole Clark stated quickly. 'I was at a party there a few years ago. It's just beautiful. All wood paneling, lots of lovely ceilings, some of them twelve feet high. You don't see that anymore.'

'Especially not in an apartment,' David agreed.

'That's for sure,' Chris Bates said, and there followed a long discussion on the housing situation in Chicago.

'How's your sister?' Beth asked David as coffee was being served.

'She's fine,' he said, then hesitated. 'Well, actually, she's been a little bit depressed lately.' Jill tried to figure out what he was talking about. She hadn't heard anything about Renee's being depressed. 'A friend of hers committed suicide.' He looked directly at Jill. 'Julie Hubbard,' he said. Jill gasped.

'My God,' she said. 'When?'

'A few days ago. The family covered it up. I don't know.' He paused dramatically, shaking his head. 'What can you say about a twenty-five-year-old girl who died?'

'*Love Story*!' Nicole Clark shrieked. 'The opening line from *Love Story*!'

'You got me,' David confessed, laughing.

'Well done, Nicki,' Don Eliot bellowed. 'Very good. You're

tied up with Jilly now. Two each.' He turned toward Jill. 'Jill, are you all right?'

Jill felt the color gradually returning to her face. 'Julie Hubbard,' she repeated slowly, 'she's—'

'Alive and well and still living in the West End,' David said, his eyes sparkling. 'Fooled you. Fooled the champ!'

'Yes, you did,' she admitted. 'Not exactly fair though. You really had me going. I went to school with the girl,' Jill explained to the others.

'I thought she was only twenty-five,' Nicole smiled.

Jill looked over at Nicole. 'I guess I was too stunned to consider logistics,' she said, thinking of how convincing a liar her husband could be.

That left only Nicole and herself, Jill realized. How appropriate. They would face each other like the gunfighters in *High Noon*, shooting their lines, like bullets, straight at each other's hearts. Jill looked around the table, feeling suddenly that it was very important she win this showdown, feeling the symbolism inherent in the situation was too heavy not to be weighted in her favor. She had to win. She had to prove to Nicole that she was still on top of things, even if it wasn't exactly clear what those things were. Neither she nor Nicole had delivered her line. Time was running out. Still, she couldn't rush. What she said had to sound endemic to the conversation. If only someone would provide her with a proper cue.

As if instinctively realizing her role, Beth handed Jill the perfect lead-in. 'That's a beautiful dress you're wearing,' she said. 'I meant to tell you earlier—'

'Oh, thank you,' Jill gushed, perhaps a touch too effusively.

'I must have changed a hundred times.'

'She always does that,' David qualified. 'But it was even worse tonight. I thought we'd never get out of the apartment.'

'Well, you know how it is,' Jill explained, feeling her heart beginning to beat faster. Could everyone hear it? Would it give her away? The words tumbled out. 'If David doesn't like what I'm wearing, I take it off!'

Nicole's husky whisper was suddenly as loud as any voice Jill had ever heard. 'I know that line!' she pounced. 'Give me a minute – I know that line, I just have to figure out where it comes from.' She threw her head back, her eyes closed. 'Just a minute. Just a minute—' Her head straightened up; her eyes opened. Her face was barely big enough to contain her smile. 'I've got it! Joan Collins to June Allyson in *The Opposite Sex*. And the exact line was, "If *Stephen* doesn't like what I'm wearing, I take it off!"'

'Bravo!' shouted Al Weatherby. 'How do you like that, Jill?' he said, turning to her. 'She got you.'

'She certainly did,' Jill agreed, good-naturedly. 'Actually, I'm relieved. I was so nervous. Am I the only one who gets so nervous?!'

'What's there to be nervous about?' Adeline asked, greatly amused. 'It's just a game.'

'And so far, Nicki's winning,' Chris Bates pointed out proudly.

'Actually,' Don Eliot said, 'she's already won! Haven't you, Nicki?'

Nicole clapped her hands in delight.

'What about your line?' Al asked her.

'I gave it,' Nicole said. 'A long time ago. When we were talking about the Rickerd divorce, and Beth wondered who'd get their gorgeous house. I said I'd been in it, which was a lie, of course. I don't even know them. And I said that it was all wood-paneled, with "lots of lovely ceilings." That was my line. "Lots of lovely ceilings." It's from—'

'*The Carpetbaggers*,' Jill said quietly, recognizing the now familiar line. 'Elizabeth Ashley to George Peppard when he asks her what she'd like to see on her honeymoon.'

Nicole's already wide smile widened even farther. 'Too late,' she chirped happily and the party adjourned to the other room.

Jill propped two extra pillows underneath the one she normally used and crawled back into bed beside her husband.

'Is that it?' he asked wearily. 'You think you're finally set for the night?'

Jill looked over at the clock. It was almost two in the morning. For what felt like the tenth time in as many seconds, she sneezed. 'It's those damn cats,' she said, hoping the extra pillows would allow her to breathe easier.

'You're sure it's not something else?' he asked.

'What else could it be?'

'Well, you didn't sneeze at all in the Eliots' dining room.'

'They don't allow the cats in the dining room.'

'You said yourself their hair gets in everything.'

'What are you trying to say, David? That Nicole is right? My allergy is psychosomatic?'

'It just seemed strange that after you lost that stupid

118

game, you started sneezing again.'

'We went back into the living room!' she said, her voice rising.

'Oh,' he said with infuriating condescension. 'Please don't yell.' She sneezed again. 'Is this going to go on all night?' he asked.

'It might,' Jill remarked, coldly. 'Why, do you have a heavy date tomorrow?'

'I have to go in to work,' he said.

'On Sunday?'

'Oh, let's not start that, Jill,' he begged. 'I'm swamped. I've told you that. I'm also exhausted. You've been sneezing for the past two hours. Why don't you just close your eyes and forget about the fact that Nicole won. It was just a game, not the goddamn Olympics!'

Jill sat up sharply in bed. 'You think I'm upset because Nicole won?' she accused.

'Well, aren't you?' he asked.

'No!' she said, protesting just a shade too strongly. 'I *do* think she got a particularly easy line to read,' she added. '"Lots of lovely ceilings" is a much easier line to sneak into a conversation than what I had to say.'

'She drew from the hat the same as everyone else,' David pointed out. 'Come on, don't you think you're making too much of this?'

Jill shrugged, knowing he was right, and knowing also that it wasn't really the fact that she had lost a silly game that was bothering her. What was disturbing her more were the implications her loss had carried to both herself and the other woman. Nicole's victory implied that there would be others; that this was merely the beginning of a long series of titles being snatched away from the reigning heavyweight, that the challenger had won the first round and was on her way to the final count. It seemed particularly ironic that the dialogue Jill had had to deliver had been of such a similar nature to their own situation: June Allyson, knowing of her husband's affair with Joan Collins, confronts the younger woman and says that if the dress Joan is wearing is for Stephen, his tastes run to simpler styles. Joan responds that if Stephen doesn't like what she wears, she – David's voice interrupted her thoughts.

'What?' she asked defensively, the child caught with her pants down.

'I said, you're not upset because you still think she's after me, are you?' His question cried out for a negative response. 'Because if you are,' he continued, not waiting for an answer, 'you're way out of line.'

'I'm out of line?' Jill questioned.

'Let's just say you're wrong,' he said, retreating. 'She hardly looked at me twice all night.'

'You sound disappointed.'

He turned over in bed. 'Let's not get ridiculous.'

Jill let out a deep breath. There was obviously no point in pursuing this line of discussion. 'Did Beth seem subdued to you tonight?' she asked instead.

'No,' he grunted.

Jill looked in his direction, wanting to hug him, to pull him close against her the way they usually slept. She was about to when she felt her stomach cramp.

'Where are you going?' he asked accusingly as she got out of bed.

'My stomach hurts.'

'What'd you have two desserts for?' he called after her as she made her way to the bathroom. 'Nobody else did.'

'I didn't realize you were monitoring what I ate,' she said, more to herself than to David as she sat down on the toilet.

She was less surprised than disappointed when she saw the blood. Right on time, she thought, searching through the cupboard for her Tampax. The one thing in my life I can always depend on.

Chapter Nine

The staff lounge of the Radio and Television Arts Department of the University of Chicago was a large, rectangular room which always appeared to be a small square, possibly because of the amount of overstuffed furniture squeezed into it. It seemed the college administrators equated mass with comfort and what was shabby with what was artistic, Jill thought, as she came inside and headed toward the coffee machine. The large percolator was already empty, which meant that if she wanted any coffee, she would have to make up a fresh brew herself. Let somebody else do it today, she decided, settling down into the nearest floral print armchair to wait, and trying to get in a suitable position for a two-minute sleep. She felt her muscles tense across her back and wondered idly if the exercise class she'd be attending that afternoon would make her feel better or worse. She also wondered if Beth would show up for this week's class, having missed the last one without notice or explanation. ('Things just got away from me,' she had told Jill subsequently, and Jill, sensing a certain reticence on the part of the other woman, had questioned her no further.) When Beth decided she wanted to talk to her – if, indeed, there was anything to talk about – she would do so.

She shifted uncomfortably on a spring whose time had come and gone and and, deciding sleep was impossible, reached over across the multi-stained coffee table to pick up the morning paper. Someone had stolen the classified section. That did it! she decided, standing up and going toward the door. No coffee, no Classified section. No justice. She thought of David. She wasn't trying hard enough, he had told her. I've been trying my little heart out, she argued with him silently as she closed the door behind her and started down the long corridor toward her class. But honest effort doesn't always change things. And facts are facts. ('Just stick to the facts, ma'am.') I know it's an honorable profession, possibly even a courageous one. But it's just not for me!

She stopped in front of the door to her classroom as several of her students pushed past her, hurrying to make it inside before the bell rang. What am I doing here? she asked herself. The bell sounded and she stepped inside.

'Documentaries have to do more than simply report the news,' Jill was saying, hearing several voices speaking just under hers. 'We have news shows that do that; we have newspapers. A documentary has several functions – one, of course, is to provide the facts. Another more important function is to give those facts some life – to put images behind the words, to illustrate – show the people just what the facts are. I've told you all this before, and it was somewhat edifying to note that your outlines reflect this. Unfortunately, what most of these outlines lack is – guts. I don't know how else to put it. You're presenting me with a lot of facts and figures and telling me how you'd visualize these conceptions, but you're not giving me any *insight* into these statistics. You're not getting to my emotions.'

'You're telling us you want guts and insight and emotion?' one of her male students asked incredulously.

'That's exactly what I'm telling you,' Jill said.

'In an outline?' he questioned, shaking his head.

'If it's not in the outline,' Jill answered, 'it won't be there in the finished product.' It seemed as fitting an exit line as any and she dismissed her students ten minutes early with a nervous wave of her hand. Something Sandy Dennis might do, and probably had, in *Up the Down Staircase*.

Jill sat down behind the desk of indeterminate wood and undeterminable color and allowed her eyes to drift over to the windows on her right. Outside, it was sunny and hot. Not too humid. Just the right kind of day for sitting in the sun in a bikini and getting the perfect tan.

Whom was she kidding? she wondered, angrily turning from the window with its teasing, almost Kodacolor view of life. When was the last time she had looked good in a bikini? Five, probably ten years ago. If ever. And that was before time and a changing metabolic rate had thickened her waistline and made her aware of how tightly she was holding in her stomach every time she went out with David. Oh, well, she thought, standing up suddenly and gathering her belongings together, that's what Rita Carrington is for. Ready, ladies? And one and two—

'I don't know, Jill,' Beth Weatherby was saying as the two women slipped out of their street clothes and into their tights and leotards. 'It seems to me that there are some basic issues you have to resolve.'

'I know,' Jill sighed in agreement. 'The problem is how to resolve them.' She watched as Beth Weatherby pulled off her panty hose and slipped into her tights, leaving her skirt firmly in place as she did so. It was strange, Jill thought, she hadn't realized Beth would be so modest. She thought back to two weeks ago, wondering if Beth had undressed in a similar fashion at that time, then remembered that Beth had already been changed when she'd arrived, and that she'd left while Jill was still waiting for Laurie to come out of the shower.

Thoughts of Laurie led to thoughts of the girl's mother. Elaine and her daughter had gone on a sudden holiday to Yellowstone National Park ('Just a little impulse thing,' Elaine had claimed when she called to explain to David that Laurie would need a new jacket and some camping equipment for the trip). Jill wondered if Ron Santini would be going along and if he'd be bringing his own infamous equipment.

She sat on the bench in front of the lockers and pulled on her pink tights. 'Damn,' she said. 'I got a run. Look at that. And I just bought the stupid things.' Jill looked disgustedly at her legs. The run ran up the inside of her left thigh. She stood up, pulling on her leotard, adjusting it at her shoulders and crotch. 'I should really get a new leotard,' she said, as Beth pulled her own into place. 'I've had this one since my second year at college.' Both women sat down on the bench simultaneously, stuffing their belongings into the locker and closing it. 'How many minutes do we have?'

'Exactly eight,' Beth said, checking her watch.

THE OTHER WOMAN

'So,' Jill said, 'you have eight minutes to solve all my problems.'

'The answer is simple,' Beth said. 'I know because I'm great at giving advice.' Jill laughed. 'You get that way after being married to a lawyer for a long time. Seriously,' she paused, patting Jill's knee, 'you have to talk to David.'

'I have talked to him. He knows I hate my job.'

'Have you discussed quitting?' Jill nodded. 'And?'

'He says it's up to me, but I know he'd be upset. My job was fine until he was married to it, then it didn't seem so glamorous or exciting anymore. It just got in his way.' She turned full-face to Beth. 'I'm afraid, Beth,' she said.

A strange look crossed Beth Weatherby's face. 'What do you mean, afraid? What are you afraid of?'

'Of losing David,' Jill confessed. 'I'm afraid of doing anything that might jeopardize our relationship. Going back into television might do that.'

'Then don't do it,' Beth advised.

'It's the same thing about having more children,' Jill continued. 'We used to talk about it. David knows how much I'd like to have a family. But lately, he refuses to discuss it. He even told Don Eliot that he doesn't want more kids. I'm thirty-four years old, Beth. I don't have a whole lot of years left for this sort of thing, but I'm scared stiff to confront him because he's liable to give me a choice I'm not prepared to make.'

'Him or children?' Beth asked.

'Some choice,' Jill said.

'What would you say?'

Jill shook her head. 'I don't know.' She paused. 'Yes, I do.

David,' she said. 'Always David. I could never lose David.'

'Even if it means losing yourself?' Beth asked her. 'What's the matter? You look like you've just seen a ghost.'

Jill said nothing, feeling the color drain slowly from her face as Nicole Clark bounced into view.

'Well, look who's here,' Beth greeted the girl warmly, not connecting Jill's pallor with Nicole's sudden appearance.

'I hope you don't mind,' Nicole said, throwing her bag across the bench and proceeding to unbutton her blouse. 'But I remembered you talking about this class and I asked Al what time it was you went, and he was good enough to tell me. I finished a little early today, so I decided to join you. I hope you don't mind,' she repeated.

'No, of course not,' Beth said, turning to Jill for confirmation. Jill made no effort to smile.

What was Nicole doing here? Jill asked herself angrily, turning away as the younger woman unhooked her bra. She is not going to dangle those tits in front of me, she thought, aware of Beth's eyes penetrating her back questioningly. She resolved not to turn around, not to acknowledge this intruder's presence in any way. The game was over whether Nicole liked it or not. There would be no more pretenses, no more ignoring or trying to be nice. This woman had said clearly and succinctly that she was after Jill's husband. She had further said that it was no joke, and more and more, she seemed to be insinuating her wormy little way into Jill's life: in court at David's side, while Jill, herself, sat several rows to the back, an observer only; at dinner at Don Eliot's, again by David's side, while once again Jill merely observed; and now, here, invading Jill's private terrain, strutting her stuff, showing off the competition, intimidating the older models. Make way for this years pièce de résistance.

Jill turned around angrily. She was going to bring things to a head once and for all.

Nicole spoke before Jill could open her mouth. 'I was wondering if we could talk after the class,' she said.

'I think that would be a good idea,' Jill answered, trying to keep her voice as steady as Nicole's.

'Good.' Nicole looked back at Beth. 'Excuse me, I'm going to try to find the john,' she said, and disappeared as abruptly as she had arrived.

'What was that all about?' Beth asked.

'I'll let you know,' Jill answered as Ricki Elfer came waddling hurriedly toward them.

'Whew, almost late,' she gasped, pulling off her dress to reveal she was already in costume. 'Did you see that gorgeous little thing that just walked out of here? I bet she's one of the new instructors. Now, that's a body to aspire to.'

Jill strode quickly toward the exercise room, feeling the knots in her shoulder muscles moving up to surround her neck, threatening to cut off her air supply and leave her breathless and gasping for oxygen, while somewhere behind her, Nicole Clark, in powder-blue leotard and matching tights, was waiting patiently to dance on her grave.

'Do you want to talk here or would you rather go out for a cup of coffee?' Nicole asked, toweling the sweat off her forehead and following Jill out of the exercise class.

'The lounge will be fine,' Jill said, wondering why, despite the sweat the younger woman had worked up, her silky black hair remained unaffected. Jill didn't need a mirror to tell her that her own hair must look as if she'd stepped on an electrical current.

'Shower first?'

'No,' Jill said, not about to compare nude bodies with the other woman. 'Let's just get this over with.'

'All right,' Nicole agreed. 'Lead the way.'

Beth Weatherby touched Jill's elbow. 'I'll go now,' she said.

'Okay. See you next week.'

'Call me if you want to talk,' Beth added.

'Thanks. I probably will.'

'Goodbye, Nicole,' Beth called before veering off in another direction. 'You did extremely well in there for someone who never exercises.'

''Bye. Thank you,' Nicole answered. 'Nice lady.'

'Yes. Very.'

'Have you been friends long?'

'About four years.' Jill turned a corner. 'This way,' she said coldly.

Nicole followed Jill into the deep purple womb of the lounge. Ricki Elfer was already there, seated at a table with two other women. She waved enthusiastically at Jill. 'Come on over and join us,' she called. 'We're talking about sex.'

'Later,' Jill laughed, indicating an empty table for two at the far side of the room.

'Now, that's what you call a body,' she heard Ricki say as

they passed, knowing the body to which Ricki was referring was not her own.

'Do they serve milk shakes here?' Nicole asked, sitting down.

'Do you sit up nights thinking of these things to say?' Jill asked, deciding to eliminate small talk altogether.

'I don't understand.'

'Look, I'll admit to a few things right off the top, okay?' Jill told her. 'I am thirty-four years old. My hair is too wild, my mouth is too wide, my features in general are far from perfect, as is my body, which I'm sure you've already noticed. It's a nice enough body, but it's thirty-four years old, and milk shakes are a thing of the past.' She paused. 'You, on the other hand, are what? Twenty-four?'

'Twenty-five.'

'Twenty-five,' Jill repeated. 'So, you're younger, you're better-looking, you're obviously in terrific shape and your innocent little remark about the milk shakes lets me know that you don't have to worry a whole lot about staying in shape. Good for you. You may stay lucky or you might wake up one morning – fat. I don't know. I hope so.' She paused. 'Anyway, I concede your youth, your beauty, your body. I give you all that. What I won't give you is my husband.' Nicole said nothing, listening intently. 'You may have it all over me in the looks department; you may even be smarter than I am. I don't know; I don't care. The fact is that *I* am married to the man you say you want and I intend to keep it that way. I was there first,' she continued, conveniently overlooking Elaine. 'That gives me some rights.' Still, Nicole said nothing. 'Now, I don't know. Maybe you've changed your mind; maybe you were a little drunk when you said those things; maybe I'm reading more into your remarks than you've intended. David thinks I am. You'll have to straighten me out, I guess. Tell me exactly where things stand. Unlike you, I hate games. They make me very nervous.'

Nicole's voice was almost inaudible. 'You told David what I said at the picnic?'

'Wasn't I supposed to? I assumed it was part of the plan.'

'What did he say?'

'He thought it was a joke. When I explained it wasn't he got quite angry.'

'He didn't say anything to me.'

'I asked him not to.'

There was a long silence. Nicole lowered her head. 'I'm very embarrassed,' she said at last. 'And I'm very sorry.'

Jill said nothing, waiting for the girl to elaborate. The apology had come so quickly, seemed so genuine, she wasn't sure how to react. She'd been right to level with Nicole, to get things out in the open. Honesty is the best policy, she could hear her mother saying. She waited. When Nicole raised her head again, Jill could see her eyes were cloudy with tears.

'What can I say?' she began. 'The whole thing is so stupid. I don't know why I said those things to you at the picnic. Maybe I *was* a little drunk, although that's no excuse.' She looked around the room, avoiding Jill's eyes. 'I'm from Maine originally. I've been here for four years now. I went to law school here and my family, my father actually – my mother's dead – he stayed back East. He got married again a few years ago and moved to New Hampshire. Anyway, I guess that's my roundabout way of telling you that I don't have many friends here. Girls have always shied away from me.' She looked at Jill. 'I know you're thinking that's no surprise. Maybe you're right. Whatever the reason, even though I know it's in vogue and all that, I've never had a strong attachment with another woman. There have always been a lot of men around, obviously. But I've never cared much for men my own age.' Her eyes froze on Jill's. 'Which brings us to David.'

Jill held her breath.

'I took one look at your husband and – well, you know. I don't have to tell you.' She looked away. 'He's quite overwhelming, isn't he? Everything about him. The way he moves, the way he talks, the way he thinks—'

'You know what he thinks?' Jill interrupted.

'I know *how* he thinks,' Nicole corrected. 'He's a brilliant lawyer. I've watched him a few times since that morning we were all in court. He's never less than incredible.'

Jill hoped her eyes didn't register the surprise she felt at hearing of Nicole's subsequent trips to observe David in court. Why hadn't David told her?

'What can I say?' Nicole asked. 'I guess it's like a high school kid with a crush on her teacher. David is everything I ever wanted.' Jill looked away, not sure she wanted to continue this discussion. She remembered using almost the same phrase when she had described David to her mother some six years before. 'I remember when my mother and I used to talk about men,' Nicole said, as if reading Jill's thoughts, 'and she always said I should find someone whom I really respected. Someone who respected me. Well, right from the first, David treated me with respect. There aren't a whole lot of women lawyers at Weatherby, Ross. Not proportionately, anyway, and when I first walked in at the end of May, well, I took a lot of kidding. A lot of the men had trouble reconciling the way I look with the way I can do my job. Except from David. He treated me like a lawyer from the start. In fact, it didn't take me long to start wishing that he'd think of me more as a woman than as an attorney, and once I thought of that, well, fantasies don't need much room to grow. I knew he was married. I heard from some of the secretaries that his wife was tall and used to work in television and that David had left his first wife to marry her – you,' she added, unnecessarily.

Jill said nothing, still pondering the secretaries' description of her – tall and used to work in television. Did that really sum her up?

'I guess I've just been watching too many soap operas,' Nicole said disarmingly. 'When I saw you at the picnic, I thought I might as well be brazen about the whole thing and come right out with my intentions. I may even have realized you'd tell David. I guess I thought he'd be intrigued enough to, I don't know, approach me, maybe. I thought that once I got him into bed, the rest would fall into place.' She stopped talking. Both women looked directly at each other. It was at least a minute before Nicole spoke again. 'Anyway, I knew how edgy you were at Don's house the other week and I decided to come today to try and explain, to apologize. I'm sorry that I said those things at the picnic.' She waited for Jill to speak, her eyes still fogged with the threat of tears.

Jill felt strangely sorry for the girl despite the open admission of her feelings toward David, or maybe because of them. She felt her shoulders slump with relief. It was over. Nicole Clark – Nicki – was pulling in her long magenta fingernails and backing away. The game was over. She had won.

'That's all right,' Jill said, finding her voice. 'I guess we all say stupid things occasionally. Things we don't mean—'

Nicole's voice caught Jill by surprise. She wasn't through being magnanimous. It wasn't time for Nicole to interrupt. Her words hit Jill with all the force of a sharp slap across the face. 'I didn't say I didn't mean them,' Nicole said, her eyes suddenly very dry – ('I'm Nicole Clark. I'm going to marry your husband.') – 'I just said that I was sorry I said them.'

Before Jill had sufficient time to recover, the other woman was gone.

Chapter Ten

It was five forty-eight when the phone rang. David reached over and fumbled for the alarm on the clock radio before he realized that the insistent ring wasn't music and that it wasn't time for him to get up yet.

'Well, answer it,' Jill said groggily, sitting up beside him. 'God, I hope everybody's all right.' It was the first thing she thought of whenever the phone rang when it shouldn't.

David picked up the receiver. 'Hello?' he demanded.

'Happy birthday to you, happy birthday to you,' the voice sang as if through a meat grinder. David looked at his wife in disbelief, holding the phone up so that Jill could hear. 'Happy birthday, dear fuckface, happy birthday to you!'

'For Christ's sake, Elaine, it's not even six o'clock.'

Jill could hear Elaine's voice clearly on the other end. 'Yes, but if I waited another few minutes, you'd be in the shower. You see, I remember all your habits. And I didn't want to miss the opportunity of letting you know how I feel.' She paused. 'You're getting on, old boy. Forty-five, isn't it?'

'Elaine—'

'No, wait, I have something to say.'

137

'You always do.'

'I was thinking about your life insurance policy.'

'What about it?' Jill and David, the phone now resting between them, exchanged puzzled glances.

'Is it all paid up?'

David shook his head in disgust. 'What are you getting at, Elaine?'

'Well,' the woman replied, 'when I realized it was your forty-fifth birthday, it occurred to me that you are, after all, only mortal, and that with your workload and your other assorted – appetites, shall we say – that it's just conceivable you might drop dead on all of us one of these days.'

David moved the phone to his other ear. 'I'm hanging up, Elaine.'

'So I think you should change your policy.' Jill heard Elaine's voice as clearly as if she were right there in the bed between them.

'You think I should change my policy,' David repeated numbly.

'To include me.' She paused, giving her ex-husband time to absorb her words. 'Because if you should suddenly die, I'd be out in the cold. I mean, the money would just stop, wouldn't it?'

David started to laugh. 'It almost gives one something to look forward to,' he said.

'Well, as the mother of your children, surely you'll want to make sure they're protected—'

'My children will be looked after, Elaine.'

'And me?'

'Goodbye, Elaine.' David hung up the phone, allowing his body to fall back against his pillow. 'Jesus,' he said. 'Can you believe that?'

'She never misses an opportunity,' Jill said, snuggling up to her husband. 'Where does she get her ideas? And at six in the morning—'

'She's been calling the office all week. I haven't answered any of her calls.'

Jill ran her hand across her husband's chest, feeling the blond hairs beneath her fingers stand up and rub against her flesh, like a cat brushing up against a pair of bare legs. The thought of cats began tickling at her nose, and she instinctively moved her hand away to block an imaginary sneeze.

'Why'd you move your hand?' he asked.

'I thought I was going to sneeze,' she answered, moving her hand back to its previous position.

'Lower,' he said.

'Happy birthday,' she whispered, stretching over and kissing him, her hand moving down his body.

'I'm getting old,' he said, almost to himself.

'Oh, don't let Elaine get to you! Forty-five isn't old. It's barely middle-aged.'

'Really?' he asked. 'How many ninety-year-olds do you know running around?'

She laughed. 'Well, they're not exactly running—' He sighed. 'Oh, God,' Jill said suddenly, sitting up but leaving her hand where it was, 'you're not having a mid-life crisis, are you?'

'If you're not going to show a little respect for my age,' he admonished playfully, 'at least make yourself useful.'

He forced her head down to where her hand was.

Jill moved herself into a more comfortable position, thinking of the man she was ministering to, remembering the first time she had seen him nude, the first time they had made love, when she thought she'd died and gone to heaven. He'd been so overwhelmingly physical. Their first two years together had been so intense. It couldn't have gone on that way forever, she realized, trying to move her head up so they could align their bodies for consummation. But his hand held her head down firmly. He was not interested in consummation this morning. What the hell, she thought, addressing herself to the task at hand (at mouth?) with renewed vigor. It's his birthday!

This thought catapulted her mind ahead to the evening to come. Jason, freshly back from camp, and Laurie, bored after a week back home with nothing to do, would be coming for dinner. As would the rest of David's family and her own parents. The first time she'd had the courage to invite everyone over together. How was she going to get everything ready on time, she wondered, thinking of the menu she'd planned and the shopping she had to do. She was even baking David's birthday cake this year. Luckily, Fridays were a light day at the university. She'd canceled her morning class, which left two in the afternoon. Hopefully, by then she'd have everything under control. She felt herself beginning to worry. Maybe she'd taken on too much. David was always telling her she bit off more than she could chew. David, she thought. My God! Biting, chewing! What was she doing to him? He groaned, his hand still gripping her head. Had she hurt him? This was awful. How could she be doing this? Thinking about menus and classes when she was supposed to be caught up in the throes of passion.

David would know. He always knew what she was thinking. He'd know her mind had been elsewhere. He'd be hurt, angry. He might not even come, she thought with dismay, which would leave him frustrated and unsatisfied, the perfect target for Nicole's subtle advances. Nicole, she thought angrily. The dear thing had been quiet again the last few weeks, no phone calls, no surprise appearances. David hadn't so much as mentioned her name. But then David hadn't mentioned Nicole's visits to court with him either. It made them even, she decided – she hadn't told David about Nicole's visit to Rita Carrington's. What good would it have done? She'd take her cue from David and act as if nothing had happened. It was better to let the whole thing rest. Let it die of boredom – What was she doing? What was she thinking about? Concentrate, for God's sake, concentrate.

She was aware of some faint groaning in the background. David. Had she hurt him? She tried to move her head but the hand held firm. The groans grew louder.

'Jesus, Jill,' he gasped, then suddenly exploded. Jill gulped several times, swallowing hard before she felt his hand relax and she was able to sit up. 'That was incredible, Jill,' he said, kissing her forehead. 'Wow. I think that was the best you've ever done.'

Wonderful, Jill thought, and I missed it.

David pulled her close against him. Jill thought of that other morning not long ago when her dream had awakened them at a similar hour and David had responded by dragging her into the shower. Perhaps he'd do the same today. She began playing with the hairs on his chest. This time they lay still and soft, a kitten well fed and purring contentedly. Her body longed to be touched, caressed—

She heard a slight click and suddenly sounds of Stevie Wonder filled the room. David reached over and turned down the volume with one hand, while his other arm extricated itself from around Jill's shoulders.

'Time to get up,' he said, moving quickly out of bed.

Jill sat up. 'Feel like some company in the shower?'

He smiled. 'Not this morning, honey, okay? I have a really busy day ahead of me.' He paused. 'You angry?'

'Just disappointed,' she admitted, trying to look brave, the way Ali MacGraw had in *Love Story*.

'I'll make it up to you.' He waited until he saw her smile. 'Why don't you go back to sleep for a couple of hours?'

'No, I'm too awake for that,' she said. 'Besides, I have a lot to do, too. It's your birthday party tonight, remember?'

'Oh, shit. I forgot.'

'You don't have a meeting, I hope—'

'No.' he assured her. 'I don't think so. I'm sure there's nothing—'

'Please try not to be late. I have the whole family coming—'

'I'll try,' he said, before disappearing down the hall.

Jill sat on the bed, the words of Elaine's caustic birthday greeting filling her head. The woman must still have so much hate inside her, she thought. After all these years. What could make a woman hang on so tightly to that much hate? A man, her thoughts responded in Ricki Elfer's voice. A man could make you hate that much.

* * *

'Let's get out of bed and go to Winston's for brunch!' she whooped, jumping out of bed and pulling the covers off his naked body.

'It's two o'clock in the afternoon,' he laughed, making no move to cover his nakedness. She could see he was already aroused.

'Well, then, we'll have lunch, or afternoon tea or something.' She moved to the window and looked out, saw her landlady and the Doberman out sunning in the backyard.

'The "or something" sounds good,' he said, coming up behind her and covering her breasts with his hands.

'What are you doing?' she squirmed, smiling widely. 'Hey – what—' He was lifting her body up, fitting himself into her from behind. 'Mrs Everly's downstairs,' she reminded him. 'What if she looks up?'

'Then she'll see two very happy people.'

'And I'll probably have to start looking for a new apartment.'

'That would suit me,' he said. 'I still don't think this neighborhood is very safe.'

'Yeah,' she agreed, feeling her breath starting to get shorter. 'You never know when someone might sneak up behind you—'

They finally went out for something to eat at around four o'clock. Jill was as happy as she could remember being in a long time. They'd had the whole day – a day of loving and talking and being together. It seemed that there were no problems in their way, no people they had to consider, feelings they had to be mindful of hurting. There was only their love for each other.

'Smile and wave,' he was saying, as he drove to the restaurant.

'What?' she asked, cognizant of the change in his tone.

'Smile and wave,' he repeated through clenched teeth. Obviously, something was wrong but this was not the time to ask what it was. She turned her head to the right, smiled at the two women in the silver Buick, acknowledging them with a nod of her head instead of a wave of her hand. The women smiled back – had the driver looked vaguely puzzled as well? – and continued driving. No one had said anything.

Jill felt all the joy drain from her body. 'Elaine?' she asked, already knowing the answer. He nodded. 'Who was that with her?'

'Her sister.'

'They're very attractive. She – your wife – is very – attractive.' Again he nodded.

'What do you suppose she thought when she saw—'

'She thinks I'm with a client all day. I'll tell her I was just driving you home.'

Jill felt the knot in her stomach twist, causing her eyes to sting. 'I'm a client,' she repeated numbly.

'Well, Jill, what am I supposed to tell her, for God's sake? That I'll be spending the day screwing my brains out?! I'm sorry. I'm really sorry,' he apologized, his voice genuinely contrite and bewildered. 'That was a dumb thing to say. Really dumb. I'm just a little shook up, I guess, and embarrassed—'

'And humiliated,' she said, adding her feelings to his. 'And ashamed.'

He pulled the car over to the side of the road. 'Oh, Jill,

please don't feel humiliated and ashamed. There's no reason for you to feel that way. I love you.'

'Then why is it her feelings you're so worried about protecting? What about mine?' He had no answer. 'You better take me home. Your wife will be expecting you pretty soon now that she knows you're all finished with your – client.'

'What does that mean?'

'Just what I said.'

'Don't play games with me, Jill. I haven't got the time or the patience to try and second-guess you. Say what you mean.'

'I mean that I want to go home,' she said, her voice devoid of expression.

'Is that all you mean?'

'I mean I'm tired and hurt and angry and humiliated and ashamed that I still can't work up enough guts to tell you to get the hell out of my life and stay there. I mean that I still love you more than I hate you and that I still want you.' She stopped. 'Look, I'm going to take a taxi home. I just don't want to be with you right now.' She opened the door and got out of the car. He made no move to stop her.

'You make me feel like such a shit,' he said.

'You *are* a shit.'

'I'll call you later,' he said, watching after her until she found a cab.

Don't bother, she wanted to yell back, but she knew – and he knew – that she couldn't.

'Hello. Is Irving Saunders there, please?' Jill held the phone tight against her ear and waited for some response, looking toward the tiny dining room at the table she had to set for tonight's dinner. How was she going to get nine people around a table which only seated four? 'What? I'm sorry, I didn't hear you. Oh, oh, I didn't realize it was still so early.' She looked up at the kitchen clock. 'What time does he get in? Eleven?' It was only nine-fifteen. 'Okay, I'll call back. No, no, wait. Tell him to call Jill Plumley, no, I mean Jill Listerwoll, as soon as he gets a chance. Listerwoll,' she repeated, spelling it out slowly as if to confirm that the name was really hers, as much to herself as to the voice on the other end of the receiver. It seemed so long ago, she thought, giving the secretary her phone number. 'It's important,' she added before hanging up.

She looked around. The cake was in the oven; the salad had already been cut up. She still had the rest of the shopping to do. Maybe now, before Irving called back. No, she couldn't run out and leave the stupid cake—

Her eyes drifted back to the dining room table. Perhaps she should try to figure out the seating arrangement. Jill went to the cutlery drawer, opened it and stared at the assorted forks and knives. 'Nine people,' she said aloud, looking back out the kitchen doorway toward the tiny end of the L-shaped living room which tried to pass itself off as a dining area. With great effort, you might be able to squeeze six around that little table. But nine? Why hadn't she thought this through before?

Jill stood in the doorway defeated. Where was she going to put nine people? Luckily, her brother and his wife were vacationing in Florida ('Who goes to Florida in the summertime?' her mother had asked repeatedly since they left) or she'd have had eleven to contend with. Maybe they could all go over to Elaine's, she thought. After all, the house had once belonged to David as well. ('Give her anything she wants, for Christ's sake,' she had urged. 'Let's just get it over with and get on with our lives!') Oh, well, it had sounded like the right thing to say at the time.

Jill left the kitchen and proceeded around the L into the living area. It was reasonably spacious, or at least the floor-to-ceiling windows made it seem so. They faced south toward Grant Park, which provided them with a beautiful view of the magnificent Buckingham Fountain. Well, we should see something for the rent we're paying, she thought. There were two bedrooms, one of which functioned as a den, although she had hoped one day to replace the television and the old, sloppy sofa-bed and leather chair with a baby crib and layette. The thought made her uneasy – she had yet to follow Beth's advice and confront David – and she diverted her attention from it by straightening the pillows of the elegantly patterned chesterfield. I could put them all in here, she thought suddenly, counting the seating capacity. Three on the couch, two on the wing chairs, and she'd bring in the four chairs from around the dining room table. Perfect. She'd set the table for a buffet and let everyone serve themselves. Hopefully, no one would spill any of the beef Stroganoff on the white broadloom. She started back toward the kitchen, absently walking into the side of a square Lucite piece of modern art from which steel sticks dangled musically against horizontal stripes. ('What is it? Some kind of air-conditioner?' her mother had asked.) The steel sticks immediately became tangled and Jill spent the next few minutes trying to extricate them from one another without much success. It would have to wait for David, she decided, straightening up and returning to the kitchen, hoping he wouldn't be late for his own party. It seemed that every time she had her parents over, he was late, causing her father to wonder aloud when it was Jill ever saw her husband. ('He works till ten every night,' she could hear him saying. 'He works Saturdays and Sundays. When is he home?') Jill always brushed such questions (accusations?) aside by explaining that David's current working hours were only temporary, the same way David had explained it to her. But how long before temporary became permanent? In the first year or two of their marriage, he'd rarely worked past seven in the evening. Of course, she'd been busy herself in those days, often working late hours at the studio, coming home to find him waiting impatiently for her return. They'd order in a pizza; he'd tease her that the only thing she knew how to make for dinner was reservations. So how did she suddenly come to beef Stroganoff and cold blueberry soup?

The phone rang. Jill picked up the receiver. 'Hello,' she said.

'Jill?' The voice was strong and masculine, bringing immediate traces of the past to Jill's ears.

'Irving?' she yelled gleefully.

'You sound surprised. Didn't you call? I have a message here that you phoned.'

'I did. I did phone. But they said you wouldn't be in until around eleven.'

'I got tired of staying at home listening to the baby cry,' he explained grumpily. 'I came in early.'

148

'Baby? Irving, I didn't know you'd had a baby!'

'Six months ago. A boy.'

'Well, that's wonderful. How's Cindy?'

'Fine. She's great. A real little mother.'

'And you?'

'Well, I already have the four boys with Janet, so it wasn't exactly new to me.'

'And everything else?' she asked. 'How's everything else?'

'Wonderful. Couldn't be better. The network is driving me nuts as usual. How about you? How's David? You're still together.'

'Of course we are. He's fine. Great,' Jill emphasized, picturing the man on the other end of the phone – fiftyish, tall and muscular, graying hair and pale gray eyes to match. Undoubtedly he was wearing blue jeans and an open-neck shirt and he was leaning against the wall in the control room, televisions blaring all around him, tapes blasting, people racing frantically around. For a moment, she felt she was right in the middle of it. 'Irving, can we get together soon? There's something I want to talk over with you. An idea I have.'

'Sure,' he said. 'I'm leaving for Africa on Monday. Africa, of all places, and I'll be there for two weeks. Why don't I call you when I get back?'

Jill felt her shoulders sinking. 'Damn, I was hoping I could see you before then. Do you have any time at all today? Lunch? How about I take you to lunch?'

'Sounds important, he said.

'It could be.'

'Lunch it is. I'll meet you at Maloney's at one o'clock. How's that?'

'Perfect,' Jill said, wondering how on earth she was ever going to get everything done by this evening. 'Perfect.'

Chapter Eleven

The restaurant was crowded. Located just across the street from the studio, it was packed with television people, most of whom Jill recognized immediately, and some of whom recognized her in return. She spotted Irving's outstretched arm near the back of the large room and made her way toward it, realizing as she pushed past the stand-up bar that there were a disturbing number of faces that she didn't know at all.

'Jill! My God, it is! Jill Listerwoll!' the voice bellowed, the arms surrounding her, hugging her close against the prickly tweed of his jacket.

'It has to be Arthur Goldenberg,' Jill said, even before she saw his face. 'The only man I know who'd wear a winter jacket in the middle of summer.'

They kissed each other warmly. 'It's almost fall,' he reminded her. 'Next week is Labor Day.' His bright British eyes twinkled at her teasingly. 'So, how *are* you? What are you doing here? Are you coming back to us?'

Jill smiled lovingly at one of the station's makeup men. 'I don't know,' she said. 'I'm here to talk to Irving. See if there's something I might be right for.'

'You're right for everything,' he said, putting his arm around her shoulders and drawing her conspiratorially closer. 'Don't look, but see that woman sitting over at the far end of the bar – don't look!' he chastised as Jill automatically moved her head in the other woman's direction. 'She was your replacement. Don't look!'

'Sorry,' Jill whispered. 'I thought Maya Richards replaced me!'

'She did, but then she didn't work out. This one was brought in from LA. Susan Timmons. She's a barracuda, let me tell you. With skin to match. Not flesh – scales!'

'Arthur! You're terrible – did you talk like that about me after I left?'

He smiled. 'Only a little bit. And that was only because I was so hurt that you left us.' He paused. 'God, I hope you come back.'

'So do I,' Jill confessed, only now putting her deepest hope into words. She patted the makeup man on his cheek and pushed past him toward Irving Saunders, who had risen from his chair to greet her. On her way, she managed to get a good look at the woman who had taken over her job at the network. She was younger, Jill estimated, by about five years, and she was attractive in a brittle, blond sort of way. No scales anywhere that she could see.

'How are you, Jill?' Irving asked, kissing her squarely on the mouth. 'Still drinking bloody marys?' He signaled for the waiter.

'I haven't had a bloody mary in years,' Jill said, sitting down. 'It sounds wonderful.'

'One bloody mary, one scotch and water,' Irving told the waiter, before turning his attention back to Jill, making no attempt to disguise his open perusal of her appearance.

'So?' she asked. 'I look okay?'

'You look terrific,' he said, and seemed to mean it. 'Marriage obviously agrees with you.'

'I hope so,' Jill said, looking back toward the bar. 'I ran into Art Goldenberg—'

'I noticed. How *is* my favorite faggot?'

'He sends his love.'

'Yeah, I'll bet he does.'

'He pointed out my replacement.'

'Did he, now?' Jill nodded. 'Yes, well, we're very pleased with Susan. She's bright, ambitious, a hard worker. As a matter of fact, she'll be on this trip to Africa I was telling you about.'

Jill tried to look pleased. 'You were supposed to say she's not working out at all and that you'll agree to anything to get me back.'

Irving looked surprised. The waiter arrived and put their drinks in front of them. Jill raised hers immediately in a toast.

'Cheers.'

'Cheers,' Irving echoed, clicking his glass against Jill's. 'Are you serious?' he asked finally. 'Do you really want to come back?'

Jill took a deep breath. 'Yes, I am,' she sighed. 'I do. Although I hadn't intended to let it pop out quite this early in the conversation. I thought we could have a little small talk first.' She laughed nervously.

'You were always rotten at small talk,' Irving reminded

her. 'It was one of your charms.'

'I was also one of your best producers,' she reminded him in return.

'Yes, you were,' he admitted easily. 'No question about that.' There was an uncomfortable silence. 'Maybe we better have a few rounds of small talk,' Irving said, forcing a laugh.

'Doesn't sound promising,' Jill said, feeling slightly embarrassed.

Irving fumbled around for words. 'Tell me – uh – you know – how come—' He gave up. 'Why?' he asked finally.

'Why what?'

'Why do you want to come back? I mean, I thought that the job was creating all sorts of problems for you. David didn't like your being away so much. He objected to your hours, the danger you always placed yourself in. Has that changed?'

'I've changed,' Jill said. She looked directly into Irving Saunders' soft gray eyes. 'When David met me,' she began, the image of Nicole Clark suddenly as close to her as Irving's face, 'I was an exciting, bright, challenging lady who was always off somewhere chasing bullets or corruption or – something. I had a career! A life! I was an independent, strong woman.' She paused, dramatically. 'Now, I'm a wife.'

'Well, you're more than that,' Irving demurred. 'You're a teacher—'

'I'm *not* a teacher, Irving, you know that! You told me that when I said I was leaving. You were right. I'm going crazy sitting behind that stupid desk. I need to be *moving* again!'

'And David? You haven't told me how he feels.'

'What's important here is how *I* feel!' Jill answered, in

154

tones so strong they surprised her.

'David's feelings were the reason I lost you in the first place,' Irving explained patiently. 'I couldn't afford to hire you back only to lose you again after a few months.'

Jill paused. 'I really don't know how David would feel. We've discussed it very briefly. He says it has to be my decision. I know, I *know*,' she repeated, 'that he might not be too happy about it at first, but, goddamn it, Irving, I was a producer when he met me! I was a producer when he fell in love with me! That's part of what he fell in love with and now that part is gone!' She shook her head, thinking out loud. 'I don't know. A man has a wife who arranges her whole life around him, and yet he gets bored. She's so predictable, after all. Her world is so insular and unexciting. He leaves her for another woman, a woman who has a job of her own, a style of her own, a life of her own. She's everything his wife isn't. So, he divorces the wife and marries the other woman. And before you know it, he starts subtly altering her image until she becomes just like the woman he left behind. Pretty soon, hubby is starting to get bored again. And so the cycle begins all over, the man always searching for what he took away.'

Irving stared at her questioningly. 'Are you reading from your autobiography?'

'Just an overly familiar scenario. I don't want it to be mine.' She took a long sip of her drink. 'Am I making any sense?'

Irving polished off the last of his scotch and ordered them each another drink. 'I understand exactly what you're saying,' he began. 'Except that I see it from the male point of view, you understand. You remember Cindy, of course,' he continued, not even waiting for her nod. 'What is it about marriage anyway that changes people?' Again, no answer was required. 'How long was I sneaking around with Cindy before Janet finally gave me my divorce? Four years? Five years? Not only was she the best damn research assistant I ever had, but she was, well, exactly what you said before. She was exciting, challenging, independent, bright. One of the few effortlessly bright women I have ever met. And now this effortlessly bright lady can spend literally hours discussing the joys of Pampers versus the drudgery of cloth diapers. I *had* all that domestic crap twenty years ago! I lived with it for more years than I like to remember. I left it for a woman who loved picking up on a moment's notice and going out for dinner halfway across the world, who loved all-night parties and last-minute decisions. Now, I have a wife who breast-feeds our new son twenty times a day and wouldn't meet me around the corner for a hamburger without two weeks' notice. I have what I left.'

'David has what *he* left,' Jill said quietly.

'David has what he says he wants.'

'David doesn't know what he wants,' Jill scoffed. 'And neither, damn it, do I.'

Irving laughed emptily. 'I don't think *any* of us knows what he wants.'

'You want it till you get it,' Jill offered. 'Then you do your best to change it.'

'Or it changes itself,' Irving said. 'Who was it that said, "Beware of what you want. You might get it"!?'

Jill smiled. 'Grace Metalious,' she answered, thinking of the now deceased author of *Peyton Place*. 'But I'm sure she wasn't the only one who said it.'

Irving was laughing in earnest now.

'What's funny?' Jill asked him.

'You are. You're the only person I know who can actually give me the answer to what was intended as a purely rhetorical question. I hope David appreciates you.'

'Do any men ever appreciate their wives?' she asked, then quickly added, 'Purely rhetorical, I assure you.' The waiter brought them fresh drinks. 'Should we order?' Jill asked Irving.

He shook his head. 'Not hungry.'

'Me neither,' Jill told the waiter, who shrugged and went away. 'She keeps looking over here,' Jill said.

'Who's that?' Irving asked.

'Susan whatever-her-name-is, from LA.'

Irving looked over toward the bar, then back to Jill. 'Word's probably reached her about who you are.'

'You think she's worried?'

'Well, I guess it's like walking into a restaurant and seeing your husband having lunch with another woman.'

'Not all other women are threats.'

'Not all other women are after her job.'

'I was there first,' Jill said playfully, recognizing her words as the same ones she had used when talking to Nicole Clark several weeks earlier, realizing suddenly how childish they sounded.

'Yes, you were,' Irving agreed, 'but you gave it up. There's always someone waiting in the shadows to grab what somebody leaves behind.'

The woman at the end of the bar stood up and came toward

them. 'Irving,' she said pleasantly. 'Jill?' she asked, extending her hand. 'Someone just told me that you used to have my job.'

'Jill Listerwoll,' Irving began, introducing the two women, 'or would you prefer Jill Plumley?' Jill shook her head as if to say that either one would do. 'Anyway, this is Susan Timmons. You all ready for Africa on Monday?'

'All packed and shot full of vaccine,' Susan answered cheerfully. 'I've never been to Africa before,' she said to Jill. 'Can't wait to go.'

'I always wanted to see Africa,' Jill confided.

'Get David to take you,' Irving said, a bit too effusively. 'A nice rich lawyer has to spend his money somewhere.'

'He does,' Jill answered, thinking of Elaine.

'Well, I hope we meet again,' Susan Timmons said sweetly, almost sincerely. 'I'll see you back at the studio, Irving.'

'I'll be there in a few minutes,' he said, watching her leave.

Jill took a quick swallow of her bloody mary, feeling her head swimming slightly. Liquid lunches were not her specialty and there was still so much she had to do. How on earth was she going to teach two classes on a stomach full of vodka and tomato juice?

'Are you all right?' Irving was asking.

'You're telling me you don't want me back,' Jill said plainly.

'I'd love to have you back, Jill,' Irving said with obvious sincerity. 'But at the moment, there just aren't any jobs available.'

'What about on a free-lance basis?'

'You know how the network feel about free-lancers,' he told her. 'It would have to be a pretty special assignment for us not to use one of our own people.'

Jill felt her eyes start to water and immediately lowered her head.

'Hey, I'm sorry, Jill,' he said quickly. 'I didn't mean to shut you out in the cold that way.'

'You can't help it,' Jill said, recovering. 'I just thought I'd try.'

He reached over the table and grabbed her hand. 'I'm glad you did. And believe me, I want you back. Look, I tell you what, and this isn't a load of bull I'm feeding you either, you know how quickly everything can change in television.' Jill nodded, thinking of the many unfamiliar faces at the bar. 'Well, I think you know what I'm trying to say—'

'If anything comes up, you'll call me,' Jill answered.

'You'll be the first one I'll call.'

Jill smiled, finishing her drink. 'Well, I guess that's a start,' she said.

'You won't say no when I do,' he cautioned.

Her smile grew perceptibly wider. 'I won't say no.'

The phone was ringing as she fumbled for her key at the apartment door. 'Just a minute,' Jill called, dropping her parcels and pushing the key into the lock. 'I'm coming!' The door clicked open and Jill raced inside just as the phone stopped ringing.

'Why do they always hang up just when you get there?' she asked aloud, retrieving her groceries and closing the door behind her.

She began unpacking her bags, putting aside the present she

had bought for David – a silk shirt in shades of blue and black, with big, artist's-style sleeves. It had been expensive, but she'd pictured David wearing it and he'd looked so beautiful that she bought it, knowing he'd love it. She looked forward to his reaction when he unwrapped it.

Jill looked at the clock. It was almost five-thirty. Dinner was one hour away, and being family, everyone would be prompt. Except probably the birthday boy himself.

She was tired already. She'd been running around all afternoon on no lunch and two bloody marys. She needed a few minutes to put her feet up and let her head settle. She decided to relax for a few minutes in the den.

The phone rang.

Naturally, she thought. If they don't get you coming in the door, they get you as you're about to sit down!

'Hello?'

'Aren't we the eager beaver?!'

The sound of Elaine's voice cleared Jill's head instantly.

'Can I do something for you?' she asked impatiently, thinking of Elaine's earlier birthday greetings, in no mood to be pleasant to this woman with whom, it seemed, she was destined to spend the rest of her life. When there were children involved, she realized, there was no such thing as divorce.

'Is my husband around?'

'Your *ex*-husband is still at the office.'

'I called there. They said he'd left for the day.'

'Oh?' Jill tried not to sound too surprised. Was it possible David had actually been able to finish early and was on his way home?

'Up to his old tricks, is he?' Elaine asked. Jill could picture the smug smile on the other woman's face.

'I'll tell him you called when he gets home,' Jill said curtly, hanging up the phone abruptly, hoping to wipe away Elaine's smile. No, she realized, looking over at the dining room table, all set up and waiting for the birthday boy, I'm the one who's not smiling. At this moment, Elaine is grinning from ear to ear in her fully equipped, newly renovated designer kitchen. 'How does she do it?' Jill asked aloud, then finished the thought in silence – no matter what the circumstances, Elaine always managed to make her feel as if she weren't worth a plugged nickel.

She picked up the phone impulsively and dialed David's office.

'Weatherby, Ross,' answered the crisp tones of the receptionist.

'David Plumley, please,' Jill asked, wondering if the woman recognized her voice. She hated wives who always pestered their husbands at work.

'Mr Plumley is gone for the day.'

So Elaine had been telling the truth. 'When did he leave?'

'About twenty minutes ago.'

'Was he going home, do you know? It's his wife.'

'He didn't say, Mrs Plumley.'

'Oh. All right. Fine. Thank you.'

Jill replaced the receiver and walked toward the den. Twenty minutes ago meant he should be home. Assuming he was coming home. She angrily picked up the morning paper, which lay in a desultory heap across the brown leather chair, and plopped herself down, determined to read what she hadn't had time for earlier in the day. Determined to relax. Damn Elaine, she thought, flipping immediately to the Birth and Death Notices. Of course David was coming right home. He hadn't wanted to come home when he was married to Elaine precisely *because* he was married to Elaine. Jill Listerwoll Plumley was a different kettle of fish altogether. 'Jill Listerwoll or Jill Plumley?' Irving had asked her. Why couldn't she be both?

She looked down the long list of birth announcements. 'It's a Boy!' one shouted, immediately followed by 'It's a Girl!' Nothing unusual there. She glanced over at the death notices. Just once, she thought, she'd like to flip open the paper and see: 'It's a Corpse!'

The phone rang again. She dropped the paper and ran to answer it. She wasn't sure why she was bothering; it was probably Elaine again.

'Hello,' Jill said.

The voice on the other end of the line was calm but carried with it unmistakable undertones of anxiety. 'Jill? Am I getting you at a bad time?'

Jill was instantly aware that the woman's voice belonged to someone she knew, but she was unable to connect a face to the words. 'Who is this?' she asked, feeling clumsy and insensitive.

'It's Beth Weatherby,' the voice said quickly. 'I'm sorry, I should have said—'

'No, that's all right. I should have known.' Why were they so busy apologizing to each other? 'Is everything okay? You sound a little – strange.'

'I'm fine,' Beth assured her, sounding more like herself. 'I called a little while ago. I guess you were out—'

'Yes, actually, I was just coming in the door when—'

'I wondered if we could meet somewhere for a cup of coffee—'

'Sure. When?'

There was a slight pause. 'I was thinking of now.'

'Now?' Jill's eyes went directly to the clock. It was almost six. Her guests would be arriving in half an hour.

'I know it's an awkward time—'

'Oh, Beth, I'm really sorry, but I just can't. I have nine people here for dinner tonight – family – it's David's birthday—'

'Of course, I understand. Please don't feel bad. I didn't think you'd be able to make it—'

'Is something wrong?'

The voice regained its strength and now sounded like the Beth Weatherby Jill was used to. 'Oh, no, of course not. I'm sorry, I didn't mean to alarm you. No, no. Al just called and said he'd be late so I thought if David was going to be late too, we could have a cup of coffee. That's all. A little old-fashioned female get-together since I missed the class again on Wednesday. I missed you. But we can do it anytime.'

'Well, I'd really like to. How about after class next Wednesday? We could make an evening of it, maybe go to dinner and a movie or something.'

'Sounds great.'

'Good.'

'So, I'll see you Wednesday. Rita Carrington's at four o'clock.'

'Perfect. I'll see you then.'

''Bye, Jill.'

'Goodbye, Beth.'

Jill hung up the phone, hastily scribbled Beth Weatherby's name in her calendar for the following Wednesday night, and ran toward her bedroom to change into something suitable for dinner.

Chapter Twelve

She had just finished serving the main course and was wondering what to do about the cake when David arrived home. Without intending to, Jill looked at her watch.

'It's ten after eight,' her father whispered loudly from his place on the sofa.

'Hi, everyone,' David said easily, coming into the room to an assortment of grunts and muffled birthday wishes. Jill sat stiffly in one of the transplanted dining room chairs and watched her husband walk toward her, bend over and kiss her on the lips. 'Sorry I'm late, sweetie. A few of the guys in the office decided to take me out for a birthday drink.'

'I called the office around five-thirty,' Jill began, again without meaning to. 'That was a long drink, two and a half hours.'

'Well, maybe it was more like two or three drinks,' he winked. Or four or five, Jill said silently, angry and yet trying to hide her annoyance from everybody else. How dare he be so late! she seethed, ruining her dinner which had dried out waiting for him, embarrassing her in front of her family and his mother (who she knew was thinking that nothing had changed since he'd divorced Elaine). His mother sat between Jill's parents on the sofa. She looked over at Jill as if to advise her to say nothing more. Probably the same advice she gave Elaine. I am not like her, Jill's eyes trumpeted toward her mother-in-law. Our marriage is completely different. Completely. He doesn't treat me at all the same way he treated Elaine.

She heard Elaine's voice suddenly whispering in her ear. 'If he treated me the way he treats you,' she began before Jill cut her off abruptly with a toss of her head. I didn't invite you to this party, she thought, banishing Elaine's earlier admonishment from her memory and directing her attention to her husband.

'Do you want your dinner now?' Jill asked.

'No,' he answered. 'I'm not really hungry. I had a huge lunch. I'll just have some cake and coffee.' He looked around the room. 'If everybody will excuse me for a couple of minutes, I'll go get out of this suit—'

'By all means,' Jill replied sarcastically. 'We've grown rather fond of waiting for you.'

David's eyes narrowed in obvious dismay. Then he smiled boyishly, kissing his daughter and tousling his son's hair before heading toward the bedroom.

Jill sat for several seconds and then stood up abruptly. She was so angry, she felt she was going to cry, which made her angrier still. She didn't want to cry. She wanted to scream and yell and carry on. 'Excuse me a minute,' she said.

'Uh-oh, f-fireworks,' she heard Jason utter as she left the room.

David was tossing off his jacket when Jill came into the bedroom. She didn't wait for him to turn around before speaking.

'I don't understand you,' she began, watching his shoulders stiffen. 'You knew I was having a party for you tonight. You knew I'd invited the whole family, and that I was cooking a special dinner, busting my ass to make everything nice. I even asked you not to be late. And what do you do? You show up at eight o'clock when everyone else has been here since six-thirty and you have the nerve to tell me you've been out for a birthday drink with the guys. Not even a goddamn meeting! Something important, for God's sake, that you could justify yourself with. Something beyond your control. Not a couple of lousy drinks!'

'Are you finished?' he asked icily.

'No,' Jill continued. 'How dare you eat a big lunch when you knew I was making a big dinner?! Haven't you got any consideration for me at all?' She suddenly dissolved into tears, sinking down on the bed.

David marched over to the bedroom door and closed it. 'If you don't mind, I'd rather keep this private.'

'What difference does it make?' Jill shot back. 'They all know what we're saying in here.'

David removed his shirt and threw it beside his jacket on the bed, pulling a fresh, more casual one out of the closet. 'Look, Jill, I'm sorry. But I got roped into it. A bunch of the guys came into my office as I was getting ready to leave and they corralled me into having a few drinks. I figured I could still be home in plenty of time but one drink led to another, and I'd had a tough day – that Rickerd woman is driving me nuts about her divorce – and I needed to unwind. It was stupid. It wasn't fair to you, you're absolutely right, but I did it. It's done. Do we have to fight about it? It's my birthday, for Pete's sake.' He tried to smile.

'Why do I feel like I should be the one apologizing?' Jill asked, pouting beneath her tears. 'You still haven't explained why you had such a big lunch,' she said.

'I was hungry,' he admitted sheepishly. 'God, I was starving!' David lowered his head and sighed. 'Jill, could you come here, please, hon.' He waited for an instant, then watched her get up off the bed. Jill was vaguely aware of voices coming from the other room, undoubtedly growing more concerned as time passed.

'Come on over here,' he continued.

'David—'

'Come on over here.'

Reluctantly, she walked into his outstretched arms. They encircled her immediately.

'Oh, Jill, I love you so much,' he said, softly kissing her hair. 'I'm sorry I'm late. Really I am. I wanted to be on time – but I just couldn't seem to break away. Please understand. Don't be angry. I love you.'

'Your daughter didn't eat a thing,' she told him. There was no point in staying angry any longer. She would only succeed in making everyone else uncomfortable and ruining what was left of the evening. She'd made her point; he'd made his apology.

'Elaine probably fed her full of cookies and milk before she got here.'

'Oh – she called.'

'Don't tell me about it.'

Jill smiled. 'Your sister and her husband loved the Stroganoff.

Apparently, they had some truly superb Stroganoff just the other day at a friend's home.'

'Sounds like a typical evening. Come here, you.'

'I am here.'

'No,' he whispered, pointing to his lips. 'Here.'

He kissed her softly.

'Are you going to change your pants?' Jill asked, moving out of his arms and back to the bed.

'Yeah,' he answered. 'Jeans okay with you?'

'Sure,' she shrugged, lifting his jacket off the bed, about to take it to the closet. 'What's this?' she asked, reaching over and picking something off the bedspread.

'A birthday card,' David answered, removing one pair of pants and putting on another. 'Some of the guys from the office.'

'The ones you went drinking with?'

'The same,' he smiled.

Jill opened it up. Under the usual Happy Birthday message were written six names. The last one reached her eyes first, staying there and blocking out all the others. *Nicki*, it curved lyrically in black ink.

'You didn't tell me Nicole Clark was with you,' Jill said, fresh anger building inside her.

David said nothing for several seconds. 'It didn't seem to merit special consideration,' he said at last. 'I didn't tell you the names of anybody else who was there either.'

'You said some of the guys.'

David raised his hands in the air as if to say he surrendered. 'Well there, you see, I consider her one of the guys. Come on,

Jill, let's not blow this thing out of proportion. It's not like I was alone with the girl.' Jill shook her head with dismay. 'You don't still believe that garbage about her wanting to marry me, I hope.' It was a statement, not a question. 'Come on, Jill, jealousy doesn't become you.'

'I'm not jealous,' Jill shot back. 'I'm mad! Can't I be mad?'

'You were over being mad until I mentioned Nicki!'

'You didn't mention her! That's why I'm mad!'

David looked at her. Jill recognized the look – it was his patient parent stare. 'Isn't this kind of ridiculous?' he asked. 'Come on, I'm home now. Isn't that what you wanted?' He smiled shyly. 'I'm not getting any younger, you know.'

Once again, Jill allowed herself to be coaxed into his arms.

The rest of the evening was as big a disaster as the first part had been. For starters, Jill's cake hadn't set properly in the middle and everyone seemed compelled to comment on it. Then David's sister, Renee, got into a heated debate with their mother and she and her husband left before the presents were opened. The presents had been uniformly awful – ('What on earth possessed you, Jill?' he'd asked, stuffing the silk shirt unceremoniously back inside its box) – and Elaine had called to see if Jason and Laurie could spend the night and the better part of the weekend with their father.

At ten o'clock, Jill's parents had left for home, and at ten-thirty, David left to drive his mother back to her apartment. Jason retreated immediately to the television and the telephone, which he used simultaneously. Laurie helped Jill straighten out the living room and stack the dishes in the dishwasher.

Jill watched the young girl as she worked, her bones protruding sharply underneath her blouse. 'You didn't eat much,' Jill said.

'The cake wasn't done right,' Laurie commented.

Jill sighed. 'I know. I meant you didn't eat much in general. Of anything.'

'Yes I did.'

'No, I watched you. You just shuffled it around on your plate all night.'

Laurie shrugged. Jill decided to try again.

'Laurie, is everything all right?'

'How do you mean?'

'I mean, are you feeling all right? Are you happy?'

'Which one?' the girl questioned, putting the last of the dishes in the dishwasher and standing up straight.

'Well, we'll start with the first, I guess,' Jill replied. 'You're feeling okay?'

'Sure.'

'No aches or pains anywhere?'

Laurie shrugged her bony shoulders for the second time in as many minutes. Jill thought she spotted a slight blush in the young girl's cheeks.

'Trouble with your periods?' she asked softly.

Laurie looked away and said nothing.

Sensing this was perhaps the problem, Jill pressed on gently. 'I remember when I started my period,' she said, feeling Laurie tense noticeably beside her in exactly the same way David's body would tense to any news he didn't care to hear. 'I used to get the worst cramps. Sometimes I'd have to stay in bed all day.

I didn't like letting something get the better of me that way, but sometimes you have to recognize when you're licked, and just accept it. My mother always used to tell me that the cramps wouldn't be so bad as I got older, and she was right.'

'My mother calls it the curse,' Laurie said, her back to Jill.

'Oh, no, it's not!' Jill said with great feeling. 'It's a wonderful thing, Laurie. It means you're growing up. That you're becoming a woman!'

Laurie turned around abruptly, her eyes suddenly much older than her years. 'Who said that's such a wonderful thing?'

Jill wasn't sure how she should respond. 'Life is what you make it, Laurie,' she said finally.

'Well, I'm fine,' Laurie responded. 'I don't have any aches or pains and my periods are none of your business.'

Jill felt the sharpness of the rebuke all over her body. 'How are things at home?' she asked softly.

'My mother's putting in a new swimming pool. It'll be ready the end of next week.'

'Just in time for autumn,' Jill said, trying to keep her voice light. 'Is she still dating Ron Santini?'

'Yes.'

Jill shook her head. It *had* to be a different Ron Santini.

'Do you like him?'

'He's all right.'

'He treats you nicely?'

Laurie looked perplexed. 'He's all right,' she repeated.

'Your mother likes him?'

Laurie's answer was swift. 'She's not going to marry him, if that's what you're getting at.'

172

'I'm just trying to get at the root of what's bothering you,' Jill said, realizing she had raised her voice.

'There's nothing bothering me.'

'Then why don't you eat?!'

'I do eat! Why don't you leave me alone?!' She stormed out of the kitchen and back into the living room, plopping herself down in the middle of the sofa, sniffing back the tears Jill could see forming. Jill sat down beside her.

'I don't want you to cry, hon,' she said, touching the child's arm. 'I want to reach you, touch you—'

'You touch my father. Isn't that enough?'

Jill withdrew her hand. 'Wow!' she said, standing up and releasing a deep breath. 'Is that what it is? That you still haven't forgiven me for marrying your father?'

'I don't want to talk about it,' the girl said.

'One day we're going to have to.'

'Why?'

'Because I'd like for us to be friends,' Jill said.

'I have enough friends,' came the reply. 'I don't need any more.'

'Do you need any enemies?' Jill asked bluntly. Laurie turned her head away. 'Look, Laurie, I don't mean to be tough on you, but facts are facts. And one of those facts is that I'm married to your father. And I intend to stay married to your father.' She stopped, suddenly aware of how often lately she'd had to defend that position. Her thoughts refocused on her husband's child. 'All I'm trying to say is that if your father's marriage to me is what's making you so unhappy, then you're just going to have to learn to live with it because it's not going to change. I love your father. Believe it or not, he loves me. And he loves you – you know that.'

'I never see him,' Laurie said, tears starting to fall.

'Who does?!' Jill answered, sitting back down beside the girl. 'He's very busy these days,' she continued. 'What do you expect from a man who's late for his own birthday party!' She reached over and took Laurie's hands in her own. 'But it's part of what we were talking about in the kitchen, part of growing up. Recognizing that there are certain things in life that we have to accept, and then making everything else as easy on ourselves as possible. Starving yourself to death isn't going to accomplish anything!'

Laurie tore her hands away from Jill's with such force that Jill was afraid the youngster was going to strike out. Instead, she jumped to her feet and began pacing back and forth in front of her. 'Why can't you just shut up and leave me alone?' Laurie yelled, her voice high-pitched and bordering on hysteria. 'Why couldn't you leave us all alone? You just took my father away. You made my mother unhappy. She cries – I can't tell you how much she cries – and it's all because of you. She's so busy trying to forget about my father that she hardly has any time for me anymore. Nobody has time for me,' Laurie cried, sobbing now, her frail body shaking like a scarecrow in a windstorm.

Jill remained seated on the sofa, slowly extending her arms toward the child. 'I have time,' she said. 'Please, Laurie, I have so much time.'

Laurie's body swayed in her direction.

'Can you cut out all the noise in there,' Jason yelled from the den. 'I can't hear the television.'

The sound of her brother's voice snapped Laurie back into her shell. Her back straightened; her arms reached up and quickly wiped away her tears. We're back at square one, Jill thought. 'Then get off the phone,' Jill shouted angrily at Jason. She looked back at Laurie, seeing pieces of Elaine in the young girl's face. It was strange, she realized, but she'd never imagined Elaine crying. The woman is a human being, after all, she suddenly found herself thinking, not just an adding machine. It was a disconcerting thought.

'Do you think that by being my friend you'd be being disloyal to your mother?'

'I already told you,' came the reply. 'I don't need any more friends.'

Jill stood up, about to leave the room. She stopped when she reached the hallway. 'I guess it's time I started to take my own advice,' she said, her back to Laurie. 'About accepting the inevitable and making things as easy on everyone as I can.' She turned to face the child. 'I won't pester you again, Laurie. I won't ask any more personal questions and I won't comment on what you eat or don't eat. But I want you to know that I will be here if you ever want to talk – about anything – or if you do decide that you can always use another friend. Whatever. The next move has to come from you.' She paused. 'I'm going to bed. I'm tired. I've had a lousy day. You and Jason can work out who'll get the sofa and who'll get the pull-out bed. I'll leave some sheets and blankets in the hall.' She started out of the room, then stopped again. 'Tell Jason to get off the goddamn phone,' she said, then walked without stopping into her bedroom, shutting the door behind her and bursting into a flood of silent tears.

She heard David's key in the door at just after eleven-thirty. He tiptoed into their room and started undressing in the dark.

'It's all right, I'm awake,' Jill said from the bed.

'You startled me,' he said, his voice noticeably strained.

'Sorry. I just meant that you didn't have to tiptoe around. You aren't disturbing me. You can even turn on a light if you want.'

'No, not necessary,' he said, approaching the bed.

'Where were you? It's late.'

'My mother doesn't exactly live next door,' he answered, crawling in beside her. 'And she wanted to talk.' He pulled Jill's body close against his.

'About what?'

'About what,' he repeated, a short laugh catching in his throat. 'About her son who should be more considerate of his wife. God, you women stick together!'

Jill moved her hands down along her husband's body. 'Want to make love?' she asked, feeling him squirm away from her touch.

'The kids—'

'Aren't they asleep?'

'I guess so.'

'So?'

'So, I just wouldn't feel comfortable making love with them so close—'

'That's ridiculous!'

'Maybe so, but it's how I feel. Come on, Jill, I'm tired. I've had a hard day at the office, I've had a hard time from you—'

'Not hard enough,' she said, trying to joke, reaching for him.

'Very funny,' he said, pulling farther away. 'Look, let's get some sleep tonight, all right?'

'I guess you're not interested in hearing about *my* day,' she said, sounding as dejected as she felt.

'To be perfectly honest, you're right,' he said. 'I'm sorry, Jill, I'm just so tired.' He suddenly sat up in bed and pounded his fist against his pillow. 'All right, goddamn it, tell me about your day.'

'Never mind.'

'No, oh no, I'm not going to be the heavy here. I insist you tell me all about your day.'

Jill turned over in the bed. 'I saw Irving today. He says there's nothing for me at the network.'

'Well, you didn't think there would be,' he reminded her.

'You don't have to sound so pleased,' she chastised.

'Sorry, I didn't mean to. So – what else happened to you today?' he asked testily.

'I had a fight with Laurie.'

'What about?'

'The fact that she doesn't eat, the fact that I happen to be married to her father, the fact that she hates my guts.'

'Oh, Jill,' he said wearily, 'leave the kid alone. She's just going through a phase. A few years ago, she was almost pudgy. I remember giving her behind a tap and telling her that there was a bit too much jiggle for my tastes.'

Jill became instantly self-conscious. 'My God, what do you think about me?' she asked.

'I think that you're a woman and she's a little girl. And I think that as much as I love you, I'm going to throttle you if you don't let me get some sleep.'

Jill let her body relax against David's. 'All right, I can take a hint,' she said, allowing her eyes to close. Things had to be better tomorrow, she thought, suddenly anxiously anticipating sleep.

The phone rang.

'What now?' she demanded, reaching across her husband and grabbing for the phone. 'If it's Elaine, she's gone too far, and I'm going to let her have it! Hello?'

She knew the voice immediately, recognizing the dark huskiness. 'Can I speak to David, please?'

'It's almost midnight,' Jill said, angrily. This was too much – the woman had made him late for dinner and now she was invading the privacy of their bedroom! It was too much.

'I'm very aware what time it is. May I please speak to David?'

'Who is it?' David asked.

Jill said nothing, stretching the receiver over to her husband. 'Who is it?' he asked again.

What the hell did she want? And why now?

'Hello?' David asked. 'Who is this? Nicki! Is everything all right?' There was a pause. Jill watched David's face change from confusion to concern to outright horror in the space of several minutes. 'My God. When did it happen? Why didn't someone call me earlier?' Another pause. He turned angrily to

Jill. 'Who the hell was on the phone?' he demanded.

Jill stared at her husband, frightened by the tone of his voice. 'Jason,' she stammered. 'Jason was on the phone for a long time—'

He had stopped listening, was back engrossed in his conversation. 'I can't believe it. Dead?'

'Who's dead?' Jill asked.

'Where have they taken her?'

'Who?'

'What? All right. What? Yes, I'll be there first thing in the morning. What? Don't be silly. You have no reason to apologize. Of course you were right to call. I'll see you tomorrow.' He dropped the phone onto the bed. Jill returned it to its proper position.

'Who's dead?' she asked again.

David's voice was incredulous. 'Al Weatherby,' he said quietly.

'Al is dead? I don't believe it! How, for God's sake?'

'Murdered.'

'What?!'

'Beth is in the hospital. The General. Apparently, whoever killed Al worked her over pretty good.'

'Beth! But that can't be – I just spoke to her! My God, no. It can't be!' She jumped out of bed and began circling the room. 'What can we do? Should we go to the hospital?'

'The police aren't allowing any visitors until morning.' He paused. 'It happened around ten o'clock, Nicki said. Don Eliot called her. Apparently, half the firm's been calling here, but the line was busy. She decided to wait and try again now.' He shook his head. 'It's incredible, the whole thing.'

'Has anyone notified their children?'

'I'm sure the police are taking care of that.'

Jill sat back down on the bed. 'Did – did Nicole say how it happened? Or who?'

'Nothing. We don't know anything. Only that Al Weatherby is dead and that Beth is in the hospital.'

Only that Al Weatherby is dead, Jill repeated to herself, and that Beth is in the hospital.

Chapter Thirteen

The hospital corridor was lined with police.

David and Jill stepped off the crowded elevator onto the seventh floor and were promptly directed toward the waiting room, where they were told to do just that. Jill felt her husband's hand at her elbow guiding her toward the designated area. She had to run to keep up with his stride.

They reached the waiting room, and, for an instant, Jill felt as if they had stumbled into one of the staff lounges at Weatherby, Ross. Half the firm was present, most of whom David had spoken to the night before, after Nicki's terrifying phone call. Most stood up to greet David, as if he were the one who could make all the jumbled jigsaw pieces fit together again. Maybe they did that with all the new arrivals, Jill thought absently. Some of the men and almost all of the women were openly weeping. David embraced as many of his cohorts as he could manage before he was approached by a policeman who asked for his name and connection to the deceased and his wife.

Jill became suddenly aware of just how many policemen there were in the reasonably small quarters. Six in uniform, possibly several more in plain clothes. Everyone was talking at once, trying to come to grips with what had happened. The morning paper, several copies of which lay opened on the various tables, had shed no light at all on the matter other than to confirm in large, ugly black lettering that Al Weatherby, one of Chicago's leading legal lights, had been brutally beaten to death, his skull having sustained massive fractures from a blunt instrument. Beth Weatherby was supposedly in deep shock, with multiple injuries to her head and body, apparently lucky to be alive. Who could have done such an awful thing? And why, for God's sake?

'Could I have your name, please?'

Jill turned to stare at the young police officer. He couldn't be more than twenty-one, she thought, quickly looking at the others. They were all about the same age, she realized. Just babies. Or was it that the older she got, the younger everybody else seemed? Right now she felt as old as Methuselah, and probably looked a good deal older than that. Nicole's phone call had made sure she hadn't gotten any sleep, just as the lady, herself, had made sure Jill hadn't had a real rest since their first meeting approximately two months before.

'Jill Plumley,' she answered, not sure how much time had elapsed between the question and her response.

'This man is your husband?' the officer asked, indicating David. Jill nodded. 'Are you a lawyer too?'

Jill shook her head. 'No. I'm in—' She stopped, realizing she had been about to say 'in television.' 'I'm a teacher,' she said. 'I can't believe this has happened,' she muttered, convinced the young man had heard this same remark a hundred times this morning. 'I just spoke to Beth last night.'

'What?' The policeman's entire posture suddenly changed. He stood up straighter; his back arched; his eyes reflected genuine interest. Jill was immediately aware of his change in attitude.

'I said I just spoke to her last night.'

'About what time?'

'About five-thirty. Closer to six, I guess.'

The policeman quickly jotted down the information. 'Excuse me a minute, please,' he said, and went out into the hall. Jill saw him conferring with an older man in street clothes who turned immediately in Jill's direction and then followed the officer back toward her.

David, who had been talking to several of his partners, sensed something was happening that he should be aware of, and returned to his wife's side.

'What's going on?' he asked, as the plainclothes police officer approached and introduced himself.

'I'm Captain Keller,' he said pleasantly. 'Mrs Plumley, is it?'

'Yes,' Jill answered, aware eyes were beginning to turn in her direction.

'Officer Rogers tells me you spoke to Beth Weatherby last night.'

'Between five-thirty and six, yes.'

'May I ask please what the gist of that conversation was?'

Jill began to speak. It was silent in the room. Jill realized that she was the center of attention and became instantly uncomfortable, as if she were center-stage and all around her cameras were recording her every move. It was a role she didn't

like, much preferring to direct the camera's point of view –
okay, Rick, see that tall, skinny policeman over there by the
door, see if you can get him to move over closer to the window
when we talk to him. Get the tree in the shot if you can. It'll
give the scene a little more color. Her cameras had allowed her
to get right into the middle of things without having to get
directly, personally, involved. Now she was definitely in the
center of things, but without her camera she felt naked and
vulnerable and a bit foolish. What she had to say, after all,
wasn't very important. It didn't matter, she realized, looking at
the faces around her. At least she had something new to report.
Something they hadn't heard before. That would be enough.

'She called and asked if I could meet her for a cup of coffee,'
Jill said simply. 'I was preparing dinner so I had to say no.'

'She wanted to meet you immediately?'

'Yes.' Jill took a minute to review the conversation in her
own mind. 'She sounded very strange,' Jill continued,
remembering now all the details she had somehow managed to
avoid the night before. 'In fact, I didn't recognize her voice
right away. She sounded – scared,' Jill said, putting a word to
what she had heard in Beth's voice but ignored because she
was too busy to want to recognize it. Oh my God, she thought,
had the killer been there when Beth had phoned? No, she
decided. Beth had wanted to meet her right away. Surely the
killer wouldn't have let her walk out to meet a friend for coffee.

'Did she say she was frightened?' Captain Keller asked.

'No. She just asked if we could meet for coffee. I asked her if
something was wrong and she said no, just that Al was going to
be late – he was tied up in a meeting – and she thought it would

be a good time to get together. She sounded fine then. It was only at the beginning of the conversation that she sounded funny.'

'She said her husband would be tied up late in a meeting?'

'Yes. We made arrangements to meet on Wednesday night instead.'

'Anything else?'

'Nothing.'

'Is Beth Weatherby a close friend of yours, Mrs Plumley?'

'We're friends,' Jill answered. 'We play bridge together a bit and we take an exercise class together. I like her a lot.' She tried to read some information from his expression but she got nothing. 'Is she going to be all right?'

'Thank you, Mrs Plumley,' Captain Keller said. 'We may want to speak to you again.' He left the room.

'What was all that about?' Jill asked, turning to David.

He shook his head. 'Why didn't you tell me Beth sounded frightened when you spoke to her?'

'I just didn't think about it. Do you think there's any connection?' she asked incredulously.

'It seems more than a bit coincidental,' he answered, a touch of sarcasm creeping into his voice.

'But how?'

'David.' The voice was soft but no less husky than it had sounded the night before. Jill turned toward it in time to watch Nicole dissolve into tears in David's arms. She couldn't believe what she was watching. In front of all these people, her husband was openly embracing another woman. Of course, no one else present was aware of all the implications – what they saw was an emotional young woman, not to mention a brilliant legal mind, who was all broken up at the death of a man everyone had loved, and was turning for comfort to the man so many of them had similarly embraced. Jill felt embarrassed. How could she be so petty as to be jealous at a time like this? Her husband's close associate and friend had been brutally bludgeoned to death and his wife was who-knew-how-seriously injured, and all she was worrying about was the stiffness of her husband's cock against Nicole Clark's tight-fitting jeans.

David backed away from the other woman's embrace gently. 'Jill, do you have a Kleenex?' he asked.

Jill reached in her purse and pulled out several crumpled tissues. 'I hope they're not used,' she said, handing them over, then watching in stunned surprise as David wiped the tears from under Nicole Clark's eyes. I hope it *is* used, she cursed silently. Did he have to make such a display of everything? She didn't remember him wiping the tears away from under *her* eyes. Then she remembered she hadn't shed any. She'd been too stunned to cry.

Jill began to feel awkward watching them, as if she were an intruder in a sacred and beautiful scene. Somehow, she found it harder to watch her husband touching Nicole than she had sighting her camera lens on the carnage and severed limbs of Vietnam. She turned away, aware now of their voices beside her, Nicole questioning, David having all the answers. A policeman approached and asked the newcomer's name. She heard him leave again, heard Nicole's whispers and her husband's soft assurances. Why had they come here? What possible good were they accomplishing?

'Davey! Nicki! How are you?'

Jill turned to watch Don Eliot approach her husband and Nicole. Tragedy had not altered his unorthodox style of dressing: He wore tight jeans and sandals along with a white shirt and green tie. He conferred for several minutes with David and Nicole before he even took note that Jill was there. 'Hi, Jilly,' he said, grabbing her hand and shaking it.

Hi, Donny, she wanted to respond. 'Hello, Don,' she smiled. 'Have you heard anything more?'

'Well, I saw Beth last night, of course, after they brought her in, but she was in a state of shock and couldn't say anything. I talked to the police, but it was too early to get much out of them. I just spoke to the doctors and to the officer in charge. Apparently, Beth is awake now and they're going to try and talk to her.'

'Are her kids here?'

'The daughter's on her way in from Los Angeles. Her older son flew in from New York last night. He's with her now. The younger son they haven't been able to locate yet.'

'You don't think *he* did it, do you?' She thought of the recent tension between father and son since the boy had dropped out of school to don flowing robes and shave his head.

Don Eliot's face grew grim. 'It's a thought,' he said.

'Oh, God.'

The room filled with the sound of fresh rumors. More people crowded into the already overcrowded area. Another policeman returned to recheck Jill's account of her phone conversation with Beth Weatherby. Don Eliot made frequent forays into the hall, conversing with several different officers. David had left

Nicole's side and was now giving comfort to one of the other wives. Jill felt vaguely tawdry about her earlier feelings and looked away. Nicole Clark was staring at her from across the room. She looked more like a frightened and confused little girl than a femme fatale, Jill thought, before reminding herself that frightened and confused little girls had a way of being dangerously attractive to other women's husbands.

She turned away, her thoughts suddenly on Beth Weatherby. Yesterday, Beth had had everything. A successful marriage, a wonderful husband, a charmed existence. Today all that was gone. Shattered by several strong blows to the skull. Wasn't it remarkable how everything could change so completely in the space of a single night, and wasn't it strange, she thought, her mind echoing a phrase Beth herself had once uttered, how nothing ever worked out quite the way you thought it would.

'Why won't they let us see her?' Jill was asking angrily. 'What are they doing for so long in there? Won't they even tell us how she is?'

No one answered her. Only a handful of people remained, including Nicole Clark, who had gone to bring everyone a cup of coffee and had returned with one cup too few. Jill had declined the girl's offer to make a second trip, claiming she drank too much coffee anyway (although she dearly would have liked a cup), and so she had to content herself with pacing the room and addressing herself to the walls like someone half-crazed and all alone. Of course I'm not alone, she told herself. My husband and his future wife are with me.

'I don't understand what's going on,' Jill continued. 'Why won't they tell us anything?'

'I'm sure they will as soon as they can,' Nicole answered, her voice sweet and soft.

If she doesn't stop being so bloody sweet to me, Jill thought, I'm going to break her bloody sweet little neck.

As if on cue, Don Eliot appeared in the doorway. 'Jilly, I'm glad you stayed. We're not getting anywhere. She won't say a thing. She just lies there—'

'Well, she's in shock,' Jill protested. 'Some lunatic beats her up and murders her husband—'

'She called you last night, is that right?' Don Eliot asked. 'Tell me exactly, word for word, what she said.'

Jill repeated the conversation to the best of her ability. 'Well, she obviously wanted to tell you something,' Don Eliot concluded. 'It's too bad you couldn't go.' He paused long enough to inspire the appropriate guilt. 'Look, Jilly, maybe she'll talk to you now. I think I can talk the doctors into giving us a few more minutes. Are you game?'

'Sure,' Jill said numbly. 'If you think it'll help.'

She knew the words out of his mouth before he said them. 'It can't hurt,' he said, and she walked down the corridor beside him, leaving her husband standing in the doorway beside Nicole Clark.

The woman sitting in the hospital bed had two black and swollen eyes, her skin was severely discolored, and large blotches of maroon, like misplaced rouge, stained her cheeks and chin. There were bandages across her nose and cheek, and one disappeared just inside her hairline. Her lips were cut and twice their normal size, her ears scratched and caked with dried blood. Still, there was something so peaceful about Beth Weatherby as she sat in her hospital bed, the blankets pulled high around her, hiding her other injuries from Jill's sight, that Jill feared in that initial instant that the woman had stopped breathing altogether, that she was being led forward to converse with a corpse.

'My God, Beth,' Jill whispered, moving toward her. 'Who did this to you?'

Beth Weatherby's eyes remained closed. Jill walked slowly to the woman's side, bent down and kissed her very gently on the forehead, on the only patch of skin which seemed untouched, her tears falling down involuntarily and wetting Beth's skin. 'Oh, I'm so sorry,' she cried. 'I'm so sorry about what's happened.' Beth's eyes flickered but stayed shut. Jill realized that perhaps the woman didn't recognize the voice. 'It's Jill, Beth. I'm so sorry I couldn't meet you last night.' She sniffed loudly, trying to stop the tears. 'It's going to be all right, Beth,' she continued lamely. 'They'll find whoever did this and then this whole nightmare will be over. That's the good thing about nightmares, you know. You get to wake up.'

Beth's eyes opened suddenly and focused on Jill. But they did more than stare, Jill realized, careful not to avert her own. They were searching. For what? Jill wondered. For answers? I don't know the question, she admitted silently. For reassurance? All I have are platitudes and empty promises. For support? You have it, Jill tried to communicate. All I have.

'I'm so tired,' Beth muttered, barely audible behind her swollen lips.

'I know,' Jill said, feeling dumb and inadequate. Just what was it she claimed to know?

'They hurt me,' she said, her words slurred.

'They?' Jill asked quickly.

'When they changed the bandages,' came the slow reply. 'I know they didn't mean to.' Her eyes closed briefly, then opened again. 'Oh, Jill, I hurt so badly.'

Jill tried to speak but couldn't. The words caught in her throat and were lost before they could find her tongue.

'Brian is here,' Beth said suddenly.

'Brian?'

Beth smiled, or tried to. 'My son, the doctor,' she said, and Jill almost smiled in return. 'I know he was here before when they were talking to me.' She raised her head and began searching the room, a look of mounting panic filling her eyes.

'Your son went out for a cup of coffee,' Don Eliot said from his position near the door. 'Do you want him?'

Beth lowered her head back to the pillow. 'They told me Lisa is on her way in from Los Angeles.' She looked toward the window. 'They haven't been able to find Michael yet. I think that's what they said. I'm not sure.' Her voice was trailing off into a soft whine. 'So many people,' she said. 'So many questions. Something to do with Al.' She looked back at Jill. 'They keep repeating his name as if they expect more than just its sound in return.' She looked puzzled. 'Poor Brian. He looks so tired and worried. I know I'm the cause. What did that policeman say to me before?' Jill could see Beth's mind racing to catch up to the scattered debris of her thoughts.

'Why don't you try and sleep, Beth,' Jill offered. 'We'll talk later.'

'Something about Al. He was trying to tell me something about Al. He talked exactly the way they do on television. I didn't say anything. I don't know what he wanted me to say. My God, Jill,' she said suddenly. 'Al is dead!'

'I know,' Jill said, a tear running down her cheek.

'Al's dead,' the woman repeated.

'Please try not to worry,' Jill pleaded, patting Beth's hand as it rested beneath the covers. 'They'll find whoever killed Al. And they'll put him away. He won't be able to hurt you anymore.'

'No, he won't,' Beth said, her voice suddenly calm, her eyes closing once again, her breath becoming less forced and more even, as she succumbed to sleep.

Jill leaned forward and once again kissed her friend's forehead. 'Sleep,' she whispered, her eyes staring straight ahead at the white of the hospital pillowcase. Slowly, she allowed her spine to straighten and her shoulders to pull back. Then she turned and walked directly to the door.

'I'm afraid I wasn't much help,' she said as she reached Don Eliot.

'You never know,' he answered. 'She said more to you than she has to anyone. That's a start, anyway.'

'The start of what, I wonder,' Jill said numbly, then opened the door to the hallway and quickly left the room.

Chapter Fourteen

If and when she ever dropped dead, Jill decided, it would definitely not be in the middle of a heat wave. It just wasn't fair to expect people to crowd into an un-air-conditioned church to mourn your demise when the temperature outside was over 90 degrees and rising. God only knew what heights the thermometer would reach inside the church itself once they were all crowded together inside. Jill wondered if Beth would be present. She had been released from the hospital just yesterday, out of danger yet still strangely quiet. In the week since Al's murder, Beth had surrounded herself with silence, speaking to no one, sleeping long hours and allowing only her daughter and sons (the youngest had finally been located) to minister to her needs. According to Don Eliot, she was almost a zombie. He could get no information out of her at all, and the doctors feared the shock might take months, possibly years, to abate. Without Beth, there was little to go on. The police still hadn't located the murder weapon, and there were no signs of forced entry into the Weatherby home, leading the police to suspect the killer had been known to his victims. Possibly even related. Jill thought of Michael. It would certainly go a long way toward explaining

Beth's silence. The shock of watching your own son destroy his father, then turn his rage on you—

Jill felt her breath becoming short and looked down at what she was wearing. David had insisted she wear a black wool turtleneck dress. It was the only black dress she had, and despite her argument that you showed respect at a funeral by your presence and not by what you wore, David had been adamant that she wear black. And so, here she was in the blistering late summer heat wearing a dress she usually saved for only the coldest days of a Chicago winter.

They hadn't even been able to get away over the long Labor Day weekend, the way they always had, Jill fretted, picturing the refreshing lake waters that framed the shore of the Deerhurst Inn, a quaint old country retreat they had stumbled across when their romance was in its infancy. She felt the loss of that weekend hideaway as acutely as a pilgrim denied his annual ablutions at Lourdes. But David had had to work all weekend, Weatherby, Ross having been thrown into an understandable state of chaos. Everyone was waiting anxiously for the police to release Al's body for burial, and the endless tests they were conducting only intensified the outrage, grief and scandal that threatened to swallow up everybody connected with the large firm. The next few weeks could only bring with them more of the same, although possibly the smothering cloak of heat which seemed to have been thrown across the city in the week since Al's death might lift. Jill tugged at the black wool which was sitting at her neck like a sleeping boa constrictor. Someone save me from this heat, she prayed silently, feeling guilty for the overwhelming triviality of her concerns in the face of what she knew Beth must be going through.

She had tried to reach Beth several times during the past week, and had met with polite but insistent refusals from her children. Their mother wasn't speaking to anyone, she was told, a fact with which Don Eliot immediately concurred. Jill repeated to all parties that she was readily available whenever she might be needed, but no one had called. Perhaps today, when she saw Beth—

The sideshow began at the front door with at least ten Hare Krishnas chanting in cacophonous unison and handing out pamphlets to the stunned mourners. Apparently, Beth had given instructions that they were not to be disturbed, this being her younger son's way of dealing with his grief. Jill and David refused the proffered pamphlets – David muttering something about shooting Jason should he ever don flowing robes – and pushed past the chanters into the interior of the church.

It was even hotter than Jill had been prepared for. The circus at the door had at least provided something of a distraction, but now the body heat of some several hundred mourners, combined with the natural temperature of the outside air, made Jill gasp for breath. For a fleeting second, she thought of the movie *Land of the Pharaohs* with Jack Hawkins and a super-sultry Joan Collins. Joan, having plotted long and laboriously to kill all those who came between her and the throne of Egypt, including her husband, the current monarch, found herself in the great tomb along with the dead Pharaoh and all his favorite slaves, concubines and horses, about to be buried alive. Such were the Pharaoh's wishes. Jill hastily surveyed the large room which was in the process of filling to capacity. Was this Al Weatherby's plan as well? Had he posthumously gathered together the modern-day equivalent of his favorite slaves, concubines and horses? Was he planning on taking them all along? Into which category did she fit? Undoubtedly one of the horses, she decided, as David pushed her toward an aisle where she was forced to climb past several sets of kneecaps, all of which seemed to have been nailed into the floor.

She felt her hair curling into tight little balls around her face – she didn't remember Joan Collins sweating – and wished now that they had accepted one of the pamphlets they had spurned at the door. It would have made a good fan.

'Are you all right?' David asked, suddenly realizing how uncomfortable his wife must be.

'Just very hot,' she answered, trying not to think about it.

His voice was soft, apologetic. 'I'm sorry I was such an ass about insisting on the black dress and makeup. I don't know why I was like that. I'm sorry.'

'It's okay.' She touched his hand, feeling a trickle of perspiration trace a line across her recently applied blush-on.

'You were very sweet about it. I really appreciate the fact that you didn't make an issue of it. I was in no mood for common sense.' Jill smiled, trying to concentrate on his words and not the heat, feeling increasingly faint. Just let me get through this and back into an air-conditioned car, she prayed silently, remembering there was still the long drive out to the cemetery. 'The makeup suits you though,' he said. 'You should wear it more often.'

It was meant as a compliment, Jill knew, so she said nothing. She'd wash her face as soon as she got home.

The minister took his place behind the podium and began the service. Jill listened as he described the man she had grown so fond of, feeling his loss more acutely now as she was forced to recall details of his life. Poor Beth, Jill thought, brushing aside a tear and straining forward in her seat to try to spot Beth in one of the front rows.

The sight of Nicole Clark just two rows ahead of them caught Jill completely by surprise. For some unaccountable reason, she hadn't expected to see her there, although everyone else from Weatherby, Ross was in attendance, and obviously, where else would the dear thing be? Nicole sat perfectly still, her hair pulled back into a neat French braid, no noticeable perspiration anywhere that Jill could see. She wore a simple black cotton sleeveless dress with just the right amount of white trimming, making it appropriate for all occasions. Naturally, Jill thought, her eyes moving down the rows of mourners, she *would* have just the right dress to wear. My God, there's Elaine, she gasped inwardly.

'What's the matter?' David asked, concerned. She shook her head and shrugged her shoulders. 'Relax, honey. We'll be out of here soon,' he said, patting her hand.

She smiled, her eyes riveted on her husband's ex-wife. Of course, she should have expected that Elaine would be here. She had known the Weatherbys a long time. It was only right that she show her respect by coming. Jill took a long moment to assess Elaine.

Her features were soft and attractive, not as perfect as Nicole's, not as irregular as her own. She was almost exactly the picture of what one imagines a lawyer would marry just out

197

of college, the childhood sweetheart who grew up without managing to grow in the same direction as her husband, who spent her hours preoccupied with bringing up her children and managing her house, forgetting – or ignoring the fact – that the work world was filling up with lots of bright and interesting ladies. Strangely enough, Jill noted, her eyes instantly taking in the remainder of the room, Elaine was also in black. In fact, they seemed to be the only three women in the entire room in the designated color of bereavement. All the other women – she still hadn't been able to spot Beth – had shunned the darker shades in favor of cooler summer prints. It seemed almost a deliberate display, the black setting them apart from the others, creating a separate entity – David Plumley and his women. It was like John Derek, she thought, conjuring up the magazine picture of the handsome former actor surrounded by his ex-wives, Ursula Andress and Linda Evans, and his current wife, Bo, all smiling, all wearing identical T-shirts, all happy to have had the privilege. My God, get me out of here, she whispered to herself, looking into her lap. Perhaps they should form a receiving line – Past, Present – Future?

Her eyes shot to David's.

'What's the matter?' he asked again, becoming alarmed. 'Are you going to be sick?' Instinctively, he edged as far as he could away from her. It wasn't very far. The knees beside him held firm.

'It's a thought,' she said. 'I know, take deep breaths,' she continued for him. Following her own instructions, she looked between her knees, concentrating all her energy on the floor, and then returned her attention to the eulogy being delivered.

She felt the tears well up inside her and was astonished when instead of crying, she felt the urge to laugh tickling its way up her throat.

The sound escaped her mouth before she could stop it and throw her hand on top of it. How could she do it? How could she laugh out loud at the funeral of her husband's mentor and dear friend? She couldn't stop, almost choking on the effort, doubling her body over to try and suffocate the blasphemous sounds. The tears filled her eyes and she felt David's protective arm around her. 'It's all right, sweetheart,' he said, soothingly, drawing her up under his arm. He thinks I'm crying, she realized, the knowledge of which was enough to bring on a fresh onslaught of giggles and cause her to bury her face deep against his chest. Around her she heard quiet expressions of sympathy and understanding. They all think I'm crying, she told herself, and for the remainder of the service she kept her head burrowed deep against David's jacket and laughed so hard that she was crying.

Jill stood waiting by the front door of the church while David went around the back to the parking lot to get the car. All around her, members of the Hare Krishna were busy chanting and dancing, shaking their tambourines against the dead air. Jill took in a deep breath of oxygen, hoping it would make her feel less faint, but there was no relief. She looked to the street, eager for the sight of the brown Mercedes. She would turn the cold air on full blast. She leaned her body against the side of the building and closed her eyes. I am walking barefoot in Antarctica, she repeated over and over, inadvertently establishing a silent rhythm with the other chanters.

'I have a bone to pick with you,' the voice said from somewhere beside her. Jill opened her eyes and turned in its direction. Elaine stood, cool and controlled, before her. 'My God, are you all right? You look like you're going to be sick!'

'Thank you,' Jill said. She couldn't think of anything else to say.

'Do you want to sit down?' Elaine asked, indicating the stone steps. 'I think we could probably make room between all these Harry and Harriet Krishnas.'

Jill shook her head. 'I'm just very hot.'

Elaine looked Jill over from head to toe. 'Well, no wonder, for God's sake. Look what you're wearing! Whatever possessed you to wear a wool turtleneck in the middle of the summer?!'

'It's September.'

'It's almost a hundred degrees.'

'It's black,' Jill told her. Was this the bone Elaine had to pick?

'So what?' Elaine asked.

'Our husband insisted,' Jill deadpanned.

Elaine's face broke into a wide grin which made her look years younger and much softer. 'You're not supposed to be funny and make me smile,' Elaine said, surprising both of them. Was this the woman David had described as humorless and unsympathetic? The whiny and shrill voice on the telephone she had come to despise?

Jill thought back to their first direct confrontation four years earlier. Courtroom C, on the second floor. Plumley versus Plumley. Divorce granted to Elaine Plumley on the grounds of adultery. The other woman: Jill Listerwoll. I know how trite this sounds, she had said to Elaine when they inadvertently came face to face in the hallway, but I really never meant to hurt you. Elaine had been unimpressed, her back rigid. It does sound trite, she had said in reply. And then she had said something else, words Jill had forced into the back of her memory until they had tried unsuccessfully to emerge at David's birthday party, which seemed now so very long ago. If he treated me the way he treats you, she had said, and treated you the way he treats me, this would be a completely different story.

Jill stared wide-eyed at the first Mrs David Plumley. Perhaps they weren't so different after all. 'You said you had a bone to pick with me?' she asked, throwing off the disconcerting thought.

Elaine regarded Jill with a blank expression, as if Jill had spoken to her in a foreign language. Then the memory of why she had initially approached her ex-husband's present wife returned and lit up her eyes. 'Yes,' she said forcefully, her voice gaining strength and purpose with each new word, 'I do. How dare you tell my daughter that I'm dating a crook!'

Jill looked helplessly around her. She couldn't believe this was happening. Where was David? Why was he taking so long with the car?

'I'm sorry,' she said finally, returning her gaze to Elaine. 'It kind of popped out before I could stop it.'

'He's in fruit,' Elaine said.

'I'm sure he is.'

'You must have the wrong Ron Santini.'

'I'm sure I do.'

'He's in fruit,' Elaine repeated, then paused. 'Even if he

were a crook, it would be no business of yours.'

'That's true. Like I said, it just kind of popped out. I don't think Laurie believed me, anyway.'

'Oh, those kids believe everything you tell them! It's always "Jill said this" and "Jill said that." It's enough to make you sick.'

'I didn't think they ever listened to me,' Jill said, genuinely surprised, ignoring Elaine's editorial comment.

'Oh, they listen, all right.' She paused again. 'For the record, even though it *is* none of your business, Ron Santini is a very nice man, and since I don't propose ever to marry again, I really don't give a damn what he does for a living.'

Jill felt the blanket of heat returning to cover her body. 'Are you so bitter,' she asked, feeling very weary, 'that you'll deny yourself happiness just so that David has to keep on paying you monthly support?'

'Ninety thousand dollars a year buys a lot of happiness,' Elaine answered. 'And yes, I guess I am that bitter. Besides, you're a married woman now! Would you really do it again?' She stopped to let the question take root. 'Not me,' she answered. 'Once was enough, thank you.' She looked across the street at her car. 'I was lucky – I found a spot right on the street. Well, I'm going to go home and lie in the sun – I guess you heard I had a pool put in.'

'I heard.'

'I'd invite you over but well, that might seem a little tacky.'

'I'd rather go to the cemetery, thank you.'

'And, of course, you always get what you want.'

'Of course.'

Each woman smiled pleasantly at the other, and Jill watched Elaine walk down the church steps and onto the street. A few days ago she would have wished for a car to come barreling down the street and knock the dear lady right out of her two-hundred-dollar shoes. But now, strangely enough, she found she had a grudging respect for Elaine. In a perverse sort of way, she had actually enjoyed their verbal fencing. The woman had more spunk than she'd previously imagined, and she made more sense than Jill had ever thought she would.

The heat must be getting to me, she thought, watching Elaine open her car door and get inside. She's getting a little hippy, Jill thought with no small degree of satisfaction. She leaned back against the church.

'Mrs Plumley?'

Jill looked over at the young, pale figure who stood before her.

'I'm Lisa Weatherby, Beth's daughter.'

Jill straightened up to shake the girl's hand. 'I'm so sorry,' she began. 'If there's anything I can do – I've called several times—'

The girl looked toward her brothers. One had his arm draped protectively around her; the other was busy chanting with his friends. Harry and Harriet Krishnas, Elaine had called them, Jill suddenly recalled, only vaguely having heard Elaine when she had said it before. That was pretty funny. She looked to the street. Elaine's car was gone.

'There *is* something you can do,' Lisa Weatherby said. Jill looked back at Lisa.

'Yes?'

'Maybe you could come up to the house one day this week and see my mother. She wasn't well enough to come today, and I know she'd like to see you. We'd hoped that by making sure she got enough rest and not letting anyone bother her she'd be all right, that the shock would start wearing off and she'd be able to tell us what happened that night, but it doesn't seem to be working. She's still not talking to anyone, and – well, you seem to be her only friend.'

'What?'

'We'd better go, Lisa,' her older brother urged. 'The limousine's waiting.'

'Will you come?' Lisa asked again.

'Of course,' Jill answered. How could she have been Beth Weatherby's only friend? The woman knew everyone; everybody liked her. What was going on? She leaned back against the church edifice. Oh, for a little ice and snow.

'Excuse me, Jill?'

What was it about the front of this building? Every time she leaned against it, someone approached her. For the third time, she straightened up and turned toward the voice, knowing before she looked who was speaking, remembering that the first time the girl had excused herself, she had called her Mrs Plumley.

'Don't tell me,' Jill said before the younger woman had a chance to speak. 'Your name is Nicole Clark and you're going to marry my husband.'

The girl lowered her head. 'I guess I deserved that.'

'You're the one who said it.'

Nicole Clark nodded. 'One of the stupider things I've said.'

'I have to agree.'

'I did apologize,' she whispered.

'You have an interesting way of saying you're sorry,' Jill told her. She felt fresh streams of perspiration running across her face. 'Look, I think we've milked this subject for all it's worth, don't you?'

'I explained to David how it all happened,' Nicole continued.

'Nothing's happened,' Jill reminded her.

Nicole ignored the well-timed interruption. 'I told him how sorry I was that I'd upset you—'

'You *do* have a way with words,' Jill said, feeling her smile stick against her cheeks, held there by the humidity. 'But I really think that David has more pressing concerns at the moment than—'

'He's been so wonderful throughout all this,' Nicole said, cutting Jill off. 'He's really been the one holding the firm together, making sure we don't all crumble and fall apart. Al meant so much to all of us.'

'I'm sure he did,' Jill acknowledged, wondering suddenly when it was that Nicole had found the time in the midst of all the chaos to explain herself to David, and when her husband had found the time to listen.

'I was trying to get some work done the other day and suddenly I just dissolved into a flood of tears. There were clients around and everything. I was very embarrassed. I could just hear everyone whispering behind my back about how women don't have the emotional makeup to be successful lawyers. All that rot. But suddenly, there was David, and he ushered me out of there and took me downstairs for something to eat, and we talked about it. He really understood how I felt about Al. He felt the same way. It was the first time I'd ever really seen David open up that way. As a man, I mean, not a lawyer.'

Jill's voice fairly seethed with fury, each word dripping venom. 'How considerate of Al, then, to have passed away so that you might have that opportunity,' she said and waited.

Nicole stared at Jill in obvious shock. Elaine would have had a smart answer, Jill thought, thinking simultaneously of her husband and Nicole Clark out for their cozily revealing lunch. So, the little pilgrim was making progress, she realized with a combination of bitterness and dismay.

The car honking from across the street diverted her attention, and she turned her head around just in time to allow the few tears that had formed in her eyes to fall and mingle with the lines of perspiration that were already streaking her face. In one deft gesture, she wiped her face clear of heat and emotion and turned back to Nicole.

'Excuse me,' Jill said, steering away from her young challenger, and heading toward the steps. Please don't let me fall, she whispered silently as she descended them carefully, aware of the girl's eyes on her back, burning a hole into the black wool of her dress. So, her dear husband had taken the sweet little thing to lunch and opened himself up 'as a man' to boot. She felt anger and indignation rising inside her. He makes *me* wear a black wool dress in the middle of a heat wave and he takes *her* out to lunch.

Her mind recalled Elaine's past admonition, rearranging it slightly to suit Nicole: If he treated her the way he treats me, she repeated wordlessly, and treated me the way he treats her, this would be a completely different story. Jill walked quickly toward her husband's brown Mercedes and angrily opened the door. Then, taking a last look at Nicole Clark, she got inside.

Chapter Fifteen

'I don't believe this is happening.'

'Relax, Jill.'

'How am I supposed to relax? I am slowly melting away before your very eyes.'

'It should only be a few more minutes.'

'You said that ten minutes ago.'

'The poor kid's working as fast as he can. He looks terrified.'

'So would you if your client was a corpse!'

'Jill, please—'

'If you tell me to relax one more time, I'm going to scream.'

'All right. Fine. Don't relax.'

'Couldn't we at least turn on the air-conditioner?'

'Sure, if you want to overheat the car. Then we'd really be stuck.'

'I just don't believe this is happening.'

Jill looked out the window at the other cars lining the side of US Highway 41. Then she looked over at the service station, where a quivering young mechanic was gamely trying to replace the fan belt that had broken on the hearse.

'I didn't think hearses had fan belts,' Jill muttered to no one in particular. 'If Al Weatherby is anywhere watching this, he must be shaking his head and saying, "What a fucking mess!"'

'Jill, please, you're not making things any better.'

'And if you say *that* again, I'm going to get out and walk.'

'Then by all means,' he said, reaching across her and opening the door, 'get out and walk.'

They sat in angry silence for several minutes. Oh, great, Jill thought. We must be playing this scene just the way Nicole Clark wrote it. She reached over and shut the door.

'I don't like ultimatums,' he said, not looking at her.

'I know,' she said, remembering.

It was late. The room was in darkness. Neither one of them had bothered to turn on a light. Underneath them, on the floor below, Jill knew Mrs Everly and her monstrous dog were fast asleep. She wished she were in bed too. Asleep. Alone. She didn't want to say what she knew he didn't want to hear.

'I can't do it anymore, David,' she began.

'What are you talking about?'

'What we always talk about. Just that this time I mean it.'

He sat across from her on the sofa. She sat on the floor, her long legs crossed in a semi-lotus position. She was wearing a long evening gown which made the position most difficult to accomplish and, once mastered, seem singularly out of place; her reddish-brown hair was pulled back into a bun from which thousands of stray hairs threatened at any second to escape; her skin was blotchy and streaked with tears. She looked as miserable and unhappy as he knew she felt. He also knew what she was going to say and he knew he didn't want to hear it. She knew the same thing but was determined to say it anyway.

'I love you, David,' she began again, pushing the reluctant words out of her mouth. 'I ache, I love you so much. But I'm tired of sneaking around, or waiting up until two in the morning, hoping vainly that you'll show up. And I'm tired of pretending that you sleep in a room all by yourself when you crawl out of my bed to go home.' She paused, sniffing loudly.

'Jill—'

'But most of all, I'm tired of having to madly scramble up a date for my cousin's wedding because the only man I've been seeing for the last two years is married and it wouldn't look nice to show up at my cousin's wedding with a married man!' She let out a loud wail, her hand reaching over to push some loose hairs behind her ears. 'Oh, shit, it's gone. I lost it.'

David looked confused. 'What's gone?'

'My flower!' she cried. 'I had a blue cloth flower in my hair. Everyone said I looked beautiful.'

'I'm sure you did.'

'I lost the goddamn flower!'

'I think you're beautiful,' he said softly, moving to the floor beside her and putting his arms around her. She laid her head against his shoulder, feeling her mascara forming little black puddles underneath her eyes.

'You must be very horny,' she smiled through the tears.

'I am,' he said, kissing her neck. 'I haven't seen you in three days.'

'And whose damn fault is that?' she asked fiercely, pushing him aside and clumsily getting up on her feet. 'Damn it, you should have seen me tonight. I really did look beautiful.'

'I'm sure you did.'

'Leon – I went out with a Leon, if you can believe it – he asked me out again. If you can believe *that!* Friday night. He wants to take me to see Second City.'

'What did you tell him?'

'I said that I usually liked to keep my Friday nights open just in case my married lover could make it over for a few hours.'

'Jill—'

'I said yes, I'd be delighted. What should I have said?'

David got up off the floor. 'What is all this in aid of, Jill?'

She shrugged her shoulder. The strap of her gown fell down across her arm. 'You have to make a choice, David.'

'Oh, Jill—'

'And I'm sorry I seem to be resorting to clichés. But we happen to be living in a cliché so I choose my words accordingly.'

'I don't like ultimatums.'

'I don't care what you like!'

They stood for what seemed an eternity in their frozen positions. Then, without another word, he turned and slowly walked toward the door. It was a month before he called to tell her he had asked his wife for a divorce and that Elaine had responded by promising to take him for every cent he had.

Jill turned the small air-conditioning unit so that it blew directly at her throat.

'Feeling better now?'

'I will feel better when I have removed this dress and consigned it to an incinerator.'

'At least they got him in the ground.'

'That was a relief. The way this day has gone, I was sure they were going to wind up dropping the coffin – as a sort of grand finale.'

David laughed. 'Quite a day.' He shook his head. 'I still can't believe any of this is real.'

'I know what you mean.'

'Al's actually dead,' he said, more to himself than to his wife. 'We watched him being lowered into the ground.'

'Well, we saw a *coffin* being lowered into the ground,' Jill corrected. 'Al may still be back at that gas station. Maybe he got a job. Even in his condition, he'd have to move faster than that mechanic.'

David burst out laughing, pulling the car to a halt at the side of the busy street. They were only a few blocks from their apartment.

'Why are you stopping?' Jill asked, then watched helplessly as her husband's laughter turned abruptly to tears. 'Oh, David,' she said, her arms encircling him, her head pressed against his shoulders. Tears suddenly filled her own eyes. For several minutes, they cried together, for the man they had both so liked and admired.

David was the first to break away, sitting up straight and drying his eyes. 'Sorry,' he said.

'Sorry? What for?'

He shook his head. 'For everything. For being such a jerk – making you wear that dumb dress—'

'That's all right.'

'No, it's not all right. Look at you, for God's sake.'

'I'd rather not be reminded about how I must look—'

'See? I did it again. Every time I open my mouth, I make you feel worse.'

'No, really. You don't. I feel terrific. Or interesting, anyway. Let's say I feel interesting.'

He leaned over and kissed her. 'You're so sweet and I'm such a prick.'

'Yes, I am and you are. So, what else is new?' She kissed his cheek. 'Come on, start the car. We'll go home; I'll burn my dress; we'll take a bubble bath and get into bed. How does that sound?'

He responded without words, nodding his head and turning the key in the ignition. The car started and they drove the two blocks to their apartment in easy silence.

A few minutes later, David pulled the car into their designated parking space in the large underground garage. He stopped, took the key out of the ignition and kept his head lowered, as if he couldn't raise it until he finished whatever thought was in his head. Jill waited accordingly, knowing there was something he wanted to tell her that was more important than getting quickly out of her clothes.

'What is it?' she asked.

Silence. Then finally, 'I owe you another apology.'

Jill held her breath, thoughts of Nicole Clark filling her mind. Had there been more than just the lunch he hadn't told her about? Don't tell me, she begged silently. I don't want to know. 'You've apologized enough already,' she said, her voice whispered and strained.

'Not for this.'

'David—'

'About your job, the teaching.'

'What?'

'About the way I reacted when you told me how unhappy you were.'

'How did you react?' Jill questioned.

'That's just the point,' he said. 'I didn't. I told you to grin and bear it. Some nonsense like that. Legal talk. Practical advice when what you needed was a little support and understanding. Damn it, Jill, if you're unhappy teaching, then you shouldn't be teaching. If Al's death teaches us anything at all, it's that life is too short, too precious to waste it doing something we don't want to do. I love you, Jill. I want you to be happy.'

'I will be.' Jill smiled through her tears. 'Something will come up. Irving will call. You'll see.'

David scoffed. 'I was really all heart that night you told me about your meeting with Irving,' he said, thinking back. 'My usual sensitive, sympathetic self.'

'All is forgiven,' Jill whispered. 'Sometimes it's better to be practical than sensitive.' She paused, then continued again, her voice soft and quiet. 'I just wish I saw more of you, that's all. Maybe then the rest of it wouldn't seem so important.'

He nodded. 'I'm sorry about that, too. I know it must seem like I'm falling back into old patterns. But believe me, Jill, the work load is extreme at the moment. Everything's gone crazy. I just can't seem to keep on top of things no matter how hard or how late I work. Now, with Al dead, it's even worse. Nobody knows what's going on. It'll be months before things calm down and we get back on a proper course.' He looked questioningly at his wife. 'Do you think you can be patient for just a little while longer? I will promise that after Christmas things should be back to normal. No more working from dawn to dusk every day. I promise. How does that sound to you?'

Jill nodded. 'Sounds good.'

He leaned over and kissed her gently. Then they each opened their respective car doors and stepped out, closing them again in almost perfect unison. They walked hand in hand to the inside elevator and waited for it to arrive.

'I wonder if Irving *will* call me again,' Jill said absently, as the doors to the elevator opened and they stepped inside.

'You were his top producer. Of course he'll call you again.'

'He was pretty negative.'

'He gets paid to be negative.'

'He said the new girl who replaced me is working out very well.'

'Nobody could ever replace you,' David said, hugging her to him and kissing the side of her face.

Tell that to Nicole Clark, she wanted to say, but she chose instead to say nothing.

'Maybe a new show will come up,' David continued.

Jill nodded. 'Something based entirely in Chicago,' she said. 'And here I would stay.'

'Until the first opportunity to see China comes along—'

'I've been to China,' she reminded him.

'I know,' he said, and then they were both silent.

They were pacing the floor, circling each other like two stray cats, their words hissed at each other across the space of their living room, their backs arched, ready to pounce at the slightest provocation.

'Why are you making such a big deal about this trip?'

'I have already given you my reasons. You've been away enough this year.'

'No more than last year.'

'You were away too much last year.'

'Oh, great. We're just going around in circles.'

Jill plopped wearily down into the soft fullness of the print sofa. 'I'm tired of fighting every time I have to go away.'

'Then stop going away.'

'I don't go away that often!'

David stopped his pacing and stared at his wife in genuine amazement. 'Jill, in the two years we've been married, you've been to London, Paris, Toronto, Los Angeles, Angola and Argentina! Now you're talking about going to China!'

Jill was quiet for several seconds. 'We once talked about going there together,' she said, emphasizing the final word.

'You know I can't go now.'

'Why not?'

'What am I supposed to do, Jill? Put all my clients on hold while I accompany my wife on a jaunt up the Great Wall?'

'Precisely. Why not?'

'Because people in the throes of a divorce don't take too kindly to their lawyers postponing court dates it's taken months, sometimes years, to set up.'

'You have partners, don't you? What are they there for, if not to help out when one of you gets busy elsewhere?'

'You know I don't like to pass off my work—'

'Some people call it delegating responsibility.'

'My clients are *my* responsibility.'

'Can't you just tell them you're going on holiday for a few weeks? I took my holidays around *your* schedule!'

'Exactly, I've already had my holidays!' David sat down in one of the large wing chairs he and Jill had recently purchased. 'What am I going to do in China, anyway? Change the film in your cameras? Be reasonable; I'd only get in everybody's way.'

Jill thought of other trips, the spouses of other members of the various crews. David was right. Whenever one of the wives (and it was always the wives, she realized) chose to accompany her husband on any such trip, there was inevitably friction and unhappiness. It was never a good rule to combine pleasure trips with business, she had long ago decided. Somehow all parties managed to feel cheated.

'Besides,' David was saying, 'we can't afford it.'

Jill took a long, deep breath. As a non-working member of the expedition, David would be required to pay his own way. And Elaine had made sure that any of the infrequent holidays David and Jill enjoyed were spent relatively close to home.

'So, where does that leave us?' Jill asked, her voice tired.

'You tell me,' David answered, no less fatigued.

'I have to go, David.'

He nodded, standing up. 'You'll miss the firm party.'

'I know. I'm sorry.'

'And dinner with the Marriotts.'

'We'll have them over when I get back.'

'What do I tell everyone?'

'The truth. That I had to go to China. It'll give the old geezers something to talk about other than the fact your first wife was prettier and what does he see in this television lady anyway?' David smiled wearily in her direction. 'If you really want to give them something to talk about, you could take a date.' A fleeting image of another woman, her legs wrapped around her husband, flashed before her eyes. 'On second thought,' she said, getting up and slinking over to David, sitting on his lap and wrapping her own legs around him, 'let them find their own topics of conversation.' She kissed him. 'Please don't be angry.'

'I'll get over it,' he said, returning her kiss.

She had gone to China, filmed the first onslaught of American tourists, and returned some two weeks later to find the apartment unchanged, the weather the same, and her husband as happy to see her as he always was whenever she returned home from an assignment. But something was different. Something intangible, caught only in passing, in a glance that didn't quite connect, or a touch that failed to linger. He'd been with somebody else. She knew it. It was as real to her as if she'd witnessed the act herself, as tangible as if he'd put it into words. He never said anything. She never asked. But it was there. A week after her return she told the network that she would accept no more out-of-Chicago assignments, and soon after, she submitted her resignation and accepted a post teaching TV journalism at the University of Chicago.

'What were you talking to Nicki about?' he asked, as they stepped into their apartment. Jill pulled the black wool dress up over her head and let it drop in a sweaty heap to the floor. 'Jesus, Jill, wait till I close the door!'

She heard the door close behind her as she walked, robot-like, toward the bathroom. From the door David heard the bath water running. When he reached the bathroom, Jill was nude and standing beside the tub waiting for it to fill.

'You didn't tell me you took her to lunch,' Jill told him by way of a reply.

David didn't require further explanation. 'She was upset. She needed someone to talk to.'

'And you were the only one she could turn to?'

'I was there.'

'Very convenient,' Jill said, wishing she hadn't.

'This isn't worth discussing,' he said, walking from the room.

Jill debated following him, but decided that the sight of her nude body would compare unfavorably in any discussion of Nicole Clark. She waited until the bath was filled almost to overflowing before she lowered herself into it and closed her eyes. Somehow, in the few minutes between the opening of their apartment door and the running of the bath water, all thoughts of bubbles and making love had been misplaced. David was in one room; Jill was in another. Nicole Clark was somewhere in between.

Chapter Sixteen

The next day, Jill drove out to Lake Forest to see Beth Weatherby.

From the street, the house looked the same as it had the last time she had visited, the green leaves of early summer still filling the trees which surrounded the large gray brick exterior, giving the lie to the silent passage of almost three months. Soon enough, she knew, the green would turn to autumn golds and reds and then, before she was ready, the color would disappear altogether, leaving the branches bare and black against the overwhelming gray of the Chicago sky. Jill stared at the rows of white and red petunias and geraniums which lined the walkway to the front of the house. Despite the fresh flowers and the surrounding heat – the temperature was only slightly down from the day before – she felt suddenly cold. It was going to be a long winter, she thought, taking the first steps up the long path toward the house.

The front door stood before her, a large, heavy oak slab, with a bronze knocker shaped like a dolphin. Tentatively, Jill reached up and grabbed the large fish's tail, feeling a sudden flush of palpable fear race through her body. Why? she wondered, annoyed at her body's reflexes. What was it she was so afraid of? That Al's ghost would materialize to answer her knock, usher her inside with his customary warmth, as he had several months ago when she and David had arrived for that misbegotten night of bridge? She remembered sitting in the comfortable living room, mesmerized by the serenity of its antiques, the room somehow implying a sense of unspoken continuance, feeling David close by her side, looking over at the photograph of the Weatherby children, and then the calm suddenly shattered by a scream in the night. Beth's scream. She saw herself racing toward the kitchen, her eyes freezing momentarily on Al's frightened face, drained white by the sudden gush of red from Beth's outstretched hand. Jill turned her head back toward the road. White and red, she thought, like the flowers.

Jill stood absolutely still, feeling her panic spreading. This is ridiculous, she thought, her self-annoyance building. She was acting like a child afraid of the bogeyman. Was it the aura of death she feared? The knowledge that a man had been murdered inside? She shook her head at her invisible questioner. No, she was not afraid of death even in its most grisly manifestations. She had often trained her cameras on the carnage of global civil wars and inner-city brutality. No, she had no fear of death – she had directed its display.

Yet she had no camera with her now to help her keep her distance. She had only herself – and her fear. For whatever reason, she simply did not want to go inside that house. Without requiring further explanation, she somehow knew that there were secrets in there she didn't wish to hear. That once she set foot on the other side of that massive oak door, her life would never be the same again.

'Oh, stop overdramatizing,' she told herself out loud, letting go of the bronze dolphin and listening as it thwacked loudly against its base.

The door opened immediately, as if whoever was behind it had known of her presence and had been patiently waiting for her to make up her mind. Jill felt her heart pumping wildly against her chest. Stop it, she told herself as she came face to face with the young girl in the doorway. Lisa Weatherby smiled wanly at her visitor. She looked much younger than her twenty-three years, Jill decided, younger, in fact, than her seventeen-year-old brother, and she'd obviously been crying. Her face was puffy and swollen, a teary mist resting like cataracts over her hazel eyes. She looked startlingly like her father. Jill quickly conjured up the image of Lisa's two brothers, both of whom she had seen at the funeral. Each had much more closely resembled his mother.

'Are you all right?' Jill asked, instantly putting her arms around the girl.

'I don't know what I am,' the girl answered, immediately bursting into tears. Jill led her quickly inside the house and closed the door. The hallway looked exactly as it had a scant few months ago. Had she been expecting blood-splattered walls? The name of the victim scribbled amid obscene graffiti in his own blood?

'Are your brothers here?' Jill asked.

'Brian's lying down,' the girl said softly. 'Michael went back to his church.'

'And your mother?' Jill wondered if Lisa had sensed her reluctance in asking the last question.

'She's in her room. Can we talk for a minute?' Lisa asked.

'Sure,' Jill answered. 'That's why I'm here.'

The girl allowed Jill to lead her into the large living room. As it was with the hallway, the room was unchanged. It still spoke of warmth and permanence, even love.

They walked together like Siamese twins joined at the hip, sharing a common leg, until they reached the sofa. Slowly, carefully, they lowered themselves down, sitting side by side, arms entwined.

'They say everybody in LA is crazy,' Lisa began without introduction, sniffing away a tear. 'You know, they say that when God created the world, he tilted it onto its side, and all the nuts fell into Los Angeles.' She tried to laugh but couldn't. 'And it's true, you know. They *are* nuts. There isn't a sane one in the whole bunch. You can't believe anyone – they lie as easily as they tell the truth. And all they talk about is money and success. Nobody ever reads or talks about anything that's going on in the world. They all drive expensive foreign cars and have houses with swimming pools, but nobody is really happy because they're never really sure after a while what lie they've told to whom. They don't even know what's a lie anymore and what isn't. It's like they're living in the middle of a big Hollywood soundstage and they're afraid that, come nighttime, someone's gonna come along and fold it all up. Nobody knows there what's real and what's make-believe.' She paused, as if trying to give her thoughts some coherence. 'I used to come home to get a sense of balance. Back here, in this house, with my mother and father, I knew there was some sanity left in this world. My parents understood who they were; they accepted

224

each other and the rest of us for ourselves. They never tried to turn us into something different.' She shook her head, her mind racing back and forth between her two worlds. 'Not like in Hollywood. Everyone's always trying to make you over into somebody else. And everyone's a star, even the ones who've been parking cars for twenty years or waiting on tables. You ask them what they are, they never say I'm a waitress or a parking lot attendant – they're all actors and actresses. They were all up for the lead in *In Cold Blood*. Do you know how many years ago that was?! They were looking for unknowns, they must have auditioned every guy between the ages of sixteen and fifty – but that doesn't make any difference. They were still up for the lead, and one day they're gonna be stars. And it happens, you know, it happens just often enough to make everybody else hang on.' She wiped at her eyes with both hands. Jill let her continue uninterrupted. 'I've been there close to four years now, trying to make it as a singer. My father didn't want me to go. Not that he didn't trust my talent. He just knew that everybody there was crazy.' She laughed a touch too loudly. 'I'm one of them. One of the crazies who's busy waiting on tables and waiting for my big break. I've been there almost four years now. Did I tell you that already? And my parents have been extremely supportive of me even though they didn't want me to go. Well, actually, my mother went along with my father when we were all together, but when we were by ourselves, just the two of us, she'd say, "Go, Lisa. Try for it. You'll never know unless you try," and I guess that gave me the encouragement I needed because my dad was really against it. But after I made up my mind and went down there, he started sending me money, and my Mom writes me a couple of times a week. We're very close. We always have been. She tells me everything. She was afraid that things wouldn't work out for me, I think, when I left: I could see it in her eyes. She looked kind of scared. I guess she was afraid she'd be lonely and she knew how much she'd miss me once I was gone, and she knew how crazy they all are there. But she was never one of those mothers who say, "Stay home and meet a nice guy. What do you want to go running off to Hollywood for? Find yourself a nice lawyer like I did and settle down!" None of that sort of stuff. She thought I had lots of time for all that. I guess eventually she wanted me to meet someone like my father. Someone kind and good and dependable, who made a lot of money and always looked after his family. You don't meet that kind of guy in LA. They're too busy looking in the mirror.' The girl took a deep intake of air. 'They were really happy, you know. They were married for twenty-seven years and, do you know something, I never heard them fight. They never even argued. Mom was so supportive of Dad. If we kids ever did anything or said anything to upset him, Mom would get really mad. She said he worked too hard all day to come home and let us upset him. She really protected him. She loved him so much. He was so funny, you know. Funny and warm. All my dates liked him. That's unusual. Guys are usually uncomfortable around fathers. But my dad never made anyone uncomfortable. Everybody liked him – loved him! Especially my mother.' A loud sob escaped her lips. 'This is killing her – you know that? She misses him so much. She walks around here like she's in a daze except that her eyes are going like crazy. Like she's talking to herself without using words. We try to talk to her but we don't know what to say! We can't reach her—' She was crying almost uncontrollably now. 'Talk about crazy,' she whispered. 'The police found the murder weapon, you know. Yesterday. One of Dad's hammers. It was stuffed into the central vacuuming system. Still covered with blood.'

Jill felt her arms tighten around the girl. Lisa cried quietly for several more minutes before straightening up again and wiping her eyes.

'I'm sorry,' she said.

'Don't be.'

'I feel like such a big baby.'

'You're not,' Jill assured her. 'Your whole life has been turned upside down. You're bound to feel you've lost your balance.'

'She seems much more settled today somehow,' Lisa continued, standing up and pacing back and forth in front of Jill. 'She wouldn't go to the funeral yesterday. She was very adamant. We had hoped that the funeral might finalize things for her, that seeing Dad's coffin being lowered into the ground might – wake her up, I guess, get her to talk about what happened. Tell us who did this awful thing. But she wouldn't go. She just sat on the bed and shook her head.'

'The shock, Lisa, of what she went through, what she saw, the beating—'

'I know all that.' Lisa stopped pacing. 'It just doesn't make it any easier.'

'She doesn't talk at all?'

Lisa stared directly into Jill's eyes. 'She talks,' she said softly. 'About the weather, how nice it is to have Brian and me home. She asks questions, lots of questions about what we're doing. She listens. She's a great listener. She even gives advice. She listened to Michael for hours about his faith. But she doesn't say a word about my father. And when you mention anything about him, her eyes get that glazed expression and her face goes blank and that's the end of it.'

Jill thought for several seconds, though there was no language to her thoughts, nothing to give them any cohesiveness. 'I guess that's the only way she can cope right now.'

'Don Eliot said that she spoke to you at the hospital, and we were hoping that maybe seeing you might, I don't know—'

'I'll do whatever I can,' Jill offered.

Lisa returned to the sofa and sat down beside Jill, allowing Jill's arms to surround her, resting her head on the other woman's shoulder. Neither woman heard the entrance of the third who stood watching them in silence from the doorway.

'Hello, Jill,' Beth's voice called softly, pleasantly.

Jill looked quickly in Beth's direction. The woman she saw was casually dressed in beige slacks and a light cotton shirt. She wore no makeup to hide her many bruises and her sun-streaked hair was short and swept away from her face. The wounds themselves had healed somewhat, their colors slightly muted, less angry, faded by time. Her right wrist was bandaged. As Beth came toward her, Jill detected a slight limp. Beneath the casual clothes, Beth held her body stiffly.

The two women embraced. When they pulled apart, Beth was smiling warmly. 'I'm so glad to see you,' she said. 'You look terrific.'

'I look terrible,' Jill said automatically. 'My hair frizzes up like steel wool in this humidity.'

'And mine goes straight as a string,' Beth laughed. 'Bet you always wanted straight hair,' she said conspiratorially. Jill nodded. 'Sure,' Beth agreed. 'And I always wanted lots of curls. That's always the way it is. Let's sit down.'

Lisa got quickly out of her way, moving to a chair across the room and letting her mother and Jill occupy the sofa.

'Hi, sweetheart,' Beth said, acknowledging her daughter as they crossed paths.

'How do you feel?' Lisa asked.

'I'm fine,' Beth said, strongly. 'You're the one who doesn't look so hot. Why don't you go upstairs and lie down for a while like your brother?' Jill saw the hesitation in Lisa's eyes. 'Go on,' her mother urged. 'Jill will take good care of me.'

'Go ahead,' Jill said. 'It'll give your mother and me a chance to talk.' That's what you want, isn't it? her eyes asked the younger woman, who seemed suddenly to comprehend. Lisa stood up.

'Can I make you some tea or anything?' she offered.

'Not for me,' Beth said with a laugh. 'They keep filling me up with tea. I've never peed so much in my life.'

Jill laughed. 'Not for me either,' she said, feeling somewhat confused, a trifle disoriented. Far from being quiet and withdrawn, Beth Weatherby was relaxed and gregarious, as animated as Jill had seen her in a long time. It was as though she had totally blocked out any knowledge of her husband's death.

'How's David?' Beth asked after Lisa had left the room and

her footsteps could be heard ascending the staircase.

'He's fine. Very busy.'

'I'm sure,' Beth said cryptically. 'The office must be in a terrible state.'

Beth's remark caught Jill by surprise. So, Beth *did* know; she was aware.'

It was as if Beth could read her thoughts. 'I don't want you to think I'm crazy, Jill,' she began. 'I know how upset everyone is around here. I know I'm the cause. But I'm just not ready to talk about it yet. Can you understand?' Jill couldn't but nodded anyway. 'I know what happened that night. I know that Al is dead. And there's a lot that I have to say. But not yet. I have to understand it all first before I can talk about it.' She paused. 'I'm sorry. I know I'm probably being infuriatingly vague about this whole thing, but I'm just not ready yet to talk about what happened. Please bear with me.' Again, Jill nodded. 'You talk,' Beth continued. 'Tell me about how you always wanted straight hair, you silly lady. You're so gorgeous just the way you are.'

Jill laughed out loud. 'I thought you didn't want me to think you were crazy,' she said, not sure if it was the proper thing to have said. The smile on Beth's face assured her that it was.

'Why do you always put yourself down?' Beth asked.

'I don't think I do,' Jill answered. 'I'm just realistic.'

'What's your idea of a beautiful woman? Go on, I'm curious. Who do you think is gorgeous?'

Jill thought for several seconds. 'Candice Bergen,' she said finally. 'Farrah Fawcett.' She paused. 'Nicole Clark,' she added haltingly.

Beth's eyes registered each new name. 'Candice Bergen, yes, lovely face, but the body is kind of ordinary; Farrah Fawcett has a lot of hair and thin lips but I guess she's pretty enough; Nicole Clark – yes, I'd have to say that Nicole is a beautiful girl.' She chuckled. 'But, who knows, Nicole Clark probably spends as many wasted hours in front of her mirror as the rest of us, wishing her hair was this way, not that, or that her nose were longer or thinner, or that her thighs weren't quite so rounded.'

'You saw her thighs,' Jill commented. 'Did they look too round to you?'

'No,' Beth confessed. 'They looked perfect to me.' She looked around the room at nothing in particular. 'Well, maybe Nicole is one of those rare people who is happy with the way she looks. Maybe everything is exactly the way she wants it.' Beth turned back to Jill. 'She looks like the type of person who gets exactly what she wants, doesn't she?'

Jill held her breath. 'She wants David.'

'What?'

'I said she wants David.'

'What do you mean, she wants him?'

'Exactly what you think.'

'Oh, Jill,' Beth said, laughing. 'What makes you think that?'

'She told me.'

'What?!'

'She told me that she wants him, that she intends to marry him, and please don't tell me she must have been joking – she wasn't. She isn't.'

Beth digested the information. 'So, that's what was going on at our exercise class that afternoon—'

'It's been going on all summer. Since the firm picnic. A real war of nerves. Only I'm afraid her nerves are stronger than mine.'

'Does David know?'

Jill nodded. 'He knows. I had to tell him.'

'Why, for heaven's sake?'

Jill shrugged. 'It just happened. If I hadn't she'd have made sure he found out. Somehow. She always seems to have an alternative course of action ready.

'And? What was David's reaction?'

Again, Jill shrugged. 'I don't know. At first I think he was partly annoyed, partly flattered. Now, I think he's mostly flattered. If he's annoyed with anyone, it's with me. And I don't know what to do about it.' Jill stood up, and began pacing in the same way Lisa had done. 'I've never felt so manipulated in my whole life. I feel like a rat in a maze. Only every path I take is the wrong one. And I'm completely powerless. I don't know. Maybe I should have let David say something to her in the beginning. He offered to.' She turned to Beth. 'Except that I know what she would have said if he'd confronted her. She'd have gone all soft and cried, told him how embarrassed and sorry she was, how she was all alone in Chicago, how much she'd admired him, how he was everything she'd ever wanted, the same speech she gave me when I confronted her. And David would have stood there looking at this poor, sensitive, terribly vulnerable girl who is not only unquestionably beautiful but who also obviously adores him, and I'd still be standing here not knowing what to do. If I make an issue, I look like a jealous, suspicious wife. If I ignore it and hope that she goes away, she'll take two giant steps forward. Either way, the result will be the same.'

'Maybe not,' Beth said. 'You're forgetting David in all this. He *does* have something to say about the outcome.'

Jill stood very still and stared down at Beth Weatherby. 'I never forget David,' she said, fighting back tears. 'Why do you think I'm so worried?' She lowered herself down beside Beth and sat helplessly for several minutes feeling the tears as they ran down her cheeks.

'Oh, Jill—' Beth began, taking Jill's hands in her own.

'I know the kind of man he is, Beth. I was there once myself, remember. He loves women. Lots of women. I knew that when I married him. Hell, I knew it the moment I laid eyes on him. A man who looks like David just has to snap his fingers and half a dozen women come running. I've seen it. We'll be at a party and he's immediately the center of attention. The women are all over him. They stare at him from across the room. Even *I* can read the smoke signals loud and clear. Do you know that sometimes it's like I'm not even there? They ignore me. It's like I don't exist. And if they do acknowledge my presence it's almost worse, because then they get this shocked expression on their faces, like, my God, what is this gorgeous hunk doing with a woman as plain as she is—'

'Jill—'

'No, all right, I'm not plain. I'm not ugly, or even unattractive. I am an attractive woman, a little different, unusual maybe. Certainly nothing that warrants putting a paper bag over my head. But I am definitely not beautiful. I wouldn't appear on anybody's ten-best list, and I know it. And David isn't blind. He knows it. And so here I am, this fairly average-looking female married to a very non-average-looking male, and sometimes I feel so – inadequate, I guess is the best way to describe it. I know that all these women are out there eyeing my husband, wanting him, wanting to make love to him, knowing that he knows it too, and I keep wondering, what is this man doing with me? How long can I keep him? How long before he starts getting restless again? And some nights when we get into bed, I'm just so goddamn grateful that he's there beside me. I feel so lucky—'

'David's the lucky one, Jill.'

Jill smiled, wiping away the tears. 'You sound like my mother.' Beth laughed quietly. 'I'm lucky, too,' Jill said.

'Yes, you are,' Beth agreed. 'David is a very charming man. I've always liked him.'

'Everybody likes him. That's my problem.'

'Everybody isn't his wife,' Beth reminded her. 'You are.'

Jill nodded. 'There's a big difference between being a man's wife and being his mistress,' she began, 'and I feel somewhat qualified to speak on the subject, having been both.' She looked away, as if searching for just the right words. 'The other woman sees only the virtues. She sees the romantic hideaways and the expensive little dinners for two, and she's so thrilled if he can ever stay the whole night that she doesn't even notice that he snores or his feet smell or he takes up the whole bed. Everything about him is exciting – even his faults – because she's never sure when – or if – she's going to see him again. It's all very – dramatic. Very high tragedy.' She paused. 'When you're the wife, it's more like a comedy, a very black one.' She laughed at her own choice of similes. 'Suddenly you're aware of all the unpleasant odors and habits and, well, like that chain letter you gave me at the picnic – God, I broke the chain, do you think this is all a direct result?' The two women laughed quietly. Jill stood up and started pacing again. 'The wife doesn't see as many of those expensive little dinners, and when she does, she also gets the Visa bill at the end of the month, and she gets to hear all the complaining about how much money they spend, and those dinners are rarely for two anyway. There are children and in-laws and partners. And reality. And suddenly when she looks at her husband, she still loves him, all right, but her eyes have lost that unquestioning adoration they once held. It's gone. And he misses it. And there are all these sweet and lovely little women out there, in the office, on the street, and they're all looking at him with these adoring eyes, and what can you do? How can you fight reality?'

There were several seconds of silence before Beth spoke. 'Has David – before—?' She broke off, reluctant to give words to the thought.

'Has he been unfaithful?' Jill asked for her. Beth nodded. Jill took a deep breath. 'I think so,' she said aloud for the first time. 'In my gut, I know of at least one time—' She felt the tears pushing against her eyes again, felt her throat constricting. 'But the whole point is that I don't know for sure! And as long as I'm not sure, then I don't have to really confront my feelings or make any decisions. Knowing – actually to know that David was sleeping with another woman – to have to live with that knowledge. Well, there is such a thing as too much reality. I don't know what I'd do. And I guess that's what scares me most as far as Nicole Clark is concerned, because there's no way she'll ever be satisfied to just have her one night with him and then quietly disappear. She'll make sure I find out, and then – I don't know.' Jill threw her head back in despair, sniffing loudly and then angrily wiping the tears from her face. 'Goddamn it,' she said, straightening up. 'I'm talking like I've lost him already. And I haven't,' she stated firmly. 'And I won't!'

Beth jumped to her feet. 'Now you're talking.'

Jill fell into Beth Weatherby's arms. 'I feel like such an idiot,' Jill said, wiping at her nose with a Kleenex she found in her skirt pocket. 'Here you are with everything that's happening to you, and here I am complaining about nothing, for God's sake.'

Beth Weatherby pushed one of Jill's stray hairs away from her face. 'You never complain about nothing,' she assured her. 'And please, don't worry about me, Jill. My problems are all over.' Her voice grew very soft. 'I did it, Jill,' she whispered. 'I killed Al. I killed my husband.'

Chapter Seventeen

Jill sat behind the wheel of her car and watched her hands shake. She was afraid to turn the key in the ignition, to start the car, unsure how her body would react once in motion. She had to get her feelings under control before she could control anything as potentially lethal as an automobile. Lethal, she thought, choosing to sit and do nothing for several minutes, to allow herself time to think, to calm her trembling fingers, to absorb what she had just been told. 'I did it, Jill,' she heard Beth repeat. 'I killed Al. I killed my husband.' As simple as that. As straightforward. No regrets, no hysteria, no tears. Just a calm statement of fact. ('Just the facts, ma'am,' she heard Jack Webb mutter at her ear.) Beth had offered no further explanation; Jill had been too stunned to ask for one. And then both Lisa and her brother Brian had suddenly materialized at the foot of the stairs and Beth's eyes had slowly closed and opened again, void of all expression. Jill knew instinctively that what Beth had just told her was not meant to be shared. Too overwhelmed even to speak, she muttered something in Lisa's direction and stumbled out of the house. She had been sitting in her car for close to five minutes, and she still felt too unsure of herself to move.

She stared down at her hands. The nails were all uneven lengths, of no particular shape or design. A few broken chips of polish clung tenuously to several cuticles. She hadn't bothered to remove them. Around the nails, her skin had been picked at and nibbled on, a habit she had often vowed to break, but one she clung to like a child's security blanket. The back of her right hand bore the trace of a small childhood scar, received when she had pulled a hot iron down on top of her. They were strong hands, capable hands. Hands a palmist had once regarded with glee, claiming he barely knew where to begin, there was such an abundance of character to be read, telling her joyfully that she was one of the world's true eccentrics and that insanity no doubt traveled in her family. Could these hands kill, she wondered?

She pictured herself digging through her kitchen drawers for a hammer. (Did they even own a hammer?) She felt herself reach for it, move down the hallway toward the bedroom where David lay sleeping, saw her arm raise the hammer high into the air and watched it fall with sickening speed, stopping just short of David's head. She closed her eyes against the image. No, she thought, she could never do what Beth Weatherby claimed to have done.

Jill looked back toward the gray brick house. It was impossible, she decided, thinking of the gentle woman inside. There was simply no way Beth was capable of such an act unless she had suffered a complete mental collapse; a breakdown for which she could hardly be held accountable. Yet she seemed so rational now, so calm and in control. The whole situation was absurd. Jill simply could not accept Beth's confession as truth. There was no way Beth Weatherby could have murdered her husband.

Feeling the issue resolved inside herself, Jill turned the key in the ignition and started the car, pulling the gray Volvo away from the curb and driving quickly away, watching the exquisite residential streets disappear behind her as she headed toward the highway. For the first time in several years, she regretted that she didn't have school to go to. The fall semester didn't start for several weeks, and even the round of loathsome staff meetings didn't begin until the following Monday, so Jill was left entirely at loose ends, feeling in need of somewhere to go, something to do. Anything to keep Beth's words from replaying in her mind.

She spotted a phone booth and swerved the car into a sweeping U-turn, stopping directly in front of the graffiti-strewn booth and fishing in her purse for change. She noticed her hands were still shaking as she dialed.

'Weatherby, Ross,' came the receptionist's familiar voice.

'David Plumley, please,' Jill stated, wondering what she was planning to tell him.

'Mr Plumley's office.'

'Diane?'

'Yes. Can I help you?'

'It's Jill.'

The secretary sounded surprised. 'Oh, I'm sorry. I didn't recognize your voice. You sounded – different.'

Jill tried to steady her voice. 'Is David around?'

'He's with a client.'

'Could you interrupt him, please? It's important.' Why did she say that? Was she planning on telling David about Beth's confession?

David's voice came on the phone, concerned, even anxious. 'Jill? Are you all right?'

'Oh, yes, I'm fine. I just wondered – whether we could have lunch together. I just noticed it's almost one o'clock.'

'I have to be in court at one o'clock,' he said, his voice becoming low, losing its quality of concern. 'Is that why you had Diane interrupt my meeting?'

'I just came from seeing Beth,' Jill ventured.

'And?'

Jill felt her shoulders slump. 'Nothing,' she said. 'I did most of the talking.'

'Jill, can't we discuss this later?'

Jill nodded, forgetting that he couldn't see her. 'What court will you be in? Maybe I'll come and watch you.'

'I don't think that would be a good idea,' he said quickly. 'It's not a very interesting case. You'd only be bored. Look – I have to go. I'll speak to you later.'

'Will you be home right after court?' she asked, realizing even as the words were leaving her mouth that he had already hung up. 'Sure,' she said, replacing the receiver. 'Call me later.'

She wasn't sure how or why she had ended up in front of Rita Carrington's exercise class, but seeing the old rusty brick building suddenly before her, Jill quickly pulled the car into the adjacent parking lot and went inside. Her adrenaline was still pumping wildly, threatening to push itself out through her extremities. Perhaps a little exercise would be a good way to get herself under control.

She was in the locker room before she realized she didn't have her exercise suit with her. 'Damn,' she said, dejectedly, allowing her body to sink down onto the waiting bench.

'Hi,' came the voice from behind her. 'Haven't seen you in a few weeks.'

Jill looked up to see a sweat-covered Ricki Elfer, nude except for a towel around her neck. 'Things have been rather hectic lately,' she said quietly, wondering whether Ricki had recognized Beth Weatherby from her picture in the paper and was about to pepper her with questions.

'You're telling me,' Ricki concurred. 'You taking a class now?'

'Forgot my leotard.'

'Great. You can join us for lunch. Me and a couple of the girls. We thought we'd go across the street.'

Jill smiled. 'Sounds good,' she said.

'Great. I'll just grab a quick shower and be right back.'

Jill watched Ricki Elfer's expansive derrière disappear around the row of lockers. It was a strange sensation, she realized, to carry on a normal conversation when one of the parties was fully dressed and the other was totally naked. She closed her eyes and tried to rid her mind of all thought except her upcoming lunch. If she couldn't exercise, she decided, the next best thing to do was eat.

'Jill, this is Denise and Terri,' Ricki Elfer said, introducing her to the two women who were already seated at the restaurant table. 'Wow, that was quite a workout today,' Ricki exclaimed, sitting down. Jill took the remaining seat and nodded hello to the other women.

'She gets tougher every day,' the short brunette named Denise agreed. 'Not even my old dance classes were this tough.'

'Well, you have to admit, she looks wonderful,' Jill offered.

'Who?' Ricki asked. 'Rita Carrington?' Jill nodded. 'I should hope so,' Ricki smiled, eyeing the salad bar.

Jill agreed. 'Yeah, I guess she should if she's teaching exercise classes half the day.'

'Exercise? Are you kidding?' Ricki laughed. 'You don't get tits like those from exercise. You get them from God or you get them from a surgeon. Last I heard, Rita Carrington doesn't believe in God.'

'If you're a surgeon, you think of the two as one and the same,' offered Terri, a slim, muscular blonde. 'My husband is a doctor,' she further explained.

The women laughed. 'Rita Carrington's had surgery on her breasts?' Jill asked.

'On her boobs, on her stomach, on her tushy,' Ricki Elfer recited. 'Everything tucked and tightened and lifted. Haven't you noticed how her boobs never move, even when the rest of her is shaking all over? That's the dead giveaway. She turns right, her boobs still face straight ahead.'

'I also heard she had a face-lift,' Denise added.

'A face-lift?' Jill asked. 'She's so young!'

'She'll never see forty-five again,' Ricki told her, as the waiter approached.

The women ordered lunch and a liter of wine. Jill chose a bowl of soup and the salad bar, eventually allowing herself to be talked into ordering dessert.

'This is delicious,' Ricki said, devouring the last of her chocolate mousse. 'I shouldn't go to these exercise classes. They give me too big an appetite! How's your fruit flan?'

'Good,' Jill said. 'Would you like some?'

'Just a taste,' Ricki nodded, her fork already on Jill's plate.

Jill took a long sip of her coffee, feeling the wine dancing near the base of her neck. Whenever she'd had just the right amount to drink – not too much or too little – her neck would begin to feel weightless, as if it were about to separate from the rest of her body. The lunch had been just what the doctor ordered. This lunch, not lunch with her husband, or watching him in court. She pictured the crowded courtroom, saw David sitting at his table, Nicole Clark at his side. Was that why he had been so reluctant for her to come that afternoon? Had Nicole Clark already made her reservation? Used up the one remaining ticket?

'What's your friend doing these days?' Ricki suddenly asked her.

'My friend?'

'The lady you usually come with. She hasn't been around lately.'

'She's kind of busy,' Jill told her. Maybe Ricki never read the papers.

'Talk about busy,' Terri piped up, pushing her dessert plate

243

away, and gulping the rest of her coffee. 'I have to get home. I'm interviewing housekeepers this afternoon.'

'Good luck,' Denise said, her voice filled with frustration and understanding.

'You know what they say, don't you?' Ricki Elfer asked. 'If she can find the place, hire her.'

'What happened to Gunilla?'

'Who?' Jill asked.

'Yes, that's actually her name. Sounds like one of Cinderella's nasty stepsisters, I know,' Terri agreed. 'She's Swedish. Twenty years old. I got her through an agency six months ago. She's supposed to help me with the housework and with looking after Justin and Scotty. A week ago, she informed me she doesn't want to be a mother's helper, that she doesn't like having to cater to a two-year-old and a five-year-old. I reminded her that on her application she specifically requested two children, aged two and five. You got exactly what you said you wanted, I told her. She said it wasn't the way she thought it would be.'

'What ever is?' Jill asked.

'Anyway, I decided to try for a housekeeper this time instead of an au pair. The first one is supposedly arriving at three o'clock, and it's almost that now.'

'My God,' Denise exclaimed, pulling some money out of her purse and dropping it on the table, 'I didn't realize it was so late. I have to pick Rodney up at school.'

'I guess we should go too,' Jill said reluctantly.

'Finish your coffee,' Ricki told her. 'I still have a few minutes.'

The women exchanged their goodbyes and made their exits. When Jill looked back, the waiter had already refilled her coffee cup. 'So,' she said, addressing her attention to the woman on the other side of the table, 'did you make any decisions about tying your tubes or having a baby?'

'Sanity prevailed,' Ricki told her. 'Paul's going to have a vasectomy.'

Jill was genuinely surprised. 'I thought you said that if Paul had a vasectomy, you wouldn't be able to fool around—'

'Sounds like something I'd say,' Ricki agreed. 'I speak a lot of rot sometimes.'

'You don't play around?' Jill asked, a little disappointed.

'No,' Ricki said, her voice suddenly serious. 'Not on Paul. I did – with the others. But when you finally get yourself a good one – and Paul is a good one – you don't take any chances. This is my third marriage, and the first one I'm really proud of. You know what I mean?' Jill nodded. 'You don't take silly chances when you finally stumble into a right decision. I like marriage. I believe in it. Christ, I'd have to – I keep doing it.' Jill smiled. 'No,' Ricki Elfer said, shaking her head, 'if you're smart – and if I'm not always smart, at least I'm not always stupid – when you grab ahold of something good, you don't fuck up.'

Both women finished their coffee and smiled at each other in silence.

That night David moved restlessly beside her in bed.

'Can't you sleep?' Jill asked him, his persistent tossing keeping her awake.

'I'm too sore,' he said. 'My whole body aches.'

Jill sat up and ran her hand down his side. 'Do you want me to give you a backrub?'

There was a second's silence, then David turned gingerly onto his stomach. 'Okay, yeah, that might be nice.'

Jill immediately straddled his back and put her hands on his shoulders.

'Ow, that hurts,' he said, his body resisting her touch.

'I haven't done anything yet,' Jill protested.

'Not my shoulders,' he told her, 'my back. Get off me, you weigh a ton.'

'Thanks a lot.' Jill moved so that she was on her knees beside him. 'Where does it hurt?' she asked.

'Where doesn't it?' came his answer.

'Just how many games of squash did you play?'

'Three – and it's racquetball, not squash.'

'Well, I think you overdid it for somebody who hasn't played for as long as you haven't.'

'You made me feel guilty – ow! Watch it, huh? – about wasting all that money, so I tried to make up for it.'

'You're trying to tell me it's my fault?'

'Exactly.'

'Figures.'

David flipped over suddenly. 'God, you give a rotten massage,' he said, smiling, putting his arm around her and drawing her to him.

'Who'd you play with?' Jill asked.

'Pete Rogers,' David answered. 'One of the students. Actually, they won't be students much longer. Another week and they're called to the bar. God, I'm sore.' He kissed her cheek. 'Sorry I spoiled the little candlelit dinner you had planned. It would have been nice.'

'Well, you didn't know,' Jill shrugged. 'I just decided to do it at the spur of the moment.'

'I'm sorry, honey, I just needed to get out and pound something. Al's funeral still has me very shaky.' He looked at his wife. 'You never did tell me what Beth had to say.'

'Nothing really,' Jill lied, wondering if, like always, he would see through her. 'She didn't say anything. I did most of the talking.'

'She's got to start talking soon,' David said, almost absently. If he didn't believe her, Jill realized, he wasn't letting on. 'What did you do for the rest of the afternoon?'

'I went to my exercise class. There's a woman there I really like—'

'Good,' David said. Jill recognized the word and the tone. It meant he wasn't interested. Nevertheless, Jill decided to press ahead.

'She'd been trying to decide whether to tie her tubes or have a baby,' Jill ventured. David said nothing. 'David,' Jill whispered, 'I think we have to come to some sort of decision on that subject too.'

'What did this woman decide?' David asked, his voice tense.

'Her husband is having a vasectomy,' Jill said, now sorry she had brought the issue to light.

'Sounds good to me,' David said, almost casually.

'Don't be flip, David. I'm being serious.'

'So am I,' he said, turning his head in her direction, his eyes searching hers. 'I've told you before – I don't want any more children. I have two already. I haven't done a very good job with. I'm sorry, Jill,' he said, catching the look on her face. 'I know you wanted children, but let's face it, I'm not a very good father, and I don't have the energy or the patience – or the desire – to do it again.'

'You sound very definite.'

'I am very definite.'

'Where does that leave me?' Jill asked reluctantly.

'Where do you want to be?'

'With you,' she said, after a slight pause, her voice barely audible.

'Then that's where you are,' he said, kissing her forehead.

'I love you,' she said, feeling her voice growing softer with each fresh remark.

'I love you, too, sweetheart,' he answered. 'Come on, turn over, get some sleep. Let me hold you.'

Jill allowed her body to be turned and held, wishing she could crawl inside him, under his skin where she would be safe. So, it had been decided for her, she thought, feeling the muscles in his legs beginning to twitch. She was not to have children. She closed her eyes. She couldn't blame David. It was something he'd already been through, something he'd already done. He didn't want to do it again. To start over from the beginning. She wasn't even surprised. She'd known this would be his decision.

His arm shifted underneath her. She felt him pulling away, withdrawing. 'I'm sorry, honey,' he was saying, 'I've got to turn over.'

Jill moved so that David was free to turn around. Normally,

Chapter Eighteen

The feeling of déjà vu was almost overwhelming. The long table, the uncomfortable chairs, the smoke and the people responsible for it, their tired voices repeating even more tired speeches, all of which Jill was convinced she had heard in their exact entirety a year before. (Welcome to the start of another school year. The fall semester is perhaps the most important term, setting, as it does, the tone for the rest of the year. We wish to welcome – etc., etc. Jill looked up and down the old, badly scarred table, the people on either side probably not much different from the network people she used to confront across similar tables during the weekly story conferences of the past. Their interests were similar; many of the teachers had, like herself, come from prior jobs in television and radio. And yet, they were not the same. Something was missing, she thought, searching the other faces, each wearing the same tired and bored expression that her own undoubtedly held. The sense of commitment, she decided, a commitment to something larger than simply getting through the day, was flagrantly absent. Though there were obviously many in the room with a deep dedication to what they were doing, there was simply not the same kind of energy flowing through everyone's veins. It was precisely that missing energy that she missed so much – the constant struggle to get your ideas heard and accepted and ultimately recorded and broadcast.

Jill looked down at the floor. She was in deep trouble, she knew, if she was thinking this way already, on this the first day of this the most important semester of the school year. It didn't bode well.

The phone call came halfway into Jack McCreary's lengthy explanation of the recent budget cuts. Jill had honestly thought she was following the familiar monotone closely, and was somewhat startled to find that the sudden tap on her shoulder brought her abruptly back from a heated story conference at the studio, where she had been bowling them over with the sheer brilliance and audacity of her ideas, to the claustrophobic confines of the crowded campus meeting room, where reality was holding court.

'Phone call for you,' one of the office secretaries confided, leaning close, trying not to draw attention. 'He said it was important.'

Jill looked puzzled, but the secretary's shrug indicated she knew nothing else, and so Jill pushed back her chair and self-consciously followed the tiny woman out into the hallway and toward the office. The secretary barely stretched to five feet and Jill felt like a giant trailing after her. Why do they always send the short ones when they want me? she wondered.

'Line three,' the woman indicated before sitting down behind her desk.

Jill picked up the phone and pressed the appropriate extension. 'Hello?'

'The shit's hit the fan,' David's voice said instead of hello.

'What are you talking about?' Jill asked, startled.

'Beth just confessed.'

'What?'

'You heard me. Beth Weatherby just confessed – she says she did it – she murdered Al.'

'I don't believe it,' Jill muttered, feeling for the chair she knew was somewhere behind her and sitting down. She noticed that all typing and other general office activity had ceased. None of the secretaries was making even the slightest effort to conceal her curiosity. 'That's crazy!' she whispered, hearing Beth's voice echo in her other ear. 'I did it, Jill,' it repeated. 'I killed my husband.'

'Not as crazy as what else she says,' David continued.

'What else does she say?' Jill found herself gripping the side of her chair.

David cleared his throat. 'She says it was self-defense.'

'Self-defense? You mean, Al was attacking her?'

'No, she admits Al was fast asleep when she started hitting him.'

'I don't understand.'

'It gets better.'

'Tell me.'

David gave an abrupt and angry laugh, strangling it in his throat before it could grow. 'She claims that he's been beating her for the past twenty-seven years, if you can swallow that one, and that the night she killed him, he'd gone to bed in a drunken rage promising to finish her off once and for all when he woke up.' Jill could feel him shaking his head. 'Can you imagine her expecting anyone to believe that garbage?'

Jill pictured Al Weatherby dancing romantically with Beth at firm parties, laughing at her jokes, displaying her proudly to his friends and cohorts, holding her hand, sitting close beside her at every opportunity, supporting her when she played badly at bridge. David was right – what Beth was saying was impossible to believe. It couldn't be true. 'She must be having some sort of a breakdown,' Jill said quietly. 'I guess Don will plead temporary insanity.'

'I don't know what Don's plans are. He's as confused as the rest of us. She didn't even consult him about her confession. Just called an impromptu press conference. Don heard about it over the radio. Not even her kids knew what she was planning. She just went ahead. The office is in a total shambles – nobody's getting anything done. I'll probably have to work late tonight.'

'Jason and Laurie are coming for dinner,' she reminded him quickly, surprised she was still capable of remembering such lesser realities.

'Shit,' he swore under his breath. 'All right, I'll try to be home.' He paused, 'Good God, what else could happen?' he asked nervously.

'She told me,' Jill muttered to herself, 'but I didn't believe her.'

There was a second's silence, then David spoke. 'What do you mean, she told you? Told you what? What are you talking about?'

Jill realized she had spoken out loud, was aware of the growing alarm and even anger in her husband's voice. 'When I went to see her last week,' she said softly, reluctantly, sensing how David would react to her admission.

'She told you what exactly?' David was demanding.

'Not anything about the self-defense or about Al's beating her,' Jill quickly explained. 'Just that she'd killed him,' she added weakly.

'Just that she'd killed him,' David repeated disdainfully. 'You didn't think that was important enough to tell me? To tell Don? Or her children? Especially after they begged you to try and help!'

'Please don't be angry, David,' Jill pleaded. 'I was so startled. I didn't know what to think. I thought, maybe—'

'You didn't think, period,' he exclaimed angrily. 'How could you not say anything, Jill? You know everyone's been tearing their hair out!'

'I didn't think it was my place to say anything to anyone,' she tried to explain. 'Beth said she needed time to think it all through. I thought maybe she'd had a breakdown, gone a little crazy—'

'Sure, crazy like a fox,' David interrupted. 'The only thing she needed to think through is this ridiculous story of hers. You gave her a week to get it down to a science. Now, all she has to do is plead temporary insanity and she'll probably never even see the inside of a jail cell. In the meantime, she'll drag a wonderful man's name and memory through the mud. The goddamn newspapers will have a field day. I mean, it's just the kind of story they love – big-shot lawyer was a wife-beater for a quarter of a century. They'll eat it up!'

'David, calm down—'

'How could you do it, Jill?' She could see the look of disbelief on his face through the phone wires. 'If nothing else, how could you keep it from *me*?'

Jill swallowed hard. 'I wanted to tell you,' she began. 'I thought about telling you. That afternoon, I called you at the office. I wanted to see you. But you were busy, and after that, I just couldn't. I'm sorry. I just knew that Beth had told me what she did in confidence, and I couldn't bring myself to say anything. I kept hoping you'd figure out I was keeping something from you, the way you usually do, and press me about it, get it out of me the way you did about—' She broke off. About Nicole Clark, she finished in silence. What were you so busy thinking about that you didn't notice I was holding something back?

David's voice was angry. 'I don't know what you're talking about, Jill! Are you trying to tell me that it's my fault for not guessing what Beth told you? That I should have figured out you were keeping something from me?'

'No, of course not,' she said. Yes, that's it exactly, she thought. You always did before.

There was a long, uncomfortable pause. 'I have to go,' David said finally. 'I only called to tell you about Beth. I didn't realize it would be old news.'

'David—'

The receiver went dead in her ear. She sat for a minute without moving, then she replaced the receiver, stood up and, pointedly ignoring the curious stares of the secretaries, walked from the room.

The mood at the dinner table wasn't much better. David had walked in just as Laurie and Jason were beginning an argument on the merits of a certain musical group and one glance at the disgusted look on his face told Jill to stay calm and quiet.

'Can't you keep these kids under control?' he had snapped in her direction, as he took his seat at the table. Jill had said nothing, noting only the surprised look on his children's faces as he spoke. He had never talked to her in such an abrupt fashion before – at least not in their presence. Jill had gone quietly into the kitchen, retrieved the food from the microwave and placed it gingerly in front of him.

'What is it? he asked, barely looking at it.

'Pork sirloin,' she answered.

'How much?'

'What do you mean? How many pounds?'

'How much did it cost?' he asked testily.

Jill looked startled, felt caught off balance. 'I don't remember,' she said, sitting down. 'I've had it in the freezer for a while.'

David looked over at his children's plates. 'You keep saying they don't eat anything! Why would you cook an expensive piece of meat when you know it'll all go to waste?'

'I'm-m-m eating!' Jason stammered.

'I'm not very hungry,' Laurie whispered.

'That's all right,' Jill said quickly, feeling her appetite disappearing. 'Neither am I.'

'Oh, great,' David barked. 'I have a good idea – next time you kids come to dinner, why don't we just burn some money?'

'Oh, Daddy,' Laurie said.

'Don't you "Oh, Daddy" me, young lady. You look like a walking skeleton and I'm sick of it. You don't leave this table until you finish everything on that plate.'

Jill watched as Laurie's eyes welled up with tears. Laurie immediately lowered her head, staring down at her plate. It seemed for several minutes as if no one breathed, and then slowly, Laurie moved her fingers to her fork and stabbed at some of the meat on her plate, bringing a forkful to her mouth. The two never connected, Laurie suddenly dropping the fork to the table and running from the room.

Jill immediately followed the girl into the bedroom despite David's loud protest. Laurie was sitting on the edge of the bed, and while the mirror was located directly in front of her and she was staring straight at it, she didn't appear to be seeing anything at all. Her eyes were stubbornly blank and dry, her lower lip quivering, her upper lip decidedly stiff.

'Laurie,' Jill began before she was cut off.

'Could you please leave me alone?' the girl asked.

Jill hesitated. 'I just wanted to tell you that you're not the one he's really angry at.'

'Could have fooled me,' Laurie pouted.

'Well,' Jill said gently, 'adults are funny people. They don't always say what they mean, and they don't always yell at the person they want to yell at. Sometimes they're not even sure why they're angry and it just comes out at whoever's available, whoever's the easiest target, which tonight happens to be you.'

Laurie continued to stare straight ahead. 'Actually, it's me your father's angry at. Some things are happening now that have everybody more than a little confused—' She tried to read something from the young girl's expression, but got nothing. 'I just wanted you to know that it honestly has nothing to do with you.' Jill stood for several seconds before moving toward the doorway.

'Thank you,' the small voice said quietly from the bed. Jill turned in surprise, saw that the girl was still staring with intense absence at the mirror, wondered briefly whether she had said anything at all, and then returned to the dining room.

Jason and his father were sitting in icy silence at the table. Jason, whether out of hunger or intimidation, had finished everything on his plate. For the first time since she had met the boy, he actually looked glad to see her.

'So, how was the first day of school?' Jill asked him, pointedly ignoring her husband.

Jason's face suddenly looked as disgusted as his father's. 'Boring,' he said. 'R-real boring.'

'The word you're looking for is "really,"' David said sharply. '*Really* boring. It's an adverb, as in *how* boring is it? It's *really* boring. I, for one, am getting *real* tired of all this California slang. *I* find it *real* boring.'

Jason regarded his father as if the poor man had lost control of his senses. 'Are you all right?' he asked.

'I'm real fine,' David answered.

'Good,' Jill piped in. 'Then we can change the subject. Who's your homeroom teacher?' she asked, smiling at Jason.

'Mr F-Fraser,' the boy answered. 'H-He's okay.'

'Your command of the English language amazes me,' David said sarcastically.

This time Jason lowered his head, obviously dangerously close to tears. Jill put down her fork in disgust and turned sharply to David. 'Don't you think you've said enough for tonight? Are you a professor of language all of a sudden? If you're still angry at me, that's fine. Yell at me. But your kids did not come here tonight for you to take it out on them. Now you've ruined a perfectly good dinner with these histrionics; you have one child very upset in the bedroom and another one here at the table. Instead of just one person in a bad mood, you now have four.'

'I'm not a child,' Jason spat flawlessly.

'Oh, be quiet,' David snapped. 'Are you so stupid you can't tell when someone's defending you?'

'I don't need her to defend me!' Jason shouted, pushing his chair back from the table, looking in rage at Jill. 'Who asked you, anyway?' he continued, furious. 'Why can't you just keep your big mouth out of everything?' He stormed out of the room. Jill pictured the two Plumley adolescents sitting side by side at the foot of her queen-size bed. She wasn't sure if she was more surprised by his outburst or by the ferocious ease with which it had been delivered.

'Well,' Jill said, starting to clear the table, 'a classic case of transference. You're angry at me but you don't want to yell at me in front of the kids, so you transfer your anger directly to them and you yell at them. Then Jason gets angry at you but can't summon the necessary courage to scream at his own father, so he does the next best thing, which is to scream at his nasty stepmother. So – you should be happy. I got yelled at, after all.' She took an armload of dishes into the kitchen and piled them inside the dishwasher.

David sat at the dining room table for several minutes, without moving, then he brought his plate, largely untouched, into the kitchen.

'I'm not very hungry either,' he said, laying his plate down on the counter. Jill said nothing. 'I guess I better go and apologize to the kids.'

'That's probably a good idea,' Jill agreed, wondering if he was about to extend the apology to herself. 'I'm sorry,' he began. Jill regarded him hopefully, ready to instantly forgive him. 'About the dinner,' he continued, then turned his back and disappeared down the hallway.

It was a little after eight o'clock when the buzzer sounded. Jill was sitting alone in the den rereading the Classified section of the morning paper ('Wanted – tall, muscular god of the Greek variety who likes dancing through golden showers and understands a little French'). David had left about fifteen minutes before to drive the kids home. He couldn't be back already, Jill thought, heading towards the kitchen. Anyway, he wouldn't buzz from downstairs. He had a key.

She approached the intercom next to the phone and pressed the buzzer to speak. 'Yes?'

'Jilly? It's Don Eliot. Is David home?'

Jill felt her heart begin to race, an unwanted cocoon of guilt beginning to wrap its way around her body. 'He just went out to drive his kids home,' she told the criminal attorney. 'He should be back pretty soon, if you'd like to come up and wait.'

'Fine,' he said. 'We're coming up.'

Jill pressed the buzzer which allowed the door in the lobby to open and walked to the door of her apartment, opening it slightly and peering out at the long corridor, listening for the sound of the elevator. Had David spoken to Don after their phone conversation that afternoon? Had he told the other lawyer of her alleged deceit, her prior knowledge of Beth's admitted guilt? Would he, too, make her feel like a traitor, an untrustworthy ally who had betrayed all their confidences?

The familiar clicking of the elevator cables interrupted the drama of her thoughts, and she heard elevator doors opening and closing down the hallway, followed immediately by the sound of voices. It was only as they turned the corner and came into view that Jill realized exactly what it was that Don Eliot had said only minutes before. 'We're coming up,' his words now echoed. We, plural, not I, singular.

'Hello, Don,' Jill said pleasantly, shaking his hand as he walked through the door into her apartment.

'Hi, Jilly,' he said, obviously upset by the day's developments but not upset enough to have already talked to David. 'You remember Nicki, don't you?' he added, almost as an afterthought.

Jill watched as Nicole Clark, stunning in shades of purple and black, put first one foot and then the other inside her front door. She's in my home, Jill thought, swallowing hard as she watched Nicole's eyes absorb everything that lay before her. She's invading my territory – looking at my belongings, passing silent judgment on my taste, touching, examining, leaving her mark like a dog pissing on the side of a lamppost, Jill thought, relishing the image. Stealing my sense of privacy like a thief in the night. That's what she is, Jill decided, satisfied with the metaphor. A thief in the night.

'I'm sure she remembers me,' Nicole said with pleasant confidence, cutting past Jill directly into the living room where she was already sitting down, making herself quite comfortable, when Jill finally summoned up the courage to join them.

Chapter Nineteen

It was almost another half hour before David returned home.

Jill moved from her position on one of the wing chairs (Don sat on the other, with Nicole between them on the sofa) as soon as she heard the key turning in the lock, and went to the door to greet him.

'Don's here,' she whispered as he walked inside.

He didn't wait for further explanation, simply moving by her into the living room, laying his wallet and his car keys on top of the stereo as he went. Jill was behind him, unable to see the expression on his face when he saw Nicole. 'Don, Nicki,' he said easily. 'When did you get here?'

Jill watched as David moved to occupy her former position on the large wing chair, feeling very much an outsider in her own quarters, not sure whether to join the three attorneys or leave them alone, retreating to the den or the bedroom like a good little wife.

'Well, what are you going to do, Jill?' asked David, reading her thoughts. 'Stand there? Sit down?'

Jill realized that the only place to sit was on the sofa next to Nicole, affording her husband a fine view for comparison.

Jill knew that her jeans-clad body and pink-slippered feet had no chance against the rich silks and high heels of Nicole Clark.

'I'll make some coffee,' she said, retreating to the kitchen.

'We got here about thirty minutes ago,' she heard Don Eliot say. 'Probably just after you left.'

'I had to drive the kids home,' David explained.

'So Jill was telling us,' Nicole offered. Jill didn't like the sound of her name on the other woman's lips.

Jill quickly poured the necessary amount of coffee and water into the coffee machine and waited for it to brew. After half an hour of numbing small talk, she was eager to hear what these two people had come to say.

'So, what's up?' she heard David ask. 'Something else happen?'

'I declined to defend Beth Weatherby,' Don said solemnly.

'He's feeling very guilty,' Nicole quickly explained. 'I suggested we come here and talk to you.'

Jill felt a sinking sensation at the pit of her stomach. She wasn't sure if it was Don's withdrawal of support for Beth Weatherby or Nicole's subsequent suggestion to see David that was responsible.

'I'm glad you did,' she heard David say. 'What happened?'

Jill re-entered the room as Don was discussing Beth's confession. 'First of all,' he was saying, 'as an attorney and her friend, I'm appalled that she would do such a thing, make a public confession without even consulting me—'

'She's very confused,' Jill interrupted without meaning to, putting a small tray with coffee mugs and bowls of cream and sugar on the square glass coffee table in their midst. 'It doesn't sound as if she knows what she's doing.'

'I think she knows exactly what she's doing,' Jill heard David say, and only a second later realized it had been Nicole who had spoken. Reluctantly, she walked around Don Eliot's chair and sat down only several feet away from Nicole.

'At any rate,' Don continued, dismissing Jill's interruption, 'it would make it very hard under the circumstances for me to defend her even if I'd never heard of a man named Al Weatherby. As it stands now, the knowledge that she says she did, in fact, murder a man who was one of my closest friends, and that she is making up such a pack of lies to try and cover up her actions—'

'How do you know they're lies?' Jill asked, again without meaning to.

'Oh, come on, Jilly, you can't believe what she's saying about Al?' Don asked in disbelief.

'I find it hard to believe,' Jill concurred. 'But I also find it hard to believe that Beth would be making all this up. I guess I just don't know at this point what to believe.'

'Well, I do,' Don Eliot said with defiant certainty. 'Take my word for it, Jilly. I've known Al Weatherby—' He stopped, correcting himself. 'I knew Al Weatherby for almost as long as Beth did. He was one of the kindest, gentlest men I've ever met. He'd take a spider outside in his handkerchief rather than step on it. You're trying to tell me that that kind of man would be capable of abusing his wife for twenty-seven years?'

'You're forgetting that Jill is a close friend of Beth's,' David explained quietly. Jill was glad for his soft-spoken support and smiled in his direction, but he wasn't looking at her.

'Well, all right, then!' Don Eliot exclaimed, as if the entire issue had been suddenly resolved. 'Did she ever, in all the time you've known her, tell you that Al was beating her? Have you ever seen her with any bruises? Has she ever given you any indication at all that she was a battered wife?'

Jill shook her head. 'No.'

'Well . . . ?' Don said wearily, leaving her to draw her own conclusions.

'Maybe she's protecting someone,' Jill said. 'Maybe Michael—'

'Michael has at least a hundred other worshippers who are prepared to swear he was with them all day and night. They never go out alone, you know. They even sleep together on the floor. No, it was Beth's nightgown that was covered with Al's blood, not Michael's flowing robes. It's her fingerprints all over the hammer. She did it, Jilly. She says she did it. I think we have to accept that.'

'What seems to be the general consensus?' David asked.

'That the woman's crazy,' Nicole answered. 'A breakdown of sorts. Anyway, most people at the office seem to believe that she cracked up and just exploded.'

'And you?' David asked her directly. 'What do you think?'

'How do you know that's not what I think?' she asked, a curious twinkle suddenly appearing in her eyes. Jill began to squirm uncomfortably.

Her husband looked right past her to stare into Nicole's eyes. 'Because it's too facile an explanation. It's too easy,'

David answered. 'I just can't believe that a heretofore perfectly healthy woman would go from sanity to madness overnight. With a breakdown, there are telltale signs along the way, even from the point of view of hindsight. There's nothing here, no evidence at all to indicate a breakdown.'

'I agree,' echoed Nicole, sipping at her coffee. 'I don't think she had a breakdown and I don't think she was battered. I think she's been reading too many novels.'

'What's that supposed to mean?' Jill asked sharply.

'Well, you have to admit, it's the current vogue,' Nicole said with just a touch of superiority. 'You kill your husband, claim he abused you for years, plead temporary insanity and get off scot-free.'

'If Al didn't beat her up, who did?' Jill demanded. 'How do you explain her injuries?'

'Some were self-inflicted,' Nicole stated confidently. 'Some were the probable result of Al waking up in mid-attack and fighting for his life.'

'You sound like you should be working for the DA,' Jill told her.

Nicole returned her coffee mug to the glass table. 'Well, it would certainly be an interesting case to prosecute,' she began, moving her eyes from Jill to David, 'since she's rejected a plea of temporary insanity and instructed her lawyers – Bob Markowitz and Tony Bower, incidentally – to plead self-defense.'

'What?' David shouted.

'She says she wasn't insane, not even temporarily. She's insisting on pleading not guilty because she says that if she hadn't killed him, he would have killed her.'

'Despite the fact that he was sound asleep at the time,' Don Eliot sneered.

'Just a minute, what is this?' Jill asked, also returning her coffee mug to the table and watching as some of it spilled onto the glass top. 'I don't believe I'm hearing this from a bunch of lawyers.' She turned directly to David. 'You're always saying that a lawyer has no right to judge his client, that his sole purpose is to defend his client to the best of his abilities, and that if lawyers tried to set themselves up as judges and juries, our whole system of justice would fall apart!'

'This is hardly the same thing,' David replied, testily.

'What you're saying is very true, Jilly,' Don Eliot added, 'and in a curious way we're saying the same thing. A lawyer has no right to be a judge. Whether my client is guilty or innocent is beside the point because my job is simply to provide that client with the best of all possible defenses, which I simply wouldn't be able to do in this instance. Aside from the obvious conflict of interest here – the man she murdered having been a partner and close friend – I believe she's lying through her teeth. The sight of her repulses me.'

'Then why do you feel so guilty?' Jill asked.

'He shouldn't,' Nicole answered for him. 'He's the one who recommended Markowitz and Bower. They were brilliant enough to get Beth out on bail.'

'What do her children think?' David asked.

Nicole shrugged. 'That she's flipped out. They're hoping, of course, that they can persuade her to plead temporary insanity before the case comes to trial.'

'She will,' David said with great assurance. 'In the meantime, the press will have a field day with this self-defense crap and by the time the case comes up, there won't be a potential juror who can read who won't be convinced she's off her rocker.'

'So, you don't think she's crazy at all?' Nicole asked.

'Crazy like a fox,' he answered, repeating the phrase he had used to Jill in their earlier phone conversation. 'I think she obviously wanted to get rid of Al, who knows why – the money, another man maybe – anyway, he went to sleep early one night. She saw her chance. Bingo – one dead husband, one instantly battered wife.' He started to laugh.

'What's funny?' Nicole asked before Jill had a chance to.

'Well, the damn thing's almost foolproof! Anyone who knew Al knew the man was incapable of the things she's accusing him of. She'd have to be crazy to think people would believe that ridiculous story! Which brings us back to square one – the crazy lady.'

'Crazy like a fox,' Nicole said, using David's words to separate the two of them from the others in the room. Jill felt as if she had just become invisible, as if the words Nicole had uttered were part of a magic spell and she and Don Eliot had just been made to disappear. The only two people in the room were her husband and Nicole Clark. She had never felt so negligible in all her life.

Jill watched in awe of Nicole's performance. The girl actually managed a tear or two as she lowered her eyes and continued to speak. 'And a man like Al Weatherby,' Nicole said haltingly, 'not only dies, but has his name and memory dragged through every dirty puddle in town. It isn't fair.' She looked over at Jill, as if trying to take her into her confidence. 'He helped me so much, you know. He was always very supportive, giving me tips on this or that, telling me the best way to make a positive impression, how to be tough. He thought I needed to be tougher.' She laughed feebly. Jill fought the urge to join her. 'He was the one to suggest I join the firm after I'm called to the bar. He was even going to come to the ceremony this Friday because my own father can't make the trip.' Her voice caught in her throat. 'How could anyone believe he was the kind of monster who would abuse his wife for over twenty-five years?!'

'No one does,' David answered, obviously moved by Nicole's seemingly impromptu speech.

'Even his children are horrified and shocked at their mother's accusations,' Don Eliot said, also impressed.

'And you?' Nicole asked, again looking over at Jill.

A neat touch, Jill thought, realizing that her reply was about to place her in absolute isolation. 'I just don't know,' she answered, opting at the last instant to stick to the truth rather than try to ingratiate herself back into the group by lying. David was always telling her that once a witness started lying, he was doomed. She looked around at the three bewildered faces, taking quick note of her surroundings. What was she thinking about? she asked herself. This was her living room, not a court of law. She was not under oath. She was not on the witness stand.

For a few minutes, nobody said a word.

'Would anyone like a piece of chocolate cake?' Jill asked, trying to break the tension. 'I made some for dessert but we never did get around to it.'

Her offer was politely declined.

'How old are your children, David?' Nicole asked.

David had to think for a few seconds. 'Jason's twelve,' he said finally. 'Laurie's fourteen. Typical teenagers, I'm afraid.' Nicole smiled as if she understood.

'You're too hard on them,' Jill said.

'*Somebody* has to be a little tough with them,' David answered.

'I guess it's hard to know when to draw the line,' Nicole offered.

'Do you have any children?' Jill suddenly asked her.

'Oh no,' Nicole laughed. 'Not even any younger brothers or sisters. Just one older sister, ten years older, so we were never very close.' She laughed again. 'No, no children.' She looked directly at Jill. 'I'm old-fashioned enough to want to have a husband first.' She smiled. Your turn, she seemed to be saying.

'Then you *would* like children eventually?' Jill asked, taking up the challenge.

'Oh yes, very definitely,' came Nicole's reply. 'I don't think a woman is really complete unless she's experienced having a baby.'

'One doesn't have a baby just for a new experience,' Jill told her.

Nicole's answer was swift. 'No, of course not. I didn't mean to imply that at all. I guess I just feel it's something no woman should miss.'

Jill said nothing, feeling smugly one-up for the first time all evening.

'Tell me, Jilly,' Don Eliot said abruptly, as if no one else had been talking in the interim since he last spoke, 'as Beth Weatherby's close friend, didn't you feel a sense of betrayal when you heard her confession over the radio and not from the woman herself? I mean, you tried to help her. You went to see her.' Jill felt her face becoming warm, knew she was beginning to blush, and hoped Don Eliot would be too self-absorbed to notice.

'Is something wrong?' Nicole asked quickly, noticing everything.

'She knew,' David's voice said softly.

'Knew what?' both Don and Nicole asked as one.

Jill cleared her throat. 'Beth told me that she'd killed Al about a week ago when I went out to her house to visit her.'

There was a moment of stunned silence. Jill looked nervously at her chewed cuticles. The jury is back, she thought. Their verdict – guilty as charged. Their sentence – death by humiliation.

'I don't understand,' Nicole was saying.

'Neither do I,' Don Eliot agreed sadly.

'You're not the only ones,' David concurred, crossing the invisible line over to their side, leaving Jill alone in a leaky lifeboat.

'It happened right at the end of my visit,' Jill tried to explain. 'She caught me completely off guard and I was very shaken, to say the least.' She searched their faces for a glimmer of understanding, but found none. 'She said only that she'd killed Al. She didn't explain the hows or the whys. I didn't ask. I didn't know what to think or what to do. So, I didn't do anything. I didn't feel I had the right to say anything.'

Don Eliot was shaking his head. 'I don't know, Jill,' he said, for the first time since she'd known him leaving out the diminutive at the end of her name, making it sound stiff and formal. 'I don't understand. I'm very disappointed in you.'

David spoke. 'Don, she didn't even tell me,' he said.

'I'm sure Jill did what she did out of a misplaced sense of loyalty,' Jill heard a voice say and turned quickly to her right, listening to the voice of Nicole Clark speaking eloquently in her defense. 'Beth is a close friend of hers, after all, and Jill is a teacher, not a lawyer. She obviously doesn't relate to the issue in the same way that we do. She felt that if she said anything, she would be betraying a friend, a confidence. It's a difficult spot to be in. I'm not sure I would have done it any differently had I been in her shoes.'

Don Eliot stood up, pulling at his yellow and black tie. 'Well, I guess you women will always find some way to stick together. Now, I really should be getting home.'

Jill remained seated, too stunned to speak. Nicole's support of her position had been as surprising as it was articulate. Why then did she feel like jumping over and throttling the young woman? She felt the sofa move beside her and looked up to see Nicole Clark rising and walking with Don Eliot toward the door. She got quickly to her feet, reaching the door just as Nicole was about to make her exit.

'I'm sorry I had to cancel our racquetball game last Friday,' Nicole was telling David. 'I booked a court for Wednesday at five-thirty. How's that?'

'Should be fine,' David acknowledged.

Don Eliot was already halfway down the hall.

'See you tomorrow,' Nicole continued. 'Goodbye, Jill. Nice to see you again.'

Jill said nothing, feeling her bile rising inside her body. If only she could keep her anger from exploding till after she'd heard the elevator depart. She walked back into the living room as David remained by the door. When he finally closed it, she was furiously stacking the coffee mugs inside the dishwasher. He paused by the kitchen doorway, about to proceed to the bedroom, when her voice stopped him.

'Where are you going?' she asked.

'I thought I'd get undressed and take a bath, if that meets with your approval,' he said, sarcastically.

'It doesn't,' she said.

'Well, you'll have to pardon me then because I intend to do it anyway,' he answered.

'I think we better talk,' she said, slamming the door of the dishwasher and following him down the hall to the bedroom.

'What's there to say?' he asked.

'There's plenty to say,' she told him, hearing her voice level rise. 'You didn't have to tell Don that I already knew about Beth! You didn't have to place me in that position!'

'What were you going to do, Jill? Lie to the man?'

'Why shouldn't I? Are you the only one in this family who gets to tell lies?'

He looked appropriately disgusted. 'What are you talking about?'

'I'm talking about your little racquetball games with Nicole Clark! Are you forgetting that you told me you were playing racquetball with one of the male students—'

'Don't yell at me, Jill,' David warned her. 'I've taken enough crap from you today.'

'You lied to me!'

He turned to her angrily. 'What was I supposed to tell you? I know how paranoid you are about Nicki—'

'I'm not paranoid! The woman is after my husband. She told me as much!'

'Oh, Jill, for God's sake. When are you going to stop using that? Didn't you hear her in that living room tonight? She was on your side, for Christ's sake! She actually defended you!'

'I don't need that little bitch to defend me!' Jill shouted, understanding now how Jason felt earlier. 'I am perfectly capable of defending myself. I don't need some little undergraduate talking about me like I'm not even in the room, referring to me in the third person, pretending to sympathize with me in order to make herself look generous and fair! She will do anything, David, to make herself look good in your eyes, and if she can make me look bad at the same time, well, then, so much the better.'

He pushed past her into the hallway. 'I'm not going to listen to this,' he said.

Jill was right behind him, shadowing him as he stormed first into the den and then through the dining area back into the living room. 'David, for God's sake, do you think it was just a coincidence that she mentioned the racquetball game just as I got to the door? You don't think that was deliberately said so that I would hear?'

'No, I don't,' he said with vehemence. 'Nicki's mind doesn't work along the same lines as yours.'

'Well, at least that much is true! David, can't you see how she's manipulating this whole situation? You and me! Can't you *feel* how you're being manipulated?' She paused, seeing the intractability of his cool green eyes. 'Or is it that you just don't care?'

'You're being ridiculous,' he said, his voice halfway between anger and sadness. 'I'm going out for some fresh air.'

'Oh, David, please don't,' Jill begged as he opened the door.

'I'll be back later,' he told her. And then he was gone.

278

Chapter Twenty

Jill looked at the clock for the fourth time in as many minutes. It was exactly eleven forty-five. David had been gone now for almost three hours.

She didn't know what to do. Whether to wait up or go to sleep. Sleep – that was a funny word. She could get into bed; she certainly wouldn't get any rest.

Where was he? Where could he have gone without his car keys or his wallet? An hour after he had left, she'd snuck down to the parking garage to make sure the car was, in fact, still there, and when she was satisfied that it hadn't moved, she returned to the apartment. His wallet and all his cash and credit cards still lay on the stereo where he had discarded them when he'd returned from driving Jason and Laurie home. That meant he had gone walking through the streets of Chicago at night alone. If he were mugged, the thieves would be furious to discover his lack of funds, would undoubtedly rough him up a bit, possibly even kill him. The thought made her panic. She debated whether or not to call the police, but knew they would tell her to wait twenty-four hours and then call them again. Instead she had called David's mother, thinking perhaps he had gone there, but after several minutes of talk about the weather it became obvious that David was not there, and Jill had been trapped into spending the next half hour listening while Mrs Plumley complained about everything from inflation to the public housing that was threatening to impinge on her neighborhood. When she was finally able to say goodbye, she quickly dialed David's sister, on the off chance Renee and Norman might know where he was. They didn't, or at least his name was never mentioned other than in the casual how-is-your-husband-my-brother category. After that, she kept the phone free in case he was in trouble and had been trying to call. If he had been, he wasn't now.

The last hour had been filled with thoughts of Nicole Clark. Jill wasn't sure which would make her feel worse – the police calling to report they'd found her husband's mutilated body or Nicole calling to announce that David was spending the night with her. It was a discomforting thought. But then, Nicole Clark was a discomforting girl. Maybe she shouldn't have said anything, Jill thought. Maybe she should have just kept her mouth shut and not taken Nicole's bait. Ignored the fact that her husband was now playing racquetball with the girl, ignored the fact that he had lied to her. But she couldn't do that. Once you agreed to accept one lie, you agreed to accept them all, to lend the lies a certain credibility. What was the legal term? To aid and abet?

And yet what had she accomplished by bringing the issue out in the open, forcing it to a head? She had simply succeeded in alienating her husband even further, driving him, tired and disgusted, out of his own apartment. Right into Nicole Clark's waiting arms?

Was that where he was?

Stop it! she told herself. It was ridiculous to torture herself this way. If he had gone to Nicole, there was nothing she could do about it now.

The whole day had been one drawn-out disaster, most of it her own making. If only she'd never confided to him about Beth's admission of guilt. She should have known how he would react to such news. She knew how much David had loved and admired Al Weatherby. He had cried over the man's death, whereas he had never cried when his own father had died. Why did she have to be so insistent about her doubts? Couldn't she simply have agreed that Al was incapable of such monstrous behavior, and then waited until another time to hear what Beth had to say? Of course David was going to take her doubts personally. What else could he be expected to do?

Jill found herself pacing the narrow hallway. She was throwing too much at David at once, bombarding him with disharmony when what he needed was a little peace and quiet. And a lot of support. He had enough problems – his ex-wife, his children, his daily grind at the office, their constant lack of funds. In the last few months, he'd had to contend with Al's death, her unhappiness with her job, and her newly organized jealousy. And now, this. Coming home had to be less than a treat.

She had to do something about it. She had to stop being so suspicious, or at the very least learn to keep her suspicions to herself, not to openly flinch whenever she heard him mention

Nicole's name; she had to back away as far as Al and Beth were concerned, learn to keep conflicting opinions to herself, at least for a while. She would refrain from making disparaging comments about Elaine and would continue her efforts to befriend his children. There must be some way to win them over. She could do nothing about what went on at his office all day. She could only concentrate on making home as appealing a prospect as Nicole Clark.

She sighed. That left only the problem about her job, and she'd just have to get used to that too. She was stuck, and there was no point in further complaints. David had to be as tired of hearing about how bored she was as she was of feeling it. But that's the way things were. David was not responsible; there was nothing he could do. The new term had begun and she was going to learn to love it.

If only he would come home—

The phone rang.

She teetered with indecision, knowing she was exactly halfway between either phone, finally racing toward the bedroom. It couldn't be the police, she assured herself, leaping across the bed, because David had left all his ID at home. Even if he were lying dead somewhere, the police wouldn't have been able to identify him and call her so quickly. Unless, of course, someone at the police department had recognized him—

'Hello?'

'Jill, I'm sorry.'

'David, where are you?'

'At the office. Did I wake you?'

282

'Wake me? Are you kidding? I've been worried half to death.'

'I'm sorry.'

'What are you doing at the office?'

She could hear him shrug. 'I don't really know. I went walking. Just kept walking. Suddenly I looked up and here I was. The night watchman let me in. I didn't have a key, of course.'

'I know. I was so worried where you could have gone.'

'I left the house without a goddamn dime, if you can believe it. That's the trouble with acting like a prima donna, I guess.'

'Are you all right?'

'Sure. Just very tired. Actually, I got a lot accomplished tonight. There was no one else around. It was quiet. I managed to take care of all my dockets. You know what a pain they are.' There was a quiet pause. 'I don't suppose you'd feel like coming down here and picking me up?' he asked sheepishly. 'I know it's a hell of a nerve but my legs are killing me and I don't have any money and—'

'And?'

'And I really want to see you.'

'I'll be there in five minutes.'

Jill hung up the phone, grabbed the car keys and raced to the doorway. Everything was going to be okay from now on. No matter what stunts Nicole tried to pull, Jill would not trip on her own feet. She'd make sure that everything would work out, and that she and David would live happily ever after.

Things started to fall apart the next morning.

For the first time that she could remember, David overslept and consequently was in a big rush to get out, which meant that she would be late because of the time he had to spend in the bathroom. At ten minutes to nine, she called the university and told the office she would be late for the morning's round of meetings because she hadn't been feeling well. She hated using her health as an excuse. Her mother had once told her it was bad luck.

'Can I make you some breakfast?' she asked him when he finally came out of the bathroom.

'Are you kidding? I'm already late.'

'That's precisely the point.'

He paused. 'Sure, why not? Scrambled eggs too much trouble?'

'No trouble at all,' she said, grateful to be given the opportunity to do something for him.

She went to the fridge as he reached for the phone.

'Diane Buck,' he said briskly into the receiver, then waited while the office receptionist connected him to his secretary. 'Diane, I'm going to be another half hour; I'm at a breakfast meeting and it's running a little later than I'd anticipated. Tell Doug Horton I'll be there as soon as I can. Okay? Thanks.'

Jill cracked the eggs into the bowl and added some milk, briskly stirring in some salt and pepper. She felt uncomfortable listening to David lie. It seemed so effortless and believable.

'Toast?' she asked, putting the eggs in the fry pan.

'Why not?' he answered. 'I've come this far. Might as well go all the way.'

A few minutes later, Jill put David's breakfast on the dining room table. David's face was buried inside the business section of the morning paper. 'Breakfast is ready,' she said, smiling.

He looked over. 'Oh, great. Thanks.' He laid the paper down beside his plate. 'Smells terrific.'

'I hope it tastes as good,' she said sincerely, surprised how much it meant to her that he be pleased.

He took a bite of his eggs and looked back at her. 'It does,' he smiled. She sighed with relief. 'Aren't you having any?'

Jill looked down at her glass of orange juice. 'I've decided to go on a diet,' she said.

'Oh? What for?'

'I thought it probably wouldn't hurt to lose five pounds.'

David looked back at his paper. 'Probably right,' he said. 'But watch that you don't starve yourself.'

Jill laughed nervously. Why was she so nervous? 'I don't think that's likely,' she said, watching him eat. 'David—?'

'Hmm?' He looked up from his paper. 'What is it?'

'I just wanted to tell you again how sorry I am about not telling you about Beth—'

'Forget it.'

'No, please. I don't want it to come between us—'

'It won't.'

'I love you.'

'I love you, too.'

They stared at each other for several long seconds, Jill desperately seeking some assurance from David's eyes. 'I love you so much,' she whispered.

'Come here,' he said warmly, holding his hands out. Jill got quickly up from her seat and walked into his waiting arms. She felt his hands pressing against her head, squeezing her hair into a tight round ball. 'I'm sorry, too,' he told her. 'I acted like a first-class prick.'

She looked at him with tears in her eyes. 'As long as it's first-class,' she said, sniffing.

He finished the last of his breakfast and Jill took his dishes into the kitchen. 'Is today a busy day?' she asked.

'Aren't they all?'

'I thought maybe we could take in a movie tonight.'

'Tonight? No chance. I've got too much work.'

'I thought you got a lot done last night.'

'I did. Unfortunately, there's lots more. I don't think you'll be seeing much of me for the next few weeks. Until I get caught up—'

'What about Friday night?'

'What about it?'

'Dinner,' Jill informed him. 'At my parents'. They invited us last week—'

'Oh, honey, I'm sorry,' he said, putting down the business section and coming into the kitchen. 'I *did* forget. I can't make it Friday night.'

'Dinner's not till eight o'clock. I could pick you up at the office,' she volunteered.

'That's not it,' he said, and waited ominously. Jill knew instinctively that she wasn't going to like the next several sentences out of his mouth. 'Please don't take this the wrong way,' he began. Jill felt her breath becoming short. David felt himself groping for words, a fact which made Jill all the more uncomfortable, knowing her husband was rarely at such a loss.

'I don't know quite how to say this because I know how you feel about her already—'

'Feel about who?' Jill asked, already knowing the answer.

'Nicole Clark,' he said.

'What about her?' Jill asked, her voice cold, flat.

'She's being called to the bar on Friday.'

'She asked you to come?'

'Her father can't be there. She has no one.'

'What about her friend, Chris whatever-his-name-was, the one she brought to Don Eliot's that night for dinner—'

'He's just a casual friend. He doesn't mean anything to her.'

'And you do?'

Jill held her breath.

'I guess I do,' he said, softly. 'Jill, please listen to me. This is the last time that I'll ever put myself in this position. I promise you that. Now, I think you're wrong about Nicki's intentions and I don't think she's the calculating, manipulative woman that you believe her to be. But I'd have to be an idiot or a blind man not to have realized by now that she *is* in love with me, and I'm neither an idiot nor blind. Nor do I regard her in any light other than that of a brilliant young attorney who's also a very sweet and lonely little girl. But that's all there is – and there'll never be anything more to it than that. I promise you.' He looked around. 'But I'm not being fair to Nicki, and I'm certainly not being fair to you, if I allow her fantasies to continue. It's flattering having a beautiful young girl like Nicki in love with me, but that's *all* it is. There's no more. There never will be. So—' He took a deep breath. 'From now on, there will be no more courtroom observances, no more lunches, no more racquetball games. I will go to her graduation this Friday because I promised that I would be there. I committed myself. But that will be the end of it.' He stared into Jill's eyes. 'All right?'

Jill turned away, wanting to tell him the answer she knew he was waiting for but unable to find the words. 'I didn't realize the ceremony was at night,' she said.

'It isn't,' he answered. 'It's in the afternoon.'

'You're taking her to dinner?' Jill asked.

There was a slight pause before he answered. 'Not just me. About five or six of us. To congratulate her, welcome her into the firm.'

'That's very nice of you,' Jill said, her voice empty of feeling.

'Jill, please understand. It's nothing. It's never been anything. After Friday, it'll be even less.'

'How can there be less than nothing?' she asked.

David looked at the floor. 'Well, what can I say? I've been completely honest with you. I've told you all there is to tell. I can't do more than that. The rest is up to you. Maybe it's too much to expect you to understand—'

'It is too much,' Jill said, feeling very old inside. 'But I'll try,' she added.

David's arms went quickly around her, hugging her tightly to him. 'I love you,' he said.

'I love you, too,' she repeated.

'And I'm very late,' he said, checking his watch. 'Doug Horton must be shitting bricks by now, I've kept him waiting so long.'

'Tell him it's my fault,' Jill said, watching David bound toward the door.

'I might do that,' he said, opening it. 'Call me later.' The door closed behind him.

Jill stood for several minutes in the middle of the tiny box that was their kitchen and contemplated all that had transpired in the last hour. She replayed David's apologies several times as if she were listening to a tape recorder. Push to start and listen, press down to reverse and rewind, push back down to start again. His voice was rich and soothing, filled with deep understanding for what she must be going through. I realize that she *is* in love with me, he was saying, or words to that effect. When was it, Jill found herself asking, that David had come to this enlightened realization? Last night in her living room? Before – over a quiet lunch perhaps? She shook her head. It didn't make any difference when, she tried to tell herself. What was important was that David was about to put an end to Nicole's little game of cat and mouse. After Friday, the weight of the world could go rest on somebody else's shoulders. After Friday, she repeated, almost aloud. It was going to be a long week, she decided, impulsively reaching for the phone.

It was answered after three rings.

'Hello?'

'Beth?'

'No, it's Lisa. Is this Jill?'

'Yes. How are you, Lisa? How's your mother?'

'My mother's just fine, thank you. It's the rest of us that are falling apart.'

'Oh, Lisa—'

'I take it you heard the news about her confession.'

'Yes.'

'And what she's saying about my father.'

'Yes.'

'Well – what do you think?' There was a slight tinge of hysteria beneath the young woman's voice.

'I – I don't know what to think.'

The girl's voice went suddenly very low and quiet, as if she did not want to be overheard. 'She's saying that he beat her, hurt her, abused her, ever since they got married. She's saying that my father was a maniac. A monster that had her in constant fear of her life. Jill,' she pleaded impassionately, 'it's impossible! I lived here in this house for nineteen years. How could I possibly live under the same roof as a monster and not recognize him for what he was? How could any of us grow up here and not have been aware of what was going on, if even a tenth of what she's saying is true? It's impossible. Three kids were brought up here. None of us witnessed anything she's claiming took place! I never heard one cry in the night, never saw my mother covered with bruises. Nothing. All I saw was a warm and loving husband and father who never even spanked us when we were bad. And let me tell you, there were times when we were really rotten. He never even lost his temper with us! God, Jill, what she's saying is absolutely impossible!'

'Is it easier for you to accept that your mother is lying?' Jill asked.

The cry was one of pure anguish. 'No!' the girl despaired. 'I don't know why she's saying these things unless—'

'Unless she's crazy,' Jill said quietly.

'She has to be crazy,' Lisa pressed. 'There's no other explanation. I know my parents. My father was no more capable of beating my mother than—' She broke off abruptly.

'Than she was of killing him,' Jill said, finishing the sentence.

'Unless she was crazy,' Lisa concluded tearfully. 'And I just can't believe that she's crazy! I don't know. You live with people, you think you know them, think that you know everything about them, and then you find out that you don't know a goddamn thing! Nothing! Zero! Zilch! And what does that say about you? About your life?'

'What does your mother say?' Jill asked.

'Why don't you ask her?' Lisa said numbly. 'She just walked in the room.'

Jill heard the phone being transferred. 'Jill?' Beth's voice inquired.

'I didn't realize before how much you sound like Lisa,' Jill told her.

'I guess we do.' Jill could feel Beth smiling. 'How are you?'

Jill laughed. 'Me? I'm all right. How are you?'

'Never better,' Beth answered. 'But the fur's really flying, I'll bet.'

'You *do* have a way about you.'

'At least I gave you some advance warning.'

'Thanks a lot.'

Both women chuckled ruefully. 'Well,' Beth began, 'what do you think? Am I crazy? Or am I lying?'

Jill could feel Beth's eyes directly on her. 'Why does my gut tell me you're neither?' she asked.

Beth's answer was immediate. 'Because you're my friend,' she said.

'I'd like to listen if you feel like talking,' Jill offered.

'How about tonight?' The swiftness of the invitation caught Jill by surprise. 'If you're busy, of course, we can make it some other time. It doesn't have to be tonight.'

Jill took a second to sift through her thoughts. David would be working late. He wouldn't be home before ten. There was no reason to stay home except for her fear. And what was she so afraid of? Whatever Beth had to say couldn't hurt her. 'Tonight's fine,' Jill said.

Chapter Twenty-one

The front door of the Weatherby house was already open when Jill pulled her gray Volvo into the driveway. She climbed out of the car, pulling her sweater around her shoulders. In the last week, a chill had abruptly descended on the city like an unwanted house guest, suitcase firmly in hand, prepared for a lengthy visit. Jill ran up the walkway to the front entrance. Beth stood waiting for her just inside the doorway.

'God, I'm glad to see you,' Beth said, her arms reaching out to surround Jill.

Jill kissed Beth's cheek. 'You look fine,' she told her.

'Every time I tell someone I *feel* fine, they get that peculiar look in their eyes like that's definitely not what I'm supposed to say. Anyway, come on in.' Jill entered the front hallway as Beth closed the door behind her. 'Lisa's in the living room waiting. She's made some tea.' Beth winked conspiratorially. 'Tea must be the Wasp answer to chicken soup. One sip and all your problems go away.'

'Wouldn't that be nice?'

'How's David?' Beth asked, leading Jill to the living room, where Lisa immediately rose to greet her.

'He's working late. Hi, Lisa. How are you doing?'

'Okay,' the girl shuffled.

'I understand you made us some tea.' Lisa nodded. 'I'd love a cup.'

Lisa moved immediately to the antique coffee table where she'd set up the tea service. 'How do you take it?'

'Black. I'm trying to diet.'

'Good God, what for?' Beth asked.

'Oh, you *are* a friend,' Jill laughed. Lisa handed her a cup of tea.

'Mom?'

'Sure. Milk and sugar, sweetie.'

A minute later, they were all sitting down in much the same positions they had occupied the previous week – Jill and Beth on the sofa, Lisa on the chair across from them. Do I look as nervous as Lisa does? Jill wondered, trying to concentrate on Beth.

'I told Lisa that you were coming over tonight to listen to my version of Life with Father. She's heard most of it before but she insists she wants to hear it again. Certainly she hasn't heard it in the kind of detail I'm about to tell you. I wanted to spare her.' She paused. 'But I've been doing that all her life. And she keeps telling me that she's a big girl now, so I guess it's time she heard the whole gruesome story.' She looked around. 'Brian is upstairs. He doesn't want to listen to any of this. He prefers to believe I'm crazy.' She looked back at Jill. 'You're sure about this now?' she asked. 'You really want to know?'

'I want to know,' Jill replied.

* * *

'I'll start right at the beginning, twenty-eight years ago when I first met Al,' Beth Weatherby began. 'Some of this you've already heard, Jill. You'll have to excuse me if I repeat myself, but I find it helps to keep things in pretty strict order, to incorporate all the little trivial details.' She paused, taking a sip of her tea and then returning the cup to her lap.

'I was very young when we got married, as you already know. I had just turned eighteen. Al was twelve years older. We met at a bank. I was a teller. He was a customer. He used to come in once or twice a week, always very nattily attired. I thought so anyway. I noticed him right away. He was so friendly to everybody. Always smiling. Everybody liked him. That never changed. Everybody always liked Al.' She stopped, taking a deep breath. 'I liked him, too. I used to sneak smiles over in his direction when I thought he wasn't looking, but one day he turned around and caught me at it, and from that time on, he always came to my window.

'I was crazy about him. Right from the beginning. He was just so appealing, I thought. And, of course, he was older. And a lawyer. God, I was so impressed when he told me that. And he seemed to be interested in me, that was the really amazing part of the whole thing. Me – who'd never even finished high school. Al was always ashamed of my education, or lack of it, but my family needed the money and working seemed more important than school at the time. After we got married, I thought I could go back to school, but the babies came along so fast and Al – well, we told everyone that I'd gone to school part-time when the children were very small, till I finally got my B.A. It was what Al wanted. He didn't want anyone to think

I was stupid, and I wanted him to be happy, and since it seemed so important to him, I went along with it. But I always worried about it. I was afraid somebody would ask one too many questions that I wouldn't be able to answer, and I'd be uncovered – a fraud with barely a high school education. So, I made it a point to read just about every book that I could get my hands on, and I kept myself well informed about current affairs. Anyway—' She paused knowing she had jumped too far ahead of herself. 'We started going out together,' she began again, returning to the beginning of her story. 'I couldn't believe I was so lucky. The only one who wasn't happy about any of it was my mother. When we got married, she was very upset. When she died, Al wouldn't even let me go to her funeral! My brothers haven't spoken to me since. Not even now.

'I don't know. Maybe she knew. Maybe she sensed the violence, the cruelty inside him. Me – all I saw was this cute guy, full of confidence, always happy, even-tempered and easygoing. Wow! So much for first impressions.

'We got married. It was a small wedding. My family didn't come. Al had no family left. A few of his old school friends were our witnesses. Afterward, we went out for dinner. Nowhere fancy. I remember I was surprised because I'd figured Al would go all out. But it didn't matter because I was Mrs Alan Weatherby and I was thrilled. It didn't matter about my family or the restaurant or even that we weren't going to have a honeymoon. I was married to the man of my dreams, as we used to say, and that's all that was important.

'The violence started on our wedding night.

'I was a virgin, of course. I'd hardly even dated before Al. But he was the one who kept insisting we wait until after we got married. I didn't care. I would've done anything he asked. He wanted to wait, so we waited. I don't know what I was expecting, but I guess I was like any other young girl. I thought it might hurt a little, but that mostly it would be wonderful. We'd hug and kiss a lot and he'd be gentle and understanding, and very loving. But he wasn't any of those things. And there was no hugging or kissing or even the slightest show of tenderness. It was awful. It was like I was in bed with a complete stranger. He was so different than he'd been even an hour before. He didn't smile. He wasn't tender. He was rough, even mean. He kept pinching me, hurting me, and when I'd try to squirm out of his grasp, he'd just do it some more. Harder. There was no tenderness. He just pushed into me until he was finished, and then when he was through, he turned me over and spanked me like a little girl. Hard, ugly slaps. They hurt and I cried, trying to get away from him. That made him angrier, so he twisted my arm until I thought he'd break it. When I pleaded with him to tell me why he was doing these things, he screamed that I'd lied to him, that it was obvious I'd been with a lot of guys. I tried to reason with him. His answer was a slap across the face. I didn't know what to do! I felt – I really felt – like it was all my fault that it was happening. That somehow I had brought it on myself. I started to apologize. I was always the one who apologized. It got to be something of a ritual.

'Every time we made love – funny term – he would strike me. At first it always took the form of a spanking. He'd use his hands. Gradually, he advanced to hairbrushes and then belts.

After we had the children and they were old enough to recognize their mother's cries, he'd put a gag in my mouth, tie my hands behind me. He was always very careful to make sure he'd hit me where the bruises wouldn't show. Unless he could make it seem like an accident, of course. He was very good at arranging accidents. I became "accident-prone", as they say. I was forever walking into things, burning myself. I was usually sporting one bruise or another somewhere, but people don't remember that now. I mean, everyone has an occasional bruise. Most of them, you can cover with clothing. If you have to be somewhere, like an exercise class,' she said, looking directly at Jill, 'you show up already properly uniformed. That way there are no questions asked that you can't answer. Anyway, I did such a good job of joking away any mysterious bruises that did turn up that I got to be a bit of a joke around Weatherby, Ross for a while. What happened to your leg? someone would ask. Oh, you know me, I'd answer merrily. I tripped again.

'I tripped over Al's outstretched foot; I burned my fingers when he held my hand down over the toaster; I cut my hand when my husband ran a knife across it after I missed a grand slam one night at bridge—'

Jill gasped, lowering her head in shame. Somehow, she had always known. Her fear had been that she would hear these exact words and know them to be true.

'When I found out I was pregnant with Brian,' Beth continued, 'I got very excited. God knows why. Maybe I thought it would calm Al down, give him the son I assumed he wanted. I guess I also thought the beatings would stop. He wouldn't hurt a pregnant woman. He wouldn't hurt his baby.

'The worst beating I ever got was the night I told him I was pregnant. He went into a rage. I don't even remember the things he said. Just the blows. Most of them to my stomach. He even threw me down a flight of stairs as a sort of grand finale. I really thought he was going to kill me that night. I think I hoped he would.

'I don't know how Brian survived that pregnancy. Somehow, we both did, even though the beatings kept up as fierce as ever. A few years later, Lisa was born. Five years after that, Michael came along. I lost a few in between. Altogether I had four miscarriages.

'Now the story gets a little monotonous. Twenty-seven years of abuse is twenty-seven years of it, and what you've heard is pretty much how it continues. Al's business began to grow. He became extremely successful, just the way he always said he would. We moved into increasingly bigger homes each year. Everyone thought he was some sort of miracle worker; they thought I was the luckiest woman alive.

'That part always amazed me about him. That he could be Dr Jekyll one minute and Mr Hyde the next. The nicest man you'd ever want to meet in public. I knew how much everybody adored him; I remember how much *I'd* adored him. He was so strong – you wouldn't have believed how strong he was, being so slight. But he lifted weights, you know. It made him very strong.' She stopped short, and laughed abruptly. 'That's what it all boils down to. The root of all our problems, all our fears. The fact that men are simply physically more powerful than we are. Even the weakest man has little trouble pinning down the strongest of women. And that's where all the injustices start and where they lie. Equal pay, better jobs, equal rights – all of it, everything women are fighting for – what we're really fighting against is sheer masculine strength. Everything else springs from that.' Beth cleared her throat and returned without further digression to her original train of thought.

'It got so that I always dreaded whenever Al would be nice to me in public. The nicer he was, the worse the beating would be when I got home. The more solicitous he was, the meaner he would be later on. You remember how he laughed about that chain letter I sent out? Well, he didn't think it was so funny in private. No, not funny at all.

'I got a real working over for that one. He wouldn't let me have any friends – you were the only real friend I had, Jill. I could relate to you instantly. It wasn't like we had to see each other a lot or speak to each other every day; we always seemed to pick up where we left off. Al couldn't do anything to stop that. And I think he sensed it would be dangerous to try.

'I can't begin to tell you what it was like all those years the kids were at home, the kind of fear I lived in that they'd find out what was going on, that he'd stop being satisfied with just beating me and turn on them. I never uttered a word against him all those years. I was desperate to protect them. I never so much as disagreed with Al in front of them. If I ever did, you can just imagine how I would have paid for it later. I centred my life around my husband, and so, of course, that's what they remember now. Why Lisa and Brian are having such a hard time believing the truth.' She stared at her daughter's tear-streaked face. 'I'm sure Lisa told you, Jill – her parents never disagreed, let alone had the kind of normal fights all married couples have. And she's right. I never dared disagree – our fights were never normal.' Beth paused, for an instant lost in thought. 'Except Michael,' she said. 'I've always suspected Michael knew something about what went on. I don't know what. I'm not sure I'm right. But I always wondered if that wasn't at least part of the reason he left school and joined that group—' She cut herself off abruptly.

'It was a mixed blessing when all the kids were finally gone. I'd encouraged them all to get out of Chicago, quietly, of course, without Al's knowledge. He'd have killed me if he'd found out. But I wanted them as far away from him as possible. I wanted them out of this house. At least I didn't have to worry about them anymore. Of course, it gave Al a freer hand, so to speak. He didn't have to time his outbursts anymore. He was like a teenager who'd had his curfew lifted. It was open season at the Weatherbys'.'

Jill opened her mouth to speak. Her words came out of Beth's mouth instead. 'You're going to ask me why I didn't leave him, I know,' she said. Jill nodded. 'Everyone asks that. It's a perfectly natural question. God knows I asked myself that a hundred times. Maybe only another woman who's lived through that kind of terror can understand. But you have to remember a few things – first, I was so young when we got married, and so confused. I thought the sun rose and set around that man. In the beginning, I thought maybe that's how all marriages were. That women accepted abuse as a natural course of events. I thought sex was like that for everyone. And I had so much pride! How could I admit my mother had been right? How could I go home after all the fuss I'd made? He swore he'd find me, anyway, if I ever tried to leave. Find me and kill me. By that time, I was absolutely terrified of the man!

'And then, of course, I thought it was all my fault. I saw this wonderful man whom everybody liked and who was terrific with everybody else but me, and so I naturally assumed I had to be to blame. God knows I tried to improve. I became a wonderful cook. I waited on Al hand and foot. But things were never done right – at least not right enough for Al. And the children – Al couldn't tell me often enough how unfit a mother I was. He threatened to take them away from me if I ever tried to leave him, that no one would believe my story.' She looked around the room though her eyes settled on nothing. 'And, of course, he was right. No one does believe it.'

Jill swallowed hard. 'I believe it,' she said softly.

There was a long moment of silence.

'So do I,' whispered Lisa, moving immediately to her mother's side and collapsing into her arms. Beth Weatherby's eyes filled instantly with tears and she hugged her daughter closely to her, rocking her silently back and forth like a baby. Without shifting her position, she moved her free arm toward Jill. Jill's hand reached out and grabbed it tightly. The three women sat without words for several minutes. When Beth finally began to speak again, her voice was stronger, more assured. The desperation that had been clinging to each word had disappeared. 'The night that I killed Al,' she began again, 'wasn't any different really from any of the other nights, except that Al had had a few drinks, something he didn't usually do. God knows he didn't need liquor to make him mean.

'It was a Friday night; I was getting dinner ready. He phoned from a bar and started yelling at me that I was a useless drain on his existence, a rotten mother, a terrible bridge player. Anything you can think of. That's what I was. Then he said he was coming home. I knew he was going to beat me. He'd been getting bolder since Michael had left; the abuse was becoming more exotic. He was becoming careless, telling lies that could easily trip him up. Like when he told you that I was upset because Lisa had a married lover. He didn't seem to care as much if anyone were to find out. It was like he was almost daring people to discover his secret. I was terrified he was going to kill me!

'I phoned you.'

Again, Jill lowered her head in shame. Beth gently disengaged her daughter and turned to face Jill.

'No, please. Don't blame yourself. How could you know? That was my mistake for years. I blamed myself! Instead of the man responsible. That's what abuse does to you. And why I don't think I'll ever be able to forgive Al. *Why* I killed him that night.

'Not for the years of being physically abused. But for what he did to my soul. For the sheer terror I lived in all those years. For the degradation. For almost destroying the human being inside the flesh – for making me feel guilty and of no more worth than yesterday's newspaper. I had no value to anyone – especially to myself. I actually felt I deserved whatever he dished out. And I'm not talking about just in the beginning now. I'm talking about later, after I became more aware, knew that things were not as they were supposed to be, that it *wasn't* my fault, that something was wrong with Al, not me— By that time, it was too late. It didn't matter anymore, which is why I never left – not even after Michael was gone. It wasn't just that I was terrified, that I knew Al would find me and kill me. It's more that there just wasn't anything left of me to go anywhere. Can you understand that? My soul was dead.

'When Al did come home that night, I was just sitting there waiting for him. He didn't waste any time. Started right in hitting me. Only this time was worse than the others. I know he was going to kill me. He had his hands around my throat and he was choking me. He obviously didn't care who saw his handiwork this time. I panicked. And for the first time, I started fighting back. Well, he thought that was the biggest joke of all. He said I was ridiculous. That's when he started scratching at me. I finally collapsed on the floor. He was kicking at my sides like I was so much dirty laundry. Then suddenly, he just stopped – he said he was tired, he was going to bed, and he'd finish me off when he got up.

'He went upstairs. I lay on the floor for a long time. My whole body was sore. Finally, I decided to go upstairs and try to get some sleep. Maybe I already knew I was going to kill him. At the time, I remember thinking he probably wouldn't wake up until the morning, and by then he'd forget about it, at least for a while. So, I went upstairs, got undressed, put on my nightgown. Actually got in bed beside Al, ready to die if that's what he wanted.

'But a strange thing started to happen to me as I lay there. I realized that I didn't want to die after all. And that I didn't have to take his beatings anymore. That I didn't care whether or not anyone would believe the truth. I knew that if I left him, he'd make good his threat to find me and kill me. Accidents happen, he used to say. I knew that the only way I could survive was to get out of bed and kill him first. In self-defense.

'That's what I did.

'I don't remember too many of the details from that point on. I got the hammer. I hit him with it. I remember looking down at my nightgown, seeing Al's blood, knowing he was dead. I remember feeling – relief. I don't remember stuffing the hammer into the central vacuuming system, but I guess I did. Or going outside, where the police found me. I just remember being there.'

Beth Weatherby shook her head. 'The lawyers want me to plead temporary insanity. They say I was crazy the night I killed my husband. Maybe I was.' She paused, looking from Jill to Lisa and then back at Jill again. 'But I really don't think so. To tell you the truth, Jill,' she said earnestly, 'and please forgive me, my darling Lisa, but I really believe that the night I murdered Al was the sanest I've been in twenty-seven years.'

Chapter Twenty-two

The phone rang just as Jill was leaving her apartment for the university.

'Naturally,' she muttered, returning to the kitchen and picking up the phone, sneaking a look at the clock. It was already ten-thirty. Her first class was in half an hour and unless she left the apartment in the next five minutes, she would be late. Since it was only the second day of regular classes, Jill didn't think such tardiness would be appreciated, and she had resolved to start this year right – with the proper enthusiasm and dedication. 'Hello?' she asked, rather than stated. Probably a survey or somebody trying to sell her a magazine subscription.

'Jill?'

'Yes. Who's this?'

'It's Irving. Irving Saunders. I hardly recognized your voice. You sounded so tentative.'

'I'm always tentative on Tuesdays. How are you? How was Africa?'

'Fraught with its customary turmoil and hot as hell. I have some great news for you.'

'Oh?' Jill found herself clutching the telephone as tightly as

307

if she had just been told the floor was about to disappear from underneath her feet.

'Aren't you going to ask me what it is?'

'What is it?' Jill repeated numbly.

'We're doing a new show,' he began. Jill took a deep intake of breath and held it. 'It's a sixty-minute news show,' he continued, 'kind of like "Sixty Minutes", in fact. A bit of muckraking and exposés, along with some issues that are concerning the people of this city. We're calling it "Hour Chicago" – Hour with an H, which I think is a great title, because it sounds like Our Chicago, without the H – which, of course, is what it's supposed to do. Anyway, are you still with me?'

'Right here.'

'Good. We want you.'

'What?!'

'Well, there's a slight hitch. A couple, in fact.'

'You want me?'

'Yes.'

'You've got me.'

Irving Saunders laughed loudly. 'I like you, Jill. You're so easy!'

'When do I start?'

There was a pause. 'Hold on a minute. We have to discuss the slight hitches I was talking about. They're important.'

Jill felt the beginnings of unease curling around her toes. She felt her heart thumping, and wanted only to seize the happiness of the previous moment and fly with it. He wanted her! He was offering her a job! She swallowed. With several slight hitches. Important ones.

'What are they?' she asked.

'Well, first, it's only a pilot. So, we shoot one show, we see how the network likes it, how it goes over with the public. I don't have to tell you. If everything clicks, we start mid-season. So, at the moment, what I'm offering you is a one-shot deal with the potential for more, but no promises.'

'I understand.'

'We go into pre-production in two weeks, which means I need a definite answer soon.'

'You've got your answer already,' Jill told him, decisively.

'What about the university?'

'They'll consider it invaluable practical experience. I can't see why they'd object. We're only talking about a few weeks. But that's my problem, and I'll deal with it.' She took a breath, her eyes returning warily to the clock. 'Why do I get the uncomfortable feeling there's more?'

'Probably because there is.'

'And you've been saving the best for last?'

'As always. You ready?'

'They can't pay my usual rates?'

'No, that's not it. The money I'm sure can be negotiated.'

'As always,' Jill said, parroting his earlier expression. 'Okay, what?'

'It's the subject matter.'

'The subject matter?'

'Of the segment you'd be producing.'

'Which is?'

There was a pause. 'Wife-beating,' Irving answered.

Jill felt her voice fall several octaves. 'Wife-beating?'

'The state of the art in Chicago,' he said dryly. 'Statistics. Reasons. The legal ramifications.' Another pause. 'Examples.' Another silence. 'Jill, it's no coincidence that I want you for this particular assignment. In fact, it's the raison d'être for this whole conversation. I'll be frank. The network wasn't interested in free-lancers. Things are tight here, as everywhere. But I went a bit out on a limb. I know how much you want to come back. I know how much I want you back. So, when the idea for this show came up, I thought about you right away. And then when this Weatherby murder thing happened and the guy's wife started yelling foul, well, it's a natural. It's your husband's firm! You knew the man! I assume you've met his wife. Now, that might get you in places an outsider couldn't; it might not. But it was an interesting hook to sell to the network. I convinced them that with your inside connections both to the Weatherbys and to the legal profession, you were the only person who could do this job. And they've agreed.'

There was another silence. 'Beth Weatherby is my friend,' Jill whispered.

'Don't get me wrong, Jill,' Irving said quickly. 'The episode doesn't have to be just about Beth Weatherby. I'm more interested in the legal ramifications. But there's no question that the Weatherbys would have to be mentioned, either as a jumping-off point, or possibly as a frame for the whole segment. That could be worked out during story conferences. But it's the Weatherbys that give this story its relevance – Beth Weatherby's claim of self-defense, not temporary insanity. Is self-defense a legitimate argument for what she did? For that matter, is

310

temporary insanity any more legitimate? Would freeing Beth Weatherby be granting all women in her position a license to kill?'

'Is a marriage certificate a man's license to kill?' Jill asked in response.

There was a satisfied pause. 'I knew you were the right person for this job,' Irving smiled. 'Think you can handle it?'

'I don't know,' Jill said quietly. 'David wouldn't be very happy under the circumstances.'

'I realize that. That's why I'm giving you a few days to think it over.' Jill said nothing. 'I don't know when I'd be able to call you again, Jill, if your answer is no,' he added, unnecessarily.

'I understand.'

'Call me Thursday afternoon.'

'I will.'

''Bye.'

'Goodbye.' Jill replaced the receiver and stood staring at the tile on the kitchen floor. How did she get in messes like this? It was almost as if they deliberately sought her out. (There's Jill Plumley and, my God, it looks like she's had two peaceful days in a row! General alert! Messes – attack!) David wouldn't like it at all. He would want her miles away from any public involvement in the Weatherby case and any of its attendant legal ramifications! And Beth herself? How would she feel?

And if she said no? Irving had made the outcome of her refusal pretty clear. There'd be no further offers, at least for some time. This was her chance, her opportunity knocking. She could take it and run, or she could run and hide. She hadn't spoken to Beth Weatherby since that extraordinary night the week before. She hadn't had time to discuss with David what Beth had told her. He'd been working late every night – the earliest evening being the Friday night he'd returned from taking Nicole Clark out for her celebration dinner – and the weekend had been lost to his work as well.

She'd needed the first few days to simply sort out all that she had heard, to come to terms with what Beth had confided. Only when it was clear in her own mind exactly how she felt would she feel free to discuss it with David. If they ever had the opportunity to sit down and really talk.

She needed to talk to both David and Beth, she realized. Irving had given her till Thursday afternoon, which meant she had to speak to both of them as soon as possible.

Jill looked up at the clock with a sudden shock. It was twenty minutes after eleven! How long had she been on the phone? How long had she been staring down at the floor?

She quickly headed for the door. If she was lucky, and the traffic was with her, she'd make it to the campus just in time for the end of her first class.

She was as surprised as he was by the way she looked.

'What did you do to your face?' he asked, getting up from behind his desk.

'I went to Saks. They were having a special today on makeup. Mr Claridge himself was there. He told me personally what makeup was right for me,' Jill laughed, finding herself embarrassed in front of her husband, 'and well, they do it for you right there in the store. What do you think? Too much?'

David walked around his wife, examining her face as if it

were a rare object. 'No, not too much. You know I like you with makeup. I'm just not used to seeing you with so much of it on.'

'You *do* think it's too much?'

'No,' he laughed, 'I think it's just right. I think Mr—'

'Claridge.'

'Mr Claridge did a first-rate job. But it's a shock, that's all, considering that you never usually wear any. But I like it.'

'He showed me how to put it on.'

'Good.' He leaned forward and kissed her. 'So, is that why you dropped by the office?'

'Well,' Jill hesitated, 'it was one of the reasons. I finished classes at four o'clock and I dropped by Saks, and then I thought, well, I'm in the neighborhood, why don't I come up and show you how glamorous I've become while you've been so busy working and see if I can't persuade my always-gorgeous husband to take his newly renovated wife to dinner.'

'Oh, Jill—'

'Please don't say no, David. We could go across the street to Winston's. It wouldn't take long.'

'Look at my desk, Jill. Can you see over that pile of paperwork?'

'Your desk was always a mess,' she reminded him.

'I can't, honey. I'm sorry.'

'David, it's important. I need to talk to you.'

There was a tap on the door and then it opened. Nicole Clark stood, regal and beautiful, in the doorway. 'Oh, sorry,' she said quickly to David. 'I didn't realize anyone was with you. How are you, Jill?'

Jill felt the makeup burning acid-like holes into her skin,

feeling like the clown in a circus when his time has been usurped to make way for the main attraction. Mr Claridge, Jill decided in the second between Nicole's greeting and her own response, could take a few lessons from her husband's newest junior associate.

'I'm fine,' Jill answered with pleasant briskness. 'I want to congratulate you on your being called to the bar, and on becoming a member of the firm.'

'Oh, thank you very much,' Nicole said graciously. 'It was very exciting. And wonderful having your husband at the ceremony. I needed support.'

'We all like support,' Jill said, smiling at David.

David's voice caught her slightly off guard. 'I'm taking my wife out for a quick dinner,' he explained to the younger woman. 'No more than an hour. Is there something you needed to discuss now or can it wait until tomorrow? Unless you'll be around later—'

Jill waited for Nicole's inevitable 'I'll be around,' but instead she heard, 'No, I'm going home now. I'm tired and this can wait. Nice to see you again, Jill. Good night.'

So, David had spoken to her as promised. And this was the result. I should have let him talk to her in the beginning, Jill thought, as David took her by the elbow and led her out of his office. It would have saved months of worry.

They sat across from each other and nibbled at their salads.

'So,' David said firmly, 'we have exhausted the weather and Mr Claridge and your new crop of students. Are you going to tell me now why we're here? I mean, your day was interesting,

I'll give you that,' he continued, smiling. 'But so far, I haven't heard anything I would describe as important.' He reached over the table and grabbed her hand. 'Not that seeing you isn't important. It is. And I'm glad I was coerced into this dinner.'

Jill smiled widely. The makeup had been a good idea. Even if it did feel like she was wearing someone else's face. It was obviously a face that David liked.

'Irving called,' she said, swallowing the last of her lettuce.

'Oh?' Definite interest.

'The network is producing a new show. Just a pilot. If everyone likes it, it would get its own time slot mid-season.'

'What kind of show?'

'Chicago's answer to "Sixty Minutes". They're calling it "Hour Chicago". Hour with an H.'

'Very clever.'

'Yes,' Jill agreed. 'It would be based entirely in Chicago, I think. At least that's the impression I got, since it's supposed to be a show about Chicago and what's concerning the citizens and everything. And—'

'And what are you so nervous about telling me?' he asked, almost laughing. 'It sounds wonderful! You'd be doing exactly what you want without a lot of traveling. I think it's fantastic!' He looked at her worried expression. 'Did I jump the gun? They do want you, don't they?'

Jill nodded. 'They want me.'

'Well, that's great. Why the long face?'

Jill reached for her glass of water while the attentive waiter removed their salad plates and replaced them with the main course. She stared at her plate of ginger chicken on a bed of green noodles and immediately lifted her fork, absently twirling the green noodles, cooked, she knew, to *al dente* perfection, around and around the sterling silver utensil. 'I love this restaurant,' she said. 'Remember when we used to come here a lot?'

'I remember. Did you forget my question.'

'No,' she said. 'I'm just not sure I want to answer it.'

'What is it that they want you to do on this show, Jill? Work nights?'

'No,' she answered quickly, wishing she could have said yes.

'You want to write it down on the napkin and slip it to me under the table?' he asked boyishly.

She laughed, her fork now fat with pasta. 'I don't know how to say this except to just say it,' she said. 'I've made too much of it already. I'm sure you won't have any objections. I'm just being silly.'

'Jill—' he said, with growing exasperation.

'The episode that they want me to produce is about wife-beating.' Immediately, she saw his eyes narrow. 'To be more specific, they're interested in not just the general phenomenon, but in Beth Weatherby. They feel her desire to plead self-defense opens up a lot of interesting legal possibilities that might make for an equally interesting television show.'

'I bet they do,' David scoffed. 'And they just happened to pick you.'

'No, they picked me quite deliberately. Irving made that very clear.'

'Well, what did he say when you told him no?'

Jill laid down her fork but continued to stare at it. 'I didn't tell him no,' she said. 'I told him I'd think about it.'

'What is there to think about?' he demanded.

'It's not so simple, David. This might be the last chance I get.'

'Baloney! There's always another chance. You know that as well as I do.'

'What would be so wrong in my doing it?'

'Everything!' he almost shouted, surprising Jill by the vehemence in his voice. 'You'd use your friendship with Beth; you'd use Al's memory; you'd use me, for God's sake.'

'How would I be using you?'

'If it weren't for me, you'd never have even met Al Weatherby!'

'You forget,' Jill reminded him, 'that I met Al Weatherby the same way I met you. Doing my job!'

'And that's all that's important to you, isn't it?' he said, angrily. 'Not me, not Beth, not Al. It doesn't matter who you hurt!'

'Who says I'd be hurting anybody?'

'Jill, for Christ's sake, you're not a child. You know that someone's going to be hurt if you do this story. Why else would you need time to think about it?'

'Because I felt I should discuss it first with you and with Beth.'

'Well, you have my reaction. I think it stinks! I think that anything that lends any credence to Beth's disgusting allegations is a disgrace and I would object very strenuously to my wife having anything to do with it. And as for Beth, how do you think she'd feel knowing you'd exploit her friendship to get yourself back into television?'

'I didn't go seeking this job, David. It came to me.'

'If you accept it, that's hardly relevant, is it?'

'I don't think Beth would view it as exploitation,' Jill ventured.

David shook his head. 'No, probably not. It might play right into her hands. You realize, of course,' he continued, after a slight pause, 'that no lawyer in the world would allow her to appear on the program.'

'Oh, obviously,' Jill quickly concurred, delighted they could agree on something. 'I would never ask that. The angle of the show, from the way I read Irving, would hinge much more on the moral and legal aspects of what Beth did and her reasons for doing it.'

'Great,' David muttered, sarcastically. Jill noticed that neither of them had touched their food. 'So, your mind's made up.' Jill started to shake her head in protest. 'Who are you kidding, Jill?' David asked her quickly. 'Your mind was made up before you walked into my office. If you think anything else, then the only person you're fooling is yourself.' He shoved his plate away. 'You don't want my opinion. You want absolution. You want me to say, sure, go ahead, destroy what's left of a fine man's reputation. Use me and my firm and everyone around you. I'm right behind you. Well, I'm not, and I can't say it. I think it's wrong, and I don't want you to do it.'

They stared at each other across the table. When Jill spoke, her voice came from deep inside her chest. 'And if I decide to do it anyway?' she asked. 'I mean, I really think I could do a good job of being fair to everyone, not blackening anyone's memory—'

'Wake up, Jill,' David snapped. 'Stop lying to yourself!'

'I don't think I am,' she protested.

'Well then maybe you're too naive for television.' He stood up. 'At any rate, the answer to your question, which I believe was "and if I decide to do it anyway?" is that it's a decision with which we will both have to learn to live.'

'What does that mean?' she asked.

'Exactly what it says,' he answered, putting thirty dollars on the table. 'Look, I have to get back to work now. There's no point in running this thing into the ground. Finish up, take your time. I'll be home later.' He bent over and kissed her forehead. 'Don't wait up,' he said.

Jill remained seated, staring down at her plate. Her appetite was gone.

'The food is not to your liking?' asked the waiter, several minutes later.

'The food is fine,' Jill told him. 'I'm just not feeling very well.'

'I'm sorry to hear that,' the waiter said with sincerity. 'Some tea, perhaps?'

Jill shook her head. 'No, thank you,' she said. 'Nothing.'

Chapter Twenty-three

Jill wasn't sure at what precise moment she realized her husband was having an affair with Nicole Clark. She was sure only that it was a fact that was now a part of her life.

She sat in the staff room between the periods of her two morning classes and tried to focus her attention on the morning paper. Two men and three women had been found in a rooming house stabbed to death. Probably drug-related, the police surmised. Another man had murdered his wife and two children because he claimed that Christ had told him to do so in a dream the night before; yet another woman had been shot to death by her insanely jealous husband because he felt she'd smiled too long at the mailman. Jill flipped the page. A woman had been given a jail sentence of two years less a day for crushing the skull of her infant son; another couple, three of whose children had already died under suspicious circumstances, was telling the courts that they considered themselves excellent parents and that they intended to keep having children until God decided otherwise. Jill folded the paper in disgust, tossing it to the low table in front of her. She had no interest in the Classified section today. Companions Wanted didn't interest her. Her husband was sleeping with another woman.

She had felt him crawling into bed beside her the night before, accepting her feigned sleep as if it were real, not bothering to try to rouse her, to snuggle against her, to warm his body against hers. She felt him moving restlessly, trying to find a comfortable position, finding it after several minutes and drifting quickly off to sleep. She heard his breathing become slow and deep. Sitting up, she looked over at the clock. It was almost 1 a.m. She'd heard his key turn in the door not more than ten minutes before. He'd come straight into the bedroom, undressed quickly and gotten into bed. And yet he smelled so clean, so absolutely odorless that she knew with certainty he had taken great pains to rid himself of any unwanted body smells. Like the smells of lovemaking, she had thought, lying back down beside him, remembering that the last time he had smelled this nondescript, this sanitary, was the night several weeks ago when he had called her at night from his office and asked her so lovingly to pick him up. She remembered her nervousness the following morning, running around trying to please him, to disguise the smell of his deceit with the odor of scrambled eggs and toast, hiding from her conscious self the knowledge that he had been with Nicole.

And so the last few weeks had all been a lie. The little scene she had witnessed the two of them play out in his office the day before – ('Is there something that you needed to discuss now or can it wait until tomorrow? Unless, you'll be around later . . . 'No, I'm going home now. I'm tired and this can wait.') – had been played strictly for her benefit and all in code. He was working late the same way he had done with Elaine. The work

322

was the same. Only the names had been changed, she thought idly, surprised by how unsurprised she felt.

She yawned and stood up, walking over to the phone at the far end of the staff room. She dialed slowly and waited as it rang. It was picked up on the third ring.

'Hello.'

'Mom?'

'Jill? Is everything okay?'

She smiled. 'Come on, Mom. You can't tell me you knew something was wrong just from the say I said "Mom".'

'Of course I could. A mother knows. Tell me. Where are you?'

'At school. In the staff room.'

'Now I know something's wrong. You never call me from work. What is it? Something with David?'

'Maybe I should just let you tell me,' Jill sighed.

'No, you tell me. What is it, darling?'

Jill looked around the room, trying not to cry. 'I'm just a little depressed, Mom, that's all. I don't know why.'

'You want to talk about it?'

'I don't know.'

'Why don't you come for dinner tonight? Your father is going to play duplicate over at the club and I'll be alone. I'd appreciate the company. I take it David's working late again.'

'Yes,' Jill whispered.

'Good. Then you'll come?'

'What time?'

'Six-thirty?'

'Fine.'

'See you later, darling.'

'Thanks.'

''Bye, sweetie.'

Jill hung up the phone and wondered what precisely she was going to tell her mother. That she'd been right all along? That David, having had no trouble cheating on one woman, was having no more trouble cheating on another? That everything was happening exactly as her mother had predicted it would so many years ago? God, were men really so predictable? Had someone taken out a patent on the situation? Were they all reacting in accordance with some divine plan, like the man who said Christ had directed him to murder his family? Was the whole world nuts? Jill looked around the room, seeking out the strange in each familiar face. Or is it just me? she wondered, leaving the staff room and walking toward her next class.

'Did you hear what happened to Sarah Welles?' her mother asked as she opened the front door and ushered Jill inside.

'No, what happened to Sarah Welles?' Jill asked, conjuring up the image of the young movie queen, Hollywood's latest attempt to duplicate the magic that was Marilyn Monroe.

'She's dead! Weren't you listening to the radio? They've been talking about nothing else.'

'I didn't have it on. What happened? Suicide? Murder?'

'Neither. A stupid accident. She was washing her hair in her sink and apparently she lifted her head and hit it against one of her solid gold faucets and it knocked her unconscious.'

'And she died?'

'Not from that. She drowned! Can you imagine? In her own

sink! Her face fell into the sink full of water and she drowned! Only twenty-six years old! I don't know! You'd think that with solid gold faucets, she could afford to go to the hairdresser's.'

'That's awful,' Jill said, following her mother into the kitchen, slowly organizing her thoughts. 'The implications are so scary,' she began. 'It means that we don't have any control at all over what happens to us. Here's this young woman with everything going for her, and one minute she's washing her hair and the next minute she's dead. Like Janet Leigh in the shower in *Psycho*.'

Her mother looked closely at Jill. 'Except that if Janet Leigh hadn't stolen that money to begin with, she'd have never ended up in that cheap motel. So – we do have some control over our lives, my darling. Accidents happen, sure. Tragic accidents. But that's all part of life. End of motherly lecture. You hungry?'

'Yes,' Jill smiled.

'Good. I have a nice stew ready. Sit down.'

Jill sat down at the round table in the comfortably wide kitchen of her childhood. 'Are you ever going to change this wallpaper?' she asked, looking at the green and brown print of clocks and country flowers that covered the room. It had been there as long as she could remember. It was still in remarkable condition.

'We did change it,' her mother said, putting a plateful of steaming stew in front of her. 'Last year.'

'You got the same paper?' Jill asked, incredulously.

'Can you imagine? They still had it in stock! I guess it's a classic.' Her mother laughed, sitting next to Jill with her own plate of stew. 'Take some bread,' she said, pointing to the bread basket in the middle of the table.

'How come you got the same one?' Jill asked, amazed.

'You father likes it,' her mother answered simply.

'And that's why?'

'It's a good reason,' her mother said.

Jill sighed, putting down her fork and looking at her mother. 'You've been married how long?' she asked.

'Thirty-eight years this January,' her mother answered.

'Thirty-eight years,' Jill repeated. 'That's a long time.'

'It's all relative,' her mother said. 'It goes by so fast.'

'You're happy?' Jill asked, knowing her question was simplistic, not knowing how else to ask it.

Her mother shrugged. 'Well, they say that the first twenty-five years are the hardest.' Both women smiled. 'How can I answer you? You know what else they say – that one couple's perfect marriage is something no one else in his right mind would want. You know – you pick what peculiarities you're going to put up with, and you learn to live with them. Sometimes you're happy; sometimes you're not so happy. In fact, sometimes you're miserable. But what usually keeps you going during those miserable times is the knowledge that it was good before, it'll be good again. Everything goes in cycles. Some years are better than others. But you have to have faith in your instincts – you say to yourself, there must have been some reason why I married him! – and usually you can remember what it was, even if it takes a little doing. You say to yourself, I loved the man enough to marry him. Surely, there's some of that love still around. You look hard enough, you can usually find it.'

'And love is all you need?' Jill asked with the proper amount of musical irony.

'Of course not,' her mother answered. 'You've been around long enough to know that besides love, you also need a high degree of tolerance, and respect and acceptance. And luck,' her mother added. 'Look at your brother. He married Emily when he was twenty and she was seventeen. They've been married for sixteen years and they still can't keep their hands off each other. They're planning a ski trip to Aspen this winter. I don't know,' she said, shaking her head, 'they go where it's hot in the summer and where it's cold in the winter. Beats me. What was I saying?'

'How Stephen and Emily can't keep their hands off each other,' Jill reminded her.

'That's right. It's embarrassing sometimes.' She looked directly at Jill. 'But physical attraction isn't the main thing. It may be part of the reason two people get married, but it shouldn't be the whole reason. There has to be more. So what if a man is good-looking? There are lots of good-looking men around. So what if he's good in bed? A lot of men are good in bed. Don't tell your father I said that.' She smiled. 'A good marriage is made up of so many things. And even good marriages are made up of a lot of very bad times. You have to decide what's most important to you, what you're willing to give to keep it going, what you're willing to give up. Sometimes people ask too much.' She paused, almost reluctant to ask the next question. 'Is David asking too much, Jill?' she said, taking Jill's head in her arms and pressing it against her breasts.

'I don't know,' Jill moaned against the warmth of her mother's body. 'I don't know.'

Jill called Beth Weatherby from her mother's house and asked if she could drive up and speak to her. Beth readily agreed and at nine o'clock, Jill found herself in front of the now familiar gray-brick exterior. She sat inside her car, her head swimming with words her mother had spoken. ('Stop talking like you're some little nobody who miraculously landed herself such a prize! You're bright; you're beautiful; you can do anything. You're the prize! Don't laugh. This is not just a mother speaking. Take a good look at this prize you've got. It might look good and it probably moves well, but what else has it done for you? I'll use your words – are you happy?') Jill closed her eyes and was immediately surrounded by images of her husband and Nicole Clark dancing around her head, their legs catching in her hair yet not tripping, still dancing, pulling her hair out by the roots with their careless feet, unaware or unfeeling of the pain they were inflicting.

Jill opened her eyes and pushed open the car door, sitting with her feet touching the sidewalk for several long seconds. How had everything gotten so turned around? She wasn't stupid. She wasn't weak. She wasn't some blithering little bubblehead whose happiness depended on having a man in her life. Or at least, she hadn't started out that way. She had begun life as a bright, secure little girl who had grown into a bright, secure young woman, independent, talented, full of natural resources. She had married at a time when she was supposedly very much her own person, someone who certainly knew the ropes and was not about to fall into all the familiar traps. And yet that's precisely where she had ended up – in the most familiar trap of all.

What was it about women that made them so eager to put themselves in this kind of position? Or worse, she thought, looking over at Beth Weatherby's house, thinking of all that Beth had endured over the years. Why are we such willing victims? Was Beth Weatherby right – did everything stem from man's superior physical strength? Did the socialization process start in the cradle? 'Damn,' she said, shaking the weight of rational thought off her shoulders. She could sit and intellectualize till dawn; she could rationalize and analyze and theorize and it would still boil down to one thing – she wanted David. She would do anything to keep him. She would make herself over, even turn herself inside out to keep him. She could outwit Nicole Clark, and if that proved impossible she could simply outwait her. And any others who came along. If David was unhappy at home, then she was at least partly responsible. She would change.

Jill stepped out of the car and slammed the door, hoping the night air would empty her head, clear away the unwanted pictures that seemed intent on driving her half-crazy. Sarah Welles had died while washing her hair. Nothing made any sense. Everything in this world was at least vaguely absurd. Why should her life be any different!

Beth had agreed instantly to the idea of her doing the show. ('Do it, Jill,' she had said. 'It's important. Tell people what I told you. Do the show. Maybe it'll wake some people up.')

Beth's easy acceptance had made the problem all the more acute. Jill had convinced herself in the time it took to walk from her car to the front door that if Beth's reaction was as negative as David's had been, she would tell Irving no. David was probably right – Irving would call her again, if not this year, maybe the next. ('Do it, Jill,' Beth had said, without any question. 'It's important. Do the show.')

Jill pulled her Volvo into the space beside the empty parking place that was reserved for David's Mercedes. She got quickly out of the car and headed toward the elevator, her keys held firmly between each finger, like a set of brass knuckles, to fend off attackers. Not that she expected anyone to be lurking around, but then, hell, Sarah Welles hadn't expected to drown in her bathroom sink either.

She reached her apartment, and despite her knowledge that David was not home, was disappointed to find the place empty. She quickly moved from room to room, turning on every light and leaving them on as she entered her bedroom and plopped down on her bed.

She picked up the phone and called David's private office number. It was just past ten-thirty. What was she going to tell him? Come home – I've decided not to do the show? Just please, stay away from Nicole and come back home.

There was no answer. Jill let the phone ring ten times, hung up and dialed again. After ten more rings she gave up. Perhaps he was already on his way home, she thought, kicking off her shoes and lying back on the bed. Maybe the whole thing was part of her imagination, something she had invented to get the old adrenaline pumping because things were starting to move too smoothly. She had no proof her husband was having an affair with Nicole Clark. Indeed, she had no hard evidence, as David would call it, that he wasn't doing exactly as he claimed to be doing each night. The firm was undoubtedly in a state of chaos because of Al Weatherby's death; the work load she had seen on David's desk was indeed prodigious. It was understandable, laudable even, that he felt he had to work this hard, this late, and this often to catch up. She had nothing but a lot of overhasty assumptions and conclusions to back up her unwarranted suspicions. David had done nothing. Was doing nothing. She was the only one who was making herself miserable.

The phone rang beside her and Jill picked it up, feeling strangely groggy.

'Hello.'

David's voice was soft and mellow. 'Hi, sweetheart. Did I wake you up?'

'I must have dozed off,' she said, clearing her throat, her eyes turning away from the bright glare of the overhead light.

'I'm sorry, hon. I just wanted you to know that I'm on my way home.'

'Where are you?' she asked.

'Where do you think?' he said, surprised. 'At the office.'

'I called you,' she said, looking at the clock. 'About half an hour ago.' She sat up.

'You did? he asked. 'Not here.'

'I let it ring ten times. Then I hung up and called again.'

'Well, it didn't ring – oh, shit, just a minute. I've got the phone turned down. There, I just fixed it. Stupid thing. I turned it off this afternoon so I wouldn't be distracted. Then I forgot about it. Sorry about that, honey.'

'No harm done,' she said, a tear falling the length of her cheek. 'See you soon.'

She replaced the receiver and sat on the side of the bed for several minutes in absolute silence. She saw David sitting in a strange room filled with nondescript furniture, Nicole Clark moving languorously in the background. She pictured Nicole as she moved to stand beside David, whose hand remained poised over the telephone, a look of doubt trimmed with a slight tinge of guilt falling over his beautiful face. She felt Nicole's hand come down gently, encouragingly, on David's shoulder. Saw him reach up and gently stroke that hand, looking back and smiling sadly in her direction. The same way he had done approximately six years ago when she had stood in Nicole's position and heard him say virtually the same words to Elaine.

Chapter Twenty-four

She checked her makeup in the mirror and then checked it again and then a third time, trying to remember everything that Mr Claridge had told her. Light under the eyes, a little highlighting at the sides, just a hint of mascara, a liberal stroke of blush-on and a finishing gloss over her lips. Why did she feel like she needed to wash her face?

She heard his key turn in the door and rushed to the mirror again to check her appearance. The negligee was new, expensive and completely out of character. Soft pink lace had been discarded with her diapers. It hadn't felt right then and it felt less right now, but David had once expressed a liking for things frilly and feminine, and despite the fact that her arms and feet were freezing and she knew she'd feel much better wearing a heavy sweater and a pair of socks, she persisted, pulling her shoulders back and trying to fill out the delicate trim of the low-cut bodice.

She took a deep breath as she heard David close the door behind him, and walked from the bedroom into the hall. David Plumley meets Total Woman, she thought as she moved, feeling like an inept understudy for an ailing Raquel Welch. What am

I doing, she wondered, wearing these clothes and this face and carrying on in this ridiculous fashion? I am trying to get my husband back, her inner voice responded. And if this approach can't help, well, then, at least it can't hurt.

'Hi,' he said when he saw her. 'What are you doing up? It's late.'

'Just midnight,' she replied, throatily.

'You didn't have to wait up,' he said, moving into the kitchen to check on the day's mail.

'Just a lot of bills,' she told him, coming up behind him and encircling him with her arms.

He patted her hands gently. 'What do I smell?' he asked.

'Oh,' she said, her heart beginning to race, 'I just took a bath. I used a new bath oil—'

'No, that's not it. Smells like chocolate.'

'Oh, I made a cake,' she said quickly.

'Sounds good,' he said, moving to the dining room and sitting down. 'Can I have a piece?'

'Sure,' she said, wondering why instead of rushing her into the bedroom, he was suddenly hungry for chocolate cake. What she was wearing couldn't have totally escaped him; he had to have noticed the way she was made up, the way she smelled. He had to realize why she had waited up. It had been several weeks since they'd made love. He had to know what she was trying to tell him.

She took the cake from its dish and cut two substantial pieces.

'Would you like some coffee?' she asked.

'No,' he said, his back to her. 'Coffee'll keep me awake, and all I want to do is sleep. I'll have a glass of milk.'

All I want to do is sleep, she heard his voice repeat. Well, he noticed all right, your face, your negligee, your whole ridiculous get-up. And this is his reply. Jill felt cold with humiliation and strode purposefully into the bathroom, turning on the hot water and scrubbing her face until it squeaked. Then she marched briskly into her bedroom, retrieved a warm sweater from her closet and threw it over her shoulders while she fished in her top drawer for a pair of heavy socks and pulled them on. Pushing her now wool-stockinged feet into a pair of tattered pink slippers and thrusting her arms inside the sweater sleeves, she headed back to the kitchen and poured her husband his glass of milk, putting the food in front of him on the table.

'Thanks,' he said absently as Jill sat down across from him and took a bite of her cake. 'Thought you were on a diet,' he said, half managing a smile. If he noticed that her appearance was in any way changed, he said nothing.

Jill shrugged. She'd been wrong when she thought disguising herself behind makeup and soft frills wouldn't hurt. It hurt plenty. She took another bite of chocolate cake.

'This is good,' he said, joining her.

'Thanks,' she said. The way to a man's heart, she thought.

'So, how come you waited up?'

'I wanted to see you,' she said, truthfully, staring into his deep green eyes, his face as beautiful to her as ever, as refreshing to her sight as a cool glass of lemonade. Would she always feel this, she wondered, this rush of pure pleasure every time she looked at him?

'Well, that's sweet, honey. But you shouldn't have. You

look tired, and God knows I'm in no condition to be much company.'

Jill looked down at the table, trying to ignore his remark about her looking tired. 'Do you have any idea,' she asked quietly, 'how much longer all this is going to go on?'

'Not much longer, I hope.'

'It seems to be getting worse.'

'I don't like it any better than you do. Christ, I'm so tired all the time.'

'Too tired to make love?' she asked, trying to sound as appealing as she could. He said nothing. 'It's been a while,' she continued softly.

'Oh, Jill, please don't start,' he interrupted. 'Can't you see I can barely stand up these days?!'

That's not my fault, buster, she wanted to yell. Instead she said, 'I'm sorry. It's just that I miss you.'

His face softened again. 'I miss you, too, honey.'

Jill finished off the rest of her cake.

'So,' he said, 'what did you tell Irving? Today was the day you had to decide, wasn't it?'

'Yes.'

'And?'

Jill said nothing, wishing now she had gone to bed early.

'You told him you'd do it,' he said for her after a pause.

'Yes,' Jill answered.

David brought his hands to rest behind his head. 'Well, what can I say?'

'I spoke to Beth,' Jill explained. 'She was very supportive.'

'I'll bet she was.'

'She wants me to do it. She feels it's an important issue.'

'I'm sure she does.'

'So do I, David.'

'That's obvious.' He stood up.

'I'd like to talk to you about it, now that we're on the subject.'

'I've said all I have to say about it, Jill.'

'I haven't,' she reminded him.

He sat back down. 'Go ahead.'

'I want you to understand why I'm doing the show.'

'No,' he interrupted. 'You want yourself to understand.'

'Please don't put words in my mouth! I know what it is I want to say. I'm quite capable of expressing myself.'

'Look, Jill, I'm really tired. Just say what you feel you have to say and let me get to sleep. You know that I'm never going to understand.'

Jill swallowed. 'I've seen Beth several times in the last few weeks. She's looking much better. Most of the bruises are gone. Her ribs are still a bit sore, but generally, she's looking pretty good.'

'Better than Al,' David said, his voice overflowing with sarcasm.

'I believe her, David,' Jill said finally.

There was silence. His look was quizzical, verging on the defensive. He would not like what she was going to say.

'You believe what?' David asked without moving.

'I believe Beth's story.' Another silence. 'I've talked to her, I really listened to her. And I believe her.'

'Believe what? That Al was beating her?! That she was a

battered wife who suddenly flipped out?'

'She didn't flip out. She says she's not crazy, not even temporarily. I agree. I don't think she's the slightest bit crazy. I think she did what she had to do. She had no choice. She was fighting for her life!'

David stood up with such sudden force that his chair fell over backward and crashed to the floor. 'What?!' he demanded. 'I can't believe I'm hearing this!'

Jill stood up, torn between comforting her husband and standing her ground. 'David, I don't want to fight about this—'

'What is it with you lately? Maybe you're the one who's gone temporarily insane!'

'David—'

'What do you mean exactly when you say that you believe her?' he demanded.

'I believe that Al did all the things she says he did.'

'What things *exactly*?' he repeated, stressing the final word.

'What do you want me to say? I'm trying to answer your questions but all you're doing is shouting at me.' She began pacing nervously back and forth.

'Jill, for God's sake, you knew Al! And not just casually. We played cards with the man, had him here for dinner, how many times? You saw the way he was with Beth—'

'In public.'

'You're saying he was a tender, loving husband in public and a monster in private?'

'That's what Beth is saying. I am saying only that I believe her.'

'A few weeks ago you didn't know what to believe.'

'I didn't understand then.'

'Understand what?'

'About Al! David, what good is this doing? We're just going around in circles.'

'You said you wanted me to understand! Okay. Go ahead. This is your big chance. Make me understand. Make me understand how Al could fool the whole world for over twenty-five years. Make me understand why my wife would believe the word of a cunning, conniving murderess and not her own eyes and ears.'

Jill stopped her pacing and lowered her voice, trying to restore calm. 'I listened to her, David. I really listened to her. She wasn't making it up. She wasn't lying. No one could be that good an actress.'

'Everyone can when their life is at stake.' David walked around the table to face his wife. 'Has it occurred to you that if what she's saying is true, that for as long as you've known her, everything else about her has been a lie?' Jill said nothing, allowing his words to find meaning in her mind. 'If she could fool you for four years, why couldn't she fool you now?' Jill was about to protest, but her thoughts were too confused. 'Why didn't she confide in you sooner? Why didn't she just leave him, for God's sake?'

Jill sank back into her chair. 'She was terrified he'd kill her. She was too beaten down—'

'Did she ever seem frightened to you? Ever seem beaten down?'

Jill's mind traveled quickly through four years of friendship.

'The night we played bridge,' she answered at last.

David's eyes reflected his confusion, then cleared, indicating he had the answer. 'She was upset about Lisa's involvement with a married man. Al explained—'

'Yes, Al explained. He always had an explanation. But it was a lie. There was no married boyfriend. There was only Al. David, Beth didn't cut herself that night – Al did it!' David was about to shout his protest; Jill kept talking. 'And now that I think about it, so much of it makes sense. At the picnic, Beth gave me some stomach pills, told me she'd had ulcers for years—'

'Oh, Christ, you're fishing at straws!'

'I believe her, David.'

'Her own children don't believe her!'

'Lisa does.'

David paused. 'If Lisa's decided to believe her mother, it's because she can't deal with what's happened in any other way.'

'Maybe she believes her because she knows it's true.'

'Oh, hogwash, Jill! I'm not listening to any more of this!'

'Why are you taking it so personally? It has nothing to do with you.'

'It has everything to do with me! Al Weatherby was my friend, my mentor, my colleague. I loved the man, damn it, and my wife, who also knew and liked the man, is suddenly willing to believe every horrible little tidbit she hears about him. Not only that, but from what you're telling me, you actually believe he deserved to die.'

'No, I—'

'If you believe Al was the kind of monster his wife says he was – do you or don't you?'

'I believe—'

'Just a simple yes or no.'

'David, stop it. I am not on the witness stand.'

'Answer the question.'

'I believe what Beth says.'

'That Al was a monster?'

'You're putting words in my mouth again!'

'You feel Beth was justified in what she did?'

'I don't feel she had any choice.'

'She couldn't pick up the phone and call the police?'

'David, you know how ineffectual the police are about things like that—'

'You feel she was right to take the law into her own hands?'

'Please lower your voice.'

'Answer my question! Do you feel she was right in taking the law into her own hands?'

'It was self-defense!'

David stared at his wife in dumb amazement. 'I just can't believe what I'm hearing.'

'David, when a man murders his wife, more often than not, his only weapon is his fists.'

'The man was asleep!'

'She had no chance against him when he was awake! He would have killed her. She had no choice.'

'We all have choices. It's part of what being an adult is all about.'

He turned from her and stared out the window at the wide expanse of the city. Jill stood for several minutes before coming up behind him and running her hand across his back.

'Please don't,' he said, without looking at her.

'David, we don't have to be angry at each other—'

He turned sharply toward her. 'Can't you see what you're doing?'

She backed off several paces. 'What am I doing?'

'You're making a mockery of my whole way of life.'

Jill was genuinely confused. 'I don't understand. How am I doing that?'

'I'm a lawyer! You're telling me that all I believe in, all I've worked for is just a big joke. That it's okay for people to take the law into their own hands—'

'What I'm saying is that I believe Beth's story. David, how can you be so damn sure that there isn't the slightest possibility that what Beth is saying is true?'

'Because I knew the man!'

'You didn't live with him.'

'I didn't have to!'

'You won't admit to even a tiny speck of doubt?'

'Not one speck! Al was a kind and decent man. There is simply no question in my mind about that. But even if there was some doubt, even if I was willing to accept these ridiculous lies as truth, it would all be strictly beside the point.'

'The point being?'

'The point being that Beth Weatherby murdered her husband in cold blood!'

'Not if it was self-defense!'

David looked back out the window then, without looking at Jill, turned and walked past her to the door. Jill's eyes followed him silently. He stopped. 'I'm going out for a while.'

'Oh, David, please don't—'

'I'm sorry, Jill, I can't stay here. My head is reeling. I'm tired and angry – very angry – and I need some time to myself. Actually,' he said, suddenly laughing, 'what I really need are a few stiff drinks.'

Jill tried to keep her voice from betraying her inner hysteria. 'Please don't go out, David. Just get into bed. I won't bother you.'

'I can't, Jill. I can't lie down. I have to get out. Walk around or something.'

'Where will you go? You can't walk around the streets of Chicago after midnight.'

'Then I'll drive,' he said simply, heading for the door.

'Can I come?'

'No.'

'David, please, you can't keep walking out on me every time we have an argument! Can't we just agree to disagree?'

He opened the door. 'Tell your good friend the next time you're talking to her that she'll stand a much better chance in court pleading temporary insanity.'

Without turning back, he shut the door behind him.

Jill felt the urge to cry and forced the tears down into her throat, returning to the dining room and righting the overturned chair, then sinking into it. Why did everything lately have to end in a fight? Why couldn't she just learn to keep her big mouth shut? Absently, she reached over and finished off the remainder of David's piece of cake. Then she walked into the kitchen and polished off the rest.

Chapter Twenty-five

Jill rolled over in bed, determined to find a comfortable position. It was useless. She'd never get comfortable. She sat up and turned on the light, looking at the clock. It was after 2 a.m. David still wasn't home.

She felt small tinglings of panic begin to spread across her body, the start of what she recognized as an anxiety attack. Calm down, she told herself, wishing she had one of Beth's chalky white tablets. Lie back. It'll be all right.

She did as her inner voice demanded, laying her head against her pillow and taking several deep breaths, telling her body to relax. Relax. David would surely come home, probably quite drunk, very apologetic. He wouldn't stay out all night. Oh please, don't let him stay out all night.

Her body immediately tensed, the tingling in the tips of her fingers and in the pit of her stomach returning. Relax, she repeated. He'll be home. He wouldn't be so obvious; he wouldn't hurt her in this way. He was just going through a very difficult time and she wasn't making things any easier for him. But he'd get over it. They'd both get over it. He wouldn't stay out all night. He had to know she'd be thinking of a night so long ago when he'd left another house after another fight and turned up drunk and searching at another door. Her door.

She opened her eyes wide, feeling her breathing becoming short and choppy. There was no point in trying to relax – she knew she'd never sleep.

Jill got out of bed and marched into the den, flipping on the television with the remote control unit. Cary Grant's youthful face filled the large screen. She recognized the movie immediately – *I Was a Male War Bride*. A wonderful, funny movie. Running quickly back to her room, she seized her heavy sweater and returned, plopping herself down inside the big leather chair and giving the TV her undivided attention, losing herself in a world where even armies were filled with innocents, and the colors of reality were not permitted to disturb the simple blacks and whites of the land of make-believe.

She tried hard to concentrate on Cary Grant and Ann Sheridan, struggled against the image of the shadowy figure who was emerging in the background, getting clearer, until she came strongly into focus, throwing everything else into the background, as if the cameraman had readjusted his lens, superimposing her face over all others. Jill watched the image become real, powerless to move or change the channel.

She saw Nicole Clark in bed, asleep. Watched her turn over, earlier smells of David still lingering against her pillow. Felt her dreaming, as she herself had been dreaming on that distant night, dreaming about a parade, a marching band. The drummers banging loudly on their drums. So loudly that she had felt her eyes open against the noise in protest. Aware now that she was awake and yet the drumming was continuing.

Now the image shifted again. Nicole getting out of bed, moving to the door, became Jill stumbling toward the window. What was going on? Who was out there on the street? It was cold. It was the middle of the night!

And now, not only banging but other sounds as well. Angry, barking noises. The great Doberman awake and alarmed, his owner's voice shrill and demanding – 'What's going on here? Get away or I'll call the police!'

David was shouting her name. 'Where's Jill?' he was demanding.

'Get out of here or I'm calling the cops, do you hear me?!' her landlady shouted through the door.

'No, wait, please!' Jill called, running down the steps. 'It's for me.'

'Not at three o'clock in the morning, it isn't.'

'Please, Mrs Everly, he's obviously drunk. We can't let him go anywhere in that condition.'

'He got here, didn't he?'

'Yes, he did,' Jill said with surprising strength. 'And he's staying here. In my apartment. Now I'm sorry he woke you up. It won't happen again. But he *is* coming inside.'

The landlady had retreated, with her dog still snarling. Only as she closed the door behind her did Jill notice that Mrs Everly's right hand firmly clutched a large, unfriendly shotgun.

'She could have killed you,' Jill explained, ushering David quickly inside and closing the door, only now thinking how she must look to him, her hair greasy, her skin sweaty with a newly broke fever, her body wrapped in flannel. Why, of all nights, did he have to pick this one?

'I came to see how you were feeling,' he said as his arms reached out for her. She let herself be surrounded by his body, smelled the liquor that permeated his skin, felt his blond hair softly whip against her damp forehead. He's in my arms, she thought.

'I look such a mess,' she whispered.

'You look so pretty,' he said simultaneously.

It was cold in the hallway despite the warmth of his body. 'Can you make it up the stairs?' she asked, reluctant to loosen her grip. He said nothing and she realized she was holding him up. 'Can you walk?' she asked. Again he said nothing, allowing her to lead him. They walked slowly, stumbling against the walls, clutching at the railing, finally reaching the top of the stairs and getting inside Jill's apartment. David collapsed onto the floor. 'David?'

He looked up at her. Jill felt like a giant. 'You're so pretty,' he said.

'Let me get you a cup of coffee,' she pleaded. He nodded. 'I'll go put the kettle on. I only have instant. Is that all right?' He smiled. She ran into the kitchen and poured cold water in the kettle, setting it down on the electric burner. Then she measured some coffee into a mug and put it on the counter. He was here; David was really here. And it didn't matter that she hadn't seen him all week or that she'd been sick with a cold and he hadn't come over; that they'd been trying to cool things and she'd been miserable; he was here now. It didn't matter that it was the middle of the night and her landlady would probably throw her out in the street come morning or that his wife was probably frantic with worry, wondering where he was so late.

All that mattered was that he was here, that this wasn't a dream. He probably doesn't know *where* he is, she thought, hurrying back into the main room. 'David, are you awake?' she asked, kneeling in front of him. His eyes were closed. He opened them.

'Yes,' he said.

'Do you know where you are?' she asked.

'In your apartment,' he said simply.

'Do you know who I am?' she asked, holding her breath.

'You're the prettiest girl I've ever seen,' he answered.

She smiled, running a hand through her hair. Why did she have to look so awful? 'Do you know my name?'

His smile grew very wide. 'I may be drunk,' he said, 'but I'm not an idiot! You're the woman I love! You're Jill,' he said softly.

'Well, I had to make sure,' she cried happily. 'You keep telling me how pretty I am. I thought you might not be seeing too straight!'

'I'm not, but you're still pretty.'

'You shouldn't be sitting on the floor,' she said, suddenly. 'You'll get a chill. Come on, let me move you over to the bed.'

She put her hands under his armpits, trying to lift him up. It was like trying to move a cement statue. 'David, do you think you could help me a bit—'

He smiled at her innocently. 'What would you like me to do?' he asked.

'Just lift your butt a little,' she said. 'Try and get up on your feet.'

'I'm very good at lifting my butt,' he said. Jill laughed.

'That's right,' she told him as he tried to follow her

349

instructions. She managed to get him to his feet and together they stumbled toward the bed. 'Okay,' she said, 'let go.'

'Not a chance,' he said, pulling them both down.

Jill lay breathless in David's arms. This isn't a dream, she kept repeating. Please don't let this be another dream. They lay completely still, David too drunk to move, Jill too afraid he might.

It was a few minutes before she realized that she couldn't breathe. Her nasal passages were completely blocked; her head was swimming. They made a fine pair, she thought, and the thought made her laugh. He opened his eyes and rolled over, his hand moving without plan to cover her mouth. Oh great, she thought, he's covered the only breathing apparatus I have that still works.

Gently, with great care, she tried to remove his arm. She touched his fingers, felt the soft hairs on the back of his hand, and very slowly pushed the hand aside. He took no notice. Jill sat up slowly in bed, careful not to make any sudden movements that might disturb him. Why had he come here now? she wondered. And why so drunk?

Possibly a fight with Elaine, she decided. Over what? She grabbed a Kleenex from the side of the bed and blew her nose as quietly as she could manage. It didn't seem to help. Her nose remained as stubbornly plugged as ever. And probably fire engine red, she thought, and flaky. Why did you have to come tonight? she demanded of him without asking. Maybe it's better that you're so drunk, she decided. But what had happened that made him that way? Was it all over with Elaine? The thought made her feel light-headed. She stood up too quickly and he sat up abruptly. Oh no, she thought. Please don't get up; please don't go home.

'Where are you going?' he asked. It was obvious from his tone that he wasn't planning on going anywhere.

'The water's boiling,' she said, her voice a hoarse whisper. 'I'm so mixed up I can't remember if you take cream or sugar.'

'Beats me,' he said, smiling.

'I think black would be best,' she told him, shuffling toward the kitchen, looking back in his direction to make sure he was still there. She poured his coffee and made herself a cup of tea, slowly adding the boiling water, feeling the steam reach up into her nose, momentarily clearing her sinuses, allowing her the luxury of breathing again, if only for the moment.

She heard him moving, the sound of his feet on the floor. Grabbing a mug in each hand, she hurried into the other room.

'Where are you going?' she asked. He was almost at the front door, although he'd left his jacket in a crumpled heap on the bed.

'The bathroom,' he muttered.

'The bathroom is over there!' Both hands being full, she used her chin to indicate direction. He smiled and came toward her, kissing her full on the lips. She felt a sinking sensation in her legs, knew that if she didn't put down the mugs, her hands would simply drop them. He pulled away from her as if in slow motion.

'God, you're sweet,' he said, then looked totally confused. 'The bathroom?' he asked again.

'Over there,' she told him, following behind and lowering

both mugs to the floor by the bed. 'Are you all right? Can you make it by yourself?'

'I've been going to the bathroom by myself since I was three years old,' he said.

'Drunk?' she asked.

He laughed and lurched forward, out of her sight. She heard the light switch click on and the door close behind him. He's going to stay, she thought. He's really going to stay. Jill reached down and brought the mug of tea to her lips, sipping slowly, allowing the steam to seep into her pores. It made her perspire more, and soon she felt trickles of sweat running across her face. She finished her tea and decided on another cup, returning quickly to the kitchen. This was crazy, she thought. It was almost three-thirty in the morning and she should be asleep in bed, not walking around her apartment, not contemplating the things her mind couldn't stop thinking about. About the possibility that he had left his wife for good. Elaine had to know he was with another woman. How could she live with that knowledge and not confront him? Staying all night meant more than just a casual affair. It meant that he no longer put Elaine's feelings ahead of hers, that he could no longer hide her existence from his wife. That he no longer cared to try.

She looked toward the bathroom. David had been there a long time. She hoped he wasn't being sick but imagined he probably was. She poured herself another cup of tea, catching her reflection in the toaster. My God, she looked absolutely awful. She ran for her purse in the front closet, searching through it and pulling out her brush. Taking another fast glance at the bathroom, she ran back into the kitchen and tried to brush her hair. The frenzied brushes only made it look more greasy, and her eyes were all puffy and as swollen as her nose. There was nothing she could do that would make her look any better short of cutting off her head. She looked down, saw the sweaty flannel nightgown and heavy wool socks and winced almost audibly. Thank God he's so drunk, she told herself, wondering if perhaps she shouldn't see if he was okay.

'David?' she called quietly, knocking gently on the bathroom door. 'David, are you okay?' There was no response. 'David? Can you hear me?' She put her hand on the doorknob and felt it turn. It wasn't locked. 'David, can I come in?' There was nothing, no sound at all. 'I'm opening the door, David,' she called, her voice as loud and strong as she could manage. She tried to push the door open but nothing happened; it wouldn't budge. There was something blocking it. Jill felt herself becoming frightened. She pushed frantically at the door, felt it give a few inches, saw David's blond hair on the floor on the other side. 'My God,' she cried. 'David, are you all right?' Had he fallen? she wondered, or simply lain down? Had he hurt himself? Had he passed out? 'David, please, can you sit up?' She pushed the door farther open, saw his eyes closed with sleep. She couldn't see any bruises or bumps; there didn't seem to be any blood. She reached her hands inside the door and awkwardly tried to pry his body loose from the other side. She succeeded in getting enough of her own body inside to give the door the extra push it needed. David rolled over lifelessly as the bathroom door opened against him.

Jill crouched down, turning him onto his back, looking over his face and head for signs of a bad fall. There weren't any. She lifted his head, examining the back of his skull. It didn't look like he'd fallen.

Jill looked hopelessly around the small room trying to decide on a course of action. She could throw him in the bathtub, try to sober him up. No, he could drown that way, she decided, choosing instead to stick him under the shower. She couldn't just leave him on the bathroom floor all night.

She stood up, having laid his head gently back on the floor, and turned on the shower. Just warm enough to wake him up a little. To be able to get some coffee into him. The first problem, of course, was getting him in the shower.

She looked at him, asleep on the floor, the most glorious-looking man she'd ever seen. Pale and blond and perfect. This is all I will ever want, she thought. She kissed him, felt his body instinctively stir. Her eyes traveled the length of his body. She'd have to undress him.

The room was starting to get warm. The noise of the water was echoing in her ears. She started to unbutton his pale blue shirt, the fair hairs on his chest coming immediately into view. She couldn't believe she was doing this, couldn't believe the excitement she was starting to feel, despite how sick she was. She finished undoing the last of the buttons and pushed the shirt aside, bending down without thinking and kissing the exposed chest. Again he stirred, his hands moving automatically to her back and then falling to the floor again, lifeless. She undid the buttons at his cuffs and pulled one arm slowly free of his sleeve and then the other. The combination of the water and her effort brought a further onslaught of perspiration. She felt tired and weak and positively elated.

She moved down to his feet and quickly discarded his shoes and socks. See, Mom, she thought, his feet don't even smell. There isn't a thing about this man that isn't beautiful. She heard her mother's voice – except his wedding ring, it said. Jill found herself looking at the thin gold band. It doesn't look very substantial, she told herself, moving on to the belt buckle of his trousers and undoing it before she could persuade herself otherwise. Then she unzipped the front zipper and yanked the pants down past his knees. Underneath he wore regular Fruit-of-the-Looms.

He groaned and opened his eyes though they were still mere slits.

'You have to take a shower,' Jill told him. 'Do you understand?'

He grunted but made no move to get up.

'I'm trying to get you undressed. Can you help me? Try to stand up.' Once again, she grabbed him under his arms. He took hold of her with one hand and the door handle with the other, and pulled himself up. His shirt remained on the floor; his slacks bunched up at his feet. He stepped out of them.

Jill looked at his body, clad only in his shorts. He looked even better than she remembered, his man's body youthful but yet not boyish. Slim, tight, sensual. She wanted him so badly she could barely move. 'Can you get out of your shorts?' she asked, not trusting herself to touch him further. He looked sleepily down at his torso and pulled down his shorts in one surprisingly smooth motion, stepping out and away from them, kicking his clothing aside. Jill tried not to look at him, coming around him instead to lead him toward the shower's spray.

355

'Step up,' she said, as they reached the bathtub. He did, though not far enough, and hit his leg, causing him to cry out. 'Try again,' she advised, guiding his legs with her hands, feeling the water hitting the side of her shoulder. Once inside, she pushed him toward the wall and directly under the water. He gasped, opening his mouth, at first hugging the wall with his back, then moving back toward the spray, tossing his head back, opening his eyes wide.

She watched him, worried he might fall, feeling herself weak with fatigue and desire. He caught her watching him out of the corner of his eye and suddenly reached over and grabbed her arms, pulling her toward him. Her legs caught against the side of the bathtub and she fell forward at the knees, feeling her hair and face hit by the sudden force of the water, feeling her nightgown grow damp and then wet. He pulled her up and inside the tub, surprising her with his sudden strength. The water pounded against her nose and mouth. She closed her eyes against the downpour, feeling his hands all over her body, on the buttons at her neck, fumbling with them, ultimately ripping them open and pulling the wet flannel up over her head.

'You're so beautiful,' he said, his words slurred, his eyes not quite focused.

'I look ridiculous,' she cried, tears suddenly mixing with the water from the shower. 'I have these dumb socks on and I'm all wet!' Suddenly, she was laughing and crying at the same time, seeing them suddenly the way an impartial camera might – David, drunk and barely able to stand, soaking wet in the shower; herself, feverish, stuffed up with a cold, her hair drenched by sweat and the downpour, nude now except for white wool knee socks hugging against her feet.

David knelt down and pulled at her socks. Jill grabbed hold of the side of the wall as he tugged the wet wool off her feet, discarding the heavy material by the side of the tub. Suddenly, she felt his hands on her buttocks and his face buried inside the wet hair between her legs. The water continued to pour down on them. This isn't happening, she thought, digging her nails into his shoulders, unconscious now of the water's steady beat. David slowly worked his way up her body, moving his hands to her breasts, catching the water in his mouth as it dropped off her nipples. He reached her lips and kissed her ferociously, as if he wanted to swallow her, make her disappear inside him. They stumbled over – she wasn't aware if she had lost her balance or he had pushed her down, but there they were on the bottom of the bathtub and he was pushing into her, sitting up and wrapping his legs around her, reaching over and wrapping her legs around him, pounding into her as the water poured hot all around them. Jill wondered for an instant if they would drown before they climaxed, then stopped caring, surrendering herself to the absurdity of the situation. Nothing in her wildest imaginings could have prepared her for this, and if she wasn't quite as comfortable as she might have chosen to be, it would certainly make for a hell of a story to tell their grandchildren. Finally they dried one another with her blue towel, moved to her bed and fell asleep.

He awoke in the morning before she did, sitting up suddenly, coming wide awake instantly, looking down at Jill, just now opening her eyes, aware of her hair damp across her face.

Automatically, she covered her face with her hands. 'Oh God, I look awful,' she said.

He pushed her hands aside and kissed her. 'No,' he said, 'you look beautiful.' He looked toward the drawn curtains. The sun was shining on the other side. 'What time is it?' he wondered out loud.

Jill sat up and pulled the clock radio on the bedside table toward them. 'A little after seven o'clock,' she said.

He rubbed his head, obviously mulling over his alternatives. 'I better go,' he said, standing up and looking around. 'Do you happen to remember where I left my clothes?' he smiled.

'I think they're in the bathroom,' she said, deciding to let him make all the moves. Did he even remember what happened last night? she wondered, arching her back carefully and rolling her neck around in an effort to relieve the stiffness. She debated what she should do, get up and make coffee or stay where she was. She decided to stay longer. What would he say to Elaine? Would he try to explain? To lie? Would Elaine believe him? She'll believe anything she wants to badly enough, Jill said to herself, realizing for the first time since early that morning that essentially nothing had changed. There would be a few more lies, that's all. Bigger ones, perhaps a little harder to deliver, a little tougher to swallow but swallowed nonetheless. Last night had been no more a declaration of independence than any other night. It had simply started later and therefore ended later. It didn't matter that Elaine had slept next to an empty space. Her eyes were closed. They were undoubtedly prepared to remain so.

David walked back into the room. He was fully dressed and ready to go.

'Do you want a cup of coffee?' she asked him.

'I better not,' he said. She nodded. He sat down on the bed beside her. 'How are you feeling?' he asked, running his hand across her cheek.

'Pretty good,' she lied.

He tucked the blankets around her. 'Stay in bed today. I don't think I let you get a lot of rest last night.'

She looked at him questioningly. 'Do you remember anything?' she asked.

He smiled, leaning forward and kissing her. 'I just remember how pretty you are,' he said, and then he kissed her again. A minute later, he was gone.

Jill opened her eyes. He was gone. Cary Grant had disappeared along with the night. David was reaching over and turning off the television.

'I'm sorry,' he said, freshly changed into a new suit. 'I went to a hotel. Slept there. It was a dumb thing to do. I hope you didn't worry too much.'

'Not too much,' she said, her voice as dead as the gray morning sky.

'I have to go to work,' he told her.

'Fine,' she answered, not looking at him.

'I'll try to be home early tonight.'

'That would be nice.'

Jill heard the door close behind him. So the lie had been fairly easy to deliver after all. Jill swallowed hard. Then, like Elaine had done before her, she closed her eyes.

Chapter Twenty-six

She saw Laurie as soon as she entered the restaurant, and rushed past the bar of familiar faces toward the table where the young girl was waiting. 'Hi, Laurie,' she said breathlessly. 'I'm sorry I'm late. These meetings can go on forever. I was afraid I'd never get out. Everyone gets so caught up in what they have to say they forget there are still a few of us around who like to eat lunch now and again. Were you waiting long?'

'Just a few minutes,' Laurie said. Jill knew from the sudden blush that appeared on the girl's cheek that she was lying. She threw off her coat and hung it over the back of her chair, sitting down and taking a long, deep breath.

'I'm really glad you could meet me for lunch,' Jill said, taking in the teenager's careless posture with a quick, subtle glance. Her arms seemed only flesh-covered sticks as they projected out from under the red-and-white-striped sweatshirt that hung, as if on a hanger, from her shoulders. 'No school today?'

'It's a PD day.'

'A PD day? What's that?'

'Professional development, supposedly. The teachers get

about one a month. Mom says they just want another day off. She doesn't believe they have meetings and stuff. She says it's all an excuse.'

Jill laughed in spite of herself. She could hear Elaine's voice as she launched into her tirade against the teaching profession. 'Did you have any trouble finding the place?'

Laurie shook her head. 'My mom drove me. She said it looked suitably shady.'

'Shady?' Jill asked, looking around the crowded room, waving at one of the network script assistants. 'No, it's just kind of a hangout for television people, because it's so close. You know, right across the road. I never thought of it as being particularly shady.'

'I like it,' Laurie offered.

'Good. So do I. Has a waiter been around yet?'

'He came. I told him to wait till you got here.'

Jill looked around, trying vainly to attract the waiter's attention. 'I think they go to a special school,' she said after several futile attempts. 'They major in lack of peripheral vision.' She smiled at David's daughter, who was obviously enjoying herself. 'So, how are you finding school so far?'

'It's okay.'

'What's your favorite subject?'

The girl paused. 'English, I guess,' she answered, unexpectedly.

'Really?' Jill asked, genuinely surprised. 'That was always my favorite subject. I used to love writing compositions—'

'Oh, I hate that part.'

'Oh.'

'It's a drag. I never know what to write about. I like to read.'

'What sort of things are you reading?'

Laurie reached for her glass of water, taking a long sip before answering Jill's question. 'I like the Nancy Drew books,' she said.

The waiter suddenly approached with the menus. 'May I get you anything from the bar?'

'A bloody mary,' Jill said, turning her attention back to Laurie. 'What about you, Laurie? Would you like a Coke or something?'

'No thanks,' she said. 'Water's fine.'

Jill picked up her menu and pretended to glance over its contents. There was no need. She knew it by heart. She hoped Laurie would eat something – it was one of the reasons she had decided that they should meet for lunch. Actually, their getting together had been Laurie's idea. In the last month, as Jill and David seemed to be pulling farther apart, she and David's daughter had begun to grow inexplicably closer to one another, and although they had yet really to trust each other with anything remotely resembling a serious conversation, there was now a certain degree of warmth replacing their customary cool. Especially in the weeks since Jill had begun her job at the network, Laurie, and to a lesser extent, Jason, had been less overtly hostile, occasionally even friendly. When David had abruptly canceled plans to take them all to a movie because of a last-minute meeting, they had willingly gone ahead with Jill and had spent several hours at its conclusion arguing about what it all really meant. It was ironic, Jill thought, lowering the menu, to be losing David just as she was winning over his children.

She cleared her throat. 'Can I recommend something for you or do you know what you want?' Jill asked.

Laurie shook her head. 'You order.'

'How does steak on a kaiser bun sound?' Jill asked, picking out what sounded the most fattening. 'It comes with a big plate of french fries.'

'Sounds good,' Laurie answered, the bones across the top of her chest protruding ominously through her sweatshirt. Jill tried not to look too surprised at Laurie's easy acceptance of her suggestion.

'Some soup to start? They make a wonderful homemade vegetable soup,' she suggested, afraid she might be pushing her luck. Laurie smiled, her face, once pretty and full, now stretching gaunt and sallow, her eyes almost sunken. Couldn't Elaine see the changes in her daughter? Why wasn't she doing anything about it? Jill remembered Ricki Elfer's solemn proclamation: anorexia nervosa. Was that it? Was Laurie really trying to starve herself to death?

'That's fine. Soup sounds great.'

'And a salad?' Jill ventured. Laurie nodded. 'Good. I'll have the same,' Jill concurred, counting up the mountain of invisible calories. 'We can order dessert later if you like.'

Laurie looked around the room, quite taken with all the network types, as Jill gave the waiter their order. God, let her eat this, she hoped, looking back at Laurie. And if she doesn't, if she just pushes the food around her plate the way she usually does, what then? Another lecture? Another bitter scene? Or another meal of looking the other way and pretending the problem doesn't exist? What was the matter with the girl's mother? Jill asked herself angrily. Or her father, for that matter. They were the ones who should be insisting that the child get some good professional advice. And where were the girl's teachers? Why hadn't one of them said anything? Jill smiled over at David's daughter. Her teachers were away being professionally developed, she remembered, thinking that it might make for an interesting target of investigation if 'Hour Chicago' got beyond the pilot stage.

'Did you ever read Nancy Drew?' the girl was asking.

'Did I read Nancy Drew?!' Jill laughed. 'Every single one. *The Hidden Staircase* was my favorite.'

Laurie's eyes grew big and wide, a smile creasing their edges. 'Mine too,' she said. 'And I love Judy Blume.'

'Who?'

'Judy Blume. She writes books for teenagers. I read all her books.'

'I don't know her work,' Jill said, feeling the name was vaguely familiar.

'Well, you're not exactly a kid,' came the reply.

'That's true,' Jill said, as the waiter put her bloody mary on the table. 'And I'm not getting any younger! Cheers!'

'Cheers,' Laurie mimicked, raising her water glass. 'Tell me about your new job,' she said eagerly.

Jill returned her drink to the table. 'Well, I'm not sure it *is* a new job yet. It's still pretty temporary. We have to see how the pilot goes first. I'll just be another few weeks here and then it's back to the university until I know one way or the other.'

'What do you do *exactly*?' Laurie pressed, obviously interested.

'Well, let's see,' Jill began, 'that's what we're having all these story conferences about right now, to try to figure out exactly what it is that we *are* doing.'

'What's a story conference?'

Jill was pleased at Laurie's questions, realizing that David hadn't asked her anything about her work since she had begun. 'It's a meeting where all the producers and researchers are present,' she explained. 'That's where you sit down and fight for your ideas. And let me tell you, there's always a good fight. You present your idea for something you'd like to see done, and then you have to pitch the fact that it's not only a good idea but a good idea *for television*. You have to show that it would appeal to a wide audience, that you can present it in such a way that it would be suitable viewing for an entire family, and that it would *look* good on television. That sounds kind of dopey, but you have to remember that television is primarily a visual medium. You with me so far?' Laurie nodded. 'Okay,' Jill continued, 'so, assuming the producer – that's me – sells her idea to the group, then she usually gets about three weeks to put the whole thing together.

'The first thing that gets decided is who's going to be your research assistant, and you can pretty well bet that whoever you dislike the most, or have the most trouble with, is who you're going to wind up being assigned. The researcher spends most of his or her time on the phone. They're the ones responsible for getting you all the necessary information. Then you have to decide, which is what we've been doing a lot of lately, just what the "breaking point" of the story is. In other words, what do you want to say and how do you want to say it?' She paused, thinking of Beth Weatherby. 'Say you're doing an exposé on people who place those ads in the Companions Wanted columns of the newspapers,' she said, abruptly shifting the focus of her thinking. 'Well, you decide your angle, maybe it's that these people aren't perverted or oversexed or any of those things, but are really just a bunch of poor, unhappy people who are desperately looking for someone to love, and you pick as your breaking point a happily married couple who met through one of these ads, and you build your show around them. You might start by contacting the various dating services, going to singles' bars and discos, maybe even cruising the park benches for some lonely people. You might even answer one of the ads yourself. You have to be *specific*. You need one example to focus on and you always have to be thinking about visualizing your story concept. You never shoot in the studio. You're always on location and you have to pray that whoever you finally do sit down to interview doesn't have a criminal record because that would blow your credibility right out of the window.'

The waiter approached with two bowls of steaming hot soup. 'Thank you,' Jill said, watching in amazement as Laurie lifted her spoon and dug right in. 'Is it good?' she asked a minute later.

'Delicious,' Laurie answered. 'Go on, tell me more about your job. What happens after you finish shooting?'

'It goes to editing,' Jill said, tasting a spoonful of the hot liquid and then continuing. 'In some ways, the editing is the most rewarding part of the whole thing. But it's also the most frustrating. That's where you see all your mistakes. You know, like the camera was out of sync or the film's defective or the best part is happening just out of range. There's a separate editor,' Jill explained, taking another spoonful of soup, noticing with great satisfaction that Laurie was already finishing hers. 'You work with the editor. Tell him what you want to keep and what you want to throw away. Anyway, what you're looking for are the sequences that flow. You're looking for moments that – how can I say it without sounding trite? You're looking for moments that illuminate. You're in a black room with no air, and you spend hours just staring at a tiny screen. You're recutting constantly. One day you're happy; you think you've done a terrific job. The next day you see it again and you hate it. It's an exhausting, exhilarating time, usually taking two days *and* two nights. It's like you're up for forty-eight solid hours.'

The waiter waited to remove their soup bowls until Jill quickly gulped down the last of hers. 'Two steaks on kaisers and fries,' he said, putting the overflowing plates in front of them, along with their salads. Again, Laurie barely waited until the plate was on the table before picking up her fork and popping a monstrous french-fried potato into her mouth.

'This is great,' she said, enthusiastically. 'So, go on. Do you keep everything you shoot?'

Jill laughed. 'Oh, no! That would be a real miracle. It's usually a six to one ratio of what's discarded to what's retained. Three to one if you're really expert, which I'm not.'

'But you are good,' Laurie said.

'Yes,' Jill answered, 'I *am* good.' She smiled widely, feeling almost smug about the successful direction that this meal had taken. Maybe this was what had been needed all along – someone to show an interest in the child, and to show that interest by not only asking the right questions but by caring enough about her to share some of *their* lives with her. By talking to her as if she were a person and not just an unruly adolescent. Jill took a large bite of her steak. 'Anyway,' she continued, almost cockily, 'at this stage, you usually have to write the script. Then you have to do the mixing, which is a real drag. I hate it.'

'What is it?'

'Well, you have to get a narrator to read what you've written. And then you need music and other sounds for ambiance. You know what ambiance means?' The girl shook her head, stuffing a forkful of salad into her mouth. 'Atmosphere,' Jill explained. 'And then you also have your interviews. They're all on separate tracks. You have a three channel audio mix, and what you do basically is to marry the picture and the sound.' She stopped, watching Laurie eat. 'Kind of a neat phrase,' she said, repeating it in her mind. 'And that's it. Then it's finished.'

'Sounds really exciting,' Laurie said, chewing.

Jill laughed happily. 'No, not exciting, really. Exciting isn't the word,' she said, groping for what the right word would be. 'It has more to do with movement,' she said finally. 'Producers of this kind of format move around a lot. We like to go around with the crew, gathering up all the news and stuff. That's what I like. I feel like for the first time in a very long while, I'm moving again! Does that make any sense?'

Laurie scooped up the last of her gravy with the remainder of her kaiser. 'I think so,' she said, pushing away her empty plate.

'Do you want some dessert?' Jill asked.

'Do they make hot fudge sundaes?'

'Is that what you'd like?' Laurie nodded enthusiastically. Jill signaled for the waiter. 'One hot fudge sundae,' she said, returning her attention to her plate as the waiter removed Laurie's.

'You met my father on one of your shows, didn't you?' Laurie asked suddenly, catching Jill off guard.

'Yes,' Jill answered, quietly.

'And you decided you liked what you saw,' Laurie paused, 'and so you went after it?'

Jill put down her fork, not happy with the sudden shift in the conversation.

'Laurie,' she began cautiously, 'I did not break up your parents' marriage. Your father was unhappy for a long time before I came along—'

'That's not what my mother says. She says everything was fine until you—'

'If everything had been fine,' Jill said, trying to defend herself, 'your father wouldn't have—' She cut herself short. She had been about to say that David wouldn't have looked at her twice. But it wasn't true and she knew it. David always looked twice. More, given the chance. And if it hadn't been for her, he might very well have stayed married to Elaine, continuing on in his already established pattern of affairs and casual couplings. 'You're right. Or at least, you're right enough,' she said. The waiter deposited the giant hot fudge sundae in front of David's daughter and left.

Laurie stared at Jill in genuine surprise. Without speaking, she raised the spoon to her lips and began to eat. She finished off the entire sundae before either one spoke again.

'You liked the ice cream?' Jill asked incredulously.

'It was delicious.'

'I'm glad.' Jill wasn't sure what to say, aware that the youngster was expecting her to continue. 'Laurie, I – when I met your father, I didn't know he was married. I thought he was separated from your mother—'

'Why'd you think that?'

She couldn't say 'because that's what your father told me.' Honesty was one thing. But a fourteen-year-old girl didn't deserve that much truth. 'I don't know. Anyway, it doesn't really matter because I found out quickly anyway—'

'How?'

'He told me. Your father told me. But by then it was too late, I was crazy mad in love with him, and I just couldn't give him up. I tried. We both tried. We didn't want to hurt you or your brother or your mother—'

The waiter retrieved the empty sundae dish and Jill's half-empty dinner plate. 'But you did, didn't you?' the girl asked. 'You hurt all of us.'

'Yes we did,' Jill quietly agreed. 'And I'm sorry.'

Laurie shrugged. 'My mom is going to re-cover the living room furniture,' she said, unaware of the non sequitur.

Jill smiled. 'Why not?' she said, wistfully.

Jill checked her watch. It was almost two o'clock. If she waited any longer for Laurie to come out of the restaurant bathroom, she'd be late getting back to work. She left an oversized tip for the waiter – perhaps he had in some way contributed to the meal's success – and pushed back her chair, striding purposefully past the stand-up bar, exchanging several quick greetings as she made her way toward the ladies' room into which Laurie had disappeared some ten minutes ago.

The smell hit her as soon as she opened the door.

'My God, Laurie, are you all right?' she called, rushing to the open stall where Laurie knelt, her arms curled around the toilet seat, her face deathly pale.

'I guess I ate too much,' she said, holding back the tears.

'It's my fault,' Jill said, kneeling beside her and running her hand gently through the child's hair. She felt that if she applied even the slightest amount of pressure, the girl's head would crack open, come apart. 'I'm always after you about how you don't eat enough.' She went to the sink and pulled a paper towel from its box, soaking it in cold water and taking it back to press against Laurie's forehead.

'I'm sorry, Jill. It was really delicious.'

'Don't talk about it. It's okay.'

She knelt beside the fragile girl and held her against her own body until Laurie felt well enough to stand. Then they slowly left the restaurant and stumbled out into the fresh air. They were immediately surrounded by the definite October chill, and they hugged their coats around them.

'Are you okay for a few minutes alone?' Jill asked her. Laurie nodded. 'I'll be right back. Wait right here.'

Jill promptly disappeared into a book store at the corner and came back several minutes later with a book under her arm. 'For you,' she said.

Laurie looked at the paperback novel. '*Wifey*,' she said aloud.

'Do you have it already?' Jill asked. Laurie shook her head, quickly rifling through the pages. 'I asked the book clerk for the best of Judy Blume. This is what he gave me.'

'Looks great,' Laurie said, still very pale.

'Are you going to be all right in a taxi?' Jill asked.

'Yeah,' Laurie nodded, looking not at all convinced.

'Laurie,' Jill broached, signaling at a passing cab which promptly pulled to the curb beside them. Laurie looked searchingly into Jill's eyes. 'You need help,' Jill said simply. 'You need to see someone who can help you—'

'A psychiatrist?' Laurie asked quietly.

'Yes,' Jill answered. 'Starving yourself for months and then stuffing yourself until you throw up is not healthy behavior and you're smart and sensitive enough to know it. I want to help you, Laurie, but I don't know how, except to tell you that you need more help than I can offer.' The cab driver opened his door and looked at them expectantly. Neither one moved. 'There's a name for your condition, Laurie,' Jill continued. 'And believe me, you're not alone. There are a lot of mixed-up girls out there doing the same thing to themselves as you are. I've been doing some research on it lately—'

'Maybe you'll do a show on it,' Laurie said with a smile.

Jill reached over and hugged the young girl, surprised by the strength with which her hug was reciprocated. 'Maybe,' Jill said. 'Will you think about what I said?'

Laurie nodded and broke from their embrace, getting quickly into the taxi. Jill watched as the car moved into the traffic and

disappeared into the general maze. Then she turned around and
headed toward the studio, a feeling of curious elation spreading
through her. 'I'm moving again,' she said aloud. 'I'm really
moving.'

Chapter Twenty-seven

She was aware of the noise for several minutes before she realized she wasn't still asleep.

'What's that?' David asked groggily from beside her.

Jill opened her eyes, focusing them on the clock. It was 8 a.m. on what she knew instantly was a Saturday morning. The noise had stopped, and for a second Jill contemplated dismissing whatever it had been as a collective dream until it began again: an incoherent Morse code repeating itself in short, staccato gasps.

'It's the buzzer,' Jill said, recognizing the sound only as she began to speak.

'The buzzer? Who the hell—' David started, but Jill was already out of bed and on her way to the kitchen. She returned to the bedroom less than a minute later, going instantly to the closet.

'You better throw something on,' she told her startled husband. 'Elaine is here. She's on her way up. She doesn't sound very happy.'

Jill pulled a long terry-cloth robe over her head and threw David's blue velour bathrobe in his direction.

'Oh, shit,' David muttered. 'What does she want?'

'She didn't say,' Jill told him. 'Maybe she can't get the top off her bottle of orange juice.'

'Very funny,' David said, running an exasperated hand through his tousled hair. He stood up, draping the bathrobe over his naked body. Jill noticed he had an erection, and felt an instant of longing sweep over her. They had made love exactly twice in the last month.

There was a loud banging at the door.

'I think she's here,' Jill said wryly.

David stood still at the side of the bed. He made no effort to move.

'We could pretend we both died,' Jill offered, hoping to produce a smile on David's sullen face. She got none. 'I'll let her in,' Jill said at last. David said nothing.

Jill went quickly to the door, debated asking who it was, decided Elaine's humor would probably be in the same state as the man's they once shared, and decided to open the door without further preamble.

Elaine brushed angrily past her straight into the living room. 'How dare you!' she began, almost instantly, turning abruptly on Jill as Jill followed her into the room.

'Hello, Elaine,' Jill said, calmly. 'Why don't you come inside?'

'Don't get smart with me,' Elaine shot back bitterly. 'How dare you?!' she repeated, fairly seething with rage.

Jill fought with all her strength to keep her own temper under control. There was no point in confronting David with the sight of two hysterical women. Where the hell *was* David anyway? 'Just what am I being accused of?' Jill asked.

'Please stop playing Little Miss Innocent,' Elaine snapped, waving something around in her hand. 'I thought we passed through that stage years ago when you admitted your adultery!'

'Oh, wow!' Jill said, resurrecting an old favorite expression as she sank into one of the large wing chairs. As long as they were traveling that far back, it seemed a most appropriate turn of phrase. Elaine moved without pattern back and forth before her, her right hand flailing out sporadically, waving what Jill now recognized as a paperback book under Jill's nose. 'If you don't mind keeping that thing away from my face,' Jill pointed out, hearing her voice rise.

'You didn't mind rubbing my daughter's nose in it!' Elaine yelled.

'What are you talking about?' Jill demanded.

Elaine hurled the book onto the glass coffee table. It bounced, then landed face up. *Wifey*, it proclaimed innocently. By Judy Blume.

'That's the book I bought for Laurie,' Jill said.

'I know goddamn well what it is! It's a piece of pure filth that even adults shouldn't be reading, let alone a fourteen-year-old girl—'

'What's the matter with you?' Jill asked, reaching over for the book and picking it up. 'Laurie told me that Judy Blume is her favorite author. She writes books for teenagers,' Jill flipped through the opening pages while Elaine turned her attention to David, who had just entered the room.

'What's going on here?' he asked in the quiet voice of

extreme agitation that both women recognized.

'Your current wife,' Elaine began, bringing the same sense of impermanence to the word that Ricki Elfer had once said she loved, 'is filling our daughter's mind with filth.' Each word was spat out with special significance.

'It's all a misunderstanding,' Jill said, standing up and unable to conceal a smile. 'I didn't realize—'

'What are you smiling about?' Elaine demanded.

'I'm sorry,' Jill apologized, 'but I didn't realize— It was a mistake.' She turned to David. 'I thought all Judy Blume books were for kids. This one is obviously not.' Her smile grew wider.

'Why are you smiling?' David asked, accusingly.

Jill's smile immediately disappeared. She turned back to Elaine. 'Forgive me, Elaine,' she said, generously. 'It's my fault, of course, but it was unintentional, believe me.'

'Was it also unintentional when you advised my daughter to see a psychiatrist?!' Elaine retorted, immediately switching tracks when she reached one dead end.

'What?!' David asked, astonished.

Jill's eyes traveled back and forth between the two angry faces.

'What the hell is she talking about, Jill?' David asked impatiently. 'What's this nonsense about Laurie seeing a psychiatrist?'

'I don't think it is nonsense,' Jill said quietly.

David was too surprised to speak.

'So, you admit it!' Elaine shouted.

'Yes, I admit it,' Jill shouted back, startling the other

woman. 'It's time somebody took an interest in what's happening to that girl.'

'How dare you—' Elaine seethed, repeating her opening line.

'Look,' Jill retreated somewhat, 'I don't mean to say that you don't love her or that you don't care what happens to her. That's certainly not the case. But I also care about what happens to her and I think I have the right to speak up when I feel something is terribly wrong.'

'You have no rights where my daughter is concerned,' Elaine announced.

'Just what do you feel is so terribly wrong?' David asked.

Jill spoke directly to her husband. 'David, all you have to do is look at her. She weighs half of what she weighed when I first met her.' She watched David's eyes cloud over, a mixture of boredom and disbelief filling his face.

'Oh come on, Jill, we've been through this. She's a typical teenager, for heaven's sake.'

'A typical anorexic,' Jill said.

'What?' Elaine demanded.

'An anorexic,' Jill repeated, about to explain before Elaine cut her off. 'It's a person, usually a teenage girl, who—'

'I don't want to know what it is! I want you to stop saying it! And to stop filling my daughter's head with filth and a lot of crazy ideas!' Jill listened without trying to interrupt as Elaine became more hysterical. 'What is it you want from my life?!' Elaine continued. 'What more can you take? I gave you my husband! Now you want my child too. Why? Can't you have any of your own? Is that the problem? That you're barren and you can't produce a child of your own so you have to try and grab somebody else's? Maybe if you had your own children you'd understand what being a mother is all about. But as long as Laurie and Jason are *my* children, you are to keep your hands off them and your filth and your crazy ideas away from them. Do you understand me?'

Jill turned to David, feeling numbed from head to toe, Elaine's words having been sprayed from her mouth as if from a can of Novocain, covering Jill's body, leaving her immune to the pain of the attack yet fully cognizant of its presence. I gave you my husband, she heard echoing in her frozen brain, colliding with words like barren and filth, words from the Middle ages, she thought, or maybe just the words of middle age. Help me, David, she thought, recognizing there was no point in trying to talk sense to Elaine. Give me some support. I'm your wife.

'Elaine's right,' he said, instead. 'This really isn't any of your concern. Laurie is *our* child,' he continued, looking over at his ex-wife. 'We'll deal with her.'

His words had the effect of a carefully aimed blow behind the knees. Jill felt herself buckling forward and grabbed hold of one of the wing chairs, allowing her body to sink into it.

'You'll also deal with all her psychiatrist bills,' Elaine said, heading toward the door. 'Laurie's decided she rather likes the idea of a psychiatrist. It'll probably give her some extra prestige at school or something. Anyway, we'll send all the bills over as soon as they start arriving.' She opened the door. 'Goodbye, Jill. Nice talking to you.'

Jill heard the door close and Elaine's footsteps retreating down the hall. She was aware that David was standing not more than two feet away from her. Still, she stared resolutely at the white carpet. She was afraid that if she looked up at her husband, she might want to kill him. It was a feeling she didn't want to know.

'Well, that was smart, wasn't it?' he was saying. 'As if we don't have enough to worry about financially—'

'I'd say our financial problems are the least of our worries,' Jill said, quietly.

'Christ, Jill,' David continued, unmindful or uncaring of the fact that she had spoken. 'A psychiatrist! Don't you think you overreacted a bit?'

'Just what is my status in this family, David?' she asked, barely audible.

'What?' he asked, testily. 'What are you talking about?'

'I'm talking about what happened in this room a few minutes ago, when I was reduced to a non-person.'

'Oh, hell, Jill, make sense.'

Jill raised her eyes to him for the first time since he had taken Elaine's side against hers.

'You don't see what you've done at all,' she marveled.

'What *I've* done?' he asked. 'I'm not the one who gave my daughter a pornographic book and told her to see a psychiatrist.'

'It's hardly a pornographic book. It's maybe mildly risqué, at best, but, at any rate, that was a misunderstanding and I have no intention of apologizing for it again. What's more important here, *all* that's important really, is your attitude.'

'My attitude?'

'Yes.' She stood up, feeling the strength returning to her legs. 'What am I doing here, David?' she asked sincerely. 'I'm your wife. I assumed that meant I was part of a family that also included your two children. It's not what I would have originally chosen for myself but I have always accepted your children because they're part of you, and the three of you belong to the same package. I assumed I'd become part of that package. God knows, I've always been included when it meant picking them up from somewhere, or cooking them dinner or looking after them for a weekend, or spending time with them when you've been busy – working late.' She stopped. 'Now, I find out that my status is no better than a housekeeper's. I can provide for certain of their physical needs but I sure as hell better not interfere in anything important.'

'Jill, you're exaggerating—'

'I am *not* exaggerating! I have just been shot down by an expert marksman while my husband stood by and passed her the ammunition. Elaine said some very vicious things to me, things one doesn't exactly expect to see one's spouse stand still for, and what does my husband say? He says, "Elaine's right." Elaine's right,' she repeated in disbelief. 'I have been thoroughly humiliated and my husband was too busy being inconvenienced to notice.' She paused. 'I guess there's nothing more to say. I've been put in my place in no uncertain terms, and so, now that I know what that place is, I can get on with my life, and start making the master of the house his breakfast.' She turned to leave.

David grabbed her arm. 'Jill, you're acting like a child! No one says you're a servant here!'

'Well, what am I?' Jill shouted, as loud now as Elaine had been earlier. 'I'm not a mother, step or otherwise, as I have been told very clearly this morning. I'm not even a wife anymore.'

'Jill—'

'Am I? Well, am I? We don't make love anymore; we don't talk anymore. Christ, how can we be expected to make love or talk when we don't even see each other anymore.'

'It's that damn TV show,' he began.

'The hell it is!' she countered angrily. 'How dare you try to blame it on that?!' she demanded, suddenly self-conscious about having used Elaine's phrase. 'Do you realize that you haven't once asked me how the show is progressing, if I like what I'm doing.'

'You know how I feel about this show.'

'Yes, I know how *you* feel. What I'm asking is if you have any idea of how *I* feel?'

David said nothing for several minutes. 'I can't fake interest where none exists,' he said, finally. 'I hate the whole idea of this show, Jill. If you want to know the truth, I think you only agreed to do it to get back at me.'

Jill stared hard into David's beautiful green eyes, their lashes fluttering nervously before her. She felt her heart sink, knowing that the moment of truth could be ignored no longer. 'Get back at you for what?' she asked slowly.

The question caught David off guard, the implications of what he had said only now reaching his conscious self. He turned away.

'Is there any point in more lies, David?' she asked, trying to grab at the retreating numbness. The next few minutes seemed to happen in slow motion. Her mind spoke each word before her ears replayed them with the actual voices attached, and then again without the sound.

She watched as David sat down on the sofa, carefully avoiding her eyes. I'm sorry, Jill. I thought it would be all over by now. 'I'm sorry, Jill,' he said with great emotion. 'I thought it would be all over by now.' I'm sorry, Jill. I thought it would be all over by now.

Jill's eyes immediately filled with tears. 'It's not?' she asked, knowing the answer. It's not. It's not. It's not.

'No,' he said, still not looking at her. No. No. No. No. No. No. No. 'God, Jill, I'm so sorry. I feel like such a bastard, but I just don't know what to do. I love you. I don't want to lose you. I'm sure that all it is with Nicki is an infatuation. She's young; she's beautiful. She makes me feel like I'm King of the Mountain—'

'I'm not interested in how she makes you feel!' Jill yelled, hurling herself at her husband and pounding him with both fists. 'Goddamn you, you son-of-a-bitch!'

She struck him one carefully aimed blow across the face before he was able to restrain her hands and force her away from him, his one hand gripping tightly to both her wrists, rendering her powerless, while her tears took away her voice and reduced her to a frenzied helplessness. She felt her nose beginning to run, tried to extricate one hand from David's grasp but was unable to, feeling him suddenly surrounding her body with his own, trying to comfort her, to quiet her. To stop her.

'Jill, Jill,' he whispered against her ear. 'Please don't cry.'

Slowly, he released her hands, leaning over her and burying

his head against her breasts. She lifted her arms to strike out at his back, to pummel his flesh. Instead, her hands moved like those of a drowning woman to grasp at a life preserver just tossed out, gripping it tightly, pulling it close against her. In a minute, he had pushed up her terry-cloth robe and discarded his own, and soon they were making the kind of urgent love that only comes from desperation, where tears replace sweat, and guilt and fear take the place of genuine passion. Both recognized it for what it was. Neither had any illusions when it was over.

'What now?' she asked, as he was pulling back on his robe. 'What happens now?'

'I don't know,' he said truthfully.

'What do you want to happen?' she pressed. 'Do you know that much?'

'I'd like things to go back to the way they were before,' he said quietly, after a pause.

'Before?'

'Before all this mess started,' he began. 'Before Beth murdered Al. Before you took on that stupid job—'

Jill couldn't believe her ears. 'Before Beth murdered Al! Before I went back to TV! David, listen to yourself. You have just absolved yourself of any and all responsibility in this matter. What about Nicole? What about the part that each of you played in all this?'

'I'm not saying I'm not responsible. I'm just trying to explain the extenuating circumstances, what made me particularly susceptible to Nicole at this point in my life—'

'Damn it, there are always going to be extenuating circumstances! You talk about wanting to go back to the way things were before. When Al was alive, when I was still teaching. May I remind you that your whole infatuation with Nicole started when things were exactly the way they were before! When the interesting career woman you married became the boring little wife at home—'

'No one said you were boring!'

'I bored myself half to death. How could I not bore you?!'

He began pacing. 'I'm sorry, Jill. I can't help but feel that it's only since you started talking about this whole television thing that our troubles started.'

Jill closed her eyes. 'I can't even talk about it now,' she said, as if from another room.

'I didn't say that. You know that's not what I meant.'

'Yes, I know,' she acknowledged. 'But you *are* saying that you want me to give it up.'

David stopped. 'I don't know,' he said. 'I don't know anymore what I'm saying. I don't mind your working in television. You know I don't. It's just this show about Beth Weatherby—'

'The show is not about Beth Weatherby,' she reminded him, 'but that's kind of beside the point, isn't it?'

'The point being—'

'The point being that my working in television doesn't bother you as long as you control my hours, my location, and now my content. That's the bottom line, isn't it, David? I stay in Chicago, work from nine to five and be careful to keep away from issues you find offensive or inconvenient—'

'Jill—'

'All right.' Jill stared wordlessly at David for several seconds before speaking. 'Okay. You win. I'll do it, I'll give it up. Now what? I've just agreed to the first of your demands. What else?'

'Else?' he asked, puzzled by the sudden turn of events.

'Well, I think we should know exactly where we stand, don't you? Children – what about children?'

Jill watched David's head sink. 'Jill, please, you know the answer to that. You know how I feel—'

'Fine, then. Okay, no children. Settled.' She stopped, biting off her next word and spitting it into the air between them. 'Nicole.'

Silence. 'What is it that you want me to say, Jill?'

'What do you think I want you to say?'

'That I'll stop seeing her,' he answered, after a pause.

'Bull's-eye.' She waited.

'I can't,' he said, finally.

Jill felt her feet burying into the thick, white carpeting the same way they had sunk into the grass at last summer's annual Weatherby, Ross picnic, holding her a prisoner then as they did now. 'You can't,' she repeated, numbly. Her eyes shot him a look of real fury. 'You expect me to give up goddamn everything – my career, a family of my own, even my husband whenever he feels the overwhelming urge of extenuating circumstances, and while I'm at it, you also expect me to keep my mouth shut about your children although I'm still expected to help take care of them, and put up with your ex-wife and all her cockamamy demands and insults and keep paying the rent on this apartment, while you divide your time and money between your ex-wife and your current mistress. Of course she thinks you're King of the Mountain! Does she realize that the mountain is made up of a stack of unpaid bills?!'

'I don't think this is getting us anywhere,' he said with infuriating calm.

'Oh, you don't?' Jill questioned. 'Well, that's just too damn bad. Because I do! I think it's helping to put this relationship into its proper perspective.' She thought over the past five minutes. 'I have just accepted all your terms. I am willing to live with your hours, your debts, your children, even your ex-wife. I am willing to live without my chosen profession or children of my own. I'm willing to do whatever you want, to be whatever you want, to turn myself inside out if necessary to keep you. I'm asking you, in return, to give up only one thing. Nicole Clark. And you're telling me you can't do it!' She shook her head in disbelief.

'I can't lie to you, Jill,' he said sadly. 'Would you rather I lied?'

'Why not?' she snapped. 'Why can't you lie all of a sudden? You've done it often enough before!' She started to cry. 'Why the sudden pangs of conscience now?' she sobbed, desperately.

'I'm so sorry,' he said, reaching for her, only to be brushed aside. 'I wish I could say the things you want to hear. I wish I could tell you that she doesn't mean anything to me, that I can just walk out of her life. But I can't. All I know is that despite the fact that I love you, and I do love you, Jill, I just can't let Nicki go. Not yet.'

'How long?' she asked.

'What do you mean?'

Jill choked back her tears. 'Not yet implies a future. A time when you will be able to let her go. How much time?'

He shook his head. 'I don't know,' he said.

'You expect me to sit here and wait for you?' she asked, feeling as she imagined Sybil Burton must have felt when confronting Richard with the years of casual infidelities.

The truthfulness of his answer surprised her. 'It's what I'd like,' he said. 'I know I have no right to expect it.'

'You're damn right, you don't!' she shouted, suddenly furious again at his complacency. 'I could really fix you, you know,' she continued, surprising herself possibly even more than her husband. 'I could take you for everything Elaine hasn't, which I'll admit isn't a hell of a lot, but it would sure teach little Nicole a thing or two about reality!' She stopped, amazed by the force of her own bitterness.

There was a long silence. Neither party moved.

'You have to do whatever you think is right,' David whispered, at last. 'It's your life. You have to live it the way you see fit. If you want a divorce, then that's what you'll get. If you want to take me for everything I've got, well, you'll do that too. I won't stop you. I'll give you whatever you want.'

'I want you,' she said, her voice cracking.

'No,' he said, his voice resonantly clear, 'the woman I just listened to wants a lot of things, but I'm not one of them.' He started to leave the room.

'Oh no, David, please,' she begged, running after him. 'I didn't mean it about taking you for everything. You know I'd never do that. Please, David, I'm sorry.' He retreated into the bathroom and closed the door behind him. Jill sank to her knees on the other side, her tears falling like drops of wet paint down the length of the door. 'I'm sorry,' she repeated over and over again as she heard the shower beginning to run. 'I'm so sorry.'

Chapter Twenty-eight

'Brother, it's cold out there!' Irving's voice bellowed as he came inside the small screening room and took off his coat. 'How's everybody?'

The room, which Jill noticed had become quiet with expectation, was suddenly full of noise again. All the old, familiar grumbles about Chicago in November were brought forth and given new life. Jill listened for a few minutes while Irving explained to the dozen people present that the client had been delayed and so the screening would be held off until the sponsors could arrive. 'Can you imagine, it's actually starting to snow out there,' she heard him utter in disbelief before she allowed her eyes to drift back toward the giant, empty screen.

She heard the door opening and closing several times behind her, knew more people had arrived, and was aware that soon every seat would be filled with not just people like herself, the drones, but by the Queen Bees themselves, the people from the network, the sponsor's representatives – the people who would be deciding whether 'Hour Chicago' would be allowed more than its initial sixty-minute run.

I should be nervous, she thought. Happy. Scared. Angry.

Confused. Something. But she felt nothing, in the same way that she was only slightly more aware of the outdoor cold than she was of the indoor heat, only marginally more aware of sound than she was of stillness, of day as opposed to night. For the past three or four weeks, she had walked through her life as if she were occupying someone else's body, a body that, like the now extinct leaves of autumn, had been drained of all its former color, shriveled up against itself, a brittle shadow of its former vibrancy, waiting only for the wheels of traffic to crush it into obscurity or for the winds to scatter its dried-up pieces into oblivion. The dried-up pieces of her soul, she thought eerily.

'So, what did you think of that?' he was asking her.

'What?' Jill asked, looking behind her to Irving, who was leaning up against the back of her comfortable chair. 'I'm sorry, were you talking to me?' she asked.

'I said,' he repeated, 'November hit Chicago with the force of a hard snowball against a car window. What do you think?'

'What do I think about what?' Jill asked, aware she was smiling, aware that it had been a long time since she had smiled.

'I made that up as I was walking over here, about November hitting like a snowball. I thought it was rather poetic.' Jill's smile widened. 'You all right?' he asked.

'Sure,' she answered.

'They giving you trouble at school?'

Jill shook her head. 'No. I explained that this screening was important. That I had to be here.'

'What's it like to be back there?' he asked.

'All right,' she said, without inflection.

He patted her shoulder. 'Well, don't let it get too all right. I have a feeling the powers-that-be are going to like what they see today and that you can dump those hallowed halls for good and get back to the world where sex and violence still have a good name. What's the matter, Jill?' he continued, without missing a beat.

'Nothing,' she said. 'Just tired, I guess.'

'Well,' he said, patting her shoulder again, 'tell that good-looking husband of yours to let you get some sleep.'

Jill turned back toward the empty screen and saw it filled with David's face. He occupied it easily and well, the warmth of his eyes and his smile only magnified by the increased size of her imaginary projection. Suddenly, Jill knew that no matter what changes time wrought, physical or otherwise, to their lives, that he would always have this effect on her, that just looking at him would make her feel weak-kneed and awkward, the nervous wallflower opening her front door to greet her blind date and coming face to face with the campus hero.

The image of her husband was like a magnet drawing her closer toward him. She wanted to run to it, throw herself into it, disappear inside it, yet she knew now that the slightest pressure would force the image to crack and break. That she would collapse empty-handed and bruised on the other side, that behind the screen – the face? – there was nothing.

The sudden intrusion of rational thought caught Jill off guard. In the past month, she had managed to keep all semblance of reality a good arm's length away. It was as if everything had stopped. Like the princess on her fifteenth birthday who pricks her finger on a spindle and becomes the Sleeping Beauty, Jill had simply waved her magic wand and suspended all time and emotion, choosing the blind path of the somnambulist, waiting for the kiss of the handsome prince to wake her up. Between pricking her finger and kissing the prince, there was nothing. The Prick and the Prince, Jill thought suddenly, surprised to find herself laughing.

She pretended to be stifling a cough, taking a surreptitious look around the room and seeing all but four of the seats now filled. The room was starting to feel stuffy, especially now that cigarettes were appearing with greater frequency than before. Years ago, when she and David had first married, he would complain that the stale odor of cigarettes clung to her clothes and hair for days after these smoke-filled meetings. Now, she doubted he would notice at all.

He was rarely home these days, his time divided between herself and Nicole, and when he chose to sleep at Jill's side it was only when he was overwhelmed with fatigue. There was no passion. Even desperation had slipped away into something more abstract. She was like a buoy in the water, conveniently marking off a familiar spot. What was it he had said? I can't fake interest where none exists? Jill closed her eyes, forcing her mind to go as blank as the screen. It was all her fault, she thought, sinking down into her seat, and laying her head back. She had forced the issue, forced everything. Now she had to wait in limbo like the sleeping princess to see if David could cut his way back through the thorns to find her.

A phone rang from somewhere beside her. She opened her eyes to see Irving picking up the red receiver and saw his lips moving, although she deliberately avoided hearing any sounds and only snapped fully to attention when she realized the room was emptying of people.

'Come on,' he was saying, leaning over her, 'I'll buy you some dinner.'

'What happened?' she asked.

'Damn winter,' Irving answered, grabbing his coat. 'People forget how to drive as soon as they see a flake of snow. The client's been in some kind of a minor highway mishap. He's all right. But he won't be here till seven o'clock.'

Jill grabbed her coat and allowed Irving to usher her into the hallway and then into the cold outside air.

'How's that stepkid of yours doing?' he asked as they crossed the road, heading toward Maloney's.

'Laurie?' Jill asked, stopping at the door of the restaurant, feeling the wind slapping against her face, as if it had been told that she was suffering from a drug overdose and needed to be revived. 'She's doing fine,' Jill told him. 'She still weighs as much as a green bean but she's seeing a doctor twice a week – her mother is actually going with her – and I think she'll be all right. I really do.'

'Sounds like it might make for an interesting show,' Irving said slyly.

Jill laughed. 'Laurie said the same thing,' she said, recalling Laurie in almost the same spot approximately a month ago, thinking simultaneously of the girl's father and how he would undoubtedly react to this fresh idea. 'Listen,' Jill said suddenly, 'would you mind if I begged off supper? I just feel like walking for a while.'

'Walking? It'll get dark pretty soon, and it's freezing out!'

'It's not that cold,' she protested good-naturedly. 'And I'll stick to the main streets.'

'As long as I don't have to walk with you,' he said. Jill moved to the restaurant door and held it open for him. 'See you at seven,' Irving added, disappearing into the inner warmth. 'Be careful.'

Jill stood for several seconds alone in the cold air. It *was* cold, she realized as she started to walk. Why had she been so oblivious to it before?

She crossed back across the street, not at all sure where she wanted to go. She felt the wind pushing against her cheeks, and moved her collar up to hug against her neck. She faced directly into the bitter onslaught of cold air, feeling her eyes sting and her nose automatically beginning to run. Naturally, she thought, wiping at her nose with the back of her gloved hand. Keep walking, she told herself, her hands now thrust deep inside her pockets. Keep moving.

What was she doing at this screening anyway? She had told David she would quit television. No, that wasn't entirely correct. She had agreed not to go back only if he agreed to give up Nicole. He had not agreed. She was still in limbo. Therefore, she was at the screening.

And if the clients, the sponsors, the people from the network liked the show? What then? If she was offered a regular position? What would her answer be – I can't tell you, I have to wait until my husband makes up his mind about his mistress?

And if he did make up his mind, if he walked in the front door that evening and announced that he had chosen her over

Nicole, over all the fairest maidens in the land, what then? What would her answer be? God, could she really give everything up? Could she remain buried up to her neck in frustrations and recriminations, knowing the branch that could have saved her had been within her grasp, only to have been tossed carelessly aside? Could she really allow herself to be shut up in some ivory tower for one hundred years because she had allowed herself to be kissed by a Prince?

She turned onto shop-lined State Street and continued.

'Hour Chicago' was good. She knew it was good. Her segment was probably the best thing she had ever done. She had torn the issue of battered women who kill their husbands inside out and upside down, and while ultimately she was providing no easy answers, she would certainly be filling the airwaves with disturbing and thought-provoking questions. 'This program is about fear,' she heard her narrator's voice intone. 'The fears of thousands of abused wives and the men who abuse them, who now see their women fighting back with often lethal results. And about the fears of many who feel that this latest trend will give new meaning to the old phrase that women get away with murder.'

Jill drew a deep breath of satisfaction and felt something falling wet against her cheeks. Opening her eyes directly into the cold of the clear sky, she saw bits of snow falling. On a sudden childlike impulse, she opened her mouth and caught several snowflakes on her tongue, feeling them disappear instantly. She was looking forward to winter, she realized with no small amount of surprise, since it had always been her least favorite season. Maybe this winter she'd buy herself a pair of skates, a thought that alarmed her, as her only two previous excursions on skates (the last time twenty years ago) had resulted in two broken wrists. ('Someone should have told you not to skate on your hands,' she remembered Beth Weatherby once telling her.)

She headed north on Michigan, thinking of Beth. She'd been so preoccupied of late, she'd neglected her good friend. Spotting a phone booth across the street, she ran, without looking, to the other side, aware of cars honking angrily behind her. She chose not to look back, preferring not to see how narrowly she might have missed death, knowing that in recent weeks she'd become almost purposely careless, as if she were leaving this aspect of her life (with all other aspects) to the will of others. She rummaged in her purse for the necessary change, fought with her memory for Beth's telephone number, and dialed. Beth's voice answered after two rings.

'Beth, how are you?'

'Jill?'

Jill nodded, then realized Beth couldn't hear a nod. 'Yes,' she answered, possibly too loudly. 'I'm so sorry I haven't called lately. I've just had so much on my mind.'

'I know,' Beth said, tangibly warm. 'How's the show going?'

'Good. Really good. There's a screening in about an hour for the people at the network, possible sponsors. My segment is the last of the three, right after welfare fraud and the Second City troupe.'

Beth laughed. 'You're pleased?'

'Yes,' Jill said. 'Your name is never mentioned. You're

alluded to only as a "recent event,"' she explained with invisible quotes.

'How quickly we become recent events,' Beth remarked with a smile. 'I'm sure that makes David rest easier,' she added.

Jill said nothing. Beth said nothing further.

'How are you holding up?' Jill asked her.

'Well, I've held up this long. I don't intend to fall apart just as I'm entering the home stretch.'

'Have the courts set a definite date?'

'Three weeks this Thursday,' Beth announced, audibly exhaling.

'Are you nervous?'

'No,' Beth answered. 'Well, maybe a little. My lawyer's the one who's a nervous wreck. He's still trying to persuade me to change my plea. I'm still clinging to my right to self-defense. Actually, I've become quite a cause célèbre in the women's movement. All sorts of money has been coming in, offers of support, letters from prominent people.' She paused. 'And Michael's come home.'

'Oh?'

'I'm not sure if he's here to stay,' Beth added quickly. 'He's still wearing his robes and there are a lot of funny-looking people hanging around outside, but – I was right, Jill. He did see something. Apparently, several times over the last few years, he'd seen Al attacking me. Of course, with my hands bound and my mouth gagged, he assumed it was some sort of kinky sex thing and was too embarrassed and ashamed to say anything about it. My mother the pervert, that sort of thing.' She laughed nervously. 'Poor baby, no wonder he prefers his chanting.' She paused. 'He's going to testify for me in court. The prosecution will undoubtedly claim I was a consenting adult, out for a little fun and games. Anyway, be prepared, I'm liable to be a hot topic of conversation for some time.'

'Does that upset you?'

'No,' Beth answered simply. 'There's nothing anybody can say about me now that can hurt me. The worst time I had since all this started was that week I was trying to come to terms with myself and with what I'd done, with what I had to do, what I had to say, knowing how many people the truth would hurt, knowing I wouldn't be believed, that I might have to spend the rest of my life in prison. But it's funny,' she continued, 'once you finally do make up your mind, the rest is relatively easy. When you finally make the decisions, and just get on with your life, well – you just get on with it.' She paused dramatically. 'It's when you don't know what to do that the panic sets in. The minute you make those decisions, it stops.'

'It's that easy?' Jill asked, knowing Beth had intended the words for her.

'No,' Beth laughed. 'But it sounds good.'

Jill joined in the laughter. 'I better go,' she smiled.

'Call me later.'

'I will. Bye-bye.' Jill replaced the receiver and headed toward the elegant shops of the 'Magnificent Mile,' glancing into the windows, crossing and re-crossing the street, continuing this random pattern for some while, aware of time's passage only by the increased presence of snow on her red coat and by the growing darkness around her. The sound of traffic seemed to be following her, and the farther she traveled the more impatient the drivers became, pushing against their horns, gunning their engines uselessly against the encroaching night. She håd gone another two blocks before she realized that the persistent honking she was hearing was intended for her. She turned toward the shiny beige and brown Seville, failing at first to recognize either the car or its driver.

'It's me, you fitness freak,' the driver yelled, lowering the tinted glass window as Jill approached and squinted inside. 'I've been following you for blocks. Where the hell are you going? Don't you know it's dangerous out here at night?'

Jill recognized the voice of Ricki Elfer before she was able to make out the face. She smiled widely. 'What are you doing downtown?'

'Put it this way,' Ricki told her. 'When I'm not at Rita Carrington's, I'm out exercising my wallet. Do you have time for a coffee?'

'What time is it?' Jill asked.

'Ten to seven,' Ricki answered.

'Oh my God, no,' Jill said. 'I have to be at the studio at seven o'clock! I didn't realize I'd been walking for so long.'

'Well, hop in, I'll give you a lift,' Ricki offered.

'Great,' Jill agreed, coming around to the other side of the car and giving Ricki directions, then briefly describing the show she was working on.

'Oh,' Ricki smiled knowledgeably, 'like that lawyer who got himself killed.' Jill nodded silently. 'How's your friend holding up?' Ricki asked, catching Jill by surprise.

Jill felt a slow grin spreading across her face. 'She's fine,' Jill said quietly.

'Wish her luck,' Ricki offered.

'I will,' Jill answered, looking around. 'This is some car,' she exclaimed, changing the subject.

'Like it?'

'Paul gave it to me.'

'Wow! Birthday? Anniversary?'

'Guilt,' answered Ricki with a smile. 'I'd been complaining a lot lately. The usual wifely complaints. Finally, Paul got fed up and he said in that special tone they all get, you know the tone, "What do you *want*?" And I said, "I want you to be more affectionate, I want you to be more loving, I want you to spend more time with me." And he said, "Couldn't I just buy you something?"' She laughed, indicating the car's plush interior with her hands. 'How can you not love a guy like that?'

The car pulled to a halt in front of the studio. 'That didn't take long,' Jill commented, opening the car door. 'Thanks a lot, Ricki.'

'Listen,' Ricki said, leaning over, 'maybe you and your husband could come for dinner one night soon. Or the four of us could take in a movie some time—'

'Sounds good,' Jill lied, slamming the door. 'I'll see you at class soon.'

Ricki honked her horn several times as she drove off. Jill watched until the new Seville disappeared from sight, and then she turned toward the building and went inside.

'This programme is about fear,' she heard the narrator begin, watching the photographs of bruised and beaten women fall one on top of the other like lifeless corpses. After that, the soundtrack became blurred, the images unfocused, and Jill wondered for a fleeting instant if something had gone wrong in the editing process, if another sound track had been improperly substituted for the correct one. She hadn't interviewed Beth Weatherby; she hadn't questioned her mother or Ricki Elfer or Elaine. Or Laurie. And yet here were all these women up there on the large screen, exchanging profiles, their lips moving in unison, their voices superimposed on top of one another, blending into each other, speaking as if from one voice, speaking as if one. So what if he's good in bed, the voice asked, as all around her heads nodded eagerly. Lots of men are good in bed. One couple's perfect marriage is something no one else would want. There are certain things in life that we just have to accept. Sarah Welles had drowned in her bathroom sink. Life is too short. The faces, blown up and expansive, registered shock, amusement and concern at the various remarks, moving easily from one emotion to the next. They separated, argued, came together again, agreed. Suddenly, a shadowy figure approached, his image growing until he all but overwhelmed everything around him. You're going to ask me why I didn't leave him, the women began as Jill felt her eyes drawn to the new presence. You have to remember that for a long time, I blamed myself. (I'm sorry, David, Jill heard herself plead under the other voices.) I kept thinking that it was my fault. (I didn't mean to say those things, David. Please, I'm so sorry.) Your pride goes first – then your common sense. (I'm so sorry, David. Please forgive me.) Soon, even your soul is dead. He killed my soul.

(Jill saw the torn pieces of her soul floating, like leaves, up past David's head.) What is there to forgive? the voices asked angrily. 'What the hell am I so sorry about?!' Jill demanded of herself.

Immediately, everyone disappeared, leaving a screen filled only with the powerful photographs of a more powerful hate. My God, what we do to one another, Jill thought, realizing that she was as bruised as any of the photographs. It was just that her bruises didn't show.

What do I want? she asked herself in silent annoyance. What is it that I want? She fidgeted in her seat, crossing one leg over the other and then returning it to the way it was before. I know what I *don't* want, she realized abruptly, sitting up very straight in her chair.

I don't want to be like Elaine, consumed by bitterness and an overriding need for revenge. I don't want to end up like Beth, driven beyond all endurance, forced ultimately to kill in order to survive. I do not want to destroy what good there *was* in my marriage, and thereby destroy both my husband and myself. I never want to hate my husband – or myself – as much as either of these women. I still believe in marriage, despite everything that's happened, but I can no longer just sit by and be a passive observer of my own life. I know what I want. I want to stop feeling guilty and unsure. I want my pride back. I want my soul.

Jill watched in silent confirmation as the episode ran to its conclusion, saw her name flash as the credits rolled quickly by, failing to note whether they had read Jill Listerwoll or Jill Plumley, discovering she didn't really care. She accepted the congratulations of the people around her, recognized in the noncommittal smiles of the prospective sponsors that it would be several weeks before the final verdict was in, and realized that that was all right too. Everything in its own good time. She hugged Irving warmly and left the studio.

Nicole Clark lived in a relatively modern apartment in a nondescript part of the city. It took Jill only ten minutes to drive there and half that time to find a place to park. Then she pulled the two suitcases she had spent several hours packing from out of the back seat and carried them to Nicole's apartment. It was late. There was no doorman, only an elaborate buzzer system which Jill was in the process of deciphering when an elderly couple returned home and held the door open for her. She picked up the luggage and stumbled through the doorway. Apartment 815, she repeated to herself as they rode up together in the elevator, watching as the old couple departed at the fourth floor. The doors closed after them, taking her up to the eighth floor in silence before depositing her at her destination.

She promptly turned right, realizing after following several of the numbers on the apartment doors that she should have turned the other way, and doubled back. The suitcases were starting to feel heavy, as if for the first time she was conscious of their weight. She released them, letting them fall gently to the floor, feeling a sudden twinge of panic. 'It's when you don't know what to do,' she heard Beth's voice repeat, 'that the panic sets in. The minute you make those decisions, it stops.' It wasn't that easy, she knew, projecting ahead to later that evening when she would re-enter an empty apartment and know for certain that David would not be coming back – but it wasn't any easier now.

She grabbed the suitcases and proceeded with renewed determination to Apartment 815, stopping when she saw the appropriate number, lowering the bags once more, wondering what she was going to say to whomever opened the door. Perhaps she wouldn't have to say anything. The sight of the luggage would undoubtedly speak for itself.

She could try humor, she thought, feeling strangely lightheaded. Hi, everyone. Since all the fun seems to be happening over at your place, I've decided to move in.

What if David had already left to return home? Suppose he'd just broken it off with Nicole and he and Jill had crossed, unknown to each other, in traffic. Strangers in the night, she said to herself.

The door opened.

Nicole Clark stood in the doorway draped in a white velour bathrobe, her skin dotted with moisture, a towel wrapped around her neck. A Siamese cat hovered shyly around her legs. 'David's in the shower,' she said, after a pause, disengaging the cat with one foot and pushing it back inside.

Jill felt her throat constrict, her nose begin to twitch. ('Hi, I'm Nicole Clark. I'm going to marry your husband.') 'These are most of David's clothes,' she said softly forcing back the itch. 'He can come by for the rest of his things tomorrow. I'll be out all day. My lawyer will get in touch with him in a day or two,' she continued, wondering who the hell her lawyer was. 'I'd rather David didn't try to call me personally.'

The two women exchanged long, probing glances.

She even looks good with no makeup on, Jill thought, allowing her glance to drop down to the other woman's bare legs. The cat had returned and was licking greedily at Nicole's damp feet. The second toe of each foot is longer than her big toe and she has a rather large corn just below one nail, Jill realized, joyously. She has ugly feet! She looked back up into Nicole's puzzled face and smiled, noticing for the first time a slight blemish just beneath the younger woman's lower lip. Perhaps it had been there all along. Or maybe it had merely been biding its time, waiting for just the right moment to pop up and announce its host's mortality.

'I don't understand,' Nicole stammered. 'You're giving up?' She paused, mentally moving the suitcases inside her apartment. 'I win?'

Jill straightened her shoulders, feeling her throat return to normal. The constriction was gone, as was any urge to sneeze. 'I guess that depends on just what you think you've won,' she answered and, knowing Nicole's eyes were watching her, turned and strode quickly back toward the elevators, confident for the first time in many months that she was not about to trip and fall.

More Enthralling Fiction from Headline Feature

═══ Joy Fielding ═══

SEE JANE RUN

THE TERRIFYING PSYCHOLOGICAL THRILLER

'*One afternoon in late spring, Jane Whittaker went to the shops and forgot who she was. She couldn't remember her own name. She couldn't remember whether she was married or single, widowed or divorced, childless or the mother of twins . . . What in God's name was happening?*'

Jane's nightmare is only just beginning. When a handsome, distinguished man, calling himself her husband, comes to claim her, she is taken to a beautiful home she doesn't recognise, kept away from the family and friends she can't remember. And despite Michael's tender concern, she feels a growing sense of unease.

Jane is in a race against time to recapture her identity before it is too late. To do that she must first remember whatever terrible thing made her lose her memory in the first place.

'Finely tuned and convincing . . . suspense is maintained at a high level . . . sharply drawn, articulate characters' *Publishers Weekly*

'Compulsive reading' *Company*

FICTION / GENERAL 0 7472 3753 0

TELL ME NO SECRETS

THE TERRIFYING PSYCHOLOGICAL THRILLER

JOY FIELDING

*'People who annoy me have a way of . . .
disappearing'*

Jess Koster thinks she has conquered the crippling panic
attacks that have plagued her since the unexplained
disappearance of her mother, eight years ago. But they
are back with a vengeance. And not without reason.
Being a chief prosecutor in the State's Attorney's office
exposes Jess to some decidedly lowlife types. Like Rick
Ferguson, about to be tried for rape – until his victim
goes missing. Another inexplicable disappearance.

If only Jess didn't feel so alone. Her father is about to re-
marry; her sister is busy being the perfect wife and
mother; her ex-husband has a new girlfriend. And
besides, he's Rick Ferguson's defence lawyer . . .

Battling with a legal system that all too often judges
women by appalling double standards; living under the
constant threat of physical danger; fighting to overcome
the emotional legacy of her mother's disappearance, Jess
is in danger of going under. And it looks as though
someone is determined that she should disappear, too . . .

'Joy Fielding tightens suspense like a noose round your
neck and keeps one shattering surprise for the very last
page. Whew!' *Annabel*

'The story she has to tell this time is a corker that runs
rings round Mary Higgins Clark. Don't even think of
starting this anywhere near bedtime' *Kirkus Reviews*

FICTION / GENERAL 0 7472 4163 5

Now you can buy any of these other bestselling Headline books from your bookshop or *direct from the publisher.*

FREE P&P AND UK DELIVERY
(Overseas and Ireland £3.50 per book)

Backpack	Emily Barr	£5.99
Icebox	Mark Bastable	£5.99
Killing Helen	Sarah Challis	£6.99
Broken	Martina Cole	£6.99
Redemption Blues	Tim Griggs	£5.99
Relative Strangers	Val Hopkirk	£5.99
Homegrown	Gareth Joseph	£5.99
Everything is not Enough	Bernardine Kennedy	£5.99
High on a Cliff	Colin Shindler	£5.99
Winning Through	Marcia Willett	£5.99

TO ORDER SIMPLY CALL THIS NUMBER

01235 400 414

or e-mail <u>orders@bookpoint.co.uk</u>

Prices and availability subject to change without notice.

ty to go
down to that asteroid, and let's look around
for our missing colonist," Kirk ordered.

"Transporting is going to be a wee bit tricky, sir," said Scott. "With conditions in this nebula, I highly recommend taking a shuttlecraft."

"Agreed, Mister Scott. In the meantime that ship, whatever its captain's motives are, can't be allowed to go anywhere. We'll have to see to that with tractor beams if we need to. If those won't work, we'll use phasers only as a last resort, as that would surely give away our position."

"Aye, sir, I'll direct all auxiliary energy to the tractor beams," said Scott. "I believe we can hold that ship, if it comes to it."

"We'll also need to sweep the surrounding area for more vessels. I don't want to get a nasty surprise that—"

A loud blast from the ship's intraship. It was the alarm that announced a ship-wide red alert!

Kirk thumbed an intraship set in the center of the conference room table. "Mister Sulu, report!"

"Captain, we have been detected and are under attack. Four pirate vessels approaching. Their weapons are hot, sir, and they are deploying torpedoes."

"Shields to maximum," Kirk immediately responded. "On our way." Kirk paused a moment, considering. "Sulu, whatever you do, do *not*, I repeat, do *not* destroy those ships!"

STAR TREK®

THE ORIGINAL SERIES

SAVAGE TRADE

Tony Daniel

Based upon *Star Trek*
created by Gene Roddenberry

POCKET BOOKS

New York   London   Toronto   Sydney   New Delhi

Pocket Books
A Division of Simon & Schuster, Inc.
1230 Avenue of the Americas
New York, NY 10020

This book is a work of fiction. Any references to historical events, real people, or real places are used fictitiously. Other names, characters, places, and events are products of the author's imagination, and any resemblance to actual events or places or persons, living or dead, is entirely coincidental.

First Pocket Books paperback edition March 2015

POCKET and colophon are registered trademarks of Simon & Schuster, Inc.

For information about special discounts for bulk purchases, please contact Simon & Schuster Special Sales at 1-866-506-1949 or business@simonandschuster.com.

The Simon & Schuster Speakers Bureau can bring authors to your live event. For more information or to book an event, contact the Simon & Schuster Speakers Bureau at 1-866-248-3049 or visit our website at www.simonspeakers.com.

Manufactured in the United States of America

10 9 8 7 6 5 4 3 2 1

ISBN 978-1-4767-6550-1
ISBN 978-1-4767-6554-9 (ebook)

For Edith Hoffman

One

Captain's Log, Stardate 6097.2. The Enterprise has reached the extreme edge of the Alpha Quadrant in a region known as the Vara Nebula sector. We are traveling to Federation science outpost Zeta Gibraltar, which is located near the main nebular dust clouds. The outpost is not answering hailing messages, and there has been no word for over a standard week. Our mission: to investigate why Zeta Gibraltar has gone dark.

Captain James T. Kirk swiveled in his captain's command chair toward Mister Spock, who was peering into his science station scope at a display of data coming in from a remote scan of the planetoid below.

"Anything, Mister Spock?"

"No signs of life, Captain, and no signs of human biology living or dead," Spock replied. "The complex's computer system and life support are still functioning normally. I'm conducting thermal regression analysis in an attempt to determine how long ago the staff was present in the main laboratory complex. I will have results momentarily."

"Will your regression provide answers as far back as the moment communication was lost with the outpost?"

"It should, sir."

"Very good." Kirk frowned. "Seven days without a word at an outpost that usually sends in a daily report," he said. He turned to Lieutenant Uhura, the communications officer on the bridge. "Any response to our hails, Lieutenant?"

Uhura cupped her hand to her earpiece and shook her head. She wore a worried expression. "No response to multiple hails, sir. No emergency signals or beacons. It's as if they've disappeared without a trace, Captain."

"We'll see about that," Kirk replied, a grim set to his jaw.

The science staff has to be somewhere, he thought. *The* Enterprise *will find them.*

Kirk glanced around the bridge, feeling pride both in the efficient manner in which everyone went about his or her job and also in the brilliance and creativity of his officers. The captain knew he was inordinately proud of his crew, but they had accomplished much together. He felt lucky to command them and responsible to make use of their skills in the best way possible. They were the best of the best, and Kirk was keenly aware that they expected no less than full engagement from him.

Besides, the *Enterprise* had a reputation to keep up as one of the best ships in Starfleet.

We will find those scientists, all right, Kirk thought. *But whether they'll be living or dead when we do—that's another matter.*

"Captain, I am picking up heat signatures in my thermal regression analysis. Small differentials in surface temperatures within the station."

"Analysis?"

"Something occurred approximately six point four days ago. These heat differentials may indicate use of energy weapons, sir. They point to disruptor technology."

"There was a firefight? This is a science outpost."

"That is how the current data correlates, Captain."

"We're going to have to find out in person," Kirk said, rising from his command chair. "Spock, you're with me. Lieutenant Uhura, have a full security team meet us in the transporter room."

"Aye, sir," Uhura said. She touched a signal pad. "They're on their way."

"Good. You're with us, as well. I'll want you to examine the outpost communications records. Chekov, you'll assist Mister Spock with his scans. Mister Sulu, you have the bridge."

Kirk turned toward the portal to the bridge

turbolift. The familiar tingle of anticipation was under his skin—the feeling he got whenever he led a landing party. This mission may turn out to be a routine sensor sweep, or it could develop into a situation that pushed him to the limits of his abilities. His rational side may hope for the former, but there was a part of him that always craved a challenge and action. Even danger.

Kirk knew that he suppressed the part of his psyche that lived for excitement at his peril. On this occasion, the captain had a feeling he wouldn't have to go looking for trouble. Trouble was about to find him.

With a shimmer of coalescing particles, the landing party materialized in the laboratory's central monitoring room on Zeta Gibraltar. It was a fairly large chamber with multiple sensor readout arrays lining a curving wall. The ceiling was a good five meters above them, and along the walls were large hermetically sealed windows, partially opaqued against the system's sun. Gibraltar was a young blue star still accreting mass in this very dusty system. The star was on the outlying arm of the Vara Nebula that intruded into Federation space. The nebula itself was a great mass of debris from a supernova that had exploded a billion years previously—creating the breeding ground for a thousand smaller stars and systems. By day, the local star brightened the sky to an almost ultraviolet purplish blue.

Zeta Gibraltar's days were only ten hours long. Although it was presently daytime on the planetoid, Kirk had been to other nebular worlds and knew the Vara would likely dominate the night sky. Perhaps he'd be here long enough to see it. Its smear of glowing light would be powered from within by the small young stars being born inside. Beautiful. Also deadly: an active nebula was an inferno of lethal radiation and a hazard to interstellar navigation for the unshielded, of course. Not that there was any run-of-the-mill traffic out here on the Federation's frontier.

Kirk looked around. Lights blinked on computer and sensor readouts. Large screens depicted various presentations from satellite feeds and ground monitors of Vara. Some displayed normal spectrum. Others flashed with garish false colors showing gamma radiation, tachyonic intensities, as well as gravimetric and chromospheric data. The nebula truly was a knotty spot in the space-time continuum, a place where ships could go in and not return.

Also a good place to hide, Kirk reflected. *If I were a pirate in this sector, it would be my first pick.*

There was no one present, not a soul. Spock and Chekov immediately began a sensor sweep with their tricorders. Kirk motioned for his security detachment—Lieutenant Graves and Ensign

Thibodeaux—to follow him. Thibodeaux, very young and obviously quite anxious on such an exotic assignment, moved to draw his phaser from where it hung at his side.

Kirk put out a hand to stay the action. "Not just yet, Ensign," he said. "Wait for the order." Thibodeaux reddened in embarrassment at being corrected by his captain. "But a good instinct to be on your toes," Kirk continued. "Stay alert."

Kirk and Graves exchanged a quick half smile between them. The kid would learn, and this was an excellent place for him to cut his teeth.

The captain followed a main corridor out of the control center and passed door after closed door on either side. All were unlocked and responded to his entry. Kirk chose one at random and went inside.

It was a personal living quarters, sumptuously large by starship standards. Someone with good taste, Kirk reflected. Abstract prints by an Earth-based artist whose work Kirk recognized adorned the walls. Several of them hung askew.

And here was something else. The sleep padding was ripped, and various items had been swept from shelves and lay broken on the floor. Spock picked one object up, examined it, then showed it to Kirk. It appeared to be a framed hologram of a family taken on a much greener and more hospitable planet than Zeta Gibraltar, where the highest form of life was a bush-like blue algae.

"Captain," said Graves from behind them. "Here."

Kirk turned to find Graves looking into a crevice formed by the curving wall and a built-in bookshelf. It would be an excellent place to hide if you didn't want anyone glancing through the door to see you. Kirk stepped over and looked to where Graves was pointing.

A handprint. It was composed of what looked like small, flaking brown leaves. Portions had fallen away, but the smeared outline of the hand—it was a left hand—was still apparent.

Kirk didn't need a tricorder readout to tell him what that flaking brown substance was. He'd seen enough of it at various times.

Dried human blood. Someone had stumbled into that wall with blood on a hand to leave such a mark.

"Not good," Kirk said. "Let's check elsewhere."

They passed through door after door, and many, though not all, of the quarters appeared to have been tossed: cushions cut, padding ripped out, items knocked from shelves to get at what may be hidden behind.

"Raiders, sir?" asked Thibodeaux.

"We don't know yet, Ensign," Kirk replied. "Somebody was certainly looking for something—or someone—in these quarters."

They entered another room, and Kirk paused,

surprised. This room was most decidedly *not* like the other personal quarters they'd examined. It was a living space, yes. There was a bed and desk. But instead of the plasto-ceramic standard furniture he'd seen elsewhere, these were made of what looked like wood.

"Mahogany," Spock said, anticipating Kirk's question. "And the wardrobe is of American chestnut."

"That must have cost a fortune to ship out here to the butt end of nowhere," said Thibodeaux.

He raised a hand over his mouth, as if he'd spoken out of turn, but a nod from Kirk seemed to put him at ease again.

On the wall was a portrait in an ornately carved frame. It was no holographic image, but an oil painting depicting a stern-looking man. He was dressed in a coat over a ruffled shirt with a cravat tied around his neck. Even more curious, the man in the portrait was clearly wearing an elaborate wig of gray hair curling down to his shoulders.

"Something odd about this furniture, Captain," Chekov put in.

"Yes?"

"It seems to be . . . well, breaking down," Chekov continued, his accent, as usual, turning the *w* sound into a *v*.

"Explain."

"I can't, sir," Chekov replied. "The chemical

bonds, they seem to be just . . . spontaneously decomposing."

"It is very strange, Captain," said Spock, looking up from his tricorder. "The process is similar to radioactive decay, but there is no matter-energy conversion. Whatever the process may be, it is accelerating. Every piece of furniture in this room will have disintegrated to dust within the next six point four days."

The walls were hung with fabrics, and a window looked out onto the planetary landscape. There were curtains framing the window. They were made of a sumptuous and beautifully printed fabric.

The mattress lay askew from the bed, and a writing desk was turned on its side since it was not physically connected to the wall.

"Interesting," said Mister Spock, who had gone to examine the drapes with his tricorder. "The woven textile fabrics are made of the finely worked pellicle coating of Earth sheep."

"Wool," Kirk said.

"Sir!" The call came from Thibodeaux. He had stepped around the tumbled desk and was staring down at something behind it. Kirk joined the ensign.

There on the floor lay what looked to be a severed arm. It was manifestly not human. There were four digits connected by folds of webbing. A chunky armband glistening with gemstones was about the wrist, but it was bare otherwise. It appeared to have been severed below the shoulder. But what was most arresting was the color.

The arm was a bright yellow.

Kirk nodded to his science officer. "Spock?"

Spock turned the tricorder's biosensors toward the arm.

"Fascinating. Most definitely a bilateral appendage," Spock said after a moment. A twist of the tricorder controls presented Spock with further analysis. "Thirty-seven chromosomes and trio-based gender determination."

"Not human," Kirk said. "We have forty-six chromosomes."

"Not Vulcan, either. Nor Romulan, Klingon or, in fact, any known Federation sentient species," Spock replied.

"Hypothesis, Mister Spock?"

"Not enough data at present, Captain," Spock replied.

"Best guess."

Spock cocked his head.

I know you all too well, my friend, Kirk thought. *Never a moment when that magnificent mind of yours isn't bubbling with one idea or another.*

"Extremely speculative, Captain. I would prefer to gather more information before hazarding an opinion."

Kirk nodded. "Very well, Mister Spock."

He turned his attention back to the room and its furnishings.

Who had wooden furniture and natural fiber curtains on a remote science outpost? This was information his orders most definitely had not included, and Kirk didn't like it.

"One thing's for sure, whoever was in this room didn't want to leave it and made someone pay a high price for intruding."

Kirk had an additional security team beamed down. He sent this detail to check every room in this wing of the complex, while he and Spock returned to the central control room. Uhura, at the main communications console, had by this time pulled up the outpost communications records—what there were of them.

"The station communication records have been wiped, Captain," Uhura reported. "Interior sensor recordings, incoming message backups, outgoing communiqués—all of it. Someone who knew their way around computers and communication equipment did this."

"Or was forced to do it," Kirk replied. "Gentlemen, it's time we venture outside."

Exterior egress was through an airlock. The planetoid was Class-M, but barely. The surface of Zeta Gibraltar was not a spot you'd want to visit for shoreleave. Or *ever*—if you didn't have to.

Atmospheric pressure was slightly lower than

Earth normal, much closer to that of Vulcan. Gravity, on the other hand, was almost twenty percent higher despite the planetoid's compact size. This was due to a dense iron core so large it even extruded through the surface in spots. It was a geology where dilithium might be found, Kirk noted, although the deposit would likely be a kilometer or more beneath the crust.

Spock remained as stoic as ever when he encountered the gravity increase, but Chekov sighed at the added weight, as did Graves, and Thibodeaux nearly collapsed at the knees, not anticipating the sudden change. The ensign stumbled a few steps before finding his footing.

Kirk felt the change immediately when he stepped out onto the gritty, dry soil of the surface.

The station interior obviously generated artificial gravity at one *g* to lighten the planetary effects. This was another odd hint of luxury for a scientific outpost. An assignment to such a frontier facility usually meant roughing it and getting used to whatever gravity you happened to find holding you to the planet or planetoid.

"*On polny mudak!*" Chekov exclaimed. "Even my eyelids feel heavy."

Kirk nodded and led the group forward. There was bright blue algae-level vegetation in clumps all about. An odor not unlike rotting seaweed filled the air—what there was of air, that is.

"The ground cover is colored blue to filter out excessive sunlight that would break down the normal photosynthetic process," Spock remarked. "Much like some desert plants on other Class-M worlds have red leaves in order to filter out intense light from a mainline yellow-red sun."

Up ahead about fifty paces Kirk spotted an area that appeared to be bare of all vegetation. "Come on," Kirk said, and directed the others to follow him toward it.

When they arrived, Kirk saw that it was exactly what he'd expected. A blast zone.

"Recent. Notice the burn marks at the outer edge. The ion signature indicates a matter/antimatter powered propulsion device was present here six point four days ago," Spock said.

"The day the outpost missed its first daily report," said Kirk.

"Precisely," answered Spock.

"A landing craft?" said Kirk.

"Very likely, Captain. However, it *is* a very peculiar ion signal."

Spock took several steps toward the blast zone, his attention still fixed on his tricorder. Kirk looked around to see if there were any other signs of what had taken place. A white flash of something tangled in one of the algae bushes caught his eye, but before he could examine it more closely, Ensign Thibodeaux's voice called out.

"Mister Spock!"

Kirk whirled to see the ensign backing away in horror from something on the ground—something Spock was about to inadvertently step on.

There was no way Spock could react quickly enough to avoid it.

Suddenly, in a streak of gold and black, Chekov barreled into Spock's torso, pushing the first officer to the side. Spock, a very difficult man to drop, merely stumbled a few steps sideways, while Chekov himself crashed into a bush. Kirk came closer and saw what it was Spock had been about to come down on.

A flat saucer shape with a pin sticking up from its top.

Landmine, Kirk thought. Outlawed in the Federation, but in use outside its boundaries by backward military regimes of various stripes—and pirates.

Spock came beside Kirk and examined the device with him.

"Whoever put this here very likely seeded the area with them to dissuade attack," he said, "or perhaps to cordon in a group."

"I'd bet on the latter," Kirk said. He turned to the others. "Be on the lookout for these landmines. There are probably more of them."

Chekov, who was on his hands and knees, extracted himself from the algae bush. He had a few scratches on his face and arms, but otherwise seemed none the worse for wear. He grinned when he saw Spock was all right.

"It seems you owe Mister Chekov a debt of gratitude," Kirk said.

Spock looked surprised. "My death or dismemberment would have disrupted the mission," he said. "It was the only logical thing for Ensign Chekov to do."

Kirk looked at Chekov with a wry smile and shrugged. The navigator returned the smile and shrugged back. They both knew to expect that reaction from the first officer and were amused rather than irritated.

What Spock lacked in emotional response, Ensign Thibodeaux made up for in buckets. The young ensign had his hands to his knees and was gasping for breath.

Kirk was about to go to him to see what was the matter, but Chekov spoke first. "Captain, allow me. I believe I know what he is going through very well. It was not so long ago that I was a green officer on his first assignment."

"All right, Mister Chekov, handle it," Kirk said. "Spock, let's see what else we can find out." He was about to leave it at that, but added: "And watch your step, won't you?"

He knew the teasing statement would likely have no effect on his first officer, but he couldn't resist if only for his own amusement.

"Indeed, Captain," Spock replied, with a raise of the eyebrow. "That type of landmine has a blast radius of fifteen point three meters, if I'm not mistaken. The ensuing explosion would likely have eliminated the entire landing party as well as myself had I activated it. I shall take care not to trigger one."

Did I get to you, Spock, or was that merely a display of routine logic? Kirk thought.

It was always impossible to tell—which was another fascinating characteristic of his friend and second-in-command.

Two

Ensign Pavel Chekov took a sip of his vodka and nodded sympathetically toward Ensign Jerry Thibodeaux, who was seated across from him at a recreation room six table.

"Go on," Chekov said gently.

"I don't know what came over me, Chekov," said Thibodeaux.

"Call me Pavel," Chekov said. "We are off duty."

And I want to give you space to speak freely without the worry that I may be filing a report.

Thibodeaux nodded that he would.

"Go on."

"I saw where Spock was about to put his foot, and I just thought, *We're all dead.* And I froze. Then I backed away even though I saw Mister Spock was in danger." Thibodeaux took a sip of his beer. "No, that's not really right. What I was thinking was that I was dead. I didn't really care about anybody else at all in that moment."

Thibodeaux and Chekov were seated at a corner table. Chekov took another sip of vodka. He noticed that Thibodeaux was now working on his second beer.

"You haven't gotten used to danger yet—real danger. It takes time. I know."

"Pavel, I spent four years at Starfleet Academy training my heart out. I was supposed to be *ready*. I requested security. There wasn't a simulation at the Academy that I didn't pass with flying colors." Thibodeaux lowered his head and put a palm to his forehead. "All for nothing."

"I believe you are not right about that," Chekov said. "The training will serve you well, do not worry. And let me tell you, you will never stop experiencing that adrenaline rush. Your mind goes completely blank for an instant, and all you feel is the urge to either flee or fight. This never goes away, my friend."

"Then I'll never be effective in a real-life situation."

"It never leaves you, but that moment of pure terror becomes shorter and shorter, the more you are used to it. And then your training kicks in. You will know what to do."

"You sure did," said Thibodeaux. "That was amazing."

Chekov shook his head. "It is something Commander Spock has done for me more than once—perhaps not in that exact manner, of course, but he has certainly prevented harm from coming to me."

Chekov gestured around himself at the others in the rec room. "That's what it means to be part of this crew. You don't just look out for one another. After a while, you owe one another your lives. Everyone understands this, and yet we seldom mention it to one another. It is a fact of life on a starship such as this." Chekov took another sip of his vodka and smiled. "Especially under Captain Kirk. He does take the mission of this vessel seriously."

"He's becoming a legend back at the Academy. And I made an idiot blunder right in front of him."

"Don't let it define you. Learn from it," Chekov said. He raised his glass. "Here's to your first real landing party mission. May there be many other adventures."

"That I don't mess up quite so badly." The navigator nodded but said nothing and took his sip. Jerry Thibodeaux would be all right, Chekov was fairly certain. They finished their drinks and headed off to their quarters for rest period. Soon it would be time to return to duty. Chekov looked forward to it. What he hadn't told Thibodeaux—because the young man would soon find out for himself—was that danger and action had their rewards as well as their costs.

The adrenaline surge went both ways. After experiencing it a few times, one might not only stop dreading it, but come to enjoy it. This was the real secret a Starfleet officer learned after a while: the fact that no other life could ever be quite as satisfying.

At least not to me, Chekov thought. He yawned as he came to the door of his personal quarters and realized he really did need that bit of scheduled downtime. Duty would call soon enough, and he planned to be ready.

———

Kirk contemplated the viewscreen on the bridge as Spock and Uhura worked together on an idea suggested by the communications officer. Communications and records had been wiped from the Zeta Gibraltar computer, but she had managed to locate what proved to be an overlooked file of meteorological events on the planet's surface. Going through this, and knowing the approximate time of the raid—or whatever had occurred at the outpost— Uhura pinpointed a momentary surge in nearby temperatures and the same curious ion signature that Spock's tricorder had picked up at the blast site.

The outpost equipment was more sensitive than the tricorder, and Spock and Uhura were narrowing down the identification characteristics by running both scans through the *Enterprise*'s state-of-the-art information comparison programs.

The planet below had no large bodies of water— most of what water there was occurred in the subsurface. This led to a planetary appearance that varied from light brown to chocolate-orange interspaced by the ubiquitous blue smears where there were concentrations of the planetary algal plants. Zeta Gibraltar was not a very inviting place when viewed from space. The planetoid did have one singular characteristic, however. It was on an extreme outlying tendril of Federation territory and was the farthest full-time inhabited planet from Earth in Federation space.

After Spock's close call, Kirk had examined the white item he'd found in those blue bushes.

A gentleman's silk cravat.

Silk. Wood. Wool. What did it add up to?

One thing he knew: he had a missing outpost crew and he had to find them.

A data slate was handed to Kirk by a yeoman and he rose and stretched before signing it and handing the slate back.

"Spock, anything?"

Spock turned from the communications console. "Affirmative, Captain. We have isolated the ion signature. It is indeed that of a craft using matter/antimatter propulsion."

"It's also unique, Captain," Uhura said. "We should be able to identify it."

Spock stepped back over to his science console. "Running sensor sweeps now, sir," he said. "It may be possible to . . . yes. There."

"What is it, Spock?"

"An ion trail leading away from the planet, Captain. It matches the signature the lieutenant and I found within the planetary records as well as my tricorder readings."

"Can we follow it?"

"Transferring path out of the system to navigation now."

"Excellent work, Spock, Uhura." Kirk sat back down. Now they were getting somewhere! "Helmsman, take her about. Mister Sulu, follow that ion trail."

"Aye, aye, Captain."

It did not take long to see exactly where the ion trail was leading them.

Out of the Zeta Gibraltar system—and straight into the glowing dust and debris of the mysterious Vara Nebula.

Three

Captain's Log, Supplemental. We are venturing into one of the great melting pots and star forges of our galaxy: the Vara Nebula. We are following an ion trail with a unique signature that we believe was left by a ship carrying the Zeta Gibraltar science station personnel. That trail has led us directly into a dangerous region of the nebula. We are being buffeted by meteoroid strikes, but we are still venturing forward in hopes of bringing home the Zeta Gibraltar staff.

Kirk was glad to see Chekov report to the bridge just as the *Enterprise* reached the nebula's outer boundaries. This was going to be a tricky passage, and Chekov had not only great skill, but something that it was impossible to teach a navigation officer: excellent intuition. Much would depend on the young ensign.

The *Enterprise* forged ahead for several hours through the material miasma of the outer Vara, shields up, but not yet at maximum. There was simply no way to journey into the nebula without encountering micrometeoroids—and quite a few that were not so "micro" at all. The ship was buffeted by several large strikes, but the shields held and had remained at full power. He could not order them to absolute maximum—because of the nebula's interference with the sensors—which meant that a portion of the energy of any large meteoroid strike would be transferred through the shields to the physical structure of the ship. This was unavoidable. They must be able to use maximum sensors to track the ion trail. But the safety of the *Enterprise* was also uppermost in Kirk's mind. It was a fine balance.

The captain touched a button on his command chair armrest. "Engineering, report. Are we still within structural limits?"

Scott's voice answered over the ship's intership. *"Aye, Captain, she's holding together. But I don't like it. There's only so much of this she can take—and then something's bound to give."*

"Keep an eye on the situation, Scotty," said Kirk. "We wouldn't be pushing forward under these conditions if there wasn't a high probability that lives are on the line."

"Understood, Captain," Scott answered, sounding only a trifle mollified. *"We'll do everything we can to hold her together. I hope we find who or what we're looking for sooner rather than later and get the ship out of here."*

"I hope so, too, Scotty. Bridge out."

Moments later, a whistle came from the command chair intraship. *"Sickbay to bridge."*

Kirk activated the intercom channel. "Kirk here, sickbay."

"We've finished analysis on that very odd surprise you brought up for us from the planetoid surface." The familiar drawl of a gentleman from the North American south let him know his friend and the *Enterprise*'s chief medical officer, Leonard McCoy, was speaking.

"What have you got for me, Bones?"

"It matches no known current species. But I seemed to recall something from a paper I read a while back about forensics research on a set of historical remains. There was a report of that DNA having an odd triplicate structure. So I ran a check, and it matched up. Jim, that arm belongs to a member of the species known as the L'rah'hane."

"The L'rah'hane? The old pirates the Federation sent packing long ago?"

"About seventy-five years," McCoy said. *"They had three sexes—'have,' I should say. That arm belongs to a hermaphrodite of the species."*

"Interesting," said Kirk. "Good work, Bones."

"Got another surprise for you, Captain."

"Yes?"

"The manner in which that extremity was separated from its unfortunate former owner," McCoy

said. He paused a moment for effect, then delivered his verdict. *"A blade."*

"As in a knife?"

"Something that could shear through it in one cut," McCoy replied. *"I'd say a battle-ax or sword."*

This was getting more interesting by the minute.

"Thanks, Bones," he replied. "Keep at it. Bridge out."

Kirk turned back to the viewscreen and sat musing as the nebular debris flew by. At least now he knew his likely quarry. L'rah'hane pirates.

The last of whom had been encountered and defeated seventy-five years ago.

A few moments later Spock turned from his constant monitoring at the science station sensor readouts. "Sir, we have lost the ion trail."

"Lost it? Can we get it back?"

"I do not think so. I have attempted to employ multiple methods."

Kirk touched a hand to his chin, considering. To have come so far, and risked lives, only to reach a dead end. Without that trail, it would be like finding a needle in a haystack. The nebula was a vast hiding place many light-years across. Yet Kirk knew he wouldn't give up the search if any chance of finding the outpost personnel remained.

"What about long-range probes, Spock? Can we send them out in a radial sweep?"

"It would require some adjustment to their

sensory programming and shielding characteristics. Ten minutes if I am able to work steadily."

"Do it, Mister Spock." Kirk turned back to the helm. "Bring us to a stop exactly where that ion trail ran out, Chekov. I want to be able to follow that breadcrumb trail back home, if need be."

"Aye, aye, sir."

Spock completed his modifications, and the probes were launched. Kirk settled in for a long wait, but, surprisingly, one of the probes soon streaked back and, when it came within close enough range that the nebula's natural radiation didn't scramble its communication channels, it sent its report.

"Captain, probe seven seems to have found something. Or multiple somethings," Uhura said, turning in her bridge chair. "It is sending a full report including images."

"On-screen," said Kirk.

The display showed faint traces of structures that looked very much like two spread hands joined together at the thumbs. Weird, but obviously created by intelligent life. Sensor readings confirmed there were beings *within* those structures.

A quick pull back and size comparison revealed they were, in fact, slightly smaller than the *Enterprise*. Four of them.

The ion trail signature was all around them.

"Those are ships," Kirk said.

"I concur, Captain," said Spock.

They were several thousand kilometers away, hidden within a cloud of dust that looked, upon examination, suspiciously globular, as if it had been created on purpose. Its center was rocky and had the readings profile of an asteroid.

So that dust globe is likely camouflage, Kirk thought. *It's a meet-up spot. Or a transfer station. A treasure island, perhaps. Let's find out what it's hiding.*

"That's enough, Lieutenant, thank you," Kirk said, indicating with a finger that Uhura could return the viewscreen to its customary exterior display. "Release a navigational beacon to mark our present position, Mister Sulu, and then let's go and have a closer look at those ships."

"Aye, sir."

"All sensors forward, Mister Spock. I don't want any nasty surprises."

"Sensors forward."

Kirk stared at the viewscreen. Nothing but dust flying past on all sides.

Like looking up into a rain storm, he thought. *If the rain were rocks moving at thousands of kilometers an hour speed.*

The globular cloud was a darker patch ahead of them.

Uhura switched the viewscreen display to infrared, and the false color imagery showed reddish bodies, with the curious handlike shapes, within a cloud of yellows and oranges.

The pirates.

"Intercepting various communications frequencies, Captain," Uhura said.

"Subspace?"

"Negative, sir. Electromagnetic. They are . . . old-fashioned radio waves."

"Please put it on bridge audio, Lieutenant."

"Switching over."

A patch of static, and then a spate of wordlike guttural sounds that Kirk could have sworn was cursing.

Spock looked up from his sensors, intrigued.

"Words, Spock?" Kirk said.

"That would be my guess, Captain, although—"

Uhura interrupted. "Captain, the signal modulation correlates with a known language."

"Don't tell me, Lieutenant. Is it L'rah'hane?"

Uhura's face took on a look of surprise. "Yes, sir, that's exactly what it is."

"Then let's have a translation."

"Working on it, Captain," answered Uhura. "The universal translator should have it . . . now."

Suddenly the sounds coming over audio began to make sense.

"You stupid foolish stumpwalker, if you don't get back here this instant with the bounty, I'm going to blow you out of the sky."

"Is he talking to us?" said Sulu, looking up from his helm console with some alarm.

"No. I don't think so," Kirk replied.

As if to confirm this, another voice broke in, replying to the first with a taunt. *"You try and make me, you virus-brained moron. The Hradrians will pay a lot more in credits for this lot than your sorry pay will ever add up to. We're leaving, and you can't stop us."*

"I'll blast you from the sky!"

"And destroy your precious slave consignment? I don't think so, Erget."

"Damn you, Splo, you won't get away with this."

"Oh, but I will! You're the one who is going to be out of luck this time, you old tyrant."

"Looks like we arrived at a bad time for *them*, but a good time for *us*," Kirk said. "Mister Sulu, find a place nearby to hide us from sensors while those two squabble. Perhaps a radiant hotspot that will conceal us in its general brightness. I want to assess this situation before we act."

"Aye, aye, sir."

Kirk turned to Spock. "Who have we got that's a twenty-second-century scholar, Mister Spock?"

"I believe Lieutenant Julia Tanner is an expert in that era, Captain."

"Uhura, report on what we've found. I want to know everything she can tell us about the days of the L'rah'hane piracy."

"Aye, sir."

"Have Doctor McCoy, Mister Scott, and Lieutenant

Tanner report to the briefing room in twenty minutes. You and Mister Spock will join us. I'll want a full situation report."

"Yes, sir."

"Also, prepare a drone to send to the edge of the nebula. I'll dictate a report for Starfleet Command for subspace transmission. We want them to know what we're doing in here, since we can't communicate with them directly due to the subspace interference."

"Drone already in the launch tube," said Uhura with a slight smile. "As soon as the nebula began to block our subspace communications, it seemed like a good idea to have it ready for immediate deployment."

"Good call, Lieutenant," Kirk replied. After handing off the bridge to Sulu, he quickly made his way to his quarters to compose his report.

Kirk reflected that he might have dictated his report on the bridge, but he planned to include a few pointed words as to his not being informed of whatever was going on at what was supposed to be a regular science outpost on Zeta Gibraltar.

———

Lieutenants Tanner and Uhura were engaged in a deep discussion when Kirk and Spock entered the conference room. Scott was present. McCoy was there as well, clearly chafing at being pulled away from his sickbay. Kirk's intuition told him he might need the doctor's advice very soon, however.

Kirk sat down at the head of the triangle-shaped table.

"Report. What do we have?"

"The language is not classic L'rah'hane, but a variant dialect," said Lieutenant Tanner. She was a petite woman in a blue science officer's uniform. Her most exceptional feature was her lustrous eyes. Kirk reflected that she must have thought so, too. She'd surrounded them with a line of dark eyeliner of an almost ancient-Egyptian thickness. "The L'rah'hane pirates roamed a large portion of the Alpha Quadrant in their day. They were taken on and resoundingly defeated in 2173. It was believed that all spacefaring technology available to them had been destroyed. Obviously we need to modify that supposition." Tanner nodded toward the triviewer, where she clicked through several blurry photographs and an artistic rendering of the L'rah'hane. They were generally humanoid in appearance, but their noses were turned upward and possessed a triad of nostrils.

Shouldn't judge by appearances, Kirk thought. *But they do look a bit like pigs.*

"The L'rah'hane were not a creative species. Instead, they specialized in either begging or stealing the technology of others. According to the few records they kept, they had originally come from a pre-warp planet when some hapless visitor crash-landed his ship. Although their homeworld was never located, after the defeat in 2173, it was believed that the L'rah'hane homeworld contained all that remained of the species. Considering their technological level, sector quarantine was deemed suitable."

"Another assumption we are going to be modifying."

"Lieutenant Tanner explained something else to me, Captain," Uhura said, cutting in. "The L'rah'hane weren't merely pirates. Primarily, they were slavers." She pronounced this last statement with disgust in her voice. "They raided worlds with their stolen technology, took away entire shiploads of the natives as slaves, and sold them."

"Sold them to whom?"

"To the highest bidder," Tanner answered. "Another unexplained datum, Captain. The ships the L'rah'hane operated were believed to be the last remnants of the Hradrian navy."

"But the Hradrian Empire hasn't existed since the twenty-first century. It was in *ruins* seventy-five years ago," said Kirk.

"This is quite true," Spock said. "There are Hradrian ruins on a broad swath of worlds across the entire Alpha Quadrant. The empire was at its zenith during Earth's twentieth and twenty-first centuries. It had a rapid decline and fall during Earth's twenty-second century." Spock cocked his head in a reflective pose. "It is fortunate that Hradrians never happened upon your home system, Captain. There would have been little chance that human technology of the time would have stood up to Hradrian firepower."

"That's very true," said Tanner. "The Hradrian Empire was based on forced labor of multiple species—slavery, in other words. Machinery and automation were kept in the hands of the upper class and ruling castes so that they could retain power. It was a system that functioned for several centuries."

"But the slaves ultimately rebelled, as I remember. It brought down the empire."

"In truth, Captain, that is one of the big questions of Hradrian scholarship," said Tanner. "Did the empire fall because of a slave revolt, or were there revolts because the empire was crumbling?"

"So the L'rah'hane flew Hradrian ships, but the Hradrians were also their best customers," Kirk offered.

"Exactly," said Uhura.

"Toward the end of the Hradrian Empire, they existed in a sort of social symbiosis," Tanner continued. She was beginning to grow a bit breathless, her enthusiasm for her subject coming to the fore. "From what we have pieced together from the Hradrian archives, the L'rah'hane pirate lanes fit neatly into the remains of the Hradrian Empire.

As the empire crumbled, the L'rah'hane preyed on Hradrian outlying worlds to provide slaves to the worlds on the interior." Tanner looked at Kirk imploringly. "Captain, we have an amazing opportunity for study. Those L'rah'hane ships are *new* and they are very likely Hradrian in origin. That means there must be a remnant of the Hradrian Empire somewhere beyond the Vara Nebula, perhaps close by."

McCoy looked like he was about to come out of his seat, so agitated was he. "Need I remind you, Lieutenant, that the Hradrians were not merely notorious slaveholders, they got rid of their elderly slaves in centralized concentration camps? I remember my history, too, and from every record the Hradrians left behind, we can infer that the empire was a vicious state built on coercion of innocent beings."

Tanner seemed taken aback. She hadn't been ready for a full broadside from the ship's doctor.

But, damn it, McCoy was right. The only reason Kirk could imagine that he'd like to rediscover the Hradrian empire would be to free its slaves and kill its leaders in horrible ways. This, he realized, was a violation of the Prime Directive.

"Captain," Spock put in, "the L'rah'hane, and not the Hradrians, are our present problem."

"Well, if they *are* these L'rah'hane pirates, then there's hope the outpost staff is alive," McCoy stated. "Assuming they were taken in a slave-gathering raid, then the L'rah'hane wouldn't want to murder the merchandise."

"Precisely," said Spock. "If the L'rah'hane still traffic in interspecies slavery, perhaps the outpost personnel are to be sold as chattel. We may also find them gathered in one place."

"Agreed," said Kirk. "Put together an armed landing party to go down to that asteroid, and let's look around for our missing colonists."

"Transporting is going to be a wee bit tricky, sir," said Scott. "With conditions in this nebula, I highly recommend taking a shuttlecraft."

"Agreed, Mister Scott. In the meantime that ship, whatever its captain's motives are, can't be allowed to go anywhere. We'll have to see to that with tractor beams. If those won't work, we'll use phasers only as a last resort, as that would surely give away our position in the nebula cloud."

"Aye, sir, I'll direct all auxiliary energy to the tractor beams," said Scott. "I believe we can hold that ship, if it comes to it."

"We'll also need to sweep the surrounding area for more vessels. I don't want to get a nasty surprise that—"

A loud blast from the ship's intraship. It was the alarm that announced a ship-wide red alert!

Kirk thumbed an intraship set in the center of the conference room table. "Mister Sulu, report!"

"Captain, the nebula detritus is no longer con-

cealing us to their sensors. We have been detected and are under attack. Four pirate vessels approaching. Their weapons are hot, sir, and they are deploying torpedoes."

"Shields to maximum," Kirk immediately responded. "On our way." Kirk paused a moment, considering. "Sulu, whatever you do, do *not*, I repeat, do *not* destroy those ships!"

Four

The firefight was intense and energetic despite the *Enterprise*'s technological advantage. The L'rah'hane weapons were no match for the *Enterprise*'s shields. Any normal fight would have been a foregone conclusion. The pirates' defenses, however, were considerably more advanced than their offensive weapons.

The L'rah'hane also understood how to fight in groups.

Three ships closed in on the *Enterprise* in an even distribution, while the fourth, the one containing one of the bickering parties as heard over the radio, broke away from the asteroid and attempted to get in a position behind the *Enterprise*.

They increased their ragged laser fire, achieving a concentration but not quite succeeding in synchronizing. The *Enterprise* shields absorbed these shots easily. More worrisome were the nuclear torpedoes. Nuclear explosions could bring down a starship's shields in time—although it would take a great many more than the L'rah'hane had yet deployed. Sulu's phasers were kept busy blasting these to pieces before they came within damaging range.

The main problem is that I can't outright destroy them, Kirk thought. *There may be Federation personnel held captive on those ships. We've got to shoot to disable.*

Shooting a starship in exactly the right spot could be done. The first problem was to identify a vulnerable system on the enemy vessel.

Kirk had Spock busily working on that.

The other problem was range. Even the highly concentrated beams of phasers spread slightly at distance. What Sulu needed was a target range of about ten thousand kilometers—that is, extremely close range for a space battle, and a position into which no sane captain would allow his ship to be drawn.

But these were bloody-minded pirates. Which gave Kirk an idea.

"Mister Chekov, establish coordinates for the thickest, most dangerous portion of the nebula that's closest to us."

"Yes, sir," replied the ensign. "Got it, Captain."

"Take us there."

"Sir?" But the hesitation was only in the helmsman's voice, not in his actions. Chekov's hands were already guiding the controls to obey his captain's orders.

"Be careful, Mister Chekov. We don't want to let a stray meteoroid do the job these pirates are trying to do on us."

"Aye, sir."

Now the bucking and pounding grew more intense. It was possible to avoid some of the debris in the region into which Chekov was turning, but not *all* of it. This was no dust cloud with the occasional rocky body either. There were some ship-sized chunks of aggregated matter slamming against the shields of the *Enterprise*.

"Steady as she goes."

"Captain, your gambit appears to have worked," said Spock from his science station. "The L'rah'hane vessels are turning and following us and closing range so as to keep us in sight in this denser region."

Sometimes it seemed to Kirk as if he and Spock actually shared some sort of continuing mind-meld. But the explanation was simpler. Clearly his first officer had reasoned out Kirk's move the moment the captain had initiated it.

"Have you isolated the L'rah'hane vulnerable systems?"

"Just completed," said Spock. "Their engine cooling system has a distinct weakness. A direct shot into the manifold vents should initiate a shutdown of propulsion without unduly endangering the ship's life support."

"How big are those vents, Mister Spock?"

"Two square meters," Spock replied. "I have routed the configuration to weapons."

"You hear that, Mister Sulu. You have a target about the size of a dinner table, and you have to make it from at the very least ten thousand kilometers, possibly more. Think you can hit it?"

Sulu nodded. His helmsman and weapons officer was extremely civilized, but Kirk knew Sulu revered and made a particular study of his samurai ancestors. He was certain he saw Sulu's lip quirk in a slight smile of warrior-like anticipation. "I'll give it my best shot, sir."

"Ships one and three at two hundred kilometers," Spock called out. "Ships two and four closing to one hundred kilometers."

"Let them get a little closer, Mister Sulu. We want all of them in range."

"Aye, sir."

"Fifty thousand meters and twenty thousand. Another nuclear device has been deployed by ship one."

"On it," said Sulu as he deftly blasted the nuke into molecules.

"Ranges on L'rah'hane vessels in meters: twenty thousand, twelve, eleven, ten thousand . . ." said Spock.

"Do you have them all, Mister Sulu?"

"Got them, Captain."

"Fire at will, Mister Sulu."

"Aye, sir."

What followed was a virtuoso performance by the helmsman and weapons officer. There was only so much telemetry a ship's sensors and computer could provide. There remained, inevitably, a terrible art to wielding the mighty weapon of a starship phaser. It was almost as if Sulu were thrusting his phasers in the precise strikes of an expert with the fencing foil and épée—weapons of which, Kirk knew, Sulu was in fact a master.

Flashes on the viewscreen as three ships were hit in turn. The fourth was struck, but either the shot had failed to strike the cooling manifold, or the ship had a slightly different construction. It came hard about almost immediately.

"L'rah'hane vessels one, two, and three dead in space," said Spock. "Ship four remains operational and is withdrawing."

"Oh, no you don't," Kirk said to the viewscreen image of the fleeing L'rah'hane. "Mister Chekov, follow that ship."

"Aye, sir."

The escaping ship streaked away through the nebula gases, seemingly heedless of its own danger of striking debris and breaking up. This was the ship that had been communicating with the asteroid base, and Kirk was fairly certain that if Federation personnel were still alive, some would likely be on that ship.

Despite the head start of the L'rah'hane ship, the *Enterprise* was rapidly closing. After a few moments, Uhura spoke up from her station.

"Sir, we are receiving a signal from the L'rah'hane ship. There's a visual as well."

"Are they trying to communicate with us?"

"I don't believe so, sir. It's a broadcast feed, perhaps a distress call sequence has been tripped."

"Put it on-screen, Lieutenant."

At first, all that was visible was a blur of moving bodies. It was difficult to make out exactly what was going on, but there were several of the bright yellow L'rah'hane struggling against what appeared to be human beings. Suddenly the contorted visage of what might be the L'rah'hane pirate leader, his upturned nose and three nostrils flaring, filled the whole viewscreen. He must be directly in front of the pick-up.

Tanner's records had not quite done the alienness of the L'rah'hane justice. It wasn't just the nose. The pirate's multiply folded, batlike yellow face was twisted in rage, and his blood-red teeth, either filed to points or naturally occurring that way, were bared as he snarled.

And then, there was a loud crack, a distinctly odd sound that Kirk half recognized, and the look of rage on the face of the L'rah'hane turned to surprise. He stumbled, and gazed down at his chest.

By stepping backward, the rest of the L'rah'hane had come into view. There was a hole in his chest about where the heart would be in a human, and he was leaking a purplish fluid that might be L'rah'hane blood.

That's an exit wound, Kirk thought. And then he realized where he knew the sound. *Gunpowder. That was the sound of an old-fashioned projectile weapon being fired.*

The L'rah'hane pirate reeled backward, but then, when it had almost covered up the device's field of vision, a bubbly froth of blood emerged from the pirate's distended nostrils. The L'rah'hane collapsed downward and fell out of view.

Behind the fallen slaver stood a tall human being. He was dressed in a long blue coat and a white shirt.

And on his head . . . a wig. There was a line of separation where the forehead met the hairline, and no doubt that this thing upon the person's head was an artificial creation.

It was long, gray, and drawn back and tied behind the neck with what looked like a black ribbon.

Like the portrait Kirk had seen, here was another man wearing eighteenth-century dress—but this man was very much alive and kicking.

"What the blazes," Kirk murmured. He blinked, making sure he was actually seeing what he thought he was seeing. In that moment, another L'rah'hane launched itself at the man, and he tumbled out of view, struggling with the pirate for his life.

Then the two rose up, now in profile. The man in the wig had drawn a long vibro-knife—

No, thought Kirk. *That's no knife. That's a sword.*

The pirate was the one with the knife. It was long, curved, and serrated—designed to maim as well as kill. The L'rah'hane thrust, but the man quickly stepped to the side and the knife whizzed by and missed. As the L'rah'hane attempted to withdraw and strike again, the man shifted his weight forward and crashed into the pirate with the sword's hilt. The pirate leaped back to regain its balance. In that moment, it flung its bright yellow arms wide, exposing its chest.

The man wasted no chance in taking advantage of the opening. With a hard thrust, and a grunt of effort, he ran the L'rah'hane through with the sword.

Purple blood welled around the wound entry point.

The pirate let out a great shriek. But the sword had probably cut through what passed for a lung in the L'rah'hane, and its shriek became a ragged, nearly airless rasp.

With a deft movement, the man withdrew the sword from the L'rah'hane's chest, then, with a wicked sideways thrust, lopped into the pirate's neck. The L'rah'hane fell—fell, Kirk was fairly certain, never to rise again.

The human victor quickly spun, looking over the situation on the alien craft's bridge. It seemed to Kirk's practiced eye to be some sort of control room, at least. The man on the viewscreen saw another man beset by a L'rah'hane and, sword held high, stormed to his aid.

With the nearby action gone, Kirk could see that the entire bridge, or whatever it was, was filled with humans fighting L'rah'hane. Some of the humans were in regulation science officer blue—the outpost was nominally under the purview of Starfleet—but others were in the garb of the man with the sword. And other, even more outlandish, costumes.

And that man with the sword . . .

It began to register on Kirk.

Not any *man*.

A man he recognized.

A man he knew from his own history lessons, his own personal studies.

A hero of his, in fact.

"Lieutenant Uhura, can you set up two-way communication?"

"Yes, sir, just a moment," she replied, her fingers nimbly touching several controls. "I believe you are on the L'rah'hane vessel's viewscreen now, Captain."

Kirk felt frustrated. Here he was visually linked to a fight—overlooking that fight as if he were some sort of disembodied referee, no less. And it was a fight to the finish, a fight in which he knew he could make a difference were he there—yet he couldn't take part, could do nothing but await the outcome.

Soon, the fighting humans overcame the last of the L'rah'hane. Several humans lay dead or wounded, as well.

The man with the sword came back into view. He bent down and picked up a hat—a tricorn hat— that had evidently fallen off in the fighting, and placed it on his head. Then the man reached over and tapped the center of his own display. It must be the size of a small monitor, Kirk reflected. His suddenly enormous finger filled up a quarter of the *Enterprise*'s viewscreen.

"*Is this one of those playback devices?*"

"*I suspect it to be a transceiver, General,*" said a voice off to the side, in a Scottish brogue that was even deeper than Montgomery Scott's. "*We are likely in communication with the man on the screen.*"

The man turned back to Kirk, his face now filling the *Enterprise* viewscreen.

There was no doubt who this person *looked* like.

George Washington.

———————

"Captain, we are detecting multiple life pods launching away on the other three disabled L'rah'hane ships," said Spock.

Kirk turned his attention from the viewscreen.

"We are out of phaser range for the moment, Captain," Sulu said.

"We're not going to fire anyway," Kirk said. "We don't know if there are any more prisoners on those pods."

"They appear to be converging and traveling in convoy deeper into the nebula."

"All right, we'll return to this problem later," Kirk said, motioning Uhura to cut the viewscreen feed from the L'rah'hane ship's bridge. "Turn us about, helmsman. Mister Spock, as soon as possible, scan those ships. I want to know if there are any Federation personnel on them."

"Coming into range in fifteen point four seconds, Captain." Spock looked down into his sensor scope. "Signs of human life aboard all three vessels."

"Get a tractor beam on those ships," Kirk said. "We're bringing them back to the other one, and then we'll deal with boarding and evacuation one at a time, but first I need to have a talk with—" Kirk shook his head. He couldn't believe he was going to say it. "—George Washington."

———

"Whom do I have the honor of addressing?" the humanoid who looked like George Washington asked, somewhat stiffly. Kirk had reestablished contact with the L'rah'hane ship, its bridge on the viewscreen.

There was no doubt. The resemblance was uncanny.

"James T. Kirk," Kirk replied. "I'm captain of the United Federation of Planets *Starship Enterprise*. Who or what are you?"

The man nodded. *"Captain Kirk, sir. Is it to you we owe the distraction of the pirate L'rah'hane that allowed our escape?"*

"We engaged in a firefight with the vessel you're on, yes."

"Please accept my deepest gratitude," said the man. *"Captain, we require assistance. Several of our number are wounded. Alas, three are dead. Also, the children of the outpost personnel are here, and they have not eaten in over two days. They are liberated, but remain in the holding area where we were kept."*

Kirk turned to Spock. "Transporter?"

"Out of the question in this particular region, sir. We are in a radiant hotspot in the nebula."

Kirk suppressed a rueful smile. "Best cover I could find at the time."

"Undoubtedly." Spock nodded in agreement, then cocked his head to indicate he'd thought of something else. "Captain, there is a risk even at this close range of radiation poisoning should we deploy a shuttlecraft for docking," the first officer continued. "But I believe the nebula's radiation can be mitigated if Mister Scott will extend our shields to encompass the L'rah'hane vessel. There are what I believe are docking collars available on the L'rah'hane craft, so a shuttlecraft would be a safe option. There is a further problem, however—"

"Yes?"

"The L'rah'hane shields remain in operation, although at depleted power. They will have to come down in order for our shuttles to approach, much less to dock."

Do they, now? said the man on the viewscreen. *"Mister Watt, can you help us with this problem?"*

I'll call him George Washington for the time being, Kirk thought. *But I won't for one minute forget that whatever* it *is,* it *cannot be Washington.*

"Aye, I can indeed, General," said the voice with the brogue. It came from the left of Washington. *"I was watchin' these birds pretty closely when they fiddled with their controls."* Yet another man in the garb of an eighteenth-century gentleman moved to a console in the background. With him was a woman in modern-day garb and with hair in a Federation style indicating she was likely one of the station scientists. Together they studied the controls and briefly consulted. The Scotsman adjusted a fader and flipped a switch. *"That should do it."*

"L'rah'hane shields are down," Spock reported.

Kirk touched a control on his command chair. "Kirk to hangar deck, ready all craft." Kirk touched another control. "Medical and security team to the hangar deck."

"We'll bring over the children and your wounded first," Kirk told the man on the screen.

The other nodded. "*We are obliged, Captain Kirk,*" he said. "*This has been a most unpleasant voyage, as you can imagine.*"

"We'll try to make it a better one back to the outpost," said Kirk. "Sir, please state for the record your name and title."

"*My title? I did not know this formality was required.*"

"It isn't," Kirk said. "Your Mister Watt called you 'general.'"

"*Yes, James may be a stubborn Scotsman, but he's loyal to the Crown. He refuses to recognize my civilian rank.*"

"Which would be—what?"

"*I can hardly refuse one whose actions released us from our holding pens. When the L'rah'hane power failed, the pen energy doors were no more, allowing our escape plan to come to fruition*"

"If you please, your name, sir?"

The man straightened up, stared a crystal-clear, gray-eyed stare at Kirk, and removed his hat. He made a partial bow. "*I am George Washington.*"

"*The* George Washington."

"*I am the president of the United States of America.*"

"*Former* president," Kirk replied.

"*For me it does not seem that way,*" the other replied. "*In my own perception, I am president still.*"

"We're talking about the George Washington from the American Revolutionary War?"

"Captain, we both know that is an impossibility."

"Then who or *what* are you?"

"Perhaps we should discuss this another time, outside of this accursed nebula, and face-to-face—"

"I want answers now!" said Kirk. "I see something that cannot be, and it makes me very wary of sending my people in harm's way."

Washington nodded. *"I take your point, Captain,"* he replied. *"Very well. I believe you have guessed who and what I am already, in any case."*

Kirk sighed.

I thought I'd seen the last of this annoying species, but I suppose it was too good to be true.

"You're Excalbian."

"Yes, Captain."

"What do you want from us this time? Is this some sort of experiment with the L'rah'hane and the outpost personnel? Are you still playing your sadistic game of torture to understand the difference between good and evil?"

"Not at all, Captain," the Excalbian Washington answered. *"That is a lesson that I, for one, learned well. Please accept my assurances that we former prisoners on this ship were truly in the slave pens of these creatures, whatever they are called. We were in need of help. We still are. I appeal to you to aid us. I*

will, of course, answer any and all questions you may have when my people are taken care of.

Kirk frowned. "You have the ability to manipulate minds and matter. Why don't you help them yourself?"

"Alas, this is no longer true. That is something I must discuss with you, Captain," Washington replied. *"You see, I have had my ability to transform stripped from me. I am, for all intents and purposes, as you see me now."*

"What I *see* is a human being. I see George Washington."

"Captain, I am trapped in this form. At this point, I am as close to being George Washington as I am to being a semi-liquid mind inhabiting the magma currents of my former planet's interior." Washington glanced to the side, and a look of concern passed over his face. *"Excuse me a moment—"*

He turned from the screen and helped a wounded man to his feet. The other clutched a hand to a wound in his shoulder. It looked to be a nasty laser burn. He was dressed in what seemed to be the garb of a Napoleonic soldier.

No, thought Kirk. *Not any Napoleonic soldier. That's Napoleon, of course.*

Washington turned to face Kirk.

The man's eyes wrinkled, and his lips curled into a smile, although he still did not open his mouth to expose his teeth. *"For the moment, whatever you* believe, I assure you that I am most happy to be free once again. I have long believed that freedom ought to be the natural state of all men."

"So it should," Kirk replied.

A light flashed on Kirk's command chair, and Scott's voice came over the ship's intraship. *"Hangar deck to bridge."*

Kirk activated his side of the intraship. "Bridge here."

"Captain, first shuttlecraft is away. Given the range, it should be docking in only a few minutes."

"Eight point nine two," Spock said.

"Thank you, Mister Scott. Deploy second shuttle-craft." He looked up again at the viewscreen, considered.

"All right," he said. "I'm prepared to talk. But this had better be good."

"The only thing I can do is tell you the truth," Washington answered. *"I have always found that sufficient to any circumstance."*

Five

The remaining humans on the other ships proved to be Federation scientists. A security team arriving by shuttlecraft had freed them out of slave pens, which were really no more than transformed cargo holds.

All that remained, it seemed, were the Excalbians on the L'rah'hane flagship. So far not one had shown up on the *Enterprise*, despite multiple runs.

Kirk had asked the outpost commander to come to the bridge immediately when she arrived. The bridge turbolift door slid open, and a tall woman dressed in Starfleet science blues entered the deck. Her clothing had seen better days. It was filthy and torn in several spots. The woman was dark skinned and had an unmistakable intensity about her that was immediately noticeable. She did not wait for Kirk to speak but piped up herself.

"Commander Imelda Contreras, director of the Federation and Starfleet joint task force stationed on science outpost Zeta Gibraltar, Captain."

Kirk stood, and Contreras quickly moved across to him and extended her hand. Kirk shook it in greeting.

"Captain James T. Kirk of the *Starship Enterprise*, Commander."

Contreras nodded. "I can't tell you how glad we all are to be on your ship, Captain."

"I can imagine. We'll arrange for quarters for all of your personnel on our journey back to Zeta Gibraltar. We should arrive in only a few hours, but perhaps you'd like the opportunity to change and freshen up."

"We would indeed," replied Contreras. "It will take a long 'fresher session to wash the stench of those slave pens off me. I don't want to be judgmental—oh hell, of course I want to be judgmental—every one of those pirates smelled like they'd bathed in a jar of ammonia mixed into a rancid tub of vomit."

"I'm sorry you had to deal with that, Commander," Kirk replied, with an empathetic smile. "I would, however, like to speak with you as soon as possible. I have . . . questions. I'm sure you know what some of those questions might be."

Contreras nodded.

Kirk's command chair intraship whistled and Mister Scott's unmistakable accent came over the speaker. "Hangar deck to Captain Kirk."

"Excuse me a moment," Kirk said to Contreras. He thumbed the intraship control. "Mister Scott."

"*Sir, we have evacuated all Federation personnel from the L'rah'hane vessels.*"

"Very good, Mister Scott."

"*I repeat: all* Federation *personnel*," Scott continued. "*Those others are refusing to come.*"

"Do they give a reason?"

"*No, sir,*" Scott replied. "*I don't know what this means, but they said to ask Mister Washington.*"

"I'm pretty sure I know what it means, Scotty," Kirk replied. "Stand by."

He shut down the audio feed, then turned back to the viewscreen.

"Uhura," Kirk said with a sigh.

———

In a moment Kirk was once again face-to-face with the Excalbian George Washington.

"I thought we were going to have our long talk, Mister President?" He let a trace of irony slip into his voice, especially when he used the man's alleged title. "Why are your people refusing to get onto the shuttlecraft?"

Instead of replying directly, Washington braced himself as if he had an oration to deliver. When he spoke, the words did indeed come out quite loud and resonant. "*Captain, may I humbly beg your permission to remain on board with my people and serve as your prize crew. I am sure that, with Mister*

Watt's able assistance, we can bring this ship back safely to the science outpost."

"Mister President, my people are trained Starfleet officers and extremely capable when it comes to handling a ship, especially through the tumultuous space of the Vara Nebula."

"Sir, I ask you to consult with Commander Imelda Contreras. She will vouch for our good intentions."

Kirk motioned for Uhura to cut the audio, then turned to Contreras. "Commander?"

"He liberated us from some very nasty confinement cells," Contreras said. "I understand your reluctance, but I trust him."

"He's *Excalbian*, Commander. Are you aware of what that means?"

"I am," said Contreras. "Next to you, I am probably the Federation's leading expert on the Excalbians."

"They have no morals. They make a point of the fact that they have no concept of good or evil."

"I believe that *these* Excalbians are different," Contreras replied. "Captain, he's a proven leader. I, for one, trust this version of George Washington— whoever or whatever he is."

Kirk turned back to the viewscreen. "Lieutenant," he said to Uhura.

"Aye, sir."

"Mister . . . President, I am sending over my helmsman, Lieutenant Sulu, along with a team of security personnel for your protection and his. There may be more L'rah'hane surprises lying in wait. Will you agree to this arrangement?"

"Of course, Captain Kirk. My highest priority is to prove the goodwill of my fellow Excalbians and our virtuous intentions toward you and the Federation."

"All right. You'll get your chance," Kirk said. "We'll be in touch. Kirk out."

Uhura expertly cut the signal. Kirk sat a moment, considering, then turned to Sulu. "Mister Sulu, I want you to keep an eye on whatever is going on over there, and be ready to take action if anything seems irregular."

"Yes sir, I understand," Sulu answered.

"Then get down to the hangar deck," Kirk said. "We need to start back before the L'rah'hane find us out here and start shooting.

"Mister Chekov, get those other L'rah'hane ships in alignment. Tractor them back with us. I want to go over those ships with a fine-tooth comb so we can find out exactly what we're dealing with should the L'rah'hane come back in greater numbers."

"Aye, sir."

"Note our location, and let's get out of here." He looked back to the viewscreen, which was now filled with a view of the nebula interior as seen from the *Enterprise*. "We need to bring our people home."

Six

Captain's Log, Stardate 6097.4. We have returned to Zeta Gibraltar after confronting and defeating a four-ship contingent of L'rah'hane pirates in the Vara Nebula. The battle was little more than a skirmish, as the Enterprise thoroughly outclassed the L'rah'hane vessels. We return with the science personnel from the Zeta Gibraltar outpost. We also have in tow three L'rah'hane pirate ships, and a fourth piloted by a prize crew led by Mister Sulu and commanded by an Excalbian who bears an exact resemblance to George Washington. I have beamed to the surface to oversee the repatriation of the station personnel and to meet the Excalbians firsthand. My first priority: secure the outpost and its personnel.

Kirk was up from his chair and stalking around the outpost conference room as he attempted to think through the situation he must deal with. This conference room was three times larger than the *Enterprise* one—so Kirk had plenty of room for his pacing.

The captain noticed some of his assembled senior officers getting nervous. Scott was pulling at the tight collar of his own dress tunic and fiddling with the edge of the ancestral tartan sash he wore on such occasions. The sight of an agitated captain was never a welcome sign, Kirk mused, but there were larger issues to deal with at the moment. Besides, walking helped Kirk think.

"All right, our mystery man who seems to be the leader of a group of fifty-eight other mystery men and women says he's Excalbian," Kirk said. "*And* that he's a replica of George Washington. Is he telling the truth? What else could he be? Opinion, Mister Spock?"

"I have no other hypotheses that do not involve preposterous assumptions or extremely unlikely occurrences," Spock replied evenly.

"Speculate, Spock."

"Captain, conjecturing that there may be, for instance, a Guardian gateway playing with the fabric of space-time in this sector does not seem a very helpful speculation." Spock shook his head. "The fact is, I currently possess insufficient data. Commander Contreras has not been particularly forthcoming, given her security instructions from the Federation Council."

"Which she claims limit what she can tell us," said Lieutenant Graves, who had led the security team that had thoroughly scanned and cleared the three captured L'rah'hane vessels, preparing them for regular personnel to come aboard. It had been a grim assignment, for there were dead bodies to evacuate, both L'rah'hane and human, and Kirk had been impressed with the professionalism with which Graves carried out his duties. "But don't we have to believe her? She *is* under Federation directive, sir."

"Indeed. Lacking more data, that we continue to consider these beings to be Excalbians would seem to be our best working theory," the first officer replied.

Kirk turned to McCoy. "I want you to give each and every one of those characters a thorough physical. I want to find out what makes them tick."

"All right," McCoy said. "I'll start as soon as they arrive. One thing we know: they seem to have no issue with beaming down to the planetoid surface. Their bodies behave as humanoid in that respect."

Although Kirk and his senior staff were on the surface of Zeta Gibraltar, they were thankfully inside the pressurized, gravity-abated science station. A security team had beamed down first to clear any booby-traps left by the L'rah'hane, and the mines that had almost claimed Spock had been swept as well. Graves had placed young Ensign Thibodeaux in charge of that operation, and from all reports the young officer had scoured the area with a metaphorical toothpick before he was satisfied all was clear.

The *Enterprise* senior officers had beamed down next, met by the security team.

Kirk had called the conference immediately, but it was clear his officers needed more information before they would be able to provide the answers Kirk wanted. "All right, people," he said. "Let's go meet the science crew and the Excalbians."

They left the conference room and assembled near the outpost's small, two-person transporter platform where Commander Imelda Contreras and her second-in-command were due to materialize any moment.

Scott went to work the console.

Kirk had not only ordered full dress uniforms for the occasion, but he had ordered security provided with bosun's whistles for pomp and flourish. Kirk had ordered an official welcome for the returning prisoners complete with color guard—exactly as he had welcomed the Excalbian Abraham Lincoln two standard years before. That had taken place thousands of parsecs away, however—on the other side of the galaxy and outside Federation space.

How these Excalbians had gotten so far from their origins was something Kirk was very interesting in determining.

Mostly I just want to know what the hell is going on at Zeta Gibraltar, Kirk thought. *And why it is such a big secret that it had to be withheld from a Starfleet captain sent on a life-and-death search-and-rescue mission.*

There were too many unanswered questions here, and if there was one thing Kirk knew about Excalbians, it was that they commanded technology far greater than anything available in the Federation, and in the past they'd had no compunction in using it to kill. They claimed not to be evil, per se. In fact, they claimed not to know the difference between good and evil.

To Kirk's way of thinking, the particulars of good and evil might be culturally or individually determined in specific cases, but there was a sense of universal justice that stretched across the galaxy and reached into every corner into which Kirk had ever ventured. Somewhere, deep inside, the Excalbians, a highly intelligent species, must know that what they had done to the *Enterprise* and her crew was *wrong*.

And yet . . . because of the Excalbians, he had personally met Abraham Lincoln. He'd spoken with Surak, the ancient philosopher who had brought peace to Vulcan by replacing barbarism with logic.

They had been simulations, of course, but so complete, so compelling, as to defy his logical thought processes. His heart, his intuition, told him that those men *were* Lincoln and Surak, no matter that his rational mind knew better.

But the very same creatures had placed him and Spock on a cruel game board purposely set up to conduct an archetypal contest merely for the so-called edification of the haughty Excalbians who were presumably looking on.

Surak, Lincoln, Kirk, and Spock had been pitted against Kahless, the founder of the Klingon Empire, murderess Zora of Tiburon, ancient conqueror of the Earth's Far East, Genghis Khan, and Colonel Phillip Green, who operated during the Eugenics Wars on Earth and ordered the slaughter of hundreds of thousands of people deemed genetically unworthy.

The game the Excalbians wanted played was life and death. Each side had access to the same primitive resources: rocks that could be used to crush, cane easily shaped into spears, and vines suited for building a man-trap or a gladiator's net.

And that is exactly what the Excalbians had staged: gladiatorial games. Good versus evil to prove nothing more than a philosophical point. Then, when Kirk and his allies refused to participate in the farce, the Excalbians had upped the stakes.

Refuse to fight and the *Enterprise* and all its crew, trapped in orbit around the planet, would be destroyed. Fight and lose and suffer the same consequences. The only way to save the ship and her crew was to fight and win. "Good" must defeat "evil," or 430 people would needlessly die.

Kirk had done what he had to do. Surak, true to his nature, had refused to fight and tried to reason with Green and his cronies. He'd been slaughtered for his efforts, then used as bait to capture, torture, and kill Abraham Lincoln.

When Lincoln fell with a spear in his back, Kirk felt as if a piece had been torn from his own heart—a portion of his spirit that would always feel the loss. It had been that moment, perhaps, that had driven Kirk to the final showdown and the defeat of the evil characters. When faced with a show of greater force, they had turned and run.

Excalbian impostors had turned and run, he must remind himself. Would Colonel Green, Genghis Khan, or any of the others have done the same?

Kirk doubted it. Evil people did not necessarily lack in courage, although good people tended to have more of it, in his experience.

No, the Excalbians had proved nothing with their nasty little show, except to learn that good people fight for reasons of self-sacrifice and altruism rather than personal gain or power. This was a truism that Kirk could have told them in a moment of conversation. It didn't need to be acted out with real lives in the balance—or even the lives of a false Lincoln and Surak.

I'm surely not the best representative of good, but lucky for the Excalbians I'm not particularly evil, Kirk thought. *If I had been, I'd have found a way to destroy those arrogant silicon monsters and send their whole cursed planet after them into hell.*

And yet . . . he'd met Abraham Lincoln. The man who led a great, flawed democracy through one of the darkest periods in human history. The man who did all he could to free the slaves and preserve the Union.

It had been a Lincoln of Kirk's own creation, yes, and so designed to meet his every expectation.

As Spock had reasoned, the Excalbians must have scanned his mind and those of the crew to create such a perfect simulation. Spock had conjectured they had similarly drawn Surak from his own psyche.

In some deep part of himself, Kirk had to admit that the nasty episode with the Excalbians had almost been . . . worth it.

"I hope we aren't going to treat them like you did before," McCoy said, "knowing what we know now."

"So you think they're Excalbians, too, Bones?"

"Unless there's a Guardian gateway, like Spock speculated, or something worse. Frankly, I prefer those scoundrel Excalbians to *that*."

"Amen, Bones." Kirk nodded his agreement. McCoy had nearly ended the history of the known galaxy at one point in the presence of the Guardian. Maddened by the accidental overdose of a stimulant drug, the doctor had leaped through the portal into Earth's past and temporarily altered the entirety of human history.

Bones was right: even the resurfacing of the Excalbians was not the worst fate one could imagine.

It's a dangerous universe out there.

A beep from the transporter panel indicated an incoming signal.

"Stand by, gentlemen. We're about to meet them, whoever or whatever they are," Kirk said. "We are giving *all* the returnees full flourish. The outpost team deserves it after what they've been through."

McCoy nodded. "I'll go along with that sentiment."

The transporter platform shimmered, and Contreras and her chief of station materialized. They took a moment to gaze around before stepping down from the platform, a look of relief on their faces.

"Never thought I'd see this place again," Contreras remarked. She descended from the platform, and Kirk stepped forward to meet her. The bosun's whistles piped a welcome.

"Welcome home, Commander Contreras. I'm pleased to report that the outpost is clear of danger, quarters are cleaned and put back in good order, and I am able to officially turn the facility back over to you."

"Thank you, Captain."

"I would appreciate the opportunity to meet those charges before the *Enterprise* departs."

"There are Federation security concerns in play here that I am not at liberty to discuss," said Contreras. "But considering the circumstances, I will personally authorize you to do so."

The forty-three outpost personnel returned first. The injured arrived on stretchers. Most seemed eager to get to their quarters and begin reassembling their lives, and a few returned to duty immediately.

Five were dead, killed by the L'rah'hane, and two others were missing and presumed dead. Two of the bodies of the dead would be beamed down to the planet for burial. A third had been the wife of a scientist, and he had requested cremation for her, as per her wishes.

After a ceremony, her ashes had been beamed into deep space from the *Enterprise* transporter room.

Finally it was time to bring down the Excalbians from the L'rah'hane vessel.

Kirk nodded and turned to Scott. "Mister Scott, lock onto the L'rah'hane temporary transporter Sulu has set up. Let's bring down the Excalbians, two by two," Kirk said. For maximum efficiency and accuracy, Sulu had had transporter components ferried over to create a makeshift transporter room in a storage hold of the L'rah'hane ship. "Energize."

"Aye, sir."

Without nebular interference, the transporter worked perfectly. "I'm certainly glad to be back to normal conditions," Scott commented.

"If by normal you mean having your atoms torn apart and flung across thousands of miles of space," McCoy added.

The *Enterprise* officers stiffened to attention as George Washington and James Watt materialized before their eyes.

The Excalbian Washington was dressed in American colonial garb from head to toe. He wore a wig, but now that he was closer, Kirk could see that he had a ruddy complexion. If he remembered correctly, Washington's real hair had been reddish-brown in his younger days.

The bosun's call ended when George Washington stepped down, followed close behind by Watt.

Abraham Lincoln, now George Washington. Am I going to work my way through all the American presidents down to Millard Fillmore?

"It is with deep gratitude and the greatest sense of personal obligation that I present myself and my people to you, Captain Kirk." Washington made a formal bow. "Your servant, sir."

Kirk played along, returned the bow. "I doubt you have ever been the servant of any man, Your Excellency," he replied with a smile.

"I am most honored, Captain," Washington said. "Please, no need to use the honorific. Although I did adopt it during my first term, I soon grew tired of the title. Cincinnatus is my model, not Caesar."

Kirk couldn't help but smile. Now he began to understand why Washington was considered charming. This was not the stern, seemingly haughty figure from the portraits, but a lively, intelligent—and subtly self-effacing—man.

He was also, reportedly, the victim of heartbreak in his younger days when his romantic attachment to the wife of his best friend had come to naught.

Kirk did not extend his hand for a handshake. Washington had never been a shaker of hands. The captain had read how much Washington disliked being casually manhandled and backslapped by his fellow officers and, especially, by politicians. There was a famous story of someone's doing just that to Washington on a bet—and living to regret the jest when the general gave him a look of complete disapproval.

It was said that George Washington's icy stare had been worth three battalions during the American Revolutionary War.

"Allow me to introduce my companion. May I present Mister James Watt."

Watt was a shorter man. He wore a rumpled tweed suit. He did extend a hand to shake, and Kirk did so.

"The man who invented the first truly functional steam engine and ushered in the industrial revolution," Kirk said. "Very pleased to meet you, sir."

Watt blushed and spoke. "Standing on the shoulders of the giants who came before me, as Doctor Swift once said." Kirk had to strain to understand him. Scott's Aberdeen brogue may have been thick, but Watt had grown up in a small coastal town on the Bay of Firth, and his speech was as Scottish as could be without actually being spoken in the ancient Celtic tongue of that land.

"This is the chief engineer of the *Enterprise*, Lieutenant Commander Montgomery Scott," Kirk said, motioning to Scott, who had left the transporter console and quietly but firmly pushed his way between Kirk and Spock.

"What a great pleasure it is, sir," said Mister

Scott. "You were a hero of mine when I was a boy." Scott turned to Kirk. "And it wasn't just the steam engine, Captain. Mister Watt was a mechanical genius, you know. He invented carbon paper and was an expert scientific instrument maker at the University of Glasgow."

"*Montgomery* Scott? You wouldn't happen to be the Montgomery Scott who is the author of the groundbreaking article on the properties and uses of transverse-g type dilithium in warp engines?"

Scott's face flushed with pleasure, but, as usual, the chief engineer was a bit tongue-tied when he was at his happiest. "Ah, it's nothing. Just a wee thing I wrote up during my shore leave on Hamish D."

"A pleasure planet, and Scott insists on touring the dilithium mines and studying the processing equipment instead of gambling at the casino," Kirk said.

"Sounds like a man after my own heart," Watt replied. "I hope we have time for a bit of conversation on warp upsilon variances over a drink, Commander Scott. I trust you like Scotch?"

Now Scott's contentment turned to pure delight. "Like Scotch? Mister Watt! I do believe we'll have lots to discuss in many regards."

"All in good time," Kirk put in. "First, Mister Scott, we have need of you at the transporter controls."

Scott straightened to attention. Duty called. He took on a serious mien and replied, "Aye, sir," before returning to his post at the console.

There were forty-two "personages" in all. That was the way Kirk had begun to think of them. Most were impressive historical figures, but there was no Surak or Kahless. All were of human origin—most had been famous, although some more obscure. There was not one whom Kirk did not recognize.

Which seems very odd in itself, Kirk thought. *Not a Vulcan among them.*

Among military leaders, there was, indeed, a Napoleon. There was Sir Francis Drake, General Philip Sheridan, and samurai Oda Nobunaga. Scientists included Galileo Galilei, Johannes Kepler, Michael Faraday, and Marie Curie. Among the civilian leaders were Harriet Tubman, Gandhi, Queen Elizabeth I, and, interestingly, her nemesis, Mary, Queen of Scots. There was Confucius, Marco Polo, and Leonardo da Vinci.

Although these personages were famous, most were well-known within a certain sphere of action. Kirk was relieved to find that there were no universal religious figures included. He didn't know what he'd do if it became his duty to order around Jesus of Nazareth or the Buddha.

Spock greeted each Excalbian with appropriate ceremony, but Kirk knew his first officer and it was clear that Spock's mind was working overtime—evaluating the circumstances, engaging with various hypotheses—

Probably computing a couple of partial differential equations on the side for practice, too, Kirk thought.

It was only when the last of the personages was presented that Spock showed real interest. When Benjamin Franklin spoke to Spock, he could tell his first officer was quite intrigued.

"A Vulcan!" said Franklin. "How delightful! I have yet to meet one of your . . . people . . . sir. I hope you do not take offense at my ignorant questions, but is it true that Vulcans depend on logic for—well, *everything*?"

"It is, Doctor Franklin," Spock replied. "We find it meets all of our needs and satisfies all of our expectations for experiencing a full life."

"Absolutely! Wonderful! I have long imagined such a state of being. In fact I wrote about it once and lamented its absence from human affairs."

"You are one of the humans who have come close to achieving such a state. I have great respect for you and what you accomplished, sir."

Was Spock capable of being ironic? Kirk considered the possibility for a moment, then dismissed it. No, Spock was genuinely impressed, even though this must be only a simulated Franklin.

Franklin smiled and waved a dismissing hand. "Hardly, Mister Spock. I am as driven by sentiment and whim as the next man. But I do admire the exercise of pure reason in others. Just as an investment in knowledge always pays the best interest, if all of us engaged in logical thinking, I have long thought the world would be a happier place."

"We are in agreement, Doctor Franklin."

"I fear we differ in one aspect, however. I believe one must take men as they are, not as we wish them to be. If you would persuade, you must appeal to interest rather than intellect."

"I believe you are correct, Doctor Franklin," Spock replied, "as far as humans go."

Franklin smiled, his eyes twinkling over his reading spectacles. "I look forward to a good chat with you, Mister Spock. Is it true you play this odd variant I've encountered of one of my favorite pastimes?"

"Three-dimensional chess?" asked Spock.

"Yes, yes. That's what it is called. I could certainly use further instruction from an expert, and I understand from your Mister Sulu that you fit the bill in that regard. I had been teaching myself this game at the outpost, when my studies were so rudely interrupted by those marauders. I was close to beating myself with a delightfully wicked move when one of those pirates stepped in and held a weapon to my chest. I'm afraid I will never forgive the fellow for the disruption . . . may his, her, or its soul find rest. President Washington later did for the creature with a single musket shot."

"I would be grateful for the chance to play you, sir," Spock replied. "Perhaps at that time you might also enlighten me as to how Mister Washington retained a musket pistol and a sword when he was taken aboard the L'rah'hane vessel, and you a walking cane."

Franklin smiled his wan, benevolent smile. "That will require some explanation, won't it? I hope we can provide it. And it will be a pleasure to engage with such a worthy maestro of that delightful game. I shall be available at your earliest convenience."

"I look forward to it," said Spock.

When Franklin strode off to his outpost quarters, Kirk gave his first officer an inquisitive look.

Spock raised his eyebrows. "A sign of respect, Captain, no dissembling intended. As my previous encounter with the reproduction of Surak taught me, even a simulacrum of a man such as Benjamin Franklin is due it."

Kirk nodded. True enough.

Sulu remained on the L'rah'hane vessel for the time being, along with a skeleton crew from the *Enterprise*. Kirk had ordered it swept for any hidden smuggling compartments, hidden weaponry—or any other modification. This *was* a pirate ship, after all.

Plus, he did not trust the Excalbians. These "people" were, after all, a highly advanced species with unknown capabilities and a very questionable history.

Finally, all outpost personnel and Excalbians were back on the planet surface, and Kirk turned to his assembled senior officers. "The *Enterprise* will be staying in orbit until I hear from Starfleet. During that time, I want you to have a close look at these personages, these Excalbians. Don't get in the way of the outpost personnel, but let's get some answers."

Kirk's communicator beeped.

"Dismissed," Kirk quickly said to his officers, motioning to them that they could go about their business. He retrieved the communicator and flipped it open.

"*Enterprise*, Kirk here. Go ahead."

"*Captain, we have inbound Federation craft. It's the* Montana."

The *Montana*? That was an *Archer*-class ship, smaller then the *Enterprise*. What's more, Kirk knew that the *Montana* was a vessel designated specifically for transporting high Federation officials. It had a reputation among Starfleet officers. Assignment to the ship as captain was considered an honor, but also guaranteed a stretch of service time filled with complete boredom. Most Starfleet captains tried to avoid it as they would the Rigelian fever.

"Establish secure communication channels with the *Montana*, Mister Leslie," Kirk replied. "Beam me up."

Seven

As much as Spock may want to play a three-dimensional chess game with Benjamin Franklin, Kirk had a feeling he might need his first officer on the bridge with him when the *Montana* arrived. Spock's effortless recall of Federation official protocol would be useful. Introduction to Starfleet Etiquette and Protocol had been one class at the Academy Kirk had been very glad to be done with.

"Captain Haynes hailing from the *Montana*, sir," said Uhura.

"Put him on the screen, Lieutenant."

Haynes was an older man, lean and tall, with a full shock of black hair graying at the temples. He had a long face and was craggy and handsome. In every way, he looked the part of Starfleet captain. However, Kirk knew of his reputation.

Haynes was known as "Showboat Haynes." He'd been passed up several times for promotion and was known to take out his frustrations on his subordinates. Nevertheless, he had commanded an outstanding voyage of discovery to the Nefertiti

Sector and had by all accounts been a brave leader and inspiration to his crew.

Kirk only hoped that whatever had led to Haynes's bitter later years did not overtake himself. In his heart, though, he knew it never would. Not with a universe out there to explore, friendships to make and hold, beautiful women to gaze upon (and engage with), and determined enemies with which to contend.

"Captain Haynes, welcome to the Gibraltar system," Kirk said. "I take it you've been sent to relieve the *Enterprise*?"

"*Thank you for your welcome, Captain Kirk,*" Haynes replied. His voice was surprisingly high-pitched, coming from such a craggy visage. "*No, we are not here as a relief vessel. We are on a Federation diplomatic mission. We are traveling with a Federation Council–appointed special representative and diplomat-at-large. I'm to deliver her safely and then await further orders from Starfleet.*"

"A diplomat? To whom? The L'rah'hane?"

"*To the special charges being studied at Zeta Gibraltar, Captain,*" Haynes replied. "*I can't say any more at present. Federation Special Representative Valek will explain.*"

"Valek? A Vulcan," Kirk mused.

"Captain Haynes, the L'rah'hane pirates have re-emerged after a generation. We are analyzing their vessels' computers for evidence that a fragment of the Hradrian Empire might still exist somewhere beyond the Vara Nebula. This is a situation with security concerns that must be dealt with. This outpost is at risk."

Haynes nodded. *"I understand, Captain Kirk."* He shrugged. *"I'm afraid I have no say in the matter, however. I'm awaiting further instructions for the* Montana, *but I do have an order for you."*

"And what is it?"

"Cooperate with the representative," Haynes replied. *"That comes directly from Admiral Howe. He was quite adamant that I emphasize the word* cooperate *to you. Use your discretion, but do all you can to support Representative Valek. She has been given plenipotentiary power over the Gibraltar system for the time being."*

Plenipotentiary. That was Federation ambassadorial slang for "next thing to a dictator." The entire system would be not only under her command, but also subject to her judicial and rule-making decrees.

"With pirates still out there, *Enterprise* is on garrison duty," Kirk said with a sigh.

"It's not so bad, Kirk," Haynes replied. Then he spoke in a lowered voice, as if talking to himself. *"Less likely to get crewmembers killed."*

Maybe that is the clue to the bitterness of old Showboat, Kirk thought. *He's seen enough death.* Kirk felt a great deal more empathy for his counterpart than he had before.

"Very well, Captain Haynes. I understand my orders."

"*Kirk, this is one Federation administrator you don't want to cross,*" said Haynes. "*She's a Vulcan, and she's a tiger about getting her way.*"

A whistled alert from Haynes's command chair was followed by a curt message delivered in an alto female voice. "*Captain Haynes, I am in the transporter room waiting. I should have been beamed to the planetoid five minutes ago. Have your crewman obey my orders.*"

Haynes touched a button. "*Chief McGillicuty?*"

"*Aye, Captain?*"

"*You have my go-ahead to beam Representative Valek to Zeta Gibraltar.*"

"*Gladly, sir . . . I mean, right away, sir.*"

"*Captain Haynes,*" came the commanding voice again, "*have the* Enterprise *captain meet me on the planetoid at 1330.*"

"*I'll see what I can do, Representative Valek. Starfleet captains can be tricky to order around like toy soldiers.*"

Kirk glanced at the bridge chrono. A half hour from now. Apparently, Representative Valek liked to move fast.

"*I do not see the problem, Captain Haynes,*" the voice said. "*The lines of command are clear. My order is clear. I hope I will not have to invoke Federation Order 1123G in this matter?*"

"*I expect not,*" Haynes replied.

"*Very well,*" the other replied, then, after a pause: "*Thank you for your cooperation. Valek out.*"

Haynes turned back to the screen. "*Good luck, Captain. Maybe you can handle her. Meanwhile, I'll be here in orbit. Very peaceful here in orbit.*" He smiled an ironic smile. "Montana *out.*"

The feed was cut, and the viewscreen flashed back to an image of the planetoid below.

Kirk turned to Spock and motioned toward the turbolift entrance. "Commander Spock, shall we prepare to beam down and, it seems, meet our fate?"

Spock raised an eyebrow and replied, "Indeed. Captain, I believe I am aquainted with Representative Valek,"

"Oh? Who is she?"

"She is someone I knew during my childhood," Spock said. "More pertinently, I believe that, at present, she works with Sarek, my father."

Kirk cracked a smile. "This is getting more interesting. Now I truly do want to meet Representative Valek. Come on."

Kirk stepped onto the *Enterprise* transporter pad considering how he was going to clearly and logically express his displeasure for keeping a Starfleet captain in the dark about a key piece of information involved with a crucial mission.

"Energize," he ordered. As always, there was no sensation of dematerialization. One moment he was on the *Enterprise*, the next . . . and there she was.

Any angry words died on Kirk's tongue.

She was Vulcan, all right. And she was beautiful.

"Greetings, Captain," Valek said. She raised her hand in the Vulcan salute. "Live long and prosper."

"Peace and long life," said Spock.

Kirk and Spock stepped down from the transporter. Valek stood next to Commander Contreras, who was a good ten centimeters shorter than the Vulcan. Contreras's utilitarian garb also contrasted with that of the representative. Valek wore traditional Vulcan dress made of a shimmering blue-black material that made her appear to be an icy empress visiting from some remote mountain kingdom.

"It has been a long time, Spock," Valek replied. "Your father and mother send greetings."

"Please deliver my own when next you see them," Spock replied.

How about that, thought Kirk. For once, a Vulcan expression he'd heard often entirely fit the current exchange: *fascinating*.

"I trust your brother prospers," Spock said.

"Varen has been appointed by the Science Academy as a tenured researcher on vertebrate extremophiles. He is doing groundbreaking work off-planet at the moment."

"Given Varen's considerable intellectual gifts, a wise choice and logical posting on the part of the Academy," Spock replied.

"Indeed," said Valek. She turned to Kirk. "You must forgive our extraneous conversation, Captain. Spock and I have previous acquaintance."

"No, no problem at all," said Kirk. "Please take the time you need."

When do I ever get to hear such . . . intimate details of Spock's earlier history? Never.

"The Varen of whom we speak, Captain, is Valek's twin brother," Spock said.

"I've never heard of Vulcans having twins," Kirk said.

"It is an uncommon occurrence among Vulcans," Valek put in. "Spock and Varen were laboratory partners during their childhood educational period."

"We were friends," Spock explained.

Valek turned her icy attention back to Spock. "You *have* been a long time among humans, Spock."

Spock ignored the jibe, if jibe it was. Kirk knew both Vulcans would deny that Valek's words had any emotional content. They were merely a statement of the obvious.

"Your brother was fortunate in his choice of Spock for a companion," Kirk said.

"Perhaps you are correct," Valek replied. Spock said nothing in reply. After an uncomfortable silence—uncomfortable, at least, for Kirk—Valek spoke again. "Captain Kirk, you, Commander Contreras, and I have much to discuss, and most of it is of a classified nature. Can we adjourn alone to a secure conference room so that I can deliver your instructions?"

Kirk glanced at Spock, who quirked up an eyebrow in response.

So that's the way this is going to be, Kirk thought. *Well then, the hell with diplomacy.*

"I'll be happy to hear what you have to say, Representative Valek. And Commander Spock will also join us as my second-in-command," Kirk replied.

"Captain, I cannot permit that."

"Representative, you may have civilian plenipotentiary power, but in times of emergency, a Starfleet officer responding to that emergency shares undisputed authority with any civilian. I hope we're clear on that."

"I was not aware we were in a declared emergency zone under Section R of the administrative code."

"I believe you will find that the conditions for such a declaration are met, Representative Valek," Spock put in. "Subparagraph three point two deals with circumstances of clear and present danger immediately following an emergency action, police response, or military engagement. I believe the present situation meets two of the criteria and any one is necessary and sufficient to constitute a *de facto* emergency zone declaration."

Valek stared at Spock, then looked away and took a moment to consider. She turned her gaze back toward Kirk. They locked eyes for a moment. Kirk did not break eye contact, and neither did she.

Her expression did not change, but after a moment she nodded. "A logical arrangement to include a trusted aid," she finally said. "Commander Spock may accompany us."

"All right," Kirk said.

Contreras let out of sigh of released tension. "If we're done staking out territory, I believe the outpost conference room will serve our purposes."

Kirk finally looked away from Valek. He smiled at Contreras, nodded. "Certainly. Lead the way, Commander."

Kirk dropped behind a few steps and allowed Valek and Contreras to walk ahead. He had thought to give Spock a bit of room to speak alone with the representative, but instead Spock also dropped back to walk beside Kirk. Fair enough, he could use the time to pump his first officer for further information. He had a feeling he was about to need a bit of leverage.

"How does she know Sarek and Amanda, Spock?" Kirk asked.

"She trained under my father," said Spock. "She now works for him as a . . . the term is imprecise, but I believe you might call her a 'diplomatic troubleshooter.'"

"She's a protégé of Sarek's?"

"Correct."

"You don't like her."

"'Like' has nothing to do with it, Captain. She once publicly spoke against my father and mother's union."

"On what she considered a completely logical basis, I'm sure," Kirk said.

"Her logic was mistaken."

"I see."

"At the time, Varen opposed her and pointed out key flaws in her argumentation."

"How old were you when this happened?" Kirk asked.

"Ten point five standard years of age."

"She was just a child."

"It is different on Vulcan," Spock said. "Childhood is quite stimulating, but less . . . playful."

"She grew up to be one of your father's favorites, while you and Sarek have over the years had . . . differences of interpretation concerning what it means to be a Vulcan."

"I might phrase it in a different manner—Sarek's choices are always motivated by logical considerations; he does not 'play favorites.' Yet your point is essentially correct. You must understand, however, that I bear Valek no ill will."

You *may not, but I'm already starting to dislike her*, Kirk thought. *But it looks like both of us are going to have to work with her, all the same.*

They arrived at the conference room, and after a DNA scan of Contreras, were admitted.

Valek wanted secure. It looked like Contreras had pulled out the stops to give it to her.

Before anyone sat down at the conference room table, Valek turned to them and caught everyone's attention with a slight bow of her head, indicating she had something she wished to say.

"I apologize if my tone seemed imperious in the transporter room, Captain, and with you when I beamed down earlier, Commander," Valek said. "I felt it would be useful to establish our mutual credentials so that our task may proceed. I am aware that humans do not always take blunt statements well. They read emotional nuances into such pronouncements that are not intended."

"No offense taken, Representative Valek," Kirk said.

"Please call me Valek. It will save time, and so long as we are clear on our hierarchical positions, the title is unnecessary."

"All right, Valek," Kirk replied. "Precisely what is 'our task'?"

"To make a decision on whether or not to admit the Excalbian refugees currently located on Zeta

Gibraltar as Federation citizens under the Federation Asylum Act."

"They *are* Excalbians," Kirk replied.

"Of course."

"And this has been verified?"

Contreras broke in. "We used the records of *Enterprise*'s visit to Excalbia," she said. "There are trace radioactive particles in our residents here that match the exact composition and distribution of Excalbian silicates as recorded by your sensor sweeps of the surface. We found, in essence, the fingerprint of Excalbian origin within them. And much else."

"Shall we sit?" Valek said, motioning to the conference table.

Kirk took his place along one side and Valek chose to sit exactly across from him.

Guess she wants to keep an eye out for any insubordination, Kirk thought, and smiled wryly. Valek noticed his expression, but said nothing. Instead, she now answered Kirk's early question.

"The Federation Council knew they were Excalbians," Valek said. "As to how they came to Zeta Gibraltar, the answer is that they were brought here. By us."

As Valek laid out the story, the Excalbians, in their present human forms, were discovered in the hold of a robotic mining transport that had malfunctioned and strayed into the exclusion zone around the Excalbian system. The craft eventually self-repaired and wound up at its destination. When the hold was opened, the Excalbians exited—all in the same form as they now appeared, as historical personages.

"Interestingly," Valek said, "there were no furnishings inside the hold. Apparently, being confined to a smaller space suppressed their regeneration capacity."

"When we gave them rooms here in the outpost," Contreras said, "the standard furnishings began to disappear. In their place were what you've seen: four-poster beds, wardrobes, tapestries. We believe it is an autonomic response. We've experimented with quarters of different sizes. The process is self-limiting."

"Fascinating," said Spock. "They seem to imprint their surroundings."

"They had very little room to affect their environment in that transport hold," Valek said. "They were a bedraggled group when they emerged. When they realized they'd made it to Federation space, they immediately requested political asylum."

"Wait a minute," said Kirk. "Asylum from whom?"

"From Excalbia," answered Valek. "They claimed to be fleeing oppression."

"And the Federation bought their story?"

Valek paused a moment, obviously not agreeing

with what she might consider simplistic wording. "The Federation did not," she answered.

"That is why they are here, at Zeta Gibraltar?" said Spock. "This is a holding place until the Federation Council can arrive at a decision on what to do with them."

"Essentially, yes," Valek answered. "Although the secondary purpose of scientific study of their physiology and culture is also being pursued by the outpost team led by Commander Contreras."

"That's why the outpost is Starfleet," said Kirk. "You need trained personnel to serve as security for the Excalbians."

"In simple terms, yes," replied Valek. "After your report on the L'rah'hane raid and capture of the Excalbians, the Federation Council has reasoned that they are not safe in this location, and a decision must be made. A special diplomatic corps commission was created by the Council Special Committee for Security and Frontier Intelligence to study the issue and provide recommendations. The commission is headed by Sarek of Vulcan and includes three other senior diplomats."

"You're Sarek's person on the ground," Kirk said. "The pointy end of the sword."

Valek stared at Kirk a moment, evidently processing and assessing his colloquialism. It seemed to suit her, and she nodded agreement. "I was chosen to assess the situation and make a recommendation.

During that evaluation process, I have been given plenipotentiary powers by the Special Committee for Security and Frontier Intelligence to include the entirety of the Gibraltar system. I shall make my recommendation, and I expect that, with suitable emendation by the appointed commission, it will be acted upon by the full Federation Council."

"Excuse me, Valek," said Spock, "your answer is somewhat vague. I must ask you to clarify what you might base this decision upon. There is no logical course of action without data on which to base it."

Valek again gave Spock one of her cold pauses.

"My task is to decide whether or not to give the Excalbians—*these* Excalbians—political asylum within the Federation and put them on a path to full citizenship. That is the action upon which I will make my recommendation. And the basis of my decision is to be my personal judgment, Spock."

"But why is this being done clandestinely?" Kirk said. "Surely this is a question that should be discussed openly by the full Council."

"There is sufficient reason for this matter to remain sub rosa for the time being."

"What is that reason?"

"I am not at liberty to discuss it."

"I hope you can see how that makes my job difficult, Valek."

"I do not follow you, Captain," Valek replied.

"Obviously, there is a threat to this outpost. Based on the firepower we observed from the L'rah'hane pirates, the *Montana* may not be enough to provide protection. Until I receive further orders, the *Enterprise* will remain right where she is, in orbit around Zeta Gibraltar, until such time as I am convinced the danger has passed. We both have a decision to make. We must work together."

"I could not agree more, Captain Kirk," said Valek. "I have every intention of working closely with you. I hope you will work with me."

"Certainly, Representative Valek," Kirk replied.

She's a bundle of contradictions, Kirk thought. *First she comes on strong to make a point, then she gets reasonable and accommodating once she's gotten her way. Yes, she's learned how to use her "Vulcan-ness" to push her agenda among humans. Not many Vulcans would stoop to do that. And she's quite good at it, apparently. She's certainly got me eating out of her hand.*

I think I'm beginning to like her.

"And Captain—"

"Yes?"

Valek put a hand on the table in front of her. Her fingers were of medium length, not long like Spock's. She had extremely well-manicured nails cut short. And was that a trace of clear polish on them? Another Vulcan first, as far as Kirk was concerned.

Thrump, thrump.

She's drumming her fingers, Kirk thought. *I didn't know Vulcans did that.*

"—there is nothing in my instructions that prohibits you from gleaning whatever knowledge you might from the Excalbians. They are free beings, free to discuss whatever they wish."

Kirk turned to his first officer. "Well, as long as we're here, there are matters on this planetoid that need taking care of. Should the *Enterprise* be called away, I would not want to leave the outpost defenseless."

"We didn't think there was any threat for thousands of parsecs when we established this outpost," Contreras said, shaking her head at Starfleet Command's misjudgment. "Only in retrospect is it apparent we were relying far too much on dated information from robotic probes."

"We have people trained in planetary defense. I want to bring some of them down." He turned to Valek. "Would that be acceptable?"

"I can . . . see how that might be useful, yes."

"I would also expect them to mingle with the Excalbians and learn as much as possible about them."

"That also seems prudent," Valek replied. "You will share any pertinent findings with me, Captain."

"Of course we will," said Kirk. "Mister Spock."

"Captain?"

"It looks like you'll get your chess game with Benjamin Franklin after all."

"Now, Captain, I have a request to make of you," Valek said.

"Yes, Valek?"

"It is time we question the leader of the Excalbians. Since they have taken human form, I believe an interrogation practice that I learned of while working for Ambassador Sarek might be of use. It is an ancient human technique. Two interrogators are required, one taking an uncompromising position, the other seeming to yield more."

"Yes, I'm familiar with it," Kirk said with a smile. "I believe it was called 'good cop, bad cop,' in the vernacular."

"A most clear and precise characterization," Valek replied.

"So how would you recommend we implement this human technique, Valek?" Kirk asked.

Valek raised an eyebrow. "I'm surprised you have to ask, Captain," she replied. "Isn't it obvious? I am the bad cop."

Eight

Kirk suggested, and Valek agreed, that putting George Washington into a bare interrogation chamber as she first proposed might defeat their purpose. Instead, he'd recommended that they meet the Excalbian in his own quarters, where he might be more at ease.

Washington had agreed readily enough. Kirk found himself sitting in the first office of an American president: a spartan room with two sturdy, unpadded chairs in front of a small writing desk no more than a half meter across. On the wall were several portraits, one of Washington's wife, Martha. There was a large American Indian tobacco pipe beside a battered powder horn, both on a sideboard cabinet.

"From two very ill-starred military campaigns," Washington said when he saw Kirk examining them.

"Braddock's attack on Fort Duquesne?"

Washington smiled broadly, but still not showing his teeth—or lack thereof. "Impressive, Captain. Yes, the powder horn is a relic of General Braddock that I kept for sentimental reasons. I see you know American history."

"I'm from Iowa," Kirk said. When he noticed a confused look on Washington's face, he added: "A state that was added to the Union after your time."

"I see," Washington said.

"And the pipe?"

Washington's face clouded. "Fort Necessity," he said. "It belonged to an Indian named Tanaghrisson. I keep it as a reminder that no matter how much success one has, disaster can be just around the corner."

"A worthwhile lesson," Kirk said.

Valek broke in. "Since I am not a product of Earth and have only an intellectual interest in its history, let's get down to our business, gentlemen."

Washington bowed his head and took one of the seats in front of the desk. Valek remained standing, and Kirk took the other. Then Valek moved around to the other side of the small writing desk, keeping the desk between herself and Washington.

"Seeing that your species threatened and brutalized the crew of a Starfleet vessel," Valek stated matter-of-factly, "I'm afraid the Federation must place the burden upon you to prove that you are different."

"Is that not guilt by association?" Washington said. "No matter." He spread his hands before him. "I hope you can see by now that myself and my people are no threat. On the contrary, we wish to assimilate into the Federation as quickly as possible."

"You'll pardon me for questioning your sincerity," Kirk replied, "but as you know, I have had personal dealings with Excalbians. I'd like to think you've turned over a new leaf, but in my experience, you like to toy with the lives of others."

Washington nodded. "Yes, you do have reason to doubt us, Captain. As a matter of fact, you have reason to doubt me in particular."

Here was something unexpected. Kirk was suddenly all ears, his intuition buzzing. He turned an inquisitive look toward Valek, but she shook her head. "Tell him," she said to Washington.

"You in particular, you say? What do you mean?"

Washington took a deep breath and sighed. "We have met before, you and I, although I never properly introduced myself. I was too busy expounding on how fortunate you were to be part of a great philosophical experiment my species was engaging in."

Recognition—and disgust—filled Kirk. "You're *it*, aren't you? The representative from the peanut gallery of Excalbians."

"I do not exactly follow all your words, but I believe I understand what the idiom means," Washington said. "You are correct. I was the one who spoke to you. My name, my Excalbian name, is Yarnek."

"I'll be damned. It *is* you, isn't it? The very same creature we met."

"Yes. I am Yarnek," said the man. "But I am also George Washington. Truly, Captain, my life, and the lives of my compatriots, depends on my convincing you that this is so."

"The last time I saw you, you were a steaming lump of magma with multiple eyes. I burned my hand when I touched you. And then you threatened to kill my crew and destroy my ship. You'll pardon me if I need something more to go on than just your word of honor, Yarnek."

Washington-Yarnek bowed his head. "You have every reason to doubt, Captain Kirk, but please hear me out." He turned to Valek. "I understand some of these matters are classified, but I wish to make an explanation to Captain Kirk, whom I have personally wronged."

"Very well," Valek said. "Please continue."

"Thank you," Washington-Yarnek replied. "All I can do is apologize on behalf of my species for that regrettable incident on my home planet." Washington-Yarnek's voice grew more solemn. "And for the other incidents that followed. I wish I could say that it did not happen again, but I'm afraid it did. I could not stop it."

"What are you talking about?" Kirk asked. "If anyone could, it's you."

"Not so, Captain," replied Washington-Yarnek. "To explain why, I must tell you of what happened after the *Enterprise* left the system."

For thousands of your years there had been unity in the Upper Stratum, the portion of planetary magma pool only a few kilometers from the surface. This was an area of complexity and change—to such an extent that consciousness itself could play upon and across its fiery surface. Here was the matrix of the Excalbian public sphere, the mental space in which individual minds could contend without burning out or absorbing their compatriots.

One million years ago, the Excalbian's ancient ancestors had evolved as silicon-based creatures on the *surface* of the planet. Then, when individual intelligence was achieved, they had discovered a way to migrate *inward*. Twenty thousand years ago, this is where Excalbian civilization was born.

That collection of rocky bits of individual consciousness within the magma, the collective, was like, and unlike, a government. The subsurface heat layer was the physical substrate where great debates were hosted, but also a place filled with competing processes, coalitions, and great confabulations of the minds that had arisen from the deep magma that surrounded the planetary iron and nickel core.

They had not discarded their bodies at that time, but rather let their thinking processes *spread out* in the volcanic heat, and had become creatures more of mind than body, churning and burning in the boiling, bubbling interior of the planet.

Heat that their furious activity brought to the surface. The planet Excalbia had not begun as a hellhole of seething lava. That had been the doing of the planet's only sentient species—and soon its only species at all.

As each individual migrated into the magmatic superstructure and began concentrating and organizing the heat, that structure had become more complex, less stable—and much more volatile. The planet had grown hotter and hotter, its interior heat released far more quickly than it would in a natural state. In the end, great magma flows had arisen and covered all the continents. The seas, which had once been beautiful and huge, evaporated or were absorbed in the planet's substrate.

All life except for the Excalbians, buried deep within the planet, perished in a holocaust of volcanic destruction.

Yet as the planet melted and boiled, its complexity grew. It took the Excalbians many thousand years, but eventually they learned how to not merely exist within the flow of heat and liquid rock, but to control the fundamental particles of matter on a quantum level. The Excalbians became manipulators of the reality around them.

For many, this seemed to be the equivalent of an ascent to godhood, and they behaved as if they were gods. Others saw the trap of solipsism and inwardness such power opened up. For if you could make anything and everything for yourself a reality, you might begin to think that thought was what formed the world, that perception was a form of *creation*. What began as a heresy over time grew to be considered common sense.

Excalbians were the only "real" thing, and the rest of the universe was a toy for the "real" people to play with.

Even in magmatic form, the Excalbians retained genders from their evolutionary past. But that was practically the only reminder that they had once been mere creatures. Good and evil as concepts melted away. Each could live in his or her virtual dream world. There was no need for morality, so concepts of "right" and "wrong" were forgotten.

Almost.

Then a strange thing happened. From the stars, a vessel arrived containing other life, other intelligences. This prompted a great debate within the complex swirl of magmatic uplift known as the collective—where presided the Excalbian ruling council. First was the question as to whether contact would be contaminating. It was decided that passive contact would likely be safe.

Reaching out to those other intelligences, it was discovered that their thoughts might be as easily read and mapped as might the churn and eddies of a magma storm or the radioactive transformation of the system's sun—mapmaking, at which

the Excalbians were already adept. Soon after contact, it became obvious that the new intelligences,
these people of the "Federation" and "Starfleet," as
they styled themselves, were not aware that their
thoughts were being charted. Even the "Vulcan"
among them, whose mental subroutines were the
most efficient and who had achieved a primitive
level of quantum information transfer known as the
"Vulcan mind meld," was unaware of the mapping.

The minds of these Starfleet officers might provide data, but they did not create understanding.
Many new concepts, many unknown perceptions
and memories of yet other ideas, were uncovered—
concepts and memories entirely new to the Excalbian way of thinking. These people were *different*.
They were *difference* personified.

A great debate arose, for this conclusion cut
at the very foundation of Excalbian existence. For
those in the starship passing through the system in
warp space, this debate would have seemed to only
take five minutes or so.

For the Excalbian mentalities, it went on for
"days."

Finally, a decision was reached. The newcomers
were either a figment of the imagination, something
like a daydream, or from somewhere "outside"
the sphere of Excalbian thought, an occurrence
deemed to be impossible by the majority of Excalbians. Most troubling of all was the alien concept of

"good" and "evil." These values implied that a world outside of thought existed and that actions within that world had weight.

Yet most were still convinced it was all a bad dream.

If good and evil proved to have observable consequences—that is, if good and evil mattered beyond being merely playthings of the mind—then humans, Vulcans, Starfleet officers might all be *real* themselves and might know something that Excalbians did not. The *Excalbians* might have something to learn from the humanoids.

The Excalbians might even have to look upon them as equals.

"Inconceivable!" declared the majority of the collective. "These are not intelligent beings, but malfunctioning mental processes within ourselves. As such, they ought to be eradicated."

"But if their reality is 'inconceivable,' then you won't mind if their ideas are tested?" said the minority.

And thus the majority was trapped by its own logic.

———

"The test," said Captain Kirk, leaning back in his chair, "was not so much to determine the difference between good and evil, but to discover whether we were figments of your imagination."

"You have the truth of it, Captain," said Washington-Yarnek. "We had to determine whether or not you could surprise us with your actions. You and Mister Spock certainly did. Abraham Lincoln and Surak, as you correctly surmised, were based upon your own ideas of those individuals, and thus were, in a manner of speaking, extensions of yourselves. All four of you—yourselves and the other 'good' forces—succeeded in surprising us. Furthermore, you awoke in many of us—such as myself—a very new feeling for having subjected you to this staged play in the first place."

"What was that?" asked Valek.

Washington-Yarnek frowned and broke eye contact with them. "Guilt, Representative Valek," he said. "If right and wrong *did* in actuality exist, then we had been wrong to bully you and to threaten your ship and your crew. I, myself, had acted in an evil manner. And there was a 'good' portion within me that was not happy with that fact."

"The classic fall from the Garden," Kirk said. "You and your species ate of the Tree of Knowledge of Good and Evil and you didn't like the taste so much."

"Captain Kirk is speaking metaphorically," said Valek. "I do not think he believes there was an actual Garden of Eden in Earth's prehistory, yet the idea of a fall from an original guiltless state is found throughout human philosophical and religious—"

"I didn't mean it literally," Kirk said. "I think Yarnek understands me."

"I do indeed," Washington-Yarnek replied. "And you are correct, at least in my case."

"Be that as it may," said Kirk, "it still doesn't explain what you are doing *here* right *now*."

Washington-Yarnek nodded.

"Captain, Representative, do you mind if I have a drink? I find a small dram of rum concentrates my mind."

"I do not mind," Valek replied.

"I wouldn't mind joining you," Kirk put in.

"I would be delighted if you would," the Excalbian said. "And you, Representative Valek? It is excellent rum from the Caribbean."

"If it were real it would be a product of slave labor," Valek said. "No thank you."

"It is real enough to do its job," Washington-Yarnek said. "But I take your point, Representative."

Washington-Yarnek rose from his chair and went to the small sideboard table that the pipe sat upon. He opened its cabin door and brought out two silver cups and a glass bottle with a golden liquid sloshing about inside. He set the cups on the sideboard tabletop. He took out a glass stopper, then tilted the bottle up and poured himself and

Kirk a healthy portion of what looked very much like rum.

And when Kirk took his cup from Washington-Yarnek, he found it smelled and tasted like rum, too. Good rum.

Washington-Yarnek quickly drained his glass in a single swallow. He stood gazing down into the empty cup.

"You look like you could use another," Kirk said.

"Indeed. Thank you, sir," replied Washington-Yarnek. He poured out another dram, then returned to his seat, cup in hand. He was a tall man, well over a meter and a half, and possessed a lanky torso matched with shorter legs, which made him seem to be a bit awkward at rest. Yet he moved with a fluid motion and, contrary to Kirk's expectations, he found Washington-Yarnek to be quite graceful, even suave and debonair in his way.

I do seem to remember learning that he was a great dancer and generally a hit with the ladies, Kirk thought. *But I didn't quite believe it until now.*

"The tale of what followed the *Enterprise*'s departure from Excalbia is a tortuous one, and, in parts, most unpleasant," Washington-Yarnek began. Then he paused and lifted his cup of rum. "But first, to your health, madam and sir."

Kirk raised his own cup and returned the gesture. Valek, meanwhile, looked on with an inscrutable expression.

Washington-Yarnek again drained his glass, and continued.

After the *Enterprise* left Excalbia, the memories of the crew and historical records gleaned from the *Enterprise* computer were retained in the silicate memory of the planet. In a further series of experiments, various Excalbians were transformed to humaniod species in the same manner as Abraham Lincoln, Surak, and the others had been.

"After we acquired the taste for pitting life against life," Washington-Yarnek said, "it proved difficult to stop doing so."

"Regrettable," Valek said.

"Indeed. We at first believed them to be a harmless indulgence, but instead, these 'games' began to consume us," said Washington-Yarnek. "Although good won out in *your* play, Captain, the idea of evil proved a very seductive philosophical position for a portion of my species. I was ordered to take part in these plays, to serve as 'host,' or 'referee,' as you might understand the concept.

"Even then, I had my doubts as to the wisdom of such so-called games. I feared they would be an excuse for callous behavior. I was proven right many times over, but I'm getting ahead of myself." Washington-Yarnek sighed. "When I refused, I was coerced into taking this form, the form of President George Washington."

"So you were made to participate in the experiments yourself," Kirk said. "You'll pardon me, Yarnek, but we humans have a saying, 'What goes around, comes around.'"

"A sentiment I very much understand, Captain," the Excalbian replied with a grim set to his mouth. "Yet not only was I given no choice in the matter—as indeed, you were not—but to up the stakes and to add more so-called 'reality' to the morality game, I was also stripped of the ability to change back into my original form. The idea was that, if I was killed, I would be truly dead."

"Barbaric," Valek said. "Continue."

"The same process was applied to all of my comrades here on Zeta Gibraltar," Yarnek continued. "We are all survivors of at least one, and often many, such gladiatorial combats. It would have gone on indefinitely until we were all dead—and thus removed from influencing politics within the collective or affecting its makeup. But, with a measure of luck on my part and a great deal of ingenuity on the part of Mister Watt, Miss Tubman, and others, a group of us were able to escape. The circumstances were extremely trying. My mate-bond—my 'wife,' in your terminology—was killed while we fled, her consciousness obliterated." Washington-Yarnek made a fist around his empty cup. "Her name was Terima. For five hundred years she lived a life of grace, beauty, and thoughtfulness. I miss her wisdom every moment of every day."

Washington-Yarnek shook his head, and his shoulders slumped.

If he's feigning his sorrow, Kirk thought, *he's the best actor I've ever seen. Which might be true, of course. He is, after all, doing a very convincing job of pretending to be George Washington.*

"I now have firsthand acquaintance with the true nature of good and evil," said Yarnek. "And with loneliness and loss, as well. Terima was a good and noble person. Without my mate-bond, I would not be here today. Others made similar sacrifices. If it were not for them, none of us would have gotten off Excalbia."

Washington-Yarnek silently contemplated his memories for a moment, and Valek took the opportunity to break in.

"Pardon me, Mister President," said Valek. "To save time and emotional epiphenomenon, I shall offer to fill in several of the details of what followed."

Washington-Yarnek sighed, then took a deep breath and nodded, relief in his eyes. "Yes, I would appreciate if you would do so, Representative Valek," he replied.

"A passing Orion-bound transport experienced a partial core meltdown and strayed within Excalbian space. The escaping Excalbians made use of the matter transmutation abilities of their unaffected accomplices and were transferred to the cargo hold of that ship. Some weeks later, they were discovered upon docking at Barlow's Planet in the Cerulean system."

Valek paused for a moment, seemingly considering how much more she was permitted to tell them.

"At the space elevator dock of Barlow's Planet, Yarnek exited the cargo hold, found a Federation official, and immediately asked for political asylum."

"Full citizenship?"

"That was the request. But at the moment, they have been given only refugee status."

"You've taken them to the extreme edge of the Alpha Quadrant, to Zeta Gibraltar for study—and to figure out what danger they might pose for the Federation."

"Precisely, Captain," Valek said, gazing at him with a sudden look of surprise and approval in her eyes.

You're not the only one who can draw logical inferences from a given situation, Kirk thought. Valek's appreciative gaze did not irritate him as much as he thought it would. Instead, he found himself enjoying her momentary approval.

"The Federation science team has done an excellent job extracting what information they can," Valek said. "In light of the recent pirate raid, I am here to make a determination on the request for political asylum so that the science outpost on Zeta Gibraltar can be closed until such time as adequate defenses are in place." She placed her hand firmly, palm down, on the writing desk, as if she were attempting to impress some truth into it. "While I am intrigued by Yarnek's explanation for his presence, I am far from convinced by it. Until I am, I deem him and the others to be a possible danger to the Federation."

Kirk feigned surprise, playing along to Valek's "bad cop," which, he had to admit, was pretty convincing. "How long do you imagine that will take, Valek?" Kirk asked.

"Unknown," Valek replied coolly. "The *Montana* and the *Enterprise* will remain in orbit until I am done here, Captain Kirk. Two ships for cover should be sufficient."

So much for retaining her admiration, Kirk thought. *She thinks we need Haynes to make up a creditable defensive force.*

"You'll excuse me, Valek," Kirk said, "but you are outside your area of expertise."

Valek looked Kirk up and down. Was that a shrewd smile playing over her features?

Vulcans don't smile, Kirk reminded himself. *Even when they believe they are being clever. But I'll bet Washington-Yarnek doesn't know that.*

"In that case, since you insist on your right to question my judgment, I am required to present to you *this*," she said.

From what appeared to be a pocket or pouch within her tunic, Valek drew forth a data card and handed it to Kirk.

Kirk felt his face redden. She'd sprung this surprise on him as well as Washington-Yarnek.

"These are orders bearing both the imprimatur of the Federation Council *and* Starfleet Command," Valek said. "I am given command privileges over any and all ships in the Gibraltar system."

Kirk rolled the card around in his hand, tempted to shatter it to pieces.

"The file is signed by Admiral Wingate, Starfleet liaison to the Council," Valek said. "I have full authority over you, your crew, and your ship, Captain."

"As pertains to your mission," Kirk replied evenly

"Your qualification is correct," Valek said. "But you will find that my mission has broad parameters." She turned to Washington-Yarnek and held him in her icy gaze. "One possible reason for denying a request for asylum is a determination that the asylum seekers have lied or misrepresented themselves in any way to Federation officials."

Washington-Yarnek looked up and met her gaze steadily. "I have not told a lie," he said in a low, clear voice. "But what would be the consequences if I had?"

"If I judge that asylum is not to be granted, one possible course of action will be to order the *Enterprise* to deport you back to Excalbia." Valek came out from behind the desk and stood beside Kirk. "Now gentlemen, if you are done with your drinks and your chat . . . Captain, I would like to consult with you as to the parameters of your orders."

Kirk stood up. "As you wish," he said. He bowed toward Washington-Yarnek. "Good day, Mister President."

Washington-Yarnek, too, rose to his feet.

"Good day to you, as well, Captain," Washington-Yarnek said. He turned to Valek. "Do you have any . . . orders for the Excalbians, Madam Representative?"

"None at present, Yarnek," said the Vulcan. "But when I do, I shall let you know."

Nine

Imelda Contreras had arranged temporary quarters for Kirk that included a sleeping area and a meeting space. Kirk had added to the space by installing a computer with a direct link to the *Enterprise*. A constant feed of scans of the system would alert the captain if the L'rah'hane returned. Kirk could remain up-to-date on ship's operations and be ready to return to the *Enterprise* on a moment's notice. Until then, however, doing *anything* beat standing hour upon hour of garrison duty.

Kirk thought, *Let someone who needs the experience use the time to learn the ropes of ship operation and sensor monitoring.*

His gut feeling that the L'rah'hane were waiting for their chance to strike back had, if anything, grown stronger.

His quarters also had the advantage of having a briefing area with chairs, a table, and the outpost's computer link. The entire suite was, he guessed, double the size of his captain's quarters on the ship.

Most of all, it was *private*—which was why he'd

retired to the briefing area with his senior staff to go over their current options.

Spock, Scott, McCoy, and Uhura, who had just finished testing the computer protocols—were seated in a semicircle around the small table. Kirk currently had the audio turned off. One less distraction.

"I didn't appreciate Valek pulling out those signed orders in the middle of our discussion with Washington, or Yarnek, or whoever he is."

"That was likely the point, Jim," McCoy said with a chuckle. "She needed a convincing and genuine reaction out of you to convince the fellow that she meant business, and boy did she get one."

Kirk nodded ruefully toward the ship's surgeon. "Yes, very clever. Unless you're the one being used as the cat's-paw." He swiveled to face his first officer. "Spock, have I got any wiggle room?" he asked.

"I have had time to examine them, and the orders and instructions on her official brief are quite ironclad," Spock replied. "But also quite specific. Valek's authority over the Excalbians is unquestionable. Beyond that, her purview may be legally limited." Spock cocked an eyebrow. "But Captain, allow me to suggest that, at the moment, we have an interest in mutual collaboration."

Kirk chuckled. "Right as rain, Mister Spock."

Spock shook his head. "A puzzling expression," he said. "Rain merely *is* or *is not*, after all. It possesses not ethical or even intellectual qualities."

"You're right as rain about that, too, Mister Spock," McCoy piped in with a smile.

Kirk turned to the doctor. "Bones, I know these people have studied the Excalbians every which way, but let's get going with our own exams. I want you to stay down here for a day or so and see if you can get a few of them to take a physical from you."

"Will do, Captain."

"Bones, down to the molecular level."

"Don't worry," said the ship's surgeon. "I'll do my best to find out what makes them tick, Jim. I already know why some of them insist on those silly wigs."

"Really? Enlighten us, Doctor."

"To hide lice," McCoy said. "They seem to regenerate those as thoroughly as everything else."

Kirk immediately felt a desire to reach up and scratch his head at the mention of the little beasts. He suppressed it. Yet McCoy, who could be a bit of a mind-reader himself, noticed Kirk's tremor and smiled.

"If I'm right, they won't pose any threat to the crew," McCoy said. "If they lived very long away from their original host, half the personnel on this outpost would be infected by now. I haven't seen many people scratching their heads around here— except in befuddlement."

"All right, then, as for the rest of us, Mister Scott, the planetoid defenses need upgrading, and

I can't help but think our James Watt Excalbian
might make—"

A greeting whistled from nearby the door.
"Visitor at entrance," said the voice of the outpost
computer.

"Identify," Kirk said.

*"Federation Special Representative Valek requests
permission to enter and speak with Captain James T.
Kirk,"* said the computer.

Kirk gazed around at his officers. "Well, let's
hear her out. Admit the representative, computer."

With a pneumatic chuff, the door slid open.

Kirk stood. "Please come in, Valek."

Valek nodded and entered. She did not seem
surprised to see the others gathered in the briefing
area. "Greetings," she said to the others, then turned
immediately to Kirk. "Captain, it occurs to me that
we should engage in a thorough debriefing following our discussion with Yarnek." She glanced at the
others. "I would also be very pleased if your senior
staff took part."

"Certainly, Valek," he replied. "How about now?"

"That would be quite satisfactory," she said with
the raise of one of her curved Vulcan eyebrows.
"May I sit down?"

"Of course."

Valek took a seat, as did Kirk. She brought her
hands together and templed her fingers on the
table. "I take it that you have observed that Com-

mander Contreras is perhaps overly in awe of her guests. I am no expert on humans, but I believe she has, in effect, accepted a subordinate role to the Excalbian leader."

"Perhaps," Kirk acknowledged with a smile. "He is, in her eyes, President George Washington, a revered figure from our past. He represents not only steady leadership, but one of the founders of democratic governance."

"Explain?"

"After America won its Revolutionary War—"

"With the aid of the country called France, as I recall."

"True, Valek, as far as it goes," put in Spock. "Yet this, too, was an event created almost single-handedly by the efforts of an American. One man: Benjamin Franklin, who was then serving as a commissioner to France."

Kirk nodded. "Franklin convinced the French to come in, and, more specifically, to commit the French navy. After that was accomplished, the British were defeated. After the formation of a federal government, Washington was elected president, an office that was held for four years at a time. There were no term limits, Washington could have served for the remainder of his life, had he chosen. In fact, he was so revered by the populace that he could have declared himself king and they would likely have gone along with it."

"That is illogical," Valek said. "The Americans had just fought to rid themselves of royal governance."

"True," Kirk said. "Being a logical man and, more importantly, a humble and strong-willed man who knew how to resist temptation, Washington reasoned that two terms were enough. He stepped down and returned to private life. In this way, he set a precedent for all those who followed. In many ways, his actions influenced the Federation Council practice of rotating, democratic leadership. Others had the idea of what it meant to be a democratic leader; Washington *lived* it."

"But this is contradictory. If he was the most logical person to lead the newly formed United States, he should not have resigned his position."

"He didn't resign his position," Kirk replied. "He decided not to run for a third term."

"It would seem to me," said Spock, "that the point was to set an example."

"That's right," said Kirk. "Eight years was enough. He went back to his estate at Mount Vernon, and he pointedly declined any further attempts to reelect him to the presidency or elect him to any other office."

"Are you saying that Commander Contreras is displacing her regard for the historical figure of Washington upon this Washington analog?"

"I don't entirely blame her," said Kirk. "The man

bears a striking resemblance to George Washington, both in appearance and in what we imagine his demeanor to be from the histories. There was a reason the Continental Congress made him general."

"Yet you understand that this is an Excalbian replica, do you not?"

"Oh yes," Kirk replied. "I have a personal history with that particular Excalbian."

Valek nodded. "That is mostly what I have come to speak with you about, Captain." She allowed her palms to spread away from their templed position, with her palms up in a gesture of goodwill and inclusion. It seemed to Kirk a very un-Vulcan motion.

"How can I help, Representative Valek?"

"Assuming I make the decision to grant the Excalbians political asylum within the Federation, there is much they will have to assimilate. For instance, you will have noticed their anachronistic garb."

"Apparently perpetually regenerating."

"It is a firm reminder that these people are not, at foundation, humanoids."

"Agreed."

"This regeneration is a special study of Commander Contreras, and I plan to closely question her on the matter. I will, of course, share any information I glean with you."

"I would appreciate that."

Valek brought her hands back together in the

familiar Vulcan templing position, which, Kirk knew, was an indicator of deep thought, contemplation, and, occasionally, Vulcan scheming—although they would never call it that.

"The Federation Council—Ambassador Sarek in particular—seems convinced there is something else behind the Excalbian explanation of their escape from the planet. That is partly the reason the ambassador chose me in particular, since I count myself a protégé of his."

"*Sarek* had an intuition?" Kirk said, amused.

"No," Valek replied. "It is comparable to seeing a puzzle mostly assembled and yet finding one piece missing—a piece that is crucial to the correct interpretation of that puzzle."

"Okay," Kirk said. "Not an intuition."

"To bend the metaphor, we have, I believe, shaken the Excalbian Washington with our conversation," Valek said. "Perhaps that missing puzzle piece will now fall out of one of his many pockets."

Kirk nodded. "Agreed."

She nodded toward the *Enterprise* officers present. "Captain, I believe it would be prudent for you to use your presence here to continue our effort to discover if the Excalbians' underlying motivation differs from that which they've stated."

"You mean find out if they've been lying to us?"

"Or telling us only part of the truth," Valek said. "You are a human with strategic and tactical experience, perhaps the closest thing Washington-Yarnek has as a counterpart in this facility. I would like you to try to win the confidence of Washington-Yarnek in order to attempt to . . . I search for the proper idiom . . ."

"Try to get him to open up to me?" Kirk asked with a smile.

"I would expect a report after each encounter," Valek said.

"I'll file a report when I have something to report," Kirk shot back.

"I will expect a verbal report," she said. "The outpost computer system is not secure, and these are extremely delicate matters."

"Very well," Kirk said. "Where do we conduct this . . . briefing."

"My quarters," Valek answered. "I have the means to adequately shield it from any eavesdropping measures likely to be employed." She cocked her head sideways. "In fact, it is likely the most private area on the outpost."

Kirk glanced over to see McCoy smiling like an amused wolf at Valek's inadvertent double entendre, and Scott blushing nearly as red as his shirt. Uhura covered her mouth with a hand to hide her smile. Only Spock seemed unaffected.

Maybe you should have studied human behavior a little bit harder, Valek, Kirk thought. *If you had, you'd know how that sounded.*

Then again, Kirk considered, *maybe she knows* exactly *how that sounded.*

Kirk found himself half hoping that such was the case.

He nodded. "All right, Representative, you've got yourself a deal."

———

"She's quite the intelligent woman, Captain Kirk?" Washington-Yarnek asked Kirk. They were in the outpost lounge. Across the room, Spock and Benjamin Franklin were engaged in what was shaping up to be an epic game of three-dimensional chess.

Kirk had entered alone, and settled down to read an analysis of the L'rah'hane ship sent to him by Sulu, when Washington-Yarnek had taken the bait and asked if he could join him.

"Please have a seat, Mister President," Kirk said.

"You may call me Yarnek if it makes you more comfortable," said the other.

"Well, sir, it . . . pleases me in some way to continue you to call you Mister President. I hope you don't mind."

"Not at all, Captain," replied the Excalbian. "I hope I am not interrupting your work?"

"I don't mind a little interruption. Just looking over a couple of reports."

Washington-Yarnek nodded. "Ah, the endless trail of paper—or nowadays, electrons—that follow a commander about," he said. "Perhaps a short break would help your concentration. I know it often did my own. I was on my way to the biolab to have a look at my experiments with a kind of winter corn that just might survive on the planet surface here at Zeta Gibraltar. Would you care to join me?"

Kirk glanced down at the ship specifications he was reading. "As a matter of fact, I would love to join you, sir. You're right. My eyes were starting to glaze over."

Washington-Yarnek pointed toward the data slate.

"Specifications for the L'rah'hane ship?"

"Yes," Kirk said. "My people have thoroughly crawled all over it and scanned it."

And found something very interesting in the process. Which I don't plan to mention to you at present, until—

"Then they no doubt came across the interesting quantum-field device in use by the L'rah'hane."

Kirk made an expression of surprise. "You know about that?"

"Mister Watt described the item to me on our voyage back," said Yarnek. "Doctor Franklin conjectured that it was some sort of information transceiver. He believed it may well be a method for communication faster than your own subspace transmissions."

" 'Your' own?"

"I mean the Federation's standard method, of course," Yarnek replied with a smile, though again carefully not opening his mouth to expose Washington's legendary bad teeth. "One day I hope to be able to include myself among its citizens."

"Perhaps you will, Mister President," Kirk said. "Shall we visit the biolab?"

They exited together, Washington-Yarnek busily describing his selection criteria for breeding wheat and corn analogs for growing during what passed on Zeta Gibraltar for spring and summer.

———

Chekov piloted the shuttlecraft *Kepler* as expertly as he performed his navigation tasks on the *Enterprise*. Sulu, in command of the mission, had taken over navigation and sensors and left the driving to Chekov for once. He occasionally served at the helm of the *Enterprise* when Sulu was away or their duty watches did not coincide. That was enjoyable. But the *Kepler*, he had to admit, was a great deal more exciting to pilot moment to moment, especially now that he and Sulu were making their way through the dense clouds and hidden pockets of solid matter inside the Vara Nebula.

Serving as the navigator of the *Enterprise* was, of course, ultimately more satisfying. To have the responsibility of plotting the course of a ship containing over four hundred people was a heady experience. But in the shuttlecraft, there was the actual experience of acceleration, deceleration, and vector changes that was lacking except in the most dire of conditions aboard the *Enterprise*. The shuttlecraft had artificial gravity built in, but this, even combined with the inertial compensators, could only dampen, but not erase, the effect of banking, turning, and racing thousands of kilometers per second through one of the universe's most challenging regions—an early-stage nebular cloud.

Chekov and Sulu were acting under orders of their captain. They were allegedly visiting a moon of the Gibraltar system gas giant Upsilon Gibraltar in order to determine if that moon was a good place for a defensive base.

They were, in fact, nowhere near Upsilon Gibraltar. Instead, they were engaged in a covert scouting and surveillance mission to determine the full extent of the L'rah'hane menace lurking within the nebula. Chekov didn't know if the scientists on Zeta Gibraltar or the Federation civilian representative that had recently arrived knew that the mission was taking place, but he figured he would let the captain worry about that.

Above my grade, Chekov thought. *And a good thing at that. Sulu and I don't have to worry about convoluted strictures, but only about Starfleet regulations when it comes to encounters with potential hostile forces. That's enough on our plate.*

Those regulations were clear: do not engage unless a threat to life and limb is imminent. Furthermore, if they got into a firefight with the L'rah'hane, that would mean he and Sulu weren't doing their job of observation and reporting.

He was flying mostly by instruments. The view out the shuttlecraft portal was similar to that of a Moscow street in a winter fog. Sulu was navigating with what information they had, and both he and Chekov were keeping their eyes on the sensors.

"I have a faint subspace signature from section 2.4, arc 247," Sulu said. "Not much to go on, but let's head that direction."

"I will bring us in slowly," Chekov replied. "We don't want to alert our quarry before we have a chance to make an inspection."

"Excellent," said Sulu.

Chekov adjusted the appropriate guidance controls, and the shuttlecraft banked behind a screen of matter—sensors showed it to be mostly ice and silicates. There was a similar field of floating debris above and to galactic west of his position. In the brief window of exposure zooming between the two hiding spots, Chekov and Sulu trained every detection device at their disposal toward the spot where the subspace signal had originated.

Safely concealed behind the second matter field, they examined the data.

Svyatoye der'mo, Chekov thought. It was a L'rah'hane vessel, all right, trailing a propulsion plume.

He looked closer. A smeared electromagnetic signal, all over the spectrum.

Primitive, he thought. Which provided the perfect opportunity for a bit of subterfuge.

"What do you think? We move in directly behind him, remain in the propulsion plume, and his aft sensors will be of no use."

"It will be tricky," Sulu replied. "That plume is going to bounce us around a good bit. Fortunately we have an Academy Double Windstar Award winner piloting the ship."

Chekov suppressed a smile. He hadn't known Sulu was aware of his record as the top navigation and flight student in his graduating class at the Academy, a distinction that included possessing the reflexes necessary to work at a helm as well as the brains to navigate. Granted, helming a deep spacecraft was nothing like flying around the Academy flitters, but Academy instructors are the best—creating starship pilots with sterling records and incredible feats under their belts.

The shuttlecraft was buffeted about, but remaining in the plume was no problem for Chekov, who had once snuck up on one of the Academy "top guns" using a similar tactic.

He'd then been rather handily "killed" by the

embarrassed instructor in the ensuing dogfight—but not before he'd gotten in the first hit.

Deeper into the Vara Nebula they traveled. It was only after the L'rah'hane vessel rendezvoused with another that Chekov pulled back and found more debris cover. By this time, the L'rah'hane vessel had slowed.

It was approaching its destination.

Chekov followed at a distance, yet always kept the quarry, and now its twin vessel, in sensor range for Sulu.

"Bingo," Sulu said as his short-range sensors lit up. "Highly active subspace chatter and multiple bogeys. Analyzing trajectory convergences. I'll have visual in a moment."

Chekov held his position and waited. Sulu's hands flew across the sensor controls. Then he sat back and let out a low whistle. "There's something out there. Something massive."

Chekov looked down at his own instrument readouts. There was a narrow gap in the debris field to starboard at two o'clock high, as the old-school pilots would say. It looked just about shuttlecraft-sized. The fit would be narrow, but . . .

"I think I can get us a better look," he said.

Carefully using side thrusters and impulse power on its lowest setting, he eased the shuttlecraft through the window—more of a narrow crack—in the thick debris cloud in which they were embedded.

As the bow of the shuttlecraft emerged into the relatively empty space beyond, Chekov fired a brief burst of aft thrusters, then shut down all accelerators.

It would take an extraordinarily accurate sensor sweep to see the shuttlecraft slightly protruding from the debris, and the searcher would likely have to know exactly what he, she, or it was looking for.

"Polarizing fields," Sulu said. "Should give us the clearest view possible."

It took a moment for the scene before them to emerge in their vision, but when it did, the sight was astounding.

They'd emerged into what was perhaps a half million kilometers of clear space.

Probably deliberately cleared, Chekov thought. The edges of the space, a decahedron, were quite exact. The kind of technology that could accomplish such a task was at least the equal to the Federation's capabilities and perhaps beyond.

No worries about violating the Prime Directive here, Chekov thought.

What occupied the cleared space within the nebula was equally impressive. There were at least ten L'rah'hane ships—and other undefined varieties of vessels with different propulsion signatures—orbiting a massive central object.

Sulu magnified.

Not an asteroid—or, at least, no longer an asteroid.

A space station, a rotating clump of technology, instrumentation, and weapons platforms perhaps five kilometers in diameter. It was covered in crenellations and superstructure that looked utterly alien to Chekov—and he'd seen a great deal of strange architecture in his travels.

"Got any idea what it is?" he asked Sulu.

Sulu shook his head, checked a readout. "That structure is approximately four hundred years old." The lieutenant gazed back out the front viewport. "Waiting for computer database confirmation," he said. "But I believe we're looking at an old space platform of the Hradrian Empire."

"That doesn't look like a relic," Chekov said. "It looks like it is still operating."

"I think we've discovered the answer to a long-standing archaelogical enigma," said Sulu.

"What is that?"

"The riddle of where the Hradrians went."

Chekov nodded toward the habitat. "You don't think—?"

"I do," Sulu replied. "Some of them came here."

Ten

The interior of laboratory C in the Zeta Gibraltar outpost was mostly dark. It was the night cycle outside, and most lights were turned down or off in the complex. In the middle of the lab, however, at a table coated with a black, anti-interactive sheath, a sort of low-level deflector shield, a pool of light from the ceiling illuminated the golden-brown surface features of a most unusual device.

The artifact, taken from a L'rah'hane vessel, was very difficult to bring into focus. It was like a blurred photo, and no matter how hard you concentrated on it, there was a smearing visual effect. And when you touched it, the surface felt as if your hand had passed through some sort of membrane or force field. Your fingers came away tingling.

In that pool of light a most incongruous pair of persons sat on stools. One was dressed in Starfleet science blue. The other wore a brown velvet waistcoat over a linen shirt. His cravat was undone and dangling around his neck, and a pair of steel-rimmed glasses hung on the end of his nose.

How they might look was the furthest thing from the two men's minds, however. They were bent over the device, prodding and poking it with a variety of instruments as well as their bare hands.

"Readings indicate that the L'rah'hane component is partially biological," said Spock, bending down to gaze at the device through discerning eyes. "Yet there are electronic logic circuits within, if I'm not mistaken. You can make them out through the translucent surface, yet analysis seems to show they serve no function."

"Difficult to believe," Benjamin Franklin said. "Obviously they do *something*. Those are not accidental structures."

"Agreed."

Spock ran a tricorder one more time across the device's surface, using a modified electron stream to penetrate deeply enough to give them a display of the interior.

"It is fascinating," said Spock.

"Now, Spock," Franklin said. "Would you agree that the living matter congealed around these electrical conduits and capacitors seems to be a power source? I don't know if you're aware of Mister Luigi Galvani's experiments with the Leyden jar and its ability to vitalize the legs of frogs." Franklin pushed his glasses up to the bridge of his nose, but they promptly slid down again to just before its tip when he leaned down to further study the component.

"It occurs to me that the process might be reversed and the frog legs used to power the Leyden jar, in a manner of speaking."

"I believe that is precisely what is happening here, Doctor Franklin," said Spock. "The living material is the power source, and it appears to be self-perpetuating so long as it is bathed in a simple sugar solution."

"And yet such might be only a secondary purpose. There is a great deal more bio-matter than would be necessary for such a function. Something else, something larger, is going on with the living components."

"The excessive bio-matter does bear a strong resemblance to nerve cells," Spock replied. He sat back and looked over at Franklin, who was grinning like a Cheshire cat. "Doctor Franklin, I believe you have already arrived at a preliminary conclusion or you would not have sent a sample to the biological laboratory for analysis."

Franklin cocked his head to look at the device sidelong. "Do you know if they have the results?"

"They do, and I requested permission to deliver them to you." Spock pointed to a pair of colored data cards he'd put upon the table between them when entering. "The analysis is on the yellow cards," Spock said. "The raw data is collected on the red one."

"Thank you, Mister Spock," Franklin said. He took up the yellow card and inserted it into the data reading device beside the console computer built onto the side of the examination table. Instantly, its viewscreen lit up with a transparent image of the L'rah'hane device. Spock reached over and pressed a button. The room lights dimmed and a holographic, three-dimensional representation of the device, with multiple layers visible beneath, appeared several centimeters out from the viewscreen, hovering over the examination table.

"Wonderful things, these computers and visual display machines," Franklin muttered. "Even if they are, sometimes, a bit distracting."

Franklin reached over and put a finger within the device image. It rotated as if touched. Franklin chuckled with delight. "Never will get used to how realistic these holograms can be," he said.

"You come from a species that is able to create entire alternate scenarios with a thought."

Franklin sat back, shook his head. "Not really, Mister Spock. I have come to understand that reality has a way of reasserting itself no matter how carefully an illusion is constructed. Witness the fact that for all our alleged great advancement, we were unable to break free of the L'rah'hane slavers."

"Point taken," Spock replied with a nod.

"Let us say the large portion of me that is Benjamin Franklin is delighted, and my Excalbian portion is just happy to be alive at present."

Spock did not reply to this, but inclined his head

toward the L'rah'hane device hologram. "It seems we have a paradox, Doctor Franklin. According to one analysis, this device cannot exist. According to another, it exists in several places at once due to quantum smearing."

"Even more marvelous," Franklin replied. He turned the device again, spread his fingers to increase magnification, poked it to zoom in, increased magnification again, and finally pointed to several clusters of indentations. "Yet these are receivers, as I had supposed. See the direction of signal flow here and here." Animated sparks appeared where Franklin touched the hologram and traveled inward toward the interior electronics.

"But *what* do they receive?" Spock said. "Nothing electromagnetic. They resemble subspace receiver nodes in some ways, but this is not their function, as the data readings make clear." Spock pointed to two other spots where there were convex bumps on the device. "These *are* subspace transceivers, and it would appear they are merely present to report telemetry, so the device can remain oriented toward galactic center."

Franklin tapped a point on the side of the device. "I'd say it is *these* indentations that are at the heart of this device," Franklin said. "My intuition tells me as much. Yet I'll be damned if my rational side can tell me how they might work."

"Might I suggest a consultation?"

"What do you mean?"

"We do have present at the outpost some of the greatest minds in history, yours included. Perhaps one of the others could shed some light on the device's function."

Franklin slapped a knee and laughed heartily. "You are absolutely right, Mister Spock," he said. "I believe I know just who we're looking for, too. He's the sort that can look at a rock or a feather—or even a dangling necklace—and see a million possibilities."

"That description would seem to fit you, sir. Who else did you have in mind?"

"Why, Galileo Galilei, of course," Franklin answered. "And if he doesn't know anything, then we can try Leonardo da Vinci."

"Two excellent suggestions, Doctor Franklin."

"And it will do Galileo good to take on a project. He's been in a funk about this church edict against his work. He knows it has been lifted for centuries, but somewhere deep inside, he still feels on trial for the very act of conducting scientific investigation! That period of captivity with the L'rah'hane seems to have dredged up some very uncomfortable memories for Galileo. His childhood was not the most stable, as I understand it."

"I was not aware that he, or any of you Excalbians, could be so affected by entirely artificial memories."

"Artificial to you, Mister Spock. They don't *feel* artificial to us, even though we know they must be. I realize this sounds quite illogical, but this is pure human behavior we're talking about," said Franklin. "And the fact of the matter is, Galileo is quite a moody fellow. He's an Italian, after all."

"They most definitely aren't human, Doctor," said Naftali Levin, the medical officer for Zeta Gibraltar outpost. He slid a data card into his office computer and invited McCoy to have a seat. "Watch this and I'll show you."

McCoy sat down in the white chair. It was more deeply padded than the ones in his sickbay, and McCoy felt for a moment as if he were sinking into a bog.

Cushy places, these ground-side exam complexes, McCoy thought. *But I'll take my sickbay any day.*

Levin activated the computer, and McCoy turned his attention to the viewscreen in front of them.

It showed an Excalbian in a sitting position on an examination table. He was just rolling up his sleeve, and Levin was putting away what McCoy recognized as an interior blood analysis tool—a specialized device that provided far more data than the usual bio monitor.

On the upper right-hand corner of the screen was a record of the stardate and time the data card was made. The seconds ticked away as McCoy continued to watch.

"Now," Levin said. "Let me show you what led up to this examination. Doctor McCoy, I give you a friendly duel between Commodore Stephen Decatur Junior and the honorable Cyrano de Bergerac."

The screen switched to a view of another room with two men in fighting stances.

The two men circled each other. Each held different swords. One was a flat-bladed sword with what looked like an inlaid silver guard. McCoy was no expert, but this was not a long sword. It had only a single-sided blade. It was the sword of a cavalryman or sailor, perhaps. Its bearer was dressed in pants of gray wool with suspenders over a white, blousy shirt. Stephen Decatur, McCoy guessed.

The other had on clothing of an older time, Renaissance Europe. He wore a leather singlet vest over a shirt and billowing pants that disappeared into high leather boots that came up above the knee. This must be Cyrano de Bergerac. He wielded two swords, or one sword and a long dagger, McCoy couldn't be certain. The dagger was flat-bladed and double-edged, but the sword was a rapier. It was longer than the other man's, thin and bladed—and it ended in what looked like an extremely sharp point.

The two men came together, and it was immediately clear that the wielder of the rapier was the better swordsman. He danced circles around the man in gray and made taunting thrusts now and again that the other could barely parry.

"Are they actually fighting with *sharpened* swords?" McCoy asked Levin.

"Oh yes," the other doctor replied. "Wait for it—"

During a particularly deadly looking thrust from the rapier-using man, the other stepped aside. The rapier thrust went wide, missing him, and de Bergerac leaned over to retain his balance.

When he did so, he exposed his head, and the other was quick to punish him. With a fast chopping motion, all in the wrist, he brought his sword down. The rapier bearer turned his head to avoid the blow—but did not turn away fast enough. The blade sliced down into his shoulder and sank into his arm like a cleaver sinks into raw meat. De Bergerac let out a scream and stumbled back.

"Ouch," said McCoy.

"I know, right?" Levin replied.

The fight did not last long. McCoy had seen enough physical brawling to know that most fights did not stretch out into long displays of skill. Usually, both parties came in bashing and whoever was stronger, luckier or, sometimes, more skilled, was the one who walked away alive.

The blow caused the stricken man not to give in, but to fight back. He began a furious fusillade of thrusts, working his blade like a sewing needle through fabric. The other fought back, but finally the rapier found its mark just over the victim's heart.

After a moment of gurgling in protest, the stabbed man fell to the ground, his blood sloshing out in great gouts as his heart pumped on.

He has *to be dead*, McCoy thought. *He* must *be dead*.

After a few moments slumped there, he stood back up. Meanwhile, the man with the rapier cleaned and sheathed his blade. Only then did he reach up to feel his neck and shoulders for injury.

The cut into his shoulder was deep enough to fit a finger into. But there seemed to be more blood than need be.

"*The ear, of course*," the man said. He had a French accent. "*You struck downward through the cartilage, you scoundrel.*"

He reached up to touch the spot, seemingly fearful of what he might find.

He found nothing. Ragged skin around a bleeding hole. The other had chopped off the man's ear.

"*Merde.*"

The rapier-bearing man began a careful search of the ground. Only after he grimaced and said "*Aha!*" could McCoy make out what he'd picked up.

It was a human ear. His own.

"*Well*," said the rapier man to the other, "that's *never happened before.*" Then the image feed went blank.

McCoy sat back in his cushioned chair. "That must have hurt."

"Oh it did, it did. That's why de Bergerac came. He wanted a pain spray to take the sting out."

"Take the sting out? That ear was *amputated* by a blade. It will take weeks of treatment to regenerate completely. Do they really fight with *sharpened* swords?"

"Have to," said Levin. "That's the only kind of swords the Excalbians have."

Not sure what he means by that, but let it go—

"Okay then, why do the damn Excalbians do it? It's obviously crazy and dangerous—"

A notification bell beeped, and Levin shot McCoy an amused glance. "Hang on to that thought for a moment, Doctor, and allow me to introduce you to Cyrano de Bergerac. You can ask him yourself."

McCoy saw from Levin's expression that something was going on that he didn't want to reveal yet. The outpost doctor turned to the door control sensor. "Enter." The door slid open, and in walked Cyrano de Bergerac. His nose, McCoy noted, was on the largish size, but was certainly not a monstrous protrusion. He was otherwise an extremely handsome man.

"Mister de Bergerac, come in, come in," said Levin. "This is Doctor Leonard McCoy of the *Starship Enterprise*."

"A pleasure, sir," said de Bergerac. He reached out a gloved hand to shake, and McCoy took it.

Odd to wear gloves in a climate-controlled environment like this, McCoy thought. *But to each his own.*

"Mister de Bergerac, I was wondering if you would mind if Doctor McCoy examined your wounded ear," Levin said.

"Not at all, not at all," de Bergerac replied. "But I think you'll find it much better."

McCoy had risen as soon as permission came and had a look at the ear.

He reached up his hands to part the curly hair around it. "Do you mind?" he asked.

"Please," said de Bergerac.

McCoy pushed back the hair, examined the ear, then thumbed it to be sure it was flesh and not some kind of prosthetic.

"It's completely healed," he said.

De Bergerac only smiled and shrugged.

"You'll find that it isn't merely healed," Levin said. "It is *exactly* the same as it was before the accident. I can show you molecular analysis that proves as much."

McCoy broke away from looking at the *perfectly undamaged* ear and turned to Levin. "Okay, what gives?"

"Tell Doctor McCoy about your gloves, Mister de Bergerac," Levin said.

"His gloves? I want to know about that ear."

Levin held up a hand. "Indulge us, Doctor." He spoke again to de Bergerac. "You took one of your gloves off this morning, did you not?"

"I had to so you could use your medical instruments to examine me."

"Yes, the compact bio monitor is very sensitive. Unlike the lab medical sensors, it can easily operate through clothing. It was the right arm, I think."

"My sword arm, *oui*."

Levin reached over and opened a drawer. "In fact, here it is," he said. He pulled out a large cuffed brown leather glove, slid the drawer shut, and tossed the glove to McCoy.

"Okay," McCoy said. "It's leather. It's a glove. Same as the one he has on now."

"Mister de Bergerac, do you happen to have a supply of those particular gloves? Replacements for when you lose one or one becomes damaged?"

"I do not need one, *Docteur*," said de Bergerac. "You know that."

"And why don't you need them?" he asked, nodding toward McCoy. "Please, enlighten the good doctor here."

"Well, because they grow back," de Bergerac replied. "This takes about an hour, sometimes two, depending. Same with the ear."

"You mean to tell me that ear regenerated in a few hours?" McCoy said.

"Not at all," Levin said. "An exact replacement formed, down to the cell level. We've documented the whole process. That glove you're holding you would find to be an exact replica of the one Mister de Bergerac is now wearing on his right hand. Exact to the molecule."

"I'll be damned," said McCoy. "What is it, nano-technology?"

"That's what we suspected at first," Levin replied. "But there is actually a holographic memory process going on. If you use quark imaging, you'll see it. There are, so help me, a tiny set of positronic instructions for constructing or reconstructing Mister de Bergerac here—might as well think of them as homunculi, because they *look* like him under the microscope. There they are, precisely situated between the molecules that make up his body, clothing, and equipment. Damage him, or simply take off his gloves, his coat, his boots? It'll come back."

"How far does this extend?" McCoy asked. "Could you—pardon me, Mister de Bergerac—could you, for instance, cut him into a dozen pieces. Would each of those pieces remake itself until you had a dozen Cyrano de Bergeracs?"

Both Levin and de Bergerac laughed heartily. "Would that it were so, Doctor McCoy," said de Bergerac. "But even I might be wary of a world full of swordsmen as good as I am."

"No, only one of those pieces would remake itself into Mister de Bergerac, but it would create him again completely, even down to his memories," Levin said.

"Spontaneous re-creation. How?" McCoy asked.

"That's something I, and the Federation, would really like to discover."

"I'll bet," said McCoy. "Mister de Bergerac, pardon me for asking, but have any of the Excalbians been killed?"

"Unfortunately, yes," de Bergerac said. "An energy weapon will do the trick. We lost some during our captivity in such a way. Also, that's why poor Marcel Proust is no more. He became incensed during a card game and attempted to draw a weapon on Bill Hickok. Hickok had equipped himself with a phaser in addition to his Colt 1851 revolver. He swears it was merely for defensive purposes. Nevertheless, he had it, and he had it set on its highest power." De Bergerac bowed his head and made a *tsk-tsk* sound. "Of course it was a mistake to draw on Hickok. There wasn't a trace left of poor Marcel, I'm afraid."

"Good Lord," McCoy said. "That's terrible! Where is Hickok now?"

"In the brig, until we can deliver him to the authorities," said Levin.

McCoy turned back to de Bergerac. "So your sword practice isn't practice at all, is it?"

De Bergerac smiled. "We cannot be truly hurt.

Decatur and I are quite used to enduring a little pain, and we do go at it rather hard at times."

"They hack one another's arms off," Levin said. "I've watched one of those matches. It's gruesome."

"All in good fun," de Bergerac said. "But that blow to my ear. . . well, I've always been sensitive there. My father used to cuff me as a boy. He used to beat the hell out of me in general, to tell the truth. But it always started with the cuffing of an ear, a hard blow that marked harder yet to come. When I am injured there the pain . . . brings back memories I would rather avoid."

"You came to get treatment not because of the injury, but because your completely sliced-off ear reminded you of your unhappy childhood?"

De Bergerac nodded with a look of melancholy. "Exactly, Doctor McCoy," he answered. "I hope I have not presumed upon our acquaintance by offering up such lurid personal details, but Doctor Levin wished me to provide a complete explanation."

"Of course not," McCoy said. "I'm honored that you'd confide in me."

"The honor is mine, Doctor McCoy. Anyone whom Doctor Levin trusts, I trust likewise," de Bergerac said. "Doctor Levin has proved time and again to be both a gentleman and a scholar."

McCoy looked to Levin.

Well, I'll be damned. The man's blushing.

"Coming from you, that's high praise," Levin said to de Bergerac.

"Completely justified," de Bergerac replied. "Now, if you gentlemen will excuse me, I have a rematch scheduled with that hot-blooded Decatur. He won't let well enough alone. As I understand it, that's what got him killed the first time. We've reserved the white exercise room with the self-cleaning walls and absorption tiles for this one. I have a feeling blood will flow copiously." De Bergerac smiled wickedly, and laid a gloved hand on the finely wrought pommel of his sheathed rapier. "Further, good sirs, I make bold to predict that the blood will be his, and only his, this time."

Eleven

"The problem is, how do we get any closer to that structure?" Sulu said. "We're close enough to know we've found something, but too far to really understand what's going on here."

Chekov nodded and smiled in what he'd been told by more than one person—many of them females—was a shrewd and boyish way. He didn't mind the implied patronizing attitude. That smile had gotten him through sticky situations more than once. Of course, his friend Sulu was immune to any charm other than Chekov's reasoning ability. He'd have to convince the helmsman with logic.

Well, I've been around Mister Spock long enough to know how to do that, Chekov thought.

"We *suspect* these L'rah'hane are slavers," Chekov said. "We don't know where they're getting them, but it has to be from some worlds hidden by the nebula. Worlds unknown to the Federation."

"True. And any subspace communication from this sector that might be intercepted is drowned by the space-time anomalies created by the nebula, as well."

"But that will cut both ways," Chekov said. "They won't know who *we* are either. Or what kind of technology we possess."

"Are you suggesting we just waltz in there and request permission to scan them?" asked Sulu incredulously.

"Not at all, my friend," Chekov said. Then he explained to Sulu what he had in mind.

———

"Unknown craft, identify, identify."

"Comrades, comrades, do not fire on us! We bring a great prize! We have looted the interlopers. They thought to take us prisoners, make us slaves, but it is we who have turned the tables on them. Now they are our slaves."

"Identify immediately!"

"The *S.S. Scottybuilt*! We bring the crew with us as prisoners, as slaves for sale! Fine, healthy slaves with knowledge of starflight. We demand top value for these."

"Scottybuilt, there is no record of your existence in the database. You will hold for scan or be destroyed!"

"Of *course* the craft is not in your database, fools. We *stole* it from those on the other side of the nebula!"

"This cannot be verified."

"Yes, it can," said Chekov. "Stand by for transmission."

Chekov turned to Sulu, who knelt beside him. Both had donned manacles on wrists and feet and knelt in the main hold. They'd had to get creative with the rations to create the look of fresh blood. But with some liberal application of sauce and crushed "lunches," Chekov had to admit that he and Sulu did a plausible imitation of two beings who had had the hell beaten out of them.

"All right, now's the time to gaze up in agony and despair," Chekov whispered to Sulu. Sulu got himself ready—he was a frighteningly good actor— and then the lieutenant activated the interior visual. For a few moments, their images as prisoners in chains went out over the subspace feed.

The shuttlecraft drew closer and closer to the main habitat.

When Sulu figured that they'd seen enough, he cut the feed and nodded to Chekov. "These two we will put on the market block first, even before we arrive!" he said. "Opening bids will start at—"

"*Fifty alons!*" came a voice over the subspace frequency.

"*Seventy-five!*" said another.

The bidding continued. The shuttlecraft drew closer and closer.

"Almost within range for complete reading," Sulu said.

Chekov pressed the communicator button. Now was the time to do some serious bargaining. Fortunately this ability flowed naturally in his Russian blood. Chekov was fairly certain that the art of bargaining was a Russian invention, first practiced by old King Rurik on his travels along the Dnieper River.

"Eighty-five alons? Do you wish to starve us? We risked our lives to bring these top quality goods, and all I hear is seventy-five." Chekov raised his voice in feigned anger. He had to admit he was enjoying getting into the act. "We demand one hundred fifty!"

"Robbery!"

"Do you wish to leave myself and my concubines destitute!"

"Unthinkable! Those are retail prices! One hundred is as high as a reasonable wholesaler can go and still turn a profit!"

Chekov turned to Sulu, who shook his head. Not quite in scan range yet.

"One hundred fifty and we will throw in the craft itself," Chekov countered. "Here, take another look at the merchandise, and see what a bargain we are offering!" He turned to Sulu and mouthed, "Ready?" Sulu nodded and activated the feed once more.

More agony. This time Sulu let out a low, loud moan for good measure.

"One twenty-five and no higher!"

"One forty, and you are stealing bread from my mouth!"

"Initiating complete scan," Sulu whispered.

"The craft, and one hundred for the tall, beautiful one. Sell the short one elsewhere."

Chekov shook his head in disbelief. Sulu! They wanted to purchase Sulu and not him. He felt an irrational flush of jealousy rise inside himself.

Hey, that's not fair! I'm strong and good-looking! thought Chekov. *I may be a bit on the short side, but I'd make as fine a slave as Sulu!*

He glanced over at Sulu, who was slyly smiling.

"What are we going to do with the little one? He'll have to be spaced. They sell as a pair, or not at all."

"One thirty-five for both, then."

"One thirty-five. Do I hear one hundred forty? Come on, what a deal!"

Subspace silence.

"One thirty-nine? No?"

"Unidentified craft, you have been acquired as a target. Stand off immediately."

"One thirty-five going once!"

More silence.

"Unknown craft, you are in weapons lock."

"Going twice!"

"Scan complete," Sulu whispered.

"Sold, for one hundred thirty-five alons! We take all forms of payment, but prefer dilithium quantum credits when possible."

"Weapons activated. All other craft advised to stand clear."

Chekov veered hard to starboard just as the station defenses began to fire. Photonic bursts exploded in the space the shuttlecraft had just occupied.

The one-hundred-eight-degree arc was brutal, and something for which no inertial compensation could correct. He felt the blood physically *push* toward one side of his body. For a moment, black spots swam before his eyes.

But then the turn was achieved. Another explosion not far off their stern. And to the side, other ships, L'rah'hane and otherwise, were converging on them.

"I've laid in the course. Get us out of here, Pavel," Sulu said.

"Working on it."

He pushed the throttle all the way forward, saw a red warning light, and overrode it. They streaked ahead.

"Feeding new telemetry," Sulu said. "It's going to be tight."

"Just like threading a needle," Chekov replied.

"When have you ever threaded a needle?"

"Never," said Chekov. "Something my grandmother used to say. Needles were invented in Russia you know."

"Right. Probably by your grandmother."

The small window in the debris field seemed to zoom toward them, but they were, in actuality, zooming toward it.

Behind them now, several torpedoes were gaining on the shuttlecraft.

Chekov pushed the engines to the red line. He kept computer control on, but any extreme movement he made would manually override the autopilot.

Closer to the hole in the debris. Closer.

It's reconfigured slightly. We're not going to—

As fast as thought, Chekov sent the shuttlecraft into a barrel roll. They entered the window.

BAM!

A shudder rippled through the entire craft.

"Contact on port nacelle," Sulu said. "Scanning for damage!"

They were through the debris and into relatively clear space.

Chekov eased back, the engines stopped protesting, and the cabin quieted.

"Damage contained," Sulu said with a sigh of relief. "We still have eighty percent."

Suddenly Chekov remembered. "The torpedoes . . ."

Sulu chuckled. "Scans indicate they were all destroyed trying to thread your grandmother's needle, it seems."

Chekov nodded. "Good old Grandmother."

"I'll proceed with full analysis," Sulu said. "Get us out of here, Ensign Chekov?"

"With pleasure, Lieutenant Sulu," Chekov replied.

He called up the subspace marker "bread crumbs" he and Sulu had dropped on the way in. He could only hope they wouldn't be followed.

Near the edge of the nebula, Sulu sat back, a look of satisfaction on his tranquil face. "The captain's going to be interested in this."

"What have you found?" Chekov asked.

"It's not a habitat or even a space station, Pavel," Sulu replied. "It's a *warehouse*. Its name translates as 'Haversack.' The computer has matched the configuration with archaeological records. That's a fully operational Hradrian robotized supply depot. According to the database, it's a vessel that is known to have been defended by multiple weapon emplacements and crewed by robots and slaves. The robots were the overseers, it's believed."

"A ghost of the past."

"I'll say. Not only that, I've finished an analysis of the subspace chatter in the vicinity. I was busy collecting it while you held that inspired slave auction of yours."

"And?"

"The L'rah'hane are massing for another raid on Zeta Gibraltar. From there they plan to raid further into Federation territory."

"What are they waiting for?"

"Two more ships are set to arrive, but that's going to take a while. Apparently they've been called in from quite far away. Where, I don't know.

But they're bigger ships that the pirates believe can take on the *Enterprise*. 'Dreadnoughts,' they are calling them. Not sure what that means in their parlance, but apparently the L'rah'hane dare not attack without them. Must be something formidable, because they've seen what the *Enterprise* can do."

"This doesn't sound like typical pirates to me," Chekov said. "Usually they are after easy pickings and avoid well-defended places and powerful opponents."

"I have a feeling it's the Hradrians, or whoever is supplying all that Hradrian technology to the L'rah'hane, who are pulling the strings," Sulu said. "We've got to get this information back to the *Enterprise*."

The adrenaline surge was beginning to dilute in Chekov's system, and he felt a wave of tiredness pass over him. *No time for that,* he told himself. Besides, he knew his own limits, and this was nothing that a cup of coffee wouldn't take care of, at least for the short term.

But he longed to be home, back on the *Enterprise*.

Suddenly a red light blinked on the console in front of Sulu. He didn't need Sulu to tell him what it was.

Nacelle malfunction.

Sulu's hands flew over sensor controls and he rapidly isolated the cause. "We've taken a hit. The dilithium matrix has been breached."

"Can we repair it?"

"No," said Sulu. He flipped another toggle, examined a scope. "But we can stabilize it.

Chekov looked at his own controls. "Speed dropping," he said. "Warp two. Warp one-point-five. Warp one." Chekov tried acceleration control. There was no response. "Nothing I can do."

Sulu looked up from his sensor. "I sealed it. Warp core stabilized."

"So at least we won't blow up," Chekhov said. He checked his power gauge. "Power levels stabilizing."

"Are we falling out of warp?"

"Negative. We are fluctuating, but maintaining approximately . . . warp factor one."

"Not good," Sulu said. "We need to get back to Zeta Gibraltar with our sensor records."

"You're telling me," Chekov replied. "At least we can send the highlights via subspace radio." He reached over to flip a switch that would do just that.

Only it didn't work. An amber warning light nearby told the story. It only came on when there was damage to the communications array.

"I spoke too soon," Chekov said. He shook his head. "Now we can't even warn them."

"If we maintain this speed, when will we get there?" Sulu asked.

Chekov called up his estimated time of arrival indicator. "Estimated time of arrival at Zeta Gibraltar system in . . ." Chekov groaned. "Five standard weeks."

"We have enough stores to make it, provided this velocity remains stable."

"Great," Chekov said. "On the positive side, we will live. On the negative side, we may not get there until the pirates have already arrived."

"Are you prepared to spend five weeks in this tub?"

"I guess I have to be."

"Maybe you can finally beat me at poker," Sulu said.

"Maybe you can finally beat me at chess."

Sulu sat back in his chair and sighed. "This is going to be interesting. But we'll have to think of a contest in which we both can participate equally."

"I will try to think of something," Chekov said. "I have plenty of time."

Sulu sighed. "Ahead, warp factor one, Mister Chekov."

"Aye, sir."

"At least we're homeward bound."

"Yes," Chekov answered. "Very *slowly*."

———

Montgomery Scott was not one given to hero worship. As much as he admired his captain, he reckoned he could withstand a few pokes at his commanding officer from some ignorant Romulan or Klingon yokel. The only matter not up for debate or challenge was the greatness of the vessel his captain commanded, the *Enterprise*. To slur her was to ask for a punch in the nose (or whatever other protuberance a species might have) from her chief engineer, Montgomery Scott.

Oh, the *Enterprise* was not flawless—no ship was. But perfect in her way? Maybe. Yet there were degrees of completion, and Scott was perpetually modifying and upgrading a function here or a component there to *add* to her beauty.

Scott felt he'd found a kindred spirit in James Watt. The Scottish engineer and inventor was almost as taken by the functional beauty of a starship as the chief engineer. He'd asked for and received permission to bring Watt up to the *Enterprise*. Within the boundaries of Starfleet security, he'd shown Watt every crack and crevice of his vessel. They'd crawled the Jefferies tubes, with Scott pointing out the slight tweaks here and there that allowed him to deliver performance from his ship that was far and above the norm. Scott's efforts were so wide reaching, her perfection was taken for granted.

The *Enterprise* was simply better and faster than most other *Constitution*-class ships, and because of that, more could be demanded of her. Sometimes Scott was afraid that those demands would prove too much. His charge, his *bairn*, had met the most severe tests a dangerous galaxy could throw at her and emerged with her colors flying, even if a little battle- and storm-torn in places.

James Watt had been rapidly catching up with modern engineering principles, and he seemed to have a natural grasp of the complex ship's systems, comparing them in telling ways to his own steam engines and astronomical inventions.

It had been a pleasure to work with Watt on Zeta Gibraltar, strengthening the point defenses for the outpost. It was impossible to create an energy shield defense—the resources and power supplies were limited, and the base, much less the entire planetoid, was much too large to cover with an energy screen.

What could be done, however, was to anticipate the likely incoming threats and have methods in place to deal with them. A kinetic-based attack—a meteoroid drop from space—always the most deadly possibility in terms of destructive energy, could be guarded against by gravitationally attuned phaser defenses. A rock might be accelerating toward the planet at even relativistic velocities, but it could never move faster than the speed of light.

There were, of course, ship-based attacks that could move faster, such as an opponent's phaser blasts, and torpedoes created with uniform energy payloads, such as photons, positrons, and other, heavier particles.

Watt, for his part, had previously made a study of the defensive works of the real James Watt's time in history and he had many useful suggestions for positioning equipment and—given the technology—appropriate lines of fire.

The outpost upgrade had proved a fruitful and most enjoyable partnership, and Watt accompanied Scott on many trips up to the *Enterprise*, where the engineering workshops were more extensive than planetside at the small research station.

The final planetary system was in place within two weeks, and Watt invited Mister Scott and several other officers from the *Enterprise* engineering team to his outpost quarters to celebrate.

They gathered around Watt's table, which doubled as a desk, and pulled up the two period armchairs—the others insisted that Watt and Scott occupy these—and a couple more contemporary chairs from a corner.

Wonderful, Scott thought as he sank into the cushion of Watt's chair. *Not too soft, not too hard.* Almost as if it had been as ergonomically engineered as the Starfleet furnishings rather than designed by Watt himself (the real Watt). Watt had told Scott his furnishings had always been custom-made articles whenever he could afford it, and Scott now appreciated what that meant: custom-made to James Watt's exacting standards. He may not have had access to modern construction techniques, but he'd found a way to substitute eighteenth-century know-how to create a chair perfect for drinking—

"Now, gentlemen—and lady," Watt said, nodding toward Ensign Mullen, who was the leader of Scott's trusted plasma-transfer tech team. "How do you all take your Scotch? As for myself, I prefer it neat."

Watt wandered over toward a cupboard near the wall. He stood on a stepstool—Watt was rangy, but not a tall man—and pulled a greenish-colored bottle from a high shelf.

The Scot then sat down in his own armchair, obscuring the label of his liquor with the fabric of the smoking jacket he'd donned upon entering.

Scott smiled and nodded toward the mystery bottle. "That all depends on what we're drinking, Mister Watt. A bit of ice can go a long way toward giving a good Scotch a momentary bump to greatness, if you understand what I'm saying, but you don't want to ruin the flavor of something that's already—"

"How about this, Mister Scott?" Watt said.

Oh my, Scott thought. *It's a Strathisla 1786.*

"What year did you come into this beauty, Mister Watt, if you don't mind my asking?"

Watt gazed upward, rubbed his chin. "I seem to remember it was 1810 or thereabouts."

Strathisla 1786.

He'd been prepared for a pleasant surprise from Watt, but this?

It's not only fantastic, it's entirely impossible.

Six-hundred-year-old Scotch did not and could not exist in drinkable form.

"A lovely replica," said Scott, shaking his head. He wondered, but did not ask what was actually inside of it.

"Oh, this is no replica," Watt answered. "At least in the way that you mean. I assure you it is authentic."

"You must be joking, sir," Scott said, not entirely seeing what was so funny about pretending a Scotch was better than it actually must be.

"Oh, it's an old Strathisla, all right," Watt said. "Saving it for a special occasion, and this certainly qualifies."

Strathisla 1786.

"You're telling me this is—"

"It comes from your own computer records and, I have no doubt, from your own mind, Mister Scott," Watt answered. "I assure you this will be the best Scotch you've ever tasted. It's the Scotch of which dreams are made. Literally." He picked the bottle up, gave it a little shake, while Scott looked on in mute astonishment. "Shall we?"

Scott nodded. "By all means," he said. "Neat, if you would."

Watt produced snifters all around. None of the others dared ask for ice after their chief had declined to do so.

Watt smiled, raised his glass. "Independence," he said, "Freedom for all people."

"I'll drink to that," Scott said.

Glasses clinked and Scott took a tentative sip.

Then he took a full, mouth-filling taste.

The thistle, the heather, the sea. They're all in there.

"This can't be real," he said, shaking his head. "It's too perfect."

"It is as real as your own conception of perfection," Watt answered. "How could it not be? It was taken from the archetype within your own Scottish soul, my friend. And now, it is part of mine."

Scott blinked, took another sip, savored this one for quite a long time. Finally he spoke. "Wherever it comes from, here it is, and if we don't drink it, we'll live lives of misery from now on longing for what might have been."

"Spoken like a true Scot, sir," Watt said. "Now set down your glass, and I'll fill you up with another."

"Absolutely. But we mustn't waste such a treasure," Scott said. "At least, not too much."

"No fear, Mister Scott, I assure you that this bottle will not run dry," he said.

Two hours later, the last of the Strathisla trickled over Scott's grateful tongue. The room was not very steady, and he wondered if the station's artificial gravity compensators were fluctuating.

I'd check in with outpost maintenance on that, but I can't quite get my feet under me.

Watt and the others seemed to have similarly diminished locomotive capacities.

"I believe we've done it, Mister Watt," Scott said. He was almost in tears. "We've drunk it all, and now there's no more heaven that awaits us."

Scott hung his head down and the motion pitched him forward. He'd have slammed into Watt's desk if he hadn't also partially slipped off his chair and, in the process of keeping himself off the floor, arranged for his head to miss getting a good knot from striking the wood. Scott pushed himself back into the armchair.

He looked back up to find Watt smiling. "Ah, but Mister Scott, if there's one true quality heaven is said to possess, it is that it is eternal."

He filled Scott's snifter once again with Scotch. He set the bottle down, and Scott watched as the level within it slowly, but inexorably, rose until the content of the bottle was complete again.

"The other quality heaven must possess is a drink such as this," Scott said, raising his glass once more. "At least the Scottish portion of heaven, eh, Mister Watt?"

The glass was moving toward his lips, but Scott realized that it was not going to arrive at the correct docking position if his arm kept wobbling as it was. It took an immense effort of will, but Scott set the glass carefully back onto the table.

Across from him Watt was bobbing from side to side in a similar manner. Scott looked around. The others were slumped in chairs in serene repose—well, except for Lieutenant Gaines's unfortunately positioned slack jaw and the tiny bit of drool leaking from the corner of his mouth.

Watt suddenly chuckled, smiled broadly, then himself crashed facedown onto the table. Scott was concerned for a moment, but then he heard Watt's peaceful snoring.

For several seconds more, Scott observed the engineer and wondered why he, too, was not in a similar position.

But then his chair unaccountably wobbled again.

Damn those gravitational compensators!

Scott found himself deposited on the floor under Watt's desk.

He'd really have to speak to outpost maintenance and have the things examined. Maybe a bit later, later . . .

Then Scott fell into a slumber dreaming of craggy mountain peaks swept by refreshing, peat-scented ocean winds.

Twelve

Captain's Log, Stardate 6099.1. I have deployed a shuttle-craft on a recon mission into the Vara Nebula to determine if there is a pirate build-up. I gave my officers complete latitude to conduct an extensive sweep, and I have faith in Lieutenant Sulu and Ensign Chekov. I am greatly concerned about the length of time without contact, but without direct evidence of imminent danger, I cannot take the ship out of this system. We continue long-range sensor sweeps looking for the Kepler.

We have now been on guard duty at Outpost Zeta Gibraltar for three standard weeks. The crew has been augmenting planetary defenses and analyzing the strange device we located on a captured L'rah'hane ship. Commander Spock and the Excalbian Benjamin Franklin have determined that the device can somehow affect the underlying structure of space-time. The crew have mingled with and studied the Excalbians. I still believe there is something missing in their explanation of their motives, but it cannot be denied that their mimicry is convincing. Federation Special Representative Valek, the plenipotentiary command of this system, has been at times contentious, but

overall, has proven effective so far. The Excalbians await
her decision.

The sickbay door swished open and McCoy looked
up from his microscope, where he was examining
the rapid decomposition of two severed Excalbian
cells belonging to Cyrano de Bergerac and Commodore Stephen Decatur.

"Doctor Leonard McCoy, I presume?" The voice
was female and had a distinct French accent.

McCoy did not at first look up. "Yes," he answered.

"My name is Emilie du Chatelet," said a woman,
the possessor of the voice, who stood in the doorway. "I have come to look through your graviton
microscope."

"My graviton—" Now McCoy did look up and see
her. A wave of recognition passed through him and
just as suddenly retreated. "Madame, have we met?"

"Never, Doctor."

McCoy stood as the Excalbian woman entered
the room, her wide dress brushing against the
doorway.

"Well then, it's nice to meet you, Madame . . .
was it du Chalet?"

"Du Cha*t*elet, Doctor McCoy, but I insist you
call me Emi. Arouet always did."

"I just had the most extraordinaire moment of
déjà vu," McCoy said. "Perhaps I've read about you

and forgotten. What is your interest in the graviton microscope, if I may ask?"

"I have long been interested in the principles of physics, Doctor. Although we only had the works of Newton and Leibnitz in my time with which to gauge the universe, I was always convinced there was more to it all, something we had not yet grasped. Now I have read Einstein, de Varlane, and Beldak and see that I was not mistaken."

McCoy came out from behind his worktable. "Well, if I'm going to call you Emi, you're going to call me Leonard," he said. "Do you often read papers on particle physics for fun?"

"One likes to understand the universe in which one finds oneself, Leonard."

As she moved across the room, McCoy struggled not to stare. She was not the most beautiful woman McCoy had ever come in contact with, but she was close. She was also the picture of elegance, seeming to glide across the sickbay as she approached him. She wore an elaborately brocaded dress of a fine blue fabric, probably pure silk, with a plunging neckline. Between her ample breasts was a blue-and-white cameo suspended on a black ribbon.

Her green eyes were deep with intelligence. On her left cheek was a slight beauty mark. Full lips, perfectly bowed.

And the scent of her! He caught it as she approached. He had never much liked perfume, but this was different. Complex, floral, yet with a touch of the exotic. Sandalwood, maybe?

Her scent was, he had to admit, intoxicating.

McCoy shook himself out of his reverie. "Step this way, Emi, and I'll give you a look. Might be of particular interest to you. I've got an Excalbian skin cell on the stage, and I was examining some very strange structures inside of it when you came in. Perhaps you can tell me their function."

"I dabble a bit and keep up with the science, but I am afraid that biology was never my specialty, Leonard," she said. She bent down to look through the scope's viewer. McCoy found himself staring at the delicate curve of her porcelain neck. "Oh, my. It's beautiful."

"Yes, it is," McCoy replied.

"And are there different wavelengths of gravitons in the same manner there are different wavelengths of light?"

"Yes, I think so. Physics was never *my* specialty, Emi."

Du Chatelet looked up expectantly at McCoy. "What else can you show me with this marvelous mechanism, Leonard?"

McCoy gestured to his sample shelf. "Would you like to see a Vulcan heart cell? Most unusual, and I'd have to say lovely, shape—though you'll never hear me admitting that to Spock. Full of copper-loving compounds."

"I'd be delighted," du Chatelet answered.

That feeling again. McCoy shook his head. "I'm sure we've never met, of course, but—"

Du Chatelet smiled. It lit up her face wonderfully. "You know, Leonard, Arouet used to always say the same thing. He swore I was the image of a dryad in a Botticelli painting he'd once seen in Italy. Silly man. He also said that while he came to me for the mathematics, he stayed for the view."

"You're a mathematician, too?"

"I dabble," she said. "My main interest is—was—in the luminous properties of fire. The books I've read tell me that I predicted ultraviolet and infrared radiation, which later were measured, but the fact that there must exist invisible spectrum was, well, as plain as day."

She covered her lips with a lace-gloved hand and snickered at her slight witticism. McCoy found it utterly charming.

"The properties of fire," McCoy said. "How appropriate."

"I don't follow what you mean, Leonard," she said. Then another smile and a gentle laugh, and she gestured toward McCoy's samples. "You were going to show me that Vulcan heart cell? I've read your paper on it, you know."

"That is the first time a beautiful woman has ever uttered those words to me. 'Read your paper on it.' I kind of like the feeling."

Chatelet blushed. "You have a tongue as silky as Arouet's. Poor man, it often got him into trouble, though."

"Who is this Arouet? Is he your husband?"

Du Chatelet gasped. "Heaven forbid, Leonard," she said. "If I'd married *him* we'd have been as poor as church mice. Especially after he came back from his exile in England." Another silvery laugh. "Oh, he should never have taunted the authorities so with his *Candide*."

Candide.

Arouet.

The real name of Voltaire.

"You're Voltaire's mistress," McCoy said. "Of course, I've read about you."

"I was," she said. "Sadly, Arouet was killed in unfortunate circumstances during our departure from the planet Excalbia."

"I'm sorry to hear that," McCoy said. "I would have liked to meet him. A rational man with a sense of humor. Could teach Spock a thing or two."

"That he was, Leonard. That he was. And kind. Perhaps the sweetest of all my lovers." There was a pause as McCoy took this in. She had stated it as if she had ample experience for comparison.

After a moment of silence, Du Chatelet brought up a delicate hand and touched McCoy's cheek.

That scent again.

"The heart cell, Leonard? Might we put it under the microscope now?"

———

"Here is the problem, Captain Kirk," said Washington-Yarnek. "The pirate raids, in some ways, woke us up to our own problem. We feel that we are locked in a perpetual limbo. If that is the case, we might as well be back in the magma of Excalbia."

Kirk and Washington-Yarnek were in the outpost recreation room, sitting near a window that looked out on the blue-orange vastness of the planetoid. It was near sunset, the purple sky darkening to a bruise brown. In the distance, a dust storm was approaching, and a huge plume from its outlying edge was beginning to darken the sky even further. The storm was to the west, and the planetoid, which had an Earth-like rotation, had its sunset in that direction. That sun, Gibraltar, shone eerily through the distant dust whorls, turning portions of the cloud a glowing bright red. It seemed as if the storm might be literally on fire.

Kirk nodded toward the exterior. "Beautiful, isn't it?" he said. "But also somewhat dangerous."

"The outpost will withstand the storm," Washington-Yarnek said. "During my time here, I've seen worse." Washington-Yarnek had ordered a Saurian brandy when they arrived (another luxury indulgence for the outpost, it seemed), and he swirled it around in its glass, then took a sip. He smiled in pleasure at the taste, but then his face became more serious. "I must tell you, Captain, this outpost has become less of a study center and more of a refugee camp. We—my people—need to get on to the next stage of our lives hopefully *within* the Federation and not on its outer edge. We are no longer residents of the planet Excalbia, but it seems that the Federation is very ambivalent about claiming us as citizens, no matter how much we may wish to become productive members of your society."

"I empathize with the way you feel, but you have to understand the position in which you've placed the Federation," Kirk replied. "You are an unknown quantity from a species with powers beyond our capabilities."

"Originally, true, but I do not know what else we can do to prove our sincerity."

"Valek would probably say that what you can do is wait out the administrative process. You want to become Federation citizens. This is how the Federation operates. Sometimes the wheels grind much more slowly than any of us would like."

"Granted, Captain," Washington-Yarnek replied. "But in the meantime, my people are getting restless. They need something to *do*. Let me tell you from experience that this is a demoralizing state."

Washington-Yarnek stared down at his brandy. "Have you had it before?" he asked.

"Yes."

"Extraordinary stuff. One could drink oneself to oblivion with this and wake up with a head as clear as day."

"There are hangover cures that work very well these days," said Kirk gently. "And one need not even choose to get drunk at all. A simple pill before drinking."

Washington-Yarnek nodded, but by his gaze Kirk could tell his mind was elsewhere.

"When we were encamped in Pennsylvania in seventy-six, there were moments when I felt in my heart that all was lost. We'd been chased like scared children through and out of New Jersey, across the Delaware. Supplies were low. The enlistments were running out. We had whole regiments leaving at once for points north and south—anywhere to get away from a dreadful winter in an ill-equipped camp. Was this what the revolution was promising?"

"A difficult situation," Kirk said with a smile. "I've read about it. In fact, we studied it at the Academy."

"The enemy held New York and Philadelphia. Things seemed truly hopeless."

"But you found a way to give the troops, and the country, hope."

"We learned from our spies that the British had garrisoned one of their most fearsome battalions of mercenaries, the Hessian warriors, in the dormitories at Trenton, New Jersey," said Washington-Yarnek. "It was extremely provocative information, but what was I to do with it?"

"You considered that they were an outlying portion of the British forces and that reinforcements would not be immediately available to them if they were engaged."

"Indeed."

"You also knew that, as poor and bedraggled as your forces were, if you concentrated them, you could overwhelm a garrison-sized unit."

"Not easily, Captain," Washington-Yarnek said with a rueful shake of the head. "When you are dealing with Hessian mercenaries, nothing is ever *easy*. But the opportunity was there."

"All you had to do was get a substantial force across the Delaware River during winter, attack, and then get back before reinforcements arrived," Kirk went on with a smile. "Not an easy task at all, sir."

"We crossed at night. I'd hoped to have the aid of the moon, but the evening proved to be cloudy. It was the middle of December and ice floes filled the water. Dreadfully cold. It seemed I could feel the suffering of my men physically."

"But they were moving."

"Yes, and though it was the Yuletide and most were far from home, they understood they had been given a meaningful task. They did not shirk it. We attacked at dawn, and the Hessians gave us quite a fight. I sent out Greene to my left, Sullivan to my right. Colonel Knox brought his cannons up to fire on the garrison. It was difficult, bloody. But, in the end, we overcame the mercenaries, sent them scurrying. We lured Cornwallis down. We then confronted him at Trenton, achieved a stalemate."

"You withdrew during the night, after that second battle."

"A tactical retreat," Washington-Yarnek said. "Sometimes it seems as if my entire military career was a series of maneuvers and tactical retreats. This was a lesson I learned well in my youth from the war with the French and Indians on the Virginia frontier. Ten years we spent losing men and giving ground. More than once, all seemed lost. Then suddenly the all-powerful French simply collapsed. Britain had won in other places around the globe, and Montreal fell to General Wolfe. It was over."

"You won for Virginia during the French and Indian War without winning a single major battle."

"In fact, I lost my fair share, two of them badly," Washington-Yarnek said. "A commanding officer's task is to win a war, not achieve victory in this or that battle."

"You won the battle at Trenton."

"Yes. We won," Washington-Yarnek replied. "Captain, I don't have to tell you: it felt *good* to win for a change." He smiled, and this time his smile, wholly unconscious, revealed the off-white surface of his set of false teeth. Kirk had read somewhere that it was hippopotamus and not elephant ivory that went into the base of Washington's teeth. This was one of those facts that stayed with you long after history class.

Not such a bad imitation for eighteenth-century technology, Kirk thought. *But I see why he doesn't smile much.*

There must be a way to modify the dentures in such a way that the form-renewing molecular activity within Washington-Yarnek would not reject the improvements. Kirk knew this was something the outpost scientists were working on. *Scotty might have a few suggestions that would help them. I'll have him look into it.*

"The effort galvanized the new nation," Kirk said. "Your manpower drain slowed—platoons, squadrons, regiments began to reenlist rather than leave for home—and new recruits arrived."

"The engagement was of little military worth. I knew this at the time. The officers were aware of the fact, as well. Most of all, we gave the men something to *do.* Something that was not obvious make-work, a small thing, but important." Washington-Yarnek took another sip of Saurian brandy and looked out the window. The dust storm was almost upon them now, and with the sun below the horizon, it seemed an ominous black cloud bearing down upon them. "What I did *not* realize until later was how important Trenton would be *strategically*, for it proved the spark in morale that reignited the fires of resistance. I got lucky."

"In my experience, a man usually makes his own luck, Mister President."

"That is why I am determined to act," Washington-Yarnek said. "*We* are determined to act."

Yarnek reached inside his dark blue jacket. Kirk stiffened. He knew this was where Washington-Yarnek's musket pistol perpetually reappeared. Was he about to face a primitive gun muzzle? Hear some sort of demand?

But when Washington-Yarnek's hand emerged, it held a scrolled piece of paper, tied with a ribbon.

"A declaration, Captain Kirk, stating our position," Washington-Yarnek said. "It has been put together by several of us. Mister Franklin and Mister Machiavelli are on the committee. They were responsible for the word-craft."

"Do you want me to deliver this to Valek? Why not present it yourself?"

"No, you misunderstand," said Washington-Yarnek with a quirk of the eyebrow and a sly smile. "I wish *you* to read it over and consider it. I don't want to make use of you as a mere messenger,

Captain. I hope to pull you into our little conspiracy."

He held out the scrolled paper, and, after a moment, Kirk took it from him and slowly untied the ribbon.

"Do I really want to see this?"

"It's just a piece of paper, Captain," Washington-Yarnek said. "What can it hurt to take a look? And, if you happen to agree with its sentiments and proposals, we've left a space on that declaration for your signature, James."

Thirteen

"Reports," Kirk said. "Mister Spock."

"A fascinating experience becoming acquainted with the Excalbian Benjamin Franklin," the first officer said. "I had expected to discover an obvious anachronism, but could not do so. My conclusion is that, if the real Benjamin Franklin were taken from his place in time and put into the present day, he would behave much like this Benjamin Franklin."

"Franklin was a genius," Kirk pressed, "and a polymath. Surely this Franklin isn't as dazzling as the historic Franklin seemed to be."

"I cannot speak to that point directly, having knowledge of the historic Franklin only through secondary sources and Franklin's own writing," Spock replied. "I would make the observation, however, that I have played *this* Benjamin Franklin eight times in three-dimensional chess. He has been victorious five of those times, and we have achieved stalemate once. I have, so far, two victories to my credit."

Kirk nodded. That *was* impressive Yet three-dimensional chess did have an element of bluffing as well as pure analytics. A human could beat a Vulcan on occasion, as Kirk himself had proved.

But five out of eight?

"Doctor McCoy, you've had a look at them on the inside. What *are* they, Bones?"

"They're human, Jim," said McCoy. "To a point. I could treat any of them with human medications, and those would be effective. If I had to operate, the organs would all be in the right places." McCoy leaned forward and scratched his head. "On the other hand, I did watch one of them regrow an *arm* in the period of twelve hours."

"Every bit of baggage and accouterments they have regenerates, Captain. Watt told me that it would limit itself to about the contents of a room," Scott said. "I wouldn't have believed it if I hadn't seen it with my own eyes, but, along with several members of my engineering team, I watched a beautiful bottle of six-hundred-year-old Scotch fill itself up." Scott put out a hand, palm side down, lowered it. "And we'd drink it down, and it would fill back up. And we'd drink it down, and it would fill back up, and we'd—"

"We get the idea, Mister Scott, thank you." Kirk turned to his science officer. "Speculation?"

"Analysis indicates a holographic engram in a matrix between every major molecular structure in both people and objects," Spock said. "This is very likely the mechanism, but we have yet to ascertain how it functions."

"They're not *really* human at all."

"Captain, I wouldn't necessarily go that far," Uhura said. "Spending time with the Excalbian Harriet Tubman has been very stimulating. She may not be a human being, but I got the sense that she truly *believed* in the cause she fought for. I have to admit that speaking with her has been . . . inspirational."

"Thank you, Lieutenant. So this is a not a conscious charade that the Excalbians are putting on, it would seem. Even if they know differently, it's clear the Excalbians *feel* as if they are who they say they are," Kirk said. "But since none of them are Socrates, do *they* know *themselves*? Might there be something within them, something Excalbian and ugly, waiting to spring to the fore? They threatened to kill us before to satisfy a whim of curiosity." Kirk paused, surveyed the faces around the table.

These are the ones I trust more than anything, he thought. *When I can feel an iota for the Excalbians of what I feel for these people, then we'll see about relaxing our vigil.*

"All right, then," Kirk concluded. "Continue to observe, and let's be on our guard. Dismissed. Spock, please remain."

The others trailed out of the room. McCoy was

the last to leave as the door shut. Spock remained sitting, looking quizzically at Kirk.

"All right, Spock," Kirk said. "Tell me about her."

"*Her*, Captain?"

"Valek," Kirk said. "You knew her. She's working for your father, whether officially or not. I feel that there is a game the Council is playing here, and I don't like being a pawn in it. I need information."

"There is not a great deal to tell," Spock said. "Varen, her brother, was my laboratory partner during our early schooling."

"Why do I think that's not all the story?"

"Varen was the only Vulcan child my age who wished to be my laboratory partner," Spock said. "There was considerable opposition to *anyone* doing so among the other children."

"I see," Kirk said. "How old were you at the time?"

"Eight Vulcan years," answered Spock. "Logic dictated that Varen and I would make an effective team. Our intellectual assets were complementary. He was gifted in his understanding of life sciences. I have certain analytical strengths."

"I'll say," Kirk said. "And Valek?"

"She concluded that Varen had made an error in judgment. She made an argument that this was the case at an institute forum before the entire student body," Spock said. "She also spoke out against the marriage of my mother and father."

"She argued that your human side would lead you to error."

"Yes, Captain, that was essentially the premise of all of the children at the time," said Spock. "There was little evidence with which to refute it. It was difficult to make a purely analytic defense of myself."

"But, boy, did you ever show them eventually," Kirk said with a smile.

"Yes, they were mistaken," Spock said. "Valek was one of the first to realize that her original premise was faulty. She wished to take a public opportunity to retract her previous statements, but I requested that she not do so. I believed, as I do to this day, that logic speaks for itself."

"But she never apologized for what she'd said before?"

"No. She merely acknowledged error."

"Yet, you forgave her?"

"Captain, you know I am incapable of feeling any ill will toward her," Spock said. "One does not *forgive* a syllogistic error. One merely notes when it has been corrected."

"And her work with Sarek?"

"This began after I left for the Academy, so I am not familiar with the details," Spock said. "Varen and I have remained in touch and still exchange occasional messages. He sometimes mentions his sister's undertakings in his letters to me."

"I realize those letters are private, but can you give me the gist of what Varen told you?"

"Certainly," Spock said. "It is unremarkable. Her parents were acquaintances of my father, therefore Sarek would have been aware that her turn of mind was geared toward the law, history, philosophy, and political science—the 'humanities,' as you might call this area of study. Varen informed me that she had achieved an impressive score on the social science portion of the Vulcan Science Academy entrance examinations and planned to study interplanetary relations. After graduation, she earned an apprenticeship in the Vulcan diplomatic service and from there went on to work for Sarek."

"And there's nothing else?"

"Captain, as you know I spent several years estranged from my father after my choice to join Starfleet. Our paths never crossed."

"I see," Kirk said. "Thank you for being so forthcoming, Spock. I appreciate it."

Spock nodded, started to leave, then turned back again. "Jim, for what it's worth, my father does not take on protégés who are not extremely gifted at what they do. Our childhood difficulties may have formed a necessary condition for her later development as an effective adult."

"One can hope."

"There is no need to hope, Captain," Spock said, raising an eyebrow. "We shall obtain evidence soon enough upon which to base our conclusion. Then we will *know*."

"In any case, it's time to make my first . . . report . . . to her, based on what we've found out. I'm looking forward to it with a bit of trepidation, to tell the truth."

"Wise," Spock replied.

Valek had on a shimmering, diaphanous dress that looked to be made of some exotic material. *Tholian silk?* It was black and reached down to her knees, where it swished about, leaving exposed an interesting expanse of Vulcan leg. It was sleeveless, and the neckline came up to her throat. Laced throughout the black of the dress was silver thread that wound into a variety of patterns which glowed faintly, lit by some sort of luminescent element within. It took Kirk a moment to grasp what the silver weavings were meant to depict.

"Constellations," he said. "Are they Vulcan?"

"Yes, as seen from the northern hemisphere, where I originate."

"Beautiful."

"Thank you, Captain," she said, motioning Kirk into her quarters. "Your call caught me unawares, or I should have gotten into more official attire."

Kirk glanced over her shoulder to the bed beyond. Her clothes were lying on the cover in a clump, twisted together as if they'd been thrown that way.

Now that's a bit puzzling, Kirk thought. *If she changed into the dress, why didn't she put her clothes into the 'fresher? Doesn't seem very Vulcan to leave a messy room.*

The alternative was that she'd quickly changed into the dress when he'd announced himself outside her quarters and hastily thrown her other clothes aside.

"Please come in," Valek said. Kirk stepped farther inside, and the door slid shut behind him.

"Shall we sit in my reception area while you report to me?"

"Certainly," Kirk answered. She motioned toward a chair, and Kirk moved to it and sat down.

Valek remained standing. "Can I get you anything, Captain?"

"No, thank you," Kirk said.

"Very well." She took a seat and crossed her legs, leaving a good portion of smooth, porcelain-pale calf exposed.

"I'll come to the point," Kirk said. "The Excalbians have decided that if you don't make your decision by tomorrow regarding their status, they're going to present to you a declaration of intent."

"What is it they intend?"

"To form their own governing entity," Kirk said. "I think the current thinking is to call it New Excalbia."

"Captain, where did you learn this?"

"Where do you think? Yarnek. He asked me to sign what he called a new Declaration of Independence for his people. It expresses a desire to form a sovereign entity among themselves, as free beings."

"And where would the territory of this proposed nation be located?"

"They plan to take Zeta Gibraltar out of the Federation along with themselves," Kirk said. "The science team would be permitted to stay, but the Excalbians would declare the planet as being under joint Excalbian-Federation law."

"Sounds rather preposterous, doesn't it?"

"I don't know," Kirk said. "They make some valid points. They have been yanked around a bit. Not by you personally, but by the people you work for."

"They are also the people you work for, Captain."

"In a general sense," Kirk said. "But there is a clear chain of command that leads from me up through the Starfleet Command to the Federation Council's Starfleet Guidance Committee. I do not take my orders directly from the Federation ambassadorial service, the Security Committee, or from any Council member who thinks it would be fun to move a starship around like a play toy."

"Interesting points," Valek said. "Did *you* sign this document?"

Kirk felt a hint of flush rise in his cheeks. "I did," he said. "Washington-Yarnek was very persuasive."

"You are aware that I could bring you up on treason charges and have you court-martialed should I wish."

"You could try, I suppose," he said. "Wouldn't be the first time."

"Yes, I know," Valek said. "I'm quite familiar with your record. Bureaucrats don't fare well when they go up against James T. Kirk." She gave a slight shrug. "In any case, I do not intend to do anything of the sort. Instead, I wish to consider your advice in this matter."

"Listen to them."

"To their demands?"

"It's not a hostage negotiation, Valek," Kirk said. "They came to me in good faith and asked that I approach you."

"Why not come directly to me?" Valek asked. A stray bit of hair fell over her eyes, and she brushed it away.

She's let her hair down, Kirk thought. *It's as black as midnight.*

Kirk smiled, pointed at himself. "Good cop, remember?"

Valek nodded. "Yes, a logical move on their part. They are becoming more politically savvy and, dare I say, more human. I've come to the conclusion that, for all their power over the material world, they were quite naïve when they first left their planet. From my observations, it seems that they expected their request for sanctuary to be immediately granted. They were, in their own minds, practically gods when compared to us."

"But now the human components have taken in more and more experience," Kirk said. "They may have developed a different idea of what is in their best interests—and how to get it."

"Precisely, Captain," Valek said. "This is one reason I have delayed my decision. I wished to give the Excalbians time to know their own minds."

"That is . . . wise, Valek. Kind, even."

"Did you not expect it of me? Sarek himself taught me this: Wisdom and mercy are the fruits of logic. When there is discord, you will find irrationality at the bottom of it."

"I must say, I had anticipated that you would take the most direct course and damn the subtleties," Kirk said. "Pardon me for misjudging you."

"Perhaps I would have, had I not spent ten years on Earth getting to know humans," she said. "I have even had a human lover. Does that surprise you?"

It sure as hell does.

"But I thought . . . what about . . ."

"The *plak tow*?" Valek leaned forward, gazing more intently at Kirk. "I am aware of your previous acquaintance with the *pon farr*. It is part of your classified file, which I was permitted to review."

"Great," Kirk mumbled. "I wonder what other marks I have on my permanent record?"

"While most Vulcans refuse to discuss the *pon farr*," Valek continued, "my compunctions in that regard have . . . loosened. Particularly with humans, who don't find passionate rage and extreme compulsions while battling for a mate especially unusual."

"But that still doesn't answer my question," Kirk said.

"I am a twin, Captain Kirk," Valek said. "Vulcan twins seldom imprint, even when forced to take part in the bonding ceremony. Our infantile mental tie with our sibling takes the place of the imprint— only in the case of Varen and myself leading to extreme loyalty, and not the sexual act."

"You're free?" Kirk said. *Spock almost killed me when the instinct asserted itself. And he would have, but for Bones's bit of subterfuge.* "Lucky you."

"There is no such thing as luck, Captain. It is, however, a convenient fact, given that most of my work is conducted away from Vulcan."

"Why are you telling me this?"

"Merely to explain my official actions to a valued colleague," Valek said. "There are many aspects of human nature that have, upon deeper consideration, far more logic to them than most Vulcans give humans credit for."

Kirk nodded. "I should be going," he said. He

stood, faced Valek. "I've made my report and recommendation. You are the civilian authority here. This is all politics now, and I've got a starship to run."

"If I release you from your current orders," Valek said. She stood as well.

"Yes."

"Which I cannot do at this time," she said. "Besides, you are still waiting for the report from your shuttlecraft reconnaissance to the nebula."

"How the hell did you know—" Kirk smiled, shook his head. "It doesn't matter. You are correct."

"We make an effective team, Captain," Valek replied.

"Good cop, bad cop?"

"I believe the relationship is more complicated than that," she said. "It would even not be out of the question for us to become friends."

She reached out her hand. It took Kirk a moment to figure out what she was doing.

She wants to shake on it.

Kirk reached forward and took her hand in his. Her handshake was warm, firm. Unexpected.

And when the door to Valek's quarters closed behind him, he had to admit he still didn't know quite what to make of Special Representative Valek.

One thing he was certain of: he must not underestimate her.

She's right that our relationship is getting quite a bit more complicated.

Despite himself, Kirk realized that he was rather enjoying the challenge.

———

Galileo casually hefted the device from the L'rah'hane ship in one hand, while gesticulating with the other. Spock was not particularly concerned at the Italian's treatment of the artifact. Even if he dropped it, Spock doubted there would be any damage to the object. It might, however, hurt quite a bit if it fell on Galileo's toe. He was wearing only sandals.

"I suspect it is attuned to certain quantum effects," Galileo said. Benjamin Franklin translated from the Latin.

"I had come to the same conclusion," Spock answered. In Latin.

Franklin began to translate, then caught himself and chuckled.

"Bless my soul, Mister Spock," chuckled Franklin. "You seem to speak Latin as well as I."

"My command of Latin is rudimentary, but it should be serviceable for our present needs."

"Ah, *eccellente*!" Galileo said. "I have spent much time catching up on your language, Sir Spock: science and mathematics. For me, these are the speech of nature. I have been so busy learning them, I haven't had time to assimilate the modern languages of men. The computer, she translates the technical material for me."

"A fortuitous use of your time," Spock replied. "What is your conclusion concerning the L'rah'hane device?"

"I am only making conjectures. There is still so much to learn." Galileo moved the device in a swooping arc, as if he were playing with a toy. "The curves of the calculus! What a wonder. And partial differential equations! The language of nature, I tell you." Galileo shook his head, smiling in what seemed to be awe.

"A conjecture from Galileo Galilei is worth the dead certainty of many a fool," Franklin said.

Galileo seemed immune to flattery, even from a master such as Franklin. "I am troubled, troubled by this, however," the Italian continued. He used a data wand to write several equations across an electronic blackboard display.

Fascinating, Spock thought. *These are advanced topographic solutions. He is using the mathematics of Lorentz transformations to attempt to describe the device's function.*

Galileo, it seemed, was either a quick study, or the Excalbian within was supplying the acumen. Wherever it came from, the math itself was genuine. Spock studied the equations.

"Pardon me if I am not reading this correctly,"

he said after a moment. "But you are predicting negative integer values for information transfer."

"Correct! Absolutely correct, my Vulcan compatriot," Galileo said, beaming.

"A negative information state is an absurdity," Spock replied. "One cannot know *less* than nothing."

"Precisely, precisely," Galileo said. "The information is going somewhere and coming from somewhere. It only seems like there is a negative state."

He made another flourish with his data wand. "Look! A two-part solution to the paradox."

"The information is being displaced by changes in quantum gravitational states," Spock said. "Information from this moment in this bit of space the device occupies is sent to one destination while information arrives from . . ."

"The future?" Franklin asked.

"This could be! This could be!" Galileo said. "And maybe also from a distance that is greater than the galaxy."

"And, if so, it arrives instantaneously," Spock said. "From a location that may very well be on the other end of our galaxy."

"Quantum physics, she is whimsical," Galileo replied. "Effervescent and beautiful, with a smile like the Mona Lisa. Leonardo, he senses this. His true mistress is the universe, you know!"

Franklin shook his head in wonder. "Do you think that's what they use it for? Sending messages to and from the future, to and from distant galaxies?"

"I do not believe the L'rah'hane use it for either purpose," Spock said. "A species that can predict the future would not find itself scrounging a living by piracy along the fringes of civilized space."

"Good point," Franklin acknowledged. "There was certainly no indication of anything of the sort going on while we were being brought aboard. Although I admit I was slightly more concerned with the constrictive shackles around my wrists and neck at the time and may have missed a detail or two."

At the mention of shackles, Galileo frowned and his animated face became so instantly sullen that even Spock recognized that an emotional transformation had taken place.

The scientist muttered a curse in Italian, then turned his back on the viewscreen full of equations. "It all comes to nothing," he said. "The moment you have a true and original thought, they lock you up and call you a heretic."

"Surely you will acknowledge that times have changed, my dear sir," Franklin replied gently.

"I acknowledge nothing," said Galileo. "There is a darkness that follows all that we do. It will swallow us up in the end, and all endeavor will come to naught."

Fascinating.

As far as Spock knew there was no record of the real Galileo experiencing emotional swings so extreme a Vulcan would notice. This behavior might be attributable to the underlying Excalbian mentality asserting itself.

And if that is true, Spock thought, *then the mood swing might have its origin in a hidden threat the Excalbian is aware of that is very real indeed.*

———————

The scent of her.

Madame Emilie du Chatelet.

Voltaire's lover.

The first translator of Newton's *Principia* into French.

What in the great galaxy is she doing with a small-town sawbones like me?

McCoy held Emi against him in his bed. He was never going to look at his quarters quite the same way again, he knew. Even as he lay in such thought, he reflected that he was glad he'd learned that she used the 'fresher to annihilate her lice, and each treatment was good for several days.

He realized he should be wary in other ways as well. He'd called Jim Kirk out on some of his lovers. There had been clones, aliens, even a robot. But he doubted Kirk had ever slept with a rock being before.

Which was nonsense. She was a human in every way that mattered. Curiosity. Intelligence. Self-awareness. Love.

Joy at the wonders of science come to fruition that she had, somehow, against all hope, returned once again to witness. She took delight in his compendium of unusual biological scans, his collection of odd and alien medical instruments, his fascination with the living body.

His fascination with *her* living body.

"Emi," he said. She rustled under the bed cover beside him, kissed his neck. "Emi, what's it like being you? I mean, really? You know you can't be her, the real Emilie du Chatelet. Is there some kind of dual awareness, some double vision, that you experience?"

She turned her head, gazed up at him with those green eyes. "Kiss me, Leonard." He leaned over and did so.

"There is no 'dual awareness' in that," she said. "I don't know about that other Madame du Chatelet. I have memories of centuries of thinking, thinking, thinking, and arriving nowhere with my thoughts. There are perhaps brilliant Excalbians. I was not one of them."

"Hard to believe. A species that can mentally transform matter."

"Yes, but what did I do with this skill? Brooding. Petty political intrigues. You have no idea what it is like to spend a thousand years thinking in circles and getting nowhere."

"I guess I do not," McCoy said. "At least not the thousand years part."

"Then, one day, I wake up and I am this brilliant *woman*. Yes, genuinely brilliant. The math that befuddled me before, it is clear. The calculation of a planet's fall about its sun, this I can now perform. Where did this come from? Was it borrowed from a mathematician when the *Enterprise* or other vessels were scanned? I do not know. What I do know is that I *like* what I have become. I glory in it. I glory in what we do together."

"It is rather glorious, isn't it?"

McCoy sat up and leaned his back against the *Enterprise* bulkhead that served as his bed's headboard.

"I know you are making a report on us," du Chatelet said. She moved up, put her head against McCoy's chest. "I came at first, maybe, to influence your report. Ask you to put in good words for us."

"All I'm doing is medical evaluations," McCoy said.

"Yes, I know," du Chatelet replied. "It doesn't matter. That's all over now. Now I want to be Emilie du Chatelet. Live in this time, this moment. Make love with you"—he tilted her head up, kissed McCoy's chin—"and learn, learn, learn *new* things.

What I could never do before as an Excalbian. What they would not let a woman do before in my imaginary past. Now I can do it."

"I think you will, Emi," McCoy said. "Whatever happens, I think you will."

"I want to learn now," she replied in a low voice, almost a whisper. "I want to learn what it is like to do this again and again."

"Do what?"

She didn't answer. Instead she took his hand and gently pulled him back down to her.

————

It wasn't exactly a strike. It was more like a series of "sick days." The Excalbians simply did not show up for "work"—their work being subjects of observation and questioning by the outpost scientists. After one planetary day, Commander Contreras was irritated. After two, she was incensed. After more than a week, she was beginning to despair.

"We're going to have to close the base down if they don't cooperate," Contreras told Kirk. "Never mind our careers, what is going to happen to *them*? Don't they realize that this study is their ticket to acceptance and perhaps even citizenship?"

"I'm not so sure they *want* citizenship any longer, Commander," Valek said.

"Then what do they want?" Contreras said. "I've been with them for months and this play-acting has got to stop. These are nanotechnologically animate silicon-carbonate *aliens*, not human beings. You take off a coat, remove a tooth, or, as we've seen, confiscate a weapon, and the thing just *grows* back, springs back into existence within a few hours. Nothing about their appearance is real."

"Yet they aren't display mannequins, Commander," Kirk said.

"I know that, Captain," said Contreras. "But every time we attempt to communicate with whatever is underneath, we run into Napoleon, or Hildegard of Bingen, or George Damn Washington." She spoke this last name more in frustration than contempt, gazing away from Kirk and the Vulcan representative.

"Commander, might I suggest that the Excalbians are not wholly aware of who they are anymore," Valek said.

Contreras looked quizzically at Valek. "Go on."

"They are stranded in this intermediate state. They cannot go back to being pure Excalbians, and yet their own memories are taken from other people—notably the captain here and other members of the *Enterprise* crew."

"So you think we ought to consider this . . . declaration," she said, gesturing at the document unrolled upon her desk. "'We hold these rights to be self-evident, that all sentient species are created equal.'"

"It's certainly an advance over what the Excalbians believed when we last ran into them," Kirk replied.

Valek looked up from her examination of the document and turned to Kirk.

"When you signed this, Captain," Valek said, "were you trying to humor the Excalbians?"

"No," Kirk said after a moment's consideration. "I agree with them."

"They wish to take Zeta Gibraltar and this star system out of the Federation," Valek replied. "They wish to set up their own *government.*"

"With the eventual incorporation as an independent state within the United Federation of Planets," Kirk said. "Talk to Washington. Hear what he has to say."

"He is proposing revolution."

"Within the bounds of what he thinks of as natural law," Kirk said. "Given his assumptions, I think you'll find that declaration to be entirely logical."

"And you, Captain, what do you think about these 'self-evident truths' Washington and the other signatories, including *you*, speak of?"

"I believe in the right to life and liberty. And when those rights are endangered, I believe in fighting for them."

"And the pursuit of happiness, Captain? Isn't this the cause of most human wars—

The placing of one group's happiness over

another's? In my estimation happiness, like all emotion, is a primitive instinct we had best move beyond."

And to think, not long ago she was arguing for the complexity and logic behind human nature, Kirk thought. *Is she trying to drive me crazy?*

"Happiness can mean a great many things, Valek," Kirk answered. "It can mean acting wisely and achieving fulfillment. I have no doubt we humans will still be pursuing that sort of happiness until the end of time."

"You will be no closer to attaining it, so long as you rely on your emotions to get you there," Valek said.

"Thank goodness for the Vulcans, then, Representative Valek," Kirk replied with a slight smile. "In my opinion, the more our species interact, the better."

Kirk was preparing to make a final argument for the New Excalbia Declaration, when his communicator signaled. The captain flipped the communicator open. "Kirk here."

"Captain, you wanted us to notify you immediately when our Upsilon Gibraltar expedition reported in," Uhura said.

Kirk's heart made a leap. Sulu and Chekov! They were all right, then.

He'd been worrying about them for weeks, but had believed and hoped they were fulfilling their mission. A trip into the Vara to locate them would have been fruitless, given the extreme sensor distortion and subspace interference—even if it would not have been a violation of orders. He'd depended on his officers to fulfill their mission and return, and so they had.

"Yes, Lieutenant," he said. "That's fine. What do we hear?"

"We received an extremely weak subspace message," Uhura said. *"It seems they had a small technical problem."*

"Are they all right?"

"Affirmative, Captain," Uhura said. *"They say they will be ready to enter the hangar deck in two point five hours."*

Something had gone wrong. They must be traveling barely above the speed of light to take so long to arrive after a signal.

But they were alive, and that was of utmost importance.

"Notify the transporter room to stand by for my signal," Kirk said.

"Aye, sir," Uhura answered. *"They said they have much to report concerning the Upsilon moon and its defensive capacities, Captain."*

"Interesting," Kirk said. "If they come through again on the subspace frequencies, be sure to tell them I can't wait to hear that report. Kirk out."

Kirk rose and started to walk away from the

conference table so that he could get a clear field for the transporter.

"I shall be interested in hearing what your officers have observed. It may make a difference on how I respond," Valek said. "Captain, I believe that with liberty comes responsibility."

"I couldn't agree more."

Valek nodded. She picked up the declaration, ran a hand over it to flatten it out, and considered its words, handwritten in a beautiful calligraphic style. "The Excalbians' wish for autonomy I find laudable. But I wonder whether they are truly prepared for the cost."

Fourteen

Captain's Log, Stardate 6099.9. Lieutenant Sulu and Ensign Chekov have returned from a reconnaissance mission into the heart of the Vara Nebula. After taking a hit, Sulu and Chekov had to limp back on their remaining power. The journey took them five weeks, instead of one day. Anxious they would be too late to deliver their warning, they have arrived in time to report a large L'rah'hane pirate operation. Special commendations to Lieutenant Hikaru Sulu and Ensign Pavel Chekov.

What do we face, and how much time do we have to prepare?

"Captain, there is some formidable firepower out there waiting to strike," Sulu said. He and Chekov had reported directly to the briefing room, knowing the captain would want to hear their report the moment they stepped off the *Kepler*. Kirk was amazed at how much of a professional appearance they'd managed to maintain after five weeks in a shuttlecraft. Contrary to regulations (although Kirk was inclined to let it slide), they had engaged in a beard-growing contest for the past five weeks. Chekov had definitely won: his thick beard gave him the appearance of a small bear. Sulu had, however, taken the mustache award. He'd even managed to put a sinister curl onto the ends of his.

"The L'rah'hane appeared to be gathering every ship they could," Chekov continued. "It was a very strange collection of vessels.

"They were waiting for something. Since we had time on our hands, we went through every piece of data we'd collected, including a few ship-to-ship intercepts. It took some doing, but one captain was apparently trying to impress another that they would have sufficient firepower to take on the *Enterprise*. They passed on a set of basic schematics for the big ships on the way, particularly indicating weaponry."

"That vessel, and the space hub, match the records for Hradrian war ships and naval installations," said Sulu. "Mister Chekov provided some excellent helmsmanship, and we were able to get extensive scans of all the exterior systems on the depot hub, as well—including its weapon systems. It's well armed, but tended by robots. We know exactly what we're up against there, sir."

"Extraordinary work, both of you," Kirk replied.

"There's something else, sir," Chekov said. "We spent much of the journey back trying to puzzle out one weapon system we believe the depot hub possesses. I could make neither heads nor tails of it. Mister Sulu may have an idea, however."

"Sulu?"

"Unsure, Captain," the helmsman replied. "There were some interesting observational anomalies in the vicinity of the emplacement."

"What sort of anomalies?"

"Puzzling difficulties in measuring specific dimensions under extreme resolution," Sulu said. "It was almost as if our view of the device was smeared, across space *and* time. My best guess based on the analysis is that this weapon array corresponds with the quantum device that Mister Spock was examining."

"Do you think that this pirate base may be using this device, whatever it is, as a weapon?"

"I'd say it's a strong possibility, Captain. And given that the ships due to rendezvous are also of Hradrian design, it would be a fair bet that they'll have the same weaponized technology."

"All right. Good work." Kirk put a hand to his chin. "Go over your data with Mister Spock. The Excalbian Franklin is on board serving as the New Excalbia Assembly liaison. Get him in on it, too. I want to know what we're up against."

"Aye, sir."

"And gentlemen?"

"Yes, Captain?"

"Be careful shaving." He turned to Chekov. "You may have to take a phaser to that rug, Mister Chekov."

"Aye, Captain."

"Dismissed." Sulu and Chekov exited. Kirk called up the Vara Nebula on the conference room triviewer and gazed at it for a long moment.

The Hradrian slave empire.

Well, if it turns out they are remerging from whatever hole they crawled into, I'm going to do my best to send them back to the land of myth and legend.

———

The Excalbians had first began beaming to and from the captured L'rah'hane ships as part of the joint project between Watt and Scott to create a point-defense system for Zeta Gibraltar. The ships were presently in orbit, but whether they would remain there, or be taken farther into Federation territory for study, had not yet been decided by Starfleet.

Yet so long as they *were* in orbit, they served as excellent surveillance platforms for threats coming from the nebula. It was only a matter of installing a simple long-range sensor in each vessel, then linking each sensor via computer to form a larger observational network. Even though the sensors were attuned to subspace, tachyonic frequencies, the principle of linking multiple antennae together to make a huge virtual lens, had been in use since the dawn of the information age on Earth.

Groups of three or four Excalbians had beamed aboard each of the four L'rah'hane ships, checked in with the vessel's skeleton crew from the *Enterprise*, then got to work. The *Enterprise* crews consisted of five duty officers taking rotating shifts. Most of the ships' orbital maintenance functions had been slaved to the *Enterprise* computer, which was remotely carrying out the basic attitudinal changes necessary to keep the ships in steady paths.

The *Enterprise* crews were spending their time scanning the few remaining bits of L'rah'hane hardware that hadn't been cataloged and analyzed. Some, when off duty, volunteered to help out the Excalbians with their installation procedures.

The comings and going of the Excalbians were soon so commonplace that no one noticed when larger groups beamed aboard each ship during one duty shift that corresponded to early morning at the outpost. In fact, except for those standing early watch, most of the L'rah'hane skeleton crews were in their temporary bunks, asleep.

In the renamed *Victory*, the L'rah'hane warship that served as the de facto flagship of the captured L'rah'hane "fleet," the Starfleet crew were quite surprised to be awakened to the sound of a phaser on overload over the ship's interior communication speakers. The weapon was one step away from explosion—something that would take a good part of an L'rah'hane ship's deck with it.

"Attention Starfleet crew," said a commanding voice over the ship's interior communication system. *"We wish no harm to come to any Starfleet personnel. We do require, however, that all Starfleet crew evacuate, as this ship is now the property of the New Excalbia Navy."*

There was no mistaking the voice. It was that of Admiral Horatio Nelson.

"We judge that, due to the placement, the overload of a single phaser will not immediately endanger you, but it will jeopardize the integrity of the ship if the phaser should be allowed to reach super-critical and explode. You would then be forced to evacuate in any case, but from a damaged ship—a ship whose orbit will decay until it burns in the atmosphere. No one wants this."

Aidan Ripoll, the lieutenant in command of the *Enterprise* crew aboard the *Victory*, rolled out of his bunk and slammed a finger into the intraship control. "Sir, with all due respect, what the hell are you trying to accomplish?"

"We are requisitioning this ship in the name of the New Excalbia Assembly for use in the defense of this system against outside attack."

"New Excalbia Assembly? What are you talking about?"

"We wish no trouble," said Nelson. *"But we are committed to occupying this ship in the name of New Excalbia and would in no way wish to bring harm to you or any other United Federation of Planets citizen. The New Excalbia Assembly wishes peace and alliance with the Federation and all its peoples."*

"You *are* its 'peoples,' as far as I knew," said Ripoll.

"This is no longer the case," Nelson replied. *"Now, if you will ready your crew, we will send you back to the* Enterprise, *no harm done."*

"Except to my career," Ripoll muttered. He rubbed his eyes, stiffened into a ready stance, then pressed the send button once again. "We will do nothing of the sort, Admiral. Furthermore, I order you to deactivate that overloaded phaser at once."

Around Ripoll in the crew quarters his three bunkmates were waking up, groggy but quickly snapping to alert once they realized what was happening.

"Lieutenant Ripoll, this is, as I believe they say, above your compensation grade," Nelson replied in a calm, almost compassionate, voice.

Suddenly the door to the crew quarters cranked open—the L'rah'hane portals were extraordinarily noisy—and five Excalbians stood in the entranceway. Sailors and military sorts. One of them was Nelson. Ripoll also recognized John Paul Jones and Captain Bligh among them. They had Ensign Gregg between them, the single member of Ripoll's team he'd left standing watch on the bridge. Bligh nudged Gregg in the small of the back, and he came into the room to join the other members of the *Enterprise* crew now gathered in a tight group behind Ripoll. They were obviously bracing for a fight.

"Lieutenant Ripoll, gather your crew immediately and prepare to depart," Nelson said. "The overloaded phaser is set to go super-critical in ten minutes."

"Where the hell did you put it? The engine room?"

"Of course not. But it does threaten critical systems," Nelson said. "You must come at once."

"What I must do is check in with my superiors."

"By all means, do so, but do it quickly."

Ripoll took his communicator and flipped it opened. "Ripoll to *Enterprise*."

"Enterprise *here, Lieutenant*," came Lieutenant Uhura's voice over the communicator speaker.

Ripoll explained the situation as quickly as he could.

"*Please stand by while I inform the captain*," said Uhura.

"Lieutenant, *please*! We've been ordered to evacuate, and I think that you should patch me directly through."

Uhura's voice grew colder. He could just see her bristling as she spoke to him. "*You tell those*

Excalbians that if they want to speak with Captain James T. Kirk, they're going to have to hold off going forward with this insanely destructive project until I can reach and notifiy him." Then Uhura cut off communication with a curt and wholly unamused, "Enterprise *out.*"

Ripoll turned to Nelson. "You heard the lieutenant," he said. "My hands are tied until I can speak with the captain."

"Very well," Nelson said, looking a bit chagrined after facing Uhura's dismissal. "In that case, perhaps we can come to an agreement ourselves. We will deactivate the phaser if you agree to allow us to occupy navigation stations on the bridge. You will retain control of all weaponry stations, so there should be no fear that we would even consider using this vessel in an offensive manner. You know as well as I do that the *Enterprise*'s computer has almost entirely taken over navigation."

"I also know that *you* know where the manual override controls are located, Admiral."

Nelson smiled. "Very good, Lieutenant," he said. "Why don't we have two men standing by in that station, one of yours and one of mine?"

Ripoll considered. "Deactivate the phaser as a show of good faith."

Nelson nodded toward John Paul Jones. "Captain, if you please."

Jones smiled slyly. He took a recording device

from his great coat pocket. It was tied to a communication receiver. "An effective sound effect, don't you think?" he said.

Nelson turned back to Ripoll and shrugged. "We needed to get your attention."

"And so you sneak aboard and attempt to commandeer my ship."

"*Your* ship, Lieutenant?"

"Yes, Admiral," said Ripoll. "I don't want to lose my first command!"

Nelson smiled sympathetically. "Of course, no captain wants such a mark upon his record. You *will* not have one if we can come to an agreement," he said. "The only way you will leave this vessel is under orders of your captain, I assure you." Nelson motioned for Ripoll to sit down in the quarters's only chair. When he did so, Nelson went and took a seat on the edge of a bed. Ripoll motioned the other members of his crew to stand down.

"Let me tell you about my own first command, Lieutenant," said Nelson. "I was a very green lad indeed at the time and made some basic mistakes that I believe you will find diverting. I must admit to finding them amusing myself, if only in the recounting."

Ripoll noticeably relaxed. "I suppose we can wait until the captain gets back to me, Admiral Nelson," he said. "So long as no harm is done. I would very much enjoy hearing about your time aboard the *Albemarle,* your first command."

"Excellent," said Nelson. "Only this was long before the *Albemarle*, oh yes. This happened when I, as a very green ensign, was placed in charge of a prize vessel. I discovered that I had brought aboard neither compass nor ship's clock, assuming I'd find both on the vessel."

"You didn't," said Ripoll with a smile.

"Indeed I did not. They were wrecked," Nelson answered. "Unfortunately my ship had by this time moved out of signaling range and was about to sail over the horizon."

"We had an emergency procedure exercise a lot like that at the Academy," Ripoll said. "I failed it three times in a row before I finally studied up on how to rig a temporary subspace radio. I know you didn't have that option, so what did you do?"

"Therein lies a tale," Nelson said. He took off his hat and placed it on his lap. His hair was curly and black, with gray beginning to mix throughout. It was long and tied back with a ribbon. "A tale—and an inadvertent adventure."

Nelson began to recount his first great adventure.

———

"You might have allowed me to approve your declaration before you made a hostile move against Starfleet," Valek said.

Her even Vulcan temperament made the point

more emphatic without yelling and screaming, Kirk thought.

They had gathered in the Zeta Gibraltar conference room as soon as Uhura alerted Kirk of the situation aboard the *Victory*.

"It was merely an attention-getting maneuver," said Washington-Yarnek. "We felt it might be time to bring the issue to a head."

"So you decided to cross the Delaware River?" Contreras said, shaking her head sadly. "I had believed you and I were friends, Mister President."

"We are friends," Washington-Yarnek replied. "And allies."

"That remains to be seen," Valek added.

"Representative Valek, the solution is simple," said Washington-Yarnek. "We want the opportunity to protect ourselves. In fact, as a new political entity represented by an elective body—"

"When did that happen?" Kirk said.

"Last night, Captain," Washington-Yarnek replied. "There was not time to inform you."

"I'll bet," Kirk said. "I'm feeling a bit used. I signed that damn declaration, you know."

Washington-Yarnek bowed to Kirk. "My apologies if I have caused offense," he said. "But as the president of the New Excalbia Assembly, I demand our right to self-preservation. The *Enterprise* and the *Montana* cannot remain on station indefinitely. The L'rah'hane undoubtedly are set to return any moment. Meanwhile, the Federation insists on keeping us on the edge of galactic nowhere until Representative Valek decides—if she decides—to give us a chance. As things stand now, we have no say in our own fate. We are ordered hither and yon without the ability to lawfully protest or seek redress for our treatment."

"I believe the Federation has been fair," Valek said. "If not speedy in its actions."

Washington-Yarnek moved forward and put a hand down on the conference room table. "Yes, you've been generous in many regards, we acknowledge this and are grateful," he said. "You feed us. You provide us shelter, in a manner of speaking. But do you believe we are children?"

"Of course not," Valek replied.

"Yet you treat us as if we were children. We once treated your kind as if you were children, to be toyed with"—he glanced at Kirk—"and you did not like it so much. Well, neither do we."

Valek nodded. "I can see how some of my government's actions can be interpreted as infantilizing you."

"The issue is the consequence of dependence. It will be far better if we treat with the Federation as equals rather than as its wards," Washington-Yarnek said. "This will serve the Federation's interests—your interests, Representative Valek—in the long run, as well."

"I acknowledge the logic of this position," Valek replied. "But I am under certain restraints."

"Are you, then, a mere mouthpiece?" Washington-Yarnek said. "I was under the impression that you had been sent with extraordinary power to decide our case."

"I have," Valek replied. "I am not a mere mouthpiece, as you put it. And I *do* have a great deal of latitude in dealing with the situation here. But there are political considerations . . . differences within the Council that must be considered and reconciled, or no accord we reach here will last very long."

Washington sighed. "Politics. Factions. I'm all too aware that you speak the truth. Alas, it is ever thus. And yet men, and women, must act as seems just or there is no point in government at all."

Valek nodded agreement. She turned to Kirk. "Captain, what is your advice?"

"I don't like that they've threatened my officers, if only with an ultimately harmless deception," he said. "The *Enterprise* fought for those L'rah'hane ships. We risked our lives to save you, Mister President."

"Yes," Washington-Yarnek replied.

"The ships are Starfleet prizes, under interstellar law."

"They are in *our* port, however," Washington-Yarnek said.

"Our?" said Contreras, irritation in her voice. "Who is this 'our'?"

Washington-Yarnek drew himself up to his full height, squared his jaw.

"New Excalbia," he said.

For a moment there was silence in the room.

Then Valek stood. She made a slight bow across the conference room table toward Washington-Yarnek.

"Very well," she said. "As a representative of the United Federation of Planets in this system, I acknowledge your representative body, the New Excalbia Assembly."

"Thank you," said Washington-Yarnek with a sigh of relief. "You have no idea what this will mean to my people."

"If they *are* people," muttered Contreras. She slumped in her chair and shook her head, her expression full of misgiving.

"And the L'rah'hane ships in orbit? We wish no conflict with the Federation, but we have occupied them for the purpose of defense, and we will not leave them so long as we perceive a threat to this system."

"I have no wish to provoke a needless conflict either," Valek said. She turned to Kirk. "Captain, you doubtless know interstellar space law better than I."

"We have every right to those ships. In a foreign

port or not, in the absence of declared hostilities, prize rights apply," Kirk answered.

Washington-Yarnek frowned, shook his head darkly.

"Hold on Mister President," Kirk continued. "We've also thoroughly studied the capabilities of those ships and have essentially poked, prodded, and measured everything aboard them. Therefore, I recommend the Federation relinquish rights to the ships to the New Excalbia Assembly."

Valek nodded. "Very well. It is so ordered."

"Again we thank you, Representative Valek."

Valek spoke a command to the room. "Computer, please put Admiral Nelson on the viewscreen."

"Acknowledged," the computer voice replied.

Kirk looked to the screen. There stood Horatio Nelson, all right. Beside him was one of Kirk's own officers.

Ripoll, Kirk thought. *With the Spanish y sound for the double l,* Kirk recalled. *He is Catalan in origin. Ship-faring family. Learned to sail on the Mediterranean as a boy. Top in his class at the Academy.*

Washington-Yarnek looked to the viewscreen as well. "Admiral, it seems we've got our navy."

Nelson smiled. It somehow looked predatory and not comforting on his beaky visage. *"Very well, Mister President."* Nelson put a hand on Ripoll's shoulder. *"Captain, my first request is that you assign your Lieutenant Ripoll as Starfleet liaison officer aboard this vessel. He has behaved with both courage and wisdom under the circumstances, and I would be proud to have him among my crew, however temporarily."*

Kirk considered. "Lieutenant, you okay with this?" he asked.

"Admiral Nelson has been telling me some very interesting stories, sir," said Ripoll. *"I'll report back to you on everything I hear."*

Kirk smiled. Now *there* was a command officer in the making, with an answer like that on the tip of his tongue.

"Permission granted, Lieutenant Ripoll," Kirk said. "Admiral?"

"Yes?"

"Welcome back to command."

Now Nelson's smile did become warm. *"Thank you, sir,"* he said. *"I shall endeavor to be worthy of the faith the Assembly has placed in me. And of your professional friendship, Captain."*

"Knowing what you did to the French navy," Kirk said, "if I were a L'rah'hane pirate, I would stay the hell away from any system over which you were standing watch."

"If you were a L'rah'hane pirate, Captain," Nelson replied, *"I have a feeling the entire Federation might be quaking in its boots."*

———

Kirk sipped his Romulan ale in the reception area in Valek's quarters. He'd come here immediately after the conference, on Valek's invitation. This time there had been no demand that he make a report, only a rather enticing invitation.

"I know that, as a human, you are experiencing the sensation of being used as a tool by others," Valek had said on the way out of the conference room after the meeting with Washington-Yarnek. "To a certain extent, that may be true, but in any case, I wish to apprise you of several details involving my presence here in the Gibraltar system."

The captain followed Valek back to her quarters to hear her explanation, or admission, or, hell, maybe it would be a confession.

At least maybe he'd get some answers about why he was being ordered to stick around in this system in the first place, even if he *did* think he ought to be here.

Valek poured herself a Romulan ale as well. She stared down at her tumbler for a moment, then knocked it all back in one gulp, as if she were a midshipman doing Lotholian shooters in a seedy bar. She poured herself another, but took this one to her chair, sat down, and sipped at it far more carefully and appreciatively. And Vulcan-like.

"Kirk, I need to tell you—"

"Why don't you call me Jim, if we're going off the record," Kirk said.

"Very well. Jim." Valek took another sip. "It sounds odd to my ears, this diminutive. As if I am assuming more familiarity than is warranted, given the situation."

"Want to try James?"

Valek considered, nodded. "James. Yes, that is better," she said.

"Am I missing something here, Valek? What is it you want to tell me?"

"The reason I was sent here, James," she said.

"I presumed that was all covered in the orders I saw."

"The real reason."

"All right," Kirk said. "Now you've got my interest."

"As you know, Vulcans cannot prevaricate nor willfully misrepresent facts in order to deceive. It is simply not in our nature."

"I know that you are quite capable of telling selective truths," Kirk said. "That fact has more than once proved a life-saver."

"That is correct," Valek replied. Another long pause. "I have contradictory instructions from two sources, both of which I consider to be my superiors."

Valek templed her fingers and stared at Kirk over them. "As you know, I am a Special Representative of the Federation Council, serving a commission appointed to deal with the Excalbians. I was put forward for this by the Vulcan representative to the Council. This is a temporary appointment. My normal position is in the Federation Ambassadorial Service. I serve in the office of Ambassador Sarek of Vulcan."

"You do seem to be walking a tightrope of sorts."

"Unfortunately, yes. The Special Committee for Security and Frontier Intelligence, the portion of the Federation Council that oversees most Federation covert activities, has been receiving very disturbing reports from its listening post nearest the Excalbian system. There is concern that a civil war is under way among the Excalbians brought on, it is believed, by your visit there."

"I didn't choose to go to Excalbia."

"I know this, James," Valek said. "It is merely a convenient shorthand."

Kirk nodded. "Go on."

"Given the great advancement of Excalbia in the manipulation of matter, it has been judged that a war between the Federation and Excalbia would lead to immense causalities, and we may lose."

"I can see the logic of that."

"The last thing the Federation would want to do is take sides in a civil war, especially considering that we know almost nothing concerning what it may be about."

"Another good point."

Valek gazed down into her glass contemplatively

for a moment, then looked back up at Kirk. "Giving sanctuary to the Excalbian refugees was deemed too dangerous a risk to take. It may appear that we are taking sides in this civil war and open us to attack by a powerful enemy. My instructions from the Security and Frontier Intelligence Committee were not only to deny the Excalbians sanctuary within the Federation, but to deport them—utilizing the *Enterprise* and the *Montana*—back to Excalbia. If they resist, they are to be eliminated. Killed. We cannot risk a conflagration with an enemy that can destroy entire starships on a whim."

"That's . . . harsh."

"Yes, and ultimately illogical," Valek said. "As Sarek put it, it is akin to running from a bully rather than confronting the bully with reason and seeking to change his ways."

"Or running from a photon torpedo. It catches up with you eventually."

"In any case, perceived weakness can lead to escalation and greater trouble." She shrugged. "It is not clear that what is going on at Excalbia is a civil war at all. The analysts are at odds with one another, and we do not have eyes on the ground in Excalbia to verify anyone's conjecture."

"But we do have Excalbians here."

"Yes, and that has been my primary function here," Valek said. "I have come to the conclusion that these Excalbians know nothing of use in that regard. Which leads me to suspect we are not seeing a civil war at all."

"Then what?"

"That I cannot answer," Valek said. "Perhaps we shall never know."

"In the meantime—"

"What is the Federation—what are you and I—going to do with our Excalbians? Yes, that's the question," she said. "I have specific instructions from the highest authority *not* to grant them asylum. So that is an option that has never been on the table."

Kirk took a long drink of his ale.

Wow, that's good. And it braces the mind instead of dulling it. Marvelous stuff.

It came to him then. "You *instigated* their little revolution."

"I may have put the idea into the air."

"You *want* them to succeed," Kirk said. "So you don't have to deport them."

"This was the back-up plan if I failed to extract useful intelligence from them."

"Whose back-up plan?"

"Ambassador Sarek's."

Kirk found himself chuckling. "Why, of all the underhanded dirty tricks." He shook his head. "And you a Vulcan."

Valek nodded. "It is *because* I am a Vulcan that it will work," she said. "When I take this solution back to the Council they will know that it was the most logical solution. As it is."

"So we don't have to kill them."

"*You* do not have to kill them, James," Valek said.

"I would never have done it," Kirk said. "I think you know that."

"Yes," Valek said. "Sarek believed this was the case after having met you on the way to the Babel Conference. I needed *your* presence. I could not count on Captain Haynes to disobey such orders. He is, as Sarek put it, a time-server."

Kirk took this in. "I'm sure Haynes would never kill those people in cold blood."

Would he? Showboat Haynes, fearful of any blot on his record that would disturb his long-anticipated retirement?

Orders . . .

"Let us never put him to the test, James," said Valek. "Let me never have to give that order."

Kirk raised his glass to her. "Here's to that," he said, and drank down the rest of the ale.

Valek rose, went to the bottle, and brought it back to where they were sitting. She leaned over to fill up Kirk's glass again, and in doing so, her hand brushed against his own.

"Valek, are you . . ."

"James, I would like to be your friend, that is all."

Kirk nodded. He wasn't entirely convinced.

But, of course, Vulcans are incapable of lying . . .

Valek poured herself another and sat back down across from him. Instead of putting the bottle back, she set it down beside her chair.

"Truthfully, I don't know how I would feel about becoming friends with Spock's nemesis," he told her.

"James," said Valek. "After all this time with your first officer, you still don't understand Vulcans, it seems."

"Meaning Vulcans never act in a way to harm others?" Kirk chuckled. "If you believe that, I'd like to introduce you to a lady named T'Pring. That'll change your mind in a hurry."

"I simply mean that our motives, while they may not be black-and-white, are ultimately logical. Logic is a tool that cuts many ways, James."

Kirk smiled. "Well, I do know that there's a great deal to understand in Spock's case. I think of it as a lifelong challenge."

Valek nodded, acknowledging, it seemed, the truth of Kirk's words. "Vulcan children are like human children in some ways and very different in others."

"Explain."

"There is play, but it is logical play. Our children are, by human standards, precocious, but they are still developing intellectually. Just as with human children, their reasoning abilities are not fully developed until later."

"So mistakes in logic, and other areas, might be possible?" said Kirk.

"Yes," said Valek. "I made such a mistake once at Spock's expense."

"You were unkind?"

"I was incorrect. There is a difference."

"Agreed," Kirk said.

"There was no malice intended. That is a human emotion. There was . . . logical frustration on my part."

"With Spock? There is no one more logical than Spock."

"With the *situation*, James."

"What situation?"

"It is difficult to explain."

"Try me. I may know more about Vulcans than you think."

Including, as you know, your bizarre, violent mating rituals, Kirk thought. He'd had to fight for his life against Spock in an effort to save his first officer from a plot by Spock's ex-wife, T'Pring, to get out of their arranged marriage by way of Spock's death. *Logic and goodwill are by no means synonymous.*

Valek took a sip of her ale. "Vulcan parents tend to lavish educational instruction and intellectual enrichment opportunities on their children, and, in many ways, the children become a project both parents are equally engaged in. This often is the intellectual connection that brings together Vulcans who otherwise would only be connected through the bonding ceremony."

"Human parents dote on their children."

"There is a difference," Valek continued. "Varen and I are twins. This is a very uncommon occurrence on Vulcan. As such, we were deeply engaged in each other's thought processes from a young age. We could be said to share the same Vulcan *katra*, or soul, although we have individually diverged. The ability of my brother and myself to mind-meld developed early, as well." Valek sat back, templed her fingers. "For a time, Varen and I were inseparable, practically a unity."

"And along came Spock?"

She nodded. "Yes, we were eight Vulcan years. Spock was treated . . . brusquely . . . by the other children. This was not intentional. It was the consequence of a faulty assumption. *Everyone* was aware that he was half human. Everyone compared him unfavorably with Sybok."

"Sybok?"

"Ah, you are not aware . . ." She shook her head. "Well, it is not my place. And, in any case, the less said about Sybok, the better." Valek's eyes narrowed, and she gazed to the side, as if lost in memory. "Oh, many specious conclusions were drawn regarding

Spock's intellectual abilities and commitment to the Vulcan way. It was a product of the restricted logic of children. It was . . . unjust of us."

"Us?"

"I am afraid that I joined in the chorus on occasion."

"That's too bad."

"What can I say? Even Vulcan children are not always analytical. My conclusions were based on false assumptions, but I was not aware at the time that the assumptions were questionable."

"I see," Kirk said. "The ignorance plea. At some point I hope you became aware."

"I did, James. Allow me to continue and I will explain how this came about."

"Please go on."

"You see, Spock had a *sehlat*—they are fascinating and somewhat dangerous beasts. For a while this seemed to be his only intimate acquaintance. My parents would not allow Varen and I to have a pet for . . . very logical reasons. At least they seemed logical at the time. Varen and I were both fascinated by Spock's *sehlat*, whose name was I-Chaya. But it was Varen who approached Spock and began speaking to him about I-Chaya. Over time, these conversations became more frequent. They both discovered a commonality in thought processes."

"They made friends."

"More than that. They became laboratory partners

in scientific experiments," Valek said. "This is an important choice a Vulcan child must make during primary education."

"Pardon me—picking lab partners?"

"It is one of the first freedoms given to children in order to exercise their newly acquired logical skills. A lab partnership is a commitment made for an entire Vulcan year. One spends a great deal of time with one's partner."

"And Varen picked Spock over you?"

"No. It is not permitted to partner with a sibling. Both Varen and I were required to find different lab partners. We knew this and planned accordingly. In fact, we made an agreement: for maximum objectivity, I would pick his partner and he would pick mine."

"How very . . . logical."

"So we thought."

"What happened?"

"He chose for me D'Hrot, a budding young chemist, who was compatible enough—although even then I was showing more promise in law, interplanetary development, and economics."

"A young envoy on the rise, even at eight?"

"Indeed," Valek said.

"And your choice for Varen?"

"There was a girl, T'Mere, very talented in mathematics, who I believed would make an excellent laboratory partner for Varen. He sometimes showed slight deficiencies in that subject—particularly in statistics, an important element of experimental work—and I was of the opinion that she might aid him in that regard."

"And did she?"

"There was no opportunity to find out. Varen rejected my choice. Instead, he told me Spock would be his laboratory partner. They were already doing research on *sehlat* intelligence and wanted to continue the project."

"This was not to your liking, I take it?"

"At the time, I felt it was extremely illogical," said Valek. She stared off to the side for a moment, as if remembering, then shook in a very human manner. "Despite his extremely high marks and clear abilities, Spock was believed by many of the children to be . . . deficient as a Vulcan. I . . . voiced these concerns to Varen. In the presence of Spock. And, to our entire school at an assembly. I questioned the wisdom of his parents' marriage, as well."

"Not exactly a nice thing to do, in human terms," said Kirk.

"I know that. It is one of my major regrets," Valek said. She picked up her ale and took a long drink from the glass. "It also served as a demonstration that I had a lot to learn if I ever wanted to be a diplomat like Spock's father. You see, even though I held a low opinion of his son, I idolized Sarek. He was an example of what I wished to become: an ambassador for Vulcan."

"I've met the man," Kirk said. "Spock is very much Sarek's son, in his way."

"This was not apparent to me at the time," replied Valek. "I believed Spock to be a sort of . . . thought experiment . . . on Sarek's part. Then all that changed. Spock's mother, Amanda Grayson, introduced herself to me. Spock had told her of my . . . disapproval. It does not take long when engaging with Amanda Grayson to realize just how formidable and intellectually adept she is, although in a human manner. In her Sarek made a superb choice."

"I agree," Kirk said.

"She is the first one who understood my intellectual propensities. It was she who later made certain that after my education was complete, I was invited to join Sarek's staff. My personal debt to her is considerable."

"Back then, did she convince you of the error of your logic as far as Spock was concerned?"

"She persuaded me to temper my judgment, yes. She also explained some of the particular difficulties Spock faced given his situation as a half-human child on Vulcan. I said no more after that."

"You didn't apologize to Spock?"

"I told him I had reconsidered my previous position regarding the lab partnership and that I now approved," Valek replied. "But I never admitted to making an error in my larger conclusions, however. I perhaps should have, but the time for such has passed."

"Does Spock know his mother took you under her wing?"

"I do not believe so," she said. "There was never a logical reason to bring this to his attention. He is aware that I apprenticed under his father, and, of course, that Sarek and Amanda Grayson were acquainted with me when I was a child." Valek shrugged. "But I am only one of the many protégés of Sarek. He is highly regarded, and a position on his staff is usually a stepping-stone to further interesting and fulfilling work on Vulcan and within the Federation. I am, perhaps, a reminder to Spock of the milieu he left behind when he decided to enter Starfleet. This is speculation on my part, but perhaps I am also a reminder of the difficulties that he and Sarek have had coming to terms with each other. There is talk of their relationship among the staff."

"Vulcans *gossip*?"

"It is logical to provide oneself with as much information as possible."

"What became of Spock and Varen?"

"Over time, Varen demanded Spock's acceptance among our peers, and I backed his position, although I never advocated for Spock the way Varen did. He and Spock remained lab partners until Spock declined to enter the Vulcan Science Academy as his father wished and opted instead to attend Starfleet Academy. You probably know the story after that. My brother, Varen, was accepted into the Science Academy and has become a field biologist doing pioneering study of vertebrate extremophiles. He and Spock have gone their separate ways, but they still correspond on occasion."

"Old friends."

"Yes. That is an accurate, if very human, assessment." Valek drained her cup. "As for Spock and myself—it is very odd."

"What is?"

"Spock and I seem to be intellectual irritants for each other. Yet I am mentally compatible with so many who are his close acquaintances. Such as you, James."

Valek leaned forward. "If you would not mind, give me your hand."

Kirk wondered where this was going, but stretched out his right hand, palm up. Valek held it from underneath with one of her hands. With the other, she lighted touched—*stroked*—the surface of Kirk's palm.

"You have experienced the Vulcan mind-meld before," she said. It was not a question.

"Yes, on several occasions."

"That is apparent," she replied. Her fingers followed the lifeline on Kirk's palm.

Damn it, she's a Vulcan, he thought. *Surely she can see the logic of avoiding—*

He wasn't exactly feeling logical at the moment, however.

"Valek, I—"

"Fascinating. I've never felt this state within a human before. There are pre-established pathways. One could almost enter into connection as one would a Vulcan—" Then he felt her, on the edge of his thoughts. It was as if she were staring into him as one might the swirls within a crystal ball. "Yet, I would not trespass without invitation."

Yes. No. Yes, but . . .

"Valek, I think you know such a thing might be dangerous for you depending on—"

The Vulcan drew her hand back and released his. "You make an excellent point, Captain Kirk."

What happened to James?

"Do I?" He did not feel quite so sure of himself at the moment. Valek was very beautiful in her icy way. Kirk sighed. He leaned back and took a long drink of the Romulan ale.

Valek moved back as well, crossed her arms. "Your pardon, James, if I transgressed. Humans have frequently been *terra incognita* for me. The opportunity to explore is enticing. Professionally."

"That's all right, Valek."

"However, you are operating on incomplete information if you believe I might be in danger of telepathic fixation. As I have told you, as a twin, I am resistant to the pair bonding that many Vulcans undergo in childhood. I would not speak of this ordinarily, but I am aware you were once present at *Koon-ut-kal-if-fee*. My choices are not dictated by a bond, they remain my own." Valek held Kirk's gaze, said nothing for a moment, then finally said, "It is best that you leave."

Kirk smiled. "I think I'll stay. If you can stand me, I can stand you. And thus we stand being around one another a while longer," he said. "I think we might even enjoy it."

Valek cocked her head in an expression of perplexity. She'd never looked more Vulcan to him than in that moment. "I can locate no logic in this remark."

"You can say that again," Kirk replied. Then he added, "But don't," just as Valek was about to do just that.

Fifteen

Captain's Log, 6100.1. I have ordered all hands back to the Enterprise. Based on intelligence secured by Lieutenant Sulu and Ensign Chekov, I'm taking the fight to the L'rah'hane. Enterprise will go to the pirate and slaver base located at the heart of the Vara.

"Captain, we're being hailed from Zeta Gibraltar," Uhura said.

Kirk signed the ship's final preparations orders on the slate handed to him by a yeoman, then swiveled in his command chair back toward the viewscreen.

"Please inform Commander Contreras that we are in the midst of readying for departure to the nebula. We'll communicate once we're under way."

"Yes, sir," said Uhura. "But it's not the commander calling."

"Who is it, then?"

"It's . . . well, it's the president, sir. Of the New Excalbia Assembly, I mean."

"The president," Kirk said. "Very well, put him on."

The screen wavered for a moment, and Washington-Yarnek's visage appeared. "Mister President, what can I do for you, sir?" Kirk said.

"*I'll just take a moment of your time, Captain Kirk,*" said Washington-Yarnek. "*I would like to formally request that the New Excalbia Navy be permitted to accompany you on this punitive expedition.*"

"You want . . . what?"

"*We wish to help,*" the president replied. "*It would be a great honor, and an historic first step for our young navy, if you would grant us this privilege. Besides, I believe that we would have much to contribute. Mister Watt and Doctor Franklin have reached an understanding of the capabilities and limitations of our vessels. Admiral Nelson is chafing at the bit to be part of the action.*" Washington-Yarnek made a slight bow of his head. "*I also would like to join you, but on the* Enterprise, *so as not to come into conflict with Admiral Nelson on his ship. I may be mistaken about whether or not I can help, but there's an old soldier still in me, and he longs to be in on this.*"

"I appreciate that, Mister President. It's the *limitations* of those L'rah'hane vessels that I'm concerned with," Kirk replied. "I don't want to endanger them, and I'd be compelled to come to their defense."

"Another incoming signal, this one from the *N.E.S. Victory,* sir," Uhura piped in.

Kirk had a feeling he knew who it was. He sighed. "Add the admiral to the conversation, Lieutenant."

"Aye, sir."

"Kirk this is Nelson," said a voice after a momentary crackle of static. Though the admiral was transmitting without visuals, Kirk easily recognized the commanding tone of the old sailor. He'd heard it a lot recently, and it was, of course, exactly how he'd imagined Nelson *had* sounded.

"Admiral."

"Captain, we will in no way be a burden to you," Nelson said. *"On the contrary, we intend to be assets. But if that proves to be impossible, I give you my word that we will pull back, and even cut and run, if we are in any way interfering with your task."*

"New Excalbia wants the opportunity to prove ourselves," Washington-Yarnek said. *"Both to you and to the Federation."*

"What does Representative Valek think about this?"

"We have persuaded her to see the logic of the proposition," said Franklin. He had just entered the bridge along with Spock. They'd come to report on their progress with the Hradrian device. Franklin's voice, as always, conveyed a tone of good humor. "She was very obliging."

"So she's in on this, too, is she?"

"I believe you will find her entirely behind us,

Captain Kirk," Franklin said. "We do not wish to present our decision to you as a *fait accompli*, however."

Although that's exactly what you're doing, Kirk thought.

"The Assembly has no wish to strain relations. We feel this is an action we must and will take," Washington-Yarnek said.

"So you're coming along whether I give permission or not."

"Damn right," muttered Nelson. *"Wouldn't miss this for anything."*

"We would much rather accompany you with *your blessing than without, Captain,"* Washington-Yarnek said.

Kirk hardened his expression. "And if I forbid it?"

Washington-Yarnek bowed his head graciously. *"Then we would not come with you,"* he replied. *"Although we might feel compelled to follow at a . . . safe distance . . ."*

"I see," Kirk said. He considered for a moment, then nodded. "I'm going to have to check in with Representative Valek. It goes well beyond my prerogatives as the senior Starfleet officer in system and becomes a Federation matter."

"This is acceptable," Franklin said mildly. "We have truly come to an agreement with her. In fact, to be perfectly honest, she is the one who made the suggestion in the first place."

"Valek? She—"

Yes, of course she did. Valek and Franklin seemed to be manipulating each other back and forth like a coin flipping across a magician's fingers.

"You'll take overall command, Kirk," Nelson cut in. *"I've been studying your record. You're a damn fine officer."*

"Thank you, sir. And thank you for your . . . faith in Federation leadership."

"Nonsense. I have faith in you, Kirk—you and your crew," Nelson said. *"You won't regret having us by your side. I'll see to that."* Nelson mumbled something, evidently to a crew member, that Kirk did not quite make out, then loudly said, *"Anchors aweigh!"*

Kirk nodded for Uhura to cut both channels. Then he turned to Spock and said with a chuckle, "How do you like that? *I'm* calling the shots, according to the good admiral."

"Noble intentions on his part, no doubt, Captain," said Mister Spock. "But he is Horatio Nelson, or at least believes himself to be."

"Let's hope there's something of the real Nelson in there somewhere," Kirk said. "Where we're going, we could use him." He turned to Uhura. "Lieutenant, get me Representative Valek, please. She has some explaining to do."

"Aye, sir," said Uhura. "Representative Valek."

"Onscreen, Lieutenant."

She appeared at her office desk, which was surprisingly crowded with unkempt data slates. It appeared she was not as neat as a pin after all.

Why didn't I notice this before? It occurred to Kirk that he'd spent a great deal more time in her quarters than he had in her workplace.

"I suppose you are tempted to say 'turnabout is fair play,' Valek? I sprang the revolution on you and now you're sticking me with its consequences?"

"Not at all, Captain," the Vulcan replied. She wore a look cool enough to turn lava to stone. *"That would be a characteristic human reaction, completely illogical."*

Kirk smiled ruefully. "I apologize," he said. "I would be interested in knowing how you arrived at your decision."

Valek nodded. *"Given our agreement with the Excalbians, the provisional governing body has established—"*

"I'm not sure they see it as provisional," Kirk said.

"The Federation now has a temporary treaty with the New Excalbia Assembly. They have not claimed the right to self-governance without responsibility, but have asserted their independence by assuming a sovereign responsibility—self-defense."

"They get to show their serious intent to form a government by standing up for themselves."

"Undoubtedly, the small armada they have assembled from the ships you captured will have a neg-

ligible effect in comparison to a Constitution-*class starship, but with it they can establish the principle of self-determination."*

"What is the Federation's interest in going along with them?" Kirk said.

"First, we sympathize with their plight. They have been shuffled to the edge of nowhere while we attempted to decide what to do with them," Valek replied. *"Second, an act of self-defense may be interpreted as the deed of a sovereign nation."*

"And it doesn't bother you that while you are legally considering them to be a refugee community *within* the Federation, they are brazenly asserting sovereign rights outside of Federation control?"

"Doctor Franklin made an excellent point about entangled quantum particles. They are intimately related to one another, even as they go their separate ways," Valek said. She hooked her two index fingers together in order to illustrate for Kirk. *"For normal particles, up is up, down is down. Positive is positive and negative, negative. But entangled particles share states. For them, up and down both exist at the same time, as do positive and negative, charm and anti-charm."*

Valek released her fingers and spread her hands *"It is when we decide to measure a particular characteristic that this suspension is resolved. If one particle is seen to be negative, then the other 'becomes' posi-*

tive. They are no longer entangled, and each goes its separate way now completely unrelated. But if one never attempts to determine a particular characteristic, but assumes that, for this pair of particles, both exist in a cloud of possibility, then those particles will travel onward and onward, bound by the laws of quantum connection. Even if particle A is on one side of the universe and particle B on the other, they are still part of one another."

"The trick is not to measure for one thing here or there," Kirk said, "but to consider the totality of the entangled set. So we don't push the issue with the Excalbians."

"Precisely, Captain."

"If we do not hang together, we shall assuredly hang separately," Kirk murmured.

"Couldn't have said it better myself," Franklin put in from his spot to the rear of the bridge.

"This reasoning I have outlined is why I agreed to let the Excalbians accompany you."

"Makes perfect sense," Kirk said.

Through the Alice's looking glass of diplomacy, that is.

———

Once out of the system the Enterprise jumped to warp 3, which was the maximum warp the L'rah'hane ships were capable of. However, their ion drive did provide them with a measure of stealth. As had been shown before, they were very difficult to track without sensors as advanced as those of the *Enterprise* and a science officer as sharp as Spock.

Inside the Vara Nebula, it was necessary to slow to impulse. The speed advantage of the *Enterprise* may have been negated, but there were other tricks that a *Constitution*-class starship was capable of.

They followed the trail of beacons left by Sulu and Chekov. These were low-powered devices, but Kirk was mindful of the fact that they might have been detected and an ambush put in place. The captain kept a close eye on the relative density of the cloud as they plowed forward. Kirk knew where *he* would likely set up an ambush.

Around the edges of a three-dimensional clearing, where I could establish lines of fire.

They had passed through several such relatively empty bubbles as they moved forward, and Kirk had called a halt before each of them and ordered a sensor sweep.

Spock reported another sparsely filled sector ahead, this one larger than any they'd encountered before, and Kirk again ordered the all stop for the *Enterprise* and the Excalbian navy.

An order that was, this time, not obeyed.

"Captain, the *N.E.S. Agamemnon* and *Boreas* are breaking away to five point three on the prime ecliptic," Spock called from his science station.

"The *Victory* and *Albemarle* have slowed, but have not halted relative to the nebula. They are drifting ahead into the less dense region before us."

"What's going on?" Kirk turned to his communications officer. "Lieutenant Uhura, get me Admiral Nelson. Immediately."

"Aye, sir." Uhura twisted a knob and calibrated her low energy subspace receiver—a secondary channel that seemed to be working far better than her primary subspace interface here in the Vara. "Captain, I have the admiral," she reported within moments.

Nelson's visage appeared on the viewscreen.

"Admiral Nelson, why are you disobeying my orders? Is there some sort of emergency?"

"No, Captain, nothing of the sort," Nelson answered. The faintest of smiles crossed his face. *"I can't take any more of this excessive caution on your part, Kirk—starting and stopping, starting and stopping. If the pirates are anywhere around this position, I intend to flush them out. I've sent two of my ships to be the trap. I myself am the bait."*

You can't fault Nelson for not having courage, that's for sure.

"Admiral, you will turn those ships around, and you will order your flagship to cease its forward motion," Kirk ordered.

"Admiral, if I may," put in Spock. "You have four ships. Three, if you are using one to lure out attackers. Space is quite large and quite three-dimensional. An attack can originate from above or below as well as from any gradient between them. You simply don't have enough ships to cover yourself unless you get extremely lucky."

Nelson nodded. *"Well, I always have been extremely lucky,"* he said. *"Although I suppose you don't believe in such stuff, Spock."*

"With all due respect," Spock said, "that was an ocean navy. This is *space,* sir."

"I'll have you know that I am capable of thinking three-dimensionally. Tell him, Captain Kirk!"

Kirk nodded grimly. "I'm sure you can," he said. "But there is one other factor you are not taking into account."

"And what is that, Captain?"

"You are not Horatio Nelson."

Suddenly Sulu spun around to address Kirk. *"N.E.S. Albemarle taking fire, sir!"*

"What, I see no—"

"Our instruments are better," Kirk said.

"I've got to help him!"

"No, Admiral, *we've* got to help him. Stand down until we've entered that sector. If you don't, so help me I'll blast that ship out from under you for putting my crew in danger—yet again!"

Nelson looked suitably chagrined by this. *"Moving to your port, Captain."*

"Very good, Admiral."

"We'll be right behind you, Captain!" said Nelson. Then he put a hand to his hat in the slightest of salutes. *"If you so order it, that is."*

"I do," Kirk said. "Now let's go."

They arrived at the firefight a moment later. The *Albemarle* was taking a beating from five attackers arrayed around her. Her shields were failing rapidly. Nelson's skirmishers, the ships that he had sent off to go around the clear sector, were nowhere to be seen.

They'll have slow going through the debris, Kirk thought.

"Arm photon torpedoes," Kirk commanded. "Lock onto our closest target. Get ready . . ."

We'll win, but we'll be too late to save the Albemarle. *We need more concentrated firepower. There must be some other—*

"Belay that order, Mister Sulu."

"Aye, sir."

"Spock, the L'rah'hane impulse drive achieves about half the speed of ours?"

"Correct, Captain."

"So if we engage, the *Victory* will be lagging behind. It will be minutes instead of seconds before they arrive to the fight."

"Correct, sir."

"Tractor beam," Kirk said, "lock onto the *Victory*. Uhura, get me Nelson."

"Yes, Captain."

"Admiral, have you ever wondered what a stone in a slingshot feels like?"

"Can't say that I have."

"You're about to find out," Kirk said. "On my command, I want you to engage all impulse power. Direct yourself to a point at the gravitational center of those attacking pirates. We're going to use our tractor beam to pull you toward us, then reverse the effect to repulse your ship. That ought to triple your speed. When you arrive at those coordinates, open fire on the pirate vessels.

"Aye, Captain!"

"We'll be right behind you, Admiral." Kirk looked to Chekov. "Mister Chekov?"

"Tractor beam locked onto the *Victory*, sir. Procedure locked into the tractor system."

"Very good," said Kirk. He glanced back at the viewscreen. The *Albemarle* was concentrating fire, focusing on the L'rah'hane disruptors on the nearest ship—but so far to little effect. "All right, initiate slingshot procedure."

"Initiating."

In the blink of an eye the *Victory* entered the viewscreen from the top and zoomed toward the fight. Within the space of a second it had arrived.

Nelson was true to his word. The moment he achieved his desired position, he halted, rolled the L'rah'hane weapons platform on his underside toward two pirate vessels, and opened fire.

"Launch long-range photon torpedoes at our target, Mister Chekov," Kirk ordered. Chekov pressed the controls and the photon torpedoes sped away, streaking toward the closest L'rah'hane pirate ship.

Spock and Scott had used their time to analyze the L'rah'hane defensive systems well. They'd located a weakness in the L'rah'hane shield frequencies and calibrated the torpedoes' frequency to overwhelm them.

The L'rah'hane didn't have a chance as the photon torpedoes slipped through its shields and both struck the engine amidships. Energy crackled, and the ship simply disintegrated.

Kirk nodded. "Mister Sulu, take us in. Phasers set to maximum, Mister Chekov."

"Aye, aye, sir."

With phasers blasting, the *Enterprise* tore through the battle sector, taking out engines on one L'rah'hane ship and, in a similar manner to the first they'd destroyed, another.

That left the two Nelson had engaged.

"Report on the *Albemarle*, Mister Spock."

"One pirate vessel incapacitated. Second engaged."

"Let's give him a hand," Kirk said. But before anyone could react the viewscreen told the story.

Nelson's *Victory* had raked the pirate ship with a disruptor broadside, leaving a ragged gash along the exterior surface. A second broadside reached deep inside, and debris erupted from the damaged area. The pirate ship hung in space, dark and battered.

"Sensors indicate last pirate ship is dead in space," said Spock. "All systems are down on the vessel except minimal life support in some areas. They're finished, Captain."

"And the *Albemarle*?"

"Her shields held. Minor damage only."

Kirk sighed in both relief and exasperation. "Uhura, get me the Admiral, please."

The exterior display of the viewscreen dissolved and Nelson's triumphant face replaced it.

"We took the fight to them, Kirk! We truly did! I haven't felt this exhilarated since Trafalgar."

"Sir, you *died* there. Let's rein in the celebrations until we reach our primary destination," Kirk said. "There's bound to be more trouble ahead." Kirk allowed himself a slight smile. "And let's collect the rest of your navy, Admiral. I have a feeling we're going to need them."

Nelson nodded, flashing an expression of suitable chagrin. *"Apologies for overstepping our command agreement, Captain. I could have cost us lives unnecessarily with my rashness,"* he said. *"It won't happen again."*

Sixteen

The scouting report of the shuttlecraft *Keplar* could not adequately convey the sheer size of the pirate base. There was a central hub, perhaps a space station, build on a planetoid. A dozen vessels surrounded it, all varying in structure. Eight displayed the characteristic slipshod repairs of L'rah'hane-commandeered vessels.

It was the other two ships Kirk was worried about.

"Spock, what are we looking at?"

"Hradrian attack ships, going by the archaeological record."

"Those ships don't look hundreds of years old, they look new."

"That assessment is confirmed by long-range sensors, sir," Spock replied. "Welding and component seals indicate this ship was constructed within the past three to five standard years."

"A new Hradrian ship," Kirk said to himself. "Remarkable." He turned back to his first officer. "Spock, why build an exact replica of a ship that was in service hundreds of years ago?"

"Unknown, sir."

"Speculate."

"Perhaps the culture and scientific knowledge of the Hradrians has not advanced since that time, Captain."

Kirk nodded, looked back at the two attack ships. "A slave-based civilization, stuck in stasis. That might explain them."

"Hradrian vessels were formidable, sir. Their propulsion and shielding were nearly equivalent to Starfleet's," Spock said. "We should not underestimate them as opponents, should they choose to fight."

"Noted," Kirk said. "Do they see us?"

As if in answer, the dozen ships began to scramble, orienting themselves toward the *Enterprise* and her small armada.

Are they really forming a line? What do they teach these guys in pirate school?

"Shields up, Mister Sulu. Take us to Red Alert."

"Aye, sir."

Kirk considered their positioning. "They really don't want us to get to that central base," he said. "I wonder what they've got stashed there."

"Captain, if I may," said the voice of Nelson.

"Go ahead, Admiral."

"They've lined up in the typical manner of ships of the line in my day," Nelson said. *"Instead of going in head on, perhaps a diagonal approach would be*

better. That way we would limit their field of fire and ability to concentrate."

"I seem to recall your doing something like that maneuver at Trafalgar, Admiral," Kirk replied. "You took out most of the French navy as a result."

"It did seem to work at the time," Nelson said. *"Of course, the enemy quickly adapted. Kept me on my toes, that's for sure. Until that sniper made sure I wasn't."*

Kirk chuckled. "Very well, Admiral, since they teach the 'Nelson diagonal' at Starfleet Academy when an enemy is so gracious as to form in a line, I believe I'll take your advice. We will, however, be engaging in three dimensions and not two."

"Of course, Captain," said Nelson. *"But speaking as one who has fought his share of sea battles in all kinds of weather, I can tell you that a raging sea is not so flat at all. Nor is it forgiving."*

"As you say, Admiral. Our computer has projected attack solutions for this maneuver. Mister Chekov is forwarding those now." Kirk paused, held out open palms in invitation. "Admiral . . . let's do this together this time."

"Aye, aye, Captain," said the Admiral, giving Kirk a rueful smile. *"Victory out."*

"Captain, power levels rising on the Hradrian vessels," Spock cut in. "They are powering up weapons."

"Get ready to return fire, Mister Chekov."

"Aye, sir."

"Give me ship to ship, Lieutenant Uhura."

"Aye, sir."

"All ships," Kirk said. "Prepare to attack."

Just as Spock had predicted, the Hradrian weaponry was phaser-like and far more powerful than L'rah'hane disruptors. The armada screamed in on five separate diagonals, cutting, exchanging fire with one or, at most, two ships at a time.

We're outnumbered, so we have to outthink them.

"Let's give those Hradrians something to consider other than swatting Excalbians," said Kirk. "Photon torpedoes away."

"Torpedoes away."

"Initiate full phaser barrage on the other one."

"Aye, sir."

The Hradrian weapons smashed into the *Enterprise* shields, and the bridge shook.

"Oblique phaser hit," Spock said. "Forward shields at eighty percent."

"Bring her about slowly, Mister Sulu. Let's give those forward shields a respite. Mister Chekov, continue barrage while we turn."

"Continuing barrage, sir."

The bridge shook again, and it was all Spock and the other standing officers could do to remain on their feet.

There will be injuries from that one, Kirk thought. *But if we get out of this with only a few cuts and broken bones, we can count ourselves lucky.*

"Aft shields took a direct hit," Spock said. "They are holding. Forward shields back to full power."

Thank you, Scotty. Kirk had no doubt the quick recovery was due to his chief engineer's efforts.

"Good." Kirk glanced at his viewscreen. One of the Hradrian ships was turning, tracking with the *Enterprise* and attempting to close.

"Mister Sulu, swing us back around and make a lateral yaw adjustment to seventy degrees. Let him get closer."

"Aye, sir."

"Chekov, arm photon torpedoes."

"Torpedoes armed."

"Range to Hradrian vessel twenty thousand kilometers and closing," Spock said.

"A little closer."

"Hradrian vessel powering up," Spock said. "Preparing to fire. She's lowered her shields."

"Torpedoes away," Kirk said.

"Firing torpedoes."

"Shields at maximum."

The Hradrian got off her shot. It struck and destroyed one of the pair of photon torpedoes. The energy interaction weakened what would have been a damaging blow. The phaser blast was easily absorbed and dissipated by the *Enterprise* shields.

The other vessel was not so lucky. The remaining

torpedo got through. Kirk watched as the ship erupted in a slow-motion, devastating explosion.

"*Nichego sebe*," he heard Chekov murmur.

"Hradrian ship destroyed," Spock reported. "Armada battle reports coming in from the *Victory*. Two Excalbian ships incapacitated, one critically damaged. Three L'rah'hane vessels crippled or destroyed."

"Which leaves us with our second Hradrian ship."

"Remaining Hradrian vessel has ceased engagement," Spock said. "She is holding position with impulse power. It seems—" A blue light flashed at Spock's station and he gazed down intently at his sensor display. "Captain, indeterminate energy build-up on the Hradrian vessel. It has a similar ion signature to that of a transporter."

"A transporter? Mister Spock, that device we took from the L'rah'hane ship—didn't you and Franklin determine that it had a transporter-like phasing effect?"

"Affirmative, Captain. The energy levels match."

"They have a weaponized version of the device," Kirk said. "Maximum evasive maneuvers, Mister Sulu!"

"Aye, sir."

The ship lurched as Sulu adjusted his controls to seldom-used extreme positions.

"Hradrian discharge imminent," Spock said.

A shimmer seemed to pass across the field of vision on the viewscreen. For a moment, there was nothing there. Absolutely nothing. The debris field in the background was simply gone. As was the view of the battle.

A flicker of energy drain passed through the ship and every control went dead.

"Total sensor fail," Spock said. "We are flying blind, sir."

Then, as quickly as it had gone off, power returned.

"Sensors and controls have returned, but power levels are depleted," Spock said.

"Options, Spock?"

"Evaluating, sir."

Kirk activated the intraship to engineering. "Scotty, what's going on down there?"

"Never seen anything like it, Captain. It's as if the entire ship just . . . reset herself. I'm overriding start-up procedures right and left to get her back up and running as soon possible."

"Estimate."

"Two to three minutes," Scott said. Kirk heard a warning buzzer go off in the background. *"Need to take care of that, sir."*

"Bridge out."

"We may not have two to three minutes before the next Hradrian discharge," Spock said. "They are initiating another power buildup."

"And they *missed* last time," Kirk said. "Spock, what *is* that weapon?"

"It seems to be a quantum disruption device," the science officer said. "The data from the aftershock indicates that gluon energy transfer is neutralized in atomic structures. The weapon, in effect, blows matter apart at the atomic seams."

"Defense."

"It is fortuitous that Doctor Franklin and myself loaded a complete data set into the ship's computer before our departure. The computer is running analysis of shield frequencies that may block the effect."

"How long will it take?"

"Unknown, sir," Spock said. "There are literally billions of possible combinations. Measuring the effect again would allow for more rapid calibration."

Which means taking another shot that we probably won't survive.

Kirk sat back in his chair. "They have us dead to rights," he said.

But it's not over until it's over.

"Continue evasive maneuvers, Mister Sulu."

"Two more L'rah'hane pirate vessels reported as defeated, sir," Uhura said.

"Well, whether he's Nelson or not, he's proving himself to be a hell of a fighter," said Kirk. He turned and gazed into the screen. "Lock all weapons on that ship, Mister Chekov."

"Aye, sir."

"If nothing else, we're going to give them a sock to the jaw that they'll remember."

"Hradrian weapon at ninety percent power," Spock said.

"Fire all weapons, Mister Chekov."

"Firing, sir."

"Direct hit on the Hradrian vessel," Spock reported. "Their shields are down."

"But we've got nothing else to throw at them at the moment," Kirk said with a shake of his head.

"Hradrian weapon fully charged," Spock said. "They are preparing to activate."

A streak of light blasted across the viewscreen.

The ship-to-ship audio crackled to life.

"Tally ho!"

The Hradrian vessel fired. Again the erasing shimmer filled the viewscreen. For a moment it illuminated the lines of the *N.E.V. Victory* as it sped by.

He's calculated it perfectly to absorb the blow, Kirk thought.

Then there was a brief flash of light, and the absolute blackness from before filled the screen.

The *Victory* was simply . . . gone.

Then the "nothingness" effect ceased, and the nebula's inner glow returned to the viewscreen.

"Computer analysis complete. Shield frequencies calibrated," Spock said. "We should be able to weather another discharge from the device with minimal effects."

"He gave us our second shot," Kirk said. "Mister Chekov, lock phasers on the Hradrian ship power generation and propulsion units. I want to disable her, not destroy her."

"Phasers locked. Their shields are still down."

"Fire phasers."

"Aye, sir."

The familiar squeal of the energy discharge filled the bridge.

"Direct hit," Spock said. "The Hradrian vessel is incapacitated. She is now operating on minimal auxiliary power." Then, after a pause, "Captain, feedbacks are building in the Hradrian vessel. They are attempting to self-destruct."

"Shields to full," Kirk said. "Back us out of here, Sulu."

"Aye, sir. Full reverse."

The Hradrian vessel exploded like a breaking melon. Debris flew in all directions. One piece zoomed past the *Enterprise,* but it was a near miss by several kilometers.

"Status report," Kirk said.

"Situation nominal, Captain," said Spock. "No damage from the explosion; however, the incapacitated pirate ships in the region were destroyed by the shrapnel effect of the blast."

"Fortunes of war," Kirk said. "How are our allies doing?"

"One New Excalbia Navy vessel destroyed by L'rah'hane disruptors, one missing, the *Agamemnon.*

Albemarle and *Boreas* have disabled the remaining functional L'rah'hane vessel."

Any fatigue Kirk felt from the battle immediately left him. "Mister Sulu, take us toward that depot," he said. "Let's end this."

"Amazing," said Scott and Watt nearly simultaneously.

The landing party exited the shuttlecraft—there was not enough power for the transporter—on the enormous Hradrian depot structure with phasers drawn and ready for action, only to find no one there.

There were no L'rah'hane pirates in sight. There was no one at all in sight.

They had docked in an atmospherically shielded bay that proved to be a loading area outside a vast storage complex. The "roof" was a double-layered atmospheric seal keeping the environment inside the structure at Class-M standards. It stretched on for what seemed kilometers, and upward for hundreds of meters.

The deck underfoot was metallic with enough crossing wires and raised ducts to cause them all to watch their steps. Otherwise, walking felt normal. Obviously, there were gravitational generators in place somewhere set to one *g*.

"Spock?"

"At first glance, one would presume the Hradrian depot serves as a warehouse for various items the L'rah'hane pirates have acquired during their raids." Spock turned in a semicircle with his tricorder. "These are storage bins. There are weapons, precious metals, jewels, and a wide range of electronic and computational devices that would take many weeks to classify and catalog."

"What Mister Spock means to say is that we have found buried pirate treasure," McCoy put in.

"Essentially correct," Spock said. "It would be a shame to destroy this structure, Captain."

"Then we won't," Kirk said. "We need to find what we're really after. Do we have a vector on those life-signs we were picking up?"

Spock checked his tricorder. "Bearing two four three point eight." The Vulcan pointed in the direction.

A four-man security team had accompanied them. The readings of vast amounts of advanced technological machinery had prompted Kirk to bring Scott. Doctor McCoy was along to attend to the medical needs of any prisoner they might come across. Spock and Chekov rounded out the *Enterprise* landing party.

As they were on their way to the hangar deck, Washington-Yarnek and Watt had confronted them in a corridor. Washington-Yarnek stated their case for the Excalbians to join the landing party.

"We are still missing two of our number—Henry Ford and Sacajawea. We presumed they were killed and spaced by the L'rah'hane. But if they are being held as slaves, it is our duty to search along with you, Captain. Also, Mister Watt might prove useful as an adjunct to Commander Scott if those sensor readings have turned up the technological hoard you and I believe is there."

Kirk held Washington's gaze for a moment.

He seems genuine enough in making his request, Kirk thought. *But then, he's been created to seem as genuine as possible.*

But it might be helpful if they did find the missing Excalbians.

"All right," Kirk said. "We'll take a shuttlecraft. There's a landing bay near our target area, I believe."

"There is, indeed, Captain," Spock said.

Washington-Yarnek and Watt were also added to the landing party. They'd been offered handheld phasers for protection, but Washington-Yarnek refused his, saying, "I will have my primed and ready musket pistol. I am afraid that, in the heat of an exchange, I might point a phaser the wrong way, perhaps back at myself or, worst of all, fumble for the firing button until it is too late."

"Point taken," Kirk answered.

Kirk had arrayed the security team around the two Excalbians for their protection.

The life-signs Spock was zeroing in on—via the tricorder—grew stronger. The science officer led them down one alley of pirated items stored on shelves. There were at least ten levels to each of the shelving units, and they did not all match. It was a motley arrangement all around. Kirk began to wonder if there was any reason to the placement of the hoard.

Weapons sat next to disemboweled viewscreens, which were next over from an assortment of machine parts and under computer components. At the end of each aisle, there was a brief perpendicular space, just big enough for one or two people to move through, then another shelving unit stretched onward until, without tricorder aid, even the most seasoned direction finder would probably be hopelessly lost. If there was order here, Kirk couldn't see it.

They located the prisoners on one of those shelves, two up from the floor. They were wrapped in a web-like substance that looked wet, but was actually shiny and hard to the touch.

They look as if they'd been wrapped for shipment by a giant spider.

"Alive?" Kirk asked.

McCoy ran his medical tricorder over the head of one of them. "Barely," he said. "Jim, these people are in some kind of suspended animation."

"They were being prepped for shipping, Captain," said Chekov. "Look down the aisle, sir."

A mechanical cart, that was four meters by two, was approaching them. There was no driver. On its rear was a crane-like appendage. Stacked in a carrying bed in the middle were several pieces of what looked like broken equipment. A maintenance drone?

"Phasers ready," Kirk said, and they all turned to face the approaching vehicle.

It approached them at the speed of a walk, then slowed down abruptly, as if it had just noticed them.

"This is Orange territory," said a voice from a small grilled opening in the front of the vehicle. "Your presence is unauthorized."

"We are . . . inspectors," Kirk said. "We hope to make a deal. We are examining the merchandise for our employers."

The vehicle/drone took a moment to digest this.

"A thousand pardons, kind master," it finally said. "Masters and slaves under direct orders from buyers must not be interfered with when conducting due diligence verification of goods. Please do not disintegrate this unit."

"We have no intention of doing so," Kirk said. "Can you answer a few questions?"

"This unit is programmed for information exchange only on a limited, utilitarian basis."

Kirk nodded. "Where is everybody?"

"This unit does not understand the inspector's question."

"The crews, the L'rah'hane and others. Your masters. Where are they?"

"Understood," said the vehicle. "There are no masters on Haversack."

"What is Haversack?"

"Here is Haversack. All that is here. The surrounding structure. The ground below."

"Why are there no masters?"

"Absolute neutrality is to be maintained between all companies paying the guild price to make use of Haversack. All merchandise must be delivered, warehoused, and retrieved by robotic means." The vehicle sounded as if it were quoting from a book of regulations.

"I see," Kirk said "Answer a question: Why are these biological units here? Why were they not already sold and shipped?"

"Records indicate that Unit T754D-559-914 and Unit T754D-559-915 arrived via fast-boat transport as pre-shipment samples for prospective buyers of wholesale lots."

"Samples?"

"For prospective buyers."

"But the wholesale lots never arrived?"

"No record of arrival. Escrow period expired. Auction suspended. Bidding disallowed."

"What is going to happen to these units?"

"Unclaimed sample merchandise shall remain in place for sixty-five auction watches and then shall be discarded."

"I see," Kirk said. "That won't happen here. We're going to take these two samples with us as testing and verification for the wholesale lot we're bidding on."

"Acknowledged," the vehicle replied. "Please present credentials for removal of items."

Kirk turned to Spock. "I thought this was going too well," he said.

"What if we don't have any credentials?"

"Those removing merchandise without authorization are subject to immediate termination."

Spock pointed upward. Kirk looked up to see round blisters that looked very much like sensors or weapons clusters. "It seems we are being watched and are covered from all angles," Spock said. "Given L'rah'hane armament, I would judge them to be disruptors."

Kirk nodded. He turned back to the warehouse vehicle. "Give us a moment to locate our credentials."

"By your command, kind master."

Chekov, standing to the side working intently with his tricorder, motioned the captain over. "What is it, Ensign?" Kirk said.

"The programming on this vehicle is silicon-based and not difficult to access. I believe I have hacked into the logic and memory processors."

"Can you provide us with fake identification?"

"I will try, Captain." Chekov's fingers flew across the dials on the tricorder, making adjustments, then he smiled. "Show it your outstretched hand, sir."

"You sure?"

"Ninety-nine percent certain."

"All right," Kirk said. He rolled his eyes upward, pointing out the weapons emplacements to Chekov. "Our lives depend on it."

Chekov's smile immediately became a worried look.

Have to go for it. Can't leave those poor souls to get spaced.

Kirk turned to the vehicle/drone and extended his hand, palm up. "Here are our credentials."

A blue light played across Kirk's palm. There was a momentary pause. The captain moved his other hand to the phaser at his side. Things might get ugly very quickly.

"Credentials accepted," said the vehicle.

Kirk glanced over to see a very relieved Chekov.

"How may this technical unit be of service?" said the vehicle/drone.

Spock leaned over and spoke next to Kirk's ear. "We could use its help to transport these cocoons back to the shuttlecraft."

"We certainly could," Kirk answered. He turned to McCoy. "Any reason they shouldn't be transported?"

McCoy checked his tricorder again. "Should be fine," he said. "Their metabolism is greatly slowed, but they seem in perfect physical shape thanks to their Excalbian regenerative power. We should be able to revive them fairly quickly once I get them to sickbay." McCoy shook his head. "I could use some help cutting them free of this packing material." McCoy nodded toward the vehicle. "Maybe that overgrown forklift knows the best way to do it."

Kirk turned back to the warehouse vehicle. "All right, technical unit," he said. "Load them up and follow me."

———

As they stood on the *Enterprise* bridge gazing at Haversack, the pirate depot, Kirk glanced over to Spock and noticed him staring at the image with something akin to Vulcan frustration. "Captain, this pirate base is a vast treasure house of technology from many unexplored sectors. It would be a fascinating project if I were to remain behind with a security team and catalog it. Even if the pirates return, they do not seem to ever set foot on the depot surface by common agreement. We should in all probability be safe from harm."

"I need you here," Kirk said. "Representative Valek wants us in the Gibraltar system. I'm sure Starfleet will want to send a team back."

"Understood, Captain," Spock replied. "Back to Zeta Gibraltar?"

"Yes," Kirk answered with a sigh.

"Hangar deck to bridge."

The captain thumbed the intraship. "Kirk here."

"All the Excalbians have been transferred from damaged vessels, sir," a technician reported. *"Deck is sealed and secure."*

"Very good," Kirk said. "Bridge out." He turned toward the viewscreen. "So ends the Excalbian navy," he mumbled to himself. The garish glow and ship-choking dust of the nebula didn't seem quite so menacing now. In fact, there was a mist-like beauty to it. "Helm, take us out of here and back to Zeta Gibraltar."

"Aye, sir."

———————

Kirk had always enjoyed approaching a planet after dropping out of warp, experiencing the relatively slow and magisterial approach toward orbit with only impulse power pushing the ship along.

There would be the revelation of how the world would appear from space. Even though he was a veteran starship captain who had visited hundreds of systems, and been the discoverer of many of them, the captain had never lost the tingle of awe and anticipation of adventure he felt when a world, and especially a world harboring life, loomed before him. Kirk had assumed he would never arrive in orbit without that brief flicker of rapture.

Zeta Gibraltar tested that assumption.

The planet loomed before them with its odd orange and blue coloration: ferrous silicates and biological variants on the bush-sized algae they'd encountered before. But the garish orange of the equator gradually faded to a deep and rusty orange toward the poles. Even from space the vegetation revealed that it was not a uniform blue, but was a patchwork of subtle differences. He could see how someone might call the planet lovely and mean it.

"Captain," Chekov said, staring up from his station at the bridge viewscreen. "The *Montana* is not in orbit."

"Perhaps she's occluded by the planet," Kirk said.

"Negative, sir."

Not again, Kirk thought. Had some outlying L'rah'hane raiders made an opportunistic foray while the *Enterprise* was away hunting bigger game? The *Montana* could be off chasing them.

"Hail the outpost, Lieutenant Uhura."

"Commander Contreras," Uhura reported after a moment.

"On-screen, Lieutenant."

A frazzled Imelda Contreras appeared before Kirk. "Commander, where's the *Montana*?"

"*I was hoping you could tell* me that, *Captain,*" Contreras replied. "*About two hours ago she left orbit. Sensors indicated a rapid departure. Shortly thereafter we picked up a burst of subspace chatter and then a mayday call. We've been going through the communications records trying to understand what's happened, but nothing yet."*

"We were inside the Vara two hours ago, too close to the nebula to be able to pick up subspace communication," said Kirk said. "Let me speak with Representative Valek, please."

"Valek?" said Contreras. *"She was on the Mon-tana. She was communicating with the Council Security and Intelligence Committee. She took the Excalbians who were not with you on board so that they could speak directly to the Council and explain their recent actions, especially that declaration of Ex-calbian independence.*

"Captain, are you going after them?"

"I can't abandon you to possible pirate attack."

"The Excalbians are our primary mission." Con-treras smiled grimly. *"The minute the Montana left, I ordered my chief engineer to charge up our new planetary defense system. It's ahead of schedule, but all systems came online and we have full function. We may not have a complete shield, but we'll be able to hold off a couple of raiders if we have to."*

She's right, Kirk thought. *It's about time some-body chooses to trust. She has to be thinking her career is in tatters. Besides, I have faith in Scotty's defenses.*

"Commander," Kirk said, "we'll be back as soon as we can. Kirk out."

Kirk turned to his first officer.

"Mister Spock?"

"Sensors show an active ion trail leading away from the planet. Analysis indicates the signature matches *Montana*. There are indications of excessive energy discharge occurring in synclinic waves. A classic indication of a ship that has all engines in full reverse."

"She was tractored away," said Kirk. "Dragged away kicking and screaming."

"Colorful, but that would be my assessment, Captain," Spock said. "The *Montana* did not leave orbit of her own accord."

"But dragged where? Toward the nebula?"

"Negative. Deeper into Federation territory."

"Let's go get her," Kirk said. "And find whatever it is that's strong enough to tractor an *Archer*-class starship."

Seventeen

Captain's Log, Stardate 6100.9. We are following the trail left by the Montana. *It appears that she was tractored out of orbit and pulled away from the system at warp speed by an unknown force. Two-thirds of the Excalbian refugees are reported to be on the* Montana *along with Federation Special Representative Valek.* Enterprise *will locate the* Montana *and then determine whoever—or whatever—is behind this.*

"Lieutenant Uhura, call President Washington to the bridge," Kirk said. He had been brooding silently for the hours the *Enterprise* had been tracking the *Montana's* ion trail, and his order startled Uhura—but she quickly recovered her usual professional aplomb and promptly summoned the Excalbian.

Washington-Yarnek arrived moments later.

"What can I do for you, Captain?" he said, coming to stand beside Kirk's command chair. He stared at the viewscreen. "I shall never get used to that sight. Racing through the stars in all their glory."

"All right, Yarnek, I want you to tell me what the hell is going on," Kirk said. "What have you been keeping from us?"

"There is nothing, Captain."

"There's something," Kirk said. "Mysterious forces do not suddenly grab starships out of orbit—at least not normally. One force I know from experience that can perform such a feat are the Excalbians. The fact that Excalbians are here and aboard the *Montana* is no coincidence. So I ask you again: what have you been keeping from us?"

"Captain Kirk, I assure you—"

Kirk turned sharply on the Excalbian. "I'm done playing games, Yarnek. Lives are at stake. Human lives, and—unless I miss my guess—Excalbian lives as well."

Washington-Yarnek was silent for a moment, considering. Then he bowed his head toward Kirk and finally spoke. "You must understand, we—my humanoid companions and myself—did not leave our native planet in the best of circumstances. We were hunted criminals, accused of treason, and we were facing"—Washington-Yarnek shuddered— "re-absorption into the planetary silicon matrix. A death sentence. I fear our pursuers may have hunted us down."

"You should have told us."

"I'm sorry I was . . . not forthcoming. In retrospect, it was obviously a grave error. But we were hopeful that if we disappeared into the vast population of the Federation—"

"Never mind that. Tell me who or what I might be facing out there once we catch them."

"I do not know for certain," Washington-Yarnek replied. "It is most unusual, although not unheard of, that members of my species leave our planetary home . . . brief expeditions, to the worlds within our system. We possess matter-manipulating technology that makes warp travel possible. Excalbians simply don't want to go anywhere else. The usual excuse is that we are far too busy exploring the inner space of our being to bother with mere physical reality." Washington shook his head. "As you know, I do not hold with such a philosophy. I believe, much as you do, in the power of exploration and discovery. It could be argued that I believe this because I am partially a construction taken from your mind, Captain Kirk. And, George Washington began as a surveyor on the American frontier."

"Fine sentiments, Yarnek. Who took that ship?"

Washington-Yarnek hung his head. "It is quite likely to be Excalbians. They possess the technology that would allow them to do this. I cannot explain how. There is much knowledge that was wiped away when I forced into this human form. But they are after us, the refugees. I believe Representative Valek and the crew of the *Montana* were merely in the wrong place at the wrong time."

"Why are they after *you*? What treason did you commit? Why not just let you go?"

"When we left, we took something with us," Washington-Yarnek said. "Knowledge. Knowledge of good and evil. They want it back."

"You're joking."

"I wish I were, Captain," Washington-Yarnek said. "You have to understand how the Excalbian collective works. All decisions are made through a series of thought experiments. Various scenarios are created and tested, again and again. I know it seemed bizarre to you when Abraham Lincoln appeared to you and we coerced you into one of our games. But to an Excalbian, it was perfectly normal. That is the way information is gathered for collective decision-making. There is no other way. Those who participate in these scenarios are, to some extent, actors in a drama. But, during the scenario, we believe we are the personas we've taken on. At the conclusion, the experiential data is collated and matched against experiential matrices from similar dramas. Conclusions are modified or reinforced accordingly. But the ones who possess this data, who retain these memories, are the individuals involved. Half-formed conclusions are not shared with the collective. In fact, the collective does not know what to do until that knowledge is shared. It is prevented from acting by the very makeup of our mental structures."

Washington-Yarnek touched his own temple

with a finger. "It's locked in here," he said, tapping his temple several times. "We escaped Excalbia with the data sets of hundreds of scenarios contained within our beings. The collective cannot act without that knowledge. It is prevented by the logical pathways of our thought processes."

"You said that the collective runs these scenarios in order to reach a decision," Kirk replied. "What was the decision the collective intended to make in this case?"

Washington-Yarnek seemed to grow tense and stood even more stiffly than usual. When he spoke, it was in a low voice, as if he were ashamed of what he had to say. "Whether or not to destroy your Federation, Captain. Excalbians do not tolerate threats to the collective's existence. They strike first and strike hard."

"How were you planning on destroying the Federation?" Kirk asked.

"By activating the planet Earth's tectonic plates. We would bury your world in a lake of lava hundreds of kilometers deep. We would then move on and repeat this process world by world. We know how to do this. We did it to our own world, after all."

"So if they want to catch you and somehow . . . reintegrate you . . . into Excalbian society . . . this would trigger the decision of whether or not to attack Earth."

"Yes, Captain."

"Yarnek, why not *tell* us this before?" Kirk asked with an exasperated sigh. "We could have helped."

"We believed that you would annihilate us rather than risk our experience and conclusions falling back into Excalbian hands," Washington-Yarnek said. "In fact, was that not the official plan?"

He's got me there, Kirk thought. *But the difference between us and them is that cooler heads prevailed.*

"I'm a Starfleet captain and a representative of the Federation. I do not annihilate people because they possess dangerous information," Kirk said. "I and my crew protect them."

"The New Excalbia Assembly had come to the conclusion that we were no longer in any danger of eradication. We were planning to inform you and Representative Valek of these facts after our return from the expedition to the Vara Nebula. It was a final test of whether you would treat us fairly. Captain Kirk, you passed with flying colors."

"Knowing what you were up to infuriates me, Yarnek."

"I completely understand, Captain."

Kirk shook his head. "I don't think you do. You still believe you can play with people's lives. Even now, when you've assumed human form, have human emotions, human beliefs. The Excalbian part of you retains this . . . arrogance."

"Doctor Franklin has been attempting to warn us of this shortcoming," Washington-Yarnek replied. "He told us it would be our downfall. He is completely correct, but to my great sorrow it may be too late."

"No," Kirk said. "It's not too late. It's never too late to learn a bit of humility. Maybe that's what the exploration and discovery of physical reality is truly for."

Washington-Yarnek put a hand to his forehead, kneaded it for a moment. "What I have told you now is all I know. I would provide to you the specifics of Excalbian capabilities so that you may better counter them, but I do not have this information. This is a portion of my Excalbian self that was wiped away to make room for George Washington. It is so with all of us. Much was lost when we became humans."

He shook his head as if to rid it of bad thoughts. He faced Kirk. "I have come to the conclusion, however, that the gain far outweighs the loss. I know you may not believe me, and I wouldn't blame you, but I tell you that I am completely on your side. I am a partisan for the human race, for the Federation, and for freedom."

Kirk smiled. "Good to hear, Yarnek. Or whoever you become," he said. "I think you've finally stopped the playacting and stepped into real life."

"I believe you are right, Captain."

"Ion trail is growing more intense," Spock suddenly reported. "Energy residue from Starfleet weaponry. Extreme energy levels would indicate that the *Montana* was engaged in combat."

"Take us out of warp, Mister Chekov. Let's see if we can make sense of—"

"Captain, ahead!" called out Sulu. He pointed to the viewscreen. "It's the *Montana*, sir."

She was spinning slowly. Her stabilizers were obviously nonfunctional. One nacelle was twisted into a jagged flower of metal-ceramics. It had blown out its forward end.

"Spock."

"Engines are nearing overload," Spock said. "Captain, the *Montana* is in imminent danger of a warp core meltdown."

"Run a scan on life signs," Kirk said.

"Faint," Spock said.

"Damn!" Kirk said, staring at the crippled ship.

"I'm sorry, Captain," Washington-Yarnek said. "I detect the hand of my former species in this."

"Scans confirm life support *is* functioning, sir."

"Uhura, see if you can get me Haynes."

"*Montana*, this is *Enterprise*," said Uhura, adjusting and readjusting her earpiece frequencies. "*Montana*, come in please."

After a moment the viewscreen crackled to life.

Red Alert lights flashed everywhere on the *Montana* bridge. Captain Haynes was busy taking a report from a red-shirted engineering officer. He turned toward Kirk.

"Haynes, what's going on?"

He answered rapidly. *"We were pulled from orbit by unknown tractor beam technology. Beam originated from a group of ships of an entirely alien design. We tried to break free and fight back, and the dilithium crystals began to spontaneously disintegrate. Condition critical. Attempting to respond."*

"Understood."

"Kirk?"

"Yes?"

"They took Representative Valek," said Haynes. *"I don't know how. Didn't look like a transporter. One moment she was on the bridge, the next moment she had disappeared before my eyes."*

"Do you have any idea who did this?"

"Not a clue. They didn't answer any of our hails. Or notice our emergency log beacon."

"Noted. Would you like to abandon ship? We should be able to get your people off."

"Negative. There was an enormous energy surge, and nonessential systems became inoperative. My engineer has a solution to prevent immediate core meltdown," Haynes said. *"It'll leave us dead in space, but should save our lives for the moment."*

"Enterprise will stand by."

"Hope we won't need it." A distraught crewman suddenly trotted up to Haynes with a report.

Haynes glanced at the data slate he was handed. "Montana *out*."

The viewscreen returned to starfield with the slowly spinning *Montana*.

Kirk lowered his eyes, shook his head in frustration. Then he looked back up, resolved. "Mister Spock, I want you and Franklin to fire up that Hradrian device and prepare it for use as a weapon."

"Aye, sir," Spock said. "Franklin and Galileo have been working on the device since our departure from Zeta Gibraltar."

"Check on their progress, Spock," Kirk said. "Do what you can speed them up?"

"Aye, sir."

━━━━━━

"Captain, multiple incoming objects," Chekov reported from the science station. "They are moving toward us at warp speed. Unknown configuration."

"On-screen."

The approaching objects looked like specks at first, but as they drew closer, their outlines began to be discernable.

"Red Alert," Kirk said. "Battle stations."

"These are the configurations of Excalbian vessels," Washington-Yarnek said with a sigh. "They have found us."

"Well, they haven't gotten you," Kirk said. "And we intend to fight for your freedom."

"That is much appreciated, Captain Kirk."

A hailing whistle from engineering broke the heavy silence.

"Mister Scott."

"Captain, Mister Watt and I have been discussing what he remembers of Excalbian science and looking through the data we acquired from our encounter with them before. We may have found a way to counter at least a portion of the Excalbian technology."

"That's the best news I've had in while," Kirk said. "Explain."

"We believe we've created a deflector shield resonance that will guard against direct matter manipulation within the ship. They won't be able to reach in and grab anyone out of thin air. Most importantly, they won't be able to mess with my dilithium crystal matrix and cause the kind of critical deterioration they did before."

"Do it, Mister Scott."

"Aye, sir."

Kirk looked back up at the viewscreen. There was an array of five ships in a star-shaped formation. They looked more like giant crystals than ships. Each was a slightly different shape, with different facets. Each ship was also a different shade, glowing faintly from within, but relatively bright here in deep space. Thousands of tiny points of light played around furiously inside the crystal ships, twinkling, moving together, and spreading apart. It resembled a bee colony, if one could peer directly inside.

"Those lights? Is that the propulsion mechanism or the Excalbians themselves?" Kirk asked.

"Both," Washington-Yarnek responded.

"Captain, I'm picking up an incoming message from one of those vessels," Uhura said.

"Put it on, Lieutenant."

The view of the crystal ships vanished and what replaced it on the viewscreen was—Valek.

She was unhurt, but her hair was disheveled and a portion of her collar was torn.

"Captain, it seems I have become a diplomatic hostage."

"Have they hurt you in any way? Where are you?"

"They have not harmed me in any permanent way," Valek answered, touching the tear. *"Although I admit to experiencing an extremely jarring mental sensation when I was snatched from the* Montana *akin to the sudden and unexpected breaking of a Vulcan mind-meld. As to your second question, they are holding me in what appears to be a small cell kept at Class-M environmental conditions. As you can see behind me, the walls of this holding cell are transparent, and what is beyond does not seem as if it would be amenable to Vulcan or human life."*

Suddenly a voice interrupted the audio feed from Valek. It was loud, of indeterminate sex, and flatly insistent. "*You will assist us in our purpose, or Valek shall be harmed.*"

"Threating a Federation representative is not a very good opening move for negotiations," Kirk replied.

"*This is no time for frivolous responses,*" the voice said. "*Valek's life and the lives of your crew are at stake.*"

"Are they?" Kirk said.

"*A demonstration is required.*"

The viewscreen went blank, then returned to the image of the five Excalbian vessels. One of them, a pale blue one, flared brightly.

The voice spoke again, sounding none-too-pleased. "*You have shielded your ship from direct matter manipulation.*"

"That's right."

"*We will proceed with the destruction of the* Montana *as an alternate demonstration.*"

Damn, Kirk thought.

He stood up from his chair. "Wait a minute," the captain said quickly. "Do not destroy the *Montana*. If you do, I assure you that we will do whatever we can to prevent you from achieving what you want."

"*Do you know what we want?*"

"I presume you've come for the refugee Excalbians."

There was a brief pause, then a crackling, as if hundreds of tiny sticks were breaking at once.

"*That's the sound of an Excalbian laugh, Captain,*" said Washington-Yarnek next to Kirk in a low voice.

"If not that, then tell us what you want," Kirk said.

"*Very well.*" A form appeared on the viewscreen. It was the rocky, barely humanoid form Kirk had seen Yarnek assume before. It had claws for hands and a circle of eyes around its head, each oval in appearance, and white with no pupils to speak of. There was no possibility of reading expression from that rocky visage. "*I am Anvit, commander of these vessels.*"

"Captain James T. Kirk of the *U.S.S. Enterprise*," Kirk responded.

"*We are well aware of who you are, Captain,*" said Anvit. "*I hope you are aware of the great trouble you have caused my people.*"

"Trouble?" Kirk said. "Last I checked, it was you who had taken myself and my first officer prisoner and forced us to fight reincarnations of some of the galaxy's worse villains. You have some nerve, calling *me* trouble."

"*If it had not been for you, we would not have initiated the morality scenarios,*" said Anvit. "*If we had not continued with the scenarios, we would be safe, instead of a people on the run.*"

Kirk was unsure about what Anvit meant by this, but first he knew he must attend to the

Montana's safety. "Anvit, I will listen to whatever proposal you have to make if you will leave the *Montana* untouched."

There was a brief pause, then an answer came. *"The collective has conferred, and this is acceptable. We cannot, however, restore the engines to working condition. The deterioration has become too great."*

Kirk made a cutting motion, and the *Enterprise*'s feed to the Excalbian was ended. "Uhura, get me the *Montana*."

"Aye, sir, a channel is open."

"*Montana*, Kirk here."

"Kirk! Good news. We've managed to retain the engine integrity and prevented a meltdown. We only have minimal impulse, but for the moment we're safe."

"Hang tight. We'll be back in touch momentarily. Kirk out."

He nodded to Uhura. Anvit reappeared.

"We have come seeking our runaways, Captain Kirk, but not to bring them back. Instead, we are going to join them. Now we have found you, as well. If you do not aid us, we will cause pain for the one you call Valek."

You almost had me on your side. Now you lost me.

"More threats?" said Kirk. "Let me tell you something, Anvit, and you can take this to your collective. We don't negotiate with those who threaten our lives or the lives of others."

"Is that so, Kirk? Behold."

The view switched back to Valek. Suddenly her cool and serenity were interrupted by a choking cough. She put a hand over her mouth, felt around for any exit from her cell.

"Anvit," Kirk shouted, "what's happening?"

Valek evidently heard him. *"The Excalbians have introduced a chemical I judge from the smell to be a copper bonding agent into the atmospheric mixture. It links with the oxygenizing metal in my blood and causes . . ."* She jerked forward, put a hand to her abdomen. She put her other hand to her head. *"Excruciating pain."*

"Valek, how long can you stand it?"

"I am attempting . . . I am attempting to . . ." Valek seemed to regain control of herself. She raised her hands and touched her fingers and thumbs together to make a triangle and stared intently at this form. *"I am attempting use of Vulcan mind control techniques to mitigate the pain."*

"Can you keep it up, Valek?"

"Unknown, Captain," she replied, her voice straining. Then the tension slowly drained from her face. Valek looked up. *"Captain Kirk, I hereby use my plenipotentiary power as Federation representative to order you to disregard any torture they inflict upon me and to not, repeat not, attempt any sort of rescue of myself."*

"Valek," Kirk said. He paused, shook his head.

"We aren't in the Gibraltar system anymore. You don't have authority here."

"James, please," she said. *"Do not let them use me to blackmail you into illogical action."*

Kirk considered. There was no way he would give up on her. But he didn't have to let the Excalbians know that.

"Very well, Valek," he said. "I will follow your instructions. And . . . I'm sorry."

"Do not be," Valek replied. *"This is—"* Another wave of pain struck her, and it took her a moment to re-center and return to her serene posture. She breathed in and spoke again. *"This is merely part of my job, Captain, as facing danger is part of yours."*

"Did you hear me, Anvit?" Kirk angrily said. "You will never get what you want from us by force."

"This response is irrational," said Anvit. An exasperated tone had crept into his voice. *"The fact that those you call 'good' act to protect others when faced with coercion through threats made upon those others to whom the good have an altruistic or romantic commitment is the prime lesson of your previous visit to Excalbia. You are not behaving as you should according to your own rules!"*

"They have learned nothing about good and evil," said Washington-Yarnek with a laugh, but a laugh filled with sadness.

"Yarnek? You are present? We did not detect you on the Enterprise."

"I noticed that," Washington-Yarnek replied. "Which means that the blocking methods of the humans has been successful."

"Yarnek, we must speak."

"I don't think so, Anvit," Yarnek replied. "You have reached an erroneous conclusion based on incomplete evidence."

Kirk raised a hand to cut them both off. "Enough of this. We will not turn over the humanoid Excalbians of Zeta Gibraltar to you, Anvit."

"You misunderstand our intentions, Captain Kirk," Anvit said. *"Whatever desire we had to capture and reintegrate the runaway scenarists has been overridden by other concerns at present."*

"So you have decided to go ahead with your plan to attack the Federation?"

"No. We shall not destroy your Federation, Captain." Anvit cocked his head and adjusted his rocky carapace to a different position.

If I didn't know better than to impute human body language to aliens, I'd say he was fidgeting, Kirk thought.

"Well, that's . . . good to hear," Kirk responded. "But the very fact that you even considered the possibility is bound to make us wary of you."

"The collective has made its choice," said Anvit, raising his hands in what seemed to be a gesture of dismissal. *"This matter is resolved. Your response is irrational."*

"What the captain is trying to communicate to you, Anvit," said Washington-Yarnek, breaking in, "is that humans have no reason to believe that the collective won't change its mind *again* should circumstances change."

"*That is entirely correct,*" Anvit replied. "*How could it not be? In the future, we may very well change our mind.*"

"You have learned nothing, Anvit," Washington-Yarnek said. "All of you have learned nothing."

"*Yarnek,*" said the Excalbian captain. "*We do not wish to dispute this with you.*"

"Then why . . ." Washington-Yarnek's look of puzzlement slowly became one of comprehension. "You are in trouble, aren't you? You have come seeking help."

"*Your assessment is accurate, Yarnek.*"

"Release the Vulcan representative immediately, and I will speak with you."

"*James T. Kirk has already refused to negotiate. Your collective has decided.*"

"I am not Captain Kirk."

"*But—*"

"Anvit, I am *human* now. Or at least I wish to be. Here there is no collective. There is no restraint but one's own conscience. There is freedom."

Anvit said nothing. Then he slowly nodded his head. "*Valek is released from coercive excruciation.*"

The view shifted back to Valek. She slumped

forward. She took a deep breath, then another, and finally stood straight again.

"Valek, are you all right?" Kirk asked.

"*I am quickly recovering,*" the Vulcan answered. "*The compound should be out of my bloodstream momentarily.*"

"*Captain Kirk, if you will lower your shield, we will send Valek back to you.*"

"I don't think so," Kirk said. "And I'm sure Representative Valek concurs."

"*I do,*" Valek stated off screen. "*Don't do it, James.*"

"*Then we are at an impasse,*" Anvit said with a shuffle of the shoulders that passed for an Excalbian shrug.

Suddenly Washington-Yarnek let out a real, unrestrained laugh. "I've just realized something," he said. "Captain, may I make a suggestion?"

Kirk looked at him. "Be my guest, Mister President."

Washington-Yarnek nodded, turned to the screen. "Anvit?"

The image of Valek, now in no apparent distress, was replaced by the rocky Excalbian. "*What is it you wish to propose?*"

"That you tell the truth, Anvit," Washington-Yarnek said. "Stop trying to bully your way to an outcome. Treat us humans as equals, and simply *tell* us why you are here."

"How will that be effective? We would thus display our weakness."

"Just trust me, Anvit."

There was a pause, then the rocky Excalbian spoke. *"Very well. We have come seeking sanctuary with the Federation. We are in dire need of your help."*

Kirk shook his head in wonder. "You . . . expect me to believe this?"

"I think he is telling the truth, Captain," said Washington-Yarnek. "Or believes himself to be."

"Go back to your planet."

"We cannot."

"Why not?"

"Excalbia no longer exists."

No one spoke for a long moment.

"We are the last Excalbians," Anvit continued. *"We are fleeing a terrible enemy."*

"And you believe you were going to *coerce* your way into our good graces?"

"We do not often deal with species unlike us. There was no time to run scenarios. We act on incomplete information. Captain Kirk, Representative Valek, please help us. We are afraid."

Kirk rubbed his temples. "How can I verify any of this?"

"Perhaps I can," Valek's voice said. *"Commander Anvit, can you create a space where you and I can coexist for at least a short while?"*

"I can."

"*If we can be in close proximity, I can attempt a Vulcan mind-meld to verify the truth of what you are saying.*"

Anvit tilted his head and seemed to consider for a moment—although his lack of a true face made any other human expression impossible. "*This will be done,*" he finally said.

On the *Enterprise* viewscreen, Valek was now standing beside the Excalbian. She'd evidently been transported to what served as the Excalbian vessel's bridge.

"*Proceed,*" Anvit said. With one of his crab-like claws, he pointed to a spot on his lower torso. "*I have cooled a portion of my carapace to a degree that should be warm, but not excessively hot, to your touch. I cannot maintain this temperature for long without damage to myself.*"

Valek nodded that she understood.

"*Clear your mind, Anvit,*" she said, "*and we shall begin.*"

Eighteen

For Valek, the experience was unlike any other mind-meld she had ever attempted. The Excalbian thought process was utterly *alien*. It was a creature of reason, but of reason turned in and around on itself so that instead of clarity there was endless convection, endless churning.

She realized she was floating in the mental equivalent of magma. For a moment, it almost pulled her under, almost burned her own mind, a small space within the massive silicon sea.

But Valek held herself afloat. Schooling her thought to perception only, so that she would not run the risk of being absorbed and dissolved. Then, slowly, she found that she could swim among the thoughts. She began to detect currents, and she followed these. The current converged. Coherent thought emerged.

She followed further, deeper—

And slowly, those thoughts formed into a story . . .

I, Anvit, remember the cause of the turmoil first. I recall the single event that resulted in the catastrophic cascade that changed everything.

The coming of James T. Kirk.

After the coming of James T. Kirk, the ground broiled without thought and conversation. Good and evil? Bravery and heroism? Greed and self-sacrifice? Treachery and honor? All of these were concepts for dealing with the outside of things, for interacting with the world of reality. They were ideas we hadn't thought about since our species had been cave crawlers, before we learned to flow through the magma.

We had spent millennia exploring our inner selves, considering and reconsidering our consciousness, our awareness, our form, and the substance of which they were made. Above all things, we were students of our own minds and thought processes. The goal of life was to find repose in order to contemplate the self and its relationship to the mind of the collective and the universal mind. To comprehend thought as a process was enlightenment. Cultivating inwardness was the goal of all philosophy.

We learned much in this manner. In so many ways, we were as far ahead of James T. Kirk and his Federation as a sentient being from a microorganism. Could we not manipulate the material world itself and turn it into thought and back again?

We captured and held the *Enterprise* with the ease of a parent plucking a nymph-child from sipping at its magma flower. These others did not even perceive matter in its atomic form directly. Their senses only apprehended surfaces. They could not even dip into one another's minds to assimilate experience or conclusions. All they had was the guttural utterances of language. They seemed to do everything the hard way.

Yet when we dipped into their minds, we found conclusions we had never considered. We found new concepts instead of the same ideas we had been turning over and over in our minds for fifty thousand years. Our curiosity grew.

Could these primitives have something to teach us?

It seemed impossible, but was it? They had ventured *out* after all. *They* had found *us*, and not we them. Could this be significant?

Could it be a threat?

We began with the most general of their ideals, the concept of good and evil.

We mined their memories and constructed our scenario, our drama. We built our stage. We assigned the first roles: Abraham Lincoln, Surak, Colonel Phillip Green, the others. We impressed the human conceptions of these beings upon those of us assigned to play the roles. We changed our actors' forms—an easy thing to accomplish—so that they wore the physical mask of the humanoids that they mimicked.

Then we lured James T. Kirk and Spock to the

surface, and the thought experiment began. But
James T. Kirk surprised us. He did not enter into
the spirit of the drama. He fought against the very
idea that he and his people should be made to act
out the very ideals they believed in.

This puzzled us. It was very strange. We forced
him back into the drama, and when he won, when
good triumphed over evil, instead of thanking us
for the privilege of participating in our elucidation,
he told us that it was *we* who were the primitives!

Unbelievable. He held *us* in contempt for what
we had done to him and his crew! He lectured *us*
about rights and fairness. What if we had destroyed
him and his ship instead of letting them go? Were
not *we*, and our right to know, more important than
this insignificant species?

Most dismissed his absurd charges, but we did
not forget them.

What if his people, his primitive Federation,
posed a *threat* to us because they knew something
we did not? As we evolved, we had learned how to
deal with threats to our own species from within
and without the planetary crust.

We wiped them out.

Ought we to do the same with this Federation?
These new concepts of good and evil and the rest
frustrated us. Many of us believed we ought to eliminate the source of that frustration before it polluted
our pure thought.

This became my faction.

But some of us—chief among them Yarnek, who had been appointed judge of the drama—began to ponder another possibility.

What if James T. Kirk was right?

What if we had been missing something, some basic truth that was right before our eyes for thousands of years?

The question must be decided, and how better to do it than to continue creating and observing even more scenarios? So we began. First we played the game among ourselves. Yarnek and his troupe of re-enactors took on many personas. Most gravitated to a particular "part" or "role."

We pitted good against evil again and again. I must admit, it became less a process of learning and curiosity and more one of amusement and diversion.

Soon, merely to play among ourselves was not enough. We began to reach out and snatch other representatives of their species to perform in our scenarios. The exclusion zone the Federation established around Excalbia did not take account of our full capabilities. Some we allowed to return home after their role was complete. Others we destroyed.

I and my faction took no issue with this. Yarnek and his faction began to believe we were committing thought-crimes against ourselves. He spoke of the concept of injustice toward others.

He spoke of murder.

Yarnek called us killers and accused himself of being the worst of all since he enabled the scenarios.

He claimed to be "ashamed" and called for the scenarios to end.

Most of us thought this was nonsense. The scenarios, in the short time of one passing of our planet around its star, had become a great source of status and advancement among us.

"No," we said, "the scenarios will continue until we have collected the requisite data and reached a satisfactory conclusion."

Yarnek seemed to us to become unbalanced, flinging about the new concepts he had encountered. He called us assassins, executioners, genocidal maniacs.

"But the scenarios serve a great purpose," we answered. "They are the means to decide whether or not we shall eliminate this upstart collection of primitives, this Federation."

Besides, we had begun to wager on the outcomes, and fortunes in prestige were being lost and won. Stop it? We were *enjoying* it.

Yarnek made his escape. He was branded an outlaw, a thought-criminal, and we made plans to hunt him down and eliminate him and the others with him.

Meanwhile, the scenarios went on. Good versus evil. Any species unlucky enough to stray near our system was lured in, captured, and forced to participate, to satisfy our curiosity.

We set our lure one too many times.

We attempted to capture the Demiurge.

The skin of the Excalbian was beginning to grow hotter—hot enough to cause Valek great discomfort. Anvit's ability to maintain the lower temperature was rapidly decreasing.

She had to maintain contact. She had to follow the tale. She had to know how the story ended.

Yet if I continue like this my own skin will be burnt to a crisp.

"Move forward. Show me the worst," Valek told Anvit in her trancelike state. "Show me the Demiurge."

The Demiurge had no problem distinguishing between good and evil or deciding which side of good and evil It embodied.

Evil.

It was a creature as at home in the world of mind-reading and matter manipulation as we were. The fact must be admitted, the Demiurge was as far above us in understanding these things as we are above the humanoids of the Federation. It was a creature of space, wholly divorced from whatever Its planetary origin might have been in eons past.

It was, in Its way, beautiful in form. Its natural surface was a changing membrane of quantum foam, and Its interior was dark matter set with a scattering of bright pricks of light, so that It could camouflage Itself as a starfield and approach Its prey unawares.

It was an opportunistic stalker. It preyed on ships, space habitats, and entire worlds.

The interior of the Demiurge was of no material we had ever seen or imagined. Somehow dark matter and space-time itself were twisted into the makeup of the Demiurge, so that there was storage capacity for enormous amounts of data, hoards of wealth gathered from thousands of pillaged worlds, and life-forms kept for amusement in zoos as big as worlds. It could do with the fabric of space-time what we can do with matter manipulation.

Although we experienced It as a single entity, the mentality was a group-mind—It referred to Itself as "we"—but one of such startling complexity and integration that It made our own collective seem like a gathering of stones compared to a mountain of granite.

In our ignorance, we created an arena in orbit above the planet in which to run one of our scenarios, a corral for the Demiurge. In truth, many of us thought it would be fun to bait such a species. We lured It in, or believed that was what we were doing, and "captured" It with field beams we thought were unbreakable.

It was toying with us all along. It allowed the greater part of the collective to gather in one easily accessed data stream.

Then It struck. It reached down to the planet. It reached *into* the planet, searching out complexity, searching out life.

Absorbing. Confiscating. Eating us alive, our mentalities added to Its own, and enslaving us to perform Its functions. For those so absorbed, there would be no more curiosity, no self-reflection, no journeying toward inner enlightenment. They would only exist to serve the Demiurge. They would not even be allowed to die.

A few of us created these crystal ships from our old, long cast-aside spacefaring technology, and attempted to flee.

We believed we had escaped unnoticed. We were fools. As we ran in terror, we received a final message from the Demiurge.

It told us to look back for a final sight of our world. Since we wished a demonstration of the nature of good and evil, It was going to give us one. It reached inside the planet and destabilized the core. We had riddled our planetary structure with great complexity from our eons of thought. Like a giant claw crushing a bit of pumice within its grasp, the Demiurge squeezed—

The planet imploded.

It crumpled. Even atoms could not exist under such conditions. It became a seething mass of quarks.

The Demiurge ate it. Pulled our world into Its maw as It had many others, incorporated the planet's former material being into Its own trans-dimensional structure.

Excalbia was no more.

We ran. As fast as we could. Because the Demiurge was not done with us yet. It told us as much.

It told us that when it eats, It finishes Its meal. When It was done digesting the mentalities of those It had captured, It would be coming for us.

It told us It was *allowing* us to escape.

Minds taste better when they've been seasoned by fear, It said. *So be afraid.* We *are coming.*

———

Valek jerked her hands away from the Excalbian, and the mind-meld broke. Her palms were beginning to blister from second- and third-degree burns. She had her answer. That was what was important.

Conscious will flowed back into her. She had her answer, and now was the time to act.

"Captian Kirk, lower your shields," she said. "We have a larger problem than the Excalbians."

Anvit nodded his large rocky head with its glowing eyes. "Valek will make you understand, James T. Kirk," he said. "You, a primitive, taught us that there was more to the exterior world than was contained within our philosophy. We have now been thrust into *your* world, James T. Kirk. We beg of you: help us to survive."

Nineteen

Captain's Log, Supplemental. The Montana *was disabled by the Excalbians in an attempt to negotiate an alliance with the Federation from a position of dominance. Their reason: they are fleeing a powerful enemy, the Demiurge. The magnitude of Its power is difficult to conceive; the Excalbians possess the ability to manipulate matter and read minds almost at will, yet they were powerless before the Demiurge.*

The *Enterprise* hangar deck was filled with an odd assortment of species: humans, Vulcans, and Excalbian humanoids. And, finally, there was the very large rocky mass of the Excalbian commander, Anvit. A conference room table had been taken apart and carried to the hangar. To accommodate Anvit, Scott had turned the internal cooling of the space as low as the Vulcans could tolerate, but the space remained uncomfortably warm.

The occupants sat or stood around the table, while a triscreen displayed Spock's status report.

"We have been measuring the gravimetric waves

issuing from the direction of Excalbia, or the system in which Excalbia existed. There is a significant spike, and it is increasing at a rate that allows us to extrapolate the speed of the Demiurge's approach." Spock paused.

He's no doubt rechecking the calculations he's already made in his head.

"We are heading at maximum warp toward the Vara Nebula, but the Demiurge is steadily gaining."

"Are we going to make it to the nebula?" Kirk asked.

"No, Captain. The Demiurge will catch up with us in five point nine hours," said Spock. "Your desire to use the nebula for cover is a good idea, even if I suspect it will ultimately be ineffective. Anyway, we will be close, but not close enough. The Demiurge will be upon us."

Anvit stirred from his resting position. His eyes flashed as he produced auditory speech from a small orifice in the middle of what Kirk thought of as his chest. "Our course of action is obvious," he said.

"And what would that be, Commander?"

"We must surrender to the inevitable. There is no rational alternative."

Kirk did a double-take. "You can't be serious?"

Washington-Yarnek turned to Kirk. "This is the Excalbian way, Captain Kirk," he said. "Anvit is speaking as would anyone in the collective."

"Surrender is not an option, Commander Anvit," Kirk said.

"There is no foreseeable action we can take that will conceivably save us." Anvit turned to Valek. "Representative, you and I have shared thoughts."

And I find myself a bit jealous of that fact, Kirk thought. *Ah well.*

"That is so, Commander," said Valek.

"You are a being who depends upon reason. Surely you see that there is no logical alternative but to surrendering to our fate?"

"I admit that a straightline algorithmic interpretation of logic does not present another answer," Valek said.

"There, you see, James T. Kirk? The Vulcan mind is optimized for logic. Even your own Federation representative agrees with me."

"I did *not* say that I agree," Valek replied, holding up a hand of warning. "When I was young, once I arrived at a conclusion, I did not consider the consequences beyond the fact that logic was on my side. But there was one who showed me that I might be mistaken in my premises, and therefore I reached incorrect conclusions."

She nodded toward the *Enterprise*'s first officer.

"Spock. He is half human. Logic dictated that his schoolmates test him to find the hidden emotion within. We claimed that we merely wished to expose his weakness for his own improvement, so that he might receive the guidance he needed. We also wished him removed so he would not annoy us and so that he would not retard our intellectual standards. We told him that he should relegate himself to a suitable position where his emotional weakness would not become a liability. Is this not so, Spock?"

"It is, indeed," Spock replied. "You and the other Vulcan children placed many obstacles in my path."

"Yet my brother, Varen, did not share our conclusions," Valek said. "He showed a wisdom beyond his years. He understood that my logic—and that of the other children—was based on faulty assumptions." Valek touched her hand to her chin and gazed downward, remembering. "We had built our premises on faulty assumptions. Varen was the only one among us who saw that in Spock were the highest ideals, instincts, and abilities of both Vulcans and humans. It was we who were lacking, and not Spock."

She's apologizing, but only admitting an error in logic, Kirk thought. *It is, however, the only apology Spock will appreciate.*

Kirk found himself admiring Valek for making the effort.

"All very interesting," Anvit said. "But I do not see how this relates to our current predicament."

Washington-Yarnek shook his head and let out a low chuckle. "She's trying to tell you to stop being an arrogant bubble-eating crawler and consider the possibility that your own rationality may be limited," he said. "Isn't the destruction of our world enough to convince you that some of your assumptions about the workings of reality may be mistaken?"

Anvit shifted, orienting himself toward Washington-Yarnek. "I hear you, runaway," he said. For a moment he and Washington-Yarnek seemed to be engaged in some kind of confrontation—perhaps a mental wrestling match—because both were stock-still. Then Washington-Yarnek seemed to relax, and Anvit rumbled into a lower position. "I hear, and I concede that you have a point, Yarnek."

"You once presented me with a convincing replica of Surak," Spock said. "I was in awe of your reproduction. Learn from your own work. The ancient Vulcans faced a similar dilemma. Nuclear war ravaged the planet. Many Vulcans died, others fled, but on Vulcan, Surak's teachings were embraced. If we had lacked the will to live, despite the devastation, Surak's philosophy would have been nullified by our own nonexistence. The dead do not think logically, for they do not think at all. For logic—or, as you put it, rationality—to have meaning, it is imperative to carry on in the face of adversity or even seemingly inevitable doom."

"Vulcans are prepared to make a stand against the Demiurge?" Anvit said.

"Captain Kirk once accused me of having, when faced with what seemed inevitable disaster, logically working out the idea that an act of irrational hope was required," Spock said. "I did not agree with his assessment at the time, but the captain had a point."

"Perhaps 'hope' is not the best characterization," Valek said. "Let us call it a random variation in the space-time continuum that we, by attempting to survive, will be in a position to take advantage of."

Anvit again stirred. "I confess I do not understand why we should not give up," he said. "But I have trust, based on evidence, that you of the Federation are capable of surprising, yet effective, behavior."

"We have much to learn from each other," Kirk said. "But we need to survive to do so."

"Agreed," Anvit said after a long pause. "I will return to my ships and ready them for a fight."

———

Another shock wave struck the *Enterprise*, nearly knocking everyone standing in the bridge off their feet and setting all scrambling for handholds.

"Gravitational and temporal disruption growing stronger," Spock reported from his sensor station. "The Demiurge entity is now one million kilometers away and closing."

A strange whine began to sound throughout the ship. It was a tone of randomly varying pitch and level.

Hard to hear myself think with that going on, Kirk thought.

"Uhura, can you clear the intership of whatever is making that noise."

The communication officer checked her board. "I think it's . . . the air."

"Confirmed," Spock said. "What we are hearing are small tears in the fabric of space-time forming in our immediate vicinity; indeed some are forming within our physical bodies."

"Can we damp it in some way so at least we don't have to *hear* our world ripping apart?"

"Difficult to accomplish," Spock said. "Perhaps if Mister Scott were to alter the resonance factor on the dilithium crystals to create a countering inner-ship vibration? I would suggest a change from frequency Alpha one six nine to Upsilon nine zero five."

Kirk punched the comm to engineering.

"Scotty, change the dilithium crystal resonance factor to Upsilon nine zero five."

"*Aye, Captain, but I have to tell you that is not in the specs,*" Scott replied.

"Do you always follow the specs?" Kirk asked.

Scott chuckled. "*On occasion. Depends on the circumstances.*" A brief pause, then he reported. "*Dilithium resonance is now Upsilon nine zero five.*"

There was a buzz, somewhat like a bad door buzzer, but it quickly died down. In its place was blessed silence.

"That took care of the problem, Scott. Bridge out."

Kirk glanced over to Spock. His first officer merely raised an eyebrow, then turned back to his station.

"Uhura, please call President Washington to the bridge," Kirk said. He shook his head in amusement. "I'll never get tired of saying that," he mumbled to himself.

———

Washington-Yarnek joined Kirk on the bridge. The two men stood and looked at the viewscreen. There was nothing to see except the five Excalbian ships.

"Five ships," Kirk said. "All that's left of your world."

"Anvit managed to save more, Captain," said Washington-Yarnek. "There are methods for preserving personalities in crystalline matrices, storing them. I believe Anvit escaped with at least a hundred thousand individuals in deep storage. He may hope to reanimate them someday if a suitable home is found." Washington-Yarnek smiled tightly. "The Excalbians like to say that what they truly are is a train of thought that inhabits a swirl of magma."

"*They*?"

"Yes, *they*, my good sir," Washington-Yarnek replied. "I no longer am one of that species. My participation in the scenarios, my time as a runaway— this has all remade me. I suspect the others of my ilk feel much like me in this regard."

"What are you now?"

"I do not know," Washington-Yarnek replied. "I could do worse than to attempt to become more and more like the true George Washington. He was an honorable man. I think he was a good man."

"He made mistakes," Kirk said. "He lost battles." Kirk paused, considered how deeply he wished to go into the matter. He owed it to Washington-Yarnek to speak the whole truth. "He also owned slaves."

"Yes, I remember," the other said. "He freed them at the end of his life." He looked down, shook his head. "I told myself I kept them for Martha's sake. It was the world she knew."

"It doesn't matter why one owns slaves," Kirk said. "He should not have."

"I agree," Washington-Yarnek said. "And I think *he* knew, too." Washington-Yarnek stepped back, considered Kirk. "He was a complicated man, yet a man of honor. He provides one with a great deal to live up to."

"Captain," Sulu said, nodding toward the screen.

At first Kirk didn't see it. It was just a ripple in the starfield, a small area darker than the other portions. As Kirk watched, this darkness began to grow larger and to take up much more of the viewscreen.

"The Demiurge," Kirk said.

"Captain, there is very little trace of the entity on our sensors. It has achieved a near perfect camouflage. We can, however, extrapolate its position by taking sensor readings of where it is *not*. This presents necessary delays," Spock said.

"Understood," Kirk said.

"Excalbians dropping out of warp, Captain," said Sulu.

"What?"

"The entire fleet is slowing. They are coming to a dead stop."

"It's almost as if they've . . . given up," Chekov put in.

"Incoming message from Commander Anvit, Captain," Uhura said.

"Put it on."

The Excalbian appeared before them. Although the viewscreen enlarged him a bit, he was almost the same size as in real life when one was in close proximity.

"*We are going to do what we should have done all along, James T. Kirk,*" Anvit said. "*We will not conduct a pointless fight. We shall allow the Demiurge to devour us.*" He paused a moment, then continued in a lower, sadder voice. "*Perhaps it will choke on us. But I think not.*" He raised a claw in emphasis. "*I know your primitive mind will never be able to accept the futility of resistance. So this is good-bye, James T. Kirk. Anvit out.*"

The screen returned to starfield.

Kirk shook his head. "Of all the boneheaded moves," he mumbled. "We are very close to the nebula." Kirk turned to Chekov. "Take us out of warp."

"Aye, sir."

"Excalbian armada at dead stop," Spock reported.

"The Demiurge has exited warp space. From sensor readings, or lack thereof, I do not think that any of our conventional weapons would do the Demiurge the slightest damage, Captain. There is nothing to lock onto, no target to acquire."

Kirk continued to gaze at the viewscreen as he returned to his command chair. "But we *can* lock onto the Excalbian vessels?"

"Yes, sir, we can."

"Well, we can't attack the Demiurge," Kirk said. "Let's attack the Excalbians, instead."

"What?" said Washington-Yarnek in surprise. "What do you mean, Captain?"

"Mister Chekov, lock phasers onto the lead Excalbian ship."

"The *Excalbian* ship, sir?"

"You heard me, mister."

"Aye, aye, sir."

"Captain," said Washington-Yarnek, "You aren't serious? You can't be intending . . ."

"Fire phasers, Mister Chekov," said Kirk.

"Firing phasers."

The phasers squealed as they erupted toward the Excalbian flagship.

The Excalbian ship had its shields down and took the fire. For a moment, its crystalline structure glowed a hot red.

"Again, Mister Sulu."

"Firing," Sulu answered.

This time the hit produced the glow, and it did not subside. "We gave him a good punch," Kirk said. "Let's see if we've made him mad."

They didn't have to wait long. Anvit's rocky visage popped up on the viewscreen. "*What's the meaning of this, Kirk? You have attacked us without provocation!*"

"We *were* provoked, Commander," Kirk replied. "By your inaction."

"*We are preparing our minds for extinction. You have disrupted our self-reflection at a most crucial moment. How dare you? You will pay for this!*"

"Not if you can't catch me."

"*What, now you flee?*" Anvit let out a sound that sounded like a steam pipe exploding. His breath-like expulsion whistled in pure anguish. "*James T. Kirk, does your arrogance have no end?*"

"I think you know the answer to that," Kirk replied. Kirk turned, and spoke to Chekov. "Mister Chekov, hit him with another. Fire phasers."

"Firing phasers, sir."

The Excalbian ship's crystalline interior shuddered slightly behind Anvit. "*You haven't badly damaged us, you fool!*" Anvit had raised his voice and was practically shouting. "*You simpleminded humans. You turn on us! You should instead be giving your lives to a species infinitely more advanced than you!*"

"Infinitely?" Kirk said. "Take a look behind

you." Kirk motioned to Uhura to cut the screen, and she did so. "All right, Mister Sulu, take us toward the Vara Nebula. Maximum warp."

"Aye, Captain."

Kirk turned to Spock. "Mister Spock, what are our friends the Excalbians doing?"

"They are in hot pursuit, Captain."

Kirk chuckled. "Excellent," he said. "Now we have them right where they want us."

"Captain, you've truly kicked the hornets' nest now," Washington-Yarnek said. "Was it merely to introduce some random factor into events?" The Excalbian answered himself. "No, it could not be."

"You heard Anvit," Kirk said to Washington-Yarnek. "Our weapons are useless against the Demiurge."

Washington-Yarnek thought a moment more. He took off his hat and bowed. His tight smile became laughter. He slapped the side of his thigh with the hat.

"You couldn't kick the big hornets' nest, so you did the next best thing," he said. "And put some fight into Anvit, to boot! Now he has an enemy he can enjoy fighting."

"The Excalbians are gaining on us," said Spock. "They are now at warp factor nine."

Kirk thumbed the intraship. "Mister Scott . . ."

". . . *more power, Captain?*"

"Everything you've got, Scotty."

"We're already in the red line heading toward a warp core meltdown."

"Keep us together, Mister Scott."

"I'll do my best, sir."

"I know you will, Scotty," Kirk said. "That's one of the things I'm counting on. Kirk out." He turned back to the helm. "Full ahead, Mister Sulu."

"Aye, sir."

The *Enterprise* shuddered. "The Excalbians are testing our shield frequencies, Captain," Spock said. "They are looking for a way to nullify our protective advantage."

"Hold them off, Spock."

"Randomizing defensive oscillations," Spock said. "There is a range of frequencies which function to block their abilities. We may be able to keep them guessing just long enough."

"What's the Demiurge doing?"

"On a vector to bypass Zeta Gibraltar," Spock answered. "Instead, it is on a direct path to run down the Excalbians."

"All right, Spock, it's time you join Doctor Franklin down on the hangar deck," Kirk said.

"On my way, Captain." Spock moved away from his post and Chekov immediately replaced him. Lieutenant Leslie took Chekov's place at navigation. The tubolift doors swished and Spock was gone.

"You reasoned that the Demiurge would only attack Zeta Gibraltar if there were Excalbians present. It goes after the most complex life as prey," Washington-Yarnek said. "It is entirely unconcerned with lowly species such as Vulcans and humans and their puny starships. It can swat you at will."

"Of course," Kirk said.

"Two superpowers pitted against one another at Yorktown."

"England and France," Kirk said. "And we're the lowly colonials that England planned to crush."

"With the French represented by the Demiurge? Wicked, Captain," Washington-Yarnek said with a chuckle. Then his expression became more serious. "I must warn you," he said. "It was a very near thing. If de Grasse's ships hadn't arrived, America would have been a mere footnote in the history books—as would I. The treasonous leader of a failed rebellion."

"American victory should have been impossible," Kirk said. "You made your own luck, Mister President."

"With a little help from Franklin, yes."

"The British were cut off from their navy. Cornwallis surrendered."

"Indeed," Washington-Yarnek said, a faraway look in his eyes.

As if he's really remembering that day, Kirk thought. *I'd like to believe that he is.*

"But remember, Captain," the Excalbian said. "I only *had* one shot. If I'd missed—"

"You'd have found another way," Kirk said with a smile. "I have no doubt of it."

"Do you think there are such things as destiny and fate, Captain Kirk?"

"And freedom," Kirk said.

"A paradox."

"A truth," Kirk said. "Chekov, report."

"We have entered the corona of the Vara Nebula, sir," Chekov said. "Recommend we slow down, sir," he added nervously. "There are a lot of things to run into out there."

Kirk nodded. "Warp one, Mister Sulu."

"Warp one, Captain."

"That's still . . . kind of fast, sir," Chekov commented. He looked back at his sensor. "First debris band dead ahead."

The ship suddenly lurched from side to side. It rumbled as if the entire vessel had been struck by a giant hammer and was ringing with the blow.

"Multiple impacts with space debris," Chekov said above the noise.

"Damage report."

"Forward shields down twenty percent," said Chekov.

"Decks eight and nineteen reporting casualties, sir," Uhura said. "Fire suppression crews headed to deck twelve."

"Excalbians near to overrunning us, Captain," Sulu said. "They are less than a thousand kilometers behind us. Already on the outskirts of our ion cavitation, Captain."

"What about the Demiurge?"

"It has entered the nebula. It is gaining on the Excalbians."

"Captain, the Demiurge is firing an energy weapon at the Excalbians. It seems to be gravity-based. Each shot is a singularity, but moving at high speed."

"A cannon," Kirk said. "A cannon that shoots black holes at tachyonic speeds. Remarkable." He turned to Uhura. "Lieutenant, viewscreen aft."

"Aye, sir," she answered.

On the main viewscreen, Kirk could see the first of the Demiurge's salvos reach the Excalbian fleet. The fleet was now lit by the ambient glow of the nebula, and its crystalline ships sparkled like diamonds.

The singularity struck one of the crystalline vessels. A burgeoning blackness surrounded the diamond-like ship like a cowl, blocking out the stars beyond. There was a moment when the Excalbian ship seemed, simply, gone—but then the shining interior of the vessel began to show through the blackness. It emerged from the obscuring dark damaged, cracked, jagged lines running throughout it. But still intact.

"We are nearing the second debris band, sir," Chekov said. "This one has got much bigger debris than the one we just passed through."

Something streaked toward them on the screen,

something so black it utterly obscured the general glow of the nebula gases.

Another bit of blackness rapidly approached from astern.

"Demiurge firing second singularity weapon," Sulu said.

The blackness grew and grew, seemed to obscure the light.

Then it was gone.

"Near miss, sir. The singularity went through the middle of the Excalbian fleet and right past us."

"Mister Leslie, do you have a navigation fix on the path of that singularity?"

"I can compute it, sir," Leslie said in a perplexed tone. Then he nodded his head and smiled. "Got it. Laying in course."

"Course engaged, Captain," Sulu said.

Kirk leaned forward and said in a low voice, "Think you can follow the path of that shot, Mister Sulu? It should have blasted us a clear path through that second debris field. But it won't be a straight path. There's too much mass to allow for that."

"I believe I can, sir."

Sulu adjusted the helm, and the *Enterprise* lurched to the side.

"Steady as she goes."

"Aye, sir. On it now."

"Excalbian fleet dropping out of warp, sir," said Leslie. "They are coming about to face the Demiurge."

"We're through the second debris field," Chekov reported with relief in his voice.

"Mister Sulu, take us out of warp," Kirk ordered.

"Aye, sir. Impulse power."

"Bring us about."

"Aye, sir."

"Mister Chekov, how deep are we into the nebula?"

"Fifty point four parsecs, sir. One-third of the way from gravitational center."

"All right, it'll have to do." Kirk touched the intraship button. "Bridge to hangar deck."

"Spock here, Captain."

"Status report."

"Doctor Franklin and I are aboard the Copernicus, *and we have loaded the modified device."*

"Are you ready?"

"Yes, sir."

"Open the hangar doors. Stand by to launch. It may be a rough exit."

"Hangar doors opening, Captain," said Spock. *"Standing by."*

Before Kirk cut the connection he could hear Franklin speaking in the background. *"Well, this is as exciting as my first trip across the Atlantic, I must say. Maybe more so."*

"Captain, the Excalbians have moved into the second debris band," said Chekov. "It would appear they are attempting to use it for cover."

"That's it," Kirk said. "Hang in there, Anvit."

"Bridge to hangar deck."

"Standing by, Captain."

"Spock, it's time to give that invention of our trio of mad scientists a try."

"To be fair, it was primarily Galileo's idea," Spock said. *"Doctor Franklin made significant contributions to the deployment arrangements of the mechanism, however."*

"All right, Spock, as you say."

Spock replied, back to business, *"Shuttlecraft is ready to launch."*

"Very well." Kirk paused for a moment. "Good luck, Spock."

Even as the words came out, Kirk knew he should have saved his breath.

"Captain, as you know, luck has—"

"Nothing to do with it," Kirk said, completing Spock's well-worn aphorism.

"Precisely, sir."

Kirk chuckled. "Launch shuttlecraft."

"Shuttlecraft launching," Spock announced. *"Clearing hangar doors."* A pause. *"We're away, sir."*

"Acknowledged. Bridge out." Kirk deactivated the comm, but stared at the receiver grill for a moment. "Good luck anyway, Spock," he quietly said.

Twenty

"Sir, I don't know exactly how to interpret these sensor readings," Chekov said. "There are massive exchanges of energy between the Excalbian fleet and the Demiurge. If we had not moved behind the debris band, we would be in the middle of it."

"What kind of energy?"

"Unknown," Chekov said. "It is produced by technological means." Chekov looked up and shook his head. "All I can say for sure is that some of it is kinetic, according to my readings. Whatever they are using against each other, it's ripping a hole in this portion of the nebula."

Spock and Franklin are out there in the thick of it, Kirk thought.

―――――――

Spock moved the shuttlecraft thruster control quickly to one side and then the other, throwing the vehicle into two stomach-lurching banking maneuvers. Debris sped by at a significant speed. The dust particle strikes were bad enough. The shuttlecraft's shields were steadily eroding. But when a larger chunk of pre-planetary matter slammed into them, there were explosions that were equivalent to the fission detonations of Earth's early atomic bombs.

The *Enterprise* shuttlecraft, although tightly built and kept in optimal state by the exacting hangar deck chief, a protégé of Mister Scott's, were not made to withstand this sort of space storm for this long.

The pounding the shuttlecraft was taking also hid it from the warring giants—the Excalbians and the Demiurge. They were beating on one another with hammers constructed by a physics that neither human nor Vulcan had even conceived of creating.

The *Copernicus* passed the Excalbian fleet, giving it a wide a berth while retaining enough fuel to reach their target: the Demiurge. As they drew nearer and nearer to that monstrosity, Spock judged their distance from the Demiurge from sensor data that was *not* there and ought to be rather than actual readings.

Active surveillance could serve to alert the Demiurge to our presence, Spock thought.

If the Demiurge perceived them, they could be swatted like a fly, then all would be lost. There was a good possibility—Spock calculated it at thirty-three point eight percent—that the *Copernicus* would be inadvertently swatted anyway, collateral damage in the titanic battle taking place.

Franklin was monitoring the battle, while Spock was busy piloting. "If I'm reading these sensors correctly, they're telling me that the Excalbians have lost another ship, I'm afraid," the doctor called out. "They are down to three."

Spock looked back to the forward viewport. Suddenly, there was a bright flash. A wave of matter shot past them at velocities such that the effects of special relativity doubled their mass. Several struck, but the greater part of the exploded fragments missed by only a few meters.

"That was cutting it close," Franklin said to Spock.

"It was not intentional. I am not attempting to pilot the craft into the conflict," Spock said.

Franklin reached over and patted Spock's arm. "I know that, Spock." Another bright and sustained explosion. "Ah, another ship gone."

Ahead, all was dark. The nebula that had previously surrounded them had vanished. "We're very close now," Spock said. "What we see, or sense, in front of us is the Demiurge entity."

"How long?"

"We must be in range to use the shuttlecraft's phasers," Spock answered. "As you know, they are extremely low powered, rudimentary, and meant for defensive use."

"It seems to me strange to sneak one's way up to a bear, and then, instead of plunging in a knife, or shooting it with a musket, we shoot a slingshotted pebble into its side."

"It is *your* plan, Doctor Franklin," answered Spock.

"Indeed," said Franklin. "I'm glad I am not a man consumed by self-doubt, or I would be gnawing upon a bone of worry at present."

Spock nodded. "One minute, sir," he said. "We can initiate the power build-up on the device."

"Yes, yes," Franklin said. He reached over and flipped a toggle. "Matter and antimatter are chambered."

"Thirty seconds."

Franklin looked down at his controls. "I believe we are ready to launch the device."

"Please do so, Doctor Franklin."

Franklin, who seemed perpetually delighted with present-day technology, reached down and pressed a green button.

There was a small *chuff* sound from the stern of the shuttlecraft.

"Device away, Mister Spock."

Spock reached to activate the controls. "Twenty, nineteen, eighteen—"

"As much as I admire the Platonic beauty of the integers, perhaps wait until *three* to count down, Mister Spock?"

Spock nodded. He continued the count in his head. *Six, five, four . . .*

"Three, two, one. Firing phasers."

"Activating device," Franklin announced. He toggled a red button. "I certainly hope we have gotten its attention."

"We have," Spock said, gazing down at his instrumentation. "A tendril of . . . nothingness, it seems . . . is moving straight for us. Hold on, Doctor Franklin. I will attempt evasive maneuvers."

Franklin pulled the restraining strap over his shoulder and slid the end into its magnetic buckle. "Spare the whip and loose the horse. Speed is our friend, Mister Spock."

"Indeed."

What?

The Demiurge felt the pinprick from the tiny craft. Or was it a craft? It seemed more some sort of the uncommon, but extremely annoying, space-evolved insectoid parasite. But when the Demiurge bent Its mind to the shuttlecraft, It comprehended that there were primitives inside. If It had not been preoccupied in toying with the Excalbians before consuming them, It may have spared a nanosecond to smear the craft and its occupants across space-time.

It could now.

No, not yet. It could always do so after It took care of the Excalbians. It would. The Demiurge was implacable and ravenous—the hunger for gorging on other mentalities was ever present. Anything intelligent outside Itself that It did not possess and dominate enraged It. The time for being eaten would soon come for the small minds inside the little, prickling craft.

Yet if It had not turned that flicker of attention toward the small craft, It would never have noticed the signaling device trailing behind in the wake of the craft.

Fascinating. In Its million years of existence, the Demiurge had, of course, encountered similar devices and similar technology. In fact, the distant descendant of a creature that had evolved to access the same physics of which this device took advantage.

The Demiurge ate information. After ingesting a sentient mentality, the Demiurge went to work stripping the properties from that mentality's sub-atomic particles, nullifying the particle, and incorporating the information into the Demiurge's own mental structure.

The more intelligent the species, the tastier they were to the Demiurge. Intelligence took advantage of such quantum properties of particles to create unique effects—most notably freedom of will in an otherwise deterministic universe. When the Demiurge ate the information from an intelligent mind, It destroyed the mind's ability to act freely as It snacked on the intelligent being's thought processes.

The Demiurge enjoyed thinking of this process as "eating souls."

As the will of the prey began to disintegrate, the prey's anguish and mental screams added to the complexity of its destruction, and thus to its deliciousness to the Demiurge.

So the more It could torture the souls as It ate them, the better they tasted.

The device the Demiurge detected had a similar effect to the Demiurge's ingestion when used as a weapon: it returned subatomic particles to their cloud state, free of formatting information. Since information followed a similar path to entropy, it ran downhill. Like energy, it could not run "uphill" by becoming more complex without the input of more information from outside the system under consideration.

Contrary to first appearances, a reformatted particle actually had *more* information than it previously had because it now contained all possible states of spin, color, charge . . . . The new information inflow had to come from somewhere. In the Demiurge's experience, such a device normally pulled such information from extremely distant galaxies where portions of scientific law that were statistically determined wound up significantly different from those same laws in the Milky Way and its local galactic cluster. The device took advantage of these variances.

Perhaps one day It would go to such places, travel to distant realms and ravage and destroy species that had an entirely different "taste" from the local cluster sentient beings.

But that was for later. There was still forage here to consume.

The Demiurge was detecting not merely the signal of distant galaxies from the device. It was sensing information flow from . . . somewhere else.

It erected a barrier to the Excalbian's puny, but irritating, attempts at counterattack and bent more of Its attention to the device.

Where had this thing come from? Surely not from the departing small craft? For a moment, the Demiurge considered reaching out and interrogating the occupants of the craft as to what they knew of the device. But the craft was so clearly inferior in technology to the device that interrogation promised to be a waste of the Demiurge's time. Anyway, to narrow one's mind down to the extent necessary to communicate with, and thus terrorize, such primitive beings caused the Demiurge discomfort, which was why It seldom worried Itself with consuming mentalities that propagated in mere carbon-based units.

It turned Its attention back to the device.

Where was this information coming from and what was its purpose? Like a predator poking at its prey with a claw, the Demiurge pushed Its non-being into the space around the device. With a ripple of space-time amusement, It cut off all possible contact with the device by enclosing it in a bubble of singularity bent into existence by concentrated dark matter. Distant galaxies with different physics or not, nothing would get through this null space containment.

The device belonged to the Demiurge now.

Yet the device remained functioning even within this pocket universe. It still created a steady "buzz" of complex noise that indicated a stream of information was flowing through it.

What could reach the device? It was, literally, in the middle of nowhere.

Then the Demiurge realized the answer to Its question, and a smug sensation of Its own cleverness propagated through It in a jelly-like quiver of space-time. This was the Demiurge's equivalent to amused laughter.

Not where. *When.*

The Demiurge snaked a sensory pseudopod into the singularity in which It was holding the device and "tasted" the buzz.

Delicious. Pure information packed into its most complex form. It had never, ever, in Its million-plus years of existence come across any morsel so tasty. No, this wasn't a mere morsel. This was an entire meal.

Although It had never been a planetary-bound

being, much less a mammal of Earth, the Demiurge, unbeknownst to Itself, felt as a bear might when it discovers a beehive filled with an immense, untapped supply of honey.

We will suck it dry. We will eat and eat. All will be ours!

Whoever the "bees" of this hive were, what they were doing with this rich supply of concentrated information was not important—certainly not important in relation to the Demiurge's desire to feed. Unlike a bear, It would take pleasure in the bees' distress when they discovered all their carefully created honey was being pillaged—and they could do nothing about it.

The Demiurge extended the pseudopod farther into the subatomic recess of the device's exterior, listening, tasting, absorbing. Yes. Signals were arriving and departing. The device was some sort of transceiver, a packet transfer station. Was there a local interface?

Indeed, there was. In a recess, the Demiurge located a nano-scaled input station with a variety of possible connection options. It was familiar with all of these input-output configurations and could mimic any of them. It did so.

For a moment, It pondered the wisdom of sticking a pseudopod into the device.

But the potential reward was too tempting.

Nectar of the gods.

And we are the closest thing in existence to a god.

Time for the next step.

This device would permit It to take that next step. Drink this nectar, and become a god. It would cease consuming mere species. It would be able to consume *galaxies*!

The Demiurge plugged into the flow.

At first, It was in ecstasy. There was so much, so much! It extended Its negative-energy pseudopod farther into the stream. As it did so, Its awareness of time, of the present moment, seemed to expand. The flow was from both the past and the future. And from . . . there was no way to conceive of it but as *elsewhere*.

This was a network! A cross-time network much like a computer network.

What was the network communicating? The makeup of the universe itself! The spin, color, charge, up-ness, and down-ness of quantum particles.

Who were the users? It reached out farther, farther . . .

It sensed presences. Multiple presences. Large. Quite large.

Larger than We are.

The presence spoke.

Hello, little worm. You really shouldn't be here, you know. But since you are, and you desire to feed— suck on this!

The large presence stuck a portion of itself, the smallest portion, like the pinkie finger of a humanoid, down the Demiurge's information-swallowing "throat."

In flowed . . .

Everything.

Like an urchin contracting upon being touched, the Demiurge squeezed Itself inward, did all It could to contract and pull Itself out of this time network, away from the presences who used It.

There, yes. Back to normal space-time. That was the escape route, it had to be . . .

But the information the presence had shoved down its throat was still flowing, expanding within the Demiurge, stretching the near-infinite folds of space-time that made up Its being to full. Beyond full.

Must get away from this device. Must disconnect.

It jerked away from the interface.

But It could not disengage. It tried again.

Stuck. The Demiurge used sensors to examine the interface plug It had used to access the device.

A trap. There was no automatic disconnect! No method for ejecting Itself! There was no way to turn the device off.

The information from the network was still flowing!

Flowing into every recess of the Demiurge.

Something It had never conceived was possible had happened. It had run out of storage space.

The information still flowed.

It began filling Its short-term memory spaces, the areas where Its own consciousness resided, with the inflow.

There was still time.

The Demiurge paused, allowed Its smug certainty of Its own superiority to settle back into its awareness.

It could handle this.

Now It understood what had happened.

The humanoids in the tiny craft. They had engineered the interface to catch It. They'd used the simplest of designs.

The harder It pulled, the tighter the grip of the device.

To escape, to loosen the hold of the device, It had to flow the other way, back *into* the device.

But to do that was to open the spigot of information to the full.

The Demiurge searched Its eons worth of memories, processes, stored procedures.

There had to be a way to escape such a simple trap! There had to be!

We will find the answer. We will search every corner of ourselves and find—

And while It searched, It filled and filled.

The Demiurge never completed Its final thought. Its mind filled to capacity.

Beyond.

And exploded.

Its insides blew outward. Information, stolen technologies, stolen sciences, species stored as algorithms—

Blew outward and congealed around, within, any material substance, any energy process it encountered.

There was a great deal of matter and star-birthing energy in the Vara Nebula.

Enough, even, to retain the gutted ruin of all the Demiurge had ingested in Its million years of feeding.

The Vara, the birthplace of stars, was now also a haunted graveyard.

———

The best vantage point for sensors to detect the destruction of the Demiurge proved to be the *Enterprise*, as it poked through its hiding hole in the Vara Nebula's second debris band. The Excalbian fleet was buffeted and another ship was lost, leaving only two remaining Excalbian vessels: Anvit's and one other.

The Demiurge had expanded within three-dimensional space as information flowed down Its gut, but the most interesting visual was a change in color from near transparency to a rusty red, to a blue, and then violet as they were turned inside out and flew apart. Its various bits and pieces took on the same colors in reverse as they flew farther away, so that the entire process resembled a slow-motion flowering firework explosion.

It was so total, and so complete a destruction that Kirk almost felt sorry for the Demiurge. Almost.

The next task was to locate Spock and Franklin.

If they could be located.

"Initiate wide sensor sweep," Kirk ordered Chekov. "I want that shuttlecraft found."

Uhura turned to Kirk and reported. "Excalbian flagship vessel hailing us, sir."

"Tell Anvit we're busy at the moment."

"Aye, sir," Uhura said. She put a hand to her earpiece. "Captain, Anvit reports that Mister Spock and Doctor Franklin are safely aboard their vessel, along with the shuttlecraft. The Excalbians were able to rescue them before the explosive effects destroyed them."

Kirk let out a long breath. Spock would probably claim that it was quite logical, given the Excalbian matter-manipulation technology.

Which was true, and not the slightest evidence disproving fortune favoring the bold.

Uhura reported. "They request permission to inspect the Excalbian vessel if time permits. Anvit says he will arrange the atmosphere and life support to oblige them."

Kirk smiled, shaking his head in relief. "Thank

the commander for saving their lives. And ask the
commander to please pass the word along to Spock
that he is hereby granted all the time he needs to
satisfy his intellectual curiosity. Ask Anvit to tell
them both job well done."

"And the thanks of New Excalbia, as well, if you
don't mind," Washington-Yarnek put in. Kirk nodded to Uhura to include this too.

Twenty-one

Captain's Log, Stardate 6100.95. The being known as the De-miurge has been destroyed by the time bomb created by Com-mander Spock and the Excalbian versions of Benjamin Franklin and Galileo. Suitably chagrined after their brush with a creature that nearly exterminated their species, the Excalbian com-mander initiated a search—using technologically advanced sensors of an unknown nature—to locate a dilithium deposit deep within the interior of Zeta Gibraltar. They delivered refined dilithium crystals to the Montana to replace those that they had caused to be destroyed. Captain Haynes of the Montana reports that repairs are proceeding, and he estimates repairs will be completed within two weeks. Commander Anvit has positioned his remaining ships on the outskirts of the Gibraltar system in order not to trip the perimeter defense. Federation Special Representative Valek, using her plenipotentiary author-ity, is mediating on Zeta Gibraltar the various claims, counter-claims, and outstanding diplomatic issues left in the wake of the Demiurge's attack. I am looking forward to witness how Valek intends to balance the various interests to reach an equi-table outcome. Once this is resolved the Enterprise's garrison duty in the Gibraltar system should be at an end.

The conference room on Zeta Gibraltar was now designated as the Council Chamber of the New Excalbia Assembly. Gathered at the moment were the *Enterprise* senior crew, Commander Contreras and her senior personnel, and Washington-Yarnek, Franklin, Watt, and as many of the humanoid Excalbians as could crowd in. The viewscreen was activated and a subspace link had been established with Excalbian Commander Anvit. His steaming, inscrutable faceless visage lent the chamber a macabre air—as if a castle hall had been hung with the portrait of an ancient relative who was rumored to have been insane.

Washington-Yarnek and Valek were at the head of the conference room table, jointly presiding, but at the moment Spock had the floor.

"We believe that the entity known as the Demiurge was not annihilated in the information blast, but dispersed. The function that best describes the effect is similar to those that describe aerosol disbursement, but in this case involving multiple dimensions beyond those that we perceive. The Demiurge has disintegrated into multiple nonsentient data-clouds that are engaged in the task of processing the absorbed information influx. My calculations are approximate, but I would estimate that at present rates the time it will take these dispersed entities to complete their task is on the order of three point five billion years, plus or minus two hundred million years."

Spock turned toward Washington-Yarnek and Valek to indicate he was wrapping up. "For the moment," he continued, "a very long moment indeed, the Excalbians and the Federation are safe from the Demiurge."

"Commander Spock, on behalf of the Assembly, allow me to extend the thanks of our new government to yourself and the *Enterprise* crew," Washington-Yarnek said. "And, since the representatives of my former species do not understand the idea of gratitude, allow me to say thank you for them, as well."

Anvit, on the viewscreen, appeared nonplussed by this, more befuddled than imposing. *"Agreed,"* he finally said. *"We acknowledge that the present situation in which we find ourselves has been brought about by a series of misconceptions on our part. It may be that we have finally come to an understanding of this thing called 'good.'"*

"Excellent," said Washington-Yarnek. "You may find, Anvit, that good may be more useful to the survival of your species than its converse, evil."

Anvit turned his head in what Kirk imagined might be the Excalbian version of a nod of acknowledgment. *"We will contemplate this,"* said the Excalbian commander. *"We have also arrived at a second conclusion that we intend to act on henceforth."*

"What is that?"

"Do not make James T. Kirk angry," Anvit replied.

"Wise," said Washington-Yarnek.

"Since any further interaction with the Federation might do so, we will disengage from any such attempt and will also relinquish any plan to destroy any planets within the Federation."

"Good to hear," said Kirk under his breath, then he stated more loudly: "That *would* anger me, I can promise you, Anvit."

"Acknowledged," Anvit replied.

Valek cocked her head and spoke to Anvit. "Commander, might I suggest that your people go to the Vara Nebula? The protean star-forming matter in the nebula may be an excellent substrate in which to release your archived Excalbian mentalities. Perhaps you can even terraform some of the rocky bodies to support humanoid life, should you ever want to try what Yarnek and the others have done."

"That is . . . an interesting suggestion, Representative Valek," Anvit said.

"Furthermore, this will allow you to keep watch over the scattered remains of the Demiurge. You might also deal with the pirate situation while you are about it."

"Quid pro quo," said Anvit. *"We will contemplate this."*

"Good," Valek said.

Valek turned toward Washington-Yarnek. "Shall we get on with other business, Mister President?"

"Please do, madam," Washington-Yarnek replied.

Valek nodded. "Very well. As a plenipotentiary special representative, I have complete latitude in all matters under the brief of my appointment. One of those matters is the granting of Federation citizenship to the humanoid Excalbian refugees." Valek gazed around the room at the gathered historical figures for a long moment, then rendered her verdict. "That application is hereby denied," she said.

There were a few murmurs of discontent, but her announcement did not cause a general uproar.

Their president has them well prepared, Kirk thought.

"There is also the matter of the Declaration of the New Excalbia Assembly presented to me and provisionally accepted by me." Valek reached down, took hold of the rolled piece of old-fashioned paper, and lifted it up. "I suggest that you make this permanent, knowing you will have the full support of the United Federation of Planets with all the previously stipulated terms, including the transfer of the Zeta Gibraltar planetoid from the Federation to the polity known and recognized as New Excalbia."

At this, a cheer went up from all the gathered Excalbians—a cheer that resonated into the remainder of the outpost as the news was communicated to those who could not squeeze into the Council Chamber.

The only one who didn't seem very happy was Imelda Contreras, who was trying to put a good face on her personal discontent over losing her post.

Washington-Yarnek rose from his seat. He reached into his blue woolen jacket and pulled forth—his musket pistol.

This quieted the room almost instantly.

Then he turned the pistol around and used its butt as a gavel. Whatever murmurs remained now cut out, and the room was silent.

"Today, I wish to declare the first act of foreign policy by this Assembly by calling for the acceptance of the representative's proposed settlement by popular acclaim."

Another cheer went up, this one longer and louder than the first.

This time it did take several bangs of the musket butt to achieve quiet again.

Kirk glanced over at Valek, who had taken a seat and was serenely directing her gaze at the president.

God, she's beautiful in her Vulcan way, he thought. *What would it be like to—*

Then he mentally kicked himself for even allowing himself to consider it.

"Captain Kirk," Washington-Yarnek said, pulling Kirk abruptly out of his reverie.

"Yes, Mister President?"

"I would like to offer a pledge to you and to Starfleet that my administration shall make it a point of honor to boldly go forth and discover whether any remnants of the Hradrian slave empire still exist. If we do find them, I will make it my personal task to free those slaves. I cannot do penance for an historical figure I do not really know, but I can certainly make amends with my own actions. We'll lick whatever remains of those L'rah'hane pirates in the bargain."

Kirk smiled and nodded. "That is *very* good to hear, Mister President," he said. "With you in charge, I'm sure the task will be a success."

Washington-Yarnek nodded his acknowledgement of the challenge. Then he turned to the assembled. "Having no further business . . . business that can't wait a few days, that is . . . I hereby declare this meeting dismissed."

Dismissed by George Washington, Kirk thought. *There's something bracing about that. Even if he is a big phony, he's my big phony after all—plucked from my expectations and my wells of inspiration.*

Emilie du Chatelet hadn't said anything when McCoy showed up in her doorway. She had just wordlessly motioned for him to come inside.

Her dressing room was furnished like an eighteenth-century dream of luxury.

Which, in a way, is exactly what it is, thought McCoy.

He sat in a marvelously soft chair while she got them both sherry in glasses with the weight of cut crystal to them.

McCoy raised his in a toast.

"Well, my dear Emi, even though in my medical opinion you are a hideous alien got up to look like a beautiful and intelligent woman, as a man, I'm still going to miss you," McCoy said.

"And I will miss you, Leonard, my master of the body in all its variations, my captain of life," Emilie du Chatelet replied.

"It's not every man who can say he slept with the woman who predicted ultraviolet radiation and translated Newton's *Principia* into French." McCoy took a sip of sherry and gazed at her. "And, of course, was Voltaire's mistress," he said, shaking his head.

"And now McCoy's," she replied. "Or you could say you were a particular fancy of *mine*."

"I could and would," McCoy said.

"Will you ever return to me, Leonard?"

"You never know with a captain like James T. Kirk," McCoy responded.

"He is your friend?"

"He is."

"As well as the reserved Mister Spock. He, too, is your friend?"

"Yes," McCoy answered. He lifted his sherry. "To us."

"To what we were and what we are," said du Chatelet.

"And what we will be," McCoy said, and drank from his glass, as du Chatelet did.

He noticed the smear of rose-colored lipstick she left on the rim and caught the faint scent of her perfume, *that* perfume, as she reached to adjust a curl that had fallen over her forehead.

"We still have an hour," McCoy said. "I'm not due back on the *Enterprise* until zero seven hundred."

"My quarters or yours, Leonard?" du Chatelet asked in a husky whisper.

"Let's stay here," said McCoy. "I'd like to feel that French feather bed of yours." He smiled ruefully. "I wish I could take something . . . a feather, a glove, a lock of your hair, anything to remember you by."

"It would disintegrate to component parts within a day or two without the animism of my presence to reinforce its molecular structure."

"'The animism of your presence,'" McCoy said. "*That* I'm going to miss most of all."

"I think I can send you away with a little of it," du Chatelet answered. She leaned over and turned her face toward him. McCoy drew her closer and planted a kiss on her perfectly bowed lips. "Or maybe more than a little," she whispered into his ear.

The bed was even softer than McCoy had imagined. And when they were finished, McCoy realized he would take something of hers with him, something of which he could never rid himself, and would never wish to.

The memory of her scent.

———

"Captain, do you think all this effort and peril has merely left us with a little slice of hell that the Federation is glad to get rid of?" Washington-Yarnek asked Kirk.

They were standing at the large windows of an outpost exterior observation room window looking out over the blue-orange vista that was the surface of Zeta Gibraltar. The sky glowed its neon purple.

"It kind of grows on you," Kirk said. "Kind of.

"I think you'll find that home is home, no matter what it looks like out there," Kirk added.

"I suppose you're correct," Washington-Yarnek replied. "Happiness and moral duty are inseparably connected, and there is much to do. We shall find happiness in maintaining what we have won for ourselves. Yet, there are times when I doubt any of this will amount to much, that I am living someone else's dream."

Kirk nodded. "Many of us feel that way," he said. "A parent's expectations. Our own youthful choices. An inherited duty. Life can feel . . . out of one's control."

"What do you do when that anxiety comes upon you, Captain?"

Kirk turned to the Excalbian and smiled. "Well, sometimes I ask myself what George Washington would do," he said.

———

It was the day cycle on the planetoid, and laboratory C was well lit from its exterior windows. Spock and Franklin bent over an experiment that the doctor had convinced the Vulcan might be worthwhile to begin together.

Franklin had called it his "gravity stove," and Spock had to admit that the idea was ripe with possibilities. Franklin had been studying the various means extant for producing artificial gravity, and he had discussed with Spock several possibilities for using alternating gravitational plates to create a kind of "current" of gravity whose feedback might created a localized warp effect.

Franklin envisioned its use to create an interstellar "flying carpet," but Spock could imagine more mundane and widespread uses, should the device prove viable.

"Galileo did the math, and he says it will work,"

Franklin said. "But in this world nothing is certain but death and debt."

In order to work with Franklin, Spock had remained on the planetoid until the final moment before the *Enterprise*'s departure. Spock's communicator signal indicated that time had come.

Spock straightened from the project before them.

"Doctor Franklin, I regret that I must beam up to the *Enterprise*," Spock said. "Before I go, I must tell you that it has been an honor and a privilege to have met and worked with you," Spock said. "I hope that our paths may cross again."

"Oh, I expect they will, Mister Spock," Franklin said. "I may do a bit of traveling myself after we get this new government settled in. Humans may have the right to *pursue* happiness, but you have the *responsibility* to catch it yourself."

"Indeed."

"Besides, I suspect both of us would like to play a truly challenging game of three-dimensional chess every once in a while."

Spock nodded. "You have a standing invitation, Doctor Franklin," he said. "Shall we make it seven out of nine?"

"Seven out of nine it is, Mister Spock," Franklin replied. "And we'll replay the stalemates. That ought to keep us busy for years."

———

The *Enterprise* transporter shimmered, and Representative Valek materialized upon the platform. She looked about and then raised an eyebrow when she saw Kirk was there to meet her.

"There was no need for you to be present," Valek said. "I no longer serve as your superior."

"I thought I might escort you to your quarters," Kirk replied.

"I hope the slight diversion to deliver me to Sandora is acceptable, Captain," Valek said. "The repairs to the *Montana* are still under way, and I am needed immediately in the territorial capital on Sandora Prime to arbitrate a dispute over asteroid mining rights. It is quite a fascinating case, actually."

"I'm certain you find it so," Kirk said. "I'd be interested in hearing why."

Valek began to speak, but then stopped herself.

"Perhaps another time," she said.

They exited the transporter room and walked to the turbolift.

"Deck five," Kirk said. Both of them remained silent until the lift door opened. They stepped out into the corridor, and Kirk pointed them in the right direction.

To the captain's surprise, Valek reached over and took his arm as they strolled down the passageway.

"In reference to our discussion four point eight days ago, I wanted to supplement a point I was making."

"By all means do," said Kirk.

Valek nodded. "It occurred to me it might add to your understanding if I were to expand more on my observations concerning Ambassador Sarek and Amanda Grayson."

"Please."

"It took me several years of being in close proximity to them, but I believe I did finally arrive at an understanding of the relationship," she said. "You humans—"

"Here's your quarters, Valek," Kirk said. He pointed to the control button on the wall beside the portal. "The activation lock is keyed to respond to your individual touch."

Valek pulled her arm away, then turned to face Kirk, her back against the closed door. She raised her right hand and held forth two fingers, the index and middle.

Where have I seen that before, he thought.

Then it came to him. This was the gesture Amanda Grayson made toward her husband, Sarek, when they had reached the limits of spoken logic and must assert the unspoken logic of the bond between them.

Kirk reached up with his own right hand, two fingers extended, and crossed the tips of Valek's fingers, lightly touching her skin.

He looked into her eyes. Not coldly logical. Just supremely rational. Rational and lovely.

"This is how we humans do it," Kirk said.

He leaned toward her, fully expecting her to push him away.

Well, what the hell—I'm tired of pretending it's impossible for me to feel this way. I do feel this way.

But she did not push him away. Instead, she moved toward him. For a moment they embraced—and it was not strange or awkward, as he had feared it might be.

In fact, it finally feels right *between us.*

Valek brushed her lips against his. The lightest touch.

And it was electrifying. Her mind, her being, almost touching his, almost sharing the same space, the same thought.

Then she pushed him slightly away and stepped back against the door.

"You *reasoned* it was time we kissed?" Kirk asked.

She arched an eyebrow. "An interesting logical paradox to explore," she said.

Kirk was about to reply, but before he could Valek reached over and pressed her hand against the button. The door to her quarters slid open.

ACKNOWLEDGMENTS

Note: any deviation from historical accuracy herein is entirely the fault of the Excalbians themselves, and does not reflect on any of the fine historians I consulted while researching this book.

Thanks to my wonderful mother-in-law, Edith Hoffmann, who provided the secluded spot where much of *Savage Trade* was written, and to Quim and Pilar Montserrat, for their excellent companionship, and for the occasional shot of whiskey, during the writing process. Thanks to editor Margaret Clark once again for her expert guidance and encyclopedic *Star Trek* knowledge. Thanks also to my lovely and essential wife, Rika Daniel, and to my kids Cokie and Hans, with whom there is never a dull moment. Never.

ABOUT THE AUTHOR

Tony Daniel is a science fiction writer and author of *Star Trek: The Original Series: Devil's Bargain*, *Guardian of Night*, *Metaplanetary*, *Superluminal*, and short stories such as "A Dry, Quiet War." He is also an editor at Baen Books. He's had multiple stories in Year's Best anthologies, one of which, "Life on the Moon," won the Asimov's Reader's Poll Award for year's best story and was nominated for a Hugo Award.